Snare

Katharine Kerr was born in Ohio in 1944 and now lives in San Francisco. Her extensive reading in the fields of classical archaeology and medieval and Dark Ages history and literature has had a clear influence on her work. Her novels, including the epic *Deverry* series, have been published around the world and she is a bestseller on both sides of the Atlantic.

By Katharine Kerr

The Deverry Series

DAGGERSPELL
DARKSPELL
DAWNSPELL
DRAGONSPELL

—

A TIME OF EXILE
A TIME OF OMENS
A TIME OF WAR
A TIME OF JUSTICE

THE RED WYVERN
THE BLACK RAVEN
THE FIRE DRAGON

Other Fiction

POLAR CITY BLUES
FREEZEFRAMES
SNARE

With Mark Kreighbaum

PALACE

Voyager

Snare

A novel of the far future

Katharine Kerr

HarperCollins*Publishers*

Voyager
An Imprint of HarperCollins*Publishers*
77–85 Fulham Palace Road,
Hammersmith, London W6 8JB

www.voyager-books.com

This paperback edition 2004
1 3 5 7 9 8 6 4 2

First published in Great Britain by *Voyager* 2003

ISBN 0 00 648039 X

Typeset in Veljovic Book by
Palimpsest Book Production Limited
Polmot, Stirlingshire

Printed and bound in Great Britain by
Clays Limited, St Ives plc

For Howard, again and always

Acknowledgments

Many thanks to: Brian Carnright, who keyboarded the first draft from a typescript; Mark Kreighbaum, who saved Jezro Khan's life; and especially, Alis Rasmussen and Amanda Weinstein, who know how to reassure a despairing author.

Author's Note

The astute reader will notice that the languages spoken by the characters in this book - Hirl-Onglay and TekSpeak, Vranz, and Kazraki - bear varying degrees of resemblance to English, French, and Arabic, which were indeed their parent languages at a remote point in the book's past. The resemblance is faint because the action of the book takes place in approximately 4200 AD. By then the parent languages have not merely suffered the usual language changes; they've picked up terms and constructions from various alien languages as well.

In the same way, the outer forms of the religions described have mutated to a greater or lesser degree. I sincerely hope that no believers will find this offensive, but if they do, I'd like to point out that the inner truths remain the same, and, ultimately, this book is labelled fiction for a good reason.

Katharine Kerr

Part One

The Faithful

The great king Chursavva of the Chiri Michi said to the leaders of the Humai, 'You have broken taboo. You have come to the forbidden country. Your power shall be deadened forever, and your trinkets smashed and broken.' Thus said Chursavva on the first day of the council, and all the Humai wept and wailed in terror. Then the captain of the Humai rose and spoke boldly to the king's face. 'We did not mean to break taboo. Yet we will accept your terms, as proof of our kind hearts and pure minds.'

And the great king Chursavva of the Chiri Michi said to the leaders of the Humai, 'You keep the spirits of many animals bound into the crystals in the jars and cabinets of your flying boat. You may choose two large ones and two small ones and two winged ones to accompany you into your long exile.' Thus said Chursavva on the second day of the council, and all the Humai moaned in confusion. Then the captain of the Humai rose and led his chiefs apart into their fort so that they might choose the animals.

Over the two small animals there was no dissension, for all loved the beasts known as the eeka and the cat. Over the two winged animals there was no dissension, for all loved to eat plump fowl and to see hawks fly. Over the first large animal there was no dissension, for all agreed that the sheep would provide clothing as well as meat. But over the second large animal there was dissension. Some wished for a beast known as the cow, which gave much milk and meat, but which required much land on which to live. Some wished for a beast called the goat, which gave some milk and some meat, but which could live in the waste places of the wild lands. And so they argued, until an old woman rose and called for silence.

'It is truly said that the cow and the goat, and yes, even the unclean pig, will give us food and give us skins for our clothes. But you are all forgetting the beast known as the horse.'

Many of the council members jeered, saying that the horse was tough and stringy and would give little food. The old woman called again for silence and continued her speaking.

'Little food, yes, but it will give us something greater, something that Chursavva can never foresee.'

'Indeed?' said the captain of the Humai. 'And what is this marvellous gift?'

'Speed.' The old woman paused and smiled. 'And eventually, freedom.'

And the council members fell silent, thinking about ancient wars in the history of the Humai, until one by one they smiled, too, and pronounced the old woman wise beyond belief. And because a woman chose the horse, to this day among the Tribes women alone may own them . . .

From the *Histories* of Ahmed, the Last Hajji

In the warm night, the scent of true-roses hung over the palace gardens. Among the red spear trees and the obsidian statuary, water splashed in fountains and murmured in artificial streams. In a cluster of orange bamboid two persons sat side by side in the lush true-grass, one a young slender woman, shamelessly bareheaded, and the other a heavy-set soldier with a touch of grey in his dark curly hair. Anyone who saw them would have known that they were lovers, but Captain Idres Warkannan was hoping that this truth would hide another, that they were also plotting high treason. Lubahva Shiraz acted her part by giggling in the most vapid way she could manage. Her gold bangles chimed as she laid a slender, dark-skinned hand on Warkannan's arm.

'Do you see why I thought you needed to hear this?' she whispered. 'Right away?'

'I certainly do. Send me another note if you hear more.'

'I will. We'll be doing the dinner music tomorrow for the same officials. They forget about us once we're behind that brass screen.'

Lubahva kissed him goodbye, then got up and trotted off, hurrying back to the musicians' quarters. Alone, hand on the hilt of his sabre, Warkannan made his way through the palace grounds. As an officer of the Mounted Urban Guard, he had every right to be in the Great Khan's gardens, but he hurried nonetheless, cursing when he found himself in a dead-end, striding along fast when he could see his way clear.

The palace buildings rarely stood more than a single storey high, but they dotted the gardens in an oddly random pattern. Beautiful structures of carved true-wood housed palace ministers and high-ranking officials. Squat huts of pillar reed and bamboid sufficed for servants. In the warm night windows stood open; he could hear talk, laughter, the occasional wail of a tired child, but no matter how domestic the sounds, he knew there might be spies behind a hundred different curtains.

Beyond the buildings, low walls of filigree moss and high walls of braided vines transformed the hillside into a maze made up of mazes. Down some turnings, the cold pale light of star moss edged broad paths that ended in thickets of bamboid. Down others, fern trees rose out of artificial ponds and towered over him, their fronds nodding and rasping in the evening breeze. Among their branches, the golden-furred eekas whistled and sang; now and then two or three dropped suddenly down to dash in front of him on their spidery legs. Once Warkannan took a wrong turn and ended up caught in an angle of mossy walls, where half-a-dozen eekas surrounded him. They joined their little green hands and danced around him in a circle, squeaking and mocking. When he swore at them, they darted away.

The outer wall at last – he'd reached it without being challenged. Gates of gilded true-wood stood open in the living walls of thorn vine, woven into bronze mesh, that guarded the compound. Two guards in the white tunics over black trousers of the infantry stood at attention on either side. When Warkannan held up his hand in salute, one stepped out to talk with him: Med, an old friend, smiling at him.

'I thought you were on long leave,' Med remarked.

'I am. Just came by to see one of the palace girls and pick up my salary.'

'Those girls don't come cheap, do they?'

'No. She's got her heart set on a necklace she saw in town, she tells me. God only knows how much that's going to set me back! It's a good thing I'm doing some investing these days.'

'Well, good luck with it, then.'

'Thanks. I'm going to need it.'

Warkannan sauntered through the gates while he wondered if his excuse would hold. Would someone high up in the chain of command learn that he'd returned to the palace in the middle of his leave?

'Charity, sir, oh charity?' A crowd of ragged children rushed forward and surrounded him. In the lamplight Warkannan could see their pinched little faces, their bony hands, the rags flapping around prominent ribs. 'Oh please sir!'

Warkannan dug into the pocket of his uniform trousers; he'd

taken to carrying small coins, these days. The children waited, staring at him. There was only one way to give charity without being followed and mobbed. He held up the handful of deenahs, glanced around, and saw a patch of well-lit grass.

'Here.' Warkannan tossed the coins into the grass. 'Go get them!'

The children dove for the coins, and he hurried downhill, jogging fast till the street curved and hid him from their sight. Every day, more beggars, he thought. When is this going to end?

The Great Khan's compound lay on the highest hill of Haz Kazrak, a city of hills. Far below to the west lay a sea-harbour, embraced by stone breakwaters where red warning torches glowed and fluttered, staining the water with reflections. In the cloudless sky the Spider was just rising in the east. This time of year the entire spiral would be visible by midnight as a swirl of silver light covering a tenth of the sky. Already it loomed over the eastern hills like the head and shoulders of a giant. Over the open ocean the two Flies, small glowing clouds, were scurrying to the horizon ahead of their eternal enemy. The rest of the sky stretched dark.

As Warkannan walked on, the Spider and its light disappeared behind a hill, but the soft glow of oil lamps bloomed in the twisting streets. The neighbourhood around the palace was safe enough. The compounds of the rich lined the wide streets, and most had lanterns at their gates and a doorman or two as well, standing around with a long staff to keep beggars and thieves away. Further down, though, the private lamps disappeared; the streets narrowed as they wound along the slopes. The squat little houses, made of bundled reeds or bamboo, stood dark and sullen behind kitchen gardens that smelled of night soil and chicken coops. Warkannan stayed out in the middle of the street, where the public lamps shone, and kept his hand close to the hilt of his sabre.

Down by the harbour the way broadened and brightened again. Here among the shops and warehouses people stood talking or strode along, finishing up the day's business or drawing water from the public wells. A good crowd sat drinking with friends in the cool of the evening at one or another of the sidewalk cafés. In the centre of the harbour district lay a large public square, and in its centre stood a six-sided stone pillar, plastered with public notices and religious dictates from the Council of Mullahs. Whores lounged on its steps or strutted back and forth nearby, calling out to prospective customers. Warkannan noticed one girl, barely more than a child, hanging back terrified. She'd been forced onto the streets to help feed her family, most likely. It happened more and more these days.

Warkannan crossed the square, then paused to look up at the velvet-dark night sky. In the north he saw the Phalanx, as the Kazraks called them: six bright stars zipping along from north to south, tracing a path between the Flies and the Spider. Since they appeared every night at regular intervals, he could get a rough idea of the time, enough to figure that he was late. In the light of a street lamp he took out his pocket watch. Yes, a good twenty minutes late. He put the watch away and hurried.

Fortunately his destination lay close at hand, where the street dead-ended at a merchant's compound. Over the woven thorn walls, the fern trees rustled as the breeze picked up from the ocean. The outer gate was locked, but a brass bell hung from a chain on the fence. When Warkannan rang, the doorman called out, 'Who is it?'

'Captain Warkannan.'

'Just a minute, just a minute.'

Warkannan heard snufflings and the snapping of teeth, low curses from the doorman, and a collection of animal whines and hisses. Finally the gate swung open, and he walked in cautiously, glancing around. Huge black lizards lunged on their chains and hissed open-mouthed as they tried to reach his legs. When the doorman waved his staff in their direction, they cringed.

'They can't get at you,' he said, grinning. 'Just stay on the path.'

'Oh, don't worry about that.' Warkannan fished in his pocket and found a silver deenah to tip him. 'Thanks.'

The gravelled path led through the fern trees to an open space around the house, a rambling structure, all one storey, woven of bundled rushes and vines in the usual style, but overlaid with a small fortune's worth of true-wood shingles. At the door, Nehzaym Wahud herself greeted Warkannan and ushered him inside the warehouse. Although she never told anyone her age, she must have been in her late forties. On her dark brown face she wore the purrahs, two black ribbons tied around her head. The one between her nose and upper lip marked her as a decent woman who observed the Third Prophet's laws of modesty; the other, around her forehead, proclaimed her a widow.

'How pleasant to see you, Captain,' Nehzaym said. 'I'm glad you could join us tonight.'

'My pleasure, I'm sure. I'm extremely interested in this venture of yours.'

'If the Lord allows, it could make us all quite rich, yes.'

Warkannan followed her across the room. Against the walls, covered with a maroon felt made of dried moss, stood a few lonely bales and sacks of merchandise left over from the winter trading season, a big desk littered with documents, some battered cabinets, and a tall clock, ticking to the rhythm of its brass pendulum. Nearby a bamboid door led into Nehzaym's apartment. She ushered him through, then followed. In the middle of the blue and green sitting room a marble fountain bubbled, pale orange ferns in bright pots stood along the walls, and polished brass screens hung at every window. Just in front of the fountain stood a low table, spread with maps of pale pink rushi, where other members of their circle sat waiting for him.

'Sorry I'm late,' Warkannan said.

Sitting on a heap of purple cushions, Councillor Indan Alwazir looked up. The old man kept his long white robes gathered round him as if he were afraid he'd be polluted by the incense-laden air. Warkannan's nephew, Arkazo Benjamil, a young man with a beaky nose and a thin-lipped grin, was sitting cross-legged on the floor and holding a good-sized glass of arak between thumb and forefinger. When Warkannan frowned at him, Arkazo put the glass down on the floor and shoved it under the table in one smooth gesture.

Standing by the marble fountain was the most important man in their venture. Tall and slender, Yarl Soutan was wearing the white shirt and loose white trousers of a Kazrak citizen, but his blue eyes, long blond hair caught back in a jewelled headband, and his pale skin marked him for the infidel stranger he was, a renegade from the Cantons far to the east of the khanate. Although he looked Arkazo's age, his eyes seemed as old and suspicious as Indan's, squinting at the world from a great distance. As always, Warkannan wondered just how far they could trust a man who claimed to be a sorcerer.

'We have been waiting,' Indan said to Warkannan. 'For some while, actually.'

'I had to go up to the palace. You're about to hear why.'

Indan raised an eyebrow. With a demure smile for the men, Nehzaym barred the door behind her, then perched on a cushioned stool near the councillor.

'All right,' Warkannan said. 'Someone's laid an information against us with the Great Khan's Chosen Ones.'

Arkazo swore. Indan went pale, his lips working. With a little laugh, Soutan turned from the fountain.

'I told you I saw danger approaching. These things always send omens ahead of them.'

'You were right,' Warkannan said. 'This once, anyway.'

'May God preserve!' Indan was trembling so badly that he could hardly speak. 'Do they know our names?'

'Calm down, Councillor,' Warkannan snapped. 'Of course they do, or we wouldn't have anything to worry about. They're wondering if we're really going to prospect for blackstone.'

'Is this anything special?' Arkazo broke in. 'As far as I can see, the Chosen are suspicious of everything and everyone all the time.'

'I don't know what they know,' Warkannan said. 'All that Lubahva heard was that someone bragged about our investment group. He implied it might be more important than it looked. The Chosen don't ignore that kind of rumour.'

'Indeed,' Indan said. 'Who was it?'

'Lubahva doesn't know yet.' Warkannan paused to glance at each member of the group in turn. 'I'm not doubting anyone here, mind, but our circle's grown larger recently. I knew we'd reach a danger point.'

The suspicion in the room hung as heavy as the incense. Everyone looked at Yarl Soutan, who strolled over and sat down.

'And would I run to the Chosen after throwing in my lot with you? The Great Khan wouldn't give me a pardon for spilling your secrets. He'd have me killed in some slow painful way for having come here in the first place.' Soutan laid a hand on the maps. 'I wonder – someone must suspect that I brought you something besides those old maps.'

'That's my worst fear,' Warkannan said. 'If they do, they'll send a man east to the Cantons just to see what he can learn about you.'

'Oh good god!' Soutan snarled. 'That could ruin everything.'

'Exactly,' Indan said. 'Why do you think I'm terrified?'

Soutan nodded. For a long moment they all looked at each other, as if the information they so desperately needed could be read from the empty air.

The Crescent Throne of Kazrajistan ruled these days by the sword and terror. Gemet Great Khan had gained the throne by sending his Chosen Ones to kill everyone in his own extended family with a good claim to be a khan, a word that had come to mean a man fit to be the supreme leader by blood and so sanctified by the mullahs. Now Gemet lived in fear of revenge, and with good reason. His brothers and half-brothers had married into the best families in the khanate, and with their murders and the confiscation of their lands, those families had lost sons and property both. Since he knew that any more confiscations would make the armed aristocracy rebel, he'd turned on the common people with taxes for teeth.

The last heir, young Jezro Khan, had been serving on the border, an officer in the regular cavalry. The assassins came for him, as they had for all the others, but no one ever found his body. With his assumed death, the khanate had settled into ten years of paranoid peace. Just recently, however, Soutan had ridden into Haz Kazrak and brought Councillor Indan a letter in Jezro's handwriting. Jezro Khan was alive, living as a humble exile far to the east. After some weeks of weighing risks, Indan had contacted Warkannan, who'd served with Jezro in the cavalry. Warkannan could still feel his shock, could taste his tears as he looked over the familiar writing of a friend he'd given up for dead. Together he and Indan had gathered a few trustworthy men and made contacts among those families who'd suffered at the current emperor's hands. Soon they had pledges of soldiers and coin to support the khan's cause if he returned. Things had been going very well indeed – until now.

'If we're going to prevent disaster, we have to move fast,' Indan said. 'We need to shelter Soutan above all else.'

'Just so,' Warkannan said. 'And we'd better do it tonight. Councillor, you have a country villa, don't you?'

'Oh yes, and my servants there are most trustworthy.'

'Good. You and Soutan get yourselves there. I'll stay in the city and keep in touch with Lubahva. If we all bolt at once, the Chosen are likely to draw some conclusions.'

Indan's face went ashy-grey.

'I'll be sending you word as soon as I can,' Warkannan said. 'Lubahva's group plays for every important man in the palace, and she hears plenty.' All at once he smiled. 'She's always complaining that they treat the musicians like furniture. It's a damn good thing, too. We'll find this traitor yet.'

'So we may hope.' Indan sighed, looking suddenly very old and very tired. 'But I see ruin ahead of us all.'

'Oh come now, don't give up so soon.' Soutan turned to the councillor. 'You forget that you have powerful magic on your side.'

'Indeed?' Indan said with some asperity. 'But if it can't read the minds of the Chosen, it's not much good to us.'

'Perhaps it can.' Soutan gave him a thin-lipped smile. 'Don't mock what you don't understand.'

When Indan started to snarl an answer, Warkannan leaned forward and cut him off.

'Patience, Councillor,' Warkannan said. 'We don't know what the Chosen are going to do. They may look us over and decide we pass muster.'

'They might,' Indan said. 'Or they may have sent one of their spies east already. Or a dozen of them, for that matter.'

'It should be an easy thing to find out.' Nehzaym glanced around the circle. 'Most of our allies are on the border. If we warn them, they'll keep watch.'

'The Chosen are very good at what they do.' Indan's voice seemed on the edge of fading away. 'Doubtless, when they send off their man, no one will suspect a thing.'

'Don't be so sure.' Warkannan got up with a nod for Arkazo. 'Let's go. Gentlemen, I suggest you leave with us. We'll walk into the town square together and talk about our maps and our profits. Remember, we want to be noticed doing ordinary things.'

Warkannan, with Arkazo in tow, headed for the door, but when he glanced back, he noticed that Soutan stood whispering with Nehzaym near the fountain. What was the charlatan up to now? Indan joined him, followed his glance, and raised an eyebrow.

'Soutan?' Indan called out. 'We'd best be on our way.'

'Of course.' Soutan strolled over to join them at the door. 'Of course. Our lovely widow was merely asking my advice about a small matter.'

Nehzaym glanced at Warkannan as if inviting comment. He merely shrugged, then turned and led the men out.

The Spider hung at the zenith on her thread of stars by the time that Soutan returned to the compound. Nehzaym was reading in the sitting room when she heard the lizards outside hiss and the chains clank. She took a lamp, hurried into the warehouse, and crossed to the door just as the sorcerer opened it. With a little bow he stepped inside, then turned to shut the door behind him.

'Well, that was a waste of time,' Soutan said. 'Warkannan's idea of acting normally is to sit around in a café and argue about anything and everything.'

'Don't underestimate him,' Nehzaym said. 'He's quite intelligent whether he acts it or not.'

'Really?'

'Really. Shall we go in?'

'By all means. I'm anxious to see this treasure of yours.'

'I just hope you can tell me what it is.'

She led the way back into the apartment. They walked down a short hallway to her tiny widow's room, which sported a window on one wall, a narrow bed at one end, a small threadbare rug on the floor, and little else. Out of habit she still kept her clothes, her jewellery, the chests of bed linens, and the like in the large room she'd shared with her husband. One of the treasures he'd given her, however, she kept here, where a thief would never bother to look for anything valuable. She set the lamp down on a wooden stand. Soutan sat on the floor, cross-legged, while she knelt by the rug and rolled it back to expose the sliding panel under it.

Inside the hide-hole lay a book, bound in purple cloth, and what appeared to be a thin oblong of grey slate, about twelve inches by nine, lying on a black scarf. As she was taking the slate and scarf out, Soutan craned his neck to look inside the hole; she slid the panel shut fast. He laughed.

'By all means,' Soutan said, 'you'd best keep that book hidden. *The Sibylline Prophecies*, isn't it?'

Nehzaym shrugged, then laid the slate down between them on the scarf. It hummed three musical notes and began to glow.

'God is great,' Nehzaym sang out. 'The Lord our God is one, and Mohammed, Agvar, and Kaleel are His prophets. In their names may all evil things be far away!'

'Amen.' Soutan leaned forward, staring.

In the centre of the panel the glow brightened to a pale blue square, which slowly coagulated into the image of a round room with a high ceiling. Floors, walls, the dais in the middle, the steps leading up to that dais – they all glittered silver in a mysterious light falling from above.

'Whenever I take it out, I see that picture,' Nehzaym said.

'Does it show you others?' Soutan said.

'Only this one. And look!' Nehzaym pointed to a narrow red bar of light, pulsing at one side of the slate. 'When this light flashes, a minute or two later the image fades.'

Already, in fact, the room was dissolving back into the pale blue glow. The red light died, leaving the slate only a slate. Soutan made a hissing sound and shook his head. 'Where did your husband get this?'

'In Bariza. He bought it in the marketplace from a man who dealt in curios.'

'Curios? Well, I suppose the ignorant would see it that way. Do you know anything about it?'

'Only that you have to feed it sunlight every day. I take it to the garden. In the rainy season it doesn't work very well.'

'No, it wouldn't. Our ancestors knew how to bind spirits into their magicks. They feed on sunlight. When they're hungry, they refuse to do their job.'

'I can't say I blame them. Are the spirits immortal?'

'What a strange question!' Soutan smiled, drawing back thin lips from large teeth. 'Everything alive must die, sooner or later.'

'And when all the spirits die?'

'There won't be any more magic, just like your Third Prophet said. No doubt you Kazraks will celebrate.'

'We've chosen to live as the First Prophet wanted us to live, yes.' She paused, choosing her words carefully. 'And how will your people feel about losing their magic?'

Soutan shrugged, his smile gone. 'Let's hope it doesn't happen for a good long while, a thousand years, say.' He pointed at the panel. 'What do you think that room is?'

'I was hoping you could tell me.'

'I can't, not for certain, but I'll make a guess. You have a copy of the Sibyl's book. Have you read the part about the empty shrine?'

Nehzaym felt her clasped hands tighten.

'I see you have,' Soutan said. 'One of these days you might see the Fourth Prophet standing on that dais.'

'If God would only allow, I'd happily die.'

'You'd be happier if you stayed around to see what happened next. Now. Let me see if I can show you something interesting. May I pick it up?'

'Certainly.'

Soutan took the slate and peered at it in the dancing lamplight. He ran one long finger down the side, paused, fingered the back of it, then suddenly smiled. He took a full breath, and when he spoke, the sound seemed to come from deep inside his body and buzz like an insect. The words made no sense to her at all. The spirit in the slate, however, must have understood them, because the panel chimed a long note in answer.

Soutan laid the slate back down on the floor. A new picture was forming of a different room, inlaid with blue and white quartz in a diamond pattern.

'Another shrine?' Nehzaym whispered.

'Perhaps. Wait and see.'

Slowly the room became clear – a half round, this time, and just in front of the flat wall stood two slender pillars, one grey, one white. Between them hung what appeared to be a gauzy veil, yet it shimmered and sparked with bluish light. Nehzaym twined her hands round each other. A pale blue thing shaped like a man appeared in the centre of the room. He waved his hands and seemed to be speaking, but she could hear nothing. Suddenly the thing's face filled the image. Its eyes were mere pools of darker blue; its purple lips mouthed soundless words.

Nehzaym shrieked, a sound that must have frightened the spirit inside the slate. Once again the red light began to flash. The image disappeared.

'May the Lord preserve!' Nehzaym said. 'A ghost!'

'Do you think so?' Soutan looked at the panel for a long silent moment. 'If I had gold and jewels to give, I'd heap them all in your lap in return for it. Unfortunately, I don't.' His voice dropped. 'Unfortunate for you, perhaps.'

Nehzaym started to speak, but her voice caught and trembled. Soutan rose to his knees and considered her narrow-eyed, his hands hanging loose at his sides, his fists clenched.

'Take it,' Nehzaym said.

'What?'

'If you want the nasty thing, it's yours. I work and pray for the coming of the Fourth Prophet, but this is evil sorcery. I don't want it in my house.'

Soutan sat back on his heels and stared at her slack-mouthed.

'I suppose I must look superstitious to you,' Nehzaym said. 'I don't care. Take it. It's unclean.'

'Who am I to turn down such a generous gift?' Soutan scooped up the slate.

'Take the scarf, too. I don't want it, either. It's touched something unclean.'

With a shrug he picked up the length of black cloth and began wrapping up the slate.

'May the Lord forgive!' Nehzaym said. 'I'll have to do penance. Necromancy! In my own house, too!'

'Oh for god's sake!' Soutan snapped. 'It was only an image of a ghost, not the thing itself.' Soutan cradled the wrapped slate in the crook of one arm. 'I'll have to look through the books in Indan's library. I wonder just whose ghost that was?'

'I don't care. You shouldn't either.'

Soutan laughed. 'I've learned so much from your scholars that it's a pity I can't stay in Haz Kazrak. But all the knowledge in the world won't do me any good if I'm dead.'

'If you bring Jezro home, you'll have an army of scholars to fetch your impious books.'

'Oh, stop worrying about impiety! You're too old to shriek and giggle like a girl.'

'I what? That's a rude little remark.'

'You deserve it. I must say that you Kazraks have the right idea about one thing, the way you train your girls to stay out of sight. But you're an old woman, and it's time you learned some sense.'

'I beg your pardon!'

'You should, yes.' Soutan shrugged one shoulder. 'I'd better get back to Indan's townhouse. He wants to leave early.'

After she showed Soutan out, Nehzaym told the gatekeeper to loose the lizards for the night. Before she went back to her apartment, she stopped in the warehouse to wind the floor clock with its big brass key. As she stood there, listening to the clock's ticking in the silent room, she suddenly remembered Soutan, talking about wanting the slate and looking at her in that peculiar way. She'd been so upset at the time that she'd barely noticed his change of mood. Now, she felt herself turn cold.

He might have murdered her for that slate.

'Oh don't be silly!' she said aloud. 'He's a friend of Jezro Khan's. He wouldn't do any such thing.'

But yet – she was glad, she realized, very glad, that she'd seen the last of him.

Beyond the Great Khan's city, true-roses rarely bloomed, and the grass grew purple, not green. All the vegetation native to the planet depended for photosynthesis on a pair of complex molecules similar to Old Earth carotenoids, producing colours ranging from orange to magenta and purple to a maroon verging on black. At the Kazraki universities, scholars taught that the plant they called grass should have another name and that the spear trees were no true trees at all, but the ordinary people no longer cared about such things, any more than they cared about their lost homeland, which lay, supposedly, far beyond the western seas.

Not far south of Haz Kazrak, on a pleasant stretch of seacoast, where grass grew green in a few gardens but purple in most other places, stood a rambling sort of town where rich men built summer villas. Fortunately, Councillor Indan's lands were somewhat isolated; graceful russet fern trees hid his hillside villa. Behind the orange thorn walls of his compound lay a small garden and a rambling house of some thirty rooms – just a little country place, or so Indan called it – arranged on three floors. When Warkannan rode up, the gatekeeper swung the doors wide and looked over the party: Warkannan and Arkazo on horseback, and behind them, a small cart driven by a servant from Indan's townhouse.

'I've brought the councillor a present,' Warkannan said. 'A carved chest from the north.'

Since wood hard enough to be carved meant true-oak, an expensive rarity, Indan's servants saw nothing suspicious about the way Warkannan hovered over the well-wrapped chest and insisted that he and Arkazo carry it themselves. All smiles, Indan greeted them and suggested they take the chest directly upstairs. Soutan helped them haul the six-foot-long and surprisingly heavy bundle up to a third-floor storage room.

The sorcerer watched as Warkannan and Arkazo unwrapped the rags and untied the rope holding the chest closed. It was indeed a beautiful piece of true-wood, sporting an intricate geometrical pattern, but someone had spoiled it by drilling a pair of holes in one narrow end. When Warkannan opened the lid, he found his prisoner nicely alive, still bleary from the drugs, but unsmothered.

'Hazro!' Indan whispered. 'I would have never suspected him. One of the Mustavas – unthinkable!'

'He bragged to someone, saying he was more important than he looked, the usual crap. Somehow it got back to the Chosen. We need to know how and who.'

'Lies,' Hazro mumbled.

Warkannan and Arkazo pulled him out of the chest. When he tried to stand, he sagged and nearly fell. When Warkannan shoved him back against the wall, he whimpered and glanced around with half-closed eyes.

'I tried to reason with him,' Warkannan said. 'Hazro, come on! One last chance. Tell us the truth. That's all I'm asking you. Just tell us the truth.'

'Nothing to tell.' Hazro tried to stand straight and defiant, but he nearly fell. 'You – how dare you – your family started out as a bunch of blacksmiths.'

Warkannan glanced at the councillor. 'This is what I've been up against. He won't tell me a thing.'

'May the Lord forgive us all!' Indan said. 'By the way, I've figured out a way to blame the Chosen for his death. We've got to keep his father on our side.'

Hazro whimpered and let tears run.

'He's still drugged,' Warkannan said. 'I'll question him later.'

'Good.' But Indan looked queasy with anticipation. 'This room has thick walls, and no one will hear a thing.'

That night they dined in a room with a splendid view of the ocean. Servants brought fresh seabuh, a spikey, six-armed creature in a purple carapace, a mixed vegetable salad, and ammonites dressed with sheep butter. As they ate, Warkannan told them what Lubahva had learned.

'The Chosen suspect Soutan of being up to no good, but they're not sure what.' Warkannan nodded at the self-proclaimed sorcerer, who was stuffing his mouth with as much ammonite as it could hold. 'They're making inquiries all over the city.'

Soutan shuddered and wiped his mouth on a napkin.

'Let's assume the worst,' Indan said. 'If they're making inquiries here, they must have sent a man east.'

'Probably so,' Warkannan said. 'But it's going to be damned hard for him to make his way east alone.'

'Who says he'll go alone?' Arkazo asked.

'The Chosen always do,' Warkannan said.

'Not that this makes life easier for their enemies.' Indan glanced away slack-mouthed. 'For us, that is.'

'Oh yes.' Warkannan leaned back in his chair and considered him. 'If the Chosen find out that the khan's still alive, we have no cause, gentlemen. They'll find a way to kill him no matter where he is. So we'd better make sure this spy doesn't find him. I'm going after him.'

'You can't do that,' Indan said. 'Your leave from the Guard's almost up.'

'I sent in my letter of resignation before we left the city. I've put in my twenty years, and I told them that this investment venture looked too good to pass up.'

For a long moment Indan studied Warkannan's face; then he sighed. 'That's quite a sacrifice,' Indan said. 'The cavalry means everything to you.'

'The cavalry I joined did. In the past few years –' Warkannan shrugged. 'Gemet's paranoia is going to poison the whole khanate, sooner or later.'

'Unless we supply the antidote?' Indan smiled, a wry twist of his mouth.

'Just that. It's a tall order, but if God wills, we'll succeed. If He doesn't, well, then, who am I to argue?'

Outside the sunset was darkening into twilight. A servant slipped in and began lighting the oil in silver lamps. While he waited for the man to leave, Warkannan looked round the table at his allies, at the luxurious room, at all the comforts of life that he might never see again. As the lamp flames grew, they sparkled on silver, on crystal, on the enormous ruby at the centre of Soutan's head-band. The fitful light seemed to be illuminating not just the room but the moment, a point of history upon which the destiny of the khanate would turn. The servant bowed and left the room.

'Warkannan,' Indan hissed. 'If the Chosen find any evidence at all to back up their suspicions, leaving the Guard will brand you as a traitor. You'll never be able to ride back to Kazrajistan.'

'Oh yes I will. At the head of an army.' Warkannan turned to Soutan. 'It's time Jezro's letter got an answer.'

Soutan considered him with a thin smile. His puzzling old man's eyes were unreadable in the shadows.

'I always intended to take someone back to Jezro,' Soutan said at last. 'And you'll never make it across the Rift alone, so I'd better go with you.'

'Someday you'll be the vizier of a Great Khan in return for all this.'

'If your God allows. But there's nothing left for an exile but one gamble after another, is there? We might as well deal the cards.' Soutan took a slice of pickled blakbuh from a silver tray and nibbled on it. 'The omens say the time is ripe for a change in the Great Khan's fortunes, and it's not a good one. A malefic current is forming a vortex around his personal symbols – a time of budding danger for him.'

Arkazo laughed. 'Then let's help the malefic along.'

Soutan favoured him with a look of contempt. 'That, my dear child, is my point and not an occasion for bad jokes.'

Indan leaned forward before Arkazo could reply. 'And what about your nephew, Captain? You'd better send him back to his father's estate before you leave.'

'No!' Arkazo slammed his hand down on the table and made the oil dance dangerously in the lamps. 'All my life I've been shut up, either on Father's lousy estate or at university. Now I've finally got a chance at some excitement.'

'My dear young fellow,' Indan began.

Warkannan raised a hand and interrupted him. 'He'll have to come with me, Councillor. He's been staying in my bungalow. If the Chosen decide we don't pass muster, he's the first one they'll arrest.'

Arkazo laughed with a toss of his head.

'Listen, Kaz,' Warkannan said. 'This isn't any joke. It's going to be dangerous, and your mother's going to curse my very name for this.'

'Not once she's got the favour of the new Great Khan's wife. Mama's always been the practical sort.' Arkazo turned abruptly sour. 'Why else would she have married my father?'

'This is no place to bring that up.' Warkannan took the silver flagon and poured them both more rose-scented water – Indan kept a pious table. 'I wish to God I'd kept you out of this.'

'You tried. It didn't work.'

'It's too late now, anyway. The dice are thrown, and if it weren't for you, I'd be glad of it. I'm sick to my gut of all this creeping round and worrying about spies.'

'Spies, indeed,' Indan said. 'Which reminds me –'

'Just so. We'd better get this over with.'

Everyone pushed their chairs back and stood, suddenly grim, suddenly quiet, even Arkazo.

Warkannan fetched a bucket of hot coals from the kitchen – he told the cook that he wanted to take the chill off his room – then followed the others up to the attic. As stiff as a rolled-up rug, Hazro lay on the floor. When Warkannan set the bucket of coals down, he whimpered and twisted in his ropes. Warkannan knelt beside him and pulled him up to a sitting position, propping him against the wall. Hazro's dark eyes flicked this way and that.

'Arkazo?' Warkannan said. 'You can leave. You don't have to watch this.'

'What are you going to do to him?' Arkazo was staring at Hazro.

'You don't need to know that.'

'But I –'

Warkannan got up and took one long stride to come face to face with his nephew. His own disgust with what he would have to do in this room turned to cold rage. 'Get out of here,' he snapped. 'Now.'

'Yes sir.' Arkazo stepped back sharply. 'I'm on my way.'

Warkannan waited to ensure that Arkazo was following his orders; then he closed the door and locked it. Indan stuffed a threadbare bit of carpet into the crack at the bottom of the door. When Warkannan knelt down next to him, Hazro moaned under his breath, then steadied himself, forcing defiance into a tight tremulous smile. Warkannan drew his dagger and looked at him over the blade.

'Listen, boy. This is your last chance. You wouldn't be refusing to tell me unless you had something to hide.'

Hazro said nothing.

'Why?' Indan stepped forward. 'Why won't you tell us?'

'There's nothing to tell,' Hazro said.

'Yes, there is,' Warkannan said. 'You've been giving information to someone. Who?'

'No one.'

'Then why do the Chosen suspect us?'

'They suspect everyone.'

'You told them about us.'

'Never. I didn't betray Jezro.'

Warkannan made a cut on his cheek, just under his eye. 'I'm

going to keep doing this till you tell me. If your face isn't sensitive enough, I'll work on your balls.'

Sweat glazed Hazro's forehead. 'I didn't tell anyone anything.'

Warkannan made another nick, then another till Hazro's face was sheeting blood. When Warkannan took the lid off the bucket of glowing charcoal, Hazro fainted. Warkannan slapped and shook him to bring him round while he fought his own honest revulsion. He hated extracting information this way, but if he didn't, what then? The Chosen might well gather them all in, and worse things would happen to his friends, his mistress, his allies, his nephew, down in some hidden room under the Great Khan's palace. Indan pulled over a wooden storage box and sat down, his eyes weary.

'Now,' Warkannan said to Hazro. 'Who did you tell?'

Hazro shut his bloody lips tight. Warkannan pulled up Hazro's tunic and made a nick on his scrotum. Hazro screamed.

'I'll put a bit of charcoal on that cut next,' Warkannan said. 'That's the procedure – a nick, then a bit of fire, all the way up your cock.'

When Hazro hesitated, Warkannan took the small tongs and fished a glowing coal out of the bucket.

'It was Lev Rashad. Rashad of the Wazrekej Fifth Mounted. I didn't realize at first he was one of the Chosen.'

Warkannan felt as if he'd been kicked in the stomach. He knew Rashad, just distantly, but he knew him. You never think it's going to be someone you know, he told himself.

'What do you think he was going to do?' Warkannan said. 'Announce it in the regimental mess?'

'I – I –'

'Wait!' Indan looked up. 'You said you didn't know he was one of them at first. This must mean you realized it later. How?'

'He must have been the one.' Hazro started gasping for breath. 'It couldn't have been anyone else.'

'Oh?' Indan said. 'He must have dropped some hint. Why didn't you come straight to us then? You were dangling us like bait in front of him, weren't you? You were using us to try to buy your way into the Chosen.'

Hazro made a small choking sound deep in his throat.

'How much did you tell him?' Warkannan said. 'Did you mention Jezro?'

'No, never, I swear it! All I said was that I was on to a good thing with this investment group. I thought he'd join us. We'd been drinking, and I –'

'You stupid little bastard!' Warkannan raised the knife. 'What did you tell him about Jezro?'

'Nothing!'

'Why did you want to join the Chosen?'

'I didn't. I didn't.'

Warkannan kept working on him until the smell of charred flesh hung in the room and Hazro was gibbering, not speaking. A bit at a time, Warkannan extracted the information that Hazro had mentioned Soutan, come from the east with ancient maps that might show deposits of blackstone. He admitted bragging, hinting that perhaps he was a man who knew important things.

'But not Jezro, never Jezro.' He was sobbing, twitching when his tears touched the open cuts on his face.

'Indeed? Are you sure of that?'

Over and over he denied having mentioned the name, even when he was at the point of shrieking and writhing at the very sight of a piece of charcoal. Warkannan finally laid down the tongs and sat back on his heels.

'I believe him. A man in this state tells the truth.'

'So do I,' Indan said. 'As for this business about his wanting to join the Chosen –'

'I didn't!' Hazro tried to shout, but he was gagging on his own blood. 'I just thought –'

'What?' Indan said. 'What were you thinking?'

'Insurance.' Hazro started to cough, then gagged again and spat up bloody rheum. 'If –'

'If they were on to us, you were going to turn informer.' Warkannan finished the thought for him. 'That's why you wouldn't tell us.'

Hazro slumped back against the wall, his bloody lips working.

'Yes,' Indan said. 'I think we finally understand.'

Soutan stepped closer to stare at Hazro's mutilated manhood, what was left of it. 'What are you going to do with him now?'

'Put him out of his misery.'

Hazro screamed, choked again, and tried to speak, but Warkannan grabbed his hair, forced his head back, and slit his throat in one quick stroke. When he looked up, he saw Soutan smiling, his eyes bright, as if from a fever. Soutan nudged the dead body with the toe of his sandal.

'Do we throw him in the ocean?'

'No. The Chosen have recognizable ways of torturing a man, and this was one of them. The councillor is going to find something big enough to hide the body. We'll take it back to Haz Kazrak, and I'll dump the corpse over the wall of Hazro's father's garden at night for the slaves to find. His father won't suspect us. He'll think that the Chosen have killed his son, and then he'll be more loyal to Jezro than ever.'

They left the body in the attic. Warkannan stayed out of sight while Indan ordered the servants to bring up a tub of hot water for his guest room. Once the tub was ready and they were gone, Warkannan could at last bathe away the stench and the gore. He only wished he could wash away his revulsion as easily.

Hazro had been a stupid young fool, a snob and apparently a coward as well. But to think that Lev Rashad – Warkannan shook his head. The very curse of the Chosen was simply that they were secret and very good at staying that way. An army within an army, they existed to spy on their fellow soldiers as well as do the Great Khan's dirty work among civilians. They lived in the same barracks, ate at the same mess, carried the same insignia as the other members of their regiments, but somewhere in their career, they'd been taken aside and initiated into a brotherhood with rules of its own.

And they force the rest of us to sink to their level, Warkannan told himself. *Maybe that's the worst evil of all.*

In the morning, when they set off for Haz Kazrak, one of Indan's servants followed them in the cart which was laden with an enormous woven basket filled with dried fruit and other delicacies, or so the servant thought. Certainly it smelled of rich spices and rose petals. Once they reached the city, the servant and the cart both headed for Indan's townhouse, while Warkannan and Arkazo went openly to Warkannan's cottage, which he kept as a relief from officers' quarters when off-duty.

Down on one of the lower hills in town lay a district full of these places, decent accommodations, complete with stables, for aristocratic officers like Warkannan, who had income from property but who weren't wealthy enough to keep townhouses with a full staff. Warkannan's little bungalow sat at the back of the communal garden, six irregular rooms bound together by vines and furnished with shabby wicker chairs and old rugs. When he and Arkazo walked in, his only servant, Lazzo, met him with a letter.

'It's from headquarters, sir.'

'Ah. I wonder if they're taking my resignation?'

Warkannan took the sheet of pale pink rushi over to the window. The letter read exactly as he'd hoped, a bland official statement of regret at losing such a good officer. He was to report one last time to determine his pension settlement.

'So that's that,' Warkannan said. 'If they're so sorry to lose me they might have promoted me.'

'I'm glad now I never enlisted.' Arkazo flopped onto a wicker sofa.

'Oh, I don't know. The discipline's good for a man. I don't regret –'

One sharp jolt like the slap of a giant hand made the room sway. The flexible walls creaked and chafed against their binding vines as they rippled in the shock. Warkannan braced himself and glanced at the wall. A long strand of blue beads hung on a leather thong attached to a plaque of true-wood, marked out in numbered, concentric circles. The beads swung back and forth against the gauge. As he watched, the quake died out in a long shiver. The beads quieted and hung steady.

'Just about a five,' Warkannan said.

'It didn't feel like much, no,' Arkazo said. 'Anyway, you've always talked about the discipline. That's one reason I don't want to join up.'

'Huh! Well, you're going to learn about discipline now. You follow my orders, or you stay at home.'

Lounging on overstuffed cushions Arkazo raised one hand in salute. 'Yes sir!' he said and grinned. 'At your service!'

'All right. For starters, you can pack my clothes as well as yours.'

They went into Warkannan's bedroom, where, in a chest woven of pale orange reeds, Warkannan kept what few civilian clothes he owned – khaki trousers, shirts to match, a broad-brimmed riding hat, worn brown boots. He dumped the lot on the bed, then looked away, startled at a feeling much like grief. Civilian clothes. Tonight he would be taking off the Great Khan's uniform for the last time. As an honourable retiree he would be allowed to keep his sabre

– *but I'm a traitor,* he thought. *I have no honour. They just don't know it yet.*

'Uncle?' Arkazo laid a hand on his shoulder. 'Is something wrong?'

'No, no, nothing. I'll just go report in to settle my pension. I want our gear properly packed when I get back. Make sure you have a hat with you. The sun's fierce out on the plains.'

Just after sunset, Warkannan and Arkazo were sharing some smuggled wine in the study when Lubahva arrived from the palace. Normally she wore modest dresses and a headscarf when she left the palace grounds, but that evening she'd draped herself with the grey veils of the ultra-orthodox, which turned her into a pious bundle indistinguishable from a thousand other women. Her behaviour, however, was far from restrained. She giggled while she tipped the old servant and made a show of lifting her veil to give Warkannan a kiss. Once the servant was gone, Lubahva sat down on a divan and pulled the veil off to reveal her black hair, done up in rows of beaded braids.

'Are you sure this is safe?' Warkannan said.

'Why not?' She smiled briefly. 'I told them I was on my way to a women's prayer service, and I am. I've just stopped by for a minute with news. A Kazrak rode out from one of the northern border forts, a merchant saying he was going to take his goods out to the Tribes.'

'Oh really? With the chance of running into prowling ChaMeech? That I don't believe. We'll leave from the north and try to catch up with him.'

'You're really going to go through with this?'

'I don't have any choice. Arkazo and I are leaving tomorrow. The sorcerer's joining us on the road.'

'Ah, Soutan!' Lubahva said with a sigh. 'Well, even fake magicians can carry letters. All right. I'll keep in touch with Indan while you're gone.'

As they walked to the door, she veiled herself, but she left the panel over her face down for one last kiss.

'Idres?' she said. 'Will I ever see you again?'

'That's up to God, isn't it? I hope so.'

'I suppose it is, yes. I'll miss you.'

'I'll miss you, too. Remember me in your prayers.'

'Every day. I promise.'

Lubahva pulled up the veil, turned fast and started off down the path to the street. Watching her shoulders tremble, Warkannan realized that she was weeping. He was honestly surprised.

Deep in the night, after Arkazo had gone to bed, Warkannan put on his civilian khakis, hid a dagger in his shirt and took a stout walking stick as well, then hurried through the dark streets to Indan's townhouse, some five blocks uphill from the compound owned by Hazro's family, the Mustava clan. At the back gate Indan's mayordomo, a man with years of loyalty behind him, met him in the darkness. Together they rolled the wicker basket down the silent mews to the Mustava garden. The white wall stood too high for the pair of them to lift or throw the grisly contents over. A porter's little hut at the back gate, however, stood empty. Warkannan rolled the basket inside, tipped the mayordomo, then hurried away, trotting through back alleys, keeping out of the occasional pool of lantern light. He met no one and returned to his bungalow without waking Arkazo.

Warkannan lingered in the city the next morning to hear the news about Hazro's corpse. It reached him early in the person of a light-skinned eunuch, Aiwaz, the supervisor of the court musicians, who knew both the Mustavas and the Warkannans. Swathed in white gauze robes he waddled into Warkannan's living room and stood shaking his head, his face deathly pale, while he repeatedly wiped his mouth with a yellow handkerchief.

'It was horrible,' Aiwaz said. 'Hazro's father found the body. He went down to unlock the back gates, and there it was.'

'What?' Warkannan did his best to look shocked. 'Just thrown onto the street?'

'No. Here's the fiendish part. There was a basket there, smelling of spice, just as if someone had left some sort of gift. Inside was the body.' Aiwaz paused, swallowing heavily. 'Mutilated. Cut and burned in the cuts. The poor old man fainted. Just let out one sob and fainted.'

Warkannan looked away fast. His memory of that night in Indan's attic rose up and sickened him. He had never thought that Hazro's father would find the thing himself.

'Yes, the poor old man.' Warkannan could hear his voice choking on the words. 'I'm so sorry.'

'So are we all.' Aiwaz dabbed his mouth again. 'Of course, none of the Mustavas could possibly know who did this.' He raised a plucked eyebrow significantly. 'But the boy's uncle swears he'll have his revenge. He seems to know whom he'd *choose* for a suspect.'

'Ah, yes, I see what you mean.'

They shared a grim smile. Warkannan turned away to find Arkazo, wearing only a pair of white trousers, standing in the hall that led back to the bedrooms. From a window sunlight fell across his pale brown chest in a stripe and left his face in shadow. The boy stood with his back against the door jamb as if he thought someone might attack him from behind.

'It's a horrible thing,' Aiwaz repeated. 'I'd best be on my way. A couple of other families need to hear the news.'

Warkannan showed him out, then turned back to his nephew. Arkazo took a couple of uncertain steps into the room, staring at Warkannan as if at a stranger.

'You're wondering how I could do such a thing,' Warkannan said.

Arkazo nodded.

'Because all our lives depended on it. Because our khan's life depends on it.'

Arkazo looked away, his shoulders high as if he feared a blow. Warkannan could hear Lazzo clattering dishes in the kitchen. The sound seemed to ring as loud as gongs.

'Do you still want to go along on this ride?' Warkannan said at last.

'Yes.' Arkazo turned back to him. 'I just –' He paused for a long moment. 'I didn't realize it was – well – real before. I mean, the whole idea of riding east and all that. It seemed like one of those stories they tell in the coffee houses.' He forced a twisted smile. 'It sure as hell doesn't feel like that any more.'

'Good. This is going to be the hardest ride of your life. Remember that.'

'I will, sir.'

'Good. Now get something to eat and get dressed. We've got to get on the road.'

Arkazo nodded and trotted back down the hall to his room.

Once they were ready to leave, Warkannan attended to one last detail while Arkazo went to fetch their horses. He wrote a letter to Indan asking him to take care of Lazzo and gave it to the old servant to carry out to the villa.

'It'll be a long walk for you, Lazzo, but you don't dare stay here once I'm gone. Indan will tell you why.'

Lazzo's pouchy eyes widened in fear.

'Don't linger, no,' Warkannan said. 'Leave before sunset, just in case. Don't worry about the furniture. The Chosen are welcome to it if they want it.'

Warkannan gave him a small bag of coins for the trip, then slung his saddlebags over his shoulder and strode out. Soon, if the Lord allowed, by bringing Jezro home he would be freeing Haz Kazrak from a madman.

Nehzaym heard about their departure later that same day. She was working on her payroll accounts out in the warehouse office when Lubahva arrived, her arms full of bags and boxes from the shops. She laid them down on the floor, dropped her grey veils on top of them, and pulled a high stool over to Nehzaym's desk. She perched on it with a sigh and wiggled her feet as if her sandals pained her.

'Idres and Arkazo are leaving today,' Lubahva announced. 'They wanted to get an early start, so I suppose they're gone.'

'Well, it's a good bit after noon now,' Nehzaym said. 'I was beginning to worry about you.'

'I know, I'm sorry. I had a lot of shopping to do for the secluded girls.'

'All right.' Nehzaym laid down her pen. 'I'm glad that things are finally moving. The longer Soutan stayed in Haz Kazrak, the more anxious I got.'

'I hope the Chosen don't suspect Idres, is all. He'd never break under torture, but I bet he'd tell them everything to save his nephew from it.'

Nehzaym felt her stomach clench. There was so much to fear, and all the time. 'That's true. Kaz has always been more like Idres' son than his nephew.' Nehzaym turned her palms upward. 'Inshallah.'

'Yes, whatever the Lord wills.' Lubahva paused, thinking. 'Are we meeting again tonight? I don't have a rehearsal, so I could come.'

'I don't think it's wise. You came here last night, and you've been out of the palace all morning. The eunuchs might wonder about you if you stay out for the evening as well.'

'I can tell them the truth. They know we meet for women's

prayers. I don't have to tell them what we're praying for.'

'Yes, but the Chosen also know that Soutan's part of my new business venture. I don't want anyone adding things up.'

'You're right about that.' Lubahva considered, sucking on her lower lip. 'The Fourth Prophet. Do you truly think she'll be female?'

'That's what the Sibyl's prophecies tell us.'

'But what if the mullahs are right, and she's a demon?'

'The mullahs condemn anything they don't understand. Now remember: we can't tell if the Fourth Prophet's meant to come in our lifetime. All we can do is watch and wait.'

'But – no, you're right. I won't carp any more. If she comes to us, she comes. Inshallah.'

'Oh yes. Inshallah.' Nehzaym suddenly smiled. 'But if she does come, she'll find us waiting.'

On their second day out of Haz Kazrak, Warkannan and Arkazo met up with Soutan in the little resort town of Samahgan, famous for its hot springs. So many people flowed into and out of its spas and medical clinics that no one would question why a retired cavalry officer and his ward would turn up at the same hotel as a foreigner like Soutan. Still, all three of them pretended to great surprise when they met in the dining room. Soutan made a show of insisting they eat with him.

'It's good to see a familiar face,' Soutan said. 'I'm leaving tomorrow, though.' He paused, letting a waiter get within earshot. 'I have to be back in Haz Kazrak to meet with the bankers.'

'We're moving on ourselves.' Warkannan spoke clearly for the benefit of a passing group of customers. 'Now that I'm retired, I'm going to visit my sister, Arkazo's mother, that is. She lives up in Merrok.'

'Give me the address. When I know how much working capital we can raise, I'll send you a letter.'

The waiter, young and shiny clean in his loose white pants and white tunic, showed them to a low table surrounded by velvet cushions. Soutan had chosen an expensive establishment. The dining room held a good fifty tables placed on fine carpets. True-wood panels hung from the reed and bamboid walls. The men all sat, arranging themselves while a young servant girl dressed in a white shift brought warm water, towels, and a large basin. The waiter rattled off the evening's menu as they washed their hands, then helped the girl carry the utensils away. Soutan leaned close to Warkannan and spoke quietly.

'We've had great luck, or else the Great Khan has had very bad luck. Either might be possible.'

'I suppose so, if you want to split hairs,' Warkannan said. 'What was it?'

'I was in the marketplace yesterday when I saw two cavalrymen ride in. They were official messengers from the look of their saddlebags, and they rode straight to the fort here in town.' Soutan paused, glancing around him. 'I have ways of learning things. They were carrying messages to Blosk.'

'I'm sure they would have told anyone who asked them that.'

'Indeed? Would they and their fort commander tell anyone who asked what the messages said?' Soutan paused for another look round. 'One of my spirits followed them into the post. They were discussing a certain officer down on the border who's about to get cashiered and turned out of the cavalry. Both of them thought the situation was odd for some reason.'

'So?' Arkazo leaned forward to interrupt. 'What does that have to do –'

The waiter came back, bowing and smiling. They ordered, he bowed again, three, four times, then strode away at last.

'If the Chosen are sending a man east,' Soutan said to Arkazo, 'he'd never make it across the Rift alone. This time of year the Tribes come to the border, and he might well be able to travel with one of them.'

Arkazo's mouth framed an 'oh'. The waiter came back with a large brass tray of appetizers and set them down with a flourish.

'Your first course, gentlemen,' he said. 'Shall I bring coffee?'

'No, not yet,' Warkannan said. 'At the end of the meal.'

With narrow eyes Soutan watched the waiter leave. 'I wonder if that boy is just a waiter,' he remarked. 'Probably so.'

'Probably.' Warkannan allowed himself a brief smile. 'We'll talk more once we're in our cottage. You can see what it's like, Soutan, to live with the threat of the Chosen.'

'Yes, I can. I can't say I like it.'

After the meal they left the dining room and walked outside, heading for the gardens and their guest cottage. Beside the outer doors crouched a woman, her face bound with the black ribbons of widowhood. Two small children clung to her.

'Charity, sirs?' she whispered and held out trembling hands. 'Charity, oh please?'

The others hurried past, but Warkannan stopped. Beggars here, in wealthy Samahgan, even here! He fished a couple of silver deenahs out of his pocket and pressed them into her hand.

'May God provide better,' he said. 'And soon.'

Out to the east of the khanate, all of the grass grew purple. No one kept a garden or tilled a field on the other side of the sunset-coloured hills that marked the khanate's border. A treaty dating back to Landfall forbade it, a pact so sacred that not even the ambitions of the Third Prophet could force the Kazraks to break it. Besides, without the open grasslands, there would be no horse-herds, and without a large number of horses the Kazraks would have no cavalry. All ambitions would become empty, then.

On the night that Warkannan was dining in Samahgan, the Tribes brought their stock into the border town of Blosk for the spring horse fair. The comnees, as the travelling groups were called, came out of the lavender grasslands, herding their horses ahead of them. Most rode, but some of the women drove rickety orange wagons, made of lashed-together bamboid, heaped with their possessions. Down by the river that flowed near town, they set up round tents stitched together in a patchwork of coloured saurskins and grey horsehair felt. In the meadows they tethered their horses with tasselled halters and drew the gaudy wagons into a circle. By the third day over a hundred tents stood in clusters out on the grass.

Children ran and played in the impromptu village while their parents brought out hoards of dried horse dung to fuel cooking fires or walked from tent to tent to greet old friends. Everyone talked about the trading ahead. The Great Khan's gold bought the necessities that only farmers could supply, such as grain, soap, and lamp oil, as well as trinkets like brightly coloured cloth and gold jewellery. Men and women both wore gaudy belt buckles, brooches, and clasps for cloaks, cast or hammered into the shapes of mythological beasts, such as the stag, the wolf, and the lion.

Ammadin picked the spot for her maroon and grey tent on the edge of the encampment, a good distance from all this convivial chaos. In silent respect, the members of her comnee, sixteen extended families in all, raised her tent, carried her possessions over from the communal wagons, then left her alone. Inside she arranged her belongings: her roll of blankets, her leather-and-wood folding stool, her two cooking pots, and the four big grey-and-blue woven tent bags that held her clothes and tools. Her most precious belongings never travelled in the wagons. In saddlebags of purple leather she carried her spirit crystals, her silver talismans, and her feathered spirit wands. The god figures of her tribe had their own pair of saddlebags, lined in fine white cloth from the Cantons far to the east.

Ammadin was arranging the god figures on their red-and-white striped rug when Maradin crawled through the tent flap. A blonde, handsome woman with skin the colour of gold, Maradin was the only person who dared enter Ammadin's tent uninvited. She pressed her palms together and bowed to the god figures, squat stone carvings, wrapped in coloured thread and decorated with feathers and precious stones. Only then did she speak.

'Dallador bought some mutton, and he's making stew. Do you want to come eat with us?'

'Yes, thanks. Have the Kazraks got here yet?'

'A couple of their officers rode up a few minutes ago. Apanador's taken them into his tent for some keese.'

In front of Maradin's tent, pieced together from mottled purple and white skins, her husband Dallador was cutting chunks of meat from a haunch and putting them into an iron kettle. Their three-year-old son sat on the ground nearby and watched him. A good-looking fellow with hair so pale it was almost white, Dallador was dressed in the usual leather trousers of the Tribes and a red-and-blue cloth shirt; his belt had a palm-sized gold buckle in the shape of a horse, its legs tucked up, its head turned as if it were looking behind it.

'I hear the Kazraks are in the mood to buy,' Dallador said. 'Are you going to sell that pair of greys?'

'If they're stupid enough to take them,' Maradin said. 'I'll give them a dose of herbs before I bring them over.'

While Dallador tended the stew pot, Maradin brought out wooden drinking bowls and a leather skin of keese, a liquor made of fermented mare's milk. She was pouring it round when Palindor strolled up to the fire. A handsome, almost pretty young man with strikingly large blue eyes and coppery skin, Palindor smiled once at Ammadin, then squatted down beside Dallador.

'I invited Palindor to eat with us,' Maradin announced.

Ammadin felt like kicking her – she was match-making again, damn her! Palindor accepted a bowl of keese with a murmured 'thank you' and looked at the ground. As an unmarried man, he had no standing in the comnee and no horses but the one his mother had given him to ride. He did, however, have a fine reputation as a warrior in the endless squabbles and raids that went on between the comnees. One of the bravest of the brave, men said of him, and as good with the long knife as he was with the bow. For the sake of that, Ammadin did her best to be pleasant to him during the meal.

By the time they were done eating, the skin of keese was empty, and Dallador brought out another. As he was refilling Palindor's bowl, he splashed keese on the back of his unsteady hand.

'Dallo?' Maradin said.

'I know. I've had enough.' Dallador handed the skin to Palindor, then began licking the spilled keese off his hand while he smiled, heavy-lidded, at Maradin, who smiled back as languidly as if she were drunk herself.

All through the camp, fires glowed like golden blossoms among the tents. Here and there, men began to sing to the dahsimmer, a three-stringed instrument, one for the melody, two for the drone. Every time he had a sip of keese, Palindor would look at Ammadin so longingly that she realized that he was in love with her, not merely greedy for the horses a wife would bring him. Ye gods! she thought. What's he doing, taking lessons from Dallo? She got up, excused herself, and went to her tent. Before she closed the flap, she listened for a moment to the clear strong voices of the men, singing of the two things they loved above all else: the hunt and war.

About an hour after dawn, the Kazrak officers rode down from the fort in Blosk to start the day's haggling. The women and girls cut the horses they wanted to sell out of the herds and brought them down to the riverbank in a snorting, prancing procession. Their husbands and brothers stood nearby to make sure the Kazraks treated their women with the proper respect. Every man had the short curved bow slung over his back and in his belt, the leaf-blades steel knife, about eighteen inches long, that marked a man as an adult. In their red tunics, buttoned tight with silver pegs, and grey wool trousers, the Kazrak officers moved stiffly, their backs as straight as arrows.

When Ammadin brought down two bay geldings from her herd, the comnee women fell back to let her have the first place in line. A dark young officer introduced himself to her as Brison and began to examine the bays. He ran practised hands down their legs and over their chests, then looked into their mouths.

'Four-year-olds, huh?'

'Yes, and halter-broken.'

'Very well. A gold imperial each.'

'Two each.'

Brison hesitated, looking at her cloak, the entire black and purple mottled skin of a slasher saur, and a big specimen at that. Even for a comnee woman Ammadin was tall, but although she had the saur's front paws clasped at her neck, the middle feet hung well below her belt and the hind set trailed behind her on the ground. Apparently Brison had been on the border long enough to know what the cloak signified.

'Very well.' He motioned to another officer. 'Give the Holy One what she asked for.'

The assistant counted four gold imperials out of a cloth sack and handed them over. Ammadin put them in the pocket of her leather trousers and walked away without another word.

During the day, other comnees rode up to join the camp. The fair would go on for weeks, though it would migrate as the horses ate down the grass. Outside the town, which lay across the only hill for miles in this part of the grasslands, booths built of bundled rushes stood side by side with peddlers who spread their goods out on old blankets and shepherds selling raw fleeces and baskets of rough-spun yarn. Women hawking food in baskets mingled with the crowd; here and there, a juggler or story-teller performed for a clot of onlookers. Round it all swarmed the tiny flying yellabuhs, scavenging on scraps and spills.

That afternoon Ammadin and Maradin strolled through the market, looked everything over before they bought anything, and stopped every now and then for a cup of Borderland wine, which tasted as light as water for someone used to keese. Since their First Prophet had specifically forbidden wine, the Kazraks weren't supposed to drink it, of course, but here and there a drunken cavalryman staggered through the fair. Ammadin bought fine coloured threads, glass beads, and dyed hen's feathers to use in making magic charms. Maradin bought lengths of striped cloth, woven from the fine light thread spun in the water-powered mills of Kazrajistan. She lingered over a tray of brass buttons.

'I should get some of these for Dallador,' she said.

'Why?' Ammadin said. 'You spoil him, you know, always fussing over him, always buying him things.'

'Well, I happen to love him.' Maradin hesitated, then turned away from the button seller's booth.

'What's wrong?' Ammadin said. 'Something is.'

Maradin shrugged, and they walked a few steps on. 'I just get so jealous when women look at him,' she said at last. 'I remember when I asked him to marry me, and Mama warned me that watching other women chase him would break my heart. She was right. He's not the most handsome man in the world, but there's just something about him. Women do flirt with him. You must have noticed.'

'It would be hard not to.'

'After all, you –'

'That was before you were married.'

'I know, just teasing.' Maradin paused for one of her wicked grins. 'It's odd, isn't it? If you looked at him and Palindor together, you'd think, oh, Palino's so handsome, Dallo's not. But there's something cold about Palindor.'

'Yes, cold and hard, like a face on a Kazraki coin.'

'But my husband –' Maradin hesitated, biting her lower lip. 'My husband's as warm as a winter fire. I was so proud when he said he'd marry me. Now, I worry all the time.'

'Has he ever taken any of these women up on their offer?'

'No. I just keep thinking he'll meet someone with more horses.'

'Maddi! Do you honestly think he'd leave you?'

'I don't know. I don't think so. I just get so jealous and sulky. And then I say things.'

'Things you regret?'

Maradin nodded, looking away.

'What about the men?' Ammadin said. 'There was that fellow the last time we rode to Nannes –'

'Oh, that doesn't bother me. He can't get them pregnant, and they don't have any horses.'

Ammadin knew two kinds of spells and charms, those that worked because they had magic, and those that worked because the wearer thought they did. Love charms fell into the latter category, but usually they did their job.

'I'll bind you a charm,' Ammadin said. 'You can wear it on a thong under your shirt. When you feel jealous, take it out and hold it in your hand, and it will soak up the jealousy.'

'Thank you!' Maradin turned to her with a brilliant smile. 'I should have brought this to you earlier.'

Before heading back to the encampment they stopped for a last cup of wine. Nearby a juggler sent four saur eggs spinning through the air, but the crowd at the wine booth was talking about a different kind of show to be held that afternoon. One of the officers in the fort was going to be publicly cashiered.

'I'll bet they waited until the fair to do it,' a local weaver told them. 'What's the good of shaming a man if there's no one to watch it, eh?'

'Well, true, I suppose,' Maradin said. 'What's he done?'

'I wouldn't know. They flog a man for any little thing out here on the border.'

When the weaver drifted away, Maradin turned to Ammadin.

'Let's go back to camp. I don't have the stomach for things like that.'

'Well, you can go back. I'm going to stay and watch.'

'Ammi! Ugh! How can you?'

'I'm curious, that's all. I don't understand the Kazraks, I never have, but I should, you know. We all should. They're dangerous.'

At that Maradin hesitated, but in the end she left, taking Ammadin's purchases back for her. Ammadin followed the crowd up to the town itself.

Out in front of the thorn walls of the big square fort lay the typical Kazraki public square, a bleak gravelled ground with a stone pillar standing in the centre. Already onlookers lined three sides, jostling for the best view. Things were dull in Blosk. To the sound of a silver horn, the true-wood gates swung open. A contingent of a dozen men marched a young Kazrak officer out to the six-sided pillar while others ordered the pressing crowd to stay back. Ammadin, who was caught against the wall of a house, climbed up on a trash barrel so she could see over the crowd.

Marked by the golden scabbard at his side and the narrow gold stripe down the sleeves of his tunic, the fort commander marched over to the unfortunate officer. At his barked orders, two of the troopers bound the officer's wrists together with one end of a long rope, then tossed the other end over an iron hook embedded halfway up the pillar. When they pulled, they strung him up like a saur carcass hung to bleed so that his feet barely touched the ground. To steady himself the officer had to stretch himself out into a perfect target. Ammadin was close enough to get a good look at him: a handsome man for a Kazrak, with dark curly hair and black eyes above prominent cheekbones. His skin was a rich brown, darker than most of his people. While the commander conferred with the troopers, he stared out in front of him, his face utterly expressionless.

When she heard someone call her name, Ammadin looked round to see Brison, walking up to her unsteady perch on the barrel. He raised his hand palm out in the Kazrak gesture of respect.

'So, the Holy One has come to watch?' Brison said.

'The show was here, so I thought I'd see it. What's he done?'

'It's a strange story. When it was time for my unit to ride here for the fair, we were told to take him with us. He'd volunteered for the horse-buying unit, and I couldn't figure out why anyone would. But a message came in that explained it all. Bad news for poor old Zayn. He'd been sleeping with the wife of this high-and-mighty court official back home, you see, and he figured he had to get out of the hot water before it boiled.' Brison paused to give Ammadin a wink. 'He didn't jump quick enough. Her husband knew about it already, and he pulled strings.'

'What? You'll flog a man for that?'

'Adultery's against the laws of the Prophets.' Brison paused for a sly grin. 'Besides, this old boy has favours to give away, like a reassignment off this damned border.'

Out in the square, the commander yelled for silence. He ceremoniously pulled the sabre, inlaid with the golden crescent, from Zayn's scabbard and threw it on the ground. Zayn set his lips tight and stared out at nothing while the commander unbuckled the sword belt and threw it after the sabre. He took a dagger from his belt, grabbed the hem of Zayn's tunic, and slit it up the back and across the sleeves so that he could pull off the last trace of the khanate's insignia and leave Zayn half-naked where he hung.

'The man who disgraces his regiment disgraces the Great Khan,' the commander said. 'A man who dishonours the reputation of the cavalry will have no honour in any man's eyes.'

Zayn allowed himself a small bitter smile. The commander stepped back and motioned to a trooper. As the trooper unrolled his long leather whip, the crowd pressed closer.

'Begin,' the commander said.

The braided leather thongs uncoiled and hissed through the air to snake across Zayn's bare back. Blood welled up in a thin, precise stripe. Zayn's eyes flickered briefly. Over and over the whip struck, lacing his back with lines of blood. Once he winced; once he made a stifled grunt; slowly his face turned from brown to a muddy grey. Other than that, the bloody stripes might have been no more than the slap of a gloved hand. At the tenth blow, Brison swore and turned away with a shake of his head, but Ammadin watched fascinated. The Tribes admired a man able to bear this kind of pain.

The whip uncurled and flew to him again and again – eleven, twelve, thirteen. Zayn's dark eyes stared fixedly at some distant point, but his face was so pale that Ammadin was afraid that he'd break yet. His back was nothing but blood; the whip bit into old wounds each time it fell. Nineteen, twenty – Zayn tossed his head and grunted under his breath.

'Enough!' the commander barked. 'The Great Khan's justice is done.'

Zayn gathered his breath in a long gulp. 'Is it?' His voice cracked and wavered, but he spoke again. 'You hypocrite!'

The commander snarled like an animal. He raised his arm and turned to the trooper, as if he was going to order a few more stripes, but Ammadin laughed loudly enough for him to hear. He shot a black look her way and said nothing. The panting trooper stepped back and began to clean the blood-soaked whip on a bit of rag. Two others stepped forward. One threw a bucket of water over Zayn's back; the other cut him down. Zayn staggered, stumbled, then pulled himself upright by an effort of will. He even managed to smile at the two troopers when one caught his arm to steady him, a cold bitter smile of blazing hatred that made them step back and leave him alone. At the commander's order, the other troopers came forward and dumped a bedroll and a pair of saddlebags at Zayn's feet. The commander shoved a tiny pouch of what looked like coins into his hand.

'There's your exile's wages,' the commander said. 'Walk wherever you want, but get out of my sight. You have three days to leave Blosk.'

Zayn looked at him, then bent over to pick up the gear on the ground. Ammadin caught her breath; she was expecting him to fall and faint, but slowly and carefully he straightened up again with the load in his arms. With the blood still running on his back, he turned and staggered off. The crowd began to jeer, yelling insults as they moved out of his way, but he held his head high and walked on. Ammadin jumped off her barrel and followed him. When she passed, the crowd fell silent.

Slowly, one painful step at a time, Zayn made his way out of the public square and turned down a narrow alley. He began panting for breath, and at times he staggered, but he kept walking until he'd left the crowd behind. He dropped his gear on the dusty street and leaned against the wall of a house.

'Zayn?' Ammadin said.

When he turned his head to look at her, he moved too fast and fell to his knees. Ammadin squatted down in front of him and spoke in the Kazraki language.

'That's your name, isn't it? Zayn?'

For a moment he merely stared at her; then his mouth twitched as if he wanted to smile. 'Yes,' he said, 'Zayn Hassan.'

'Do you have anywhere to go?'

'No.'

'Come with me if you want. I can use a man like you to tend my horses.'

He reached out a hand twined round with a runnel of blood and touched the edge of her saurskin cloak. 'A witchwoman. Why would you bother helping the likes of me?'

'Because you've got guts. And it seems a little harsh to be treated this way for bedding a woman who wanted you.'

Zayn managed a thin smile.

'I thought so.'

He fainted, falling at her feet. Ammadin got up and went to the mouth of the alley. Out in the street four young comnee men hurried along, heading for the centre of town. She recognized none of them.

'You!' Ammadin called. 'Come over here!'

They stopped, scowling, turned, hands on knife hilts. The tallest of them suddenly smiled.

'It's a spirit rider,' he said. 'We're coming, Holy One. What do you want us to do?'

'Carry this man and his gear back to my camp.'

The four trotted over and did what she asked.

Ammadin had them lay Zayn face-down in the grass behind her tent, then sent for Orador, the man who knew wound lore. He was a portly man, Orador, with a long drooping moustache, mostly grey, and a round face to match his belly. A young apprentice brewed herb-water at Ammadin's fire while the master looked over Zayn's wounds. Carefully he washed the blood off Zayn's back with the herb-water, then poured keese over the stripes. When the liquor hit, Zayn's fingers dug into the grass like a saur's claws, but he made no noise at all.

'That'll keep the evil spirits away,' Orador said cheerfully. 'No bandages for you, boy. Air's the best thing for these shallow wounds, and the bleeding's stopped already.'

With a long sigh, Zayn turned his head and looked at Ammadin, hunkered down near him in the grass. His eyes were as distant from his pain as if he were merely taking the sun.

'How soon can he ride?' Ammadin said.

'Today if I have to,' Zayn whispered.

Orador laughed under his breath. 'I like your guts, but you'll need to rest for a couple of days, at least.'

'Easy enough,' Ammadin said. 'The comnee won't be riding for a while. When we do leave, Zayn, we'll be heading east.'

'Good.' Zayn smiled briefly. 'I've always been curious about the east.'

All at once, Ammadin felt danger, an odd intuition that seemed to rise out of no particular cause. For a moment she considered Zayn, lying utterly still in his exhaustion, his back as raw as a piece of freshly butchered meat. The warning came to her as the scent of anger. Puzzled, she stood up and found Palindor standing nearby with his arms crossed tightly over his chest. When he caught her glance, he turned on his heel and strode off. So that's it! Ammadin thought. Well, I can handle a jealous young colt like him easy enough. She left Zayn under Orador's care and went to find Apanador to tell him that she had a servant and the comnee a new rider.

After they left Samahgan, Warkannan led his men north rather than straight east, just as if he were indeed going to visit Arkazo's family in their country villa. In this province, Zerribir, the larder of Kazrajistan, the land stretched out flat in a broad valley, all gold and red with crops – wheatian, oil beans, breadmoss, vegetables – tended by farmers who lived in white-washed cottages set among the rosy fields.

Graceful mosques, built of white-washed true-oak and adorned with minarets, rose out of the magenta view. Five times a day they heard the call to prayer, either carried on the wind from a distant spire or close at hand from a wayside shrine. They would dismount and stand in the road, holding their horses' reins in one hand while they raised the other to point towards the sky, just as the Second Prophet had taught his people to pray when they were outside. Soutan would stand to one side, watching. One late afternoon Warkannan had enough of seeing him sneer.

'And just what are you smirking about?' Warkannan said.

'Nothing.' Soutan wiped the smile off his face. 'Tell me something, Captain. Do you know what you're pointing at?'

'Of course. The holy city of Mekka.'

'Which exists up in the air, floating along?'

'Don't be stupid! It's a symbol of Paradise, where Mohammed's soul went when he died.'

'Ah. What would you say if I told you it was a real city, made of wood and vines like any other?'

Warkannan considered a number of blunt insults but discarded them. 'Of course it was,' he said instead. 'Back in the Homelands somewhere. In a desert, if I remember rightly. That doesn't mean it can't have some sort of symbolic meaning as well.'

'Yes, it was in a desert.' Arkazo joined in. 'And it was made of stones and mortar, not vines. They didn't have as many earthquakes back in the Homelands.'

'Very good.' Soutan favoured him with a small smile. 'There may be more to your mind than I thought.'

Arkazo's face brightened with rage, but Warkannan cut him off. 'Let's get going,' he snapped. 'I want to make a few more miles before sunset.'

In this flat country the well-kept roads made travelling easy. Warkannan and his men managed a good twenty-five miles a day at a smooth, steady walk. Now and again they pulled their horses to the side of the road to allow a closed carriage to clatter past, drawn by four matched horses, carrying the womenfolk of some rich man behind its curtained windows. More often the roads ran beside canals, where they saw horse-drawn narrowboats glide by, piled high with produce.

'It's peaceful here,' Soutan remarked one morning. 'Peaceful and prosperous.'

'For now it is,' Warkannan said. 'If there's another round of new taxes, I don't know what people are going to eat. The salt tax has damn near broken the farmers as it is. They have to work out in the sun, and salt's no luxury to them. That's something that Gemet will never understand, the greedy bastard – hard work and what it does to a man.'

'Unfortunately, you're quite right. I have no doubt that Jezro will take a very different view of the matter.'

'Neither do I. God blessed us when He spared Jezro.'

'As he damn well should, considering all the trouble you people have gone to for his sake.'

'Now just what do you mean by that?'

'Only that you left the Homelands to come here. Haven't you ever wondered about those Homelands, Captain?'

Warkannan considered as they rode past a long maroon field of vegetables. Out among the rows farmers were harvesting, cutting leaves and piling them high in baskets. He could hear them singing as they worked.

'From what I understand,' Warkannan said at last, 'we're a lot better off here. The Homelands were filled with infidels and evil magic. It was so bad that the great Mullah Agvar was afraid the true faith would be lost.'

Soutan rolled his eyes heavenward. 'No doubt that's what you've been taught. Don't you ever wonder if it's true?'

'No. Why would I? The mullahs are the ones who have all the old books and such. They'd know the truth.'

'Maybe. What if they're not telling the truth, though?'

'Why wouldn't they?'

'To keep you from regretting what you've lost, the Homelands, I mean.'

'Why would I regret a pack of filthy infidels and their tame demons?'

Soutan looked at him for a long moment, eyes wide in exaggerated amazement. 'You belong in a museum, Captain,' he said finally. 'A pure example of a pure type.'

'Now, watch it, Soutan!'

Soutan flinched as if he expected a blow. 'Sorry. Didn't mean to be insulting.'

Warkannan snorted, then changed the subject.

As they travelled north, they stopped now and then at a cavalry fort to see if they could pick up gossip or news that might point them to the Chosen's spy. Warkannan's twenty years of service had left him with plenty of friends, many of them stationed at one or the other of the chain of cavalry forts that bound the khanate together. It was at Haz Anjilar that he heard more about the officer cashiered out at Blosk.

Warkannan had left Soutan and Arkazo at the inn and gone alone to pay a courtesy call upon the commander, a colonel named Hikko who had once shared a border posting with him. Over glasses of arak, they agreed that the cavalry wasn't what it used to be, that the young officers nowadays were slack and ill-educated, and that the enlisted men lacked a proper respect for authority.

'What we need,' Hikko said, 'is a war. A good long campaign against the ChaMeech – now that would weed out the unfit. There'd be none of this lying around the barracks and arguing with the sergeants then.'

'Can't blame the men, I suppose,' Warkannan said. 'When you consider what they've got for officers.'

'Now that's true.' Hikko shook his bald head sadly. 'I've got a story along those lines. A fellow named Zayn Hassan. Everyone said he had a brilliant career ahead of him. He was stationed in Bariza, on his way up, but he couldn't keep his hands off of some official's wife.'

'What happened to him?'

'He ended up cashiered, that's what. Down in Blosk, they flogged him and turned him out. A comnee took him in, apparently. But you know what's damned odd? No one knows the name of this very important cuckold or his wife. You'd think the womenfolk would have spread the gossip over half the khanate.'

Warkannan found himself very sober very fast. 'Yes,' he said. 'You'd think so. How many lashes did this Hassan get?'

'Twenty.'

While Hikko poured himself more arak, Warkannan considered the matter. Twenty stripes – the thought made him wince. Would the Chosen inflict them on one of their own just to make his story more convincing? Possibly, considering what they were, but not likely. When Hikko offered him the bottle, Warkannan shook his head.

'I've had plenty, thanks. You know, the husband in the Hassan case could have spread money around to keep his name out of it. Who wants to be known as a cuckold?'

'Now that's true. And the fellow must have been rich as a khan to get the cavalry to take his revenge for him.'

'Rich or well-connected.'

'That too. Damned poor way to run an army, letting civilians meddle with discipline, but there you are.'

Warkannan found himself thinking about Zayn Hassan as he walked back to the inn. Something about the story nagged at him. He kept coming back to the lack of names and realized that the tale required more detail to be fully convincing as juicy gossip. Still, Blosk lay nearly four hundred miles to the south, while Haz Evol, where their other suspect had turned up, stood only a hundred and eighty to the east. Warkannan decided they'd best stick with their original plan.

On the morrow they left Haz Anjilar early. Some five miles along the khan's highway they rode up to an intersection where a square-cut stone pillar stood in a little island at the cross of the roads. Carved arrows pointed north to Merrok, west to Kazrikki-on-Sea, south back the way they'd come, and east to Haz Evol and the border. They paused their horses beside the pillar, and Warkannan pointed to the north road.

'All right, Arkazo,' he said. 'What do you say you keep riding north and take some letters to your mother for me?'

'No!' Arkazo's face flushed scarlet. 'You said I could come! I mean, with all due respect, Uncle.'

Warkannan laughed. 'Respect, huh? All right, Nephew. I wanted to give you one last chance to stay out of this.'

Arkazo shook his head, glaring at him all the while.

'All right,' Warkannan said. 'I'll just have to pray that your mother forgives me.'

They reined their horses to the east and rode off, heading for the border. Not far along the east-running road the land began rising in a long slope. Ahead a ripple of purple hills stood at the horizon like a fort wall, guarding the civilized life they were about to leave behind.

'And beyond them lie the plains,' Warkannan said to Arkazo.

'And the ChaMeech. It's a damned shame the Third Prophet didn't wipe them out when he had the chance. Kaleel Mahmet, blessed be his name of course, but I can't help wishing he'd driven them across the plains and slaughtered the lot.'

'Indeed?' Soutan snapped. 'They're not animals, Captain. They have language, they have feelings.'

'So?' Warkannan turned in the saddle to look at him. 'They also have weapons, and they'll use them on any H'mai they can.'

'Horseshit! Do they ever attack the Tribes?'

'Oh all right, then. They use them on any Kazrak they can.'

'Now, that's true enough. Of course, they feel they have reason to. Your southern provinces were theirs, originally.'

'Well, hell, they weren't using the land. They turned up there maybe once a year if that.'

'They don't farm. Their culture needs land for other things.'

'Like what? Strolling around admiring the ocean view?'

Soutan rolled his eyes heavenward and sighed with great drama. 'No, but I doubt if I can convince you,' he said. 'There are advantages to seeing things simply, I suppose.'

'And what's that supposed to mean?'

'Think about it, Captain, think about it.' Soutan smiled, then nudged his horse with one foot and pulled ahead to end the conversation.

Warkannan exchanged a look of disgust with Arkazo. They rode on without speaking.

Like all members of the Chosen, Zayn Hassan – whose real name was Zahir Benumar – possessed odd talents that set him apart from normal human beings, but something prosaic had recommended him for this particular mission. Before the Chosen had discovered his existence, Zayn had spent six years on the border in the regular cavalry, where he'd known Idres Warkannan well, a useful thing in the eyes of his superiors, and the reason that they hadn't simply arrested the circle around Councillor Indan and his mysterious sorcerer. When Zayn had insisted that Warkannan would never involve himself in anything the least bit illegal, his superior officers had accepted his opinion, then decided that he was the ideal person to piece together information about Yarl Soutan and Warkannan's investment group.

Zayn had also learned the Tribes' language, Hirl-Onglay, which he spoke with no noticeable Kazraki accent. He had a knack for learning that went far beyond any abstract intelligence. Just from meeting comnee women at the horse fairs he had soaked up more information about their customs than ten Kazraki scholars might have done. He knew, for instance, that the comnees admired a man with endurance and that they'd see his supposed adultery as no crime at all. All his superiors had to do was to ensure that his little charade got itself played out at a horse fair. So far, the plan was working splendidly; he'd even had the sheer good luck to be rescued by a shaman, a spirit rider as the Tribes called them.

But many times in the following days, Zayn had to admit that he had never realized just how much that flogging was going to cost him. He had seen men flogged during his days in the cavalry, but they had endured a few quick stripes, four at the most, delivered by a man who knew them and who kept the lashes as light as he could while his commander watched. Their ordeal had been nothing like his.

That first day Zayn could barely stand, and in fact, Orador insisted he lie prone. The pain burned on his back like a fire dancing on oil. Although he could keep control of his own actions, the world around him ceased to make much sense. People came and went, their voices came and went, the sunlight fell or shadows deepened. Orador's round face would suddenly swim into his field of vision. His broad, scar-flecked hands would shove a piece of leather between Zayn's teeth for him to bite on, then drizzle stinging keese over the wounds. When Zayn came round from the resulting faint, the apprentice's hands, slender but still calloused and scarred, would hold a bowl of water so he could drink. Afterwards Zayn would sleep, only to dream of the flogging all over again and wake in a cold sweat.

Finally, somewhere around noon of the second day he realized that the pain was lessening. He was lying on his stomach in Ammadin's tent when Orador came in, looked over the wounds, and told him that they were scabbing up 'nicely', as the healer put it. While they throbbed, they had stopped burning.

'Don't sit up yet,' Orador said. 'I don't want you breaking them open again.'

'Don't worry,' Zayn said. 'Thank you, by the way.'

'You're welcome. I'll be back around sunset.'

'Wait – can you tell me something? I had a bedroll and some saddlebags when I left the fort.'

'It's all right here.' Orador glanced around, then pointed. 'Over there by the tent flap. Nobody's opened them.'

'Thanks.' Zayn let out his breath in a long sigh of relief. He carried things in those bags that he wanted no one to see, lock picks and other tools better suited to a thief than a soldier. During his initiation into the Chosen, he'd learned that they'd started out back in the Homelands as special military personnel called commandos during dangerous wars that threatened the existence of entire countries. Now, the battles all seemed to be against their own people, though always, or so he'd been told, in service to the laws of the Great Khan.

After Orador left, Zayn stretched his arms out to either side and laid his face against the blanket under him. He found himself wondering yet again what had made him come up with this wretched idea. It's for the Great Khan, he told himself, and for the honour of the Chosen. The Chosen had become his whole life and his reason to live. Before his initiation he had been nothing, worthless – worse than worthless, a man set apart by evil secrets. They had rescued him, or so he saw it, and he owed them any amount of suffering in return. He fell asleep to dream that once again he stood bound to the pillar of blue quartz in the fiery room, a masked officer's glowing knife at his throat, to swear his vow to the Chosen and the Great Khan.

Voices – women's voices – woke him from the dream. Just outside Ammadin was talking with someone, discussing the horse fair. In a few minutes the other voice stopped, and the Spirit Rider lifted the tent flap and came in, carrying a roll of cloth in one hand. She knelt beside him with a thoughtful glance at his back.

'Orador says you're healing,' Ammadin said.

'I am, Holy One,' Zayn said. 'I can think again.'

'That's always good.' She flashed a brief smile. 'Don't push yourself too hard.' She laid a blue-and-green striped shirt down by his head. 'This is for you. Don't put it on until you can stand the feel of it, though.'

'Thanks. I won't, don't worry.'

'Those cavalry trousers of yours are stained all down the back with blood. Other than that, are they still wearable?'

'Oh yes. I'll wash them when I can. I've got another pair anyway. And I've got a hat for riding.'

'Good. I'll let you get back to sleep now.'

Zayn stayed awake, however, to rehearse his new identity. He'd invented all the details of his supposed affair with the official's wife, just in case someone demanded them. He spent a long time drilling himself on the story, along with his new name. Over and over he repeated, both silently and whispered, 'Zahir Benumar is dead. I am Zayn Hassan.' By nightfall he believed it.

When Orador finally allowed him to walk around, Zayn discovered that eighty-three people rode with Ammadin's comnee, ranging in age from two infants to white-haired Veradin, who at ninety could still ride a horse, provided her great-granddaughter helped her mount. With the single exception of Ammadin, all the women were closely related, but the adult men had all come from other comnees. Even so, the men tended to look much alike. To the eyes of most Kazraks, the people of the Tribes all looked alike, men and women both, with their light-coloured hair and pale eyes, fine noses and thin lips, but a trained observer like Zayn could see plenty of differences.

Zayn pretended to make mistakes anyway and endured some good-natured laughter at his expense. One mistake, however, was an honest one. He came out of Ammadin's tent and saw a young man walking past – Dallador, he thought, and hailed him as such. The fellow turned and laughed.

'I'm his cousin,' he said. 'Name's Grenidor.'

'My mistake!' Zayn said. 'I'm sorry.'

As they shook hands, Zayn studied his face. He could have been Dallador's twin.

'Your mothers were sisters?' Zayn said.

'No, we're much more distantly related than that.' Grenidor frowned, thinking. 'Our grandmothers had the same mother. I think. You'd better ask Dallo.'

'Oh, doesn't matter.'

And yet, Zayn felt, it did matter, that two men so distantly related would look so much alike.

After two more days of doing very little, Zayn's back healed enough for him to take over the job of leading Ammadin's horses to water; she owned a stallion, fifteen brood mares, four saddle-broken geldings, and twelve colts and fillies. One of the geldings, a sorrel with a white off-fore, would be his riding horse, she told him, for as long as he was her servant. When, some few days later, the comnee packed up and left Blosk, Zayn could ride well enough to keep up with the communal herd and watch over her stock.

Like all comnee men, he was expected to do the cooking for those in his tent. Since Dallador had gone out of his way to befriend him, Zayn asked him to teach him.

'I don't know a damn thing about cooking. Back home food is women's work.'

'You can't eat very well, then. What do women know about preparing game?'

'Well, we don't eat much game. Sheep and chickens – that's about it for meat.'

Dallador rolled his eyes in disgust. 'Not much of a cuisine. Well, come watch me when I'm cooking. You'll catch on quick enough.'

'Thanks. I appreciate it. I don't even know what's edible out here. We had servants in the officers' mess who took care of all that.'

Dallador laughed. 'First lesson: don't eat anything until I've told you it's not poisonous.'

Since the comnee was hurrying to reach the summer grazing grounds, they never made a full camp at night, but they always raised Ammadin's tent, because it housed the god figures, they told him, and the chief's splendid white and red tent, because he was the chief and no reason more. After a meal at one fire or another, Zayn would take his bedroll and go sleep in the summer grass. In the morning he would return, toss his bedroll into a wagon, and make a fire to cook breadmoss porridge. Ammadin would join him, eat in silence, and then, after a few words about the horses, she would leave, saddling one of the geldings and riding alone in advance of the comnee.

In their brief times together, Zayn studied her. Unlike the rest of the comnee women, she wore little jewellery, only a true-hawk feather hanging from a gold stud in one ear. Her long, blonde hair was bound up in heavy braids, like a crown over her soft, bronzed face, oddly pretty and sensual for such a solitary soul. Her eyes, however, showed nothing but the hardness of someone who keeps a distance from the world. Fittingly enough they were the pale grey of steel.

Zayn had no idea of what to think of her magic, but everyone in the comnee believed in it. Ammadin would at times make them charms out of coloured thread and the chitinous portions of various native insects, 'bugs' as the first settlers had indiscriminately called the smaller life-forms that came their way. Most of the horses in the herd had bluebuh-claw charms in their halters to ward off lameness and colic; the children in the comnee all wore thongs full of reebuh charms around their necks to keep them healthy and free from evil spirits. Since the good health of the Tribes was legendary, and they had nothing between them and illness but the charms, Zayn could only conclude that somehow or other, the magic worked.

The comnee had been travelling nearly a week before he saw hard evidence that Ammadin did know things beyond the reach of ordinary people. Although the sun shone warm in a clear sky, she announced that it was going to rain.

'When that happens, we'll make a real camp and set up all the tents. You can sleep in mine, but you sleep on your side and me on mine. Understand?'

'Never would I offend you, Holy One.'

During the day's ride, Zayn would occasionally look up at the clear sky and wonder what Ammadin would say when the sunset came dry. He never found out, because in the middle of the afternoon the wind picked up, rushing in from the south and making the tall grass bow and ripple like the waves of a purple sea. Ammadin galloped back to the comnee; she rode up and down the line of march to shout orders to make camp. When Zayn looked to the south, he saw clouds piling up white and ominously thick on the horizon. By the time the comnee found a decent campsite near a stream, the sky was filling with thunderheads, racing in before the wind.

Everyone rushed to set up the tents and bring the wagons round into a circle. They unloaded the wagons, piled everything helter-skelter into the tents, then ran to tether the horses. The rain began in a warning spatter of big drops. The women as well as the men kept their shirts dry by stripping them off and tossing them into a tent. Just as they finished tethering the stock, the rain began to fall in sheets, sweeping across the open plains like slaps from a hand. The women clustered around Ammadin to ask her if there was going to be lightning that might panic the herds.

'I don't know yet, but I'll find out. Zayn, you can go get dry.'

Zayn trotted back to her tent. He crawled in, stripped the worst of the water out of his hair, and let himself drip a bit before he put his dry shirt back on. Although a few drops came in the smokehole in the centre of the tent, the leather baffles kept the worst of it out. Zayn was pleased with the tents. About twelve feet across, they were solid, dry, and good to look at, too. It wasn't a bad way to live, he decided, owning only what you could carry. He set to work sorting out their bedrolls, the woven tent bags that hung from hooks on the walls, the floor cloths of thick horsehair felt. When he tried to lay the floor cloths out, the tall grass sprang up and made them billow. He was swearing and trying to tread it down when Dallador joined him.

'I thought you'd need some help. There's a sickle in one of the tent bags. You cut the grass and pile it up under your blankets.'

Although the sickle had a bronze blade, not a steel one, it cut grass well enough. Thread-like leaves, tipped with red spores, fringed each long violet stalk. Dallador showed him how to grab a handful of stalks at the ground and harvest them in a smooth stroke. By the time Ammadin returned, they had the tent decently arranged.

'Will there be lightning?' Dallador said.

'None,' Ammadin said. 'I've already told the women.'

Dallador bowed to her and left.

Ammadin laid two pairs of saddlebags down on her blankets, then knelt beside them. From one set she pulled out a red-and-white rug and the god figures. Zayn saluted them with hands together, then turned his back. It wasn't his place as a servant to watch her set them out.

'You've got some idea of how we live, I see,' Ammadin said.

'Well, I served on the border before. Before this last trip out, I mean.'

'Ah. All right, I'm done now.'

Zayn turned back. Ammadin sat down on her blankets and undid her braids to let the long tangle of golden hair spill over her shoulders and breasts. Zayn had to summon his will to keep from staring at her. She began to comb out her wet hair with a bone comb while he got an oil lamp and set it on the flat hearth stones under the smokehole. Matches he found in a silver box inside one of the tent bags. As the light brightened, he sat down opposite her and noticed a strange pattern of scars on her left shoulder.

'How did you get those scars?' Zayn said. 'They look like some kind of claw mark.'

'That's exactly what they are. The slasher I killed to make my cloak? He got a good swing on me.'

'You killed it yourself?'

'Of course. It wouldn't have any power if someone else did it for me. Spirit riders have to get everything they use for magic by themselves.'

'Makes sense, I suppose. How did you kill it?'

'Arrows first, then a couple of spears to finish him off. He broke the first one.'

Zayn looked her over with a curiosity that had nothing to do with lust. She was about as muscled as a woman could get, he supposed; her shoulders and arms were strongly and clearly defined, heavy with sinewy muscles.

'What's wrong?' Ammadin said. 'You mean your women back home don't kill saurs?'

'Not that I ever heard of.'

'Huh! Your women couldn't even kill a yellabuh if it flew their way.'

Since she smiled, he allowed himself a laugh. She turned to look at him, and as the lamplight caught them her eyes flashed blood-red and glowed. Another movement, and they returned to their normal grey, leaving him to wonder if he'd imagined the change.

'You have to do a lot of difficult things if you're going to ride the Spirit Road,' Ammadin went on. 'I knew that from the moment I decided to ride it.'

'When do you make a decision like that?'

'When you're a child, but they give you plenty of chances later to back down. I left my mother's comnee when I was five to ride with the man who trained me.'

During a lull in the rain, Orador came by to invite Zayn to join the men in Apanador's enormous tent. After the chief's wife left to visit friends, the men of the comnee filed in and sat down round the fire burning under the smokehole. The married men sat in order of age nearest the chief; the unmarried men, Zayn among them, sat farthest away with their backs to the draughty door. Apanador opened a wooden box and took out a drinking bowl, gleaming with silver in the firelight. He filled it from a skin of keese, had a sip, then passed it to the man on his left. As it went round, each man took only a small ritual sip before passing the bowl on. When it came to Zayn, he saw that it was a human cranium, silvered on the inside. Zayn took a sip, then passed it to Palindor, who looked him over with cold eyes.

Once they'd emptied the ritual cup, Apanador filled ordinary ground-stone bowls and passed them round. The men drank silently and looked only at the fire unless they were reaching for a skin of keese. This was the right way to drink, Zayn decided, with neither courtly chatter nor the kind of bragging men do just to be bragging. Finally, after everyone had had three bowls, Apanador spoke.

'It's time to make some decisions about this summer.'

The unmarried men laid their bowls down and got up to leave. When Zayn followed them out, Palindor caught his arm from behind in the darkness. Out of sheer reflex, Zayn nearly killed him. He had his hunting knife out of his belt and in his hand before he even realized what he was doing, but just in time he caught himself, stepped back, and sheathed it. Palindor smiled at the gesture.

'Listen, Kazrak. The Holy One was good enough to pick you off the street like a piece of garbage. Treat her with the respect she deserves, or I'll kill you.'

'I have every intention of treating her the way I'd treat the Great Khan's favourite wife.'

'Good. I'll make sure you do.'

His tone of voice challenged, but Zayn had trained his emotions too highly to take offence. With a shrug, he walked off in the rain and left the comnee man scowling after him.

In the tent Zayn found Ammadin sitting close to the flickering lamp. Beside her, on a piece of blue cloth, lay four smooth spheres of transparent crystal, each a good size for cupping in a hand. The lamp light shone through one sphere and cast on the tent wall curving shadows of numbers and strange symbols. He focused his mind and captured a memory picture of them. When he returned to the khanate he would draw it for his superiors. Ammadin noticed him staring at the shadow.

'There are tiny numbers engraved all around each crystal, like a sort of belt,' she said. 'That's what you're seeing.'

'Interesting,' Zayn said. 'But should I be looking at them? I'll leave if I'm breaking one of your Banes.'

'It's perfectly all right. They're just glass at the moment. They don't have any power unless you know the incantations that wake their spirits.'

As he sat down on his bedroll, Zayn tried to look solemn instead of sceptical. In the dim light, the crystals glittered as if they were faceted, but their surfaces appeared perfectly smooth.

'Can the spirits answer questions?'

'Oh yes, but only certain kinds.'

'Can they tell me why Palindor hates me?'

'What?' Ammadin looked up with a laugh. 'I don't need spirit power to answer that. Palindor wants to marry me, and here you are, sleeping in my tent.'

It was just the sort of thing that might get in the way of his mission.

'I can sleep outside under a wagon.'

'Why? I'm not going to marry him, and he'll have to get used to it. If he gives you any trouble, just tell me. I said you could sleep here, and that's that.'

'Look, I'm totally dependent on the comnee's charity. I don't want to cause any trouble.'

'You're a strange man for a Kazrak. Which reminds me. I've been meaning to ask you something. Every other Kazrak I've ever known prayed to your god five times a day. You don't. Why? No one here would say anything against it, if that's what's bothering you.'

Zayn froze. He could never tell her the truth, could never admit that men like him were forbidden to pray, that prayers from such a polluted creature would only offend the Lord.

'Uh well,' he said at last. 'I do pray, but silently. Usually we're riding when the time comes, and I don't want to advertise my piety or anything like that. The Lord won't mind.'

'The Lord? I thought his name was Allah.'

'That's not a name, it's a title. It just means "the lord," in the sacred language.'

Ammadin nodded, then took pieces of cloth from her saddle-bags and began wrapping up the spirits. She laid each crystal down in the exact centre of a cloth, then folded the corners over in a precise motion while she murmured a few strange syllables under her breath. Once wrapped, each went into a separate soft leather pouch; while she tied a thong around the mouth, she chanted again. As he watched this long procedure, Zayn felt his body growing aware of her. There they were, in the dim tent together, with the rain drumming a drowsy rhythm on the roof.

She was a comnee woman, not one of the chastity-bound girls at home. Ammadin raised her head and looked at him.

'No.'

Zayn nearly swore aloud. What had she done, read his thoughts? When she looked him over as if she could see through his eyes and into his soul, all his sexual interest vanished. He got up and busied himself with arranging his bedroll on the far side of the tent.

The rain came down intermittently all night. When the morning broke grey with clouds, the comnee decided to stay in camp. After he tended the horses, Zayn went to Dallador's tent mostly because Ammadin had told him to leave her alone – to work, she said, and he wondered what strange ritual she had in hand.

A fire burned on the hearth stones under the smokehole, and Dallador sat near it, carving slices of a red animal horn into the little pegs used to fasten shirts and tent bags. His small son sat nearby and watched solemnly and silently where a Kazraki boy would have been pelting his father with questions. Zayn joined them and studied the way Dallador cut peg after peg with no wasted motion.

'Can I ask you something?' Zayn said at last.

'What?'

'It's about Ammadin. Uh, is there something odd about her eyes?'

'Very.' Dallador looked up with a quick grin. 'You've seen them flash, I'll bet.'

'Yes. I certainly did.'

'That's the mark of the spirit riders. It shows up when a child's about as old as Benno here. That's how the parents know their child's going to be a spirit rider.'

'What if a person didn't have those eyes but wanted to study the lore anyway?'

'They wouldn't have a hope in hell. No one would teach them. It's a sign that they can see things ordinary people can't. If they have the spirit eyes, then they have spirit ears, too, and they can hear spirits talking.'

'Hear spirits? How?'

'How would I know?' Dallador smiled briefly, then laid his knife down and considered the little heap of horn pegs. 'That's enough to last us a while. Now let me show you how to shell land-shrimp. I found a whole nest of them this morning, and if they're cooked right, they're pretty tasty.'

When Zayn returned to Ammadin's tent, he brought her a skewer of grilled land-shrimp and some salted breadmoss in a polished stone bowl. He found her sitting cross-legged on her blankets with her saddlebags nearby.

'That smells good,' Ammadin remarked.

'Dallador's teaching me how to cook.'

He handed her the food, then laid his palms together and greeted the god figures before sitting down opposite her. She plucked a shrimp off the skewer, bit into it, and smiled.

'Very good.'

While she ate, Zayn considered the god figures, sitting on a multi-coloured rug opposite the tent flap. There were six of them in all, most about a foot high, carved of different coloured stones, then decorated and dressed with cloth and feathers. One figure was obviously human, but the others – he'd never seen creatures like them before. Two were roughly human in shape, but the green one had scales and a wedge-shaped head like a ruffled lizard's, and the small black one had what appeared to be fish's gills pasted on either side of its chest. Another seemed to be only half-finished: a torso, studded with bits of gold to represent what might have been eyes, rose from an ill-defined mass of grey stone. The fifth had furled wings of stiffened cloth, huge in relation to its frail, many-legged body, and the sixth, the largest of them all, resembled a worm with leather tentacles at one end and paddle-shaped chips of shell stuck at the other.

'What do you think those are?' Ammadin said abruptly.

'Well, your gods. Or representations of them, I should say. I know you don't worship the bits of stone, of course.'

'Of course.' She smiled, but only faintly. 'Why do you think our gods look so strange?'

'I have no idea.'

'Neither do we.'

He waited for her to say more, but she merely finished her meal. When she handed him the dirty bowl he went to wash it out in the stream. Night had fallen, and the storm clouds had broken up. He could see the last of them off to the north, a lighter smudge on a dark horizon. When he turned to the east he saw the Spider glittering in the sky, a huge spiral of distant light, but the Flies had already set.

Zayn hunkered down at the stream bed and scrubbed the remnants of food out of the bowl with the side of his hand. Little flashes of blue light in the water greeted this gift from the heavens – tiny fish, dotted with luminescence, snapped at the crumbs as they sank. As a boy he'd wondered if the animals in grass and stream believed that their gods were the humans, those baffling beings who fed them or killed them according to some whim. We'd look just as strange to them as those bizarre little fetishes do to me, he thought. And what of Ammadin's remark? *Neither do we.* Somehow, he knew, it held a challenge.

With the rising of the pale sun the comnee struck camp and moved on. Since the day promised heat, Ammadin folded up her saurskin cloak and put it away in its special tent bag. She had Zayn saddle her grey gelding, then rode out ahead, where she could think away from the noise and dust of the herds and wagons. No one, of course, questioned her leaving. Her people assumed that on her lonely rides Ammadin worked magic for the good of the comnee, perhaps invoking spirits to gain hidden knowledge or maybe driving away evil with powerful spells. In one way she was riding alone for their good, she supposed. How would it affect her people if they knew that their spirit rider, the guardian of their gods, their defender from dark forces, their healer and spiritual leader, was rapidly losing her faith in gods and magic both? Better that she take herself away than let her doubts show.

All around her the lavender grasslands stretched out to an endless horizon. As she rode, the grass crackled under her horse's hooves. Yellabuhs swarmed but never bit. Now and again turquoise-blue winged lizards leapt from the grass and flew off, buzzing furiously at these huge intruders. Otherwise, nothing moved in the summer heat, nothing made a sound. Here and there she saw a cluster of blood-red pillars rising from the grass that meant distant spear trees and thus water. Eventually, when the sun was reaching its zenith, she headed for one of the groves to give her horse and herself some relief from the sun.

Along a violet stream bank, the red spears leapt from the earth and towered, far taller than a rider on horseback. Close up they appeared to have grown as a single leaf, wound around and around on itself to the thickness of a child's waist, but down at the base, hidden by a clutter of mosses and ferns, were the traces of old leaves that had died back and withered. The spears grew in clumps from long tuberous roots, spiralling out from a mother plant. How the mother plants got their start, no one knew.

Ammadin unsaddled her gelding and let him roll, then led him to the stream to drink. When he finished she got a tin cup from her saddlebags and scooped up water for herself. She drank, then took off her floppy leather hat and poured a couple of cups of water over her head. While the horse grazed she sat on the bank in the blessed shade and gazed into the stream, running clear over pale sand. In a little eddy grew skinny reddish-brown leaves, trailing in the current, and among the leaves lay a clutch of spirit pearls, milky-white spheres about the size of a closed fist, that were absolute Bane for anyone, even a spirit rider, to harm in any way. Rarely did one find them in a stream this small and this far west of the Great River.

Ammadin ached to know what lay inside them. Something alive, like a lizard chick in its egg? It seemed a good guess. The name, spirit pearl, made no sense. Down at the southern seacoast there were Kazraks who dove to bring up shells with pearls inside – hard little things, no bigger than a fingernail. But since spirits had no bodies, they could never lay eggs, no matter how much like eggs these seemed. At times, when the sun struck the water very late or very early in the day, and a spirit pearl sat in just the right place, the light would seem to flow through it, and then she would see the faint shadow of something that might have been a curled chick. If she could only lift one out and hold it up to the light of a lamp, like the farmers on the Kazrak side of the border did with the eggs of their chickens and meat lizards, she would be able to settle the question once and for all, but the Bane upon them stopped her.

Bane ruled the life of the plains. This plant must never be eaten, that stream must never be forded. If anyone found a pure white stone, he had to leave it in place. Spirits lived in certain fern trees and might offer a shaman help. Other spirits in other trees were pure evil and had to be avoided at all costs. If anyone found a green plant, whether grass or flower, growing outside of Kazraki gardens, she had to pull it up immediately and throw it onto the next fire she saw. For years as a child she had memorized lists of these Banes and learned how to place them into her memory in such an organized way that she could sort through them at need. She remembered the boredom of those years so well that she felt like weeping still.

Why not just write them down, as the Kazraks wrote their lore? That, too, was Bane. The lists of Banes existed only in the spirit language, which could never be written down.

And why did that particular Bane exist? Her teacher had told her that the spirits disliked having their language frozen into letters, something that made no sense to Ammadin, not that she would have dared to say so. After all, the spirits never minded that shamans spoke their language to talk together about the most mundane things; some even used it to tell funny stories about Kazraks. Still, Bane was Bane, beyond argument.

Who laid down the Banes? The gods, of course. Of course. She remembered Zayn, making a clumsy attempt to hide his bad manners. At least he'd tried. Every other Kazrak she'd ever met had dismissed the tribal gods as stones and sticks and nothing more. Idols, they called them. But what if they were right? Just whom, or what, did those figures represent, then?

Ammadin got to her feet and looked out over the purple grass, shimmering under the summer sun. If there were no gods, then there were no spirits. If there were no spirits, then how could there be magic? Yet the magic worked. The Tribes people rarely fell ill, the spirit crystals told her things she needed to know, the holy herbs had exactly the effects they were supposed to have. How could there not be spirits and gods?

Or so thought every other shaman out on the grass. None of them shared her doubts, and yet her doubts remained. She could think of only one remedy – to find another spirit rider to watch over her comnee while she herself rode off alone on a spirit quest similar to those she had undertaken as part of her training. If she suffered enough, if she mounted a vigil for long enough, if she had the right dreams, if she saw the right visions, perhaps they would answer the question that had come to consume her life: who were the gods? why did they give us magic?

If she could see them, if they would come to her in vision, once again she could believe. But if they didn't? If she discovered that her doubts were true? Fear clotted in her throat like dried moss.

*   *   *

By late afternoon the heat had grown so bad that the women began to worry about the pregnant mares and new foals. Along a good-sized stream they made an early camp. While the men raised the tents, the women drove the herd into the shade of a stand of spear trees. After the herd had drunk its fill, they tethered the vulnerable mares and foals in the shade and the rest of the herd, as usual, out in the grass. When Zayn offered to help, they laughed at him and sent him back to Dallador's fire.

In a few minutes Apanador joined them, and Dallador brought out a skin of keese and three bowls. In daylight it was allowable to talk over drink, and Dallador and Apanador discussed the long summer ahead while Zayn merely listened.

'When we reach the Great River,' Apanador said, 'we'll have to be careful. We can't turn directly south. Ricador's comnee will be coming up from the coast about then.'

'They'll want another fight, that's for sure,' Dallador said. 'We beat the shit out of them last time.' He glanced at Zayn. 'They tried to steal some of our women's horses.'

'Ah.' Zayn had heard of the feuding out on the plains. 'Do they always ride north the same way?'

'Yes, they have a Bane on them.' Apanador hesitated, then shrugged. 'You don't need to know more.'

'Whatever you say.' Zayn bobbed his head in the chief's direction.

'The hunting should be good this summer.' Apanador changed the subject. 'We'll have to teach you how to handle a bow from horseback.'

'I'd like that,' Zayn said. 'I've always loved hunting.'

'The wild saurs came with us from the spirit country at the birth of the world,' Apanador went on. 'In time you'll learn all about them, Zayn. The gods gave horses to women, and the saurs to us. Horses are fit for women, because they come when they're called. But a man has to hunt his gifts, with the bow we received from the Father of Arrows, back in the dawn of time.'

'I've heard a little about him. He's not a god, is he?'

'No. He was the first comnee man, and his wife was the first comnee woman – Lisadin, Mother of Horses. So you see, there's a lot for you to learn.'

'I'm just grateful you'll teach me.'

'You're the first Kazrak I've ever met who admitted he had things to learn.'

'Well, the only people you've come across are the cavalry. I'll admit it: we're an arrogant lot. Or I was, until I learned what it means to own nothing but dishonour and the charity of strangers.'

Apanador nodded in silent sympathy.

'Ah, you can't judge a herd by the geldings,' Dallador remarked. 'You can't all be like that. I've heard about Kazraki poets, and wise men who write in books, and beautiful women.'

'But they don't come to the border. Come to think of it, I don't suppose any other Kazrak has ever ridden with a comnee before.' Zayn was only speaking idly, but the answer he got sent his mind racing.

'There was one once,' Apanador said. 'I can't remember his name, because he rode with another comnee in the south grazing, and he only stayed with them one summer.' He glanced Dallador's way. 'You were still a boy then.'

'If I heard the story, I don't remember it.'

'Kind of interesting, though,' Zayn remarked. 'What kind of man was he? Another cashiered officer?'

'No.' Apanador thought for a moment. 'Stranger than that. A hunting party found a half-dead Kazrak, just lying there bleeding in the grass. His wounds looked like they'd been made with a ChaMeech spear, but when they took him back to the tents, he told them that he was an enemy of your great chief, and the chief's assassins had tried to kill him. He kept saying that he wanted to die because he had nothing to live for, but they bound his wounds and told him he'd change his mind later. So then, some of the young men found his horse. It must have fled when its rider fell, you see, and it was wandering around half-starved thanks to those metal bits you people use. Once he had the horse back, this Kazrak suddenly decided he wanted to live after all, because there was a piece of jewellery in his saddlebags that meant the world to him. If he ever said what it was, I never heard.'

'That's a damned strange story. Was he a travelling merchant, then?'

'Oh no, one of your cavalry officers, which makes it even stranger.' Apanador paused for a rueful sort of smile. 'He was still afraid, though, that the great chief's men would find him and finish their botched job, so when the comnee went east to trade, he found a patron in the Cantons and stayed behind.'

'Well, let's hope the poor bastard's happy. He's a long way from his enemies now.'

Unless of course one of them was, all unwittingly, coming after him. His superiors would want to know about this Kazrak, Zayn figured: someone who'd angered the Great Khan, someone who should have been killed, but a clumsy paid murderer had let him get away – and then there was that mysterious piece of jewellery.

'Apanador?' Zayn said. 'Do you remember when that happened?'

'When Dallador was still a boy.'

'I know, but what year?'

Apanador blinked at him.

'Sorry,' Zayn said. 'How big a boy?'

'Let me think.' Apanador did just that for a long moment. 'It would have been right before he gained his rightful name.'

Dallador laughed. 'Ask the Spirit Rider,' he said. 'She's the only person I know, anyway, who can reckon years the way you Kazraks do.'

As soon as Ammadin returned to camp, Zayn jogged out to meet her, catching up to her when she was turning her horse into the herd. She listened patiently while he explained.

'I heard that story at the time,' Ammadin said. 'When was it in years, you want to know?'

'Well, if it's not too much trouble. I'm curious about this fellow.'

'I can't blame you for that. Carry my saddle back to camp for me.'

He picked it up, but she took the saddlebags herself. As they strolled back to the tents, she suddenly spoke.

'Ten of your years ago, that's when.'

'Ah! Thank you. It would have nagged at me, not knowing.'

'Really?' She stopped walking and turned to consider him.

'Well, yes. I like to get things straight, that's all. In my mind, I mean.'

She smiled, shrugged, and resumed walking. As he trailed after, Zayn was considering the date. Ten years ago Gemet Great Khan was purging his bloodlines to remove any disputes about his right to rule. That piece of jewellery might well have been the zalet khanej, the medallion that proved a man had been sanctified as a khan and thus as a rival for the Crescent Throne. Maybe. He knew nothing for certain, but that simple date shone like one of

Ammadin's crystals: hold it up, and it sent light sparkling in all directions.

When Warkannan and his men had turned east, they had left all of their plausible reasons for being on the road behind. They also traded the public roads for narrow dirt paths, and the constant rise of the land slowed them down as well. As long as they travelled through Kazrajistan proper, they rode at night and by day either camped well off the road or bribed some farmer to let them sleep in his barn. They avoided every town that was more than a village and kept clear of the military posts and courier stations that stood along the Darzet River.

After some days of this slow riding, they reached Andjaro, a province that had gone from being ChaMeech territory to an independent nation until, a mere hundred years ago, the khanate had decided that an independent nation on its border was a threat. The low hills angled from the north-east towards the south-west, so soft and regular that they reminded Warkannan of the folds a carpet forms when pushed and rumpled by a careless foot. Among these rolling purple downs, Warkannan had allies, and the allies, large landowners all, had private armies. Each night Warkannan and his party stayed in compounds surrounded by thousands of acres of purple grass, dotted with flocks of sheep. At each, Warkannan received coin for the journey, supplies of food and fuel, pack horses when he mentioned needing them, and the assurance that Jezro would have a place to hide when he came home.

Early on their third day in Andjaro, they crested a down and saw, stretching below them, a valley filled with green, billowing in the wind like clouds. Arkazo reined in his horse and stared, his mouth half-open.

'What is that?' he stammered. 'Water?'

'No,' Warkannan said, grinning. 'Trees.'

'I've never seen so many in one place. All that green! And they grow so close together.'

'How observant of you,' Soutan drawled. 'The word for a lot of them in one place is forest. That university of yours seems to have taught you little of value.'

'We studied the works of the Three Prophets,' Arkazo said. 'Nothing's of greater value. Not that an infidel like you would understand why.'

They had reached the tax forests, stand after stand of true-oak, planted in regular rows and watched over by foresters. As part of their most solemn duty to the Great Khan, the border landowners put as many acres into the slow-growing forests as they could afford – more, in some cases. Although in the volcanic mountains every metal imaginable lay close to the surface in rich veins, fuel for the smelting of it was another thing entirely. So far at least, no one had ever found any of the fabled blackstone or blackwater that were supposed to burn twice as hot as true-oak charcoal. As a result, while any peasant could pan the easily-melted gold from a stream and work it, it took a lot of that gold to buy a little steel.

'It's a pity about our prospecting venture,' Soutan remarked. 'If we'd actually found blackstone we could have been as rich as a khan ourselves.'

'If,' Warkannan said, grinning. 'Those maps of yours show likely spots, not sure things.'

'Ah, but they're copies of ancient maps – spirit maps, the Tribes would call them.'

'Well, Nehzaym will take good care of them. As far as I'm concerned, we'll have better odds backing Jezro Khan than looking for blackstone.'

Soutan turned in the saddle and considered him for a moment.

'I'm inclined to agree with you,' Soutan said at last. 'Ancient writings exist that present strangely disturbing implications concerning the black marvels.'

'And what's that supposed to mean?'

'Your manners are painfully bad, Captain. I see no reason to speak further and be mocked.'

Soutan kicked his horse to walk, passed Warkannan, and headed downhill. For a moment Warkannan considered returning the insult, then shrugged the matter away. Most likely the sorcerer thought talking in riddles impressed people. Damned if he'd encourage him in it.

Entering the forest felt like plunging into the ocean, all cool air and deep green light. All along the narrow road grew ancient trees, twining their branches overhead. In a few minutes Soutan paused his horse in the dappled shade and let them catch up. They set off again, riding three abreast with the sorcerer in the middle.

'A question for you, Captain,' Soutan said. 'Arkazo says that nothing's more important than the books of the Prophets. Do you agree?'

'Well, it seems extreme, I know, but actually I do.'

'I suppose it's a question of following the laws of God. But other prophets have written books of those laws for other peoples, after all.'

'True. But our books, our way – that's what makes us who we are. We follow the Three Prophets, and that sets us apart from people who follow other religious leaders. If I stopped following the laws, I wouldn't know who I was any more.'

Soutan frankly stared. 'You must love your god a great deal,' he said at last.

'I don't know if I'd call it love, not like love for your family or for a woman. It's more like – well, what?' Warkannan thought for a moment. 'More like a sense of mutual obligation. I have a duty to serve God but in return, that duty gives me a place in His universe.'

'God as the supreme commander of a celestial cavalry?' Soutan drawled. 'It would make sense to you, I suppose.'

'I don't like your tone of voice.'

'Sorry.' Soutan shrugged. 'Just a figure of speech.'

Two nights later they arrived at the last Kazraki villa. Kareem Alvado's compound stretched out like a small town, with his mansion and gardens, the cottages of the craftsmen, the barracks for his private troops, and the dormitories for the workmen who tended the flocks and the tax forests. Since Warkannan had served on the border with Kareem, and Kareem's son Tareev and Arkazo had attended university together, they stayed for two full days.

On their last evening, the men sat finishing their dinner around the true-oak table in the dining-hall, a long room with walls of purplish-red horsetail reeds, twined together with pale yellow vines. At regular intervals ChaMeech skulls, bleached white and bulbous, hung as trophies. The older men had been reminiscing about Jezro Khan when Tareev interrupted. Like many Andjaro families, Kareem's had some comnee blood that gave father and son both pale grey eyes and dark, straight hair, and they turned to each other with the same tilt of the head, the same crook of a hand.

'A favour to beg you, sir,' Tareev said. 'The captain's going to have a hard time guarding our khan with just a couple of men. Let me go with them.'

Kareem's heavy-set face turned unnaturally calm.

'Why should Arkazo get all the glory?' Tareev went on. 'It's unfair. Let me go and invite the khan here personally.'

'Now listen, boy,' Warkannan broke in. 'This isn't going to be some pleasant little ride.'

'I know that, Captain,' Tareev said, still grinning. 'That's why you need me along.'

'It's up to your father. There'll be plenty for you to do once the war starts.'

Kareem had a sip of wine, his calloused fingers tight on the goblet.

'What about that girl you promised to marry?' Kareem said at last.

'What would her father want with a coward?'

Kareem smiled, a weary twitch of his mouth. 'Very well, then. But you're riding under Warkannan's orders. What he says, you do. Understand me?'

'Yes sir, I do.'

Warkannan glanced around the table. Arkazo was leaning onto the table on his elbows, watching, unusually solemn, while Soutan lounged back in his chair.

'This might be a good time to make something clear to everybody,' Warkannan said. 'It's dangerous out on the grass. I spent fifteen years of my life there, and I know. When we ride out, I'm the officer in charge of this little venture. Understood?'

'Of course, sir,' Arkazo said.

Soutan sighed, long and dramatically. 'I was waiting for this,' he remarked to the air, then looked Warkannan's way. 'Someone needs to be in charge of the boys – oh, excuse me, our young men, I mean – but no one orders me around, Captain. Understood? If not, you can try to find Jezro on your own.'

Warkannan took a long breath and let his anger ebb.

'Let's hope we don't get ourselves into the kind of trouble where orders are necessary,' Warkannan said at last. 'But if there *is* trouble, sorcerer, then I'll have to put the safety of the other men first, Jezro or not.'

Soutan got up, bowed to Kareem, and strode out of the room. He slammed the door behind him so hard that the wall bounced. Kareem let out his breath in a long whistle.

'I don't envy you this ride,' Kareem said.

'Thanks.' Warkannan managed a smile. 'The Cantons aren't that large. If worse comes to worst, we should be able to track the khan down sooner or later.'

'Well, inshallah.' Kareem spread his hands wide. 'All right, Tareev and Arkazo. You'd better have weapons with you. Let's go to the armoury and see what's there.'

Later that evening Kareem invited Warkannan to his study for a glass of arak. They settled themselves in comfortable chairs while servants lit oil lamps and bowed themselves out of the room. Once they were alone, Warkannan asked Kareem if he regretted putting his son in danger. Kareem shook his head no.

'If he'd wanted to stay home safe, I'd have had some harsh words for my wife. I'd have known he wasn't mine.'

'I'll do my best to keep him out of trouble.'

'Let's pray you can. If the Chosen have taken a hand in this –' Kareem shrugged. 'Who knows?'

'That's true, unfortunately. That reminds me, I've got something I want to leave with you. Suppose the Chosen decide to eliminate me and Soutan – I don't want them getting their ugly paws on this.'

From his shirt pocket Warkannan took out a roll of rushi, protected by a leather cover stamped with a design of two crossed swords below a crescent: Jezro Khan's crest. Kareem kissed it, then slid the rushi free with a snap of his wrist that unrolled the letter. The sheet had one long torn edge, as if the khan had ripped a blank page from a book in his haste.

'It's Jezro's handwriting, sure enough,' Kareem said. 'Thanks be to God, merciful as well as mighty!'

Warkannan had read it so many times that he knew every word by heart.

'To Indan, Warkannan, and all my friends in Kazrajistan,' the letter began. 'That is, of course, assuming I have any friends left. I wonder what you'll say when you find out I'm alive. Will you celebrate, or will I only be seen as a damned nuisance, a ghost who should have stayed dead? I don't even know what things are like in the khanate now. Warkannan, do you remember me? Consider this an invitation to come have a couple of drinks with me. I have some interesting things to tell you. I don't dare say where I am, but Yarl Soutan has agreed to help me. All I can do is pray to God that he'll bring you back with him without my brother finding out. Maybe a couple of men can slip over the border unseen. Yours as always, Jezro.'

The signature had touched Warkannan deeply, just a simple name, no longer the honourable and regal titles, just Jezro. With a sigh, Kareem finished the letter and began rolling it up.

'Well, he's going to find out what loyalty means, isn't he? From what you've been telling me, Warkannan, we can count on four thousand men the minute he crosses the border.'

'At least. And there'll be plenty more as soon as we start marching.'

'Should pick the khan's spirits right up. I never thought to see the day when he'd sound so dispirited.' Kareem tapped the roll on his palm. 'But exile's hard on a man.'

'So it is,' Soutan said. 'And Jezro loves his homeland.'

Warkannan stifled a yelp and turned to see the sorcerer standing by the door. Soutan had a way of gliding into a room that set Warkannan's teeth on edge.

'The last time I saw the khan,' Soutan went on, 'he talked about Haz Kazrak as if it were Paradise.'

'Well, there's something about the place a man's born in.' Kareem glanced at the letter in his hand. 'But it's a shock to see him so hopeless. Especially since you were going to deliver his letter.'

'He thought I'd never reach the khanate alive.'

'I wouldn't have bet good money on it, either.' Kareem smiled, then turned thoughtful. 'Ah God! When we were all young and on the border, if someone had told me that I'd end up a traitor to the Great Khan I'd have slit his throat!'

'I'd have done the same,' Warkannan said.

Soutan stood hesitating, then found a chair and sat down uninvited. Warkannan decided that the only way to smooth over the incident at dinner was to pretend it hadn't happened; he handed the sorcerer a glass and the bottle of arak. Soutan smiled in what seemed to be a conciliatory manner and poured himself a drink.

'I take it you served with our khan, too?' Soutan said.

'I did, and proudly,' Kareem said. 'The stories we could tell, huh, Warkannan?'

Perhaps it was the arak, or the shadows dancing around the ChaMeech skulls on the wall, but they ended up telling a lot of those stories that night. Soutan sat unspeaking, seemingly profoundly interested in tales of too much fighting, drinking, whoring, and the resultant hang-overs or disciplinary actions.

'What surprises me,' Soutan said at length, 'is that the khan seems to have been treated just like any other officer.'

'Exactly like,' Kareem said. 'When you're riding down a pack of screaming ChaMeech, there's no time for giving yourself airs.'

'Imph, no doubt.' Soutan tented his long pale fingers and considered Kareem over them. 'Back in the Cantons we tend to think of the Kazraks as rigidly hierarchical – everyone knowing their place, everyone afraid to leave it, that sort of thing. What I've seen and heard while I've been here makes me think we're wrong.'

'Well, yes and no.' Warkannan waggled a hand in the air. 'The cavalry is one place a man can rise above his birth.'

'And the university,' Kareem put in. 'Get a good religious education, and the faith will take you far.'

'True,' Warkannan said. 'In the cavalry you get your education the hard way. At the end of a spear.'

The pair of them laughed while Soutan smiled, thinly but politely.

'Jezro told me once,' Soutan said, 'that a man can rise from an ordinary trooper, get himself commissioned, and then be accepted as an officer.'

'He can, yes,' Kareem said. 'And you can start off as an officer and get yourself broken down to the ranks, too, if you don't obey orders. What counts in the cavalry is whether or not you meld with your unit. There's no room for individual heroics or individual slackers, either. A lot of young aristocrats can't seem to understand that.'

'Quite so.' Warkannan glanced at Kareem. 'Men from the ranks – they know they live or die together. If they're smart and capable, they can rise far. Remember what's his name? The sergeant from First Company.'

'Yes, I do, the man with only three fingers on one hand.' Kareem looked exasperated. 'Damn my memory! His name's gone right out of it. And then there was Zahir Benumar. A damn good sergeant who made an even better officer.'

'Ah,' Soutan put in. 'That name rings a bell. I think the khan may have mentioned him.'

'Probably he did.' Kareem turned in his chair to speak to Soutan. 'Now if Zahir were drinking with us tonight, we wouldn't be having all this trouble with people's names. He had a phenomenal memory, Zahir.'

'He certainly did,' Warkannan said. 'Unlike mine. Do you know where he is now, Kareem? He was transferred off the border, of course.'

'Suddenly, too, now that you mention it. To the Bariza Second Lancers, wasn't it? I lost track of him about then.'

'So did I, and I'm sorry I did.' Warkannan considered for a moment. 'I did write him care of his new unit. Either they didn't forward it, or he wasn't interested in answering me.'

'Don't be an idiot!' Kareem snapped. 'The letter must have got lost somewhere along the way. Men who endure what you two went through together don't forget each other that easily.'

'I'd like to think so. When Soutan first turned up, I had thoughts of trying to find Benumar, to let him know the good news if nothing else. Zahir, Jezro – the three of us. We were a good team as officers. Worked well together.'

'That's one way of putting it.' Kareem paused for a smile. 'Well, if you bring Jezro back, Zahir's bound to hear of it quickly enough. I did hear he was transferred again, out of Bariza, I mean. I can't remember where. Must be the arak. Can't be middle age.'

They shared another laugh, but Warkannan set his glass down. 'I've got to get up before dawn,' he said, 'I think I'll call it a night.'

'Yes, tomorrow it starts.' Kareem turned solemn. 'And may the Lord guide you every mile of your journey.'

Just at dawn, they assembled in front of the villa, Warkannan, Soutan, the two young men, all holding the reins of their riding horses, who stamped and snorted as if they too knew that the journey ahead promised great things. After a last handshake all round, they mounted, took the lead ropes of the pack horses from the servants, and headed for the gates. When Warkannan glanced back at the house, he saw figures at the windows of the women's quarters. Curtains fell, and the figures disappeared. Tareev turned in his saddle once to wave farewell to his father, but Warkannan never saw him look back again.

The road brought them free of the oak forest by noon, and by mid-afternoon they rode up to the crest of the last high hill. In front of them the downs of the north border fell away. Beyond, the view faded to a lavender haze, spreading endlessly, it seemed, under a harsh sun.

'There they are,' Soutan remarked. 'The plains.'

'Yes indeed,' Warkannan said. 'I started hating them after I'd been on the border for maybe a week.' He turned in the saddle to glance at Arkazo and Tareev. 'Very well, gentlemen. Let's ride.'

The road dropped down through waist-high vegetation, purple and orange, red and russet, a tangled mass of thorns and fleshy leaves fighting over sun and air. Here and there hill trees – thick fleshy trunks topped by huge flabby pink leaves – rose above the chaparral and sparkled with beads of resinous sap. Over them insects swarmed like pillars of smoke. As the men rode through, they now and then heard the rustle or squeal of small animals fleeing the noise of their passing. Occasionally a chirper, a lizard about the size of two clasped hands, broke from cover and flew on a whir of turquoise wings.

The road would settle into shallow valleys, then rise again to another hill crest, but each stood lower than the last. Just at sunset they climbed the last rise and saw below them Haz Evol, a straggle of town along the reed-choked banks of a stream. The fort, a tidy square of thorn walls, stood just beyond.

'Is it safe to ride in?' Arkazo asked. 'What if someone recognizes you?'

'It's a chance I'll have to take. We need information.' Warkannan ran his hand over his burgeoning black beard. 'The last time I was on the border, I was clean-shaven and in uniform. It's funny, but when you're in uniform, no one much looks at your face. I'll bet I can slip through.'

Haz Evol, a small rambling town, existed to serve the military and little more. Warkannan hired quarters for his party at a shabby little inn, made of stacked trunks of spear trees bound together with vines. He went immediately to their cottage while the others tended the horses and brought in the gear. They ate in, rather than risk letting someone get a good look at them in the public common room.

'Now tomorrow, if anyone asks you why I don't come out, tell them I've got some kind of a fever,' Warkannan said. 'That'll keep people away.'

'Just so,' Soutan said. 'We need to buy gift goods – charcoal, wheatian, matches, things like that. The Tribes are hospitable, but it's very rude to not have gifts to give them in return. Besides, spending money will get the townsfolk feeling friendly towards us.' He glanced at Arkazo and Tareev. 'Let me do the talking. Neither of you has impressed me with his subtlety.'

When Tareev opened his mouth to snarl, Warkannan waved him silent. 'Soutan's right.' He turned back to the sorcerer. 'Go on.'

Soutan did so. 'We need to find out if anyone remembers anything about this merchant we're tracking. I consulted the oracle last night, and it said that we're in grave danger of being deceived.'

Tareev and Arkazo snickered.

'I wish the oracle had told us this earlier,' Warkannan said.

'So do I,' Soutan said. 'It has its little ways.'

'Well, let's hope we're not on the wrong trail. If one of the Chosen's already heading east, time's short.'

'Oh, there's plenty of time. I don't care how dedicated or highly trained this spy is. He can't get across the Rift alone. He'll have to talk a comnee into escorting him. Have you forgotten about the ChaMeech?'

'I never forget the ChaMeech. Let's hope they eat him.'

'They will, if he tries to ride alone. There's only one thing the ChaMeech fear, and that's magic. A spirit rider can scare them off, and I've no doubt this Chosen One knows it as well as I do.'

'And what about us?' Arkazo said. 'Do we have to attach ourselves to the stinking barbarians, too?'

'Of course not,' Soutan snapped. 'You have me.'

All the next day Warkannan paced back and forth or sat near the window to keep watch. Now and then he would try to read – he carried a copy of *The Mirror of the Qur'an* everywhere with him – but doubts distracted him, even from the beloved teachings of the First Prophet. Fortunately, Arkazo and Tareev returned early in the afternoon with their armloads of supplies.

'No one seemed to be following us, sir,' Arkazo reported. 'No one told us much, either. Soutan sent us back. He had the gall to say that we talked too much and got in the way.'

'Ah.' Warkannan thought that for once, the sorcerer was probably right. 'Well, why don't you two go out and get our horses some water? I'll pack these supplies.'

Soutan came back late, bringing with him a skin of keese and a girl, a mousy little thing whose clothes reeked of grease and strong soap. Warkannan wondered about Soutan's taste in women until the sorcerer announced that Vorika knew things of interest.

At that, Warkannan sat her down in the best chair and poured her a cup of keese. Vorika, it turned out, worked as a kitchen girl in a local caravanserai that served the merchant trade. She was also flattered enough by all this unaccustomed attention to giggle, hiding her stained teeth behind one hand.

'Well, I saw this merchant, but I didn't know him. Everyone talked about him for days. He was crazy. I mean, just absolutely everyone said he was crazy, because he went out onto the grass with only a couple of men along.'

'A merchant, huh?' Warkannan said. 'What kind of goods?'

'Oh, axes and swords, stuff like that. Just absolutely everyone told him he was carrying ChaMeech bait – that's what they called it, ChaMeech bait – but he wouldn't listen.'

Warkannan and Arkazo exchanged a significant smile.

'Come now, girl,' Soutan said. 'Tell them what happened to this merchant.'

'Oh yes, sir. Well, you see, about a week after he left – I think it was a week, anyway – no, I tell a lie – it was ten days after he left, but anyway, he came back. His men said they were going to leave him out there alone if he didn't. So he rode south somewhere for the next horse fair. A couple of the men who stay regular-like in our inn saw him there, you see, and they say they teased him ever so much about it.'

Warkannan swore so vilely that the girl flinched. He apologized, soothed her feelings with a couple of silver deenahs, and ushered her out. He returned to an uncomfortable silence. Tareev and Arkazo sat on the floor, looking at the carpet. Soutan had flopped into an armchair, and his smile carried barbs.

'The oracle may be ambiguous at times,' Soutan remarked to the empty air, 'but it never outright lies.'

'It doesn't, huh?' Warkannan sat down on the divan. 'Well, I wonder if the Chosen sent this merchant as a deliberate false trail.'

'Maybe they didn't have to.' Soutan glanced at Arkazo and Tareev. 'Fools abound, after all.'

Arkazo started to speak.

'Shut up,' Warkannan said. 'Now let me think. It's possible that our spy's slipped over the border without anyone knowing, of course, but that possibility gets us nowhere.'

'There's that cavalry officer,' Arkazo said. 'The one who was cashiered.'

'Yes.' Soutan drawled the word. 'How providential, wasn't it, that a comnee took him in? Are we going to ride along the border and ask about him?'

'No,' Warkannan said. 'We're heading out tomorrow. Sooner or later, we'll find a comnee. If one of the comnees has taken in a Kazrak, the news will spread. They're like that, passing things along. We'll track him down.'

'And what then? Ask him ever so politely if he's one of the Chosen?'

'No. We're going to kill him. If he's not the right man, well, I'm sorry for the poor bastard, but I don't dare take any chances, not with Jezro Khan's life.'

'The Chosen aren't so easy to kill, from what I hear.'

'No, they're not. We're going to have to try, though. If God wills it, it'll get done.'

Soutan rolled his eyes, then laid a hand on the copy of *The Mirror* that Warkannan had set down on the table.

'What is this?' Soutan said. 'Not the Qur'an itself?'

'No. No one can touch the holy book unless they're ritually pure, so you can't carry it around in your saddlebags with you. That would be sacrilege. This is just a translation into Kazraki.'

'So it is a Qur'an.'

'No, because it's not in the old language.'

'But the thoughts are surely the same.'

'Maybe, but God spoke in the old language, not in Kazraki. That's why the real Qur'an is so holy.'

Soutan raised a sceptical eyebrow. 'What do you think would happen if you touched a copy when you weren't pure, whatever that means? Fire from heaven?'

'Of course not! The law's just a sign of respect.'

Soutan had the decency to look abashed. Warkannan changed the subject.

They rode out from Haz Evol in the cool of dawn. Warkannan led his small caravan of four mounted men and four pack horses due east, heading for the Great River, where the comnees congregated during the summer. The last of the downs dwindled behind them until the plains stretched ahead, mile after mile of grass, turning from lavender to a deep purple here at the end of the spring rains. The grassland ran to a horizon as straight as a bowstring. Here and there a few orange and magenta fern trees or a stand of blood-red spears rose up to point at the sky; otherwise, there was only grass.

By their first night's camp, the plains were beginning to get on Tareev and Arkazo's nerves. It happened to men, their first time out; the cavalry called it border fever, a twitchy way of riding, a certain way of turning the head, staring this way and that, a certain slackness about the mouth as men realized that there was simply nothing and nobody out in the grass but the wandering comnees. Tareev and Arkazo had all the symptoms. At night, they hugged the pitiful excuse for a campfire, flinched at every strange sound, and talked much too loudly when they talked at all.

In the heat of summer, raiding parties of ChaMeech rarely travelled any distance from the Rift, but still Warkannan kept a careful watch as they rode. Thanks to the Tribes, the big predatory saurs – the longtooths, the slashers, the grey giants – who once had ruled the plains were scarce these days, at least in the Tribal lands, a huge area from the northern headwaters of the river system south to the seacoast.

'You never know, though,' Warkannan told Tareev and Arkazo, 'when you'll run across one of the meat-eaters. The Tribes haven't wiped them out by any means.'

'They can be scared off,' Soutan put in. 'It takes several men to do it, but shrieking and clashing sabres together gives the saurs something to think about. They've learned they can find easier meals than H'mai.'

'Good,' Arkazo said. 'But I wouldn't mind seeing one.'

'From a distance, I wouldn't either,' Soutan said. 'The greater the distance, the better the view.'

They did regularly see the six-legged grassars, the herds of grazing saurs who provided meat to the Tribes and the predators both. The females stood about four feet high at the shoulder, the males as much as six, and where the bright red female heads were slender, the piebald males had broad skulls crowned with three long horns. Both sexes had thick pebbled hides and long tails ending in a spike of bone. Whenever they smelled the horsemen, the males would raise their massive heads, snort a warning, and slam their tails against the earth. In answer the females shrieked to call their young hatchlings back to the safety of the herd.

Warkannan would always halt his little caravan and let the grassars lumber away. Despite their solid size, their six legs gave them a surprising agility; they could begin a turn on the forelegs, stabilize on the middle pair, and swing the hind legs around to follow while the spike on their tails slashed any predator close behind them.

'How do the Tribes kill them, anyway?' Tareev asked.

'With arrows and spears,' Warkannan said. 'They weaken them with arrows, then move in with the spears for the final kill.'

Tareev rose in his stirrups to watch the herd trotting off. He was grinning as he sat back down. 'I'd love to join one of those hunts,' he said. 'Kaz, are you game?'

'You bet,' Arkazo said. 'If we find a tribe that'll let us ride along.'

'The point of this trip,' Warkannan broke in, 'is to reach Jezro safely and get him home the same way. Charging around hunting saurs isn't in the itinerary, gentlemen.'

'Yes sir,' Tareev said with a martyred sigh. 'The way we're going, we might not ever see any Tribesmen anyway.'

'Oh we will,' Soutan said. 'I'm keeping a good look out. We need information.'

Every time they stopped to rest the horses or to camp, Soutan took a strangely-wrapped object from his saddlebags and walked off alone to stare into it. When one morning Warkannan asked about it, Soutan unwrapped the silk pieces to reveal a polished sphere of heavy glass, engraved with numbers and strange marks around its equator.

'It's a scanning crystal,' Soutan said.

'What do you see in it?' Arkazo said, grinning. 'Spirits and demons?'

Tareev snickered.

'That's enough, gentlemen,' Warkannan snapped.

'Thank you, Captain.' Soutan looked the two young men over, then shrugged. 'I see your university didn't teach you good manners.' With that he stalked off into the grass.

Warkannan turned to Arkazo and Tareev. 'Front and centre, you two,' he growled. 'Soutan believes in his damned sorcery. We need his help. Hell, without him, we'll get nowhere. I want you two to treat this magic business with every show of respect. Do you hear me?'

'Yes sir,' Tareev said. 'I'm sorry.'

'It just goes against the grain, somehow,' Arkazo muttered. 'But of course, sir. Whatever you say.'

When Soutan returned, Tareev and Arkazo apologized.

'Accepted,' Soutan said. 'By the way, there's a comnee some ten miles ahead of us.'

'You're sure?' Arkazo said.

'If I hadn't been sure, you young lout, I would never have mentioned it.'

'I'm sorry. It's just hard to believe that bit of glass is magic.'

Warkannan started to intervene, but Soutan smiled.

'Why?' the sorcerer said.

'Because of the engraved numbers, I think,' Arkazo said. 'It makes it look like a tool or something.'

'Very good! It does, yes. Think about that.'

Soutan walked over to his saddlebags and knelt down to put the crystal away. Tareev leaned close to Arkazo and muttered, 'Huh! We'll just see if this comnee ever shows up.' If Soutan heard, he never responded.

All three Kazraks were in for a surprise when, after some hours of riding, they saw the comnee right where Soutan had said it would be. Warkannan and his men saw the horses first, and only then the sprawl of tents along a stream. Against the brightly coloured trees and the wild grass, the tents, so gaudy in themselves, blended in so well they almost disappeared. The comnee insisted that they eat the evening meal with them and brought out skins of keese to drink with the guests. When Warkannan asked his carefully prepared questions, he found that several of the men had indeed heard of a Kazrak exile who rode with a comnee. Somewhere to the south, they told Warkannan, and a spirit rider was the one who took him in. When Warkannan and his men were ready to ride out the following morning, Warkannan gifted their hosts with a sack of grain and received warm thanks in return.

'No, no, I should be thanking you,' Warkannan said. 'For your company.'

And for your information, Warkannan thought. And yet, as they rode away, he felt heavy-hearted, to be hunting a man down like a saur. He's one of the Chosen, he reminded himself. They're more vicious than any beast alive.

In summer every comnee travelled to the Great River, which flowed, wide but shallow, from the north through the heart of the

Tribal lands all the way to the distant southern sea. Apanador's comnee arrived in the middle of a sunny day. Once the tents were set up and every scrap of fuel in the area scrounged and set drying, the men put out snares for small game. Along the riverbanks grew fern trees, spear trees, brushy shrubs, and mosses in a riot of orange fronds and yellow threads. In this thick vegetation lived the turquoise chirpers, the purple and grey spotted snappers, redboys, and a dozen other kinds of meaty reptiles. They'd supply meat until the grassars came to the river to drink.

Ammadin had never thought of Kazraks as hunters, but Zayn had brought with him a perfect weapon for snaring tree lizards – three brass balls connected with leather thongs. Down by the river she saw him stalking a redboy. It scrambled up a fern tree, then made the mistake of shimmying out onto a frond, where it stood squawking on its six skinny legs. Zayn swung the balls around his head and made them sing like a giant insect, then let them fly from his open hand. The balls wrapped the cords around two pairs of the redboy's legs and dragged it writhing from the tree. Zayn scooped it up with both hands and snapped its neck.

'That's amazing,' Ammadin said. 'You've got a good eye.'

'For this kind of thing, maybe. I hope I can do as well with comnee weapons and bigger game.'

Handling a spear came to him easily, because he knew the lance from his time in the cavalry, but the bow was another matter. In the morning Ammadin rode out to watch him practise with the short bow, made of layers of horn and wood. Dallador had stuffed an old saurskin with grass and set it up as a target. Ammadin sat on her horse and watched as Zayn galloped by, guiding the horse with his knees and nocking an arrow into the bow. Zayn twisted easily in the saddle and shot three fast arrows next to, above, and beyond the target. With a whoop of laughter, he turned his horse and trotted back to Dallador. When he dismounted, Ammadin joined them.

'There's nothing wrong with the way you ride,' Dallador said. 'But you're going to have to practise shooting dismounted for a while. You know, one step at a time.'

'All right,' Zayn said. 'At home we hunt with a longer bow, and you hold it vertically, not across your body like this.'

On the morrow, the men rode out early. The women began their part of the food work: milking their mares, churning butter, setting yogurt to cure and keese to ferment. Ammadin saddled her grey gelding and rode out alone in the opposite direction from the men. Spirit rider or not, a woman would bring bad luck to the men's hunt if she tagged along. She ambled south until she found, some miles from camp, a place where a shallow stream joined the river. She watered her horse, then tethered it out to graze.

On foot she pushed her way through the tangle of trees and ferns to the riverbank, where yellabuhs swarmed. Now and then a slender brown fish would leap open-mouthed from the water and scoop some of them up before falling back. The survivors would fly madly around for a few moments, then resume their swarm, only to fall prey to the next leaper. Ammadin knelt down and peered into the water to look for spirit pearls. Sure enough, they lay thick among the orange mosses and the red-brown river weeds, but it seemed to her that there were fewer this year than she was used to seeing in the Great River.

She sat on the bank and for a long while watched the pearls. Most lay inert on the river bottom; then suddenly and inexplicably one would float free and catch the current, only to sink again farther downstream. As she watched, most of the clutch jerked itself into the current and floated out of sight. Two, however, never moved, and they seemed wrinkled as well. Could they be dead? If so, there'd be no harm in her taking one out of the water, would there? She got up and considered the underbrush around her. Nearby she found a poker tree, so-called because its skinny orange branches stuck straight out from its fleshy squat trunk. She cut off a pair, then stuck them into the mossy bank next to the shrivelled pearls as a marker. If they hadn't moved on by morning, she promised herself, she would consider examining one.

When Ammadin returned to camp, she found the men back already; they'd had splendid luck and surprised a herd of grassars as it left a stream. Out behind the tents they hunkered down to skin and clean the two kills, both of them fat from the summer forage and a good seven feet long from nose to the base of the tail. The children clustered round to watch with eager eyes for the fresh-roasted dinner ahead of them. Three of the men had already skinned one saur and were butchering the meat with their long knives.

Off to one side Zayn was kneeling beside a three-horned male with a skinning knife in his hand. Orador was standing over him and telling him how to separate the red-and-purple striped hide from its previous owner. Ammadin strolled over to join them.

'What's this?' she said. 'Did Zayn make his first kill?'

'More or less,' Orador said, smiling. 'Someone else's arrows crippled it – Grenidor, I think it was – but Zayn's the one whose spear finished it off. Took some doing, too, so we awarded the kill to him.'

Zayn looked up, and she noticed the left side of his face, swollen maroon and purple around a bruise in the shape of a grassar hoof.

'His first kill is an important point in a man's life.' Ammadin dabbled her forefinger in the bull's dark blood and marked a cross on Zayn's forehead. 'You've brought home food for the comnee. The gods will honour you.'

'Thank you.' Zayn ducked his head in acknowledgment. 'The Wise One honours me as well, and I'm pleased I could help feed us all.'

He'd answered as nicely as any comnee boy. Ammadin suddenly wondered just how and why he knew so much about Tribal ways.

While Orador taught him how to draw the carcass, Ammadin hung around and watched. Zayn was starting to attract her, with his exotic Kazrak features and lean well-muscled body. Years before, she'd taken a few casual lovers, just as any girl of the Tribes would do, but she'd always found them irritating after the first few nights. They followed her around, they got in the way of her spirit journeys, they begged her to marry them, they wanted sons. Dallador had been different, but she'd felt that having sex with him was like eating a good meal – fine while it lasted, but ultimately meaningless. He was so sensual that he could attract anyone, but when it came to keeping them, Maradin was the only person who'd ever really loved him. Ammadin only hoped that Dallo knew it.

Zayn, on the other hand: the easy set of his shoulders, the slow way he smiled, the sense of privacy, the reserve in his dark eyes – they intrigued her. She had to remind herself that he'd only be a nuisance during the day. As if he were aware of her study, Zayn looked up and smiled at her.

'Do you want these horns? I've noticed that you people use them for all sorts of things.'

Orador laughed, a little whoop of mockery that made Zayn blush. So. Here was one bit of Tribal lore the Kazrak didn't know.

'I don't think you understand what you're offering,' Ammadin said. 'A man gives a woman the horns of his kill after she asks him to marry her.'

Zayn sat back on his heels and looked at her in pleasant speculation, as if he wouldn't mind receiving such a proposal. Orador made a great show of cleaning his skinning knife on the grass. Ammadin turned and strode away, annoyed with herself far more than with Zayn for allowing this embarrassment to develop. He was only a man, after all, and men were always angling for a good marriage and the horses it would bring them.

That night the camp feasted. The men dug a pit and used some of the charcoal bought on the border to roast half of Zayn's bull grassar. All afternoon the comnee smelled it baking, and by the time it was finished, a hungry crowd milled around the pit. In the gathering twilight the men hauled the meat up and laid it on the tailgate of a wagon. With his long knife Apanador set about cutting it up; the slow-roasted meat fell apart into rich brown chunks. He fed Ammadin first, then the other women, then the children, and finally the men. The keese flowed as everyone sat down in the grass to eat. Zayn brought his share over to Ammadin and sat down next to her. They were just finishing when Apanador and Dallador joined them, hunkering down in the grass.

'Your servant's going to be a good hunter, Holy One,' Apanador said. 'He can stay on a horse like a comnee man, too. It's time for him to think about the future. I'll offer him a place in the comnee if you agree.'

Zayn caught his breath.

'What do you say, Zayn?' Apanador said. 'Do you want to return to your khanate and live as a shamed man?'

Zayn hesitated, thinking hard. 'I'd rather ride with you,' he said at last. 'If you truly think I'm worthy.'

Apanador looked at Ammadin for her opinion.

'You're welcome to stay,' she said to Zayn. 'But only if you're willing to become a man. I know you're a man among your people, but to us, you're still a boy. You haven't gone on your vision quest and learned your true name.'

'I've heard about that. Will the Spirit Rider tell me what to do?'

'Of course. It's one of my duties.' She glanced at Apanador. 'I'll consult the spirits and find an auspicious day.'

'Good,' Apanador said. 'Then we'll head to the Mistlands when we break camp.' He turned back to Zayn. 'Our boys go to the Mistlands for their vision quests. Do you know about them?'

'Every officer on the border has heard of them, but I've never had a chance to see them.'

'You're going to now,' Ammadin said. 'Boys vigil there in the summer.'

'What about the girls?'

'Girls quest in the winter, down in the swamp-forests by the ocean.'

'That's interesting. May I ask why there's a difference? Did the gods –'

'No.' Ammadin paused for a smile. 'It's just not safe to go into the Mistlands in the winter. The lakes are swarming with ChaMeech then. They must come from all over.'

'Why?'

'I haven't the slightest idea. Maybe they send their children on vigils, too.'

'You can talk later,' Apanador broke in. 'Let's put this matter to the comnee.'

Near the smothered fire-pit Apanador gathered the comnee together and put forward his proposal. Every adult had the right to speak out, either for or against allowing Zayn into the comnee; the majority vote would decide. One at a time, everyone agreed to allow him in, until Apanador turned to Palindor. Ammadin was far from surprised when Palindor spat out a futile no.

'And what do you have against Zayn?' Apanador said.

'He's a Kazrak. Isn't that enough?'

'No, it isn't. He's a Kazrak smart enough to leave his bizarre khanate and come to us.'

When the rest of the comnee laughed, Palindor rested his hand on the hilt of his long knife. 'He's also a man who offended the great chiefs of his country. He broke his own laws. Who's to say that he won't do the same to ours someday?' Palindor looked around, appealing to the crowd. 'Do you really want to ride with a man who'd lie to a chief?'

'I never lied.' Zayn stepped forward. 'He never even asked me if I was sleeping with his wife, and by God Himself, if he had, I would have told him to his face. She was that beautiful.'

When this drew a good laugh, Palindor's hand went tight on his knife's hilt.

'Palindor, the comnee's already agreed,' Apanador said. 'If someday Zayn betrays us, well, then, you'll have the wonderful satisfaction of saying I-told-you-so to all of us. You'll have to be content with that.'

'And if I'm not?' Palindor snapped.

Some of the women gasped.

'Then you'll have to go back to your mother's comnee,' Apanador said. 'Maybe your sister will let you guard her horses.'

Blushing a furious scarlet, Palindor strode off into the darkness. When Dallador started after him, Apanador caught his arm.

'Talking to him right now won't do any good. After he's had a chance to think, I'll take him aside. Zayn, let's go drink in my tent. There's a lot you need to know.'

In a group the men surrounded Zayn and led him off. All sly smiles, Maradin hurried over to join Ammadin.

'Now isn't this interesting? So you want to have Zayn riding with us, do you?'

'You're being tedious. It doesn't take the spirit power to know what you're thinking, Maddi, and no, I have no intention of marrying him.'

'Hah!'

'Oh, shut up! Why are you always trying to get me to marry some lout?'

'Well, for the children, of course.' Maradin seemed honestly surprised that she'd ask. 'What are you going to do when you're old, and you don't have any granddaughters? Who are you going to leave your horses to?'

'Your granddaughters, probably. You don't understand. The spirit knowledge is all I've ever wanted, and it'll be more comfort than a hundred daughters when I'm old.'

Maradin thought this over. 'Well, maybe so – for you,' she said at last. 'But come on, you've got to admit that Zayn's a handsome man.'

'Take him as a lover if you like him so much. I'm not going to.'

'Hah!'

'Oh, stop saying hah!'

Ammadin turned her back on Maradin and strode away. She was beginning to regret ever picking Zayn up off the streets of Blosk.

Out away from the camp, in the quiet, her anger ebbed away.

She lay down on her back in the crackling grass and considered the night sky. Just overhead hung the Herd, as the Tribes called the spiral of light that the Kazraks had named the Spider. Galloping down fast from the north came the Six Riders, silver and bright against the dead, dark sky. Shamans like Ammadin knew lore lost to the Kazraks, that there were actually sixty riders, ten groups of six apiece, that galloped in formations whose return and permutations were as predictable as the rising of the sun. These flying lamps – or maybe they were tiny worlds; opinions differed – controlled the spirits of the crystals.

And just what, she wondered, was the Herd? She sat up, considering. Her teacher had told her that powerful spirits had gashed the heavenly sphere to allow light from the spirit world to shine through and give the Tribes light in the darkness. Loremasters in the Cantons claimed that suns, thousands and thousands of them altogether, had clustered together to form the Herd. The points of light looked so small only because they lay at some unimaginable distance in the sky. Why would spirits perform such a mighty act of magic just to help the lowly H'mai? Or, if there were other suns, did other worlds circle them? Wouldn't they bump into each other, in that case? Neither theory made sense.

In the morning, while the rest of the comnee packed the wagons, Ammadin rode back to the stream to check her spirit pearls. She found the sticks, and when she knelt on the bank she saw the two shrivelled pearls still lying where they'd been the day before. They had definitely grown smaller and more wizened overnight. The smooth spherical pearls that had lain near them had disappeared, twitching themselves downstream, she assumed. Why would the gods object if she took a dead thing out of the water? Despite the logic of her own argument, she had to summon courage before she could reach into the stream and pick up one of the dead pearls.

The surface felt like a saur's eyeball, cold gel in a membrane. She brought it up and laid it on the flattened leaves of a red fern, but as soon as the air touched it, it began to shrink and pucker. She drew her knife and slashed it in half. The interior liquid spilled and ran, leaving thin milky husks to shrivel in the air. In the centre lay something as small as a bead. She slid the point of her knife under a little clot of tissue, touched with pale orange blood.

'Exactly like the lizard eggs!'

Ammadin used her free hand to dig a tiny grave on the bank, then laid both embryos inside and covered them. She washed the blade of her knife clean, dried it on her tunic, and sheathed it. Apparently the spirit pearls were nothing but the eggs of some animal – a fish, perhaps?

'But why would they be Bane?'

Witchwoman, help me! Our gods they leave us. Our children they die.

The voice rasped and hissed. She heard it not with her ears, but with the bone of her skull just behind her left ear – or so it seemed. A spirit voice, then. She crouched on the bank and listened.

Witchwoman, please hear me.

'I do hear you.' Ammadin spoke aloud. 'Can you hear me?'

Please hear me. Please help me. I be Water Woman.

The voice disintegrated into a long hiss and crackle, then faded away. Ammadin sat back onto her heels.

'Her children? Does she mean the pearls?'

It was possible that spirits were trying to be born into this world, and that the eggs were their means of taking on bodies. The theory struck her as clumsy. Questions, more questions, and the cold bite of doubt – the spirit's voice made them urgent.

'Water Woman!' she called out. 'Water Woman, can you hear me?'

No answer came, not even the hissing. Ammadin got up, rubbing her arms, chilly with gooseflesh still. She decided that she would supervise Zayn's vision quest, then start looking for another spirit rider to tend her comnee. The questions would give her no peace until she tried to answer them. Besides, if she left on a quest of her own, her absence would keep Palindor from Zayn's throat. But the trouble came too fast, flaring up like a spark in dry grass when she returned to camp. Most of the wagons stood packed and ready to move out, but the men were still breaking down the last few tents and stowing a few last pieces of gear where they could find room. Ammadin was putting her bedroll into a wagon when she heard someone shout in alarm. As she ran towards the sound, she saw Dallador and Grenidor grabbing Palindor by the arms and hauling him back. Zayn faced him, his hands on his hips. Just as Ammadin reached them, Apanador ran up. She stepped back and let him settle this men's matter.

'And what's all this?' Apanador growled. 'How did it start?'

'Over something really stupid,' Dallador said. 'Palindor said Zayn shoved him when they were loading the wagon.'

'I won't have this kind of trouble in the comnee.' Apanador looked back and forth at Palindor and Zayn. 'I can see that we need to do some hard talking.'

Palindor's handsome face twisted. He shook free of the restraining hands, but he sheathed his knife.

'I'm willing to settle this once and for all,' Zayn said. 'Let's have our fight but with bare hands. The one who loses leaves the comnee.'

Apanador turned Palindor's way and raised an eyebrow.

'I'll agree to that,' Palindor said. 'But you won't have a horse and a sabre on your side, Kazrak.'

Zayn merely smiled.

The entire comnee came to witness the fight, held on a stretch of ground where the horses had cropped the grass down to good footing. Palindor handed his long knife and Zayn his Kazrak dagger over to Apanador. Ammadin was furious with both men; no matter what the rest of the comnee might think, she knew they were fighting over her like studs over a mare in heat. Apanador left the two standing about three feet apart and carried the weapons back to the waiting comnee.

'Very well,' the chief called out. 'Begin.'

They dropped to a fighting crouch and began to circle round each other, hands raised, eyes narrowed. Zayn kept his hands open, not in fists, and moved as smoothly as a cat. They feinted in, testing each other, dancing back fast; then Palindor charged, swinging both fists. Zayn ducked, feinted, dodged, then landed a solid punch. The comnee shouted as Palindor staggered back with his mouth bleeding. Zayn closed in and landed a quick series of blows. When Palindor tried to dodge, his foot slipped, and he went down to one knee. Zayn waited as Palindor got up, gasping for breath, his face so dark with rage and blood that he looked like a demon.

The fall taught Palindor something. This time, he feinted in cautiously, keeping his hands low, aiming for Zayn's stomach, not his head. Zayn danced in, slapped him across the face, and danced back before Palindor could hit in return. With a howl of rage, Palindor charged. Zayn let him close, then struck with half-closed hands, punching him in the face, blocking Palindor's every blow while Palindor struggled and fought, swaying where he stood but still game. Suddenly Ammadin realized that Zayn could kill him with his bare hands if he wanted. She ran to Apanador and grabbed his arm.

'Stop it! It's gone far enough.'

With a nod of agreement, Apanador trotted out and yelled at them to stop. When Zayn stepped back at the order, Palindor threw one last punch. Zayn grabbed his wrist and swung him around, pulling him back against his chest with Palindor's arm twisted in his grip. Palindor dropped to his knees and bit his lower lip so hard that it bled again.

'He said stop.' Zayn let him go with a shove.

Gasping for breath, rubbing his arm, Palindor refused to look up when Apanador walked over.

'All right, saddle your horse,' Apanador said. 'Ride out.'

Palindor nodded, then staggered off, heading for the wagons to retrieve the few things he owned. For a few minutes Zayn stood alone, rubbing his bloody, swelling knuckles, until Orador brought him some herb paste to treat them. Together they went back to loading the wagons as if nothing had happened.

Ammadin waited until Palindor was ready to ride. When he led his bay gelding out, loaded with saddlebags, she joined him at the edge of the camp. He refused to look at her, merely twisted his reins round and round his bruised fingers while the horse snorted and tossed its head.

'Find a woman who wants you,' she said. 'You're too good a man to demean yourself this way.'

Palindor shrugged and twisted the leather tight. 'When he betrays you, remember that I love you.'

He turned away and swung into the saddle. Ammadin watched him till he rode out of sight, a tiny figure, disappearing into the purple grasslands like a stone dropping into the sea.

When they were still some two days' ride away from the Great River, Warkannan and his men came across another Tribal camp, an unusually small comnee led by a chief named Sammador. They rode in, dismounted, and found themselves in the middle of a swarm of young children, who stared at them silently with solemn eyes.

'Where are your fathers?' Warkannan said in Hirl-Onglay. 'Hunting?'

The children said nothing. From one of the tents someone shouted; from another an older girl crawled out. When she called, the camp came alive, and adults surrounded the Kazraks. The girl, or young woman, really – Warkannan judged her to be fifteen or so – hooked her thumbs into the waist of her saurskin trousers and stood off to one side, staring at Tareev and Arkazo with undisguised interest.

Warkannan addressed himself to the young chief. After the usual greetings, Warkannan asked if anyone knew a Kazrak travelling with a spirit rider to the south. Luck favoured him. Sammador's comnee had travelled to the Blosk horse fair, and they gave him names: Zayn was the Kazrak, and Ammadin, who rode with old Apanador's comnee, the spirit rider. With this information, however, came ominous news.

'Ammadin is a really powerful woman,' Sammador told him. 'All the other spirit riders say so.'

'Really? Well, I'll count myself honoured if I ever meet her.'

'Good, good.' Sammador glanced around at his people. 'But I'm forgetting my manners. Will you join our camp for the night?'

'Thanks, but no,' Warkannan said. 'I was hoping to make a few more miles before sunset.'

With a wave of his arm, Warkannan gathered up his men, mounted, and led them back out into the grass. When they'd gone about a mile, he stopped his small caravan; the other men guided their horses up to his.

'Listen,' Warkannan said. 'We're going to have to plan Zayn's death carefully. If we kill the servant of a witchwoman, the Tribes will take it as an insult, and they'll be crying for our blood. The Tribes practically worship their witches.'

'It's much more likely that she'd take her vengeance on her own,' Soutan said. 'This is a damned nuisance, Captain. I've never met a witchwoman yet who didn't have the greatest power. They look primitive, these people, but their magic isn't.'

'I take it you know something about it, then,' Warkannan said. 'Their kind of magic, that is.'

'There's only one kind of magic.' Soutan paused for one of his teeth-baring smiles. 'The kind that works.'

That afternoon they made camp by a stream deep enough for

bathing. The three Kazraks stripped off their clothes and waded in, passing a bar of soap back and forth. Soutan sat on the bank, however, and read a book he'd been carrying in his saddlebags.

'Don't you want to come in?' Warkannan called to him.

'Later perhaps.' Soutan kept his nose in his book. 'Not right now.'

His choice, Warkannan supposed. When Tareev and Arkazo lapsed into horseplay, threatening to drown one another and yelling mock insults, Warkannan left the water. Still naked he knelt on the bank and washed out his undershirt and shorts, then put them on wet. In the heat of late afternoon, they'd dry fast enough. He washed his socks and shirt, too, and laid them onto the grass to dry. Soutan looked up and shut his book.

'Where did you get that scar?' Soutan said. 'The long one on the back of your leg.'

'From a ChaMeech spear.'

'It looks like you're lucky to be alive. A few inches higher, and you'd have bled to death.'

'Yes, that's certainly true.' Warkannan reflexively reached down and rubbed the scar. 'But that's not the worst thing they ever did to me.'

'Oh?' Soutan cocked an eyebrow.

'I was taken prisoner by the slimy bastards – me and Zahir Benumar. Kareem and I mentioned him, if you remember. He was one of my sergeants, then; he was commissioned later. Anyway, we caught a pack of them trying to steal our horses, and they outnumbered us.'

Soutan winced. 'That must have been unpleasant.'

'You could call it that. They tied leather thongs around our wrists, tied ropes to those, then took off at a lope in the hot sun.' Warkannan held up his hands so Soutan could see the scars, thick as bracelets, around each wrist. 'Benumar has a set to match these.' He lowered his hands again. 'They dragged us along when we couldn't run any more. Now and then they'd stop, let us rest, then take off again.' Warkannan shook his head to clear it of the memory. 'If it weren't for Jezro Khan, we'd have been killed for their amusement. Very slowly.'

Soutan winced again, then put the book down on the grass beside him. 'Jezro was an acknowledged heir then, yes?'

'Acknowledged and sanctified. He had the zalet khanej around his neck.'

'Ah yes, the medallion. He showed it to me once. He seemed quite proud of it, but it ended up being his death warrant.'

'Once the old khan – his father – died, yes.' Warkannan felt his rage, rising sharp in his blood. 'Gemet turned out to be a murderous little swine.'

'Indan told me that it wasn't technically murder, that the oldest son has some sort of legal right to clear away excess heirs.'

'That's true, but it's a very old law. Most great khans find positions at the palace or in the army for their brothers, or at least for the ones who are willing to swear loyalty. The recalcitrant ones are usually just castrated. Gemet had every single one of them killed, loyal or not, even the bastards.'

'Except Jezro.'

'Yes, except Jezro. The Lord is merciful, blessed be His name.'

Soutan glanced away, his lips pursed as if he were thinking something through. Out in the stream Tareev and Arkazo were still splashing around like schoolboys.

'All right,' Warkannan called out. 'That's enough. Out of the water! Get your stinking underwear clean, will you?'

Still laughing they climbed out to follow his orders. Soutan picked up his book again and ostentatiously began to read. Soutan's loose trousers had once been tan, and his tunic blue, but they were spotted and stained with grass and sweat both. His face, oddly enough, looked both unstubbled and clean, but the rest of him stank.

'Soutan?' Warkannan said. 'You can bathe in peace now.'

'Thank you, but no.' Soutan kept his gaze on the book. 'I prefer to bathe in complete privacy. I know this seems strange to you Kazraks, what with your public bath houses and all, but I detest the idea of someone watching me.'

'To each his own.' Warkannan raised his hands palms upward. 'It'll be dark soon.'

After the evening meal, Soutan did indeed borrow the soap and take himself off downstream. As they sat by their fire, they could hear him splashing and even, at odd moments, singing.

'Tell me something, Uncle,' Arkazo said. 'That girl this afternoon?'

'What girl?'

'The one in the comnee's camp. The pretty one.'

Warkannan suppressed a smile. 'Most Tribal women are pretty,' he said.

'Yes sir,' Arkazo went on. 'It's really something, isn't it, how all these people look alike? But we meant –'

'Sir, the one who –' Tareev interrupted. 'Well, I thought she was looking me and Kaz over. Those stories you hear about comnee women? Are they true?'

'That they're good with a bow when they have to be?'

'You're teasing, aren't you?' Arkazo was grinning at him.

'Yes, of course I am,' Warkannan said. 'If you mean, do they sleep with men they fancy when they want to, yes. But here's another true saying – make a comnee man jealous, and you'll have a knife fight on your hands. Kindly don't go propositioning girls who belong to someone else. We don't need any more trouble on this trip than we have already.'

Warkannan was about to say more when he heard someone approaching through the raspy grass – Soutan. He was wearing clean clothes, pale khaki in the same loose cut that the Kazraks were wearing, and carrying his other things wet.

'There is just something about a bath,' Soutan announced. 'Here's your soap back, gentlemen, and I thank you.'

On the morrow they reached the Great River, where, late in the afternoon, they ran across an unusually large comnee of some thirty families. Their chief, Lanador, greeted them as hospitably as always, but he warned them that the comnee would be riding west on the morrow.

'You're welcome to ride with us, of course, if your road takes you that way.'

'Well, thank you,' Warkannan said. 'But we're heading south. I'm looking for someone, you see. Zayn the Kazrak. Someone told us he rides with Apanador's comnee.'

Lanador blinked twice; then his face went expressionless.

'Ah. Well, come have a bowl of keese with me.'

Lanador took them in to his enormous tent, where blue-and-green tent bags hung on the orange and red walls. The chief sat them down on leather cushions, then poured keese into the ritual skull-cup. Warkannan took a sip and passed it to Arkazo, who ran a finger over rough bone and nearly dropped it. Tareev grabbed it from him just in time.

'Drink from it,' Warkannan whispered in Kazraki. 'Skull or not.'

Arkazo took it back, forced out a smile, and drank. Much to Warkannan's relief, the chief raised one broad hand and pretended to cough, covering a laugh rather than taking insult. Lanador was just handing round the ordinary bowls when an old man lifted the tent flap and came in to join them. He was gaunt, with prominent cheekbones and long bony fingers; his grey hair hung down to his shoulders in greasy strands. The saurskin cloak and the true-hawk feather in his ear marked him for a witchman. He refused a bowl of keese and squatted down next to Warkannan.

'Why are you looking for Zayn?'

'He's a friend of mine. I want to see if he'll come home with me instead of living in exile.'

The old man's eyes caught him. Warkannan could neither move nor speak until the spirit rider looked away, his mouth twisted in something like disgust.

'Do you know where Zayn is?' Warkannan said.

'No.' The spirit rider got up and left the tent.

Lanador rose, muttered a few excuses, and followed him outside. Soutan leaned over and grabbed Warkannan's arm.

'You idiot!' Soutan spoke in Kazraki. 'You never should have lied to him. Witchfolk can practically smell lies.'

'What was I supposed to say?' Warkannan shook his hand off. 'That I'm going to kill Zayn when I find him?'

'Imph, well. You have a point –' Soutan broke off.

Lanador was lifting the tent flap. He came in, smiled vaguely at his guests, and sat down. As the afternoon wore on, he was as gravely courteous as if the incident had never happened. A few at a time, the other men in the comnee came in to take their place in the circle and drink. Warkannan noticed one of them studying him. A handsome, almost girlishly pretty young man, he carried the long knife in his belt that marked him for a warrior, and on his face were the green and yellow marks of old bruises.

That evening, to honour their guests the comnee cooked a communal feast over several different fires. Everyone ate standing up, carrying bowls of food with them while they drifted from friend to friend to talk. Warkannan noticed a pair of comnee girls, both in their teens, staring at Tareev and Arkazo and giggling behind raised hands. As the feast wore on, the two girls began to follow the two young Kazraks, always at a discreet distance, always giggling. Warkannan eventually pointed them out to Soutan.

'Where are their mothers, I wonder?' Warkannan said.

'Trying to ignore the whole thing, most likely,' Soutan said. 'Do you know what they're giggling about?'

'No.'

'Neither do I.' Soutan shrugged. 'Doubtless nothing in particular. We should be asking questions about this Zayn, not worrying about other people's morals.'

'True enough.'

But when Warkannan mingled with the comnee, everyone he asked claimed never to have heard of Zayn – not that he believed them. Since the comnees despised lying, their lack of practice showed. Warkannan let the matter drop and talked only of the weather and the ChaMeech. Some of the men in the comnee had sighted ChaMeech a few days past, but only three females.

'Three females without any males?' Soutan said. 'That's really peculiar.'

Their informant, a beefy young comnee man, nodded his agreement. 'We left them alone,' he went on. 'They weren't likely to give anyone any trouble.'

'They wouldn't, no, not females,' Soutan said. 'And travelling this time of year? Odd. Very odd.'

The comnee man drifted away, and Warkannan glanced around – no one within earshot. There was also no sign of either Arkazo or Tareev.

'We need to talk about things,' Warkannan whispered in Kazraki. 'I'll just collect our young colts.'

'They can find our camp on their own,' Soutan said. 'I have no doubt that those girls are satisfying their curiosity.'

'Their what?'

'I finally heard what the little sluts were giggling about. Both of our boys have big noses. The girls were wondering if other – er – features are commensurately large. You know, the old folk superstition about organ size.'

'Shaitan!' Warkannan felt himself blushing. 'Of all the immodest –! Their mothers should beat them within an inch of their lives.'

'I quite agree. The mothers wouldn't. Shall we go? The boys will come staggering back at dawn, most likely.'

Warkannan led the way downriver to their little camp, which he'd set up out of earshot of the comnee. While Soutan lounged on the grass, Warkannan built and lit a tiny fire of dried horse dung around a few pieces of oak charcoal, then sat down near it for the light.

'There's one good thing,' Warkannan said. 'If Zayn's still with this comnee, he's not off in the east, stumbling over Jezro Khan.'

'If he really is the spy from the Chosen. We can't be sure.'

Warkannan was about to answer when he heard footsteps crackle in the grass. He was expecting Arkazo, but the comnee man with the bruised face stepped into the pool of firelight.

'Come walk with me,' he said to Warkannan. 'I can't risk being seen here.'

Warkannan followed him through the dark night to the fern trees along the river. The comnee man leaned close to whisper.

'My name is Palindor. Why do you want to find Zayn? The Spirit Rider says you're lying when you say he's your friend, so don't tell me that again.'

When Warkannan hesitated, Palindor laughed, a cold mutter under his breath.

'I hate him, and I think you do, too.'

The venom in his voice rang so true that Warkannan decided to trust him.

'Yes, I do. The woman he dishonoured was my sister. I'm going to kill him when I find him.'

Palindor laughed. 'He's about twenty miles south of here, and riding this way. Look, he's going to make a vision quest out in the Mistlands. Do you know what that means?'

'Oh yes. He'll be alone out there, in a place where it's damned hard to see someone coming. Huh – if his comnee's riding upriver, it'll camp on the southern edge.'

'Where the river flows out. The quests always start there.'

'Good.' Warkannan laid his hand on his coin pouch. 'A hundred thanks. Can I give –'

'Keep your money, Kazrak. Just help me kill him.'

In the middle of the grasslands lay a vast swamp, a semi-earth of bog and stream nearly eighty miles across, fed by underground springs. The Kazraki scholars taught that God had created the Mistlands to provide water for the horses no matter how hot the summer. When Zayn repeated this theory to Ammadin, she laughed, much to his annoyance.

'I guess that means you don't believe me,' he said.

'You're not the person to believe or disbelieve,' Ammadin said. 'You're only repeating what you've been told.'

'Who do you think created them, then?'

'I don't have the slightest idea, myself. Now, in the Cantons some of their sorcerers are called loremasters. One of them came to buy a horse from me some years back. When we talked, she told me that in the Mistlands, the earth's beginning to tear apart. There's water underneath, and it comes up through the holes.'

'That's ridiculous!'

'Is it? Consider the earthquakes. The ground moves then, doesn't it?'

'Well, yes, but –' Zayn paused, thinking. 'Well, I hadn't thought of it that way before.'

Whatever their origins, and Zayn was by then thoroughly caught between the conflicting theories, the Mistlands breathed an aura of the holy. Not the comfortable holiness of a gilded mosque, but the stomach-wrenching trembling holiness that bespoke the left hand of God – or the dark gods, if the Tribes had the right of it. On the day that the comnee reached the Mistlands, Zayn saw the fog from miles away, a grey brooding, blending into the purple horizon to the north. The closer they rode, the more the air turned damp, and the dampness became a smell, a foetid coolness of mud and rotting things. Like clouds piling up for a storm, the grey canopy grew larger and larger as the riders approached. At the place where the comnee stopped to make camp, the canopy seemed to arch over half the sky. With sundown it grew larger still, spreading grey tendrils like reaching fingers into the twilight.

Since he was fasting, Zayn walked to the edge of the camp while the others ate. When he looked into the mist, he saw points of bluish light drifting close to the ground – spirits, or so the mullahs would call them, gennies and evil spirits. Ammadin called them spirits but nothing evil, just spirits, who existed as men and animals did, with neither malice nor good will. She had been teaching him the ways of her gods, to prepare him for his quest. In the darkening swirls of mist, it seemed he saw vast figures striding and drifting: Ty-Onar, the god of the swamps, all green and crested like a lizard; Hirrel of the high places, slender and black, with bright pink gills along his sides. Deep within the mists other figures seemed to gather, but never close enough for him to identify. Tomorrow he would be among them, asking for a vision.

Sharply Zayn reminded himself that he was a Kazrak and a follower of the one true god. He was only undergoing this ordeal to keep the confidence of the comnee, because if he lost that confidence, he would have a hard time reaching the Cantons. To a fifteen-year-old boy, he supposed, the quest would be terrifying, the first and likely the only time in his life that a comnee boy would be alone. Doubtless the terror blended with the fasting and the simple pride of becoming a man to produce the visions they were supposed to see out there. Thanks to his studies of Tribal customs, Zayn could make up a convincing vision to tell Ammadin, something that would satisfy these primitive people. That was all there was to it. Superstitious nonsense. Of course. But out in the mists the blue lights danced, brighter in the thickening night. He felt a cold seep into his heart that had little to do with the dampness of the air.

Zayn hurried back to Dallador's fire, but since he was fasting he refused the usual keese. Maradin and the child were visiting friends. They sat together silently and watched the pale flames. After some while Dallador went into the tent and came back with a long knife in a sheath inlaid with red leather. He handed it to Zayn.

'Your father's not here to give you one,' Dallador said. 'Take it.'

'Thank you. I can't thank you enough – I mean that.'

Dallador merely smiled.

'I didn't think a comnee man would have an extra knife,' Zayn went on.

'I won that one in a fight. Some loudmouth from another comnee insulted Maradin.'

'Ah. To get this away from him you must have killed him.'

'Oh yes.' Dallador smiled at the memory. 'No one's said a wrong word to her since.'

Zayn unbuckled his belt, slid off the sheath of his Kazrak hunting knife, and replaced it with the long knife. Settling this new weapon at his hip made him feel like a different man. As for the old knife – he picked it up and offered it to Dallador.

'It'll be a curiosity to show around, if nothing else.'

Dallador hesitated for a moment, then took it. He looked so solemn that Zayn realized they'd just bound themselves together in some ritual way. It was a mistake, he supposed, making a friend, but he refused to go back on it now.

That night Zayn took his bedroll and slept outside far from the camp. Just at dawn, Apanador and Ammadin came to waken him. Since he'd slept fully dressed, Zayn started to pull on his boots, but Apanador stopped him.

'The rocks are too slippery. Your boots could drown you out there.'

'All right.' Zayn laid them aside. 'Can I take my knife?'

'Of course. At the end of this, you'll either be a man or dead. If you die, we'll bury you with the knife so you can protect yourself in the spirit world.'

'All right,' Zayn said. 'I like that way of thinking.'

'Good.' Ammadin handed him a long, smooth pole, sharpened to a point at one end and bound at the other with a blue thread, two true-hawk feathers, and a silver talisman. 'This is a spirit staff. Don't lose it. Now kneel on the ground for a moment.'

When Zayn knelt, she held up a tiny ground-stone jar.

'Go to the gods. Beg them for your true name.' She paused to dip a bit of rag into the jar, which turned out to hold a pale pink ointment. 'Either return with your vision, or pray that Ty-Onar drowns you. How can a man with no vision live his life? How can a man with no name be a man?'

She marked his forehead with a smear of the ointment, then rubbed it into his skin. The warmth of the rag – or was it the ointment? – was disturbing, far too hot for normal cloth. Zayn felt as if the warmth were boring into his forehead and spreading through every nerve in his body. She dipped the rag into the ointment again and wiped it across his lips. Reflexively he licked them, and she smiled, pleased. Slowly the warmth faded, but he saw with different eyes. Every blade of grass, every detail of her face and clothing, were so vivid that he nearly cried out. He turned his head and saw that Apanador seemed to be standing in a cloud of bright light.

'Walk in as a boy,' Apanador said. 'Then ride as a man ever after.'

Alone, carrying the spirit wand in both hands like a quarterstaff, Zayn headed towards the Mistlands. He was just out of sight of the camp when he came to the first stream, running slowly, clogged with purple tendrils of weed and pale, lavender scum in little backwaters. He stepped in cautiously, but the bed proved to be firm sand and stone. As he crossed stream after stream, the ground began to turn spongy. Even when the ground rose above the water, his bare feet made a sucking, squelching noise on the short hummocky grass. He used the spirit staff to tap his way through the marshy ground, where here and there stagnant pools of water oozed among lush red-orange lichens. Slowly the mist came to meet him, arching up and covering the sky like a tent, the torn edges gleaming in the sunlight. When he walked under the cool greyness, he could see it lying on the ground ahead as thick as a wall. The air turned cold; drops beaded on his shirt. His view shrank as the greyness built an ever-receding wall some yards ahead. Near him everything looked abnormally clear and significant: each hummock of grass, each ooze of water carried an urgent if unreadable message. His hearing, too, seemed sharper than ever before. From the mist came the sound of water slapping and splashing in slow movements, each sound like the cry of some live thing.

As he was tapping his way along, the mist swirled to reveal a darker grey. Ahead stretched one of the lakes, a flat rippled sheet of shallow water, disappearing into the white drift. Red rushes grew sharp and dark, like strokes drawn with a scribe's pen. Among them stood a grey flying creature of the species called cranes. With a squat body, a long slender neck, and enormous wings of naked skin, furled close to the body at the moment, it perched on one thin, pink leg and looked at him with beady yellow eyes.

'Little brother,' Zayn said. 'Ask the gods to bless me.'

Even as he spoke, Zayn wondered why he'd say such a thing – him, a rational man, educated at the best school in Haz Kazrak. The crane, however, bobbed its head to him, then spread great wings to reveal the pair of vestigial arms that dangled underneath. It flew off with a slap against the heavy air, its pink feet and lashing tail trailing awkwardly after. Zayn followed as it circled the edge of the lake, but soon he lost it in the mist. He began to wonder how many boys camped right here and never dared to go further into the unnerving not-quite-silence.

He stopped at the place where the lakeshore bulged out in a muddy spit of land, pointing to a hummock out in the water. Testing his way with his staff, Zayn stepped off the spit and into the lake. He nearly cried out in surprise: the water was warm. So was the muddy bottom as it clung to his bare feet. He slogged his way out to the hummock, and from this higher ground, he could see a good ways out into the mist-shrouded lake.

Lumps of sodden land lay like a chain of tiny islands and seemed to lead to deeper water. He was debating whether to go further when he saw the crane, perched on a hummock just at the limit of his sight. He stepped off and began making his way towards it, going from hummock to hummock, but spending most of his time in the turgid water, which grew warmer and warmer the farther in he went. It was hard going, fighting the water, testing every inch of muddy ground, clambering from one soft lump to another. Every time he grew close to the crane, it would fly off again, leading him further. As the water grew warmer, a strange kind of slimy plant, dark red and no more than half an inch high, replaced the purple grass.

What felt like hours passed before Zayn paused to look back. The shore had disappeared, wrapped in mist. Ahead, the water stretched out smooth and empty, rippling in the light wind, but to his left stood a hummock big enough to qualify as a tiny island. Zayn splashed his way over and climbed onto the stretch of slimy moss-covered rock, about fifty yards long and maybe twenty at its widest point. On the far side grew a huge stand of a different sort of reed, of a mottled purple-brown colour, each one about as thick as his wrist. Zayn knelt down and cupped water in his hands; it tasted medicinal and sharp, full of mineral salts, he supposed. He drank it sparingly.

When he looked up, the mist swirled and lightened, and this time, he did cry out. For a moment he thought that he was seeing a city looming out of the endless fogs: shining towers, great mounds of houses, some pale green, some horizontally striped in browns and tans, but most as white and shiny as salt. Huge billowy domes, edged in opaque icicles, loomed over flat terraces. Crazy-tilting roofs hung, caught in mid-fall over what seemed to be open squares while rope ladders and twisted balconies marched down glittering walls. Far larger than even Haz Kazrak, on and on this broken cityscape stretched, reaching back into the surging clouds and walls of mist, reaching up into the temporary gilding of the sun beyond the fog. As he stared in open-mouthed awe, he found himself remembering every old tale or fable he'd ever heard as a boy about the wondrous cities and huge flying ships of the Ancestors, lost forever, or so everyone said, in their ruined homeland.

Then, when the entire wrapping of mist blew sideways for a few brief moments, he realized that water was trickling out of the towers and sheeting down, that the supposed buildings were vast deposits of minerals and salts, accreted over the Lord only knew how many endless centuries or aeons, from the outlets for the mineral springs under the Mistlands. He grunted aloud in sheer disappointment as the mists came back, a blanket raised by the wind's hands and just as quickly dropped.

His reason reasserted itself. The hot springs would boil up inside those deposits, he supposed, to produce the huge quantities of fog when the steam hit the cooler air. The moisture would then run down its own accretions, leaving a further residue of salts. How far the travertines stretched he couldn't see – a long, long way, far beyond the limit of his mist-shortened view. For a moment he considered wading over to explore, but the crane came flapping back. It settled, plopping into the water, and turned to block his way. When it opened its beak, he saw tiny spikes of teeth.

'You want me to stay, don't you, little brother? All right. I'll make my vigil here.'

The crane tucked up one leg and began to study the water, head a little to one side, long beak ready. Zayn sat down on the rocks nearby and shivered in his soaked clothes. He looked at the spirit staff in his lap, ran his hands along it and found it comforting that Ammadin's hands had bound the thread and tied the talisman. Just beyond the mists, she and the members of the comnee were waiting for him with food and warm blankets. He wondered how long he was going to have to stay out here to prove his manhood to the comnee.

'They have a hard way with their boys, these people.'

The crane bobbed its head as if agreeing.

'My father had the usual ceremonies done over me. Now, my uncle – he took me to a whore-house when he figured I was old enough. The old man was furious enough to kill us both, but my uncle was bigger than him. Good thing, too.'

Zayn found himself remembering his father's face, but as a young man, not as he was now. He jumped to his feet and swore, because it seemed Father was standing in front of him, vivid and solid. The vision lasted only a moment, but Zayn saw the anger in his eyes, the sharp twist of a mouth that was about to spit curses on his son. Then the vision faded, leaving only the rock, the water rushes, and the crane, raising its head to look at its restless neighbour.

'I saw that look on his face the whole time I was a child,' Zayn said. 'And you know what the worst thing was? I agreed with him. I knew it already, you see, that there was something wrong with me. I was just too young to know what.'

The crane seemed to be considering all this seriously. Zayn started to laugh at himself for talking to a bird, but with a sharp cry, the crane leapt and flew away, leaving only silence and empty water behind it.

'Come back!' Zayn called. 'I'm sorry I laughed at you.'

Well, he'd driven away everyone else who'd tried to befriend him, hadn't he? He'd always been terrified of letting anyone close. After all, he might have let something slip in some relaxed moment. They might have come to see what he was, barely human at all, an outcast and a pollution.

'What are you doing?' he said aloud. 'Letting your mind run this way!'

You're just tired and hungry, he told himself. Men do see things when they get that way. Perhaps. There was a cold ripple down his spine that had nothing to do with the damp air. Suddenly he was sure he felt spirits all around him. He knew it, couldn't talk himself out of it, felt them circling him like a cold wind. He held the spirit staff up like a weapon and stared out into the mist.

In a pale, translucent progression, drifting like bits of torn cloud, they came walking across the water towards him. Smoke-shapes with human faces, they drifted nearer and nearer, staring at him with demon-slit eyes. In the rippling water he heard voices.

'Zahir,' they whispered. 'Zahir Benumar! We see you, Zahir. We know your real name now. Death taught us a good many things.'

'Who are you?' Zayn snapped. 'What do you want?'

'Don't you remember me?' One smoke wisp resolved itself into a middle-aged man, fat and naked. 'I hanged myself after you went to the Chosen with your tales about me.'

'You were a traitor!'

'No, no traitor, only a man who wanted justice for his daughter. Better I died fast than at the hands of the Chosen.'

With a howl of laughter, the spirit disappeared. The others stayed, prowling round and round the island.

'What do you want with me?'

With a sigh, an inarticulate reproach and murmur, they pressed closer.

'Remorse.' A woman appeared out of the smoke. 'Zahir, don't you ever feel any remorse?'

'We all died because of you.' This spirit seemed to be a young man. 'For some of us, our dying was a long slow thing.'

'That had nothing to do with me! I'm just a pair of extra eyes for the Great Khan. I'm just a pair of ears.'

'Listen to him!' The spirits began to laugh. 'Listen to him!'

'It's true! I never killed any of you.'

'You killed all of us.'

One at a time, with a last whisper, the spirits dissolved like a mist before a wind, until only the lake stretched in front of him, rippled and dark. Zayn lowered the staff. For a long while he merely shook. He was so desperate for the sound of a voice that he spoke aloud.

'This isn't the kind of vision I can take back to Ammadin, is it? I wonder what she'd think if she knew the truth?'

Zayn sat back down and tried to think of some tale to convince her and the comnee that he'd seen a proper vision. Not the slightest idea came to him. He could at least claim to have seen a spirit crane. Suddenly he wondered if such a claim was the simple truth, because the bird came back, settling into the water nearby.

'Little brother, did you send those ghosts to me?'

The crane cocked its head and looked at him with oddly intelligent eyes. It was just a bird – it had to be just a bird – but he saw a light around it, a glow like sun in a mist emanating from its scaly skin. The golden eyes seemed to pierce him with a stare like Ammadin's cold scrutinies.

'Little brother, send me a vision.'

With a soft cry, the crane flew, circled the island once, then disappeared into the mists. Zayn clutched the spirit staff and sat perfectly still. The hard slimy rock under him, the cold, his hunger – they were nothing to him, who could crouch for hours on his hands and knees in order to overhear some conversation between suspect officers or to see some forbidden meeting. The fog above turned a brighter silver to signal that noon had arrived in the world beyond the Mistlands. The warm and bitter-scented water lapped and splashed at the edge of the island. Zayn waited, staring into the mists.

He was floating in a room or seeing it in a dream; he was never sure which, but the room looked as vivid as if he stood in some sort of brothel, a handsome well-appointed place, anyway, where men sat in a haze of hashish smoke, and unveiled women moved among them with plates of food on silver trays. Sitting in one corner was a man with a military posture and thick streaks of grey in his hair, not a bad-looking fellow for his age, but Zayn hated him the moment he saw him. He looked sober, barely touched by the smoke in his safe little corner, while he peered out at the room with such a knowing little smirk, such a look of contempt for the people he watched that Zayn wanted to kill him. He would be doing the world a favour if he removed this empty husk of a man, who reminded him of nothing so much as a scavenger lizard, feeding off the deaths of others. His hand on the hilt of his knife, Zayn moved towards the fellow, who turned and looked him straight in the face. At that moment, Zayn recognized him: it was himself, the same face that he saw every morning when he shaved, merely some twenty years older.

The sound of a cry broke the vision. Zayn was on his feet, his knife in hand, before he realized that he'd made the cry himself.

'No! God forgive me! No!'

A terror that he couldn't understand clutched him as he paced back and forth on the rocky islet. Maybe he should throw himself into the lake to drown, if his life was going to come to that, those sunken eyes, possessed by a simple ugly emptiness, a man with nothing to live for but revenge.

'I'll get back at you. I'll get back at all of you.'

Whom was he talking to? He didn't know, only knew that he'd lived the promise in that voice for years now, four long years that he suddenly saw as an arrow, flying straight into the future and leading him to the brothel of his vision.

'It isn't true. You're tired. You're hungry. This place is enough to drive any man crazy. It's just a kind of dream, like you get when you're feverish.'

But the memory of the smirk stayed with him, and the bright little eyes of a scavenger – some scrabbling land crab, collecting the droppings of stronger beasts and pushing them back to its lair, as proud as it could be of its collection of dung. His own metaphor made him shudder. He walked round and round the island and looked for the crane.

'Come back, little brother! Don't leave me here alone! Please come back, please.'

The water splashed on the rock like one of Ammadin's incantations, a constant murmur of sound. For all that he desperately tried to talk himself round, Zayn felt magic all around him. It was as if magic were a person who was watching him, spying on him, following every move he made. He felt it as a coldness down his back, a prickling of his skin such as a wild animal must feel when the hunter stalks close.

Abruptly he realized that the noon-glow was long gone and the mists were turning a steely grey. When he thought of staying out all night, he was so frightened that his stomach clenched, and he dropped to his knees to vomit. Since he'd eaten nothing in a long time, all that came up was the lime-bitter water. This spasm of fear convinced him to stay. He'd conquered a hundred other fears; he could conquer this new one, not of death or torture, but of seeing too much. He went to the edge of the island and knelt down, scooping up water in his hands to wash the foamy vomit from his mouth. All at once he heard the crane, shrieking what sounded like a warning overhead. Out of sheer reflex he threw himself to one side.

The arrow sped by him.

It came so fast, hissing through the air, that he thought he'd imagined it until another shaft sped out of the mist and struck with a clatter on the rock just behind him. Zayn screamed a gurgling imitation of a death-cry, then pitched himself head-first into the water. The warm darkness enveloped him, as languid as a bath. In the shallow water he could not swim, but he forced himself down to the bottom and, crawling more than swimming, managed to reach the spread of water rushes. Among them he could half-stand, half-crouch on the muddy bottom with just his face out of the water – an imperfect shelter if his unknown attacker chose to send a volley his way. For a long time he heard nothing but the splash of water; then distantly came the sound of someone laughing. So. The fool thought he'd killed him, did he?

Smiling to himself, Zayn began to crawl sideways, dropping to his knees under the water and holding his breath until his chest ached like fire. At last he risked coming up in the shelter of rocks and water weeds. Out in the lake on the other side of the island, a man was slogging towards him. Even in the mist, he recognized

Palindor. The old border adage was holding true: insult a comnee man – fight for your life.

Zayn slipped the long knife free of his belt, then crouched again, leaning back so that his face was barely out of the water. He heard splashing as Palindor climbed onto the island and the wet slapping steps of bare feet as he walked across. When Zayn risked another look, Palindor was standing some twenty feet away.

Slowly, carefully, Zayn began to climb up the rocky bank of the island. His back towards him, Palindor unstrung the bow and began using it like a staff to poke amongst the rushes. Zayn gained the ground and straightened up, his knife ready in his hand.

'Looking for me?'

When Palindor spun around, Zayn charged, racing across the rocks. Palindor dropped the bow and grabbed at the knife at his side, but Zayn reached him before it was out of the sheath. In a futile attempt to protect himself, Palindor flung up his left arm. Zayn grabbed it, swung him around off-balance, and slipped with his enemy. As they went down, Zayn wrestled him round and fell on top of him. He stabbed with the long knife at the base of the neck, one quick blow that severed the spine. Palindor whimpered, twitched convulsively, then lay still.

'You stupid little bastard! I'm not even the reason you couldn't have her.'

Zayn wiped his knife on Palindor's shirt, then sheathed it. He decided that he'd better not tell the comnee about this, but then it occurred to him that Palindor had committed a grave crime, stalking a man during his vision quest. He took the dropped bow and unbuckled the quiver of arrows hung on Palindor's belt. They were solid evidence that Palindor intended to murder, not challenge him.

Far off in the mists came a rasping cry that was doubtless meant to sound like a swamp lizard's croak. Zayn froze, his hands tight on the quiver. That Palindor could find allies for an impious murder was the last thing that Zayn ever would have suspected from the Tribes, but the cry came again, seemingly closer. In the mist and wind it could have come from any direction. Zayn strung the bow and stuck the quiver down the front of his shirt. Crouching low, he trotted to the edge of the island and slid off into waist-deep water, but he held the bow up to keep the bowstring dry. Moving as silently as he could, slipping a bit on the muddy bottom, he started back for the hummock that marked the path to the lake shore. All he wanted was to get out of there before he was forced to kill another comnee man. He heard the false lizard cry again, desperate now, insistent for an answer.

When he reached the first hummock, Zayn stayed in the water. It was too dangerous to clamber up and expose his back to an arrow. But how deep did the water lie here? At that he remembered the spirit staff, left behind on the islet. All his instincts told him to leave it there and run for his life, but he felt that to lose the staff meant losing the manhood he'd come here to gain. He crouched low, holding the bow free of the water, and waited. The mewling cry came loud out of the mists on the far side of the islet. When he looked back, he could just see the dark shape of Palindor's corpse.

Keeping the island in sight, Zayn circled round in the direction of the cry to stalk the man stalking him. The wall of mist receded ahead of him as he waded through the lake, and slowly there appeared dark shapes that had to be another chain of hummocks and rocks. All at once he saw the spirit crane, standing on a small, sharp rock. The crane spread its wings, bobbed its head, and danced a few threatening steps – guarding a nest, maybe, but Zayn took it as a warning. He crouched down, the water lapping around his chest, but kept the bow up and dry. He waited, fighting the warmth of the water, a drowsy mineral warmth that soothed and relaxed every muscle in his body. He was stifling yawns by the time he saw the man-sized shape, slipping through the water ahead of him some thirty feet away and headed for the islet.

Zayn let the man get a good head-start, then drew and nocked an arrow in his bow and followed him, keeping well back on the edge of his enemy's visibility. Sliding in the muck, cursing under his breath, the man reached the island and clambered up the rocky bank. Zayn saw him kneel down by Palindor's body and lay his bow aside. Zayn stood up, the bow ready, and waited. He had no hopes of actually hitting a target with the unfamiliar Tribal bow; he merely hoped to distract the enemy with the shot, then dodge to one side and approach from a new direction. At last the enemy rose, his bow dangling in his hand. Zayn loosed. Much to his shock, the arrow hissed home and struck its target in the side of his chest. The man screamed, twisted and clawed at the shaft, and fell to his knees. By the time Zayn made his way over to the islet, he lay dead with bloody foam crusting on his lips and chin.

Zayn slung his bow over his back, then crouched down by the bleeding corpse and turned him over: a Kazrak. His eyes were pale grey and his straight hair dark, but he was a young Kazrak, all right, with a beaky nose and dark skin, wearing a tunic over his leather trousers. Zayn had never seen him before in his life.

He ran across the island, grabbed the spirit staff, and kept running to the farther bank. He slipped into the water and started back across the lake. He was half-way to the first hummock when he heard another false croak, coming from the opposite direction of the first, as if there were a net of men being drawn around him. As fast as he could, Zayn slogged on. Every now and then he would crouch down and look back, only to see nothing but mist.

By the time he gained the lake shore, it was growing dark. Tapping his way with the staff, desperately looking for the traces he'd left in the morning, he picked his way through the swamp. In the twilight, the only sign of treacherous bogs were little glimmers of silver from standing water. When he realized that he had miles between him and safety, his exhaustion caught him. He would find another islet and sleep. If he died of exposure, then he'd never have to wake up, and at the moment, that seemed a blessing. When he looked back, he saw the bluish lights drifting in the mists behind him, soft round balls, drifting like watchers for the gods. The sight drove him onward.

Zayn went about half a mile on before he saw the light ahead of him, a pale blue fire bobbing as if it were a lantern held in someone's hand. He fell to one knee, laid the staff down, and nocked an arrow in his bow. As the light came closer, he suddenly wondered if it were an evil spirit; if so, the bow would be useless.

'Zayn?' Ammadin called out. 'Is that you?'

Zayn sighed aloud, a sharp hiss of relief.

'Yes. Stay where you are! You could be in danger.'

Zayn put the arrow back in the quiver, picked up the spirit staff, and went on, stumbling on the mossy ground. When he finally saw Ammadin, he swore aloud. She was holding her hand shoulder high, and from her fingers streamed a pale bluish light like cold fire. When she spoke, he couldn't answer: all he could do was stare at the light on her hand.

'I had the feeling you'd be back at sunset,' she said. 'Here – what? By the gods, where did you get that bow?'

Zayn could only shrug and watch the streaming light.

'Tell me.' Ammadin grabbed his arm with her other hand. 'What danger? Are you hurt?'

'No. The bow? I took it from a man who tried to kill me with it. Someone was hunting me out there.'

'Who?'

Zayn made an effort and looked away from the magical fire. How could he tell her the truth? Palindor had loved her once.

'Someone I don't know. Kazraks.'

'Don't lie to me.' Ammadin's voice turned hard. 'Who?'

'Very well, then. Palindor. But he had a couple of Kazraks with him.'

Ammadin went stiff and still, her hand still tight on his arm.

'I'm sorry,' Zayn went on, 'but he had this bow. He was trying to kill me. I swear it. I'm sorry.'

'No need for apologies. I believe you. Come along. We've got to get back to the others.'

'But he – I mean Palindor. Aren't you sorry he's dead?'

'I'm sorry he broke the law. There's no time for chatter. Come on!'

Once he was sitting by a fire with a bowl of stew in his hands, the day turned so dream-like in his mind that he was almost grateful to Palindor, because the death threat at least seemed real, preserving the other memories with it. In a silent grim crowd, the comnee crowded close to hear about his quest. While Ammadin, her hand now stripped of the magical light, told the story, Zayn gobbled stew and let the fire-warmth soak into him. When she finished, Apanador took the captured bow and studied the decoration on it.

'It's Palindor's, all right,' the chief said. 'Well, his mother's comnee is going to have some harsh words about this.'

'Why should they?' Dallador rose from his place. 'Palindor acted like an ugly little coward. He went out there to murder a man with all the odds on his side.'

'I know that. But will his mother see it that way?'

'She'll have to.' Ammadin turned to Zayn. 'He broke the laws of the gods as well as our law. When a man goes to vigil in the Mistlands, his life is as sacred as a spirit rider's. Who would go seek a vision if he thought his enemies would be waiting for him in the holy places?'

The comnee nodded in grim-faced agreement. Dallador sat down, satisfied.

'And as for these Kazraks,' Apanador said, 'they're no concern of ours. If they come hunting a comnee man, they'll have to pay the price. Zayn, do you have enemies in the khanate?'

'I must.' Zayn picked his words carefully. 'Maybe it's that chief whose wife I took. But I don't understand. That Kazrak I killed? I've never seen him before in my whole life. Maybe he was just a friend of Palindor's who offered to help him.'

'If another Kazrak were riding with the comnees,' Apanador said, 'we would have heard about it long before this. Let me think. Palindor's mother rides with Lanador's comnee. I don't even know where they are – west, I think. Holy One, should we seek them out?'

'No,' Ammadin said. 'She's better off without a son like that. If the gods will that her path crosses ours, I'll offer her a horse in restitution. One is about all he was worth.'

'Do you think she'll take it?' Zayn asked.

'Why not?' Apanador glanced his way. 'I know her, and she'll be pleased to get any kind of blood price. By rights, we don't have to offer her anything at all since her son was bent on murder.'

'Zayn?' Dallador broke in. 'But do you want retribution? For the broken vision quest, I mean.'

'No,' Zayn said. 'I just wish it hadn't happened. I didn't want to kill anyone, much less him.'

Ammadin and Apanador exchanged a satisfied glance. As the crowd broke up, Dallador came over to Zayn and laid a friendly hand on his arm.

'Not bad,' Dallador said. 'A man's hunting you with a bow, and you've only got a knife, but you managed to kill him anyway.'

'You gave me a good knife, that's why.'

Dallador grinned.

'Palindor used to eat at your fire, didn't he?' Zayn went on. 'Am I still a friend of yours?'

'What happened was between you and him, and he was in the wrong, anyway.'

'Thanks, but still –'

'Let me tell you something.' Dallador held up his hand for

silence. 'The comnees don't count cowards as men. Palindor was a coward, so he's no friend of mine, and he's not worth mourning. Let me warn you: the comnees demand more from a man than you Kazraks ever would.' He waved his hand vaguely at the encircling darkness. 'Out here, mistakes mean death. A man who makes mistakes has no place in the comnee. Do you understand?'

'Oh yes. And I'll tell you something. I like it.'

They shared an easy smile.

In Ammadin's tent a ball of pale light hung on the ridge pole like a lantern. As part of the ritual, Zayn had to describe his visions, and as she waited, watching him, her eyes seemed to look through, not at him. Safe, warm at last, well-fed, Zayn was too blurry with sleep-longing to think of any convincing lie.

'I saw a spirit crane. It met me on the lake shore and took me to the island for my vigil. Then later it kept coming back.'

'Wonderful! Did it leave you a gift?'

'No, but I was going to stay all night until the arrows started flying.'

'Ah, damn Palindor! The crane would have given you a gift if only he and his Kazraks hadn't got in the way.'

'Got in the way? That's one way of putting it.'

'From now on, cranes are Bane for you,' Ammadin went on as if he hadn't spoken. 'You must never kill one – never, do you hear me? Don't disturb a nest, either. Any crane you see means an omen, and you must greet them and speak to them. If you find a dead one, you must bury it properly.'

'I promise, and I mean it, because that crane saved my life out there. It showed me a vision, too. My father came to me.'

'His ghost? Is he dead?'

'No. I guess it was just an image of him.'

'That's good enough. Did he have some advice for you?'

'You don't understand. My father hates me. I was nothing but one disappointment after the other.'

Ammadin stared, visibly shocked. 'Did he curse you?' she said at last. 'In the vision, I mean.'

'No. He had the usual look on his face, like a man who's just stepped in fresh horseshit with a bare foot.'

'Why did he hate you?'

'The Lord means everything to him. He kept our household as pure as he could make it, until I came along.'

'Your people can be harsh, when it comes to your religion. It must be that book you read.'

'He read it all the time, that's for sure. He wanted me to memorize it, you see, and so I did.'

'Wait a minute. Why would he get angry if you did what he wanted?'

Zayn felt cold fear clutch him. He'd blundered, and badly. Back in the khanate that lapse might have led to his unmasking and, ultimately, his death. Ammadin raised one eyebrow but waited for him to speak. He wanted a lie, could think of none.

'Uh well,' Zayn said. 'I did it in a single afternoon. I mean, I read through it, and I knew it off by heart, all of it. I was eight, maybe.'

'Well, so?'

'Don't you know what that means?'

'No. I should think he'd have been proud of you, a child that young, laying up holy words in his heart.'

'But –' He hesitated.

'But what?' Ammadin leaned forward, staring into his eyes. 'What does it mean, then?'

Caught – how could he tell her? But how could he refuse? She waited patiently, her expression gentle, concerned.

'Ah well,' Zayn said at last. 'It means I'm demon spawn, of course.'

'What? That makes no sense at all.'

'A memory like mine, it's one of the twelve times twelve forbidden talents. So Father tried to exorcize the demon part of me, and when that didn't work, he took me on quite a journey. We went to mosque after mosque, holy man after holy man. He was trying to find one who had the power to cure demon blood, you see. Finally I realized what he wanted, and so I pretended I was cured. But he never really trusted me.'

'I still don't –'

'You must have heard of the forbidden talents.'

'No, I haven't. Are they like Banes?'

'Yes, exactly. But –' Zayn caught himself just in time. Why was he babbling like this? The face of the man in his vision rose in his memory. For a moment he thought he saw it floating like a mask in front of him, a smug face, twisted and gloating over secrets held too long.

'What's wrong?' Ammadin rose to a kneel. 'Are you going to throw up?'

He shook his head. 'The talents, they're Bane, all right,' he said. 'But you're born with them. If you have one, it marks you as demon spawn. Most fathers kill children like that, but I was his only son. So he didn't. I learned to hide it.'

'Demon spawn? What's that supposed to mean?'

'Back in the old country, across the sea where we came from, there were demons. They were impure, and they had the forbidden talents. But some of our women slept with them and had children, impure children. That's one reason we left the old country and came here, so we could be pure again.'

'Are the demons supposed to have come with you?'

'No. It's just that those women must have hidden some of their children, you see, so the mullahs couldn't kill them. And those children would have grown up and passed the taint on to their children, and so on. And now, people like me still have demon blood in us. My mother must have carried it.'

Ammadin considered him for so long that he assumed she, like all the others, despised him. Finally she shook her head and spoke. 'That is the stupidest thing I've ever heard. Demons can't sire children. They don't have bodies.'

He gaped, knew his mouth was hanging open like some idiot child's, tried to find words, and realized at length that he was shaking.

'Don't you believe me?' Ammadin said.

'Of course I do. The mullahs and my father – they always warned us against demons, the gennies, they called them. They could look like real people, but they weren't. They were spirits, and their bodies were just illusions.'

'Well, then, how is one of these illusions supposed to get a woman pregnant?'

He could only stare at her. He wanted to say 'of course they can't, you're right, it's ridiculous,' but his mouth refused to form the words. He hadn't seen. Why hadn't he seen? He hadn't dared to see. What if he'd tried this piece of logic on his father? The old man might have killed him. He'd come close to killing his tainted son as it was, with his beatings and periods of forced starvation.

'What a waste!' Ammadin went on. 'Your people could use a memory like yours. They've got so many laws and prayers.'

He nodded. 'Look, Spirit Rider, Wise One, if I'm not demon spawn, then what am I?'

'A man like any other, I suppose, with an odd turn of mind. Some men are good with a bow; others can't shoot to save their lives but ride like they're half-horse. Some men would forget their own names if they lived alone; others can remember every horse their wives have sold to the Kazraks in the last thirty years.'

'But the forbidden talents –'

'– are on some list one of your holy men made up a long time ago. I have no idea why he did it or why he put having an amazing memory on it, but I think he was born a few pages short of a holy book, if you take my meaning.'

Zayn laughed, softly at first, then louder, realized that his eyes were filling with tears, but the laughter kept coming, making him tremble until Ammadin reached over, grabbed him by the shoulders, and shook him.

'I'm sorry, Wise One.' He was gasping for breath. 'I don't know what's wrong with me.'

'It's the shock. You've spent your life guarding this evil secret, haven't you? Wondering what would happen if someone knew?'

'Just that. Yes.'

'And now I tell you that it's not evil and shouldn't be a secret. Why wouldn't you be shocked?'

'I see your point, yes.' Zayn managed to smile. 'I wish I could go back to the Mistlands. I never thought I'd say it, but I want to see more.'

'It's too dangerous. I haven't forgotten about those other voices you heard out there. Apanador thinks that we should ride east. Maybe we can throw them off your trail.'

'I've brought you nothing but trouble, haven't I? It's good of you to ride just for me.'

'And wouldn't we ride for anyone in the comnee? Zayn, you belong to us now.'

Ammadin spoke so quietly that Zayn felt his lies eating at him, simply because her words were perfectly true: part of him would always belong to Apanador's comnee. He wanted to wash the lie away, to warn her that he'd have to leave the Tribes to fulfil his duty to the Great Khan. But the Chosen – his vow – he could say nothing. Ammadin laid a maternal hand on his arm.

'You're exhausted. Go to sleep. We can talk in the morning.'

When he looked at her hand lying on his arm, Zayn shuddered, remembering the way it had dripped fire.

'What's wrong?' Ammadin said.

'Well, it's just the light. I mean, the light you had on your hand when you met me. I'm not used to strong magic.'

'That?' She paused, laughing at him. 'It's the juice of a plant. It only grows in the Mistlands, or you would have seen it before this. When you crush it, the sticky stuff inside glows for quite a while before it fades. Look! I wiped it off onto a rag and stuck it on the ridge pole.'

When Zayn looked, he blushed. The rag was one of those that he used to wash pots and bowls, and here he'd been so sure that the light sprang from magic that he'd never recognized it.

Later, when he was rolled up in his blankets, Zayn remembered that he'd failed to find his true name. He knew that he should tell Ammadin, that in fact he should get up and go find her immediately, but exhaustion took him over, and he slept.

Zayn was well on his way back to the lake shore by the time Warkannan found the bodies. The captain was about half a mile away from Tareev, keeping in contact with Arkazo by croaking like a swamp lizard while he fought the muck and the stinking water. When he heard Arkazo calling, a frantic little string of signals, Warkannan called back and splashed his way through an empty stretch of lake and mist. He finally found him crouched on a muddy hummock.

'I heard someone scream,' Arkazo said. 'Over to the left.'

It was either a good omen or the worst one in the world. For some minutes, Warkannan sent lizard cries through the mist, but no one answered. He nocked an arrow in his bow, told Arkazo to do the same, and set off in the rough direction of the scream. Although he and Arkazo kept calling, they heard nothing from Palindor or Tareev. At last, looming in the mist, Warkannan saw a long rocky stretch of islet, and on it, two dark mounds.

'Stay here and cover me until I call for you.'

Holding the bow out of water, Warkannan splashed through the waist-deep lake. Constantly he turned his head, looking for a possible enemy, but he saw only a grey crane, perched on one pink leg amongst the tall rushes. Then, from a few feet away, he saw the bodies. Rasping like a fly-lizard struck him as sacrilege.

'Arkazo! Get over here!'

Without a word, Arkazo came splashing through the water. Together they climbed up the rocky bank.

They lay in a pool of blood, Palindor with his spine efficiently severed, Tareev dead from a Tribal arrow. In his shock, it took Warkannan a moment to realize that Palindor's bow was gone. Somehow Zayn had killed him with only a knife, taken the bow, and started a hunt of his own.

'He's one of the Chosen, all right,' Warkannan said. 'We've got to get out of here.'

Arkazo made no reply. He was crouched down beside Tareev, his hand on his dead friend's face, staring into Tareev's unseeing eyes as if he could bring him back to life by force of will.

'I'm sorry, Kaz,' Warkannan said, as gently as he could. 'I know it's hard, but the only thing you can do for him now is to swear vengeance.'

Arkazo looked up, his mouth set, his eyes blind.

'Come on now,' Warkannan said. 'There's a dangerous man out there in the mists with a bow. We can't do a thing for the khan's cause if we're dead.'

'We can't just leave him here.'

'We've got to.'

Arkazo shook his head in a stubborn no. Warkannan left him, grabbed Palindor's corpse by the shoulders, and dragged it to the edge of the islet. When he slung him in, Palindor sank into the dark water that would be the only grave he'd ever have. With a long cry of mourning, the crane flapped up from the rushes and flew away. When Warkannan returned for Tareev, Arkazo got up, his hand on his sword hilt, and barred his way. Warkannan slapped Arkazo across the face so hard that the boy staggered back.

'You're following my orders, you stupid young fool. We've got to get out of here. I don't like doing this any more than you do. Now get out of the way.'

His hand on his cheek, Arkazo moved. As he was lowering Tareev into the water, Warkannan felt a tightness in his throat, but many another good man would die before the khan claimed the throne. He allowed himself a brief thought of Kareem, who would never see his son's grave.

'Come on,' Warkannan said. 'We've got to get back to shore. We'll deal with Zayn later.'

Sullenly Arkazo followed when Warkannan stepped back into the lake. Bows at the ready, they slogged their way across the open water, heading roughly north-east. Warkannan stayed on guard, listening for every small sound, watching for every small trace of movement in the shifting view. At last, when the twilight was turning the Mistlands grey and featureless, they staggered out of the water onto the spongy lake shore. In this relative safety Warkannan turned to have a word with Arkazo and found him in tears. He left him alone with it and led the way down the bank.

A few miles down the shore stood a tangle of orange and russet fern trees, bent and twisted by the constant wind. Nearby, on a stretch of drier ground, the horses were tethered, and Soutan paced back and forth. When he saw them, Soutan hurried forward to meet them.

'Zayn's our man, all right,' Warkannan said. 'Palindor and Tareev are dead. The Chosen teach their men how to defend themselves.'

'That's horrible.' Soutan was whispering. 'So horrible about Tareev – I'm sorry, Arkazo. Truly sorry.'

Arkazo stared at him as if he hadn't heard.

'Well,' Warkannan said, 'we'll get our revenge for this. It's the only comfort we're going to have, but we'll get it.'

'Oh yes.' Soutan nodded firmly. 'You see, before Zayn went under the fog cap, I saw him. I know what he looks like now.'

'Which is?'

'Mostly he looks Kazraki.' Soutan paused, thinking. 'A somewhat flatter nose than usual, and darker skin. Deep-set eyes. Tall, very straight back. I'm assuming he was in the cavalry.'

'A lot of the Chosen were, yes, or still are. I'm glad you've got him pegged. I want another shot at him. But this time, we're going to be damned careful.'

That night they made a miserable camp a few miles out of the swamps proper. Overhead the fog turned the dark dome of night into a ceiling, hanging close above their heads. After they finished eating, Arkazo went some ten feet out into the grass and sat unmoving, staring out into the dark plains. Soutan took a book and a small cloth pouch out of his saddlebags, then sat down by the fire.

'What's that?' Warkannan said.

'The oracle.' Soutan smiled with a flash of tooth. 'I see no harm in showing it to you. It requires no particular magic to cast.'

Warkannan leaned forward for a look. He could see the title, stamped in black on a pale leather cover, but he found it incomprehensible.

'It's written in the old language of the Cantons,' Soutan said. 'Which was, in fact, its original language, but a Kazraki translation exists. It's *The Sibylline Prophecies*.'

'Shaitan! But I don't know why I'm surprised. It seems logical, using heresy to work sorcery.'

Soutan laughed, then opened the pouch and shook out six bronze discs. 'Ordinary coins,' he remarked. 'Heads count one, tails two, and there's a way of adding them up.'

Warkannan watched while he shook the coins in both hands, then strewed them on the ground. In the firelight the sorcerer leaned forward, peering at them, muttering to himself. He repeated the throw six times, then opened the book, flipped through the pale pink pages, and finally laid one finger on a passage.

'Could you put a bit more fuel onto that fire?' Soutan said. 'This print is large, but still –'

'What? I thought you sorcerers could make light when you needed it.'

Soutan ignored him. Warkannan added more dried horse dung and blew on the fire to bring up the flames. Soutan hunched close, his lips working as he read over the passage the coins had indicated. Finally he swore – in the language of the Cantons, but Warkannan could guess his frame of mind well enough.

'Bad news?' Warkannan said.

'No, merely completely irrelevant. I must be too tired.' He shut the book with a snap. 'Or else I misread the coins in the bad light. I'll try again after sunrise.'

'What did it say?'

'Oh, some rambling drivel about the Fourth Prophet being close at hand. Do you know about that? No, I see you don't, pious soul that you are. The oracle claims that a fourth prophet will come to the people of Kazrajistan just as the others did, arising out of humble circumstances amid signs from God and so on in the usual way of prophets.'

'Well, I suppose it could happen. Prophets do appear now and then.' Warkannan held up one hand and ticked the names off on his fingers. 'Mohammed, blessed be he, who wrote the true faith into a book. Agvar, who led us out of our bondage in the demon-lands. Kaleel Mahmet, who carved a khanate in our new home with the cavalry for his knife.' He lowered his hand. 'And there have been plenty of minor prophets over the years, too many to count, really.'

'Indeed, whenever the khanate found it convenient to be prophesied at.' Soutan paused for an unpleasant smile. 'But this one is supposed to be a major prophet, the final fulfilment of the law, and a woman as well.'

'Oh. It's nonsense, then. Drivel, as you said.'

'You're sure of that? Your women pray, they read the holy books.'

Warkannan hesitated, thinking. 'That's true,' he said at last. 'But it strikes me wrong. Men aren't going to listen to a female prophet. Why would God waste His time?'

'You Kazraks are amazing, really amazing.'

'What do you mean by that?'

'The things you attribute to God, such as worrying about wasted time. Do you think he's always winding his clocks like you people do?'

Warkannan caught himself on the verge of bad temper. 'Ah well,' he said instead. 'You're right, if you mean that ordinary men can't understand what God may do or what He's like. But the true prophets –'

'– may be just as wrong. Consider Hajji Agvar and this business of living as the First Prophet lived, for instance. You don't do anything of the sort. The First Prophet lived what? just over thirty-six hundred years ago, by your reckoning, when H'mai lived disgustingly primitive lives. Do you think his tribe had printing presses and carriages and all those other fancy things you people use every day?'

'What do carriages have to do with it? I can't imagine that God cares if our women ride in carriages.'

'Oh, indubitably. Then what were your ancestors fleeing when they chose to come here? What did they want?'

At first Warkannan thought the sorcerer was merely baiting him, but Soutan was waiting for the answer, his head cocked a little to one side, his eyes perfectly serious.

'Well, a simpler life than we had back in the Homelands,' Warkannan said. 'Huh, I begin to see your point about those carriages. But it wasn't just the luxuries that drove us out. It was the evil magicks and pollutions of the blood.'

'Magicks like what? Your books do mention "unspeakable practices", but since they never speak about them, I don't have the slightest idea what the authors mean.'

At that Warkannan had to laugh. 'I had the same reaction when I was a boy,' he said. 'One explanation I heard was the infidels back in the Homelands bred demons.'

'Bred demons?'

'Yes, they learned how to mingle the blood of men and animals, somehow, to produce new creatures. The mullahs called these demons.'

'I see.' Soutan thought for a long moment. 'I wonder what that really means?'

'What it says, I suppose. The mullahs don't lie.'

Soutan shook his head in mock despair.

'Well,' Warkannan snapped. 'Do you think they're lying?'

'No. I merely think that they don't know what they're talking about.'

'Now here! You're getting close to blasphemy.'

'Oh, no doubt, no doubt. I'll stop. God forbid I make you think!' Soutan rolled his eyes, a gesture that Warkannan was beginning to hate. The sorcerer stood up, then looked across the fire and out to Arkazo's silent back. 'Will he be all right?'

'Eventually. He's never seen a dead man before.'

'Ah.' Soutan considered this for a moment. 'Well, if we do bring Jezro back to Kazrajistan, he'd better get used to it.'

The sorcerer walked over to his gear and squatted down to put his book away. Warkannan reminded himself several times that he needed Soutan to get across the Rift. Strangling the irritating little bastard would be counter-productive.

That night Warkannan dreamt of Tareev's body, floating to the surface of the shallow Mistlands lake. He and Kareem stood together and watched as it drifted out of sight, and Kareem wept as bitterly as a woman. When Warkannan woke, he felt as exhausted as if he'd not slept at all.

Zayn woke from a long dream of the Mistlands to a light so cold and grey that for a moment he thought himself still dreaming. He rolled over onto his side and lifted the tent wall a few inches for a look out. Over the patchwork tents and orange wagons the fog lay thick. He sat up, pushing his blankets back, and glanced around.

Ammadin's bedroll lay neatly rolled under her tent bags. From outside the noise of the camp filtered in – dogs barking, children laughing and calling, adult voices passing by. He had slept late, then. He got up, pulled on his trousers, and noticed the rag stuck on the ridge pole where Ammadin had left it the night before. In the morning light he could see the reddish-brown streaks of sap, congealed and dry, their phosphorescence long gone.

The night before. Ammadin. The memory of their talk came back like a slap in the face; he tossed his head as if to shake off the blow. He had told her everything. He had been an utter fool. He started to shiver, grabbed his shirt and put it on, still felt the gooseflesh run down his back. You're not in the khanate, he reminded himself. You're safe here. No one cares about the damned demons and their talents. But Ammadin might mention his secrets to someone else, and that someone might talk about them in front of a Kazrak at the next horse fair.

The tent flap rustled, shook, and lifted. Ammadin came in, then let the flap drop behind her. She set her hands on her hips and studied his face.

'What's wrong?' she said. 'Did you have bad dreams?'

'In a way,' Zayn said. 'Uh, what I told you? About the demon spawn and all of that?'

'I'm not going to mention it to anyone else. I don't want to see you stoned at a horse fair because someone slipped and told your secret to a Kazrak.'

The fear left him, and he managed to return her smile. 'Thank you,' he said. 'That was on my mind, all right.'

'I thought it might be.'

'But they wouldn't stone me. They'd turn me over to the Council, and I'd be burned alive.'

'It's hard to say which would be worse.'

'Well, yes. I'd just as soon not have to choose.'

Ammadin smiled briefly. 'Tell me something,' she said. 'Your father. You said he was still alive, right?'

'Yes. He's become a hermit.'

'A what?'

'A holy man. He lives in the hills near the border, in fact, in a hut. It's near a mosque, and the men in charge bring him food and keep an eye on him.'

'How very strange! Why did he do that? Do you know?'

'Yes, I asked him when I went to see him. He says it's in penance for having fathered me.'

'Oh gods! I'll never understand you people.' Ammadin paused, her mouth twisted in disgust; then she shrugged. 'About your supposed demon blood – is your memory for words your only talent?'

'No. I can draw pictures, too.'

'So? A lot of people can do that, some badly, some well.'

'I mean, I can glance at something like a diagram in a book or a decoration on a wall and then draw it again months later. It's odd. I can see the design in my mind, and then if someone hands me some rushi and a pen, I can sort of push the design out through my eyes onto the rushi and copy over it.'

Ammadin considered this for a moment. 'That is odd,' she said at last. 'Not demonic, mind, but odd. It's still a memory talent, though.'

'Yes. I can learn just about anything fast. I can repeat whatever it is, word for word, picture for picture – even if I don't understand it. And music, if I hear a song or something like that once, I can sing it back.'

'What else is on that list?' She paused for a smile. 'I'm assuming you can remember.'

Zayn laughed, astonished that he could laugh, and so easily, over a joke that would have seemed deadly just the day before.

'I can, yes,' he said. In his mind he could see the page in one of his father's holy books, black letters, as curved as sabres, damning him. 'The twelve forbidden talents of memory, the twelve forbidden warrior talents, the forbidden talents of perception, and so on. I can recite them all, if you'd like.'

'I would. I – what's that?'

Outside someone was calling her name. She raised the tent flap and peered out.

'Maddi, he's awake, yes,' Ammadin called in return. She dropped the flap and turned back to him. 'They want to strike this tent and pack it. You'd better go eat. We're riding out as soon as the wagons are loaded.'

'All right.'

As he left the tent, Zayn was hoping that she'd just forget about the rest of the impure talents. Merely thinking of them filled him with a profound unease, born of long years of fear and scorn.

You're a man like any other, just with an odd turn of mind – or so she said. He looked up at the silver sky.

'Oh God,' he whispered. 'Can it really be true?'

No answer sounded in a booming voice, no lettered banner appeared in the fog. He laughed at himself and went to find Dallador.

The Great River ran shallow where it issued from the Mistlands, allowing the comnee to ford safely and head east. As usual Ammadin rode at some distance ahead, but she kept watch for Zayn's enemies. One of her spirit crystals, the one she'd named Sentry, made a humming sound whenever the Riders appeared in the sky, even during the day when no one could actually see them. At the sound Ammadin would halt her horse and dismount. She'd take another crystal, Spirit Eyes, out of her saddlebags and unwrap it. For as long as the Riders were overhead, Spirit Eyes would show her a vision of the territory around her, as much as a walking person might cover in a morning. Once the Riders had passed below the horizon, the spirit in the crystal would fall asleep and refuse to wake, no matter how many times she chanted the magical commands.

In the crystal Ammadin would see a circle of purple grassland, overlaid with pale yellow numbers that seemed to float in the air. She would see her horse and herself as a tiny black dot in the centre of the field of vision. The moving comnee, a tiny blotch of herds and wagons, would appear just at the edge, under one of the spirit numbers etched around the crystal's equator. If she called that number, the view would shift, and the comnee would re-appear in the centre of the circle. She could then see the country around them on all sides, or she could refocus her eyes and magnify the image in the centre until it seemed large enough to show every detail. Once she'd finished her scan, she would carry the crystal in one hand as she rode on, holding it up to let the spirit feed on the sunlight as its reward. A shaman who forgot to feed her spirits would soon find herself with dead crystals.

Three days out from the Mistlands, Sentry sounded his alarm not long after she'd left the comnee behind. As she stared into Spirit Eyes, Ammadin thought she saw a group of figures, or their smudged, tiny images, riding and leading pack horses at some long distance from the comnee. When she tried to transfer the vision to look straight down at them, Spirit Eyes made a sharp chirping little cry.

'You can't see that far?' Ammadin said. 'Or is nothing really there?'

Once more she tried to scan; once more the crystal chirped.

'Never mind,' she said. 'If they're that far away, they're not a real threat anyway.'

The next time that the Riders appeared overhead, Ammadin saw a far stranger sight than the men who might have been Zayn's enemies. Her crystal showed her three ChaMeech loping along through the grass, again, at the very edge of its range. Although she coaxed the spirit with commands and praise both, it simply could not show her more than three tiny ChaMeech shapes moving fast. From then on she kept a watch for them as well. That afternoon, not long before sunset, they reached the Blue Stone River, running from the north-east to the south-west. Near the river lay a regular Tribal campsite, but the surrounding grass, standing high and untrampled, told them that no one had passed that way for months. While the women tethered out the horses, the men began cutting down the grass to clear the areas around the stone firepits. The comnee would be making a full camp and raising all the tents. Apanador and Ammadin walked into the meagre shade of a stand of spear trees to talk.

'My wife says that some of the mares are ready to drop their foals,' he told her. 'And there's no meat left. We'll have to stay here for a couple of days.'

'Good. I have some work I need to do.'

'What about those Kazraks? Zayn's enemies.'

'They're following us, but they're clever. I only catch glimpses of them now and then.'

'I'll tell Zayn to stick close to the other men when he goes hunting.'

Once the men finished raising the tents, Ammadin carried her saddlebags into hers. Zayn had already laid the floor cloth and spread out her blankets on one side of hearth stones under the smokehole and his own bedroll on the other. She set up the god figures on their rug, then sat down on her blankets and took out her crystals.

She owned eight, each etched with a belt of different symbols. Five had been gifts from her teacher, though normally she only used four of them – Sentry, Spirit Eyes, Rain Child, and Earth Prince. The fifth, Death Chanter, she brought out only when a person had been gravely injured or lay ill with extreme old age. If Death Chanter glowed when she laid him on the victim's chest, the sufferer would most likely recover. If he remained dull, it was time for her to start instructing the victim about the road to the Deathworld.

The last three crystals she had found in the trading precinct over in the Cantons, one at a time and at intervals of years. Where the merchants had got them, they refused to say, but they had known their value and bargained hard over them. These three still glowed with life every time Ammadin took them into the sunlight, but since she didn't know their command words, the spirits had stubbornly stayed asleep.

The work she'd mentioned to Apanador involved the three crystals and Water Woman, the spirit who had called to her some days past. Perhaps here, near another river, Water Woman would do so again, and perhaps one of the sleeping crystals might let her answer.

'Spirit Rider?' Zayn lifted the tent flap and stuck his head in. 'Do you want me to bring you some light?'

'Please, yes.'

In a few minutes Zayn returned, carrying a stone oil lamp that he'd lit at someone's fire. He set it down on the hearth stones. By the flickering golden light she began wrapping the crystals and stowing them in their usual saddlebag. He sat down opposite her and watched.

'Are you hungry?' Zayn said. 'We've got some jerky left, but Dallador's down at the river, catching fish.'

'I'll wait, then,' Ammadin said. 'He's really good at finding food, Dallador.'

Zayn nodded, smiling a little as he watched her wrap her crystals. He was sitting cross-legged, his hands resting on his thighs, broad hands but somehow fine, with long fingers that might have belonged to a craftsman or even a scholar back in the khanate. Soon enough they would become scarred, calloused, and blunted, she supposed, as the hands of all the comnee men did, sooner or later. For the first time, though, she noticed his wrists. At first she thought them tattooed, then realized that a thick line of pale scar tissue circled each, as if his hands had been bound together by something that had rubbed him raw.

'We haven't had much chance to talk, this last few days,' Ammadin said. 'Have you been thinking about your vision quest?'

'Every day. A lot.'

'Good.'

Ammadin put the last crystal into the saddlebags, then set the bags down at the head of her bed.

'Tell me something,' she went on. 'Your father, did he threaten to kill you?'

'Often.' Zayn looked down at the floor cloth as if he found it suddenly fascinating. 'Whenever I slipped. That is, whenever I did something that showed I had the talents.'

'But you Kazraks have laws against murder. Or didn't you realize that as a child?'

'Of course I did. But they wouldn't have applied to me. I wasn't human. I was demon spawn, and killing me would have been like killing an animal.'

'How horrible! Is that why you didn't go asking him awkward questions about demons and the like?'

'Yes. I don't suppose you blame me for keeping my mouth shut.'

'No, I don't. Zayn, it's hard to blame you for anything after the things you've told me.'

His reaction took her utterly off-guard. He sat stone-still, and the scent of fear wreathed around him.

'What's wrong?' Ammadin said.

'Nothing.' Zayn scrambled to his feet. 'I just remembered that I promised Dallador I'd help him net those fish.'

In two strides he reached the tent flap and ducked out without looking back. Now what had brought that on? She considered asking him outright – no one in the Tribes would have dared refuse to answer such questions from a spirit rider – but she had seen real pain in his eyes. She would wait and watch, she decided, rather than press on some old wound. Still, she got up and left the tent.

Outside the sunset still glimmered in the sky, and the air was turning cool. Since there was no Bane against a woman watching men fish, she walked down to the river, flecked with light like gold coins, and saw Zayn and Dallador working side by side in the waist-deep shallows among dark red water reeds. Their clothes lay on the bank. As she watched they began hauling in the net, heavy with fish to judge by the silver roil in the water. With each pull they took a step back, dragging the fish to their doom in the open air. Water streamed down their shoulders and backs and highlighted the criss-cross of whip scars on Zayn's dark skin. Dallador's pale hair gleamed, fiery in the sunset light.

From behind her she heard someone walking up and turned to see Maradin, bringing a stack of big baskets to carry the fish to camp.

'Oh, it's you, Ammi!' Maradin smiled in obvious relief. She set the baskets down and laid a hand on her shirt, over the charm that protected her from jealousy. 'I didn't know who was down here.'

'And you thought she was watching your husband?' Ammadin smiled at her.

'Well, yes, I know I'm awful. The charm has really helped, though.' Maradin gave her a sly smile. 'I'll bet you came down to watch Zayn.'

'No, I came down because I'm worried about Zayn. A broken spirit quest is a really dangerous thing.'

'I just bet.'

'Maddi!'

'Oh all right, I'll stop, I'll stop.' Maradin turned her attention to the river. 'You know, I think we'd better go back to the tents. Zayn's not going to want to come out of the water while we're here. He's a Kazrak, after all.'

'You're right. Let's go.'

In the morning Ammadin left the camp and rode a couple of miles upstream to look for spirit pearls. Where purple rushes grew high in the water, she dismounted and began searching, but although she walked a good distance along the bank, she saw none. Normally, this early in the summer, she should have found several clutches or at the least the occasional lone specimen. She unsaddled her horse and let him roll, then slacked the bit to let him drink. She set him to graze, then sat on the bank beside her saddle and saddlebags and considered the swift-flowing water, murmuring as it trembled the thick stands of reeds. Occasionally she saw a flash of silver or brown as a fish darted among them.

Without spirit pearls nearby, would Water Woman try to reach her? Would she even be listening if Ammadin called out to her? There was of course only one way to find out. Ammadin took the three sleeping crystals out of her saddlebag, unwrapped them, laid the wrappings on the ground, and set the crystals carefully upon those, not the ground itself. Sunlight fell across them and flashed like lightning as the spirits began to wake. Within each crystal she could now see the spirit as a fine silver line spinning around the device's centre. While they fed, she considered how to phrase her command. To make a spirit serve her, the shaman had to chant the exact right words in the spirits' ancient language in a particular way, sounding each syllable in a deep, vibrating voice.

Ammadin could remember how Water Woman had addressed her and decided to try turning her words into the command formula. She rose to her knees, took a deep breath, and began to intone.

'Spirit, awake! Open hear me. Open hear me.'

Nothing. All three spirits merely spun, feeding on the sunlight. What exactly am I trying to do? Ammadin asked herself. She tried again.

'Spirit, awake! Open call out. Open call out.'

In one crystal the spirit swelled into a silver spiral, but it chirped rather than singing a note. A start, at any rate – Ammadin wrapped the other two crystals up, slipped them into their pouches, and put them safely away into her saddlebags. By the time she finished, the third spirit had returned to the shape of a spinning line. She let it feed for a few minutes, then tried a variant of her previous chant.

'Spirit, awake! Open call for. Open call for.'

The spirit sang a note and formed itself into a silver sphere, turning slowly inside the crystal. Ammadin felt like laughing in triumph, but the sound would only confuse the spirit.

'Open call for,' she repeated. 'Call for Water Woman.'

The spirit made three loud angry chirps. It wouldn't know who Water Woman was, Ammadin realized. But when Water Woman had called to her from some long distance away, no doubt she was using a spirit crystal, too. There was a good chance that the two spirits would recognize each other and respond – if Water Woman made the first move.

'Spirit,' Ammadin chanted. 'Open take name. Open take name. I name you Long Voice.'

The spirit chimed in answer. There! Ammadin thought. That's one of them tamed, anyway.

It was close to noon when the Riders returned to the sky.

Ammadin took out Spirit Eyes and looked into it, focusing first on the camp. At the edge of the circle of tents stood four tethered horses, and beside them their saddles, laden with gear, sat on the ground. Horses she'd not seen before – strangers had come to the comnee. Zayn's Kazraks?

Ammadin packed up her crystals and rode back to camp as fast as the heat would allow. She realized that she'd been right to hurry when she found Maradin waiting, pacing back and forth at the edge of the horse herd.

'I'll take care of your horse,' Maradin said. 'There's some men from Lanador's comnee here, asking about Palindor. They're in Apanador's tent.'

When Ammadin entered, she found four young men sitting stiffly across from the chief, who was pouring keese as casually as if this were only a friendly visit. She recognized one of them, Varrador, the husband of Palindor's sister.

'Ah, there you are, Spirit Rider,' Apanador said. Ammadin sat down beside the chief and accepted a bowl of keese. Apanador handed out the other four bowls before he continued. 'Our friends here have a problem,' Apanador said, 'and I think you can solve it for them.'

'I hope so, anyway.' Varrador seemed more puzzled than angry. 'My wife's brother has disappeared. I thought maybe he'd come back to your comnee.'

'No,' Ammadin said. 'He's dead.'

Varrador winced, then had a sip of keese to steady his nerves. The other three men leaned forward and watched him as if they were waiting for a signal.

'Why did he leave your comnee?' Ammadin said. 'Do you know?'

'No,' Varrador said. 'He rode away about two weeks ago, but he didn't tell anybody where he was going. Just before that, some Kazraks came to our comnee and said they were looking for your servant, Zayn. Our spirit rider – Makador, I'm sure you know him – anyway, he told us to keep our mouths shut, so we did, and in the morning they were gone. The next day Palindor left. A little later, one of the Kazraks brought Palindor's horse back. He said they'd found it wandering near the Mistlands. He said he didn't know whose horse it was, but then why did they bring it straight to us? The Kazrak mentioned that he'd heard your servant was questing in the Mistlands. My wife tells me that Zayn and Palindor hated each other.'

'Yes, they did. Palindor attacked when Zayn was questing. He broke Bane, and Zayn killed him for it. Apanador, give them back Palindor's weapons.'

The chief reached behind him, retrieved the bow and quiver, and handed them over. Varrador examined them, his face immobile, his eyes expressionless. His men turned to him, their hands tight on their drinking bowls.

'Those Kazraks were lying to you,' Ammadin went on. 'I think we can all figure out what must have happened. Palindor must have seen that they meant Zayn no good and ridden off with them. They tried to kill Zayn; they failed. When that fellow brought Palindor's horse back to you, he was probably hoping you'd want vengeance, so you'd do his murdering for him.'

'Sounds like Kazraks, yes.' Varrador tossed his head once. 'My poor wife!'

'It'll be worse for her mother,' Ammadin said. 'You don't want to think your son would do something as rotten as this.'

'I wanted to take the Kazraks prisoner, but the chief said we didn't have the right to.'

'Sooner or later we'll deal with them,' Apanador broke in. 'Together, I hope.'

'That's not for me to say.' Varrador laid the bow aside, then finished his keese in one long swallow. 'But I can't believe that Lanador would turn that offer down.'

Apanador smiled and saluted him with his bowl.

'Let's go out to my herd,' Ammadin said. 'Pick out any mare you want and take her back to Palindor's mother.'

Varrador chose a chestnut four-year-old. Ammadin waved farewell as they rode away, then returned to camp. At Dallador and Maradin's tent she raised the flap and stepped inside. On the far side of the hearth stone, Zayn and Dallador were sitting on the double bedroll, or rather Zayn was sitting, cross-legged and stiff-backed, while Dallador was lounging on his side, his shirt off in the heat. A naked little Benno lay asleep in the curl of his arm.

'You can come out now,' Ammadin said. 'They're not holding anything against you.'

'Thank God!' Zayn said. 'I didn't want to cause trouble for the comnee.'

'What about trouble for yourself?' Ammadin said. 'You were in a lot more danger than the rest of us.'

'Well, I –' Zayn paused and glanced Dallador's way, as if asking for help.

Dallador, however, laughed. 'Yes,' he said, 'what about yourself? I've never met a man who worried less about his own safety.'

Zayn started to speak, then shrugged.

'Never mind,' Ammadin said, smiling. 'I'm going back to our tent to work, so leave me alone until the evening meal.'

In the grass behind her tent Ammadin took out her crystals. Much to her relief, the Riders were still above the horizon. At the northern edge of Spirit Eyes' range, grey smoke stained the sky – a campfire. Nearby, tethered horses grazed, and men stood talking, two men with dark curly hair, one of them with a full black beard: Kazraks. Beyond them by about a hundred yards, she could see someone or something sitting in the grass.

At her chant, Spirit Eyes moved the vision directly over a middle-aged man with shoulder-length grey hair, bound by a jewelled headband. A peculiar bluish light sparkled around his body and danced on his clothing, a pair of dirty white Kazraki trousers and a loose shirt. He was sitting cross-legged and staring into another crystal, which he held in bony, wrinkled hands. So! He was a witchman, or as they called his kind in the Cantons, a sorcerer, and Zayn's enemies had magic on their side.

Sentry began to hum, then rang a soft note, over and over – his warning of magic turned her way. Most likely the sorcerer was watching the comnee even as she watched him and his Kazraks. Sure enough, she saw him pick up a pouch lying in the grass beside him and slide a second crystal out. She picked up Long Voice.

'Open listen to, open listen to.'

Only an angry chirp answered her command.

'Open listen for. Open listen for.'

The spirit sang out. At first she thought she'd once again given it the wrong command, because she heard a humming sound like a second Sentry. Then she realized that she was hearing the sorcerer's crystal and then, his voice.

Open hide me. Open hide me.

Spirit Eyes showed only grassland. Long Voice fell silent.

'You thrush-foot gelding!' Ammadin muttered. 'But I wonder –'

She took a deep breath and chanted. 'Sentry, open hide me. Open hide me.'

The crystal sang three joyous-sounding notes. Although she had no way of testing her theory, Ammadin was guessing that she'd hidden herself from the sorcerer just as he'd hidden himself from her. An impasse, then – neither had lost, neither had won.

'But I did win something,' she said aloud. 'I know a new command.'

She'd also gained ideas as valuable as steel: her spirits owned powers beyond those her teacher had identified, and the Cantons sorcerers knew more about crystals than spirit riders did. In Nannes, the trading precinct, she'd seen a bookshop, which might have books on magic. Such treasures had always lain beyond her reach, because she couldn't read. But now she had a Kazraki servant, who could.

Thanks to Soutan's scanning crystals, Warkannan and his men had been keeping track of the comnee from a safe distance. Rather than follow, they were riding parallel, some four miles north of the comnee's course, in the hopes that the spirit rider wouldn't look their way. When the comnee camped, they camped; when it moved on, so did they. Regularly during the day, Soutan would go off alone into the grass to scan, then return with news. On this particular afternoon, however, he came back ashen and shaking.

'Well, that was alarming,' Soutan said, shuddering. 'That spirit rider – I told you she had to be a woman of great power, didn't I? Well, she's seen us, and for a moment I thought she'd managed to kill one of my crystals.'

'Sounds serious. What should we do about it?'

'There's nothing you can do. I need to be much more careful, is all. Especially once the comnee starts riding again.'

'I hope to God they get on the road soon! How far are we from the Rift?'

'A hundred miles or so.'

'This damned comnee we're following, by the Prophet's name! They're the slowest of the slow. They can't be travelling more than ten lousy miles a day.'

'Maybe we can use the time to our advantage. It would be better to kill our spy before we reach Jezro.'

'If we can.'

Warkannan waited for him to go on. Soutan inserted an unsanitary-looking fingernail under his gold headband and began scratching his forehead.

'That headband must be rubbing you raw,' Warkannan said. 'You're always scratching.'

'Oh damn you!' Soutan stalked away without another word.

All that afternoon Soutan kept to himself. Even after he returned for the evening meal, Warkannan at times caught him peering up at the sky, as if he were expecting to see eyes there, looking back. Every now and then, he would start to scratch under the headband, then jerk his hand away as if by force of will.

Before the evening meal Ammadin and Apanador walked together along the riverbank. In the cool twilight frogs called back and forth, lizards buzzed and rasped. Clouds of greenbuhs rose over the magenta fern trees and swarmed so thickly that they looked like thunderheads.

'There's trouble on its way,' Ammadin said.

'Zayn's enemies?'

'Yes. I finally got a good look at them. Two Kazraks –'

'Is that all?'

'– and a sorcerer from the Cantons.'

Apanador swore and turned to spit into the river. 'This sorcerer – why haven't we heard of him before? How did he manage to get all the way to Kazrajistan?' The chief sounded personally affronted. 'Magic or not, he should have ended his trip in a ChaMeech stomach.'

'You'd think so. He must be pretty powerful, with a lot of spirits to protect him. I'll keep an eye on him from now on.'

'Speaking of Zayn,' Apanador glanced away with studied casualness. 'The men are riding out to hunt tomorrow. They might well find a good-sized bull grassar. The horns this time of year –'

'I am not going to marry Zayn. By all the gods at once! Have you been talking to Maradin?'

'Oh, just a few words, here and there.' Apanador was trying to suppress a smile. 'And to my wife, of course.'

Ammadin turned on her heel and strode off.

When she reached her tent, Zayn was kneeling in front of it and cleaning a pair of fish with his long knife. She sat down and watched. He'd chop off the head with its two shiny pairs of eyes, then slice off the six long fins, slit open the belly, and pull out the thick white strip of cartilage and nerve tissue that connected the tail to the brain node lying above the heart.

'Roasted in the coals?' he said. 'Or seared on a hot stone?'

'Roasted would be fine. You're getting to be a really good cook.'

Zayn looked up with a quick grin that was almost shy. Ammadin had to admit that she found it pleasant to sit with him, sharing a companionable silence in front of their tent, instead of being a guest at someone else's fire.

'How long will we stay in camp?' Zayn said.

'Not very. We'll be heading east soon.'

Zayn smiled, a sudden flash of anticipation.

'Are you as curious about the Cantons as all that?' Ammadin said.

'Oh well.' He was concentrating on wrapping the gutted fish in leaves fresh from the riverbank. 'You hear such strange tales about them back home.'

'I suppose you would, yes. Do you know their language?'

'Only a few words. In school we didn't study the Cantons much, so most of what I know is just hearsay – tales of evil sorcerers, that kind of nonsense. I do know that they're people of the book.'

'What? Does that mean they use writing?'

'That too.' Zayn gave her an easy grin. 'But it really means that they believe in only one god, like we do. It must be the same god, no matter what they call him. If there's only one, then there's only one, right?'

'If there's only one.'

'Well, true.' Zayn ducked his head as if apologizing. 'But anyway, they have a holy book about God. Mohammed, blessed be his name, read it back in ancient times and said that it was worthy of respect.'

'So you Kazraks still respect it? After all these years?'

'Well, of course. The teaching doesn't change. It's eternal.'

'But wasn't your First Prophet a H'mai?'

'Of course he was, but the Qur'an comes from God. Mohammed heard His words from an angel.'

'Wait a minute. When you say heard, you mean the angel came to him in a vision?'

'No, the angel Jubal came to him and dictated the verses, and the Prophet spoke them to his companions, who wrote them down. But he heard the voice of God, too, not just the angel's.'

'He actually heard the voice of his god?'

'Yes. I suppose this all must sound pretty strange to you.'

'Strange? No.' Ammadin looked away, her mouth slack. 'I envy him. I can't tell you how much I envy him.'

For a moment she felt close to tears. Zayn tactfully looked away; he picked up a long spine from a poker tree and began using it to dig trenches in the coals of the fire. Ammadin waited till he'd laid the wrapped fish into them.

'So, in this holy book the Cantonneurs have,' Ammadin said, 'did God speak to their prophets, too?'

'So I've been told. I've never read it. Which reminds me. Do you know the language of the Cantons?'

'Daccor.' She paused to smile at him. 'That means yes, you see. I know enough to trade and ask polite questions. It's called Vranz.'

'If you wouldn't mind teaching me what you know, I'll pick the rest of it up fast enough.'

'The reading part, too? If I bought a book there, would you read it to me?'

'Daccor.' It was Zayn's turn for the smile, but his face suddenly darkened. 'Well, uh, if I can. If someone can help me learn how to read Vranz, I mean.'

He meant a great deal more than that. Ammadin smelled lying, a sudden acrid burst that made her nose wrinkle.

'I forgot to get salt from the wagons.' He stood up fast. 'I'll be right back.'

'Don't!' She scrambled up after him. 'Zayn, come back here.'

He stopped, stood hesitating in the broad space between the back of Maradin's tent and the front of hers. In the glow of the cooking fire she could see him shaking.

'Zayn?' She softened her voice. 'Come back and tell me what's wrong.'

He turned around and walked back as slowly as he could manage and still be moving. He was smiling, perfectly composed from the look of him, but she smelled fear so strongly that she half-expected his shirt to be stained with it like sweat.

'I seem to keep saying things that upset you,' Ammadin said. 'If something's wrong, tell me.'

'I can't.' He was looking her straight in the face. 'Please! Don't –' His voice trailed away.

'Don't pry?'

He tossed his head, looked away, then nodded yes.

'My first responsibility is always to the comnee,' Ammadin said. 'This secret of yours? Will it harm them?'

'No.' He looked at her again. 'You know, I think I'd rather die than bring harm to any of you.'

'You really mean that, don't you? I can hear it in your voice.'

'I do, yes.'

'All right,' Ammadin said. 'Then your secret's no business of mine. You have my word on that.'

He hesitated, shifting his weight from one foot to the other, then came back and knelt by the fire.

'I lied about that salt,' he said. 'We've got plenty.'

'Somehow I figured that.'

They shared a smile, but Ammadin felt that something dangerous had just taken place. She merely wasn't sure what it might be.

On the morrow the comnee packed up its tents and set out east, travelling steadily but slowly. The weather had turned so hot and dry that the whine of insects in the grass made Zayn think of fat sizzling on a griddle. Every morning, after the horses finished grazing, they would saddle up and ride until mid-afternoon, when they would make camp. Zayn fell into the long rhythms of driving stock, as soothing as drinking, and felt his life shrink to the motion of his horse and the rising and setting of the sun. He found himself thinking a traitor's thoughts: I could spend my life this way, I could stay here forever. Whenever they rose, he shoved them away.

Inadvertently Ammadin reminded him that the Great Khan's will still ruled him. They were sitting together in front of the tent when she mentioned that she'd been scanning.

'Your enemies are tracking us,' she said. 'Two Kazraks, one older with a beard, one young with a truly magnificent nose, and then a sorcerer from the Cantons.'

'A sorcerer?'

'Just that. A middle-aged man with long grey hair.'

Soutan? Zayn thought. Out here in the plains? But Soutan was young and blond. 'I don't know anyone like that,' he said.

'Well, then, he must have some reason of his own for joining the Kazraks. Maybe they hired him to help hunt you down.'

'Maybe.' Zayn turned his palms up and shrugged. 'I really don't understand. I thought the people who live in the Cantons didn't leave them.'

'Not often, no.' Ammadin thought for a moment. 'I've never heard of a sorcerer travelling west, never.'

Zayn's superiors had never heard of it, either; they'd sent him to gather information about Soutan for just that reason. Now here was a second sorcerer travelling around and following him to boot, along with the two Kazraks who had already tried to kill him.

'No more ideas?' Ammadin was watching him, waiting for him to speak.

'I'm baffled,' Zayn said, and quite honestly. 'I don't know who these men are, or why they're following me.'

'Here's something that's even stranger. Three female ChaMeech are following them.'

'Good God!'

'Unless they're following you, too.' Ammadin suddenly smiled. 'If they are, I don't think it's adultery that's on their minds.'

Zayn laughed. 'I hope not,' he said. 'But ChaMeech are supposed to be fascinated with magic, aren't they?'

'That's true.'

'Maybe they know this sorcerer has some, then.'

'Maybe. I –' Ammadin suddenly paused. 'Sorry,' she said at length. 'I just had a thought about something else. Anyway, I'm not sure what we can do about the sorcerer.'

'I guess there's nothing to do, except wait. I'm grateful you'll keep a lookout for me.'

'Why wouldn't I? Every single person in this comnee is my responsibility.'

'All right. But thank you anyway.'

'You're welcome.' Ammadin stood up. 'I've got work to do. I'll be down by the stream if anyone needs me.'

'Will you be safe?'

For an answer she smiled.

'Sorry,' Zayn said. 'Stupid of me.'

With a little wave of her hand she walked off. He watched the fire and considered a new sensation: he cared enough about a woman to worry about her.

* * *

The Herd had just risen above the horizon, and in its silver light, Ammadin picked her way through the various roots, rocks, and thorn bushes that would have tripped an ordinary person. She sat down beside a stream and watched the water, glinting in the sky's glow. Zayn had given her an idea, preposterous at first thought, but just possible upon a second. What if Water Woman were a ChaMeech who had managed to tame a spirit crystal?

By keeping careful track of how much of a spirit's power she was draining, Ammadin had learned how to use the crystals in darkness. They disliked going hungry all night, but once she'd finished, an oil lamp or fire would feed them enough to tide them over till sunrise. She brought out both Sentry and Long Voice. She'd done some hard thinking about Long Voice's possible abilities and commands, culled from the lore her teacher had told her as well as from her experiences with Spirit Eyes. She was guessing that the Riders were due to appear, and sure enough, in just a few minutes Sentry began to hum.

'Long Voice!' Ammadin said. 'Open listen for.'

The spirit sang out. In the bone behind her left ear Ammadin heard a strange whispery sound, like sea waves hissing over gravel. She waited, listening to the distant waves rise and fall while the Herd eased itself higher into the sky and the Riders galloped far above her. She was just thinking that they would be setting soon when she heard the voice.

Witchwoman! Witchwoman!

'Long Voice!' Ammadin said. 'Open lock on.'

The spirit sang three bright notes.

'Long Voice! Lock on!'

Another note, and she smiled. 'Water Woman,' she said, 'can you hear me?'

I hear-now you, Witchwoman, I hear, but faintly.

'You're too far away. My name is Ammadin.'

Ammadin. I hear you, Ammadin. Please, talk-soon-next. Water Woman's voice was growing fainter, fading.

'Yes, I will. Look to the Riders in the sky.'

Riders – Her voice vanished, swallowed in the long hiss of the strange sea, far off in the land of spirits.

'Water Woman! Can you hear me?'

No answer, just waves, turning distant gravel. Ammadin closed down her crystals.

Back at camp, out in front of her tent, Zayn had already started a fire. When he saw her coming, he ducked inside and returned with cushions.

'Good,' she said. 'The spirits will need feeding.'

'I thought so,' Zayn said. 'That's why I made the fire.'

'Thank you.' Ammadin smiled at him.

He was beginning to see her needs, a good thing in a servant. And yet, she was so pleased to see him smile in return that she began to wonder if she truly did see him as only a servant. He knelt down and arranged the cushions, then sat back on his heels and looked up. From his scent she knew that lovemaking was very much on his mind. Reluctantly she realized that it was on hers as well. He was watching her with half-closed eyes, smiling a little, as if perhaps he knew that she was weakening.

'You can go drink with the other men,' Ammadin said. 'I won't need anything more here.'

'As the Holy One wishes.' His smile gone, Zayn stood up. He nodded once in her direction, then hurried off into the camp. As she watched him go, she realized that she was as disappointed as he was. You don't need entanglements, she reminded herself. Especially not when you're planning a spirit quest. With a long sigh she sat down by the fire and began to unwrap her hungry crystals.

Warkannan woke just at dawn and found Soutan gone from the camp. Beside the dead fire Arkazo still slept, rolled up in a blanket, so sound asleep that Warkannan decided against waking him; they could say their morning prayers a bit late and not offend God. Warkannan pulled on his trousers and his boots, then stood for a moment winding his pocket watch, a morning ritual that dated from his first days on the border. It was comforting, somehow, to know the time, to measure the time, even out here where space seemed so endless that time became irrelevant.

This early in the day the air was cool; he could hear the nearby stream chortling over rocks; a breeze trembled the long purple grass that stretched to the horizon. The silver dawn caught a few streaks of clouds and turned them as crimson as the distant trees. Frogs croaked; tree lizards, as bright as jewels, sang to each other; the hum of constant insects sounded in the brightening light.

'God, I hate it out here!' Warkannan muttered. 'Give me the city any day!'

He seated his watch in his pocket, clipped the chain to his belt, and went to look for Soutan.

Warkannan found him just a few hundred yards away, muttering over his crystals. At Warkannan's approach, he looked up.

'What would you say to an old-fashioned ambush?' Soutan said.

'Of Zayn, you mean? What did you have in mind?'

'The comnee seems to be heading due east, and I suspect they're on their way to the Cantons. They'll have to pass through the downs to get to the Rift. Comnees always stop in the downs to hunt before they cross over. When we get there, you'll see what I mean about the terrain – plenty of places to hide and wait for a hunting party with Zayn in it to come along.'

'All right. I take it you couldn't come up with some mighty magical spell.'

'Sneer all you want, but the crystals will give us all the magic we need. When we see him ride out, we can set our trap.'

And that, Warkannan had to admit, was true enough.

As they continued east, Zayn took to riding at the rear of the herd, where he could turn in the saddle now and again to keep watch for his enemies. The land began to rise and fall in long low downs, as if the ground were buckling under the push of a giant hand. In the shallow valleys streams ran through tangles of orange ferns and gold pipeplants.

During the day the high-pitched chitters and whip-lash calls of the bush lizards would fall silent as the comnee approached, only to pick up and swell into a chorus of warning once they passed. Night brought a cacophony of frogs. Zayn learned to separate out the chirps of tiny six-legged hoppers and the booming of the big squat watertoads with their red double tongues. Whenever he heard a crane calling, he would turn in its direction and try to answer. At those moments the Chosen and the khanate both seemed things he had dreamt once, a long time ago.

This slow travelling eventually brought the comnee to a long, broad valley and a chain of small lakes, pale blue against the deep violet of spring grass. Here they set up a full camp to prepare for the journey across the Rift. Zayn was assuming that the danger from ChaMeech would be on everyone's mind, but much to his surprise no one took it very seriously.

'They're a nuisance, sure,' Dallador told him. 'Sometimes they try to raid our herds, but they save their bloodlust for the Kazraks. I don't know why, but they hate your guts.'

'Yes, we've noticed.'

Dallador flashed him a smile. 'The real problem with going east is taking our own hay for the horses.'

'Isn't there grass in the Cantons?'

'Of course. But there's a Bane. The horses can eat Canton grass while we're there, but on the journey out they can only eat hay from the plains.'

'Why?'

'We can't carry any seeds out of the Cantons and into the plains. If the horses ate Canton plants just before we got back and then shat, there could be seeds in it.'

'That's damned strange, Dallo. Why –'

'I don't know why. It's just Bane.'

To keep down the amount of hay they had to carry, only part of the comnee would travel east; they would take only their own mounts and the horses to be sold. The women got together to decide who would travel and who would stay. Those leaving appointed trusted friends to tend their children while they were gone; in exchange, they would take along the horses that those staying wanted sold. Some of the men would ride with them as guards, and the spirit rider would bring the gods to keep her people safe from foreign magic in a dangerously different land.

'At times I still think like a Kazrak,' Zayn said to Dallador. 'It's strange to see the women doing the buying and selling.'

'Why would men want to? Haggling is women's work.'

'But doesn't it trouble you to have nothing to leave your son?'

'A man always knows who his mother is. But his father? Who knows what women will do in the dark? So they're the only ones who know who the blood-kin are, and it's your blood-kin who should have your horses.'

Preparations for the trip took days. While the women cut grass and spread it to dry into pale blue hay, the men hunted. The big grassars avoided this rough shrubby terrain, but a smaller species, the orange-and-grey striped browzars, flourished in the valleys. Every time someone made a kill, the men stripped the carcass down to bone and smoked the meat into jerky. Zayn spent several days learning how to cut the raw flesh – a job that he found irritating beyond belief. It was tricky work, using the long knife to slice leather-thin strips of meat. Sweat ran down his forehead and got into his eyes. Shiny magenta flies and the ever-present yellabuhs swarmed around, stinging and stealing.

His turn to hunt came as a welcome relief. In the downs, the browzars sought shelter in the valley thickets; once they got into the underbrush, the men would have to take their spears and follow on foot – a dangerous kind of hunting, thanks to venomous snakes and other such creatures in the dense thorn thickets. The best tactic, or so Dallador told him, was to look for a herd that was grazing part-way up the slope of a hill, then get below and chase them towards the crest and open land.

They left camp just at noon. Riding single-file the six hunters worked their way upstream along the riverbank. In a shallow valley, they spotted at last a small herd. The men looped their reins around their saddle horns, then took their bows from their backs. With their quivers on one hip, they walked the horses, guiding with their knees, until they were close enough for the noise to alarm the dominant bull.

It threw up its orange head and bellowed, slapping the ground with its tail. The hunters kicked their horses to a gallop and charged, shrieking a warcry. The browzars lashed out with striped tails, then bounded away, turning uphill. The men loosed their first volley and grabbed for second arrows while the well-trained horses sped after the fleeing prey.

Zayn loosed an arrow, missed badly, and rode hard for the main herd. Arrows arched overhead as the other men shot again. Bleeding and howling, a young female browzar fell. Zayn aimed for another, missed again, and pulled another arrow as they raced up the side of the hill. He swore under his breath – his reflexes were simply all wrong for this sort of bow. Almost directly in front of him a young bull, smarter than most, broke from the herd and headed downhill. With a curse Zayn loosed, missed, and shifted his weight in the saddle to turn his horse after it.

Down through the treacherous tall grass they raced. Zayn was hoping that the thorny brush along the stream would stop the bull and force it to stay in range. He was determined to hit at least one target for the day, and the determination got the better of his common sense. When they reached the flat, Zayn's horse gained ground, but even from this close a distance Zayn's arrow sailed wide. The bull gave one last leap and charged into the tangled cover. Cursing, Zayn let his horse come to a halt and swung himself off.

Shrubs rose waist-high among the nodding frond-trees in an infuriating orange and red tangle. Zayn could see the bull pushing its way through ahead of him as it struggled to reach the stream. He would have gone after it with his last two arrows, but from behind him he heard someone yell.

'Stay right there!' Dallador shouted. 'Don't go in!'

Zayn obeyed. He mounted his horse, but he let it rest while the others rode down. They surrounded him, and he could see the concern on all their faces.

'What's wrong?' Zayn said.

'Firesnakes, that's what,' Dallador said. 'Don't you remember what I told you? We've already made a kill. You don't need to risk getting bitten and poisoned to make another one.'

'Sorry. It just makes me so damn mad that I can't hit anything with this bow.'

'You'll get it eventually. Come on, let's get the kill back to camp.'

When the men left for the hunt, Ammadin had taken her crystals and walked out into the grass. Over the past few days, she'd been trying at every pass of the Riders to contact Water Woman, but so far she'd failed. On this occasion as well she heard nothing but the mysterious ocean waves that seemed to emanate from somewhere inside Long Voice. Finally she gave up, took Spirit Eyes, and scanned, sweeping outward from the camp in a spiral. Off to the east, at the very limit of the spirit's power, she saw three figures who looked like ChaMeech, but the image was too indistinct to reveal their gender.

Ammadin did, however, find the hunting party. On one of her sweeps she saw the tiny figures of men on horseback, driving browzars along the crest of a down. All at once a bull broke free and charged downhill with one of the men riding hard after it. She recognized Zayn's sorrel gelding.

'Closer!'

Spirit Eyes obliged. The view shifted, and she was looking down as if from a height of some fifty feet. It was Zayn, all right, risking the horse's legs and his own neck. By the time he reached the flat, the browzar had plunged into the brush, just under mark twelve on the crystal. Zayn started to follow, then pulled up to wait for the other men, riding more cautiously down the hill after him.

'Go to twelve.'

In the red and gold tangle of foliage she saw the bull shoving its way through the brush. It tossed its head from side to side, raised its muzzle as if it were bellowing, and thrust with its thick shoulders. At last it splashed across the river, burst out on the other side, and rushed off into the grass. The hunters had lost it. Some yards downstream, however, something moved. Someone stood up – a Kazrak, the same older man with a black beard she'd seen before. He held a hunting bow, and he was visibly angry.

'Long Voice,' Ammadin said. 'Listen for.'

Dimly she heard his voice, humming in the bone behind her left ear. *Arkazo, come on, we might as well give it up.*

Another Kazrak, the young man with the beaky nose, rose from his hiding place some feet away. Although he spoke a few words, his voice was too faint to understand. Apparently Spirit Eyes could see farther than Long Voice could hear. When she shifted the focus back in Zayn's direction, she saw that he and the other men were riding away, leading a pack horse burdened with a dead browzar cow. They would be heading back to camp, most likely. She closed the vision down.

In about an hour the hunting party rode in. Ammadin hurried out to meet them and watched while they turned their horses into the herd. The younger men, carrying their saddles over one shoulder, led the pack horse with the kill back to the tents. Zayn and Dallador followed more slowly, their arms full of horse gear.

'I need to talk with you, Zayn,' Ammadin said. 'I happened to scan you, and that bull you were chasing? It was leading you into an ambush. I saw your enemies on the far side of the stream.'

Zayn muttered something in Kazraki under his breath.

'One of them is named Arkazo,' Ammadin went on. 'Do you know him?'

'I don't, but I've heard the name. It's not all that common.' Zayn paused, thinking. 'I can't place it, though.'

He looked at her blandly. She could smell the change in his scent, but she would have known he was lying even without her shaman's talents – Zayn with his phenomenal memory, not remember where he'd heard a name? In front of Dallador she said nothing, but she was beginning to regret her earlier gesture, when she'd promised Zayn that she wouldn't pry into his private affairs.

As for the sorcerer, she had been spending every available moment on working with her crystals, trying out new commands and exploring different ways of using them. Sooner or later, she knew, she would have to test her new knowledge and challenge him.

'He was so close!' Arkazo was scowling at the bow in his hands. 'We had a shot at him. Why –'

'Five other Tribesmen just happened to be close, too,' Warkannan said.

'They were still on top of the hill! And they would have had to dismount, and we could have been out of the underbrush and across the stream before they could come after us.'

'You've forgotten that they have bows. The arrows could have crossed the stream easily enough.'

Arkazo winced and looked down at the ground.

'Listen, Kaz,' Warkannan softened his voice. 'I know how much you want to avenge Tareev, but you won't do his memory any good if you're dead.'

Arkazo threw the bow on the ground and strode off to tend to the horses. Warkannan shook his head and turned to Soutan.

'He's young,' Warkannan said in a near-whisper. 'But he'll learn.'

'This is true,' Soutan said. 'Well, now what? If Zayn's going to go everywhere in a pack of Tribesmen, we're not going to have much of a chance at him.'

'Yes, I have to agree.' Warkannan paused, thinking, but no clever ideas occurred to him. 'We may have to leave him be and ride on ahead. He doesn't know about Jezro, after all, so if we reach the khan first, we can give him the slip and head back to Andjaro by a different route.'

'Maybe, but that sounds risky to me. Risky and extremely stupid.'

'Oh, does it? Suppose you tell me why.'

Soutan merely smirked. Warkannan took one step forward. Soutan squeaked and flinched.

'Oh very well,' Soutan said. 'This Zayn, suppose he finds out about Jezro. Will he try to kill him?'

'Mostly likely, yes. Do you think he will find out?'

'If he asks the right questions of the right people, he could. That's why it would be better to dispose of him now.'

'Of course it would be better. The question is, can we? If not, we've got to reach the khan before Zayn does.'

'Well, yes.' Soutan hesitated, his eyes rolling like a spooked horse's. 'But –'

'We can't leave the khan unguarded.' Warkannan interrupted him. 'Now, if you figure out a better way to kill our spy, just let me know. I'll give you one more day. If you can't think of anything, then we're leaving the comnee behind.'

Zayn had been working at learning the language of the Cantons with a zeal that surprised everyone in the comnee. All the adults and older children knew some of the trade talk; many had picked up words and phrases beyond those necessary for the selling of horses. Veradin, who had travelled east often in her long life, spoke it very well indeed. Zayn went from one person to another, learning what they knew and badgering everyone to let him practise. Finally Ammadin asked him why he was putting so much effort into learning Vranz.

'I hate to be in a strange country and not understand a damned word,' Zayn told her. 'A man could be insulting you, and here you wouldn't even know.'

'It sounds like you travelled a lot before you joined us.'

'The Great Khan's business keeps his cavalry on the move.'

'Oh? How many languages do people speak along the border?'

Caught – Zayn gave her a sickly sort of smile. 'Ah well,' he said at last. 'I was just speaking generally.'

'I see.'

He arranged a fake smile, she waited. At length he muttered something about helping Dallador prepare jerky and walked away fast. If I only hadn't given him my damned word I wouldn't pry! Ammadin thought. With a growl of irritation she got up and fetched her saddlebags.

Ammadin left the camp and found a quiet spot near a stream, where she could sit in the cover of a pair of frond-trees to wait for the Riders. Lately she'd had no luck scanning for Zayn's enemies. Every time she focused the crystal upon them, the sorcerer would chant command words that clouded her crystal. She had, however, managed to hear his chant of power several times, a strange triad of words in the ancient spirit tongue.

It was time, Ammadin decided, that she tried using her new magic against him. She opened her saddlebags and took out not only the spirit crystals, but four brass cases. Each held a wand about a foot long, carved from Kazraki oak, wound round with red and gold threads, and decorated with two hawk feathers and three golden spirit beads. She left the shade and cleared a place to work out in the full sun. While she chanted a prayer to the six gods, she stuck the plain ends of the wands into the ground to mark a square, roughly four feet on a side. In the middle she laid Long Voice and Spirit Eyes close together, each on top of their pouches, to let them feed while they waited. She laid the other crystals out in the sun, too, but beyond the wand-marked square so they could feed in peace.

Exposed to the sun the spirit beads began to glow. At first they merely glittered as any gold would in sunlight, but after a few minutes they seemed to catch fire. A pale blue spirit danced upon the surface of each one like a flame fanned by some hidden breeze.

'Link,' Ammadin said in the spirit tongue. 'Link and reroute.'

The spirits bound into her crystals sang aloud to welcome the unbound spirits of the beads. Abruptly Sentry chimed. The Riders were beginning their long gallop through the sky above. Ammadin knelt on the ground in the centre of the square formed by the wands and opened Spirit Eyes. Inside the sphere she saw the Kazraki camp as if she floated high above it. Another command, and she sailed down close. With the wand-spirits lending their power to those bound in her crystals, she could see more detail than before and hear better as well.

The heavy-set bearded man stood arguing with the sorcerer. Ammadin opened Long Voice and heard them clearly through the bone just in back of her ear.

Have you come up with some way to kill our spy? the Kazrak was saying.

I'm afraid not. Not yet, anyway. I have the germ of an idea, but –

We don't have time to waste on fancy ideas that might not work.

The sorcerer drew himself up to full height and glared at him.

We're moving out tomorrow, the Kazrak said. *Whether you like it or not.*

The bearded man turned and walked away, leaving the sorcerer scowling after him. All at once his sentry crystal chimed, and the sorcerer threw up his head like a startled horse. He grabbed his belt pouch, fumbled briefly, then drew out a spirit crystal and held it up to the sun. Ammadin saw him lick his lips as if to loosen them for work; he was beginning his chant. She got in before him and chanted the stolen command.

'Oh Verr Ride!'

She heard the sorcerer's snarl, an animal sound of pure rage. Without being told, Spirit Eyes swooped down close enough for her to see into his crystal. The spirit inside shrank to a silver line.

'Sleep,' Ammadin intoned. 'Sleep till wakened. Wake to my voice only.'

The spirit shrank further; she could barely see a faint line like a captured hair. The sorcerer snarled again and began chanting commands. At his voice, the view widened as her spirit flew up high to escape him.

'Oh Verr Ride,' Ammadin intoned. 'Oh Verr Ride all.'

Ammadin's spirits swooped down close to the enemy crystals. She saw the sorcerer throw back his head and heard him howl like a wounded animal. The bearded man spun around and ran back.

Are you all right? What's wrong?

Oh shut up, you stupid fool! The sorcerer shook his mane of grey hair back from his face and turned to face him.

Well, for the love of God! You screamed. Do you need help?

As if you – The sorcerer stopped, breathed deeply, and began again. *I'm sorry, Warkannan. But leave me alone, will you? I have important work to do.*

Have it your way, you wretched infidel!

The sorcerer turned on his heel and strode out of the camp. The man called Warkannan raised a fist, then shrugged, as if calming himself. Ammadin could guess what the sorcerer meant by work to do. She considered fighting another skirmish, then decided to leave him wondering about her strength. She closed down Spirit Eyes, then picked up Sentry and began to chant the 'hide' command.

'Wait. Can cell.'

At the new command the spirit chimed and spun to show it understood. If she hid herself from magic, Ammadin realized, Water Woman would be unable to reach her. She picked up Long Voice and settled in to wait.

Weary and haggard, especially about the eyes, Soutan came back to camp at sunset. Warkannan and Arkazo had already eaten, and Arkazo was building a fire when the sorcerer walked slowly out of the high purple grass.

'What's wrong?' Warkannan said.

'Nothing,' Soutan snapped.

'Really?' Warkannan raised an eyebrow. 'You're damn near staggering.'

Soutan merely scowled for an answer. Arkazo sat back on his heels and watched, his head cocked to one side.

'I think I understand,' Warkannan said. 'That spirit rider's pulled some trick on you, hasn't she?'

'You bastard.' Soutan's voice sounded more tired than angry. 'But you're right. She's taken steps of some kind.'

'Steps? What do you mean?'

'You don't have the slightest ability to understand such a recondite secret.'

'Am I the only one who can't?'

Soutan swore at him – in Vranz, Warkannan supposed, since he couldn't understand a word of it.

'I warned you that these people were powerful, didn't I?' Soutan went on. 'She's managed to injure the spirit in my crystal.'

Warkannan allowed himself a moment of inappropriate gloating, then squeezed out a few sympathetic noises.

'This is very bad,' Soutan said. 'I won't be able to scan till I can heal it.'

'Not even for ChaMeech?' Arkazo joined in.

'Not even for ChaMeech.' Soutan paused, glancing Arkazo's way.

'We can stay on guard,' Warkannan said. 'We'll take turns standing watch at night, then. Soutan, that means you too.'

'No, it doesn't,' Soutan snapped. 'I need my energy for working with my crystals. If I can heal the wounded one, we won't need guards.'

Warkannan considered enforcing his orders with a fist but decided against it. 'Have it your way, then. Arkazo, you'll take the first watch, and we'd better get to sleep early. We're riding out at dawn. These damned horseherders can follow in their own sweet time.'

'Very well. From now on, we have to make all possible speed. I –' Soutan stopped speaking and suddenly smiled.

'What is it?' Warkannan said.

'A happy thought. Once our spy leaves the comnee, the spirit rider won't be able to hide him.'

'What makes you think he's going to leave the comnee?'

'He'll have to, if he's going to poke his long nose into my business. The Tribes never ride into the Cantons themselves. They go as far as the trading precinct and no farther.'

'I see. But if you don't have your crystal –'

'It won't matter. Once we reach the Cantons, I have allies. I can use their eyes until I can get another crystal.'

In the cool of twilight Zayn was lying on the grass beside the tent, sound asleep with his head pillowed on his saddle. Without thinking Ammadin knelt down beside him. In one smooth motion he twisted around and sat up, his knife springing to his hand. Ammadin swayed back out of his reach barely in time.

'Lord preserve!' Zayn's voice shook, and he stared at her wide-eyed. 'Never wake me up like that again, will you?'

'You have my solemn word on that. You're pretty quick with a blade, aren't you?'

He shrugged and sheathed the knife.

'I woke you because I've got some information for you,' Ammadin went on. 'I finally got a good look at your enemies. There's the sorcerer, and that Arkazo fellow, and the third one's name is Warkannan.'

'Warkannan? Good God!'

'Do you know him, then?'

'Well, I know a man by that name.'

'Does he have a son or nephew named Arkazo?'

'Arkazo and Warkannan are both common names at home. It's probably not the man I'm thinking of.'

'You're lying.'

Zayn glared at her. She smiled and crossed her arms over her chest to wait.

'By Iblis!' he said finally. 'All right, then, this Warkannan could be the man I know. He's got a young nephew named Arkazo. But I thought we were friends. I don't know why he'd want me dead.'

'You don't *know* it, maybe, but you could make a really good guess if you wanted to.'

'What is this?' Zayn scowled at her. 'I always heard that spirit riders can smell lies. Is it true?'

'Of course. Most people smell different when they're frightened or worried. Telling lies worries most people.'

'But what if someone was a hardened liar, and it didn't bother him?'

'Then I couldn't smell it, probably. But you're not like that.'

Zayn started to speak, then turned his head and stared out at nothing. 'Guess I'm not,' he said at last. 'Huh. You learn something every day.' He got up, but he kept his gaze on the middle distance. 'I'd better make a fire. You must be hungry.'

'Sit down.'

Zayn froze, hesitated, then turned back and sat.

'When you speak like that,' he said, 'you sound like a cavalry officer. A colonel at least.'

'Why, thank you!' She allowed herself a brief smile. 'Now look, Zayn. I promised you I wouldn't pry into your private affairs, but this Warkannan and the sorcerer were talking about killing a spy. The sorcerer's known for a while now that I've been scanning him out. He must want to get rid of me so they'll have a better chance at you.'

'Oh my God! You've got to stop riding off alone. I'm sorry. This is all my fault.'

She could smell a fear that bordered on terror.

'There's no need to panic,' she said. 'I'm not an easy person to kill. But you're right about not going off alone. If I really need to, I'll bring you and a couple of the other men along for bodyguards. It'll be a nuisance, but I have no intentions of riding in the Deathworld before my time.'

'Good.' His voice was shaking. 'I'm sorry.'

'You don't need to keep apologizing.'

'I'm sorry – I – oh horseshit!'

For a moment she considered him and wondered whether to prod him further. Even in the dimming twilight she could see him shaking. She decided upon mercy.

'Why don't you get some fuel and start a fire?' she said. 'I'm hungry.'

'So am I.' Zayn stood up, looking away. 'I've got some hard thinking to do.'

'About Warkannan?'

'Yes.'

She waited, he said nothing, nor did he look her way.

'Zayn? How many people will Warkannan be willing to kill to get at you?'

'I don't know. He's the kind of man who won't use violence unless he thinks it's absolutely necessary.'

'If he's set on killing you, then he must feel it's necessary.'

'That's true, isn't it?' Zayn paused for a long moment. 'One thing, though. I'm willing to bet that he'd never attack against hopeless odds.'

'And that's what he'll have if he tried to give us trouble. Very well. But if you think that he and that sorcerer are going to try to murder anyone else –'

'I'll tell you. I promise.'

And from the quiet way he spoke, she knew she could believe him.

His face was slipping. Zayn found himself thinking of his situation with that metaphor, that his carefully created false face, the mask he wore when he was serving the Great Khan, was sliding off, or splitting or cracking or any one of a number of words that indicated a slow but imminent destruction. In the Mistlands he had seen what would happen if he let the mask grow into his face. After his vigil, talking with Ammadin, he had wanted nothing more than to be rid of it. Apparently he was getting his wish – now, when he was going to need the mask more than ever.

All that evening, during the dinner he made for Ammadin and himself, during the hours when he drank with the other men in the chief's tent, he found himself returning again and again to the metaphor. His face, his mask, his careful distance from the world – he was on the verge of losing them. If he did, he would – would what? he asked himself. Die? Go crazy? Or simply change so much that he'd be useless to the Chosen? In that case, he might as well kill himself and spare them the trouble.

The dark thoughts finally drove him out of Apanador's tent into solitude. He walked a little way from camp and stood at the edge of the horse herd, where he could look up and see the night sky, so smooth and dark, unblemished at this hour by any speck or trace of light. Once he would have found the darkness soothing. Now it seemed to send fear like rain down from the sky. With a shudder he turned back to the camp. A few cooking fires still burned between some of the tents, while inside others oil lamps were blooming. The saurskin panels glowed against the night in red-and-purple mottling or stripes of orange, more brilliant than coloured glass. He hurried back, drawn to the light.

Ammadin was sitting out in front of her tent and tending a small fire. She'd laid her crystals out to feed, and they lit her face with glints and flickers of reflected flames. She looked up and nodded his way. Her eyes flashed red and glowed until she turned her head again.

'Good,' he said, 'nothing's happened to you.'

'And what can happen to me, here in the middle of the comnee?'

'Nothing, I suppose, but aren't you frightened?'

Ammadin laughed.

'All right,' Zayn said. 'Sorry. Guess I had too much to drink.'

'I can smell it on you, yes.'

Zayn sat down near her. In truth he'd drunk very little, but he'd taken care to spill keese on his shirt in the hopes of masking those smells of fear and deception that she could read so easily.

'When I was in the chief's tent,' Zayn said, 'I was thinking about that sorcerer. What if he tries to kill you with magic?'

'I've tested his strength.' Ammadin smiled briefly. 'Don't worry about him.'

'All right, but –'

'There isn't anything to worry about, Zayn. Now drop it.'

Zayn bit back a nasty retort. She did have the right to give him orders, he reminded himself. Ammadin got to her knees and began fussing over the crystals, turning them and placing them at different angles to the firelight. Zayn considered what she'd told him about Warkannan's remark. 'Kill our spy' might mean Ammadin, it might mean himself, or perhaps even both. Now that he knew that Warkannan stood behind the Mistlands attack, things were beginning to make a painful kind of sense.

Zayn had to admire the wisdom of his superiors. They'd guessed right when they suspected Councillor Indan's so-called investment group of having more in mind than finding blackstone. Someone in the group must have discovered that the Chosen had sent out a spy, and most likely Warkannan had ridden to the plains to dispose of him. I was wrong about Idres, Zayn thought. I never should have talked the officers out of arresting the whole damned pack of them. Warkannan's attempts to kill a member of the Chosen proved Indan's little cabal had some sort of criminal intent. Not, of course, that Warkannan knew who this spy was – and what would he say if he ever found out? It would be a bitter sort of joke on them both.

'You look troubled.' Ammadin had finished with her crystals; she sat back down.

'I am. I was thinking about Warkannan, and the way he's trying to kill me.'

'Well, it must be troubling, yes, since he was a friend of yours. Where did you know him, in the cavalry?'

'Just that. I was a soldier in his troop.'

'I thought you were an officer?'

'I am – I mean, I was. I came up from the ranks and earned my commission.' Zayn hesitated, caught by memories.

Ammadin leaned forward, watching him, her lips half-parted. What kind of grief had shown on his face, that she'd look so troubled for his sake? He arranged a bland smile, and she scowled at him.

'I told you I wouldn't pry,' she said, 'but this is getting annoying. First you look like you've swallowed a mouthful of rebbuhs, and then you smile.'

'Well, sorry. I was just thinking about Warkannan, and about a friend of his. Another one of my superior officers, and a damned fine one. He got himself killed by ChaMeech.'

'Well, that's very sad, yes.'

Zayn started to make some dismissive remark about soldiers expecting that kind of fate, but he found himself turned cold by a sudden insight. In truth, Gemet's assassins had killed Jezro – or so they said. They might have failed, might have lied to hide their failure. What if Jezro Khan were the man the Tribes had found bleeding out in the grass? Ten years ago in summer. The date was right, but Apanador had told him that the wounds came from ChaMeech spears. On the other hand, the mysterious Kazrak had claimed to be an enemy of Gemet Great Khan – your great chief,

Apanador said, and his assassins. If the assassins had known how popular Jezro was in the cavalry, and it was no secret, they might have used ChaMeech weapons to avoid a possible border mutiny over his murder.

And what could matter so much to Warkannan that he'd try to murder one of the Chosen? Only something overwhelmingly important could override the loyalty that came so naturally to him, some greater loyalty such as, perhaps, to Jezro, his friend, the man who'd saved his life? Zayn reminded himself that he didn't even know if this other Kazrak was an heir or not, or if the piece of jewellery that had meant life itself to him was the zalet khanej. Making assumptions in his line of work often proved fatal. He repeated the reassurance over and over in his mind: he knew nothing for certain, nothing.

The fire was burning low. Ammadin rose to her knees again and began gathering up her crystals. Zayn made a great display of yawning.

'I'd better go to bed,' Zayn said between yawns. 'Unless there's something you want me to do?'

Ammadin hesitated, and for a brief moment she smiled at some private joke. 'No,' she said at last. 'Not right now.'

At dawn Warkannan and Arkazo broke camp. While Arkazo watered the horses, Warkannan opened one of the big canvas packs and brought out hardtack and white cheese for their breakfast. Soutan lounged in the grass and watched them work. Every now and then he would reach up and scratch under the gold headband.

'We must be getting near the Rift,' Warkannan said to him.

'Yes, indeed,' Soutan said. 'Once we're across, we'll reach Nannes in another day or so. That's the town with the trading precinct, dead east from the Riftgate in Bredanee Canton. From there we'll head north.'

'North is where Jezro Khan is?'

'In Burgunee Canton, yes.'

Warkannan waited, but Soutan let no more information slip. Warkannan found himself wondering how big this Canton was, and if he could possibly find the khan without Soutan's help, once they were safely out of ChaMeech country. Unfortunately, he knew only a few words of Vranz. He got up and walked out to meet Arkazo, who was leading the horses back to camp.

'Tell me something,' Warkannan said. 'Did you study any Vranz in that university of yours?'

'No. I wish I had,' Arkazo said. 'I only took Hirl-Onglay.'

During their morning meal, Warkannan began to worry about his nephew. Ever since Tareev's death, Arkazo had withdrawn into a silence punctuated only by flashes of anger, but that morning he babbled constantly, rehearsing every horrible rumour and old folktale he'd ever heard about the strange lands beyond the khanate.

'So I was wondering about the Cantons, just supposing we live through this ride.' Arkazo came to the end of his breath just as Warkannan was reaching the end of his patience. 'Do you think everyone in the Cantons really is an evil sorcerer like they say?'

'No, I most certainly don't!' Warkannan said. 'That's just the kind of nonsense people make up about places they don't know.'

'For a change, Captain,' Soutan said, 'you're quite right. My kind of skills are quite rare, but useful, especially when it comes to crossing the Rift. I'm not making light of the real difficulties, mind, but I have things with me that will ease our path considerably.'

'Magic, I suppose?' Arkazo started to sneer, then hesitated. 'I shouldn't – I mean, ever since you started finding comnees out here, I –'

'You started to believe in magic?' Soutan smiled more warmly than Warkannan had ever seen him do before. 'What if I told you that some of the things we call magic are just clever devices, like your uncle's pocket watch?'

'One of my teachers at university said the same thing, but he never mentioned the crystals like you showed us.' Arkazo looked away, chewing on his lower lip. 'He talked about pottery that couldn't be broken. Some people said it was forged by spirits, but he made fun of the idea.'

'Good for him. What else did he tell you?'

'Not much. He didn't want to get caught teaching us heresies.'

'Heresies.' Soutan rolled his eyes. 'I am amazed at how blindly you Kazraks believe –'

The earth shuddered beneath them, a weak tremble only, but Soutan swore and clutched the ground with spread fingers as if he could steady it by brute force.

Warkannan laughed. 'I think the Lord is sending you a message.'

'Spare me your superstitions, Captain,' Soutan remarked with some asperity. 'Your god has nothing to do with it.'

As if to agree, the earth stayed quiet for the rest of the morning. Once they were finally in the saddle and riding east, Arkazo's nerves seemed to settle down as well, until, at noon, they came across a reminder of worse dangers than earthquakes. They'd stopped to rest their horses, and Arkazo wandered off down a small gully to look for water, then shouted. Warkannan drew his sabre without thinking and ran while Soutan followed more slowly. Arkazo was standing by a rivulet in the purple grass and pointing to a pile of human bones, stacked up like firewood with a flat stone on top.

'ChaMeech work,' Soutan remarked. 'That stone is supposed to keep the dead man's ghost from wandering. I wonder who was stupid enough to ride this close to the Rift alone?'

'Don't they ever eat their own kind?' Warkannan said.

'Only rarely. Generally they bury their dead, and there aren't enough bones in this pile to make up a ChaMeech skeleton. This was either a comnee man or someone from the Cantons. Notice there's no skull. They eat the brains first, you see, to get an enemy's magic, then grind the skull up for potions.'

Arkazo made a retching sound deep in his throat. Warkannan laid a hand on his arm.

'We've got a sorcerer with us,' Warkannan said. 'Magic is the one thing that terrifies these creatures.'

'Creatures again.' Soutan shook his head. 'They can also, my dear captain, be reasoned with.'

'Huh!' Warkannan said. 'As long as a man has cold steel in his hand, maybe. Now let's get some food in our bellies. The faster we get out of here, the better.'

In the middle of the morning the comnee had started to break camp. The men and women who were going east to trade cut horses out of the herd or stowed a spare selection of their belongings into saddle packs. Those who would stay behind began loading the wagons for their trip south to new grazing.

Off to one side, Apanador and his wife, Gemmadin, stood conferring. She would stay behind and lead the comnee while he took the trading party east. They each held a calendar stick – the dry white leg-bone of a saur. Every day at dawn, they would each cut a notch into their sticks. Gemmadin would bring her people back to this camping ground in twenty days, while Apanador would try to return with the trading party in the same amount of time. If he should be late, Gemmadin would move the comnee a day's ride west for fresh grazing, and he would know to catch up with her there. If he were early, he would wait for her until he had to move to the fresh grazing.

Ammadin started over to join them, but Zayn came hurrying up to her. He was carrying a lead rope in one hand.

'I've roped the two geldings into the pack train,' he said. 'Do you want to take that young buckskin mare?'

'Yes, I do,' Ammadin said. 'She's never been accepted by the bell-mares. We might as well sell her.'

'We?' He smiled, his head cocked a little to one side.

Ammadin found herself utterly tongue-tied. She really had started thinking of them as a 'we', she realized, not as 'myself and my servant'.

'Just go get the horses,' she said.

Zayn laughed, but he jogged off, heading for the herd. She reminded herself that such thoughts could be dangerous, especially about a man who kept secrets. She realized that morning that if Zayn weren't constantly lying to her – or speaking on the edge of lying, at any rate – she might well have given in to her attraction and slept with him. As it was, she had no intention of letting him close to her.

When the time came for the two halves of the comnee to separate, everyone felt a profound reluctance to do so. People went back and forth, saying farewells and reassuring their tearful children. Packing up the last of the gear caused squabbles within families over who was going to take what. All of this cost the travellers hours. The pale sun had climbed high above the purple horizon before the long line of horses and riders formed up, followed by a single wagon carrying Ammadin and Apanador's tents. Twenty-two humans and three times that many horses set out, heading due east, to one last round of goodbyes from those left behind.

Every time Sentry chimed, Ammadin would get out her crystals and scan for Zayn's enemies, but she learned nothing of interest until the next morning. In the first light of dawn, Warkannan and his nephew still slept, but Soutan was sitting out in the grass, bent over something he held in his lap – a thin slab of slate, she thought at first, but a peculiar blue light flickered on its surface in what looked like random patterns. Although she watched for some while, she could make no sense of them. Finally, when she heard Maradin calling her from camp, she gave the puzzle up and shut down her crystals.

'What the hell are you doing now?' Warkannan said.

From his seat in the tall grass, Soutan looked up, swore, and clutched some flat thing to his chest with both arms.

'Sorry,' Warkannan went on. 'But we've got the camp struck. We're just waiting for you to come back so we can load the pack horses.'

'Surely you don't expect –'

'You to do some actual work? May the Lord forbid!' Warkannan resisted the urge to heap up sarcasm. 'I want to wait till the last possible minute to saddle up, is all. We can't afford to be caught out here with galled mounts.'

'That's true, yes.' Soutan laid the object into his lap again. 'I'll just shut down.'

'Good. What's that? A writing slate?'

'No, of course not! Do you see a pen in my hand?' Soutan ran a finger along the long edge of the slate. 'This was a gift from Nehzaym, may your god bring her joy. It produces visions, and I was hoping to get a vision of how to fix my injured crystal.'

This explanation sounded even more peculiar than most of Soutan's chatter. The sorcerer frowned at the slate, tapped the short edge with one finger, then picked up a length of black cloth from the ground beside him.

'I'll wrap this up and put it away,' Soutan said. 'Then we can ride out.'

'Good. I'll get the horses saddled.'

They set off on a morning so achingly hot that a pale gold mist hung at the horizon. No matter how badly he wanted to make speed, Warkannan coddled the horses. Every time they reached water, he called a halt to let the stock drink, and at the top of every low rise they paused for a brief rest. Warkannan would dismount and walk a little away from the others to look back, shading his eyes against the sun. In the middle of the afternoon he saw the sign he'd been looking for – a plume of dust rising. He pointed it out to Arkazo and Soutan.

'The comnee,' Warkannan said.

'It must be, yes,' Soutan said. 'I cannot tell you how infuriating this is. That wretched witchwoman has a living crystal, and I don't. Good god, she can spy on us whenever she feels like it, and there's not a thing I can do about it.'

'That worries me, too, but you're right. There's nothing we can do about it, so it's in God's hands.'

'Inshallah,' Arkazo murmured.

Soutan pursed his lips in a scowl, then shrugged.

'I suppose that's as good a way to think about it as any,' Soutan said. 'We should reach the Rift tomorrow, if they don't catch up with us, anyway. That would be a damned nuisance.'

'Can't we go across by a different route?' Warkannan said.

'There's only one way across. The Riftgate. You'll see when we get there.'

'Will I? Then we'd better get moving.'

Warkannan kept up his rearguard watch all afternoon. Some three hours before sunset, the dust plume disappeared. He could assume the comnee had made camp. A soft wind sprang up, bringing with it cooler air. Warkannan decided to risk pushing his own stock and kept his men riding for another couple of hours. When they camped, though, he found a spot well out of sight of the trail.

After they ate their evening meal, Soutan carried his mysterious slate out into the grass to mutter spells where they couldn't overhear. Warkannan and Arkazo unloaded the canvas packs to take an informal inventory. They had food left, dry hardtack, cheese, some flasks of oil, some saur jerky. Charcoal they still had as well, and cracked wheatian for the horses.

'We could travel another week easily,' Warkannan said. 'Soutan tells me we'll reach the trading precinct before then.'

Arkazo nodded, then looked away, his eyes full of tears. Warkannan found himself remembering the time Arkazo had fallen off a pony – he must have been no more than six – and broken his wrist. He had stood the same way, desperately trying not to cry, afraid to catch his uncle's eye for fear he would.

'Kaz?' Warkannan said. 'What's wrong?'

'I was just thinking.' His voice shook badly. 'We've got extra because Tareev isn't –' He broke off.

'Isn't here to eat his share. Yes, that's true.' Warkannan laid a hand on his shoulder. 'I'm sorry.'

'Are you?' Arkazo spun around and looked him in the face. 'You don't act like it's bothering you in the least. You've forgotten all about it, I'd say.'

'I'm a soldier, Kaz. I don't think you realize what that means. I've lost friends out on the border. I've seen plenty of dead men who weren't friends. You never get used to it, never that. But you learn to keep it inside and get on with the jobs that need doing.'

Arkazo caught his breath with a noise that might have been a sob, might have been a sigh.

'I'm sorry,' Warkannan repeated. 'This is why I didn't want you to come. This is why I didn't want Tareev to join us.'

Arkazo concentrated on wiping his eyes on his shirt sleeve. Warkannan waited, saying nothing more. At last Arkazo looked his way.

'We'd better get this stuff packed up.' Arkazo's voice was steady again.

'I'll do it. You build a fire, and make it bright if you'd like. We've got the fuel.'

In the last of the daylight Warkannan repacked the supplies, distributing the weight among all the packs so that no one horse carried more than the others. Arkazo laid a fire; when the light rose up, he crouched in front of it, but Warkannan stayed standing, looking off to the long purple grass where Soutan sat hidden. Against the darkening sky a flock of cranes flew overhead, soaring on naked wings – he could see the dotted stripes of phosphorescence along their thin necks and dangling legs. They shrieked, banked and wheeled, then flew off back the way they came. Arkazo shuddered at the sound.

'I have a bad feeling about this place, too,' Warkannan said. 'Tell you what. Go bring the horses into camp. Hobble and double tether them.'

Arkazo got up and trotted off to follow orders. When he returned, and the horses were secure, Warkannan brought their weapons over to the campfire and laid them within easy reach.

Not more than two hours later, Warkannan's intuition proved itself true. They were just thinking of putting out their fire when Warkannan heard a cry that sounded like a distant howl of laughter out in the dark downs. He and Arkazo were on their feet in an instant, but Soutan knelt and began fumbling in his saddlebags.

'What is it?' Arkazo said.

'What do you think?' Warkannan said. 'ChaMeech.'

In little bubbling shrieks, the cries came closer, circling round the camp, calling back and forth, closer, ever closer, ringing them round before they could think of running. Warkannan drew his sabre and made a silent pledge that they'd pay high before they brought him down.

'Grab that axe,' he snapped at Soutan. 'It'll be better than nothing.'

'I have all the weapons I'm going to need.'

Soutan got up, holding a long tube of silver metal. When he barked a nonsense word, one end of the tube glowed with a warm yellow light. Soutan twisted a metal band at the other; the glow turned into a beam. He flung up his hand and sent a spear of light into the sky. Out in the dark grass the ChaMeech fell abruptly silent. The ruby on Soutan's headband flared red as it caught a splinter of the unnatural glare.

'They recognize this wand, you see,' he said, and his tone was peculiarly off-hand. 'It holds an ancestral spirit, and it means I have magic.'

Soutan called out another incomprehensible word. Golden light spewed like a fountain from the tube and flooded the camp. The horses tossed their heads and danced, but fear kept them silent and their double tethers kept them in place. Trapped in the light stood six mottled red and purple ChaMeech, crouched with their weight thrown back on their hind pair of legs, their mid-pair propping them tense and leaving the front pair, the pseudo-arms that ended in a single finger and opposed thumb, free to handle their long spears, edged at the point with obsidian flakes. At the end of the long graceful necks the bulbous heads turned this way and that, while their doubled pairs of eyes blinked against the glare.

'Their heads!' Arkazo was shaking where he stood. 'They're so big.'

'They're big all over,' Warkannan muttered. 'And remember: you can only pierce their hide along their necks and stomachs.'

Holding his lightwand up high, Soutan began to chant in a language Warkannan didn't recognize. Slowly, a few at a time, the ChaMeech fell back until they hovered at the edge of the pool of light. Only the biggest remained, an individual about ten feet from his flat, fleshy snout to his stub of rudimentary tail. Around his loins hung a red tattered kilt made out of captured cavalry tunics, and at his throat hung a foot-long tangle of charms, beads, and coloured strips of cloth. When Soutan stepped forward, the ChaMeech lowered his head slowly and submissively. The purple sac of skin on his throat filled and deflated, over and over, in a steady silent pulse. Soutan's lips moved, but Warkannan could hear nothing.

For a long time the pose held: the sorcerer with his shaft of light held high, the monstrous warrior crouched before him. Suddenly, with a long hooting cry the ChaMeech flung up his head and spun round, shockingly graceful, and bounded off into the night. Shrieking and mewling, his men followed. Warkannan let out his breath in a sharp grunt and Arkazo frankly whimpered. Golden in the unnatural light, Soutan looked them over in cold contempt.

'Well, Captain, do you see now what magic can do?'

'Oh yes.'

Soutan smiled, a cold twitch of his mouth. 'Let me make something clear right now. Once we put Jezro on the throne, I shall expect to be treated as I deserve.'

'I don't think you need to worry about that.'

With a laugh Soutan snapped out another peculiar syllable. The light in the tube went out, leaving them all blinking as badly as the ChaMeech. Only later did it strike Warkannan just how easily Soutan had won his battle of wills, as if in some silent way he'd been communing with the ChaMeech instead of fighting with it.

Ammadin woke long before the rest of the comnee. In the pale, reddish light of dawn she took her crystals and walked out into the grass, though she stayed well within sight of the camp. A soft wind blew from the east, bringing a faint scent. She tossed her head back and breathed deeply, catching the all-too-familiar smell of male ChaMeech, acrid with rancid musk. If any females travelled with them, the male stink would cover their softer scent. Still, she opened Long Voice and tried calling for Water Woman. When she received no answer, she opened Spirit Eyes and began to scan.

Eventually she saw the ChaMeech in the shelter of a ring of spear trees, six warriors, lying asleep in their usual fashion, huddled and heaped half on top of one another, with their spears, body decorations, and sacks of food strewn around them on the ground. The sorcerer and the two Kazraks she found camped only a few miles away. Either they'd been lucky, or the sorcerer carried magic powerful enough to scare off the warparty. When she went back to camp, she told Apanador that the trading party needed to stay in camp for the day.

'They're probably hoping to drive off a few horses,' Ammadin said. 'If the herd's hobbled, they can't.'

Apanador nodded his agreement. 'Six ChaMeech?' he said. 'That's a good-sized warband, but it's not big enough to attack the camp in daylight. At night – well, we'll post guards.'

'Good idea. I'd better prepare a few surprises of my own, just in case.'

At last! Warkannan thought, and in a way, the sight was worth waiting for. He stood at the edge of the Rift with Arkazo and stared, simply stared for a long time. At their feet lay dusty bare ground, which sloped down some hundreds of yards to a straight drop. In turn the cliff plunged down so far that he could only guess at the distance – a mile, perhaps. On the far side mist rose and hung across the cliff face like smoke. He could make not even an educated guess about the width of the canyon, though he could see that it yawned here at the top and narrowed at the bottom. From his viewpoint the floor looked like a carpet woven out of orange and purplish-brown foliage, brushy and tattered, perhaps fern trees, perhaps not. Water gleamed through the occasional breaks in the cover.

'Uncle?' Arkazo turned first north-east, then south-west. 'How far does it run? From here it looks like it goes on forever.'

'Not quite.' Warkannan smiled at him. 'But far enough. Over a thousand miles, if those maps Soutan had are correct, all the way from the southern ocean to the northern one.'

Arkazo whistled under his breath and shook his head. Warkannan returned to studying their route down. The Cantons would have been cut off from the west irretrievably had someone not carved a road out of the cliffside at this spot. In switchbacks wide enough for three riders abreast it snaked down, each slab laid into a cut at a gentle angle like big steps made of tan rock. Down the middle of each slab ran ruts, ground out of the rock by generations of comnees and their horses.

'Ah, there you are.' Soutan came strolling up. 'Impressive, isn't it?'

'It lives up to its reputation,' Warkannan said.

Arkazo smothered a laugh. Soutan, surprisingly enough, smiled as well, then turned back to Warkannan. 'We'd best get on our way,' the sorcerer said. 'We need to get out of the Rift before nightfall. The ChaMeech present no problem, but every now and then you run across a longtooth hunting in those trees.'

'If we end up having to run for our lives,' Warkannan said, 'I'd just as soon do it in daylight. I take it there's another road on the other side?'

'Just like this one, yes. This is the Riftgate I told you about. The Ancients made it.'

'I've got to hand it to them. They were pretty damn good at building roads.'

'They were good at building a great many things, Captain.' Soutan paused, staring across the Rift, and for a moment he looked close to tears. 'Ah well, time to get moving!'

'Good. Now, we can't ride down. We need to be on the ground and leading the stock in case one of them panics. Each man will lead his riding horse. We've got four pack horses, and Tareev's horse, too, so that makes eight horses for three men. We'll rope them up like this: three for me to lead, three for Arkazo, and Soutan, two for you.'

Soutan nodded, then began scratching under his headband again. A drop of blood trickled down his forehead.

'Take that thing off,' Warkannan said, 'and let me treat that sore under it. We've got a first-aid kit in the packs.'

'I never take this off.' Soutan's voice snapped with rage. 'Don't you ever try to lay one filthy finger on it, do you understand me?'

'Shaitan! I try to help you and all you do is bite like a wounded animal.'

Soutan snarled like one, too, and marched off, heading for the horses, which they'd left tethered nearby.

'God give me strength,' Warkannan muttered. 'God, don't let me throw him off the cliff on the way down.' He took a deep breath, then turned to Arkazo. 'Let's get going. The climb up won't be easy on the horses, and I agree with our sorcerer on one thing: we don't want to be in the Rift when night falls.'

The horses proved nervous when it came to stepping down onto the first switchback. They snorted, rolled their eyes, and danced back from the edge. Like most cavalrymen, Warkannan had more patience for horses than he did for H'mai. With soft words and the touch of his hand he finally managed to coax his own grey gelding down. Seeing one of their own start the descent gave the others some courage. They followed – reluctantly, tossing their heads, pulling at the lead ropes, but they followed. The first turn in the road gave the horses more trouble, but in the end they swung themselves around and kept on walking. From then on, herd mentality took over, and in a line the horses marched calmly down the switchbacks with the men at their bridles.

After the first few turns Warkannan had the leisure to look around him. Alternating stripes of dark dirt and pale stone streaked the Rift walls; little plants grew in the occasional crevice. At each turn he looked out at the vast stretch of the Rift, fading into mist far beyond the reach of his sight. By about half-way down he could see the canyon bottom clearly. The orange mass proved to be fern trees, a veritable forest of them, growing out of murky water. After a few more turns of the road, the noise rose to meet them: the chirr and whine of insects, the croaking of frogs, the sharp calls of lizards. Farther down still, the air turned moist and heavy with decay. Warkannan realized that they were descending into a swamp like the sea-coast marshes far to the south.

'Soutan?' Warkannan called out. 'Is there a road through this swamp?'

'Of course!' Soutan called back. 'How else would the Tribes get their horses across? Think, for God's sake!'

At the bottom of the switchbacks the road levelled out onto rocky ground, bare except for a reddish-brown moss, gently furred with spore stalks. Only the middle of the canyon would get enough sunlight for trees, Warkannan supposed. The forest cover overhead threw shadows over the oozing water and the dark red horsetails that grew along its edge. Crusted with pale orange algae, water lapped onto stone. Now and again a russet fish leapt from the murk and caught one of the iridescent needlebuhs hovering over the surface.

They had just got the last horse to level ground when Warkannan heard the sound – a thrumming or boom, so deep in pitch that he felt it as much as heard it. The frogs and lizards fell silent, as if in fear.

'Do you hear that?' Warkannan said to Soutan. 'What is it?'

'Just the wind blowing up in the high canyon,' Soutan said. 'There are some peculiar rock formations a few miles in.'

'They must be pretty odd, all right. It almost sounds like drums.'

'Are you sure it's wind?' Arkazo put in. 'I don't see how rocks could make that sound.'

Soutan smiled vacantly and looked away. In a few seconds the thrum stopped, and the frogs picked up their chorus again.

Warkannan gathered his men and horses on the edge of the brimming swamp and let the horses rest. The horses pulled on their reins and lead ropes, reaching towards the water, then snorted and tossed their heads in disgust.

'It's brackish,' Soutan said. 'There's sweet water on the other side. Some underground springs surface there.'

'Good.' Warkannan could see, among the scaly stalks of the fern trees, some flat grey thing running along the ground. He pointed. 'What is –'

'The approach to the bridge,' Soutan said. 'It rises some three feet above the swamp in most places, a little higher in others.'

'All right. Let's get moving. The horses need water more than they need rest.'

Soutan led the way onto the grey surfacing of the road, which was wide enough for at least four horsemen to ride abreast. Underfoot the road felt slightly spongy but solid enough that the horses stepped right onto it. Through the trees Warkannan could see that after some hundred yards the roadbed rose free of the ground on dark grey pylons, driven into the water. Thick clots of brownish river weed grew around them and spread lazily on the slow current.

Warkannan had just led his men onto the rise of the bridge when stinging rebbuhs swarmed to the attack. The horses stamped and swished their tails, tossed their manes and stamped some more, a strategy that seemed to convince the rebbuhs to attack the men instead. Warkannan slapped at the swarm, killed a few, and slapped and swore at the rest. Arkazo was frantically trying to wave them away with his riding hat.

'That won't work,' Soutan drawled. 'Wait a moment.' He tossed his horse's reins to Warkannan, then went round to rummage through the saddlebags. 'Here we are.'

Soutan drew out a cylinder about eight inches long and an inch in diameter, then intoned one of his nonsense words. Immediately the rebbuhs began to fly away, rushing off in clumps as thick as mist. Warkannan could see the big drones zig-zagging through the air as if they were drunk.

'What is that?' Warkannan said. 'Some kind of poison vapour?'

'No.' Soutan bared his teeth in a smile. 'It's magic, of course.'

'Wait a minute!' Arkazo said. 'It's vibrating, isn't it? What's it doing, making some kind of high-pitched noise?'

'Exactly right.' Soutan handed him the cylinder. 'You have better eyes than your uncle.'

Arkazo examined the cylinder, found some sort of button, and pressed it a couple of times with one finger.

'That turns it on and off,' Soutan said.

'Yes, I could feel it stop vibrating, then start again. You don't need to say one of those commands?'

'No.' Soutan glanced Warkannan's way and seemed to be suppressing a smile. 'That's only for magical objects.'

Warkannan snorted like one of the horses and tossed Soutan's reins back to him.

'Let's go,' Warkannan said. 'I don't want to breathe this filthy air for a minute longer than I have to.'

Towards sunset Ammadin scanned and found that the male ChaMeech had seemingly disappeared – worrisome, since they might be hiding deep in the Rift, lying in ambush for the trading party and its tasty horses. The Kazraks she found easily; they'd crossed the Rift and were making camp some miles east. There remained Water Woman. Ammadin had given up hope of hearing from her again, but out of habit she opened Long Voice and sent out its call note. A familiar voice answered immediately.

Ammadin. You have-power-now to hear me? Ammadin. You speak-soon to me?

'Yes, I'm here. Water Woman, is that you?'

I be she who bear that name. I speak-again-now. You tell-then me the Riders. I know-then these not.

'In the sky –'

Yes, I know-now. I know-then not. I be-then confused. We call them Deathbringers.

'Deathbringers? Why?'

They come-then with Canton people. They bring-then death.

'I don't understand. Can you tell me more?'

Much more when they fly-next. Silence needs be mine now. I needs-be hide.

'From whom?'

Others, some of our men, but not my spear servants, other men. They be near, I know-not them, but I have-now many many suspicions.

'Who do you – wait! You're ChaMeech, aren't you, Water Woman?'

Ammadin heard a sharp hiss; silence followed. She wondered if she'd been too blunt, but at the same time, she felt triumph like keese in her blood. She had guessed right, she was sure of it, and in a few moments, Water Woman confirmed it.

I be true Chiri Michi. I lie-not. Hate-not me. Fear-not me. I beg you.

'I neither hate nor fear you.'

I give-now you thanks. I mean-not you harm.

'Then we can bargain. You don't harm me, I won't harm you.'

A bargain, yes. I agree.

'Tell me – your males, they who hunt, the warband. Are they in the Rift? Are they waiting for my people?'

They be in the Rift. I know-not if they wait to attack you. Her voice paused. Another spoke distantly in her own language, as if another ChaMeech hovered near to listen to her crystal. *They wait-maybe. We know-not.*

'You're not alone there.'

No, I have two servants to walk with me. I be true Chiri Michi. I walk-not alone.

For a moment Ammadin could say nothing, wondering why this simple idea, that Water Woman had servants, struck her as so amazing. She had always seen the ChaMeech as animals, she supposed, somewhere deep in her mind. Even though she had known that they had a language of their own and could learn others, she had fallen into the common trap of thinking them wild, roaming like beasts at the edges of the plains. But those servants – their existence spoke of a world of laws and customs.

Ammadin, Water Woman said. *You hear-still me?*

'I hear you. Tell me – why ask me for help? Something made you look for a spirit rider.'

Yes. The Sibyl tell-then us, go into the grass and search for a witch-woman.

'The Sibyl?'

You know-not her? She teach-then us your talk.

'No, I don't know her. Is she a ChaMeech woman or a H'mai woman?'

Woman like you but not like you. She be H'mai, but a stone woman. She live-then-now-next-soon.

'I don't understand. Do you mean she's old?'

Very old, yes. Live-always.

'You mean she's a god?'

No no, god be-not she, but stone H'mai. Sibyl say-often, if there be gods, then they be-not what we think, no big people in Silverlands. We all fear, our people, that our gods be dead.

'What? Why?'

Troubles fall upon us. Everything change-now. We all pray-then-many-times. They help-never us. Sibyl say, if there be gods, they have-not ears to listen with.

'And you believe Sibyl?'

I know-not if I do or not. She be wise, but she be-maybe wrong, too. I go-soon now. They be too close, the males. Maybe they hunt-only, maybe they spy. I promise you this. I try-soon to learn if they attack not attack. I tell you-next-soon I know. This be a treaty gift between you and me.

'Thank you. I'd be grateful for a gift like that.'

I go-now.

She had not merely stopped speaking; she had taken her voice away. In the bone behind her left ear Ammadin heard only the illusory sea, tumbling waves over its gravelled shore.

For some long while she knelt, watching the sunset light fall golden upon the purple grass, listening to the familiar sounds of the camp behind her. So: the ChaMeech divided themselves into servants on the one hand and on the other, true Chiri Michi, whatever Water Woman may have meant by that. The phrase reminded Ammadin of the Kazraks and their true-oak and true-hawks and all the rest of it. What startled her the most, however, was that the ChaMeech could use crystals. And who was this Sibyl, the stone woman? She must live somewhere in the ChaMeech lands, deep in the east. Ammadin felt her previously small interest in the ChaMeech and the east both beginning to grow.

That evening Apanador called the men to a council round his fire to discuss the possibility of ChaMeech lurking in the Rift. All night they stood guard over the herd. Each time that Sentry pealed,

Ammadin woke; she'd go to the tent flap and look out to see the dark shapes of the men coming and going as the watch changed. Yet never did she hear a shout of alarm, and she decided that if the ChaMeech were going to attack, they would most likely do so down in the Rift itself. At length she slept, only to dream of a huge stone statue of a woman, rising from the purple grass to speak like thunder: 'There are no gods'.

Sentry's chimes woke her one last time at the morning. She dressed and went yawning to the tent flap. At the western horizon, silver dawn broke among high clouds. All around her tent the members of the comnee lay asleep, wrapped in their blankets. Ammadin fetched her saddlebags and walked out into the grass.

When she opened Long Voice, Water Woman was waiting.

Ammadin, Ammadin, I know-now. They walk-now in the Rift, they hunt-now, yes, but they most likely harm-not you.

'Thank you! That's very good news.'

The men walk-then up ways Rift. I send-then speech to them. I say: I am true Chiri Michi. I say: harm-not the horsefolk.

They be outlaws, but I be true Chiri Michi. They tell-then me they go uprift, go-next home. They say-then: we harm-not horsefolk.

'You mean, there's another way through the Rift than the Riftgate?'

Yes. We have a secret way, but it be no good for horses. You ask not more, please.

'All right. As for the hunters, thank you for the information. If I can ask, why were you so afraid of them yesterday?'

I be afraid-then-not of them, precisely. I know-then not who they be, but I know-now, and so there be-not a reason to fear.

'It might have been some other group of males?'

Yes. If so, trouble. These – they be outcasts and weak. Sibyl tell-once me a grand word. Despicable. They be that.

Ammadin decided that prying further would be rude if nothing else. 'We'll see if they attack or not.'

Yes, we see-soon-next. Now, there be need for me to ask you again. You help us not help us?

'What do you want me to do?'

Stop Yarl Soutan, the sorcerer. He bring-then trouble already when he come poking around our lands. He bring-next-soon more trouble.

'Soutan the sorcerer? Do you mean the man with grey hair who's been following my comnee?'

Yes. He chase-now you and travel-now with two Karshak men. In my sky spheres I see-then that he follow you. I figure-then that you be-might the witchwoman help-maybe us – She paused briefly. *If Soutan chase-now you, then Soutan be your enemy.*

'Wait. You call them Karshak. Do you mean the Kazraks?'

Long back-then, we call them Karshaki. When they come-first to our lands.

'I see, yes. The sorcerer's my enemy, all right. Stop him from doing what?'

There be a need that we meet. There be a need that we talk for a long time. We all cross-soon the Rift. I talk-next you when we leave the Rift.

Ammadin heard the hiss of that peculiar crystal sea; Water Woman had gone. Could she trust the ChaMeech and her talk of a treaty gift? Soon enough she'd know. She ran back to camp to find everyone up and busy: eating breakfast, tending the horses, packing up their gear, preparing generally for the difficult ride across the Rift. She hurried into her tent and knelt down in front of the god figures. After the proper salutations she began to pack them into their carrying bag.

'Ammadin?' Apanador's voice called from outside. 'Are you in there?'

'I am,' she called back. 'Come in, will you?'

The chief ducked under the tent flap. 'Did you spot the ChaMeech?' he said.

'No. That doesn't mean they're not there, hiding under the bridge or in one of the caves.'

'That's true. Well, if they want trouble, that's what they'll get.'

Apanador hurried off again. Once she'd packed the god figures, Ammadin went looking for Zayn.

When he woke, Zayn had got right to work, watering Ammadin's horses. He stripped down the tent, but when he went to look for the wagon, he found Dallador and some of the other men unloading it.

'Everything's going down on horseback,' Dallador said. 'You can't drive a wagon down the Riftgate.'

Zayn helped stow the contents of the wagon in the pack saddles, then watched as the others took apart the wagon itself. He understood, finally, why the Tribes made their wagons of flimsy bamboid. The sides and the tailgates came off and were roped to big pack frames along with the wheels; the wagon bed would be slung between two horses. With the heavy work done, the men discussed the possible ChaMeech attack while the women examined every inch of every piece of lead rope and repaired even the tiniest flaw.

'Zayn, remember,' Apanador told him, 'the horses carrying the wagon are your responsibility. Don't go running off to join the fight if there is one. You don't have any armour, and that's that.'

'No one's going to consider you a coward,' Dallador put in. 'After this trading trip is over, we'll have to get you started on making some.'

'I could still use a bow –' Zayn began.

'A waste of arrows,' Apanador said, and firmly. 'ChaMeech hide is too thick. You don't shoot well enough to put an arrow into an eye or throat.'

There was no arguing with the chief, but Zayn felt decidedly envious when he watched the other men putting on their long shirts of armour, made of mottled red and white grassar hide and studded with metal beads in a diamond pattern. They would turn a sabre blade, he supposed, most of the time, or stop anything but a full-force slash from a ChaMeech obsidian blade.

'Zayn!' Ammadin's voice, and he turned to see Ammadin herself, standing some yards away with her saddlebags slung over one shoulder. 'Zayn, come over here, will you?'

'I'm on my way.'

She turned and began walking away, gesturing for him to follow. They'd gone well out of earshot of the other men before she stopped and turned to face him.

'I have some information for you,' Ammadin said. 'That sorcerer's name is Soutan. Does that mean anything to you?'

Lying, Zayn decided, was a waste of time. 'Yes,' he said, 'but didn't you tell me that he was middle-aged and had grey hair?'

'That's what he looks like, yes.'

'The Soutan I know is young and blond.'

'A father and son, maybe?'

Zayn shrugged and turned his hands palms upward. 'I honestly don't know –' he began.

'Oh, I believe you.' She smiled, briefly. 'This other Soutan, the one you know. Is he a sorcerer, too?'

'I've been told he is.'

'Ah. Two sorcerers from the Cantons, but don't you know them both?'

'I told you, no.' He glanced around, searching for some way out of her questioning.

'Look at me! I'm sick as I can be of the way you nibble the edges of the truth.'

Zayn swallowed his burst of fury and looked. She's a spirit rider, he reminded himself. You don't dare argue with her, not in front of the comnee. Ammadin had her arms crossed over her chest, and her silver eyes were as cold as rain clouds. 'I don't know who the older sorcerer is.' Zayn forced his voice level. 'The Soutan that I know about, the young man with blond hair, he's a business acquaintance of Warkannan's. I heard that they're prospecting for blackstone.'

'What's that?'

'Something that probably doesn't exist. It's a black substance as hard as a rock, but it's supposed to burn, and burn really hot, at that. That's probably why they're out on the plains. I guess. I don't know. All the old stories about blackstone say you find it in the mountains.'

'I've certainly never heard of it. But they're trying to kill you, not find this blackstone.'

'Well, I don't understand it either. I'm as frustrated as you are with all these damned riddles.'

'Like why Warkannan's trying to kill you?'

'That, too.'

Ammadin's mouth twisted as if she disbelieved him, but she turned her head and looked over his shoulder, as if something behind him had distracted her. 'I've got to talk with Apanador,' she said. 'We can discuss this later.'

She stepped around him and walked off. He waited, letting her get well ahead of him, then went slowly back to camp. He reminded himself that he needed to act the part of a servant, that screaming in rage at a spirit rider would get him kicked out of the comnee at the very least. As soon as you're across, he told himself, you'll be leaving her behind.

The sun had risen well above the horizon by the time the comnee rode out. Zayn had always imagined the Rift as a deep gorge, narrow, craggy, perhaps even forbidding, but when they reached it, the reality shocked him. He stood for a long time staring down at the ribbon of orange foliage far below, laced with the gleam of water, at the mists that hid the far wall, at the vast length of the thing, and remembered Ammadin's remark, that here the earth was tearing apart. He could no longer argue the point.

'Zayn?' Ammadin walked up beside him and handed him a rag, damp and faintly sticky with plant sap. 'Rub this on your face and neck, your hands, too, or the rebbuhs will eat you alive.'

'Thanks.' Zayn took the rag and began rubbing. 'What about the horses?'

'The rebbuhs won't bother them. They only like the taste of H'mai.' She paused, glancing down into the Rift. 'It's quite a sight, isn't it?'

'It's amazing. I'm glad I've seen it. The descriptions I've read don't do it justice.'

'I thought your wise men would have drawn pictures of it.'

'No, they never do that. The Prophets forbid making images of God's creations.'

'You and your prophets! Your people are always looking backwards, aren't they? The first prophet, the second – they all lived hundreds of years ago.'

'The laws are eternal.'

'That sounds like something from one of your father's books.'

'It is.' Zayn gave her a rueful smile. 'It goes on: the laws are eternal and universal, for God is everywhere in time and space.'

'He must be busy, then, running around everywhere with no one to help him.'

Zayn thought at first that she was teasing him, but she looked solemn, her lower lip caught between her teeth as she stared down into the Rift. She had uncoiled her long blonde braids and let them hang down her back. Uneven wisps of hair stuck to her sweaty face. He found himself wanting to reach out with his fingertips and smooth them away, but she looked up and considered him so coldly that he wondered if she'd read his mind.

'It's time to get moving,' Ammadin said. 'I consulted my crystals earlier, and the earth is going to stay quiet for the trip down. Can you imagine what would happen if there was an earthquake when we were on the Riftgate?'

'I can, yes,' Zayn said, and he shuddered. 'Are you going to be riding at the head of the line?'

'Yes. Why?'

'Isn't that dangerous? You don't even have an armour shirt.'

'The ChaMeech are just as likely to attack from the rear.'

'Maybe more likely, yes. I should have thought of that.'

The Tribal horses knew the Riftgate, and his pair of charges showed not the least concern when it came to taking the slab road down. Zayn was glad of their calm company. The possibility of a ChaMeech ambush had made him alert to a preternatural degree. All the colours brightened; the striping of the canyon walls seemed precisely etched. The sounds of the horses' hooves, the voices of the comnee's members, calling back and forth, seemed both loud and isolated, each a stroke of noise on the bell of the swamp air that rose to meet them. Slowly the air grew warmer, turned humid, until Zayn was sweating so hard his shirt was soaked through. The swamp stench, a compound of mud and rotting things, nearly made him retch.

When they reached the bottom of the Rift, Ammadin and Apanador paused their horses on the strip of rocky ground directly beside the cliff but some yards away from the last step down. As the others arrived, they fanned out behind them with the orderly ease of people who had been making this difficult manoeuvre all their lives. While they gave the horses a few minutes' rest, Zayn studied the swamp. He could find no clear view between the thick scaly trunks of the fern trees, the red horsetails, and the tangles of vines. No more could he hear anything but the hum and hiss of insects, the calls of turquoise chirpers and the many frogs. A perfect place for an ambush, he thought. Four of the armed men, spears at the ready, jogged forward and joined the chief. Much to Zayn's relief, Ammadin let the warriors have her place at the head of the line and dropped back to ride just in front of him and the wagon horses.

With a yell and a wave of his hand, Apanador signalled to the comnee to move out. They walked their horses slowly along the water's edge, and once the line spread out, Zayn saw their destination, the smooth grey road and the pylons of a bridge, threading its way through trees. Rebbuhs swarmed around the caravan, hovered over bare hands and faces, then flew off fast when they smelled the plant-juice repellent.

'Ammadin,' Zayn called out. 'Who made this road?'

She turned in the saddle and glanced back at him. 'The Ancients,' she said. 'But I don't know how.'

The horses stepped up onto the road eagerly, and as soon as he followed, Zayn understood why. The grey surface seemed soft yet firm at the same time, far easier underfoot than stone or the orange muck at the edge of the water. On either side of the wide roadbed stood a railing, held up by supports some three feet high. Once, no doubt, these supports had stood straight, but the long centuries of earthquakes had pulled them off true and left them twisted. Here and there cracks ran across the roadbed, most the mere thickness of a blade of grass but ominous nonetheless. No one in the khanate could mend this material, Zayn knew, much less replace it. Some hundred yards in, the road began to rise on squat pylons. A few yards more, and it became a bridge. Here too cracks laced the edges, and some of the supports for the railing had disappeared, leaving broken stumps behind.

At the high point of the bridge, Apanador turned in his saddle and called out an order. 'Everyone move over to the right.'

In a murmur of voices the order travelled along the line of march. Zayn urged his horses over, glanced back, and saw everyone doing the same to clear a space to the left, wide enough for armed riders to pass. If the ChaMeech attacked at either head or rear of the line, reinforcements could join the battle. And yet the comnee crossed safely. At the far end of the bridge the road debouched onto another long expanse of dusty stone. The comnee once again spread out behind Apanador. As soon as everyone had got into position, Apanador set off again, leading the comnee south, parallel to the cliff towering above them.

The horses tossed up their heads, sniffed the air, and walked faster. In a short while Zayn saw what they had smelled: fresh water, bubbling up from springs at the base of the cliff. Here, Zayn realized, was the danger point. With so many horses, the comnee would have to water them in pairs, a long slow process, but the horses needed to drink in the clammy heat.

The line of march had just halted near the springs when Zayn heard the sound, a deep vibration of the air, a thrum or hum, he supposed he could call it, something like distant thunder. Out in the swamp the animals fell silent.

'Ammadin?' Zayn called out. 'What's that noise?'

'ChaMeech, damn it!' Ammadin dismounted fast. She led her dun gelding back to Zayn and handed him the reins. 'Hold him, will you?' she said. 'I'm going to scan.'

The spectral thunder again rolled down the Rift. Ammadin rummaged in her saddlebags and came out with a pair of pouched crystals; he could hear one of them chiming like a Kazraki clock. Ammadin carried them to a spot where sunlight broke through the forest cover, then turned her back on the comnee and knelt on the ground. Everyone else, Zayn noticed, was pointedly looking away to give the Spirit Rider what privacy they could. Although he watched, fascinated, he realized soon enough that he wasn't going to see any peculiar act of magic, just Ammadin crouching over a crystal sphere, unmoving, speaking now and then in a language he couldn't understand. Finally she stood up and walked back, shaking her head.

'I don't see any ChaMeech,' she called out. 'They could be hiding in caves or out in the water, but then again, the thrumming we heard sounded pretty far away, and it was even fainter the second time.'

Apanador turned in the saddle and called for Dallador, who trotted his horse up the line to join him. While they sat on horseback together and discussed how to dispose the armed guards, Ammadin walked back to Zayn and her gelding. She put the crystals away in her saddlebags, then laced the flap down.

'I'm really surprised,' Zayn said, 'that you'd work magic where everyone can see you.'

'There's no reason not to,' Ammadin said. 'No one can just mimic what I do and work the magic. You've got to know the spirit language and all the correct command words, and the right way to say them. The only way to learn those is to become a spirit rider.' She paused, suddenly distant.

Zayn waited.

'I'm sorry,' Ammadin said at length. 'I was just thinking of something else.'

'What? Well, if I can ask.'

'Why not? I was wondering who would teach a ChaMeech how to use a crystal.' She paused, smiling. 'There. Now you know, but you're none the wiser.'

By the time the horses were all watered, and the comnee on its way again, long shadows filled the canyon. The sunlight gilded the edge of the south-west rim, then slowly faded. Out on the plains the ChaMeech would have attacked at just this time, when the dark was beginning to gather for the night. The comnee, however, reached the road up without hearing the bubbling yip of a war cry. An ambush at the top, maybe – but Ammadin would have seen them in her crystals. They'd crossed safely, Zayn realized, and he devoted what was left of his energy to the long hard climb up.

In the long light of afternoon the comnee travelled a bare half-mile from the Rift to set up camp between a fast-running stream and a strange rock formation. Eight large boulders, placed a few feet apart, sat in a straight line; at one end, three smaller rocks formed an arrowhead pointing east. About five feet apart, two shallow trenches, thick with moss, ran parallel to the rocks; they looked like the ruts left by some gigantic and gigantically heavy wagon.

As Zayn followed these marks along the line of boulders, something caught his eye, and he squatted down for a closer look. A ring of ashes and spent charcoal, a few spilled grains of wheatian, lay on grass that had been beaten down, probably by feet walking back and forth – Warkannan's camp, most likely. Zayn stood up, looking off to the east. He felt personally betrayed that Idres of all people would somehow turn against the Great Khan and force them to become enemies. And what, Zayn asked himself, will you do if your duty to the Great Khan demands you kill him? He realized that he could give no answer. With a toss of his head, he hurried back to camp.

Zayn put the two wagon horses on tether ropes and took them out to the herd. Maradin brought him two pairs of leather hobbles.

'Can I ask you something?' Zayn said. 'This Bane about the horses eating Canton grass on the way home. Dallo told me about the Bane on bringing seeds to the plains, but why would that be forbidden?'

'No one really knows,' Maradin said. 'My mother tried to find out. She asked every spirit rider she ever met until they got sick of her asking. Mama was a stubborn woman, just like me.' She paused for a smile. 'Finally she met one old woman who told her that the problem was the green grass, not the normal kind, and the other green plants the Cantonneurs have in their gardens. It's part of the Bane against having green things growing on the plains. Ammi told you about that, right?'

'Yes, she did, but I don't understand that Bane either.'

'Don't try to understand Banes. They never make sense.'

'That's good advice, I suppose. Whose comnee does your mother ride with?'

'Oh.' Maradin looked away. 'Of course, you wouldn't know. She's dead.'

'Forgive me! I shouldn't have –'

'There was a grass fire last summer.' Maradin went on as if she hadn't heard. 'You've not seen one yet, and I hope to the gods none of us ever do again. When the grass is dry, fire travels fast, like a wall moving across the plains, and all you can do is get into water. We'd almost made it to safety, some of the comnee was already in the Great River, I mean, but Mama looked back and saw her favourite mare panicking. She turned back to try to save her. The fire took them both.'

'I'm so sorry,' Zayn realized he was whispering. 'What a horrible thing. You saw it?'

Maradin nodded, her eyes stark with remembered horror, an expression that reminded Zayn of his father's when he spoke of the death of Zayn's mother. Then Maradin shrugged, again as his father used to do, to bring herself back to the present moment. 'Well, it's not safe out here, you know. People die all the time, especially the men. You need to know that.'

'Yes, yes, I do. I'm still sorry about your mother.'

'So am I. I'll miss her always.'

The awkward silence hung between them. Zayn began glancing around for Ammadin in the hopes of finding an excuse to leave.

'You're looking for Ammi, aren't you?' Maradin said.

'Not particularly.'

She raised one eyebrow and grinned at him, back to her usual teasing self.

'Well,' Zayn said, 'I need to know if those ChaMeech are going to attack. Did the Spirit Rider say anything about that?'

'She told Apanador that they were long gone.'

'Good. But we'd better mount a guard over the horses anyway.'

Late that evening, when the Spider lay silver at zenith and flooded the sky with pale light, Zayn took his turn at riding herd. As he sat on horseback, a comnee spear tucked under one arm, he found himself thinking about Idres. He remembered the first time they'd met, the raw recruit of a trooper and the accomplished officer, newly appointed captain of their company. Why did you enlist so young? Warkannan had asked him. Zayn had mumbled something about wanting to serve the Great Khan and see distant lands. How could he have told his captain the truth?

'I joined up to get myself killed,' he said to his sorrel gelding. 'That was the real answer. It nearly worked, too. Twice.'

The horse stamped and snorted. Zayn clucked to it, and they ambled off, making a half-circuit of the drowsing herd, then turning and ambling back. He rose in his stirrups and looked off to the east. Where was Idres tonight? he wondered. Camping somewhere miles ahead on the road to Bredanee, most likely, and I'm here, right behind him on guild business.

'I joined the Chosen to get myself killed, too.'

The sorrel tossed its head with a long ripple of mane. The real question, Zayn knew, the one that tormented him, was whether or not he had started wanting to live.

That night the ChaMeech came again to Warkannan's camp. The Spider had passed zenith when Warkannan heard the horses whinny an alarm. At the same moment the unmistakable acrid stench of male ChaMeech reached him. He jumped to his feet, picked up his scabbard from the ground and drew his sabre, then yelled at Arkazo and Soutan.

'Come on! ChaMeech are after the horses!'

Arkazo scrambled up, reaching for his sword, but Soutan yawned and stayed sitting.

'Calm down, Captain,' Soutan said. 'The horses are hobbled, and they're in no danger. Despite the stink.'

Soutan leaned back, grabbed his saddlebags and pulled them over, then took out the lightwand. Yips, bubbling shrieks, a ghastly sound like a parody of human laughter – the ChaMeech were coming closer.

'Soutan,' Warkannan snapped. 'Get on your feet and ready.'

'Don't you give me orders.' Slowly, amazingly slowly, Soutan stood up.

For a moment he fiddled with the loose ring around the wand; then at last he raised it and chanted. As before, a fountain of light sprang into the sky. The glare trapped the warband of six ChaMeech, but tonight they were crouching in a wedge-shaped formation behind their leader. With a toss of his huge head, the amulet-bedecked ChaMeech ambled forward a few steps, then bent his front legs and bowed to Soutan while his pseudo-arms flapped and fluttered. He whined and lowered his head still further; his throat sac filled and throbbed.

'It's the same one,' Arkazo muttered. 'Look at those tunics he's wearing.'

'I see them,' Warkannan said. 'And I see something else, too.'

Once again Soutan's lips moved silently as he stared at the ChaMeech leader. Once again the ChaMeech suddenly howled, swung himself around, and bounded away. His men followed, yipping softly on a single high-pitched note.

'I know that sound,' Warkannan said to Arkazo. 'It means they accept defeat.'

Soutan chanted another incomprehensible word. The glare dimmed to a pleasant glow, and he lowered the wand, holding it point down, to send a crisp circle of light over the ground around him. Warkannan could feel himself trembling with rage. He sheathed his sabre, took a deep breath, and crossed his arms over his chest to keep his fists under control.

'All right, sorcerer,' Warkannan growled. 'You're colluding with the ChaMeech, aren't you?'

'It would be more accurate, my dear Captain, to say that they're colluding with me.' Soutan paused to draw his lips back in a toothy grin. 'Most of their people don't approve of their helping me, no, not at all.'

The last thing Warkannan had expected was a confession.

'For all the good they were, damn them!' Soutan went on. 'I wanted them to attack the comnee and rid us of our spy and that wretched witchwoman both. They had the gall to tell me that they'd been ordered off by a true Chiri Michi – as if females would be running around out here! The real reason, I suppose, is plain cowardice. The comnee has too many fighting men for their taste.'

'Just wait a minute!' Arkazo snapped. 'They didn't say anything at all.'

'Oh yes they did.' Soutan looked at him. 'You simply don't have the ears to hear it.'

Soutan barked a command, and the light died. Warkannan stood blinking in the sudden dark and struggled to control himself. You don't know enough Vranz to get by, he reminded himself. You still need this stinking infidel's help. He turned away, orientated himself by the light of the tiny campfire, and strode over to throw on an extravagant handful of fuel. He knelt down and watched the tinder catch, then blew on the thinnest sticks of charcoal till they glowed red and gold.

'Well?' Soutan said. 'No questions?'

Warkannan looked up to find him smiling nearby.

'Just one,' Warkannan said, as calmly as he could manage. 'Do you realize how close you came to dying just now?'

Soutan went pale and stepped back. It was Warkannan's turn for the smile.

'I've got to be alone,' Soutan said. 'I need to, uh, er – I need to consult with my spirits.'

He trotted off, stopping only long enough to scoop up his saddlebags, and headed out into the darkness. Arkazo joined Warkannan at the fire.

'Uncle?' he said. 'Do you know what he meant, about the ears to hear, I mean?'

'I don't. More of his damned magic, I suppose. I don't much care. It turned my stomach, watching that filthy infidel trafficking with ChaMeech! I –' Warkannan took another deep breath. 'Well, no use in carrying on about it. It's over and done with.'

Soutan stayed away until long after Warkannan and Arkazo went to sleep, but in the morning, Warkannan woke to find him snoring in his blankets on the far side of the dead fire. Arkazo still slept as well, with one arm thrown over his face to block the hot morning light. Warkannan got up, pulled on his shirt, then took his pocket watch out of his saddlebags, where he stowed it at night. Winding it soothed him.

Warkannan was just chaining the watch to his belt when Soutan woke, sitting up with a long snort and a yawn. He rubbed his face, then let his hands fall into his lap and looked at Warkannan, merely looked for a long moment. Warkannan waited.

'Good morning,' Soutan said finally.

'Morning,' Warkannan said.

Soutan got up, fished in his blankets, and produced his shirt. He shook it out, then put it on, smoothing the white cloth down over his chest.

'I'm sorry you disliked our company last night,' Soutan said without looking his way. 'They have their uses.'

'Are these the allies you were telling me about? If so, I don't much care for your choice of friends.'

'I have a great many allies, Captain. Also a great many enemies.

I can't afford to be fussy if we're going to get Jezro Khan safely back to Andjaro Province.'

'You have a point.'

'Yes, and it's the only point.' Soutan took a step towards him, but he was looking off somewhere over Warkannan's shoulder. 'Do you understand, Warkannan? Everything depends on Jezro. Everything.'

'Well, of course,' Warkannan said. 'We'll never get rid of Gemet without an heir to put in his place.'

'That too, yes. But that's only the beginning.'

'Beginning of what? Tax reforms, I suppose you mean.' Warkannan was about to say more when he realized that Soutan was no longer listening. The sorcerer's eyes had gone very wide, and he stared unblinking at the distant view. He smiled, but it was a gaping sort of smile, on the edge of viciousness. Warkannan felt the hair on the back of his neck bristle. Suddenly he saw that he had ridden half across a continent with a madman.

Part Two

The Lost

We have been betrayed, outnumbered, and outvoted. We knew that the mullahs would give us trouble, but we weren't prepared for the treachery of the contingent from Ruby. Sixteen of their wake-berth leaders sided with the mullahs, which left five to vote with me and the other fleet commanders, all six of us. We should have expected trouble from a bunch of terrorists. The Ruby defection meant that when we negotiated the terms of settlement with Chursavva, our chief speaker was the so-called great leader himself, Mullah Agvar. The old boy has charisma; you've got to hand it to him. He even charmed Chursavva's harem, and thanks to them, the Ruby contingent got their damned horses, all right, and the plains to pasture them on.

How long the native culture here can hold out, I don't know. We Shipfolk will do our best to protect the Chiri Michi, but there are three thousand of us against sixty ships' worth of our charming Karashiki emigrants and the Ruby deportees. We've thrashed out a plan that might give the Chiri Michi a fighting chance, because Mullah Agvar will back it. This whole thing would give the Councils back on the Rim screaming fits, but what the hell, they'll never know what we've done. Every time I realize just how far from home we are, I want to cry.

From the log of Admiral Zhunmaree Raynar

'Tell me something, Dallo,' Zayn said. 'How far are the Cantons from here?'

'It depends on which one you mean,' Dallador said. 'There's five of them. We're heading for Bredanee Canton and Nannes, the town where the trading precinct is.'

'Five cantons, huh? I thought there were only four.'

'Four live ones. There's Dordan north of Bredanee, and I think it's Burgunee to the north-east of there. And then south of Bredanee is Pegaree. The dead one was a long way away, straight east of here, and it had a weird kind of name before the ChaMeech took it back. I forget what.'

'N'Dosha. We learned about it in school. The ChaMeech pretty much slaughtered everyone who lived there, right?'

'That's what I've heard. Did that school of yours ever tell you why? I'd like to know.'

'No, they told me there wasn't any reason. The ChaMeech just kept coming and killing, year after year.' Zayn felt his fists clench and with an effort made himself relax. 'It's like the slimy bastards. They kill for the fun of it.'

Dallador cocked his head to one side and considered him for a moment. 'I don't know if I'd say that,' he said at last.

'You haven't fought against them the way I have.'

'True. But they left the other cantons alone.'

'So far.'

Dallador seemed to be about to speak, then shrugged. 'Let's go put the wagon back together. We'll be getting on the road soon.'

The comnee set off east across grassland, but when the sun hung on the horizon, they came to a massive round pillar and behind it what had once been a road, a wide stripe of spongy grey material running due east as far as Zayn could see. Just to the north of the road stood another line of huge tan boulders, nine of them this time, forming an arrowhead pointing east like the one at the head of the Riftgate.

When Zayn investigated the pillar, he found to his surprise that rather than being made of blocks of stone, it was all of a piece, smooth, white, and so hard that when he flicked it with a fingernail the finger hurt. On the westward side, he found rows of writing in characters unknown to him but precisely carved by some master craftsman. He took a moment to tuck the inscription away in his memory against the day he learned to read Vranz.

Around the other side, a white roundel, moulded directly into the pillar in low relief, displayed a spiral pattern with several arms curving out of a central circle, an image that seemed oddly familiar. Zayn ran a finger along the relief, as slick as a glazed pot and just as hard as the pillar itself. Tracing it made him realize where he'd seen it before: in the night sky, the Spider. A religious symbol, perhaps? He went to look for Ammadin on the off-chance that she'd know.

He found her standing at the edge of the camp. With her saddlebags slung over one shoulder, she was staring up at the sky as if she were waiting for something to appear.

'Ammi?' Zayn walked up to her. 'Say, those arrows on the ground. Do you know –'

'Nothing about them.' She smiled as she interrupted him. 'I'm assuming the Cantonneurs made them, but I suppose it might have been ChaMeech.'

'They're damned strong when they work together, yes, but I'll bet they didn't make that pillar with the Spider on it. Sorry, I mean the Herd.'

'I doubt it, too.'

'But you don't know who did make it? And what about that white stuff, what is it?'

'By all the gods at once! I have never met a man as curious as you.'

'A lot of people have told me that, over the years. All right, here's an easier question. When do you want me to make dinner?'

'I'm not particularly hungry.' Ammadin stopped her survey of the sky and looked at him. 'Go ahead and cook, though, if you are. Just save me some.' She started to say more, but something inside her saddlebags began chiming – one of her crystals, he supposed. 'Sorry. I'll be back later.'

With a nod his way she jogged off, heading for the line of boulders. Zayn walked back to camp to lay a fire; she'd need the light for her spirits when she returned. As he was chopping saur jerky to mix with breadmoss in a kind of porridge, he realized that he had begun to think like a servant as well as act like one. The realization should have pleased him. The Chosen learned to live their false identities down to the level of instinct, a necessity in their line of work, where one false step meant exposure and death.

But as he scraped together fuel for a cooking fire, Zayn realized that he felt angry, not pleased. I'm not her servant, damn it! Yet he and no one else had decided to act as if he were. He'd lived his entire life taking other people's orders, his father's, the cavalry's, his guild's, and the orders had never chafed before. But no matter how he argued with himself, the resentment remained. You're not the same man who rode to Blosk, he told himself. Who he actually might be was a question he couldn't answer.

Witchwoman. Ammadin Witchwoman. You hear-now me?

'Yes, I hear you.' Crouched behind a boulder, Ammadin smiled at the sound of the ChaMeech's voice. 'I need to thank you for your help. The warband never attacked us.'

Good, good.

'Now, what's this about Soutan? Why do you want him stopped?'

Great Mother, Sibyl, I, we all fear-now. Soutan want-now to bring many Karshak men east to our country. They take our land-soon-next.

'Why does he want to do that?'

Water Woman said nothing. Ammadin waited for some minutes, then decided to prod. 'Water Woman, if you want my help, you have to tell me what the trouble is. I feel like you keep hiding something. You walk up to the edge of the truth, and then you draw back. Are you lying to me?'

No no never that. I be afraid. H'mai kill-then-now many of my people. Will your people kill-soon-next me?

'No. You have my word on that. I don't suppose you have any reason to trust my word, but it's all I can give you.'

Sibyl say-then witchwomen never lie.

'Sibyl was right. Trust her if you can't trust me.'

I trust-then-now-soon-next Sibyl. I want meet-next you face to face.

We talk-that-time. I give-next you a token of good faith. You give-next me a token. I have two servants, you bring-next-soon two servants.

'Very well. I'll agree to that. Where will we meet?'

You know the White Ruins? The sleeping tower?

'I do, yes.'

East of the White Ruins be a big white stone. Not far east, just a little ways to walk. I wait-now there, you come when you come-next-soon.

'Do you mean you're there already?'

I be-now there, yes.

'You people can move really fast when you want to, can't you? That's two days' ride away for us.'

Oh, well, we keep-always going on. Come-next-soon when you can. I wait-until.

'I will yes. Tell me something now, though. Did Sibyl teach you to use magic?'

Sibyl teach-then the great mother who find-then her. This be long time ago when the great mother find-then her cave. Great mother teach-then-later the new great mother, and she teach-then and so on. This Great Mother now-with us teach-then some true Chiri Michi. Sibyl give-then sky spheres.

'Sky – You mean the crystals? The ones you talk into?'

Yes. I have-now a big sphere that I talk-now into. I have a little sphere I hear-now-with – the Great Mother pierce-then my skin. Put-then little crystal into cut, like Sibyl tell-then her. I hear-then hear-now. Sibyl own many sky spheres-then-now. She give-then some to us.

'Where did Sibyl get all these crystals?'

They come-then with her, when your people come. She be H'mai.

'Do you mean the people in the Cantons? My people have been here since the creation of the world.'

No no, your people come-then with the Karshaks, long time past now, but the world be here for a long time already. The plains be-then ours, and the western sea, too. When the Karshak people come-then, my people pity-then them. Karshak people take-then north sea coast. Chursavva give-then plains to your people. Chursavva say-then that you horse-people keep-next Karshaks away from our side of border Rift. Horses come-then to the world and iron spears and the sky spies, the Deathbringers. Your people arrive-then too.

'That can't be true!'

It be true. The great mother see-then, she tell new great mother who tell-then new great mother. Down long years they tell-then. My people see your people come-then-way-back. It be true.

'But our spirit riders say that we've been here always.'

I understand-not. We sign-long-time-ago a set of promises, everyone call-then the Landfall Treaty. You know about this yes no?

'Yes. But did my people sign it too?'

Great Mother say-always so. Horse People keep their promises. Not Karshaks.

'That's fascinating, but –' Ammadin glanced at the sky and realized that the sun was setting. She brought her attention back to the problem at hand. 'Why does Soutan want to bring a lot of Kazraks east?'

To hunt-next-soon something he call-then the Covenant Ark. This happen-four-years-back. He say-then he want Ark, and only this Ark, and he talk-then with some of our young men. They say-then that they help Soutan find Ark so you H'mai people go-next-soon away.

'I don't understand. What are your men saying? That if they help Soutan find this Ark thing, we'll all go away?'

Only some men say this. Not all of our men.

'All right, but where are we all supposed to go to?'

I know-not. Not Yarl Soutan, not our men say-then. We argue-then in front of the Great Mother. Many raise-then their heads high and screech-then at one another. Finally, the Great Mother say-then she believe-not Yarl, not one word. So, others of our men drive-then Soutan's supporters away. The Great Mother pronounce-then judgment: they belong to us no longer. When they stand in front of us, we see-not them. When they speak, we hear-not them. When they mark, we smell-not them.

'Are these men the men who were in the Rift?'

Yes, but only some of those that follow-now Soutan. They believe-still Soutan when he say all you H'mai go away. I believe-then-now-next-soon not not not.

'Neither do I.'

I believe-then-now, the Karshaks, they take-next-soon our land. Chursavva give-long-time-back them land, but they say, they need more land. They take-then-next more of our land on the north sea coast. They take-then-next the south sea coast, too. They drive-then us away and build-then forts in the hills to keep us out of our land. We go-then east, find new land. Now they come-maybe and take-next-soon this new land.

'That sounds more like them, yes. And then my people will be trapped in between two groups of Kazraks.'

This be true. You help-next-soon me?

'Yes, I will. Neither of us wants to see the Kazraks take more territory.'

True. And I thank you.

'There's something else I'd like to know. You told me the men in the Rift were outcasts. But you were afraid there might be another group of your men there, ones that were dangerous.'

This be true.

'Should I be afraid of this other group? Will they harm my people, my comnee, and our horses?'

Here they harm-not you. Dangerous men at home, our country. Water Woman fell briefly silent. *Witchwoman, my people, we be divided. Once not-long-time-ago all my people agree. Not now. Soutan bring-then trouble when he ride-then into our land. Some few, they believe-then-now him, but many many more people agree that he lie. This many many, we say Sibyl help-maybe us. I go to Sibyl – you know-now all this. But there be third group, many more people than follow Soutan, but not many many. They say go-next-soon to Sibyl, ask-next-soon her for weapons, magic spirit weapons, like the H'mai have-then-long-time-past. They say, go-next into the cave and get-soon weapons.*

'And this group, you're afraid of them?'

Afraid no. Worried yes. In my country many many agree with me, and this group have little power. Out here – things be different in the Borderlands. I know-not what they do if they be out here.

'Ah, I understand now. At home they aren't powerful. Would Sibyl give them weapons?'

No, she say-not. She say-then, there be no spirit weapons here, I have-not power to give them weapons. I tell-then this group that Sibyl have-not weapons. They believe-not me. They say, we ourselves go-next to her cave and grab the weapons, Sibyl no Sibyl. But they know-not where her cave be. Only a few of us know, and they all be true Chiri Michi. Ammadin, the sun set-soon. The darkness kills-next-soon my sky sphere.

'Yes, mine too. We'll talk more when we meet, which will be at the big white stone east of the White Ruins.'

I be there. You come-next-soon.

'I will. Very soon.'

Ammadin let her crystals soak up the last of the sunlight while she considered what Water Woman had told her: more mysteries, more questions, and all of them leading her east.

It was after dark, and all through the camp small fires were blooming, when Ammadin finally returned to her tent. Zayn had been keeping her share of the porridge warm in an iron pot near the fire. He scooped it into a clean bowl and handed it to her. For a few minutes she ate steadily, then set the half-full bowl down beside her.

'Isn't it all right?' Zayn said.

'It's fine,' Ammadin said. 'I'll finish it in a bit. Tell me something. When your people came to Kazrajistan, did the Tribes come with them, or were we already here?'

'What?' Zayn sat back on his heels and smiled at her. 'Now you're the one who's being curious. That's a strange question.'

'True enough. But do you know?'

'I was always told that when our people came, they met the ChaMeech first, and then, once we'd explored to the east, we found your people. But –' He hesitated and looked away. In his mind he could see the pages of a book and mentally turned them, flipping through till he found what he needed. 'Most people believe that you were already here, but some historians don't. They say they have evidence that we all came at the same time, but the book doesn't say what the evidence was.'

'Here's another strange question. Do your people ever call yourselves Karshaks?'

'Not that I know of. But the old country was called New Karashi. Why?'

'Someone told me that you did.'

'Well, they've got it wrong, then. We're Kazraks.'

'But were you always? A lot of lore seems to have changed, over the years.' For a brief moment Ammadin looked furious; then she shrugged. 'That list of the forbidden talents. I never asked you to recite the whole thing.'

'I can do it now, if you'd like. They're divided into groups, so each entry starts out with the words, the three forbidden talents of . . .'

'You can skip that part.'

'All right. It doesn't make sense, anyway, because there's generally a lot more than three in each group.' He looked away and saw, floating between him and the landscape, a pale pink area much like a page of rushi. Upon it words formed. 'I'll tell you the main headings first. Memory. Perception. Warfare. Illness.'

'Start with the ones for perception.'

'Talents of vision. The hearing of sounds. Talents of the sense of smell –' He stopped, struck by his own words.

'That sounds like something that applies to me, doesn't it?' Ammadin said. 'Do they break them down further?'

'Yes. The forbidden talents of vision. Seeing at night but not in complete darkness. The seeing of heat from living things. The seeing of things too small for other men to see. The seeing of small things as if they were large things. Hearing. The hearing of faint sounds. The hearing of voices from the world beyond. The hearing of voices too low or too high for other men to hear.' He paused, thinking. 'Here's one I've never understood. The hearing of words when other men hear only babble.'

'I don't understand it either. Go on.'

'Smell. The discrimination of bodily odours. There's one I didn't understand before, but I sure do now.'

Ammadin smiled faintly.

'The perception of smells from a far distance,' Zayn continued. 'The discrimination of natural odours. The discrimination of chemical odours.'

'What an odd lot!'

'Yes, it is. Do you match them?'

'I suppose so. I have no idea what they mean about words from babble, and I've never run across anything called chemical odours, but as for the rest, yes, they fit me.' For a long moment she was silent. 'I know perfectly well that there aren't any demons among my ancestors.'

'Do you want to hear the rest of the list?'

'Not right now. The holy men who branded them impure and forbidden – they lived in ancient times, right?'.

'It was Mullah Agvar himself, blessed be he.'

'Well, then. If your people and my people have some of the same talents, we're more alike than we think.'

'Yes, that's true.'

'And maybe it means that we all arrived here together. But arrived from where? Do you know?'

Zayn shrugged. 'Over the seas somewhere. I've never much thought about it. We're here now, and the mullahs say we can't go back because the demons destroyed Karashi, so that's that.'

'It's odd that you're so curious about so many things, but never thought to question the mullahs about your homeland.'

'I did ask when I was a child. Questioning the mullahs was a good way to get into trouble, so I learned to keep my mouth shut. I'd already embarrassed my father enough.'

'I can't say that my heart bleeds for him.' Ammadin picked up her bowl of porridge. 'This is all becoming very interesting.'

Though Zayn waited for her to go on, she merely ate her dinner. After a while he got up and went to drink with the men.

In the morning the comnee packed up and followed the crumbling road east, but they travelled only until some hours after noon. To let the horses have a long graze and a rest, they camped for the night near a ruin that Ammadin called simply 'the fort'. When he'd finished his chores, Zayn walked over for a closer look.

Behind a crumbling wall of corroded brass wire tangled with dead thorn vine stood a pair of grassy mounds that marked, by their precisely rectangular outlines, the remains of buildings. Zayn jumped the knee-high wall and walked into the middle of the compound, where a square, white building stood, some hundred feet on a side and pierced with regularly placed narrow windows. He found an opening that once had held a door and walked in. Fire had gutted the place quite recently to judge by the smell of rot and mildew that greeted him. Through a hole in the thatched roof, the light streamed in and picked out heaps of charred rubble, scattered with animal droppings and hung with white strands of fungus. Rain, however, had washed the exposed parts of the walls, both inside and out, back to a smooth and pristine white, as slick yet metallic as the roundel on the pillar he'd seen at the end of the road. When he ran a hand across it, the material felt more like a saur's scales than metal, but despite all the evidence of a really horrendous fire, he couldn't find a trace of charring or blistering.

'Zayn!' It was Ammadin's voice. 'Zayn, where are you?'

She came jogging across the compound and joined him inside. 'Have you lost your mind?' she snapped. 'You shouldn't wander off alone.'

'I just wanted a look around. Looks like the ChaMeech have been raiding.'

'Maybe. The last time I saw this place, there were five families camped in here.' She poked at a pile of charred rubble with the toe of her boot. 'They'd built bamboid walls to divide the space up, and then they had cooking fires, and so you can imagine how easy it would be for the whole thing to go up.'

'Why were they camping here?'

'They had nowhere else to go, they said, because they had no money. There are people like that in the Cantons. They lose their farm or money or something, and they end up drifting around, dragging their children with them.'

'Doesn't anyone give them charity?'

Ammadin shrugged with a profound lack of interest. 'The loremasters say that the ancestors of the Cantonneurs used this building to guard the Riftgate when they were building it. That's why it's still called the fort.'

Zayn gaped.

'Sounds like nonsense, doesn't it?' Ammadin said.

'That would have been what, eight hundred years ago at least, when they arrived here. You'd think it would have all crumbled into dust by now.' Zayn touched the nearest wall with the flat of his hand. 'But I don't think there's anyone alive today who could make this white stuff.'

'Eight hundred years, yes, a Cantonneur told me once that they'd been here that long. They came with your people.'

'Well, so I was told. The demons had destroyed their part of the homeland too.'

'You and your damned demons! That doesn't make any sense.'

'How's this? They also taught us in school that the Cantonneurs came here in flying ships.'

'Oh please! If you Kazraks believe that, you'll believe anything.'

'I didn't say I believe it. I said my teacher told it.'

'That's an important difference, yes. My own teacher told me a few things that have turned out to be untrue. But look, if the Tribes did come here with everyone else, why have we always thought that we didn't?'

'Vanity?'

Ammadin laughed and nodded her agreement. 'Maybe so,' she

said, still smiling. 'It's very flattering to think that the gods went out of their way to create your people.'

When she smiled, her face softened. Her long braids were slipping from their coil; she reached up and began pulling out the bone pins to let the braids tumble down her back. The gesture made her shirt ride up, exposing a stripe of pale skin. Zayn stepped closer, expecting her to move away, but she merely shoved the handful of pins into the pocket of her leather trousers. Another step – she looked up, still smiling. He raised his hand and touched her cheek with his fingertips. For a moment she hesitated, but when he bent his head to kiss her, she turned away.

'Neither of us should be standing out here,' she said. 'Let's get back to camp.'

'Ah damn it!'

'What?'

'You know damn well what.' He stepped up behind her and put his hands on her shoulders. 'Ammi –'

He could feel how tense she was, tense and wary, but when he pulled her a little closer, she rested in his grasp.

'Are you really as cold to me as you act?' He softened his voice.

'No.' With a sudden twist she broke away and walked a few paces off. 'But it doesn't matter.'

'What do you mean, it doesn't matter?'

'Just that. I'm not going to sleep with you.'

'What? Why not?'

'Because you keep lying to me. Or not really lying, but you dance along the edge of the truth. I can't trust you.'

Zayn winced.

'I promised you I wouldn't pry,' Ammadin went on, 'and I won't. But if you can't be honest with me, then I'm not going to let you close to me.'

'All right.' He could think of a hundred arguments, but he knew she'd demolish them all. 'That's fair.'

'Now let's get back to the comnee. When I scanned this morning, I didn't see that sorcerer and his murderous friends, but for all I know he's got another crystal and can hide himself again.'

As he followed her back to camp, Zayn realized how right her worry was. He turned a little cold, wondering why he'd risked his life by wandering off just as if he hadn't an enemy in the world. It was an elementary mistake that no member of the Chosen should ever have made, and a mistake that he'd never made before. He felt safe in the comnee, he realized, and a feeling of safety was the greatest danger in his world.

'I have got to get a new crystal,' Soutan said. 'This is ridiculous! For all I know our stupid barbarians could be one mile away or a hundred.'

'It's a bad situation, all right,' Warkannan said. 'What can we do about it?'

Soutan shrugged and sat down on the far side of their campfire. He took his saddlebags into his lap and opened them. Arkazo was kneeling in the pool of firelight, sharpening his hunting knife on a small flat whetstone.

'That noise!' Soutan snapped. 'It could drive a man crazy.'

'What?' Arkazo looked up. 'Isn't it too late for you?'

'You insolent young lout!'

'Shush!' Warkannan said. 'Both of you, just drop it.'

Soutan ostentatiously scowled into his saddlebags. Arkazo went back to work on the blade.

They had camped for the night some twenty miles east of the fort. Soutan had led them to a clearing in a forest the like of which Warkannan had never seen. Ancient true-oaks, twined round with orange vines, grew amidst a wild tangle of purple and red ferns and shrubs. In the deep shade yellow fungi sent swollen fingers up from the litter of decaying leaves. The oldest oaks, too big for a man's arms to reach around, sported festoons of dark red strands beaded with orange swellings. The nodes gave out a phosphorescent light, as if this stretch of forest were a nightmare version of the Great Khan's gardens. Soutan had warned them to leave both growths strictly alone, particularly the festoons, which the Canton people called Death's Necklace. High up in the trees, small maroon reptiles with six legs and long, narrow heads chirped and clambered – eating the leaves, Warkannan assumed, or chasing the shiny blue insects that swarmed around the fungus. At irregular intervals something in the deep forest shrieked, a ghastly half-human sound that made Warkannan jump every time. Whether it was predator or prey he didn't want to know.

'Well, what about that crystal?' Warkannan said. 'I don't suppose you can just find one in the marketplace.'

'Sometimes you can, actually,' Soutan said, 'especially in the trading precinct. Spirit riders will pay high for them.'

'Well, then, we should ride into town and ask around.'

'I can't!' Soutan's voice rose and squeaked. 'I cannot go into any town in Bredanee, you idiot! I told you that.'

'You did, but you never told me why.'

Soutan looked away, his mouth twisted in a pout. Warkannan waited without speaking.

'It's because of my enemies,' Soutan said at last. 'They laid false charges against me, and there's a warrant out for my arrest.'

'What kind of charges?'

'They induced one of my students to lie and say I'd raped her.'

'Students? This is the first time I've heard about any students.'

'I used to teach in a school run by the sorcerers' guild, but this lying little bitch lost me my job. Rape!' Soutan snorted in disgust. 'She seduced me, the little whore, and then she lied when her mother found out about it. They must have bribed her to stick to her story before the magistrates.'

'They?'

'My enemies!' Soutan snapped. 'The people who envied my position in the sorcerers' guild.'

'And this was in Bredanee?'

'No, in Dordan. But all the Cantons have an extradition treaty.' Soutan paused to take the lightwand out of a saddlebag. 'I do have an ally of sorts who lives near here. He may be able to procure a crystal for me, he may not. At the least, he'll put us up for the night.'

'What is he, another ChaMeech?'

'Oh no, he's as human as we are, except on Sevenday.' Soutan suddenly laughed, a cackling sort of sound.

'And what is that supposed to mean?'

'It's his holy day, Sevenday.'

'What are you talking about?'

'Don't you try to interrogate me, Captain.' Soutan scrambled to his feet. 'I need to be alone. I have work to do.' He grabbed his saddlebags and stalked off.

At the edge of the clearing Soutan snapped out a word that started the wand glowing, casting a dim circle at his feet. Warkannan watched the light swaying through the trees until it shone more faintly than the pale blue beads of light among the oak leaves. Arkazo tested the knife blade on his thumb, then sheathed it with a satisfied nod.

'Uncle, do you think he really raped that girl?'

'I have no idea. A young woman who's caught polluting herself with a man often does lie about it, trying to save her honour.'

'Are the Canton women like ours or like the comnee girls?'

'Good point. If there's no penalty for losing her virginity, why would she lie? I don't know their laws, but they're infidels here – people of the book, mind, but infidels nonetheless.'

'That's true.' Arkazo sounded hopeful. 'Maybe their women see things like comnee women do.'

'Maybe, yes. But if he did commit rape, I'd just as soon carry out the First Prophet's law and be rid of him. On the other hand, we need him, Jezro needs him, and so, Kazrajistan needs him. I'll have to leave his head on his shoulders whether he's guilty or not.'

The comnee left the fort about mid-morning on a day so sweaty-hot with the approach of a summer storm that no one felt inclined to hurry their balky horses. To make matters worse, the land here began to rise – not much of a slope, but noticeable, turning the road into a long slow climb up. It was another reason, Dallador told Zayn, that the comnees brought only essentials with them when they rode to the Cantons.

'There must be mountains farther east,' Zayn said. 'Or at least hill country.'

'So I've been told,' Dallador said. 'You can't see them from Nannes, though.'

Riders and horse herd both ambled down the road in a line so untidy that Zayn caught himself wishing, with a grim kind of humour, that Warkannan could see it – their slovenly progress would have had him scarlet with rage. Around noon, Zayn noticed a dark mass on the horizon ahead, too static to be storm clouds. He rode up next to Dallador and pointed it out.

'It's a forest,' Dallador told him. 'I've heard that the Cantonneurs planted it when they got here, but they sure haven't done much with it since. We scrounge dead wood at the edge, but no one ever goes into it.'

'Why?'

'It's dangerous. Bandits, for one thing. Every now and then one of the people who live around here just disappears.'

Some hours before sunset the comnee reached a spread of

purple meadow crossed by a clear-running stream. Apanador called for a halt, then gathered the comnee, still mounted, around him.

'We'll make camp early,' the chief said. 'The spirit rider has some business to attend to at the White Ruins.'

In a swirl of confusion, the members of the comnee spread out to dismount. Zayn rose in his stirrups and looked around for Ammadin, finally spotting her at the wagon, where she was searching for something in the load. He dismounted and led his horse over to join her just as she pulled her saurskin cloak out of a tent bag.

'Oh, good, there you are,' Ammadin said. 'You're coming with me to the White Ruins.'

'Glad to hear it,' Zayn said. 'I was afraid you were going to go off alone.'

'No, I promised you I wouldn't. I'll need another guard, too, Dallador probably. We're not going far.'

'All right. Can I ask you what you're going to do? If you're wearing your cloak, it must be important.'

'It is.' Ammadin was rummaging in her saddlebags. 'Ah, here we are.'

She held up a brooch about the size of her palm and shaped like the spiral of the Herd, made of transparent tubing filled with blue liquid. As the sunlight touched it, the liquid turned a deep cobalt blue and glowed.

'What is that?' Zayn said.

'Something from the Ancients. It must be magic, but I don't know what it does exactly. The person I'm giving it to might know.'

'And that person is?'

'Do you remember when I told you about the three female ChaMeech who seemed to be following Warkannan?'

'Yes.'

'Actually, they were following me. They need my help, their leader told me, against Soutan, so we're meeting to discuss it.'

'ChaMeech? You're going to traffic with ChaMeech?'

'Traffic with?' Ammadin looked up, puzzled.

'Yes, just that. Collude with them, scheme with them –'

Ammadin laid a firm hand on his arm. 'I'm sorry,' she said. 'You smell furious.'

Zayn realized then that he was trembling, his jaw set tight, his hands clasping into fists. The memories of his ordeal as a ChaMeech prisoner were rising beyond his power to stop them: the endless run through the grass, panting, gasping, his lungs burning, the searing pain of leather thongs biting into his wrists and the sound of ChaMeech laughter screeching around him. His memory – his damned foul memory, he termed it – had preserved every minute of those days, vivid, agonizing still. Ammadin shook his arm hard.

'Zayn, what is it? You've gone off somewhere.'

He looked around, dazed, panting for breath, then found he could still speak. 'I *am* furious,' he said. 'How could you have anything to do with slime like that?'

'What do you mean? My people – your people now too – don't have any feud with the ChaMeech, just with some of their young males. If you Kazraks hadn't driven them off their land, they wouldn't be feuding with you, either.'

'Oh? It's not just the Kazraks. What about N'Dosha? How many people did they kill there?'

'Well, yes, hundreds. That's very true. But if this ChaMeech is telling me the truth, she's trying to avoid more wars and more deaths.'

'Truth? ChaMeech? You must be naive if you think –'

'Stop it!' Ammadin held her hand up flat for silence. 'Are you even capable of thinking clearly about this?'

'Probably not. I've spent a lot of years hating them.'

'Well, consider this. This particular ChaMeech is a female, a true Chiri Michi with her two female servants, and she considers Soutan her enemy.'

'All right. That's a point in her favour. But how do you know she's not just bait, drawing you into an ambush?'

'Because if she were, I'd have seen the ambushers in my crystal.'

Zayn winced; he was forgetting the obvious, a dangerous symptom.

'But now that I know how you feel about the ChaMeech,' Ammadin went on, 'I'll take Dallador and Grenidor, and you can stay here.'

'What? No! It's my job, protecting you.'

'Since when?'

'Since my being here put you in danger.'

Ammadin considered for a moment, then shrugged. 'I don't want you doing anything stupid,' she said. 'You hate the ChaMeech, so fine, I'll get someone else.'

'What in hell do you mean, do something stupid?'

'I'm not sure. Charge them maybe, or insult them.' Ammadin tipped her head to one side and stared at him through half-closed eyes. 'I can smell rage pouring off you. It's amazing.'

Zayn took a deep breath, then another, calling on all his training to calm himself, to bury the rage deep, to lock the memories back up where he would no longer feel them. Ammadin waited, saying nothing, until he finally could force his voice to stay steady.

'I'm sorry, Spirit Rider,' Zayn said. 'You're right. I'll stay here and take care of the tent and the horses.'

'Good. Later we can talk. Were you wounded in a fight with ChaMeech? Or lose a friend to them?'

'I don't want to talk about it.'

'It'll eat you alive until you do.'

Zayn turned on his heel and strode off. He kept himself busy with the horses until he could be sure that Ammadin and her guards had ridden away.

The White Ruins lay a few miles off the road at the edge of the ancient forest. Huge slabs of the same ceramic that the Ancients had used for the fort lay one on top of the other in a heap as high as a man's head. Purple grass grew tall around them; orange puff fungus clung to the free-hanging edges of the slabs. A few feet away lay the sleeping tower, as Water Woman had called it, a white tube nearly a hundred feet in diameter and a good two hundred feet long. Over the years since the Ancients had abandoned their project, drifting leaves and grass had filled the tower, rotted, and collapsed to make room for more drift until it had become a warren of peat for tiny orange snakes.

As Ammadin and her two guards dismounted nearby, she could hear the tunlers shriek warnings against these intruders. In the hot humid air the tower colony stank like fresh excrement, but over that scent she could smell female ChaMeech, pungent but cleaner, somehow, than the male stink of a warparty. The horses also caught the smell and tossed their heads with a flourish of mane. From the way Dallador wrinkled his nose she could guess that he'd picked it up as well.

'They're close,' Dallador said.

'They said they'd be at the white stone,' Ammadin said.

'All right. Grenno, I'll take the rear.'

'No,' Grenidor said. 'It's too dangerous, and you're a married man. You go on ahead, and I'll take the rear guard.'

Leading their horses, they walked on. Beyond the tower a narrow path took them into the forest, gone feral and tangled over the long years. The great oaks crowned far above them, their branches twined into a canopy that cast a deep and welcome shade. In the canopy, maroon leaveeders chirped and called. Bluebuhs swarmed in mid-air, darting from tree to tree. In the tangled ferns and vines, tiny grey skitters hissed as they passed. Big red pounzers rustled through the debris on the forest floor as they fled the humans.

In less than a quarter of a mile the path snaked to the right and debouched into a clearing, bright with sun. In its centre sat a lustrous white sphere, four feet in diameter, half-buried in the earth and drifting leaves. On the far side three ChaMeech were sitting haunched, their pseudo-arms held up high, their people's way of signalling peace. Two smaller grey females sat a little behind a larger, whose skin gleamed, oiled to a deep purple – Water Woman, Ammadin supposed, the true Chiri Michi.

In general they looked much like their males, but taller, stockier, in every way more solid, somehow, with their heavily muscled necks and strong legs. They had the same bulbous heads as the males, but a sharp thrust of cartilage defined their faces; their mouths and noses came to a point much like a beak, though their thin plates of lips were flexible enough to mimic human sounds. The two grey females wore nothing but strands of wooden beads and charms around their necks. Water Woman had tied blue-striped trade cloth around her midriff to form a loose skirt that covered her hindmost legs and fell to the ground. Instead of thongs, she wore around the base of her neck a scarf of red trade cloth, pinned with a long gold needle-like ornament. When she spoke, her throat sac pulsed scarlet.

'I be Keevashartalchiri, Water Woman in your way of speaking. You come-now, Ammadin.'

'I've come, yes, just like I said I would.'

Water Woman lowered her head and stretched her arms forward. 'There be a great need for talk. I be very pleased to see you.'

'I'm very glad to meet you as well. As you see, I've brought my two servants.' Ammadin glanced back at Dallador and Grenidor. 'Can you hear her?'

'Just,' Dallador said. 'It's almost too low but not quite.'

'It's more like I feel it,' Grenidor said. 'Like her voice is a humming sound or throbs or something.'

Water Woman stamped a front foot on the ground, the ChaMeech equivalent of laughter. 'Your voices sound like the flying ones, I think you call them bluebuhs? A whine, very high.'

'Bluebuhs, yes,' Ammadin said, smiling, then turned back to the men. 'Unsaddle the horses and let them rest.'

When Dallador and Grenidor led the horses away, Water Woman's two servants retreated to their side of the clearing. Behind them, in among the trees, sat a heap of sacks and baskets.

'Ammadin, come sit.' Water Woman pointed at the white stone with one pseudo-hand. 'You be-then as tall as I.'

Ammadin expected to slog her way through heaps of windblown detritus, but the leaves and suchlike turned out to be barely deep enough to rise above the soles of her boots. The sphere held other surprises. Despite its gleaming surface it felt rough, not smooth, and when Ammadin swung herself up, she felt it rock under her. Water Woman slumped a bit more so that their heads were level, and Ammadin could see her doubled eyes – a pair of ovals in each socket, with, in her case, the upper a solid pale blue, the lower a solid green. Whenever she blinked, the lids over the lower eyes flicked downwards, but on the upper eyes, lids of translucent membrane rolled up.

'Neither of us knows the customs of the other,' Ammadin said. 'If I say something rude, please tell me.'

'And if I say some rude thing, you tell-next me. Yes.' Water Woman clasped her two-fingered hands together on her broad chest. 'I repeat: I be so grateful you come-now to talk.'

'Because of Soutan?'

'Because of the Karshaks he bring-then bring-soon-again to our land. The Karshaks take-then-long-time-past so much land, kill so many of our men. They come-now east, and if so, hundreds die, not just us but Karshaks. Our men, they say-now they fight this time, no more pity, no more concessions.'

'I can't blame them, but I can understand why you're frightened.'

'And if our men, they lose-soon this war? Karshaks take-next our land, drive-next us east to the mountains.' Water Woman leaned forward. 'Beyond the mountains, farther east – there be no rivers. It be very dry land, little to eat, little water, much sand that the winds blow in huge storms. So: soon, there be-not Chiri Michi, there be-not Chur either.'

'Which is something that would please most Kazraks. Did Soutan say he wanted to bring an army into your territory?'

'No, he talk-then only of finding Ark. Our men, they who help-then him, insist he take-only Ark and go-next home. Maybe it be true. But if not true, then there be no more Chiri, no more Chur.'

'It would be a huge risk to run. Why didn't you just kill him? Soutan, I mean.'

'Some want-then to do just that. But his followers from our men stand-next in the way and threaten-next bloodshed to protect him. We want-not deaths. Ammadin, there be less of us every year. We want-not a war. So, we let-then Soutan leave and keep-then a watch to make sure he come-not back. Sibyl watch-then too. Just-now-summer she see him coming back with Karshaks. I go-then with servants to find help.'

'Wait a minute. Sibyl lives in your territory?'

'Yes.'

'But she saw Soutan riding on the grasslands?'

'Yes. Sibyl have powers to do much that you, I have-power-never to do. I bring-now a token to prove this.' Water Woman turned to her servants. 'Bring the gift!'

One of the greys trotted forward, carrying a red and white grassar-skin sack in her pseudo-hands. She bent the knee of one foreleg and offered it to Ammadin.

'This be from Sibyl,' Water Woman said. 'She tell-then me, give this to the spirit rider who helps-soon-next you. Tell her: if she come-some-time visit me, I give her more.'

Ammadin took the sack, opened it, and slid out a silver tube, about three feet long and a palm's width in diameter, banded top and bottom with stripes of bright red metal.

'The spirit command be "light",' Water Woman said. 'Its spirits feed-must on sun, like all spirits. It has power to shine much light and for a long time. You say, light. You say-next, much light, little light. It give-next what you wish.'

'A thousand thanks!' Ammadin held the tube in one hand and

with the other fished her gift out of her pocket. 'And this is a token for you, a thing my teacher in magic gave me.'

'Very precious!' Water Woman took the glowing spiral brooch in both hands. 'Beautiful and precious. I give you a thousand thanks.'

While Water Woman's servant pinned the brooch onto her mistress's red scarf, Ammadin examined the tube. The two metal bands sat loosely in some sort of track; they would turn one way for a few inches, then back the other. Under her hands the metal felt cool and almost oily. The servant bowed again, then scurried back to the edge of the clearing.

'Water Woman,' Ammadin said, 'Sibyl must be rich to give away things like this.'

'Very rich, and she be very eager to meet you. I too wish you come-might see Sibyl. If you want to come, I lead you there.'

'I want to meet Sibyl, but the comnee, the H'mai I ride with, I can't just ride off and leave them. I need to find another spirit rider before I can leave.'

'I puzzle over your words.'

'My comnee must have a spirit rider to guide them. I am the one, their only spirit rider. I cannot leave them because I am the only –'

'I understand-now. Then I wait till you find second spirit woman, but I have-not the power to travel with you now. Danger lie-always in the town, Nannes. I go-not there. I go-not close there.'

'I know that the Cantons don't welcome your people.' Ammadin tapped the light tube against her palm while she thought things through. Honesty, she decided, was crucial. 'Not all of the killing's been done by the Kazraks, has it? Four hundred years ago, your people destroyed one of the cantons.'

Water Woman moaned, a long, deep throb of her throat sac, so low-pitched that Ammadin felt rather than heard it. 'Yes,' she said at last. 'It be for the sake of our children, who die-then. We had-then no choice.'

'You told me once that the children are dying now, too. What do you mean?'

'We be-must on the sea beaches to get our children back again.' Water Woman paused for a long moment. 'I tell-next a secret. Please, promise me you tell-never any other comnee person and never never a Karshak. Sorcerers in Cantons, they know, but that matter-not. If Karshaks learn this, disaster!'

'All right, I promise. You have my word before all of our gods.'

Still, Water Woman hesitated. She reached up and caught the edge of her scarf between her finger and thumb, twisted it tight in an oddly human gesture, then let it go.

'Our children begin life in the Great Swamp, the one you call the Mistlands,' she said at last. 'We birth them in the warm waters. They travel-next to the sea.'

'Spirit pearls!'

'You know-then them, yes. We, true Chiri Michi, give birth in the place you call Mistlands. Hundreds of children each, thousands of children we birth there. The rivers take them to the southern seas. In the salt water they change. The pearl splits, they swim out. They stay some few years, but many die there. There are the zalotlan, there are the silamintrinik, our names for the enemies who eat them. Only the best children, the most intelligent, the strongest, survive. One summer they come-then back to us, the strong ones, the smart ones, they who survive-then the sea. Some hundreds, not thousands, come back to us. They are very small, and we need-then greet them. Without us, the kri altri – you call them birds – come to the shore to hunt them.'

'And they kill –?'

'Kill and eat, yes. Now, if we be-not there, there be a few children who be smart enough to dodge the birds and reach the trees. But most – they die.'

'Do you remember any of this? Do you remember being in the sea and breathing water?'

'Only a few –' Water Woman paused to wag her pseudo-hands in the air as if the gesture helped her think, '– a few broken memories. Like dreams. Your people, they dream not dream? When they sleep?'

'Oh yes, we dream, too.'

'Good. Then you know-now what I mean. Water memories they be like dreams, very small and very hard to see, just pictures, pieces of pictures. But the air memories, riding waves and breathing air, yes, they stay-now with me. I remember-too the terror I feel-then, when I see at last how dangerous be the waters. Something inside me said-then, go to land, hurry to land. I remember the sand, and the seeing of my people, and knowing, somehow I know-then they were mine – I have-then-not speech or words, but I know-somehow they be mine, and I run so very hard and they run to me, waving spears to scare off the birds overhead, the birds, nasty nasty birds!' She shuddered with a toss of her massive head. 'So you see, we be-must there when the children, they come out of water.'

'I do see, yes.'

'So.' Water Woman held up one pseudo-hand. 'We have-must coast land. We have-must roads to coast land. Karshaks took-then the south coast, the north coast. They keep-then us from coast of the west lands. We have-must roads in our east lands, like you see-now.'

'And the Cantonneurs closed the roads?'

'Not exactly. Those years you speak of, many earthquakes come-then, and finally the earth give birth to a mountain of fire. The rock blood pour-then and cover-then all our roads. Death air spew-then too. We can-then-not travel-then on old roads. You see? We need-then travel on Canton roads. We ask-then them. They say-then no.'

'The Cantonneurs say your people never asked them anything. They say they just attacked.'

'Then they lie.' Her throat sac swelled out huge, turning gold in fury. 'They lie and lie. We send-then emissaries to N'Dosha farm lands. Canton people treat-then our people like beasts. They wave-then sticks, they call-then names, they throw-then things.'

It was possible, Ammadin thought, that H'mai leery of the ChaMeech had refused them access to their roads. It was also possible that each side had misunderstood what the other asked, whether out of hatred or contempt or from simple ill-luck and fear. Water Woman stretched her neck and swung her massive face close to Ammadin's own.

'We have-then no choice, or so we feel-then. You see not see? No time, we have-then no time to think, talk. They turn-then us back.' Water Woman moved her head a little closer, her throbbing voice urgent. 'We try-then to reach the coast lands, where we know our children wait. They turn us back.' She took her hand away from her scarf and flapped it in the air, a helpless-seeming gesture. 'The children, they die-then. So: our men call war. Two year they fight-ever.'

'Two years? I was always told it was five years.'

'They lie-again. I swear-now to you: they lie and lie.'

'All right. After two years' war, what then?'

'Our men force-then the roads and claim them. The Great Mother send-then females and many males with spears to reach-then the coast land. But they find-then no children alive. They find-then nothing that-year-way-long-back. The children all die-then-before we reach-then them. Next year after they find-then nothing again.'

'That's terrible! All your children, dead!'

'You see-now. Good. The third year after the war, we find-then some children on the coast. Every year next-then we have roads, but they lead-only to a small strip of coast.'

'You can't travel down the Rift, can you?'

'No. Near the sea, it be deep deep river. My people, we swim well, but this river, the current, it pull you way out to sea, and you drown-maybe.'

'I should have thought of that, yes.'

'So, some children find us. Others leave water I know not where.' Her throat sac filled, she tossed her head back, and wailed a long sobbing note that brought tears to Ammadin's eyes. 'They find-never us. They die-always.'

'I've seen them.' Ammadin paused to wipe her eyes on her shirt sleeve. 'Small grey creatures, all wrinkled, walking on four legs, with little arms, and they have pink gills all round their necks.'

'Yes. The gills drop-next-soon. They breathe-already air, but the gills cling-still to their necks.' Water Woman lowered her head and with a twist of her neck looked straight into Ammadin's face. 'They come-now up on your coast?'

'Sometimes. We've never harmed them. Long ago our gods marked them as Bane to us. But they just wandered off, somewhere.'

'They die-then.' Water Woman pulled her head back and moaned. From their place among the trees her servants added their voices to hers in a long howl of pain.

'We have to work out some kind of treaty, so you can come take them home.'

'Be this a real thing? Your men, they agree not agree?'

'I don't know, but I don't see why they wouldn't. They don't hate your people. They just like to fight with your young men when they try to steal our horses. The other spirit riders will help me, too. But if Soutan brings the Kazraks to your lands, it won't matter, will it?'

'No, it matter-not-then if Chiri and Chur, we all die in the mountains. Please, you come-soon meet Sibyl?'

'I want to, but it's likely that I won't be able to find another spirit rider until we go back to the grass. This will take time. I'm sorry, but I can't just ride off. The comnee, the families I ride with, they're like my children.'

'I understand-now. I wait-next near Rift. You go-next to plains, I follow-next you.'

'That will work, yes.'

'Very well. But we talk-next-soon with sky spheres?'

'Yes. We'll talk often.'

'And you come-soon meet Sibyl?'

'As soon as I possibly can.'

Water Woman held out her two-fingered hands. Ammadin clasped them in hers.

'You have my word,' Ammadin said. 'First we'll talk with Sibyl, and then we'll see about the coast lands.'

'My heart sing-now aloud. I help-next-soon all ways I can help.'

'Good. And as for Soutan, he's tried to murder a man who rides with my comnee. We'll see what we can do about him and his Kazraki friends both.'

'I be happy, and Sibyl also be happy when she know-soon. We honour-next-soon spirit of Chursavva.'

'Chursavva was true Chiri Michi, wasn't she?'

'She be-then-long-time Great Mother, yes.'

'And then, when you say, true Chiri Michi, it means?'

'One who give living children to the rivers.'

'Ah. I thought so. I just wanted to make sure. And then, the Chur are your males?'

'Yes, males and females who give-never children to the rivers.' She turned and waved a pseudo-arm at her servants. 'They be Chur. But there be true Chur, Chur Vocho, males who –' She paused, lowered her head, and fluttered her pseudo-hands.

'I understand.' Ammadin spoke fast to end Water Woman's embarrassment. 'No need for details. So, if I need a name for all your people, what is it?'

'Chof. In your language, it mean "us".' Water Woman stamped a foot to show her amusement. 'Just us.'

* * *

After Zayn took care of the horses and pitched the tent, he had nothing to do but wait. He paced up and down in front of the tent while his imagination wove images of treacherous ChaMeech killing Ammadin or taking her hostage. Finally, when the sun hovered low in the sky, Maradin unknowingly saved him from his black thoughts by joining him.

'Are you hungry?' Zayn said. 'I can cook for both of us if you'd like.'

'Well, thank you, but they should be back soon,' Maradin said. 'The White Ruins aren't very far off.'

'You think she'll be safe there?'

'Of course. She'd know if something were wrong. She's a spirit rider.'

'Of course.' Zayn managed a smile and hoped it was convincing.

'While Dallo's gone,' Maradin continued, 'there's something I want to talk to you about.'

'All right.'

'You know an awful lot about Tribal ways, but I wonder if maybe you've missed something. You and my husband are great friends, aren't you?'

'Well, yes.'

'I see you together a lot, and I can see how close you've become.' She paused, thinking something through. 'If you want to have sex together, it's all right with me. As long as he's not siring children on someone else, what he does is his business, not mine.'

Zayn felt his face burning. He turned away, realized that the gesture made him look foolish, turned back to find her watching him in concern. She laid a hand on his arm.

'I'm sorry,' Maradin said. 'I didn't mean to embarrass you.'

Zayn tried to speak and cleared his throat instead.

'We look at things like love differently out here,' she went on. 'Since you're one of us now you need to know that.'

'Yes.' Zayn cleared his throat again. 'Guess I do.'

'Now, look, Dallo's never said anything to me about you or anything. I was just trying to sort of clear things up in advance.'

'Thank you. I suppose.'

'Oh gods, I hope I haven't make you uncomfortable around him or anything.' Maradin caught her lower lip in her teeth for a moment. 'Me and my mouth again!'

'No, no, you haven't. It's fine.'

'All right, then. Don't men have affairs with each other back in Kazrajistan?'

'What? No! It's against the laws of all three prophets.'

'You Kazraks do lots of things your prophets forbid. Why not that?'

'Probably some men do. They don't talk about it, though, especially not with their wives.'

'What? And let them think they're off with other women? That must make their wives worry, if you ask me.'

'Didn't.'

Maradin tossed back her head and laughed, then patted his arm with a maternal gesture. 'Poor Zayn! Well, you'll get used to us sooner or later.'

'Let's hope it's sooner.' He tried to smile, then gave it up as a bad job.

With one last maternal pat on his arm, Maradin took herself off. Zayn sat down in front of the tent and hoped he could look Dallador in the face from now on.

The Herd was rising in a sweep of silver clouds by the time Ammadin and her guards returned. Zayn was so relieved to see them riding up that his relief turned to rage. Damn her anyway, for making him worry! Ammadin came back to the tent alone, leaving Dallador and his cousin to tend her horse as well as theirs. She was carrying her saddlebags slung over her shoulder, and in her hands she was holding a long metal tube. Zayn held open the tent flap to allow her in, then followed her. She laid the saddlebags down on her bedding, but she kept the tube.

'What is that thing?' Zayn said.

'Watch.' Ammadin held it up, took a breath, and intoned a single word. Yellow light sprang from the tube and turned the tent bright. Zayn gasped and took a step back. She chanted a brief phrase, and the light dimmed to the glow of an oil lamp.

'I don't want to exhaust the spirits,' she said. 'This was a gift from the ChaMeech woman.'

'Maybe there's something good to say for the females. I've never seen any, after all. How would I know?'

'You don't have to pretend for my sake. Were you worried?'

'No, of course I wasn't worried.'

'I just wondered. It took us a while to get back to camp.'

'Well, I'd thought the ruins were closer, yes, from what everyone said.'

'I stopped to scan.' Ammadin frowned at the tube in her hands. 'It was the strangest thing. We left before Water Woman and her servants, and we hadn't ridden far at all when I stopped, which means they couldn't have gone far either. But I couldn't see them anywhere.'

'They might have been hiding in the forest.'

'I suppose.' She shrugged the problem away. 'But it was interesting, talking with a Chiri Michi. Which reminds me –'

'I do not want to talk about ChaMeech.'

Ammadin raised an eyebrow. Zayn grabbed his bedroll from the floor.

'I'm going to sleep in the grass. If it rains, too damn bad.'

Before she could answer he left the tent. He strode across the campground, walking fast, and if she ever called him back, he didn't hear it. In the middle of the night the rain came, soaking him awake. He lay in his sodden blankets and listened to the others rushing back and forth, finding a space to sleep in one tent or the other. Once the camp fell quiet, he got up and went to sleep under the wagon, or to drowse, really, shivering in his wet clothes.

By morning, a warm wind was scrubbing the sky clear of clouds. Zayn draped his blankets over the wagon tree to dry, then went back to Ammadin's tent. He was expecting some comment on his damp clothes, but she said nothing about them. While he was cooking breakfast and packing the tent away, she never mentioned the ChaMeech, either. Zayn decided that he'd made his point.

When the comnee rode out, Zayn walked his sorrel gelding into his usual place in the riding order, beside Dallador at the head of the line of pack horses, even though the memory of his conversation with Maradin made him profoundly uneasy. Dallador seemed to notice the change in his mood. For a couple of miles they rode in silence; then Dallador turned in the saddle to look at him.

'Something wrong?'

'No.' Zayn realized both that he'd snarled and that he had a plausible explanation close to hand. 'Sorry. It's the damned ChaMeech. It really gripes me, thinking of Ammadin having anything to do with them.'

'She mentioned that you had a grudge against them.'

'Me have a grudge? They're the ones who raid our borders and lay traps for our cavalry and kill our horses. Why the hell wouldn't I hold it against them?'

'Our cavalry?'

'Well, it was mine once. I lost two of the men under my command to ChaMeech. It still hurts.'

'Now that I can understand.'

'Thanks. I figured you would.'

Dallador answered with an easy smile, affectionate enough to make Zayn look away. He leaned over his horse's neck and pretended to be fussing with a snarl in its mane to cover the gesture. Damn Maradin anyway! he thought. Just like a woman! Ahead on the horizon he could see the dark swell of the forest, rising nearer.

'Dallo?' Zayn said. 'Nannes is on the other side of that forest, right?'

'Yes, about half a day's ride. We'll make camp once we're through the forest and then ride into Nannes the next day.'

'How far past Nannes will the comnee go?'

'What?' Dallador turned in the saddle to look at him. 'We never go anywhere but Nannes. It's the trading precinct.'

'I didn't realize that.'

'It's like the horse fair at Blosk. Anyone who wants horses comes to Nannes to buy them.'

'Makes sense.'

'It's not just that, though,' Dallador went on. 'The people of the Cantons don't like foreigners. When I was a boy my grandfather told me about the way things were in the old days. If the Canton people caught a foreigner out of the trading precinct, they killed him. Just like that – no trial, no nothing. But by the time Grandfather was a child, nobody cared that much any more. A lot of people have forgotten the old laws, I guess.'

Zayn considered for a moment. He was afraid of showing too much curiosity, but Dallador had no reason to be suspicious of his interest. 'So anyway,' Zayn said, 'they'd let a single comnee man travel around, now, I mean?'

'Maybe even two or three. They sure don't want an entire comnee riding past Nannes. Apanador says they're afraid of us.'

'Stands to reason. They're just farmers and town folk.'

Dallador nodded his agreement. So, Zayn thought. Soon he'd be leaving the comnee behind, heading out on his own again – alone, the way he liked to be. He was damned glad of it, too, or so he told himself, although he had to repeat the thought a good many times before he believed it. He would be free at last to learn the truth about this sorcerer, who must have somehow or other corrupted Warkannan. Zayn simply could not conceive of Idres turning against his old loyalties on his own, not Idres, who had risked his life again and again to protect the khanate.

Earlier in the same day, Warkannan and his men had left the forest, but instead of heading east to Nannes, Soutan had led them south along a dirt road. On either side, fences woven of vines and bamboid marked out fields of wheatian and other food crops. Now and then they saw in the distance a white-washed farmhouse or barn. Once they passed a farmer in a long dirty-brown smock as he was strolling through a wheatian field, pulling a seed-head here and there to test for ripeness. When he saw the horsemen coming, he ran to the fence to lean over and stare until they'd ridden by.

'These fields all belong to my supporter,' Soutan remarked. 'Or to his father, to be precise, though Alayn will inherit them when the old man dies.'

'He must be pretty well off,' Warkannan said.

'By the standards of the Cantons, yes. By Kazraki standards, no. You'll see. We're almost to the manor house now. But even though they don't live in luxury, Alayn's family is an important one. His father is what they call a zhay pay, a local magistrate. He can try petty criminals and remand the more important cases to the ruling council in Nannes. He also keeps a cadre of private soldiers.'

Late in the afternoon they reached the villa, or as Soutan called it, the estate. About half a mile from the forest edge, a thorn and vine wall set off a long lawn of green grass. Behind it stood a cluster of plain, square buildings, made of woven bamboid and sticks of true-wood with pale blue roofs of bundled thatch. A gravel path led them to an iron gate, all twisted and rusty, and as they dismounted at the fence, noise broke out – some animal, Warkannan assumed, yapping and making a sharp sound rather like *ar ar ar*. Sure enough, when he looked over the fence he saw a pair of four-legged animals, covered in close-cropped tan fur, charging straight for them. They had prominent muzzles, long floppy ears, and skinny tails that waved back and forth as they ran.

'Those disgusting shens,' Soutan said wearily. 'They bark like this all the time. We'd better wait till someone comes to see why they're making this racket before –'

The barking shens threw themselves against the gate. They had lustrous black eyes, black noses, and black lips, pulled back to reveal sharp white fangs. Warkannan's cavalry-trained horse stood its ground, but one of the pack horses whinnied in terror and tried to rear, a gesture that started the others dancing. It took all the men's attention to keep them from bolting as the shens yapped and howled. Warkannan was ready to draw his sabre and slap the shens down when a young man came running out of the nearest building. As he raced up, yelling something or other in Vranz, the shens quieted, and in a few minutes so did the horses. With a laugh the young man began to untie the gate. He was slender, with pale skin and an untidy shock of red hair, and dressed in a pair of blue leggings and a white shirt made of coarse-woven cloth. He should have been handsome with his fine features, but there was something unsettling about his pale eyes. They glittered in deep sockets above dark circles, so livid that it seemed he'd not slept in days. At one corner of his mouth hung a brown wart the size of a fingernail.

'Yarl!' The young man held out his hand, then asked a question that sounded like 'say too?'.

'Daccor!' Soutan shook it, but briefly. 'Alayn!'

Warkannan understood nothing of the flood of Vranz that followed. Eventually Alayn turned to the Kazraks and smiled.

'Come in,' he said in heavily accented Hirl-Onglay. 'The shens, they not hurt you. You are my guests.'

'We came at the perfect time,' Soutan said in Kazraki. 'His father is away, so we won't have to make any awkward explanations.'

'About what?' Warkannan said. 'The reason we're here?'

'That, and about the false charges against me.'

Although they were reluctant at first, the horses walked through the gate after Alayn sent the shens racing back to the house ahead of them. As they approached the cluster of buildings, four men came trotting out of the house.

'Ah, some servants,' Soutan said. 'They'll take our horses for us.'

Alayn flung open the door of the manor house and ushered them inside to a big room, plain and airy. Four long trestle tables with benches stood at the near end, along with a big ceramic stove and wooden bins filled with grains and produce. At the far end, wooden chairs and a divan woven of purple rushes stood under the windows. On the divan a woman with long, grey hair, tied back with a thong, sat reading. She wore a loose blue dress, sleeveless and pulled in at the waist with a belt made of linked gold coins. As Alayn led his guests down the length of the room, she looked up, smiled, and rose to greet them. Alayn began speaking fast in Vranz.

'Alayn's mother,' Soutan whispered in Kazraki. 'You address her as "mada" and bow over her hand if she offers it to you.'

Mada did indeed offer Warkannan her hand. Painfully conscious of her bare arms, he took it, smiled, and bowed. Arkazo did the same, and she smiled at them both, then sat back down on her divan and picked up her book. Alayn led them on through the room, out into a hallway, and on down.

'Guest tents,' he said in Hirl-Onglay and flung open a door to reveal not tents, but a sunny room with a further room visible beyond. 'I have the maid bring water. Food?'

'Yes, thank you,' Warkannan said.

Arkazo contented himself with nodding vigorously. Warkannan glanced around the room – a pair of narrow beds, covered with blue blankets, a pair of woven-rush chairs before a long window with a view of the lawn, and between them, a low table. Opposite the window an open door led into another room with a third bed.

'This looks very comfortable,' Warkannan said in Hirl-Onglay. 'Thank you very much, sinyur.'

Alayn smiled, then left with a wave of his hand. Soutan followed him out, talking fast in Vranz.

Warkannan sank gratefully into a cushioned chair. 'That was quite a shock, seeing a woman of position just sitting there half-dressed.'

'Yes,' Arkazo said. 'But look, we've got real mattresses, real pillows! I'm going to lie down and take a nap.'

Arkazo was still asleep when Soutan came snarling into the guest room and slammed the door behind him. Arkazo woke, looked around yawning, then turned over and went back to sleep. Soutan threw himself into a wicker armchair and glowered at the view outside. Warkannan joined him at the window.

'What's wrong?' Warkannan said.

'I had the perfect plan,' Soutan said. 'But Alayn wouldn't carry it out. I wanted him to go into Nannes and see if he could buy me some crystals. I told him I'd give him a gold coin for running the errand, but no, no, it's not the money, he says. His father's suspicious of certain things. The old man's at the law courts in Nannes, and he'll be there for days. If he sees Alayn buying a crystal, he'll be more suspicious than ever.'

'Can't he avoid his father?'

'Nannes is a good bit smaller than Haz Kazrak.' Soutan paused for a dramatic sigh. 'And everyone knows Sinyur Alayn and his father the Zhay Pay.'

'If we ride straight to Jezro, you won't need a crystal.'

'Don't be stupid! Of course I'll need one with this wretched Zayn following us along.' Soutan scowled at the lawn for a long moment, then continued. 'Alayn did come up with something of an idea. There's a group of – well, I'm not sure what they are, but they call themselves priests. Their head man's collected a number of crystals, Alayn says. He might be willing to make a trade.'

'Sounds like a good idea to me. We have Kazraki coins, and there's at least one extra horse.'

'Exactly. Surely we can work something out – provided he has the right crystals, of course.'

'I take it they're not all alike.'

'No, I've catalogued twenty kinds. You see, they were –'

Someone rapped on the door. Soutan called out in Vranz, and Alayn stepped in, closed the door carefully behind him, then leaned against it for an extra measure of safety. As he and Soutan talked, Warkannan realized that Soutan was looking more and more frightened. Finally the sorcerer turned to him.

'Our luck has definitely gone bad, Captain. The comnee's camped just off the main road not more than five miles from here. One of Alayn's tenants saw them just now.'

'Then we'd better stay where we are till they've moved on,' Warkannan said. 'If that's all right with the sinyur here.'

'Oh yes, that's fine with him and his mother. But I hope that those beastly barbarians move on tomorrow. All this waiting is getting on my nerves.'

About a mile past the forest the comnee had found an unfenced meadow that provided decent pasture for the horses. While the men were raising the tents and starting the evening meal, Maradin and two other women went to the forest edge to hunt for fallen wood. With the Riders due to appear in the sky, Ammadin took her saddlebags and went with them. While the women spread out to forage, she scanned.

Spirit Eyes swept over the countryside, but found no Kazraks and no Soutan, either. If the sorcerer had somehow woken his sleeping spirits, he would have been able to hide from her, of course, but she was expecting him to attack her as soon as he had weapons, and so far, no attack had come. Finally Spirit Eyes showed her a cluster of buildings behind a thorn-vine wall that stood about five miles south of the camp. To one side of the compound lay a paddock where eight horses were grazing. Those she recognized immediately: the Kazraks' riding mounts and pack horses. Soutan apparently had an ally who was sheltering them.

By then the women had gathered armloads of deadfall oak, and together they returned to camp. In front of her tent Zayn had started a fire. He was kneeling behind it and using his long knife to shred saur jerky into a pot of simmering breadmoss.

'Smells good,' Ammadin told him. 'My news isn't so good – your enemies are about five miles from here. It looks like they're staying with one of the local landowners. I can't be sure, because I didn't see them. They must be inside his house.'

'You can't scan inside buildings?' Zayn said.

'No. The crystals can't see when the Riders are hidden by clouds, either. All they show then is clouds.'

'Nothing but clouds?'

'Yes. They won't look at the ground then for some reason. What's odd is you'd swear you were looking at the clouds from above.' Ammadin shrugged the problem away. 'Spirits have their quirks. Still, I'm certain that Warkannan and the others are close by, and that's what matters now. Make sure you don't get out of sight of the comnee from now on.'

'All right.'

Zayn was concentrating so hard on stirring the porridge that she realized he was hiding something from her again. She considered probing, then decided that she was tired of trying to dig the truth out of Zayn. She went into her tent and devoted herself to arranging the god figures on their special rug.

In the morning, when Ammadin scanned again, she found

another comnee and their horses camped beside the grey road at the very limit of Spirit Eyes' range to the west. Someone else had decided to cross the Rift early in the trading season. Since they appeared as tiny figures with no detail, she had no idea of whose comnee this might be. She made a point, once she'd returned to camp, of telling Apanador about them.

'I hope it's not someone you men are feuding with,' Ammadin said.

'So do I,' Apanador said. 'We've got enough to worry about as it is, with Zayn's enemies and all.' He paused, glancing over her shoulder. 'I'll be glad to get back on the road. That forest – you can feel the evil, even this far away.'

'Too many people have disappeared into it.' Ammadin suddenly shivered. 'And their spirits still walk. When we're here, I see them sometimes, slinking through the trees.'

'You'd think the local authorities would have put an end to those murders a long time ago.'

'So you'd think. I can't say I have a lot of respect for them. Well, it's probably no business of ours.'

Dallador was grooming his favourite horse, a coppery-coloured gelding with a blaze and a white off-fore. After he finished with the curry comb, he pulled a long twist of the purple grass and began rubbing the horse's coat down, making it shine in the early morning sun. As he worked on the horse's legs, his pale hair would fall into his eyes; he'd toss it back with a laugh. Zayn stood some distance away, in the shelter of the wagon, and watched him. In the night he'd dreamt about Dallador. He could not get his conversation with Maradin out of his mind, either. The dream and the memory added up to an insight he could no longer hide from himself. He found himself wondering what it would feel like to kiss that generous mouth, and to feel Dallo's hands – Zayn turned away with a shake of his head. It would do him no good to follow out that line of thought.

When the comnee rode out, Zayn volunteered to bring up the rear, the dustiest and least desirable spot in the riding order. He did actually feel that it was his turn to do so, but even more, he knew that Dallo wouldn't want to join him there.

That morning they rode through farming country, rich fields of ripening wheatian, long rows of some leafy plant, stippled red and white, that he didn't recognize, all set off from the road by pale yellow fences. The land rose slowly but steadily, as if they were plodding up a giant ramp, forcing them to pause often to let the stock rest in the summer's heat. Towards noon the road finally levelled out. Zayn could see across the fields to scattered true-oaks and the low straight roofs of yellow and white buildings.

Nannes lay on either side of a shallow river, flowing north to south, crossed by four wooden bridges that led to the town on the east bank. The comnee camped on the west bank in a long meadow fronting the river but upstream from the town – land set aside for visiting comnees, Ammadin told him, and their horses.

'We probably won't get any customers today,' she told him. 'It'll take time for the local horse dealers to find out that we're here.'

'All right,' Zayn said. 'I don't suppose a town like this would have a bookshop.'

'Yes, they do. I've seen it. It's a trade town, after all, and they have a lot of craftsmen. Why?'

'I was thinking of trying to find a book that would teach me how to read Vranz. So I can read that book to you one day.'

'There's money in the blue tent bag. Take what you need.'

She waved an arm in the direction of Nannes. 'Cross that second bridge and follow the street down. In a few blocks you'll come to a market square. You can't miss it. It's hung with banners.'

After the monotony of the plains, Nannes came as a relief to a city-raised man like Zayn – not that it was much of a place. Perhaps some three hundred houses and craft shops lay along dirty cobbled streets. The houses sagged and rambled, built from tree-fern trunks, bundles of rushes, and long reddish poles cut from some plant Zayn couldn't identify. Vegetable gardens flourished out in front of each; here and there chickens scratched and clucked behind woven fences. Trees grew everywhere, both true-oak and a species he'd never seen before. The graceful maroon trunks ended in a spray of branches, delicate and long enough to hang almost to the ground. On each branch were clusters of yellow leaves as narrow as needles, growing from a central stem. Skinny yellow lizards clung to the trunks and chattered as Zayn passed by.

Two-storey buildings that seemed to be both house and shop edged the market square. Although they drooped and leaned, from their upper storey bright banners flapped in the breeze, announcing with pictures a shoemaker, a candlemaker, a blacksmith, and other such artisans. Zayn walked slowly, glancing around him. One time through, and he would have the entire town tucked into his memory, ready to become a map if he should need to draw one.

Zayn had just spotted the bookseller's shop when he heard a noise that sounded like drums. He paused at a corner and listened – yes, drums, a deep bass, a chatter of snares. The sound of horns, similar to cavalry bugles but sweeter, drifted on the wind. A crowd of small children tore past him, laughing, and headed towards the music.

'Where are you going?' Zayn called out in Vranz.

'The Recallers!' a little girl shouted. 'Their last parade.'

Recallers. The word tore at his memory. He should know what it meant; he had heard it before. Where? He trotted after the children, but he was barely conscious of the streets around him. His reflexes kept him from crashing into walls and bumping into townsfolk while his mind searched, running down the corridors of his memory, throwing open doors, looking into rooms he hadn't opened in twenty-five years.

And he saw at last the small boy, himself, crouched miserably on the black-and-white tiled floor of a mosque between his father and the healer they had come to see. Tall in white robes, his head wrapped in sleek blue, Hakeem Abbul spoke softly, urgently.

'The boy is half a demon, yes. There were once a class of men named –' Here he spoke a foreign word, one beyond Zayn's understanding then, though he knew it now: Recallers. 'These Recallers made a blood pact with demons in order to learn secret knowledge, forbidden knowledge.'

'What must I do with him?' His father's voice was a mutter, a sigh.

'You know the answer to that.'

The crouching boy felt as if all the warmth of his body were draining into the tiles. He was going to die before sunset, he was sure of it, and yet, when his father held out his hand, he got up and took it, let his father lead him from the mosque and back to their room at the shabby inn.

And of course, his father hadn't killed him.

As he stood, all those years later, on a street in a town far from Kazrajistan, Zayn or Zahir – at that moment, with the memory so vivid, with himself so changed, he was no longer sure which was his real name – grasped for the first time just how peculiar it was, that his father had never done what so many holy men had told him to do. His father had at times beaten him, at others starved him, all in hopes of ousting the demons within him, but never had he let his son actually come near to dying. Why not?

'I guess because I was the heir, and the only one he was going to get. I guess.'

Zayn realized he'd spoken aloud, shook himself, glanced around, but no one had heard, not in the racket coming down the street. A long line of men and women were prancing and dancing as they drew near. Some carried drums, some played horns, some jingled straps sewn with tiny bells. All of them were dressed in red and yellow clothes; all had long red ribbons braided in their hair and dangling from their sleeves. Just behind the musicians other men and women came dancing, dressed in a variety of bizarre clothes – sleek one-piece outfits embroidered with spirals, billowing dresses patched together from scraps: blue, purple, green. In among them children wearing long white dresses with purple hoods ran and shouted. Some of the adults, dressed entirely in black, carried bundles that Zayn at first mistook for blankets.

As they came closer, he could see that the bundles were imitation ChaMeech – draped red and purple cloths topped by big ChaMeech heads made out of some kind of shiny material. As they walked they slipped one hand into the heads and made them look around or bow to the crowd. Bringing up the rear of the parade were children carrying baskets. They ran back and forth across the street and shoved the baskets at the watching adults, most of whom dug through their pockets and handed over coins. A little girl with gold hair ran up to Zayn; he fished a couple of Vransic copper souz out of his pocket and dropped them in. She smiled brilliantly, curtsied, and trotted off again.

Once the procession had gone past, the crowd began to break up and drift away. So, Zayn thought. Those are the Recallers, are they? A bunch of buffoons, noisy musicians and bad dancers. Obviously the hakeem had meant something entirely different. As he walked back to the market square, the diversity of the townsfolk struck him – some had pale skin, others dark, though none as dark as his; he saw every possible colour of hair and eyes, thin lips, full lips, curly hair and straight. He found it surprising, but somehow intriguing as well.

When he opened the door to the bookseller's, silver bells rang out. A long room, crammed with books on shelves, books on tables, books stacked on floors – the light was dim, and the smell of dust and old rushi overwhelming, like the rich perfume of a beautiful woman, or so it seemed to Zayn. Back in Kazrajistan, books though common enough were expensive, run off a page at a time on a press powered by the printer's apprentices. That a small town like Nannes would have so many amazed him. Out of the murk appeared a skinny young man with short brown hair, wearing a green apron over a shirt and narrow blue trousers.

'This is a surprise,' he said. 'You're a Kazrak.'

'Daccor, but I ride with a comnee now.' Zayn smiled pleasantly. 'You must not get a lot of Kazraks through here.'

'We don't, no. In fact, I think I've only ever seen one before. When I was still a child, a fellow rode through here.'

'Really? I don't suppose you remember much about him.'

'I don't, no, but ask the older people. They might remember. Now, what can I do for you?'

'I want to learn how to read Vranz, and how to speak it better, too.'

'You could use a little help there, yes.' The fellow laughed, but pleasantly. 'Come back to the counter, and I'll show you what we have.'

On the counter, inside a glass box, lay an oblong object about six inches by ten. Some shiny blue substance formed a case around an even glossier grey rectangle.

'That's an ancient book,' the young man said.

'How do you read it?'

'No one knows any more, but we do know it's a book.' He shook his head. 'The Ancients had whole libraries of these.'

Zayn spent a pleasant half-hour, learning how to associate the Vransic alphabet, which was completely different from the Kazraki version, with the sounds of Vranz. Learning anything new, whether it was the layout of a town or a language, brought him physical sensations of ease and comfort, the same as many men got from a few bowls of keese. Once he knew the alphabet, he bought a children's reading book and a dictionary with the luxurious joy others would have found in handling gold.

Yet as soon as he left the shop, his cheerful mood evaporated like spilled keese. As soon as he stepped into the street, he felt eyes watching him. He spun around and caught the gaze of a youngish man with pale hair, a clumsy spy, who bolted and ran the moment he realized Zayn had seen him. Zayn held his ground. In broad daylight he might find the fellow, but what then? He could hardly beat the truth out of him here in a foreign country. As he hurried back to camp, he stayed on guard, but he never saw the fellow again nor any other suspicious person.

Zayn went straight to Ammadin's tent. He listened for a moment, then raised the flap cautiously and looked in. She had left and taken her crystals with her. Although he'd been planning on merely putting his new books away, he ended up lying on his blankets for the rest of that day in an extravagant orgy of memorizing words in Vranz.

'I have news,' Soutan said. 'One of the Zhay Pay's men has come back from Nannes. The comnee rode in yesterday just after noon.'

'And Zayn was still with it?' Warkannan said.

'Oh yes. The fellow made a point of telling me that he'd seen the Kazrak down in town. Zayn was still there this morning. Our informant saw him grooming the spirit rider's horses.'

They were sitting at the long window of the guest room, drinking a pale brown liquid, served hot, that Soutan called 'tay'. Outside, Arkazo was playing with the shens on the green lawn. One of the servants had given him two leather balls. In the cool morning light he threw them for the shens, who chased them down and brought them back, drooling and prancing, to beg Arkazo to throw them yet again. Shens, Warkannan decided, were not intelligent animals.

'My worst fear,' Soutan continued, 'is of Zayn leaving the comnee immediately and getting a head start on us.'

'He won't. He's got to make his inquiries about you, hasn't he? The Chosen probably don't even know which canton you came from. You certainly never told us.'

'The fewer people who knew, the better.' Soutan frowned into his cup. 'If your god is kind, Zayn may not even hear about Jezro, but that's a bit much to hope for.'

'Yes, I'm afraid so. I guess we'd better see about getting you those crystals. How far away is that priest you were telling me about?'

'Not very. A couple of hours' ride. Alayn says he'll take us there.'

'He knows these people well, I take it.'

'Too well. I'll explain when I'm sure he won't overhear us.'

'Good.' Warkannan got up and looked out the window at the sky. 'We should get on our way before the day gets too hot.'

When they rode out, Alayn led them straight into the forest by a path just wide enough for two horses to walk abreast. The pack horses turned nervous, pulling at the lead ropes and tossing their heads. Even Warkannan could smell the rank scent of decay, of animal droppings and dead flesh, of peculiar growths and fungi; to the horses the forest would reek of danger. The light fell broken through the canopy and gave no clear view ahead or to either side. Some sort of tiny black insect swarmed on the path, and while they never bit either horse or man, the horses stamped and switched their tails, tossed their heads and laid their ears back whenever they were forced to walk through the insect clouds.

After two hours of this dank travelling, the trail brought them free of the trees and into a clearing so large that it must have been man-made. Roughly circular, it stretched for several hundred yards across. Behind a thorn-vine fence, it housed a cluster of buildings and a wide lawn of true-grass. Alayn led them straight into the compound. They halted and dismounted in front of the largest building, a two-storey affair with a peaked roof, built entirely of true-wood. Behind it and off to one side stood smaller buildings and a scatter of sheds, mostly woven from rushes and vines reinforced with wood here and there.

When Alayn called out a greeting, the double doors of the true-wood building swung open. Two men trotted out, wearing rusty black smocks over torn and faded blue leggings. The younger began talking with Alayn in Vranz while the older crossed his arms over his chest and studied the rest of the party. He was a tall man, abnormally thin and quite bald, with narrow blue eyes and pale eyebrows, but what caught Warkannan's attention were the growths on his face. Brown and spongy, some round, some dangling – they clustered around his mouth and spotted his cheeks. A few were as thick as a thumb and crusted in pale grey. The younger fellow carried a scattering of brown warts around his lips to match the growth that hung at the edge of Alayn's.

'I'll explain later,' Soutan whispered in Kazraki. 'Disgusting, isn't it?'

'I'm afraid so.'

The older man looked at them sharp-eyed for this bit of

conversation. Soutan arranged a smile and spoke in Hirl-Onglay. 'Ah, Father Sharl! How pleasant to see you again! Alayn told me that you've acquired some crystals.'

'Yes,' Sharl said, and he spoke Hirl-Onglay with no accent. 'None I want to part with.'

'We can offer you Kazraki gold and a horse.'

'No. I'm not haggling, Soutan. I mean it. No.'

'Ah.' Soutan paused, considering. 'You're sure that there's nothing we can offer you? They say everyone has his price, don't they?'

Sharl smiled, and the growths around his mouth danced and twitched. 'The only price I have,' he said, 'is one you won't want to pay.'

'You can't be sure of that until you tell me what it is.'

'Good point.' Sharl thought for a moment. 'My little flock here is getting restless. It's been a long time since we had a proper ceremony for Sevenday.' He pointed a bony finger at Arkazo. 'What about that fellow for the altar?'

Warkannan opened his mouth to snarl but Soutan got in ahead of him.

'Of course not!' Soutan snapped. 'If you need a sacrifice that badly, we can offer you a horse.'

'Animals won't do.' Sharl crossed his arms over his chest. 'Too boring, too ordinary.'

'You're joking, aren't you?' Soutan smiled, then let it fade. 'Or no, I don't think you are.'

'I'm completely serious. The congregation likes some thrills when they're under the influence. Bring me a sacrifice, and you take your pick of my crystals. Three of them, say.'

'It would have to be five at least, but I'm certainly not going to –' Soutan stopped talking, glanced at Warkannan, and smiled. 'Wait. Let's think about this. We actually know someone who might do, someone who's just passing through, no family to try to find him, no employer to demand that the zhundars do something about his disappearance.'

'Really?' Sharl grinned, revealing black gaps among brown teeth. 'Three crystals if you get him here.'

'Five,' Soutan said firmly. 'How many assistants do you have here now?'

'Only three I can trust with an errand like this.'

'Ah. So Alayn will have to help.'

At the mention of his name the sinyur turned to join the conversation, and all three men began talking in Vranz. Warkannan and Arkazo took a few steps back to stand among the horses and speak softly in Kazraki.

'Does this mean what I think it does?' Arkazo said.

'Probably, if you mean catching Zayn and handing him over to these – well, whatever they are. Priest doesn't seem like the right word to me. Idolaters, more likely.'

'Yes. That Sharl – Uncle, he must be a comnee man. Or he was.'

'Shaitan! You're right, aren't you? I wonder how he ended up here?'

The conversation between Alayn, Sharl, and Soutan grew louder. All three men were waving their hands in the air and looking heavenward as if to invoke various gods – gods of haggling, Warkannan assumed, and quite rightly. Eventually they all shook hands. Smiling, Soutan walked back to the two Kazraks.

'Well, there we are,' Soutan announced. 'I get four crystals, Alayn gets the extra horse, and Sharl gets Zayn. Or rather, Alayn, the younger priests, and I get our hands on Zayn somehow and turn him over to Sharl. Hence the payment to Alayn.'

'Makes sense,' Warkannan said. 'Are they going to kill him?'

'Of course. There's only one real drawback,' Soutan continued in Kazraki. 'We have to wait till Zayn leaves the comnee. In order to find him once he does, I'll need to use the crystals. Sharl insists that we stay here. He doesn't want me taking the crystals and just going on my merry way with them.'

'Would you do that?' Arkazo said.

'I wouldn't have the slightest compunction. Let us go to the guest house Sharl offered us, and I'll explain. Oh, and we're giving Alayn the horse now. He won't back out, and this way the temple won't have to feed it.'

'Temple?' Warkannan had had enough mysterious remarks for one day. 'What in hell is this place anyway?'

'Let me show you.' Soutan was smiling, but the smile was forced. 'The young priest there – Gee is his name – he'll stable our horses.'

'What kind of a job will he do? I'd rather take care of that myself.'

'Ever the cavalryman, aren't you, Captain? Very well.' Soutan turned and called out in Vranz.

Gee answered, waved, and turned and walked off.

'He's just as glad to let someone else do the work,' Soutan said. 'But let me show you the temple while it's still light. You won't want to be in there in the dark.'

Warkannan tied the horses to a long wooden rail and left them under Alayn's watch before he and Arkazo followed Soutan into the true-wood building. Sharl brought up the rear. The double doors opened into a narrow porch of sorts, empty of furniture. On the far side another set of double doors brought them to a long room, dimly lit by small glazed windows on either side. They walked down an aisle between two sets of rough wooden benches, enough for a good fifty people, Warkannan estimated. At the far end three stone steps led up to a dais. A pair of dirty dark curtains covered the wall behind it. As they approached the dais, Warkannan became aware of a stink rather like rotting meat, but faint and stale.

In the middle of the dais stood what at first appeared to be a wooden table. As Warkannan's eyes got used to the gloom, he realized first that it was topped with a slab of stone and second that it was long enough to hold a human being. Down the middle ran a blood gutter reminiscent of a butcher's shop. Underneath stood an ordinary tin washtub streaked with what might have been rust. Judging from the smell, it was nothing so innocent. Arkazo made a choking noise, as if perhaps he was suppressing the urge to vomit.

Warkannan felt less than well himself. To kill an enemy in a fight was one thing; to put him on an idolatrous altar, quite another. It's your duty, he reminded himself, and sharply. Soutan turned to Father Sharl and spoke in Vranz. Sharl laughed and trotted up the stairs, went round the altar, and picked up a coil of rope. When he pulled, the curtains creaked back, revealing a statue some eighteen feet high by Warkannan's rough guess. Carved of a greenish, slippery-looking stone, an enormous male ChaMeech glared down at them; his eyes gleamed with red gemstones. He sat haunched, and in his pseudo-hands he held a wooden spear edged with obsidian.

'May God protect us all!' Warkannan muttered in Kazraki. He switched to Hirl-Onglay and said, 'May I ask who that's supposed to be?'

'Aggnavvachur,' Sharl said. 'The ChaMeech name means Hunter of Souls.' He threw back his head and made a high-pitched yipping noise on a single note, echoing in the empty room. 'Do you know what that sound means?'

'Yes,' Warkannan said. 'A ChaMeech surrender.'

'Exactly. Sooner or later, Captain, we all submit to his rule.' Sharl stressed the word 'submit' and smiled.

'Oh yes,' Warkannan kept his voice level. 'Briefly. Before our souls go on to the place appointed for them by God.'

Sharl seemed to be about to say more, but Soutan stepped forward with the brisk cheer of a banquet host stepping between two drunken cavalrymen. 'I know you're worried about the horses, Captain,' he said. 'Shall we go get them stabled and fed?'

'Good idea,' Warkannan said. 'Going to help me, Kaz?'

'Of course, sir. Let's go.'

Soutan led them outside through a side door near the dais and marched them quickly along, too, until they were a good ways away from the temple.

'Sharl's not following.' Soutan glanced back the way they'd come. 'What was that odd exchange about?'

'The name of our faith goes back thousands of years to the sacred language.' Warkannan paused, steadying his voice. 'One translation of Islam is "submission".'

'I see. My apologies, Captain. I never expected he'd be so belligerent.'

'It strikes me that your friend there thrives on doing things people don't expect.'

'He's not my friend. You're right about the rest of it.'

'Soutan?' Arkazo broke in. 'Where did they get that statue? How did they get it inside?'

'It was here already, actually,' Soutan said. 'They built the temple around it. In better light you would have seen that it sits on bare ground, not a floor.'

'Then there were ChaMeech in this forest?' Warkannan said.

'Not precisely. There were ChaMeech here before the forest. The Cantonneurs planted the trees, and then realized it was some sort of sacred ground in ChaMeech culture. That's why they let the forest go wild.'

'What? And waste all this wood?'

Soutan let out his breath in an exasperated puff. They were at the stable door before Warkannan realized that the breath was the only answer he was going to get.

The stable turned out to be decently clean and well-aired. Warkannan and Arkazo unloaded and unsaddled the horses, watered them, and helped themselves to the temple's stacked hay. Arkazo found a couple of sacks of wheatian; they parcelled that out among the horses as well. While they worked, Soutan actually condescended to carry some of the gear into the guest house, though he left the heavy packs for Arkazo and Warkannan. Still, as Warkannan remarked, it was a nice change.

The three of them were hauling the last of their gear when they spotted a young man walking into the compound from the forest. He wore the usual smock and leggings, but he'd bound a white kerchief over the bottom of his face, and he wore thick leather gloves that reached to his elbows. He was carrying a shallow basket, about three feet across, heaped up with dark red strands of Death's Necklace.

'Don't ask, don't say a word,' Soutan murmured. 'Let's get inside.'

Fortunately the guest house was only a few yards away. They hurried in and dumped their loads onto the plain wood floor. Soutan shut the door firmly behind them, then for good measure closed the wooden shutters over the unglazed windows.

'Poisons?' Warkannan whispered.

'Not quite,' Soutan spoke just as softly. 'Though they might as well be. They have some way of processing the stuff. Then they eat it. It gives them visions, they say, and it's supposed to enhance all sorts of sensations and make them into wondrous experiences. Very sexual, they say, and exciting.'

'Experiences like watching a man stabbed to death on that butcher's table of theirs?'

'Exactly. Some of their customers are quite highly placed, Alayn among them, so they can get away with things. The drug – it's terrible stuff, Captain. You've seen what it does to their mouths.'

'How can they keep on eating it?'

'It's addictive, of course. Very very addictive.'

'Good God! Does Alayn's father know?'

'No. That's why he refused to go buy me the crystals in Nannes. If his father started asking questions about how he was spending his leisure time – well, you can guess what would happen.' Soutan shuddered again. 'Sharl and his underlings support themselves by selling this wretched stuff.'

'Those sores,' Arkazo said. 'Or cancers or whatever they are.

Don't they give the customers away? I mean, you'd think someone would ask about them.'

'Of course. Everyone believes it's something in the local water that causes the growths, but only on those people who have a predisposition to getting them. Or something like that – it's rather a garbled story. Every now and then the addicts will have the growths removed, but they always come back.'

'They don't sound very bright,' Warkannan said.

'No, they're not, but let's face it, most members of the H'mai race are stupid.' Soutan wrinkled a contemptuous lip. 'Arkazo, what do you think of this?'

Arkazo tossed his head as if trying to shake off an insect. 'It's horrible,' he said. 'It's going to eat their faces away, sooner or later.'

'Oh yes,' Soutan spoke softly. 'Eventually, I suppose, it'll kill them. Good riddance.'

Doubtless because of those highly placed customers, the guest house was comfortable enough. The room in which they stood sported white walls, bright carpets on the floor, a scatter of comfortable-looking wicker chairs, and a cushioned divan. Through an open doorway Warkannan could see a long dormitory-style room with a row of narrow beds covered with clean blankets.

'I hope no one else is going to be sharing this with us,' Warkannan said.

'Don't worry,' Soutan said. 'The last thing they want is for us to learn the names or see the faces of their regular visitors.' He sighed in a martyred sort of way. 'I have to go back and talk with Father Sharl. I need to see these crystals of his and pick out the four I want.'

After Soutan left, Warkannan and Arkazo arranged the packs, saddles, and their other gear against one wall. Warkannan took his copy of the *Mirror* out of his saddlebags and sat down in one of the chairs. He wasn't in the mood to read, but he wanted to have his hands on God's words, even in translation, for the comfort of them.

Some hours later Soutan returned in an expansive mood. He was carrying a wooden box and smiling so broadly that Warkannan figured it must hold the crystals.

'They're in excellent condition.' Soutan confirmed his guess by patting the top of the box. 'I've identified their primary functions, but I'm sure there are secondary ones I've missed.' He set the box down on a low table near the divan. 'It will take me a while to train them, but I should have plenty of time, unfortunately, while we're waiting here.'

'Here's hoping that Zayn leaves Nannes soon,' Arkazo said. 'This place makes my skin crawl.'

'Good.' Soutan took a chair opposite Warkannan. 'It shows you've got a brain in your head.'

Arkazo sat up, cross-legged on the divan. 'I don't understand the drugs, the murders, any of it,' he said. 'Soutan, what do these people think they're doing?'

'Amusing themselves,' Soutan said. 'I can only suppose that they're very good at lying to themselves. They keep having the growths taken off their faces and go right on eating the vines. Or the nodes, rather. Those swellings on the Necklaces are what contain the drug.'

'How is worshipping some idol amusing?'

'Well, amusing may not be the right word.' Soutan thought for a moment. 'Frisson, that's more like it. A thrill, a shudder, from fear or pleasure or both. Their lives are dull, they long for something more. That's true of most people in the Cantons, actually, but only the weak souls engage in foolishness like this. Some of the stronger souls worship in the Church of the One God. They say it gives their lives meaning. Others just drink too much and chase each other's wives. And to be fair, sometimes the wives chase each other's husbands.'

'What?' Warkannan put in. 'This doesn't sound like much of a place.'

'It isn't,' Soutan said. 'It's a dying culture, Captain. Dying, decaying, falling apart, however you want to put that, and people who live in dying cultures do desperate and silly things.'

Warkannan could only stare at him. Arkazo started to speak, then shrugged as if trying to shake the words off.

'There are reasons for it, of course.' Soutan stood up. 'But I'm not ready to tell them to you.' Soutan scooped up his box of crystals. 'I need to go feed the spirits.' He strode out, slamming the door behind him.

'One of these days,' Warkannan said, 'I'm going to lose my temper, and Soutan is going to lose a lot of blood. May God keep me from doing it until after we've reached the khan.'

* * *

The comnee that Ammadin spotted on the road turned out to be friendly, a small group led by the youngest chief on the grass. They'd been fording the Great River in the winter rains when a sudden swell of water from upstream had pulled half their people and most of their horses under, including their chief and their spirit rider. The survivors had elected Sammador chief for his bravery in rescuing two children. When Ammadin had seen them at the spring horse fair, they had just found a new spirit rider to guide them, Kassidor, who had finished his apprenticeship only a few months before.

Sammador led his people into the trading precinct a few hours before sunset. Everyone in Apanador's comnee helped them unload their wagons and set up their tents. Ammadin and Kassidor stood off to one side, out of the way, and watched the others work. He was just about her height, but built solidly, with a barrel chest and heavy thighs. He had the silver eyes of a spirit rider, of course, and wore his hair, a darkish sort of blond, shaggy and thick.

'Did you have a safe trip across the Rift?' Ammadin said.

'Yes, actually,' Kassidor said. 'Didn't see a single ChaMeech.'

'Good. We spotted a warparty when we crossed. I'm glad they moved on before you got there.'

'So am I.' He had an engaging grin. 'Very.'

'You crossed early.'

'Yes, we were following you, actually. We've been trying to catch up to you for weeks.'

'What? Why?'

'Something odd happened when we were still back on the grass. Three Kazraks and a Cantonneur rode our way. They were asking for information about you.'

'Oh were they? One Kazrak was older, rode like a cavalry officer?'

'That's right, yes.'

'The Cantonneur, he was middle-aged, right? Long, grey hair?'

'No, he was young and blond.' Kassidor thought for a moment. 'He was wearing a jewelled headband. Something about him irritated me, but I couldn't put my finger on it. Then later we heard that they were somehow responsible for the murder of a comnee man named Palindor. Apanador's comnee was supposed to have something to do with it, too. We didn't believe that for a minute. So Sammo and I thought you'd better hear about the rumours.'

'Thank you, it's important, all right. I've got a story to tell you about these people.' Ammadin shaded her eyes with her hand and looked over the camp. 'Zayn! Come here, will you?'

Zayn, who had been helping unload a wagon, put his burden on the ground and trotted over.

'Kasso, this is my servant, Zayn,' Ammadin began.

'Actually I remember him from the horse fair,' Kassidor broke in. 'You won't remember me, Zayn. You were in pretty bad shape at the time.'

'I don't remember much from those first few days, no.' Zayn smiled, but his eyes were guarded.

'Kasso's met your Kazraks,' Ammadin said. 'And his description of Soutan tallies with yours, Soutan as a young, blond man, that is. Kasso, I've seen him in my crystal, but there he looks old and has stringy grey hair. The headband's the same, though.'

'You're sure it's the same man?' Kassidor said.

'Just how many Cantonneur sorcerers are there riding around the plains? Yes, I'm sure. When I scan, I also see a strange bluish light that dances around him.'

'Ye gods!' Kassidor's eyes grew wide. 'He must be a shape-changer.'

'So it seems.' Ammadin turned to Zayn. 'That's one mystery solved anyway. There aren't two sorcerers, only one. He uses magic to change his appearance, that's all.'

'That's all?' Zayn said with a choked sort of laugh. 'Sorry, I can't be quite that casual about it.'

'Well, neither am I, really.' Ammadin turned back to Kassidor. 'Let's talk about this.'

'Definitely. I've never actually seen a shape-changer before.' Kassidor began speaking in the spirit language. 'I'm beginning to remember more about the fellow, too, and his friends. The older Kazrak was asking about Zayn.'

'I'm not surprised.' Ammadin answered in the same. 'They've been trying to kill him all summer.' She glanced at Zayn and spoke in Hirl-Onglay. 'I'm sorry, I didn't mean to leave you just standing there. Don't worry. Kasso and I will figure out what to do about this.'

'Thanks,' Zayn said. 'Your spirit language? It's related to Hirl-Onglay, isn't it? I could understand a few words here and there.'

'You what? How?'

'Hears words where other men only hear babble.' Zayn grinned at her. 'Remember that talent on the list?'

'I do, yes.'

'Well, that's how.' He looked away, his smile fading. 'Another forbidden talent! I'm damned in a lot of ways, aren't I?'

Before Ammadin could answer, Zayn strode off, heading back to the work party. Kassidor watched him go with puzzled eyes.

'I'm glad you're here,' Ammadin said. 'I've been wanting to talk with another spirit rider for some time.'

'So have I.' Kassidor glanced away; when he spoke, his voice shook. 'Sammo and I are both too damned young. I can't sleep nights sometimes, Ammi. I'm so afraid I'll do the wrong thing and let everyone down.'

'I remember that feeling.' Ammadin was about to say more when an idea struck her. 'Do you think Sammador would agree to ride with Apanador for a while?'

'Merge the comnees, you mean?'

'Just for a little while. Till winter, say.'

'To tell you the truth, I think we'd both be relieved.'

'Good. I'll come with you while you seat your gods. Then we can talk things over. I've also learned a lot about crystals lately. You'll want to hear that, too.'

As she followed Kassidor to his tent, Ammadin was thinking about Water Woman. She would need to contact the Chiri Michi soon, while they were still in range of each other's crystals. If the two chiefs agreed, she might be able to leave the comnee and ride off on her quest a great deal sooner than she'd hoped.

'Uncle?' Arkazo said. 'If you wouldn't look at your watch every five minutes, the time would go faster.'

'You're right, aren't you?' Warkannan snapped the case closed and put the watch into his pocket. 'Sorry.'

'It's getting too dark to read,' Arkazo went on. 'We have oil for the lamps, don't we?'

'There's some in that big clay jar,' Soutan said. 'The one under the window. I saw some wicking in that drawer over there, too. Father Sharl likes to supply everything his fancy clients need. At least at first, before they've become addicted.'

Warkannan filled and lit as many lamps as he could find, then set them together on the table to pool their light. Arkazo hooked his thumbs over his belt and stared into the flames.

'What's wrong?' Warkannan said.

'I just keep thinking about Tareev.' Arkazo walked back to the divan and sat down. 'I wish we could get on the road.'

'Me, too,' Soutan said. 'All of this business with Chosen Ones tracking us down –' He shuddered and flapped his hands in the air.

'Another day here,' Arkazo said, 'and I could end up demented.'

'Yes, it's wearing.' Soutan thought for a moment. 'I have my work with the crystals, your uncle has his beloved book, but there you are with nothing to do.'

'Well, yes.' Arkazo tried to smile. 'I didn't think I'd need a hobby on this ride, or I would have brought one.'

'How would you like to learn some Vranz? From now on, I'll have to be extremely careful. I don't dare go into a town to buy supplies. I don't even want to go into a farming village.'

'There's a reward on your head?' Warkannan said.

'Just that, and rather a large one.' Soutan looked sincerely aggrieved. 'That lying little slut!'

'Yes, it's too bad.' There was little genuine sympathy in Arkazo's voice. 'But yes, I'll learn Vranz. It'll pass the time.'

'Not me,' Warkannan said. 'You people sound like you're talking out of your noses.'

'Better than gargling every other consonant, like you Kazraks do.' Soutan gave him a sour smile. 'But trayb yen, Arkazo. That phrase means "very good". Let us begin.'

Listening to one person drill another in the basics of a foreign language was not a pastime that Warkannan found congenial. After some minutes he walked over to an unshuttered window. He put his hands on the sill and leaned out, staring into the night. Beyond the compound he could see the dark mound of the forest, shot here and there with the glow from Death's Necklace. He could hear animals calling out among the trees and, closer to hand, chanting coming from the temple, a reedy whine of voices drifting on the warm night air. He turned and perched on the sill to look out.

The chanting stopped. In a few minutes he heard the distant creak of opening doors and then footsteps, crunching on the dry grass, heading more or less in his direction. He leaned out a little further and saw someone walking not directly towards the guest house, but at an angle that would take him past it. At first he thought the fellow was carrying an oil lamp, but the bobbing glimmer of light accompanying him shone pale blue, not yellow. As he came closer, Warkannan saw the truth: the man's lips and the skin around them were glowing with phosphorescence. Warkannan pulled his head in and closed the shutters.

For the first time in weeks he remembered Hazro, and what he'd been forced to do to their traitor up in Indan's sealed room. Now he was condemning a man to a death that might well be worse. Not a man, he thought. One of the Chosen. A man who'd inform on his brother officers, a man who'd turn a friend over to torture if he thought it would please the Great Khan. Not a man at all. He hoped he could make himself believe it.

Whenever Zayn asked about Ammadin, he was told that she was in Kassidor's tent, and interrupting spirit riders at their work was of course Bane. Zayn disliked the way he'd seen them talking together, standing so close, sharing a language he couldn't understand. Still, if Kassidor could figure out how to handle Soutan, he could put up with his jealousy. A shape-changer, a man who could transform himself, who could change his face the way a normal man changed his shirt – the thought turned Zayn cold. Once he left the comnee, he might be looking straight at Soutan and not recognize him. He could imagine passing some stranger in the street only to feel a knife in his ribs the next moment.

Zayn spent the evening drinking with Dallador and some of the men from Sammador's comnee, but he found himself a place to sit where he could keep an eye on Kassidor's tent. Eventually, when the silver Herd hung low in the east, Ammadin and Kassidor came out, laughing together. Zayn watched them cross the camp and go into Apanador's tent, where the two chiefs had retired to talk about the trading ahead. With her safely in someone else's company, Zayn could relax. He felt even better at the end of the evening, when he went to her tent and found her there alone, studying one of her crystals by the light of a single lamp.

'Do you want more light?' Zayn said.

'No, I'm about ready to go to sleep.' Ammadin began wrapping the crystal, then paused to sniff the air. 'Are you drunk?'

'Almost. Do you mind?'

'Not particularly, but you might want to stay sober with your enemies so close.'

'Yes, you're right.' He sat down on his blankets. 'About that shape-changer –'

'I'm still not sure what to do. Kasso's no help. He's young, you know. He was an apprentice till last winter.' She frowned down at the wrapped crystal. 'Huh, I wonder if Water Woman knows more?'

'The ChaMeech?'

'Yes. We talk regularly through our crystals.' She looked at him, one eyebrow raised as if she was expecting some hostile response.

Zayn made none. He pulled off his boots, then lay down, a bit too suddenly, on his blankets. He heard Ammadin laughing at him, but he fell asleep before he could answer.

Zayn had been planning on hunting up information about Soutan, but with the morning the professional horse dealers arrived at the trading precinct. The long hours of haggling left him no time for the hunt. Whenever a customer expressed interest in one of Ammadin's horses, Zayn would hook a lead rope onto its halter and bring it out of the herd, then run alongside the horse as it displayed its gait. Afterwards he'd walk the horse cool, then lead it to the river to drink. In the intervals he did manage to find out a few useful things; for instance, that the Cantons lay in a long broad valley between the Rift on one side and mountains on the other.

'The damned ChaMeech pretty much own the mountains,' one of the men told him. 'And the foothills, too. If you ever ride that way, don't get lost up there.'

'Don't worry,' Zayn said. 'I'm not planning on getting anywhere near the hills.'

When the horse-traders left, they took the best mounts with them. The local people would come to look over the remaining stock on the morrow, Ammadin said.

'You've had quite a day of it,' she went on. 'You must be tired.'

'A little,' Zayn said. 'Dallador was talking about going into town. Would it be all right if I went with him?'

'Certainly. Do you still have some of the money I gave you? Spend it if you want. We're doing pretty well.'

'Thanks. Yes, we are.'

Only when he was walking away did he realize how easily both of them had said 'we'. Ammadin may have been keeping herself sexually aloof from him, but she was seeing them as a pair. If I could stay, he thought. If only I could stay! Impossible, of course, but he felt heartsick. He had never been happy before, not even in the cavalry. There he had managed to feel secure, competent even, but happy, no. He felt like a starving man who'd been given a few bites of bread only to have the loaf snatched away.

Walking into town with Dallador only made his heartsickness worse. They walked side by side, so close that their shoulders nearly brushed, and talked idly of the trading and the road ahead. Dallador's easy assumption that Zayn would be riding back west with the comnee made him sick with shame. He'd lived his whole life as a series of lies, curling around one another like the furled trunk of a spear tree. Once he'd been proud of carrying it off, but it hurt to lie to Dallador. They went to the market square, where Dallador spotted a jeweller's shop. Zayn leaned against a rough wooden counter and watched while his friend picked over some heavy silver pins, made to the Tribal taste in the forms of various animals.

'I want something for Benno's winter jacket,' Dallador remarked. 'As much as I love my wife, she can be tight-fisted when it comes to spending for the boy. I hope we get a daughter soon. I'd hate to have her divorce me.'

'Oh come on, she wouldn't do that!' But Zayn felt a twinge of worry that made him realize just how much he'd started thinking like a comnee man. 'You take good care of her.'

'Sure, but how much is that going to count in the long run? It means everything to women, having a daughter.' Dallador shrugged the problem away. 'Well, the gods will give us a girl or not, and there's not a damn thing I can do about it. When we're done here, want to go to a tavern? They make this peculiar drink here called kerrv.'

'Good idea. Ammadin gave me some money, so let me buy.'

They left the shop and stepped out onto the street, crowded with passers-by, most of them hurrying about their own business. Some yards away a pale young fellow leaned against a building. A loiterer maybe, but he seemed to be watching the two Tribesmen with more than ordinary curiosity. When Dallador followed Zayn's glance and looked his way, the young man strolled off with a studied indifference – a less clumsy spy, this time.

'I hope he doesn't mean trouble,' Dallador said. 'Sometimes the Cantonneurs can be downright unfriendly.'

'Nothing like picking a fight to give you some excitement, huh?' Zayn said. 'Small towns are like that back home, too.'

When they found a tavern, down a side street near the edge of town, they hesitated a moment, wondering if they should just go back to camp, but the place was nearly empty and seemed safe enough. The room was more of a shed, a tottering draughty affair of bundled spear-trunks with one wall open to a muddy yard out back, but the tavernman spoke passable Hirl-Onglay. At a high table the old man poured kerrv into pottery mugs and handed them over when Zayn paid. Zayn took one sip and nearly spat it out – it was bitter, dark, and oddly thick. Dallador was drinking his, however, with a small smile of appreciation. Zayn took another sip and decided that eventually he'd grow to like it.

Although the tavern offered a few chairs and a couple of tables, the two comnee men stayed standing – and near the door. Wiping his hands on a rag, the tavernman strolled over to join them.

'Kazraki, aren't you?' he said to Zayn.

'Yes. Something wrong with that?'

'Not in my opinion, but you know what opinions are like. You can always find someone who doesn't share yours, if you get what I mean. Now, I mean that in a friendly way.'

'I'll take it the same way, then. Thanks. Huh, I didn't think you people would see enough Kazraks to have opinions about us one way or the other.'

'Um, well.' The tavernman paused, sucking his teeth. 'You'd think so, wouldn't you?'

'Has someone been asking around after me?'

'Not about you, exactly. About Kazraks, if I'd seen any.'

'Ah. And he didn't seem to like my kind much?'

'Don't know about that.' He paused for a long time. 'A pale sort of fellow with brown hair, and I don't know . . . there was just something about him that put your wind up. Wouldn't want him asking for me.'

Zayn and Dallador exchanged a glance, handed their mugs back, and left the tavern. As they were walking back across the bridge, it occurred to Zayn that he'd managed to forget to ask about Soutan.

Late that night Zayn went back to the tent to sleep and found Ammadin there ahead of him, studying her crystals. She'd lit a pair of oil lamps and laid the crystals in a semi-circle around them. Zayn sat down on his blankets and began pulling off his boots. In a moment Ammadin looked up.

'When you were in town today,' she said, 'did you notice anything wrong?'

'What makes you ask that?'

'I'm not sure.' She smiled faintly. 'Just an odd feeling.'

'Well, I noticed someone following me and Dallo around. And then a tavernman told me that some brown-haired Cantonneur was asking around about Kazraks.'

'I don't like the sound of that at all. I'm glad we're leaving soon.'

Zayn managed a casual nod and lay down on his blankets. A thin, black line of smoke from the lamps was circling up to the smokehole. Even though he tried to concentrate on it, he was painfully aware of her, so close by but so far away. Finally he turned over onto his side and watched while she wrapped the crystals and put them away. Trust his luck to bring him to the one comnee woman who valued her chastity as much as any Kazraki girl! Never once in his life had he made love to a woman he liked and respected, Zayn realized, only bought sex from the sort of whore who hung around the cavalry. Single officers like Warkannan, with aristocratic connections and independent incomes, could arrange pleasant liaisons with girls from the palace troupes of musicians and dancers, but not men from families like his.

Zayn wasn't even surprised when Ammadin realized the drift of his thoughts. She laid the last crystal down and scowled at him. 'Zayn, I said no.'

'I never did.'

Much to his surprise, she laughed. 'Fair enough,' she went on. 'I'll offer you a bargain – you tell me the things you're hiding, and maybe I'll reconsider.'

Zayn came close to betraying every secret he had. It was as if the words were live things, desperate to escape his mouth. Ammadin leaned forward, her smile gone.

'Something's really wrong,' she said. 'What is it?'

The moment ended. 'No,' he said, 'I'm just generally miserable and lovesick.'

'Oh ye gods! Then you'll just have to suffer.'

'I figured you'd say something like that.' Zayn sat up. 'You know, I think I'll go sleep outside.'

'It'll probably be easier for you.'

'Damn it, Ammi! You can't be as cold as –'

'Yes, I can. Haven't you got that through your thick skull yet?'

Zayn stood up and grabbed his blankets. 'Go to hell!' he snapped, then ducked through the tent flap and stalked off. He'd gone about ten yards when he realized that he'd left his boots behind, but he decided against going back. He laid his blankets out under the wagon, then crawled onto them. For some while he lay awake, feeling foolish, wishing he'd thought up something better to say as he left. Eventually sleep rescued him.

In the morning Ammadin treated him as if nothing had been said between them. For that alone, he decided, she was worth desiring, hopelessly or not.

In the morning they had few customers, and none of those bought a horse. Zayn began thinking about going back into Nannes. He could use finding a book for Ammadin as his excuse and start his hunt for information about Soutan, but first he decided that he needed to feed their riding horses some grain. After that, he watered all their stock, then fixed a loose cinch on Ammadin's saddle. The morning eased itself into afternoon before he realized that he was avoiding all thoughts of Yarl Soutan. Finally, however, the hunt came to him. A customer arrived, a man in his thirties, Zayn guessed, who wore a black smock as long as a Kazraki woman's dress and a round little cap of black felt. He announced himself as Reb Donnol.

'I lead the congregation here in town,' Donnol said. 'The Church of the One God, that is. Now, my congregation's given me the money for a riding horse, but, er, I do hope you've got a gentle one.'

'How about a mare?' Zayn said. 'A young buckskin mare.'

'I'll look at her, certainly.'

Zayn went out to the herd, caught the buckskin by the halter, and led her back to the rabbi. Ammadin had joined him to do the haggling. Zayn broke into a run and let the mare trot back and forth, then slowed her down and brought her over. When Donnol held out his hand, she whuffled into his palm.

'She likes me,' he said, beaming. 'How much do you want?'

Ammadin briefly considered. 'Twenty of your silver vrans, and

I'm not haggling. It's a low price for a horse like that.'

'Yes, it is,' Donnol said. 'Some of the men in my congregation primed me, you see, and told me what to pay. I'll take her.'

'Zayn?' Ammadin said. 'Get that extra bridle for His Holiness. We'll give it to him as part of the deal.'

As Zayn followed the order, he was aware of Reb Donnol studying him. He bridled the mare, then handed the reins to the rabbi, who handed over the money. By then, Ammadin had walked away; Zayn pocketed two big silver coins, each worth ten vrans.

'A Kazrak, are you?' Donnol said.

'I was once. I think of myself as a comnee man now. You must not see many of us out here.'

'Almost never. But there was one other fellow through here once, years ago now.'

'Someone else mentioned him to me. His name wasn't Jezro, was it?'

'You know, it certainly was! He was some sort of political exile. I gather your leader had tried to have him killed. He asked for asylum and stayed with us at the seminary for a few months. That was before I was called to Nannes.'

'I see, yes. Does Jezro still live around here?'

'No, he headed off to the north-east, probably to Burgunee, since that's the only civilized place out that way. Our abbot gave him a letter of introduction to a seminary there, if I remember rightly. I have no idea what happened to him after that.'

'I take it he was a religious man.'

'Well, he hadn't been before, no. Before almost dying, I mean. He told me that it had had a profound effect on the way he saw the world.'

'I suppose it would. Interesting. Well, thank you, sir. I hope our little mare serves you well.'

For a long few minutes Zayn stood watching the rabbi lead his new horse away. He felt cold, and it seemed ridiculously hard to think. So. It was true. Jezro Khan was alive, after all these years of thinking him dead. Jezro's alive, and it's my job to kill him.

'Zayn?' Ammadin had walked up to him. 'Are you all right?'

'Of course.'

'You look ill.'

'Do I?'

'Grey and sweaty, yes.'

'Oh. Maybe I'm hung over. I feel like hell, actually.'

'Why don't you go lie down for a while in the tent?'

'Thanks. I will.'

Zayn ducked into the tent like a hunted animal reaching its den. He sat down on his blankets, pulled off his boots, then lay down on his stomach and buried his face in his arms. He felt so physically sick that he was almost able to talk himself into believing he'd eaten spoiled food and nothing more. Almost. He knew better. I cannot kill the man who risked his career to save my life. I can't. But if I don't – I swore a vow to the Great Khan. I swore a vow to the Chosen.

He turned over onto his back and stared up at the tent's grey ceiling. From outside he could hear voices and footsteps, members of the comnee calling back and forth – his friends' voices. Maybe he could just stay with the comnee. If he avoided the border horse fairs, it would take the Chosen a long time to hunt him down. He'd have a few years, a few good years, before Fate caught up with him.

'Zayn?' Dallador lifted the tent flap and ducked inside. 'Maddi told me you were ill.'

'I'm all right now. Just tired, I guess.'

Dallador sat down next to him and stretched out his long legs. He smelled of horses and sweat, but the smell was somehow clean, even inviting. Zayn felt his closeness like a slap on the face, waking him from a kind of sleep. When he remembered the dreams he'd been having, he could lie to himself no longer. Dallador held out his hand. Zayn somehow knew that this was the moment for him to sit up and move away, and that if he did, Dallador would never allow such a moment to develop again. He could not move, was afraid to move, was afraid to stay, wanted to speak, said nothing. Dallador leaned forward and ran his hand through Zayn's hair, then bent over and kissed him on the mouth. Zayn flinched, then felt his body ease of its own accord. The kiss seemed like the most normal thing in the world.

With a supple twist of his body Dallador lay down next to him. Zayn rolled into his arms with barely a thought.

'Ammi, you really mean this?' Maradin said. 'You're going to leave us?'

'Not forever,' Ammadin said, smiling. 'But I have to ride this quest. I'm sorry, Maddi, but it's crucial. I'm not even sure why, but I know I absolutely have to ride east with Water Woman. I've been having spirit dreams.'

'Well, that settles that, then. But –'

'There isn't anything more to say.'

Maradin sighed, a defeated little noise. In the late afternoon sun they were walking among the horses, taking count of their stock. Ammadin had sold every horse she'd brought to market except for one black two-year-old, and he was a horse that she had no objections to taking back to the grass with her. Maradin had done equally well.

'I saw you giving the little buckskin to that rabbi,' Maradin said. 'Well, not giving but you could have got about twice the money for her.'

'I know, but I've met Reb Donnol before, and he's a good man. His church does a lot of good, too, even if they do think there's only one god.'

Their stroll had taken them to the far side of the tethered herd, upriver of the camp and the town. For a moment they stood at the edge of the meadow, where a cluster of fountain trees offered some shade. They leaned on the fence and looked east across fenced fields of wheatian, pale gold and bowing in a summer breeze.

'Does Water Woman know?' Maradin said.

'Oh yes,' Ammadin said. 'We've decided that we'll meet north-east of here. She can't travel openly in the Cantons, of course, but the Chiri Michi have their own roads – or so she told me. Secret roads, she called them.'

'I suppose they must. It was their land first, after all.' Maradin paused, thinking. 'You know what amazes me the most, though?'

'No, what?'

'Finding out that Chursavva was a woman. Well, a ChaMeech woman, but still! After all those legends and things that said she was a king. I wonder why they made a mistake like that?'

'ChaMeech females are bigger than their males, and they do most of the talking.'

'I can see how the Kazraks thought that meant she was male, yes, but I'm surprised at the Cantonneurs.'

'Maybe they had different attitudes, all the way back then.'

'Could be. You sure you'll be all right? I mean, you'd know, wouldn't you, if you couldn't trust Water Woman?'

'Well, no, not if you mean can I smell if she's lying. They have different bodies, so all their scents mean different things.' Ammadin considered for a moment. 'She's not telling me everything. I don't need spirit powers to figure that out. There's some other faction or group back in her homeland that she mentioned once, but when I ask her, she turns evasive. But if you mean, do I feel she won't harm me, yes, I do, because I'm too valuable. She really needs H'mai on her side for some reason. I'm just not sure what.'

'Well, it sounds risky to me, but I know you. If your mind's made up –'

'Nothing you say will change it, yes.'

Maradin laughed, then turned to look at the distant tents. Smoke from cooking fires was rising among them. 'We should get back. Does Apanador know you're leaving?'

'No. Kasso and I will talk to the chiefs this evening.'

'You know, Kassidor's awfully good-looking –'

'Oh stop it! I can't think of a worse marriage than one between two spirit riders. They'd fight all the time over whose visions were better. That's why there's only one spirit rider in a comnee, after all.'

'Well, yes, that's true. I'll bet Zayn's going to be just sick when he finds out you're leaving.'

'Why? He's having an affair with your husband.'

'So? He's in love with you, not Dallo.'

'Oh? I don't think so.'

Maradin laughed again. 'Of course he is! You understand spirits, Ammi, but I understand men.'

'You're right, aren't you?' Ammadin grinned at her. 'But I've got the better bargain.'

He would have to ride away before he stayed forever. After Dallador left, late that afternoon, Zayn lay on his blankets and repeated that bitter truth. He would have to ride away, and it would have to be that night, or he would stay with the comnee till one of the Chosen came to kill him. He sat up, listening to the normal sounds of the camp outside, the talk, the laughter. Through the smokehole a long shaft of sun fell upon the hearth stone in the centre of the tent, his tent as he'd started thinking of it, the tent where he'd been given a place. He got up, stretching, then dressed. He spent a few minutes putting the things he owned into his saddlebags. He would have to smuggle them out as soon as it grew dark.

In the meantime he would have to act as he were thinking of nothing but returning to the grass. Zayn left the tent, glanced around for Ammadin, and saw her nowhere. Some of the other men were lighting cooking fires, some of the women were out among the herd. No one seemed to take particular notice of him. They would wonder tomorrow, he supposed, why he'd gone. In the bright sun of a hot afternoon he strolled down to the river, flowing smooth and brown between its purple banks. Although he considered going into town to hunt up information about Soutan, he knew that if he found Jezro Khan, he would find Soutan with him. Nothing else would have brought Idres across the plains.

The orange-mottled water reeds, stirring in the light wind, made him remember his spirit crane. Out in the water a flock of animals swam back and forth; they were squat and grey, flecked with purple and magenta, and about the size and shape of true-hens. Like the hens they had tucked-up wings, but of pink scaly skin, not feathers. Their long necks ended in bulbous heads and mouthfuls of teeth. Zayn sat down on the grass and watched them dive for black river crabs, which they brought up kicking and crunched down alive.

Tomorrow he would be alone again. He would be hunting not just information, but a man's life. Jezro Khan had to die – his duty and his common sense both told him so. The thought rose in his mouth like the taste of vomit. If only there were more time! He could simply ride back with the comnee, then head for Haz Kazrak and tell his superiors what he'd learned. They could send someone else to make the actual kill. But there was no time. Idres was ahead of him on the road.

Zayn heard footsteps behind him and turned to see an old man, leaning on a long true-wood staff as he shuffled along. Dressed in a dirty patchwork smock and threadbare brown trousers, he carried a small cloth sack in one hand. In a voice cracked with age he sang to himself, wavering from one song to another. When he saw Zayn, he stopped singing and smiled, revealing that half his teeth were missing.

'Good afternoon,' he said. 'Have you come to watch the ducks?'

'Well, not exactly. I'm a comnee man, you see, and I just wandered down from the camp.'

'Ah.' The old man sat down next to him. 'Don't mind if I join you, do you?'

'Not at all. Do you live in town?'

'Well, off and on, off and on. I have a daughter here, and I live with her most times, but I like to wander around the country during the summer.' He waved vaguely at the animals he'd called ducks. 'I make lists of beasties, you see. I count 'em and write down what they look like. I'll bet that strikes you as a peculiar way to spend your time.'

'As long as you enjoy it, it's none of my business, is it?'

'I wish more people saw it your way. And I look for old books, too. Know what a book is?'

'Daccor.'

'Well, that's a surprise. A lot of comnee men have never seen one.'

'I wasn't always a comnee man. I'm from Kazrajistan. Ever heard of it?'

'Oh, heavens, yes! They're supposed to have wonderful libraries there, filled with books so old we've forgotten the titles in our part of the world. When I was young, I used to think about making the trip, but I waited too long. Too old, now, to travel that far.' He sighed, a long rattle of sound. 'My name's Onree, by the by.'

'Mine's Zayn.'

'Pleased to meet you. Ah, you Kazraks! After all, you were never invaded.'

'Um?'

'To lose your books, I mean. When the ChaMeech took N'Dosha, they burned a lot of ours, all they could find, or so the story runs. They came for the books, you see, or well, that's what some people say. For the books and for the – well, the magic.'

'What would ChaMeech want with books?'

'Nothing. That's why they burned them. Or that's what the story says. I wouldn't know. I wasn't there myself. I mean, I know I'm old and all, but not that old.'

'Not by half, no.' Zayn paused for a smile. 'You travel all over, you say?'

'Yes, I certainly do. Every spring and summer. When the weather gets wet, I go home.'

'I was wondering if you'd ever run across a man named Yarl Soutan.'

The old man tossed his head back and laughed. Out on the river the ducks turned towards shore and laughed with him, or at least, they cackled and whistled.

'Uh, what's so funny?' Zayn said.

'Do I know Soutan? Oh yes, I know him. Rotten little bastard, that's what he is. Why are you asking?'

'Well, it's a long story. The man I'm really looking for is another Kazrak, named Jezro. Someone told me that Soutan might know where he was.'

Onree laughed again. 'Maybe he does,' he said at last. 'But asking Soutan a favour is a little like asking a longtooth saur for the time of day. Maybe he knows it, maybe he doesn't, but he's likely to bite your head off before he tells you either way.'

'All right. I'll keep that in mind.'

Onree cocked his head to one side and considered Zayn for a long moment. 'Do you think I'm crazy? Just a crazy old man with a wandering mind?'

His stare was disturbing, an unblinking gaze from surprisingly clear and shrewd blue eyes.

'Not in the least,' Zayn said.

'Thank you.' Onree brought out a thin wooden tablet, coated on one face with thick wax, and a thin pointed stick. 'Time to count these ducks.'

'Nice to have met you.' Zayn stood up. 'I'd better get back to camp.'

As he walked away he glanced back and saw Onree writing on the wax with the stick. Out on the river the ducks sailed back and forth, teeth and jaws green with crab blood.

Zayn had been dreading having to cook for Ammadin and chat as if nothing in particular was on his mind, but when he returned to the tent, she was gone. One of Sammador's men told him that she and Kassidor were eating with the two chiefs in Apanador's tent.

'She might have told me, damn it!' Zayn snapped.

'Well, you know what spirit riders are like. Always off on a cloud somewhere.'

Zayn stayed inside the tent until the twilight turned thick and grey over the camp. He could not bear seeing Dallador. All it would take, he knew, was one of Dallo's slow smiles, and he would never leave. He waited until everyone in the comnee was eating at one fire or another, then slipped out, carrying his saddlebags. At the far end of the meadow stood a cluster of fountain trees. Zayn cached the saddlebags among them, then went back to camp and hid in the tent again. The evening wore on, darkened. The other men began to sing, a sure sign that they'd drunk enough keese to blunt their eyesight. Zayn took his saddle and his bedroll out to the fountain trees and laid them down with the saddlebags.

This time, when he returned to camp, he paused at the edge of the darkness and looked at the fire-lit tents, the wagons, the people who sat among them, laughing and talking. He had been planning on hiding in the tent for a while more, but he knew that he had to leave right then or never. He got his bridle and the last of his gear from the tent and strode out to the horse herd. No one seemed to notice, or if they did, they assumed that he was doing some errand that needed to be done. He found the sorrel and led him into the fountain trees.

Picking up the saddle nearly lost him his nerve. Once he rode out, he'd never ride back. He would find Jezro, kill him, and then return to the khanate, where his superior officers would doubtless shower him with praise he didn't want and a promotion he'd despise. The sorrel gelding nuzzled his shoulder.

'We've got to go,' Zayn whispered to the horse. 'I'm sorry. I'll find some way to get you back to Ammi, all right?'

The sorrel made no objections. Zayn saddled and bridled him, hung and tied his gear to the saddle, then mounted and rode out, skirting the edge of the meadow until he reached the road that ran due east, deeper into Bredanee. At first it ran through fields of wheatian, an odd yellowish-grey in the light from the silver spiral of the Herd. Some miles on, though, the fields gave way to rough pasture, and ahead Zayn could see the dark mound, shot with glints of blue light, that marked the forest edge, curving round to intersect his path. Had the road run among the trees, he never would have followed it, but it turned to skirt the forest edge, then continued east, running about twenty yards away from the verge.

The Herd was just reaching zenith when the road brought him to a fast-flowing river and a wooden bridge. When Zayn started to ride across, the sorrel balked, tossing its head and fighting the bit. The hollow sound of hooves on wood had spooked it, Zayn realized. Tribal horses never crossed bridges in the normal course of things. He let the horse turn and walk back a few paces on the road.

'Steady on, old boy,' Zayn said. 'I'll lead you across. How's that?'

Zayn dismounted, then shortened up on the reins to walk right beside the sorrel's head.

'Now,' he said, 'let's try this again.'

The sorrel walked forward calmly enough, but just as they reached the edge of the bridge, something shrieked in the river below. A crane! The sorrel tossed its head and began to back up. With one last cry the crane rose from the river and flapped off. Against the dark night, the phosphorescent dots along its legs gleamed.

'We'd better get out of here,' Zayn said. 'I don't know why, but we'd better.'

Ahead on the road someone laughed, a human voice this time, jubilant. Riders were coming out of the forest, blocking the bridge, blocking the road. Zayn grabbed for a stirrup and started to mount, but sudden light flared, blinding him. He managed to swing himself into the saddle, but when he looked back, he saw two more riders cutting off his escape. Seven men altogether, from his hasty count, and all of them were wearing cloth hoods, slit for their eyes. Zayn pulled his long knife.

'If you're going to rob me, you're not going to get very much,' Zayn said. 'I don't carry enough coin to make dying worthwhile, and I'll get at least one of you before you bring me down.'

One of the hooded men laughed under his breath and raised his hand. Zayn felt something brush his shoulder from behind – a lasso. He twisted around and tried to grab it, but another one flew and snared the gelding around his neck. Zayn leaned forward and tried to cut it away. As the horse began to prance and snort, another came from the side and caught him around the shoulders. Zayn writhed, trying to get free, but it was pulled tight by a man on horseback, and a second one followed from the other side, tangling him round like a bird in a wire snare. All at once he went limp, slumping in the saddle. When he felt the ropes relax around him, he ducked and grabbed, had one off and the next slipping half-way up his body before the third rope fell around his neck and jerked tight. He dropped the noose he was holding and grabbed the deadly loop, but it was too late. The long knife slipped from his fingers as the noose pulled tight, then tighter still. He heard an ocean roaring in his ears and saw a black wave rising up in front of him, to sweep down and tumble him into darkness.

In the darkness he heard voices. He opened his eyes to a world turned upside-down and realized that he'd been slung face down over his saddle and tied like a dead browzar. Other riders surrounded him, but he could only see the legs of men and horses both. The pain in his throat was a stab and a thirst all at once. Every step his horse took made his head throb.

'Sinyur Alayn, I think he's awake,' someone said in Vranz. 'Better let him sit up. Father Sharl won't be happy if he dies on the way.'

'That's true. Here, let's get him down.'

In a jingle of tack the bandits – or whoever they were – came to a halt. Zayn heard men dismounting; then hands lifted him down from the horse. As soon as his feet touched the ground his knees gave way; he staggered, then fell. Hands hauled him up to a sitting sprawl. A torch flared, and he could see hooded figures all around him. One knelt in front of him and held up a bottle.

'Drink this,' he said in Kazraki. 'It's not poison. It will help your throat.'

When he held up the bottle, Zayn drank from it. The thick liquid tasted bitter, but the pain in his throat did ease. When he tried to raise his hands, he found them bound in front of him. The man kneeling in front of him pulled off his hood.

'Hot in these things,' he remarked.

The torchbearer came closer, holding up – not a torch at all, but a long metal tube, pouring out light, similar to the one Ammadin had got from the ChaMeech. In its glare the blond man's face loomed, and the jewelled band round his head sent out long glints of glare like knives.

'Drink some more.' Soutan spoke Kazraki well. 'These idiots nearly crushed your windpipe.'

Zayn gulped down another mouthful of the acrid stuff. After a few attempts, he realized that he could talk, though his voice rasped and caught.

'Well, Soutan,' Zayn said. 'Looks like we've finally met.'

'Oh yes, all good things come to him who waits, or however that goes. How do you know who I am?'

'You were pointed out to me in Haz Kazrak. I doubt if you even realized it.'

Soutan shuddered, then got up and turned to the other men. 'He'll be able to ride now if you tie him to the saddle. We need to get back.'

'So we're agreed?' Ammadin said.

Sammador and Apanador said yes at the exact same moment, then laughed. They were sitting in Apanador's tent, passing round a bowl of keese to seal their bargain: the two comnees would ride as one while Ammadin rode her quest.

'That's a good omen, the way you answered in unison,' Kassidor said. 'I certainly agree. Now remember, Ammi, you've got to tell me everything you learn. Maybe you should take that servant of yours with you, if he's got such a good memory.'

'No, I think I'd best ride alone.'

With handshakes all round, the conference in Apanador's tent broke up. Ammadin and Kassidor walked across the meadow together in the pale light of the Herd. They said little; Ammadin was thinking of ways to tell Zayn that she'd not be riding back to the plains with the comnee. Someone called out. Maradin, flickering lamp in hand, came trotting to meet them.

'Ammi! Something's wrong. Zayn's gone.'

'He's what?'

'Gone! Dallo went to your tent to invite him over to our fire. He was gone, his gear was gone, and the sorrel's gone, too.'

'That rotten little gelding!' Ammadin burst out. 'Stealing one of my horses!'

'Ammi!' Maradin held up the lamp and cast light on both their faces. 'That sorcerer! He must have lured Zayn away somehow. Dallo's frantic.'

'It's possible,' Kassidor joined in. 'The Canton sorcerers have a lot of power at their command.'

'I think he left of his own free will.' Ammadin realized that she was close to snarling and paused for a long deep breath. 'He's been lying to me – or partly lying – ever since the day I brought him into camp. I'm beginning to see that those lies had something to do with the Cantons. He used us to get here, and now he's stolen a horse and ridden off.'

By this time Apanador and Sammador had caught up to them.

Ammadin left Maradin to explain and ran back to her tent. She looked through all her tent bags, half-expecting to find that Zayn had stolen something else.

'Ammadin! Please!' The voice belonged to Dallador, torn between rage and grief. 'Aren't you going to do anything?'

Ammadin opened the tent flap and stepped out to find a small crowd gathered. Dallador, Apanador, some of the other men, all stood waiting, and Kassidor hovered off to one side.

'We're better off without him,' Ammadin said.

'I don't see it that way.' Dallador tossed his head. 'Besides, I *can't* see it that way. We traded knives.'

Ammadin let out her breath in a long sigh. No matter what she thought of Zayn at the moment, Dallador and his bond-oaths were her responsibility.

'Oh all right!' she snapped. 'Light a fire. Make it a good bright one. Kasso, will you help me? We need to scan.'

Fortunately, the Riders still hung overhead. Once the fire was producing plenty of light, the two spirit riders knelt in front of it, each with their own scanning crystal.

'He must have ridden east, further into the Cantons,' Ammadin said. 'That's the way the sorcerer and the other Kazraks were riding.'

'We'll start here, then. I'll take north-east. You take east to the south.'

In the spirit language they summoned their spirits and sent them racing out over the dark landscape. They both talked aloud, telling each other what they were seeing, while Ammadin's comnee clustered together, a respectful distance away. At last, in the dark forest, a glint of yellow light caught her attention.

'A torch on the forest road,' she said to Kassidor. 'Start at your ten.'

'All right. I – yes, got it. Oh by the gods!'

Deep in the crystal Ammadin saw torchlight, illuminating a bridge, sparkling on a river. Men on horseback, one mounted man in their midst – something flew through the air. Magic? No, ropes! She saw Zayn, roped and struggling like a wild horse. Men surrounded him, he nearly slid away, they were choking him. She heard herself swear, caught her breath – at last they released the noose.

'He's still alive,' Kassidor whispered.

'Of course he is. They can't sacrifice a dead man to the old gods.'

He laid his crystal down on its pouch, then turned to look directly at her. 'Aggnavvachur?' he said.

'Who else, in that forest?'

Kassidor shuddered and got up to signal to the others. Ammadin laid her crystal out to feed on the firelight, then rose, listening to Kassidor tell the men what they'd seen. Apanador listened gravely, his fingers rubbing the hilt of his long knife, but Dallador – even in the uncertain light Ammadin could see him turn pale in cold rage.

'I'm riding after him,' Dallador said. 'Even if I have to ride alone.'

'Calm down, Dallo,' Apanador snapped. 'You won't be riding alone, and you know it. Get a warparty together and go after Zayn with the spirit riders. I'll go wake up the mayor. He hates these priests, or so I've heard, but we don't have time to let him do the riding for us. The women will load the wagons and strike camp. If you have to kill someone to rescue Zayn, so be it, but if you do, we'd better be ready to leave.'

When Dallador called for volunteers, both comnees responded. In fact, every man available would have ridden with him, but Apanador insisted that some remain behind to help the women pack up the camp. The warparty raced for the herd and began frantically saddling horses while Ammadin and Kassidor put their crystals away. Although Ammadin had thoughts of scanning again, she refused to risk killing a crystal over Zayn.

By the time they reached the bridge, the Herd had set. The dark line of the forest billowed against the darker sky, shot with the eerie glow of Death's Necklaces strung in the oak crowns. Finding a path in took time, while Dallador swore and chivvied the two spirit riders to hurry. Finally Kassidor recognized a path from their scanning. 'I'm pretty sure,' he said, 'that this is the one.'

'Well, we've got to start somewhere,' Ammadin said. 'Dallo, if you don't calm down I'm going to hit you over the head with something. It'll be sunrise soon, and the Riders will be back. We'll be able to scan again.'

'It could be too late by then,' Dallador growled.

'Just be quiet!' Ammadin turned her horse's head towards the path. 'Let's go.'

At sunrise, however, they found something they'd never

expected: a guide. In the pale grey light of dawn, they reached a fork in the path and paused their horses. Down one fork Ammadin saw some glimmery thing; she rode a few yards closer and realized that it was a white sphere similar to the one near the sleeping tower. She rode back to find Kassidor and Dallador arguing furiously while the others kept yelling at them to make up their minds. Grenidor let out a sudden yelp.

'What now?' Ammadin snapped, then turned in the saddle to look where he was pointing.

Ambling down the path marked by the white stone came an old man, pausing now and then to lean on the stick he carried. He was dressed in brown leggings and a dirty smock patched together from bits of different colours of cloth. He carried several misshapen sacks slung over his shoulders and some sort of bundle under one arm.

'Good morrow, Wise One,' he said. 'You and your men seem to be lost.'

'One of our own's been kidnapped. Can you help us? You look like the kind of man who knows more than he lets on.'

'Maybe so, maybe not,' the old man said with a half-toothless grin. 'But the spirit rider has sharp eyes. I haven't seen anyone riding by here, if that's what you mean.'

'Oh, they're well ahead of us in that forest by now. The man we're looking for is a Kazrak and a comnee man both, and I'm afraid that the priests of Aggnavvachur have taken him.'

The old man swore under his breath in Vranz. 'I've met your friend,' he went on. 'A polite fellow, too polite for a nasty end like that. He was looking for Soutan the sorcerer if I remember rightly.'

'Soutan's behind this, one way or the other. He's been trying to kill Zayn all summer.'

'Really?' The old man's eyebrows rose to a peak, then dropped. 'Well, you know, if Soutan's involved, I think I'll just travel with you a little ways. I have some idea of where the temple stands, not that I'm going to go anywhere near it.'

'That's fine.' Dallador leaned over his horse's neck. 'Just show us the right road, and we'll do whatever else needs doing.'

For the rest of the night Zayn's captors led him through the forest. As his head cleared, he tried to watch for landmarks along the route, but the narrow paths twisted and branched in a pattern too intricate to untangle. By the time the dawn light penetrated the forest canopy, he was hopelessly lost – not that he was going to let his confusion keep him from trying to escape. Once among the sheltering trees, his captors pulled off their hoods and revealed themselves as Cantonneurs, led by a red-haired young man who rode next to Soutan.

Dawn was turning into morning when they reached the clearing and the compound of wood and vine buildings behind a thorn-hedge fence. As they rode through the gate, Zayn saw a bald man, dressed in a short black smock over leggings, standing in front of the largest building. His captors dismounted and led their horses – and Zayn – over to him.

'Here he is, Father Sharl,' the red-haired fellow said. 'Safe and sound. For now.'

Father Sharl laughed. The crust of growths round his mouth bobbed and quivered. 'Yes,' he said. 'For now. The ladies in the congregation are going to enjoy watching this one squirm, aren't they?' He raised one hand and saluted Zayn in the Kazraki manner. 'Welcome, oh blessed one of the gods. You have come to your haven. You have come to gain a glory greater than any on earth. Blessed be your name, and you will live in splendour for the ages of ages. Or that's what I tell them during the service, anyway. You're the one who's going to see if it's true or not.'

Zayn's ankles were tied to the stirrups only. He kicked out sideways and nearly caught Father Sharl in the chest. The priest ducked back and spun out of the way.

'I'm not as old as I look,' Sharl said, then turned to the redhead. 'Alayn, cut him down, will you? Let's bring him inside to meet the god.'

Zayn's stomach twisted in dread. Two of his captors brought him down, but they left his hands bound in front of him. Sharl and Soutan led the way, while the others surrounded Zayn and marched him into the temple. Morning sun streamed through the windows and lent some of its light to the dais at the far end, enough for Zayn to see the altar. Glittering next to the blood gutter on the stone lay a long bronze knife.

The priests burst out chanting – a deep, rumbling sound that rose and fell in a broken rhythm. They dragged Zayn up the steps and to the front of the altar, then forced him to kneel by kicking him in the back of one knee. This close, he could see the streaks of dried blood on the altar stone. Behind it loomed an oily green statue of a ChaMeech, haunched and holding a spear.

'Aggnavvachur,' Zayn whispered.

'You'll meet the old boy tonight,' Father Sharl said, grinning. 'In the darkest hour, being as my congregation only comes here when no one can see them arriving.'

Zayn looked at the long bronze knife and began to calculate if he could spring forward and grab it. When he glanced around, he saw that the red-head – Sinyur Alayn, he assumed – had his sword out and ready, and that the three younger priests had fanned out in a semi-circle, ringing him. Apparently this cult had seen other victims become sceptical about the glory ahead of them. Soutan seemed to have gone off somewhere, but a side door opened, and he returned, leading two Kazraks, Warkannan and a beaky young man that Zayn recognized as his nephew.

'Let's have a look at him,' Idres was saying. 'Is he in here?'

'Oh yes,' Soutan said. 'In front of the altar.'

Warkannan strode over, stepped through the half-circle of guards, and stopped so fast he nearly tripped. For a long moment he stared, simply stared, his lips half-parted.

'This would be funny,' Zayn said in Kazraki, 'if it weren't going to be fatal.'

Warkannan swallowed heavily, started to speak, glanced at Soutan, at the priests, and finally found his voice at last. 'No. Not you, Zahir,' he said. 'There must be some mistake.'

It was such a perfect Idres remark that Zayn did laugh, a chuckle on the edge of hysteria. He choked it back while Warkannan went on staring at him.

'No mistake,' Zayn said at last. 'I'm the man the Chosen sent, all right, but just to learn something about Yarl Soutan. We didn't know about Jezro Khan then, and come to think of it, probably no one else but me does now.'

'Zahir.' Warkannan took a deep breath. 'Why?'

'Why what? Why did I join the Chosen?'

Warkannan nodded.

'It's a long story, and I don't think I have the time to tell you. Do me a favour. Kill me clean, will you? Don't let the priests hack at me. That knife looks dull.'

'This is ridiculous!' Warkannan burst out. 'Soutan, talk to these damned priests. They've got to let Benumar go.'

'What?' Soutan stepped forward, his voice rising in alarm. 'You can't do that! We've got to protect the khan.'

'Don't be stupid! Benumar's not going to harm Jezro.'

'Besides,' Soutan went on as if he hadn't heard. 'They'll demand another sacrifice to put in his place. Your nephew, probably – the khan needs both me and you, after all.'

Warkannan's face drained to ashy grey. He raised his hands and rubbed his eyes, then turned back to Zahir. 'Why?' he said again.

'Why do you even want to know?' Out of the corner of his eye Zayn could see that Alayn had lowered his sword. He let his voice fade, as if he were so exhausted that he could barely speak. 'I've dishonoured myself, I've betrayed you, I was hunting down the khan. For God's sake, just let them kill me, will you? It's better all round if they do.'

Warkannan sighed sharply and shook his head. Soutan laid a hand on his arm. The priests turned towards this argument in a tongue they couldn't understand. Zayn lunged up from his kneel and grabbed the knife from the altar. He had to clutch it awkwardly in his bound hands, and before he could swing it at Alayn, the priests grabbed him from behind. Calmly, in dead-silence, they wrestled him around with the strength born of long practice. Zayn kicked out, broke free, and lunged at Sharl, who lurched to one side and fell. His sword reversed, Alayn rushed over. Zayn tried to dodge, but the heavy sword hilt struck a glancing blow on the side of his head. Alayn had judged his force precisely. Zayn fell, dazed but still conscious and alive. A young priest snatched the knife from his hands.

'Take him away,' Sharl snarled. 'Lock him in the holding cell.'

The young priests surrounded him, lifted him up, and hauled him off. A door behind the altar proved to lead to a stairway. As they started to climb, Zayn looked back and caught one glimpse of Idres, watching with his face twisted in honest anguish.

'Let me see if I've got this right.' Soutan's voice dripped sarcasm. 'You want to let Benumar go and ruin everything.'

'Shut up!' Warkannan snarled. 'You'll get your damned crystals, don't worry. I won't insist on taking your trade goods away.'

'It's not just the crystals.' Soutan came close to shouting, then calmed himself. 'Captain, please! I know you're upset, but I am telling you the exact truth when I say that we cannot cheat Sharl out of his victim without giving him another one. He'd never let us leave here alive if we tried.'

'I suppose I believe that.'

'Damn you! It's true.' Soutan leaned forward, his eyes wide, his hands shaking. 'Why do you think Alayn's two men are still here? Alayn would have sent them home if it weren't for you talking about sparing Benumar. Sharl knows enough Kazraki to figure that out.'

'All right, I believe you,' Warkannan said. 'Let's see, there's the three young priests, Sharl himself, and then Alayn and his pair of bodyguards. Then there's me and Arkazo. I don't much like those odds.'

Soutan made a gargling noise deep in his throat. His face had gone pale and sweaty.

'I'm trying to tell you why I'm not going to start a fight,' Warkannan said. 'Get control of yourself! The khan needs us, and you know I'd never risk harming Arkazo, either.'

Soutan sighed and wiped his face on his sleeve. They were sitting in the guest house, watching Arkazo pack up their gear. The boy's shoulders were set, his mouth twisted in a hard line.

'Kaz?' Warkannan said. 'I'll pack if you don't want to.'

'No, I'll do it.' Arkazo paused, though, and turned to look at him. 'I wanted to kill Zayn. I want revenge for Tareev's death. You know that. But may merciful God forgive me, not like this!'

'Good for you.'

Arkazo shrugged and went back to work. Warkannan stood up. 'I'm going to go talk with Zahir,' Warkannan said. 'I won't let him out of his cage, don't worry. But I've got to talk with him, now that I've had a chance to think of what I want to say.'

'I'll come along and explain things to Father Sharl.' Soutan rose and joined him at the door. 'Kaz, I'll be right back, unless Sharl tries to wiggle out of our bargain. Then I'll have to stay and argue.'

Arkazo nodded and concentrated on stuffing a shirt into one of the packs. Warkannan hesitated, but he could think of nothing to say that would be a comfort. With a shake of his head he followed Soutan out.

Only later did it occur to him that Soutan had used Arkazo's nickname.

* * *

Zayn had been expecting some sort of filthy cell, but Alayn's men threw him onto a bed in a small room up above the temple. One of them cut his hands free while another stood guard with raised sword. They walked out backwards, watching him all the while. The young priest slid a barred grate over the doorway, locked it, then stepped back and slammed shut an outer door, made of true-wood. Zayn heard locks snap there, too.

With a grunt of pain Zayn sat up and examined his aching wrists. Red bruises, bloody where the skin had rubbed away under the bindings, ran next to and over the old scars that the ChaMeech had given him. His hands prickled and stung. When he tried to stand, he nearly fell. His head throbbed. He perched on the edge of the bed and began shaking his arms to get the blood flowing into his hands.

Sunlight came through a barred window and cast a pattern of stripes on the red and gold carpet. On the walls hung tapestries of geometric designs in blue and white. A silver pitcher of water and a silver cup stood on a small table, inlaid with mother of pearl. Either the priests wanted their sacrifices to leave life with pleasant memories or they used this room themselves at times. He suspected the latter. Once his hands had recovered their feeling, Zayn poured himself water, hesitated, then drank. He was too thirsty to worry about possible drugs, and the water tasted sweet enough. It helped settle his head; he poured more, tried standing, and found he could walk if he did it slowly.

Cup in hand, he went to the window, which proved to be some twenty feet above the ground. He could see the buildings of the compound, a priest strolling across the lawn in the sunlight, and then the dark encircling forest, rising up higher than his prison. Above, the sun shone in a clear sky. The dark hours of the night, or so the priest had said, would see his death. He had a while yet to figure some way out.

Zayn was just finishing a third cup of water when the outer door swung open. Warkannan stood behind the grate, a nervous Sharl at his elbow.

'Come to say farewell?' Zayn said. 'One last curse before we part?'

'Stop it, Zahir!' Warkannan snapped. 'This is no time for your stupid jokes. Do you think I like this?'

'No, of course I don't.'

'Good. I came to apologize. No man should have to die like this, least of all you. I'm sorry.'

It was so like Idres, that apology. Zayn turned away and with some effort managed to set the cup down. His hands were shaking again.

'I should apologize to you,' Zayn said. 'Idres –'

'Don't! Just tell me why.'

Zayn walked over to the grate and held out his hand.

'A bargain,' Zayn said. 'I'll tell you why if you answer my question.'

Warkannan reached through the bars and clasped his hand. 'Fair,' he said. 'Go on and ask it.'

They shook hands, then stepped back apart.

'Are you going to try to put Jezro on the throne?' Zayn said.

'Of course. You don't need me to tell you that.'

'True enough. So you're taking him to Andjaro, right? You'll have no trouble raising troops there.'

Warkannan nodded, staring at his face as if he could read secrets upon it. 'The most peculiar thing about this,' Warkannan said, 'is that I wanted to find you. Back home, I mean, when I heard that Jezro was alive. I figured you'd want to join us.'

Zayn winced. 'It's a good thing you didn't.'

'A good thing? For us, yes, but I'm surprised you'd see it that way.'

'You know something? So am I. You know something else? I'm the reason you weren't arrested. My officers – they asked me about you. I told them that you were the last man on earth to turn traitor. Guess I was wrong.'

For a moment Zayn thought Idres would break down and weep.

'Gemet turned traitor long before I did,' Warkannan said at last. 'He murdered his own brothers. He's betrayed every precept the Prophets ever laid down for a ruler. And now he's bleeding the common people white. I can't stand for that.'

'You, from your family? Worrying about farmers and shopkeepers?'

'The family doesn't come into it. I'll tell you something, Zahir. You're the one who taught me to respect the so-called common people. After I got to know you, I had to change my ideas about who was worthy of what.'

Zayn winced and looked away.

'Gemet's done a good many more disgusting things than we have time to list,' Warkannan went on. 'You know it as well as I do.'

'Including using the Chosen? Well, in a little while there'll be one fewer of us for you to worry about.'

'If I had the slightest bit of choice, I'd never leave you here. Do you believe me?'

'Yes, I do, actually.'

Father Sharl grabbed Warkannan's sleeve as if to break into the conversation. Warkannan shook the hand off and gave him a look of such contempt that Sharl backed away.

'All right, it's my turn for the question,' Warkannan said. 'Why, Zahir? In the holy name of God! Why would you let yourself get sucked into that slimy pack of paid informers?'

'God comes into it, all right, or at least His mullahs. Now, how do I put this?'

Warkannan crossed his arms over his chest and waited.

'You know about the forbidden talents, don't you?' Zayn began. 'The twelve times twelve demon-spawn talents?'

'Yes, who doesn't?'

'Well, I carry them, or some of them, I should say. They're the mark of the Chosen Ones. Everyone thinks the name means chosen by the Great Khan, but no, that's not it. We were chosen by Iblis, or so they told me.'

Warkannan grimaced at the mention of that evil name. 'Your memory,' he said. 'That damned phenomenal memory of yours.'

'That's one of them, yes. And damned is the right word.'

'I – no, go on.'

'Do you know how it feels,' Zayn continued, 'realizing you're unclean, an affront to God, someone who by rights should have been smothered the day he was born? Do you know what it's like to live with a secret like that?' He started to shake again, whether from anger or fear he couldn't tell. 'Always hiding, always lying, always sick to your guts with fear! I would have been killed if my father had allowed it. He used to threaten me with it, too. Burned alive. Can you imagine it, Idres, being eight years old and terrified of burning alive?'

'Not really.' Warkannan spoke so softly that he was hard to hear. 'But in the abstract I can understand. Are you telling me that every man in the Chosen –'

'Every single one of us. We're all marked by some forbidden talent.' All of a sudden it became hard to breathe. Zayn forced his voice on. 'We're all demon spawn, or so we were told, anyway. We know what it's like to lie and live lies and have no choice but lies. That's why we're all so good at what we do. When we were children, we all thought we were the only one, too, the one and only damned little soul in the whole saved world.' Zayn paused, searching for words. He found it bizarrely difficult to think, but then, he reminded himself, he'd just been concussed. 'And then years later we found out we weren't the only one. They offered me a place in a legion of the damned. Why wouldn't I enlist?'

'I see. I mean that, I do see.' Warkannan's voice choked. 'No wonder you were such a hard man to befriend.'

'Yes. I had to be. Are you sorry now you –'

'No! Don't be an idiot, Zahir.' Warkannan paused for a long moment. Tears were running down his face. 'I'm just sorry that – well, that things have worked out like this.'

'So am I. Believe me, so am I.'

Warkannan raised his arm and wiped his face on his sleeve. 'I'll pray for you,' he said. 'I can't believe that God would condemn anyone to Hell for something they were born with.'

'Don't you? I know He can. I've lived with it for years.'

'No!' Warkannan stepped forward. 'There's something very wrong here. I don't care what they told you. The Lord is the all merciful, the compassionate. What do you think? that He'd pull wings off yellabuhs to watch them crawl?'

Zayn felt his head start throbbing again, a regular pulse of pain. In his ears something was hissing, bubbling like water boiling in a kettle. 'No,' Zayn could barely speak. 'I don't suppose He would.'

'Then ask yourself why He'd treat you worse. Ask yourself if He'd torture children the way you were tortured. They lied to you, Zahir – the Chosen, I mean. For the love of God, please, think about it. They had to have been lying to you.'

'Oh? The mullahs said the same thing, you know. Long before I'd even heard of the Chosen.'

'Then the mullahs were wrong, and God will make them pay for it, one fine day.'

The hissing turned to a roar like water drowning the world. Zayn could barely see Warkannan's face, swimming beyond the bars.

'I don't know,' Zayn whispered. 'I can't believe in your god.'

'Then I'll pray for you doubly.' Warkannan's voice cracked. He turned on his heel and walked away.

The priest slammed the outer door shut. Zayn took one step and fell to his knees. He sat down on the carpet, merely sat for a long while, staring at the door beyond the bars. The pain in his head slackened off, and the boiling hiss first receded, then vanished, from his hearing. When he tried standing, he found his balance back to normal.

For a long time Zayn stood at the window and stared out at the forest, but in his mind he was seeing fog and water, lapping around the island in the Mistlands. Once again he saw the image of himself grown old and empty, a husk of a man floating through his double life. He was going to be spared that fate, at least. Maybe it was better to die now than to end up drifting like a ghost through what was left of a life that never should have been lived. Maybe God was merciful in some ways, anyway. All at once he realized that he couldn't remember what Idres had been telling him, except, vaguely, that it had something to do with God's mercy.

'Alayn must have hit me harder than I thought.'

Outside, the sunlight was dancing on green trees, impossibly beautiful, all of a sudden, impossibly beyond his reach. Someone was leading horses across the green lawn. He turned sideways in order to watch this simple moment, when men who were going to live led horses into the sunlight. Men – it was Warkannan and Soutan, and the nephew, ready to ride out, leading pack horses, leaving the temple behind. He should have known that Idres would refuse to watch him die.

Others joined them, Alayn's two bodyguards as far as he could tell, but he didn't see the red-haired sinyur among them. Most likely Alayn was going to stay and enjoy the ceremony. From the way Warkannan was gesturing and pointing, it was clear that he'd taken charge of everybody, and that they were obeying his orders, just as most men did obey Idres when he set his mind to it. Zayn watched as they mounted up. He stayed at the window until the little caravan disappeared among the trees.

Zayn left the window and lay down on the bed. The pillow was hard and scant; he grabbed it and shook it to soften it. With a waft of perfume a pale brown hair fell from the covering. He caught it, dropped the pillow, and stretched out the hair – long, very long, most likely a woman's. He decided that he wouldn't wonder what these so-called priests had done to her before her death. He threw the pillow onto the floor and lay down without it.

His head throbbed, he ached with the bruises his capture had given him, but above all, he felt drained of all life, all feeling. He fell asleep to dream of his initiation into the Chosen and the tall pillar, a single crystal of quartz, a pale blue quartz. Some sort of light glowed inside, points of light, pale fire rippling in its depths. They'd bound him to it – it stood taller than he did – and administered their oath of silence with a crystal knife held at the side of his throat.

Crystals. Ammadin. She stood by a fire, swearing at him for stealing one of her horses. You're one of us now, she said. Why did you sneak off like that? She held up a scanning crystal. Deep inside it he saw a tiny image of himself, riding through the night. Suddenly he found himself awake and sitting up. Very real, that dream, so real – for the first time it occurred to him that Ammadin could find him if she wanted to. He felt a surge of hope, as palpable as a shudder of sexual desire, that drove him onto his feet and to the window.

Heat shimmered on the empty lawn. The lie of the shadows told him that he'd slept till afternoon. Awake, Zayn saw no reason why Ammadin would want to rescue him, unless perhaps to retrieve the sorrel gelding. He felt himself start shaking again, and cold sweat ran down his back. He gripped the windowsill with both hands and considered the second thought that came to him: he didn't want to die. After all those years of playing games with Death, Death was finally going to win, just when he'd decided he wanted to live.

'Now listen,' he told himself aloud. 'It'll be quick. You've never been a coward before, and you're not going to die like one.'

The sound of his own steady voice reassured him. He knew he could face it when the time came, just as he'd faced the flogging down in Blosk. No doubt this would hurt a good bit less. He went to the table and poured himself more water. Judging from the position of the sun, he had only a few more hours before the priests came for him. He sat down on the bed and stared out at nothing.

The sun was hanging low in the sky when he heard the sound. At first he thought he was imagining it out of simple despair: hoofbeats, and someone yelling a couple of words in Hirl-Onglay. Yet the sound came closer, grew louder. Zayn ran for the window in time to see mounted riders erupt out of the forest and swirl around the temple. Comnee men. Zayn saw Father Sharl run out, hands up in supplication, but two men swung themselves off their horses and grabbed him. Over the yelling, screaming mob, Zayn couldn't hear what the old man was saying, but he could guess it was curses.

'Oh my God!' Zayn said. 'Saved.'

He tossed back his head and laughed like a maniac, then swung around. Footsteps were pounding up the stairs outside his door, and it was too soon for them to belong to his rescuers. The outer door swung open; a priest began wrestling one-handed with the lock on the iron grate. He held the long bronze knife in the other hand, and right behind him stood Alayn with his drawn sword at the ready.

'You're not going to be giving evidence,' the priest snarled. 'Not against us!'

The priest swung the grate open and rushed in with Alayn right behind him. Zayn picked up the flimsy silver cup and hurled it straight at his head. With a yelp the priest ducked, then lunged, brandishing the knife. Zayn grabbed the pitcher in one hand and swung it up, throwing the water straight into his attacker's eyes, then hurled the pitcher after it. The manoeuvre bought him a split second, long enough to grab the priest's arm. Zayn swung him around like a shield, slammed him from behind, and forced his chest onto Alayn's naked blade. With a scream, the priest arched backward as the sword bit deep. Howling with rage, Alayn pulled the blade free. Zayn grabbed the bronze knife and thrust the dying man straight at Alayn, who staggered back to the doorway from the force of the dead weight. Alayn shoved the corpse to the ground, then glared at him, panting for breath. His pale eyes glittered as he stepped over the corpse, then paused, listening.

Muffled voices were shouting in the shrine below.

'Dallo!' Zayn yelled at the top of his lungs. 'Dallo, up the stairs.'

Zayn heard footsteps pounding, but Alayn heard them too. Swearing under his breath, he charged, the blade flashing. Zayn caught it on the bronze knife. For a moment they struggled; then the bronze snapped under the steel. Zayn leapt, dropped, rolled and kicked out with both legs. His feet slammed into Alayn's knees and knocked them both to the floor. As he fell, Alayn lashed out with the sword and nearly caught Zayn across the face. Zayn rolled again and found himself up against the wall. Alayn scrambled to his knees and raised the sword in both hands, ready to slice down with all his strength.

With a howl of rage Dallador appeared in the doorway and threw his long knife. It tumbled end over end in a glitter of caught light and sank its point into Alayn's face. Alayn screamed and fell back, dropping the sword, screamed over and over while his hands pawed at his face. The long knife had bitten deep into his right eye. Dallador ran in and grabbed the sword. He held it two-handed and high, then plunged it into Alayn's throat. The sinyur's body twisted, writhed, and lay still.

Zayn clambered to his feet and stood panting for breath. Dallador knelt on one knee, looked at Alayn's face, and turned so pale that Zayn thought he might vomit. Instead he pulled the long knife free, shook himself once, then wiped the blade off on the hem of Alayn's smock. He rose, sheathing the knife in one smooth motion, and turned towards Zayn.

'I'm damned glad you called for me,' Dallador said.

'So am I,' Zayn said. 'Somehow I figured you'd be here.'

More footsteps came pounding up the stairs. 'Dallo!' Grenidor yelled. 'Are you in there? Where's Zayn?'

'In here!' Zayn called out.

Long knife in hand, Grenidor ran into the room, then stopped, staring at the bodies on the floor.

'Oh gods!' Grenno blurted. 'You've killed a priest.'

'And a sinyur, too,' Dallador said. 'We'd better get out of here.'

'Dallo, listen.' Zayn laid a hand on his arm. 'Let me take the blame. I killed that stinking priest, so outside the comnee, let's just say that I killed Alayn too. They can only hang me once if it comes to that.'

'It's not going to come to that even if we have to fight our way back through the Rift,' Dallador said. 'I'm not going to let you take the blame for my kill.'

'Don't be a fool!' Grenidor broke in. 'You've got a child to think about.'

'Yes, you do,' Zayn said. 'And a wife.'

Dallador hesitated, then nodded his agreement. They hurried down the twisting dark stairway and came out into the shrine.

Four comnee men were standing in front of the altar. Sitting on the steps of the dais were the other two young priests with their hands and ankles bound. The side door swung open. Kassidor strode in, and behind him Orador and another man were dragging Father Sharl, bound hand and foot as well. They threw him down on the steps next to his assistants. Orador turned to Zayn and held up a long knife.

'Yours, I believe?' Orador said, grinning.

'It is, and thanks.' Zayn took it and sheathed it. 'Where did you find it?'

'On the belt he's wearing.' Orador pointed at Sharl. 'That stack of horseshit shaped like a man.'

'Isn't this something?' Kassidor said. 'Charlador turns up at last, and he's still no damned good for anything on this earth.' He glanced at Zayn. 'He was a spirit rider once, back when I was a child. We were all hoping he was dead, but we weren't lucky enough.'

Sharl hauled himself up to a sitting position. Hatred burned in his eyes and set his grotesque mouth quivering.

'All right, renegade,' Kassidor went on. 'You'd better hope that some of your ever-so-civilized friends find you before you die of thirst.'

Sharl started to speak, then stopped himself.

'You should have known better than to kidnap a comnee man,' Zayn said to Sharl. 'But don't worry. I killed Aggnavvachur a sacrifice. Sinyur Alayn is dead.'

Sharl snarled and spat straight at Zayn's face. The drops fell short.

'Let's go,' Kassidor snapped. 'Their god can come rescue them if he wants.'

Kassidor, Grenidor, and the rest ran down the long room and headed out. In his exhaustion Zayn followed slowly and Dallador stayed with him. Just inside the temple doorway Dallador paused; his face had gone pale again.

'What's wrong?' Zayn said.

'That was a shit ugly way to kill a man.'

'I'm sorry you –'

'Don't apologize!'

'All right.' Zayn flung his arm around Dallador's shoulders and pulled him close. For a moment Dallador let himself rest against him, sharing warmth, sharing strength. Zayn was tempted to kiss him, but Dallador stepped away, turning to look out. He shaded his eyes with one hand to study the crowd outside.

'What arc –' Zayn said.

'Wondering where the spirit rider is,' Dallador said. 'Huh! She's probably looking for the sorrel gelding.'

'She's going to want my hide for taking him.'

'She said something along those lines.' Dallador turned to him and managed a smile. 'But you'll live through it.'

'I'll even enjoy it. It'll mean I'm not dead. You know, I never thanked you.'

'No need. We've got to get out of here fast. That sinyur keeps paid soldiers at home, and they might be coming back for him.'

Outside, the rest of the comnee men had spread out across the lawn, some to hold the horses, others ready for possible trouble. Kassidor and Orador stood together, talking urgently.

'There's Ammi.' Dallador pointed across the compound. 'She's found the sorrel.'

Zayn saw Ammadin leading the gelding, which she'd saddled and bridled. She was heading right for them. Her mouth was set in a tight line of fury, her face was smudged with dirt, but to Zayn she looked more beautiful than ever. All his old desire for her was still alive – the realization shocked him, that he could stand next to Dallador and yet realize how much a woman meant to him. For a moment he had such trouble forming a coherent thought that he felt as if he'd drunk himself into a near-stupor. Dallador muttered something cowardly and trotted off, leaving Zayn face-to-face and alone with Ammadin. When she threw the horse's reins at him, he caught them in one hand. The sorrel tossed its head and snorted as if it were glad to see him.

'Spirit Rider,' Zayn began, 'I'm sorry –'

'You should be,' Ammadin said. 'You're going to tell me the truth when we get back, Zayn. And I mean every last word of it.'

'Anything you want. You know something? I never thought you'd come after me.'

'You idiot! What do you think being a comnee man means?'

'I didn't understand before. I do now.'

'Good. Try to remember it from now on.' She suddenly frowned. 'Why are you looking at me like that?'

'I never thought I'd see you again, and you're beautiful.'

'Oh, stop it!' Ammadin took a deep breath, as if she were stocking up plenty of air to list his sins.

Kassidor, however, saved him. Just as Ammadin was launching into a tirade, Kassidor called her name and, with a couple of men in tow, came running up.

'There you are, Ammi,' he said. 'Charlador's inside. He was the man in charge here.'

'Oh was he?' Ammadin's voice went flat and cold.

'Yes, he made a point of telling me when he was trying to make me let him go. Is there anything you want to say to him before we ride?'

'Say?' Ammadin blinked rapidly. 'Not precisely.' Ammadin turned on her heel and headed for the temple. Zayn flung the sorrel's reins to one of the comnee men and hurried after her, as did Kassidor. They caught up with her as she was striding down the aisle, heading for the dais, where the three so-called priests sat flopped like fish on the riverbank. Sharl started to speak, then let the words fade. Ammadin stopped in front of him and looked him over for a long hard minute. He scowled, let that fade, started to speak again, stopped, then slowly went pale. The growths stood out, lurid against his sweaty white skin.

'Zayn?' Ammadin said. 'Come here.'

When Zayn joined her, she turned and pulled the long knife from the sheath on his belt before he was truly aware of what she'd done. Sharl screamed, twisting this way and that, and flung himself off the steps in his desperation. Ammadin knelt beside him. In one smooth motion she shoved her left hand flat against his forehead and pinned his head to the floor. With the other hand she cut his throat. Blood sprayed, soaking his smock, dappling her face, but she neither flinched nor spoke. My God, she's strong! Zayn thought. She cleaned the knife on his trouser leg, handed it back to Zayn, then wiped her face on her shirt sleeve.

'Let's go,' she said to Kassidor. 'The other two, they're no concern of ours.'

As they all hurried out, Zayn glanced back. One of the young priests was sobbing; the other, white-faced, sat as still as the idol behind him.

'Ammadin?' Zayn said. 'Why –'

'He was a renegade, but he was still a comnee man. We're all responsible if one of our own does something criminal. Now save your breath. We've got to get out of here.'

Zayn reminded himself to wash the knife first chance he got and followed her outside.

When, earlier in the day, Warkannan had led his caravan out of the temple compound, Soutan had found them a winding dirt path that led more or less east. A scant mile along, they came to a fork, and there Alayn's men left them. As they trotted off, one turned in the saddle and shouted something back.

'He says the other path will take us to the Burgunee road,' Soutan said.

'Can we trust them?' Warkannan said.

'Of course. They've sworn their loyalty to Alayn, and we're his friends.'

'They have more honour than me, then.'

'Captain, are you still fretting over Benumar?'

'Fretting? No, I'm not fretting. I'm sick to my guts over it. May God forgive me, but I wish I could go back and –'

'You can't!' Soutan's voice rose to a squeal.

'I know that.' Warkannan took a deep breath and steadied himself. 'Let's get out of this forest, shall we? I've come to hate it.'

'On that we agree.' Soutan managed a sickly smile. 'Forward!'

By mid-afternoon the path had brought them free of the trees and back to the east-running road. Farmland stretched out on either side, peaceful and bright in the sunlight, fields of gold wheatian striped with red and orange fields of vegetables. Now and then they passed a windbreak of true-oaks, sheltering white-washed houses and red barns.

An hour before sunset, Warkannan called a halt. He and Arkazo needed to make their evening prayers, and Soutan announced that he wanted to scan. Warkannan asked Arkazo to hold his horse, then knelt in the dust of the road. Ordinary prayers wouldn't do, he decided, not with Zahir's soul hanging in the balance. Words came hard. He could only mutter, 'Dear God, please!' over and over. God would know what he meant, he decided, or so at least he could hope.

All at once, Soutan shrieked, howling in rage. Warkannan finished with a hasty word, then leapt to his feet. At the side of the road the sorcerer was sitting on a strip of purple grass and staring into his crystal. Soutan's lips moved, but he made no sound, and his head trembled, shaking in a silent no no no.

'What is it?' Warkannan snapped.

'I don't know,' Arkazo said.

'Soutan!'

The sorcerer looked up, his face dead pale. 'I cannot believe this,' he whispered. 'The comnee. They're in the compound. They've taken over the temple.'

Warkannan tensed in a surge of hope. Soutan stared at the crystal again and whimpered.

'They've got him,' Soutan went on. 'I just saw them bringing Zayn outside.' He looked up, pale, his mouth half-open as if he were too weary to close it.

Warkannan flung his arms into the air and stared up at the blue dome of the sky. He wanted to speak, could not, but he felt his heart overflow with gratitude towards God, who had His own ways of working mercy. 'Thank you,' he whispered; then his voice choked.

'Warkannan, what are you doing?' Soutan was shrieking again. 'You're glad, aren't you? How can you! This murderous little bastard is going to try to kill the khan.'

'He can try all he wants,' Warkannan said. 'I don't intend to let him.'

Scowling, Soutan got up, clutching his crystal in both hands. Warkannan stared at him until Soutan looked away with a muttered curse.

'Ah well,' Soutan said. 'I have to admit that I'm hoping they've killed Father Sharl. At least that would be something to the good.'

'And you've got the crystals,' Arkazo said.

'Yes.' Soutan's smile was so joyful that it almost seemed innocent. 'Four very good crystals indeed.'

They had all been in the saddle for half a night and most of a day, and the horses were dangerously weary, yet Ammadin and Kassidor agreed that they could never camp safely in that forest. When the warparty left the compound, they dismounted and led their stumbling-tired stock to spare the horses their weight. Once night fell, they might well have lost the trail if it weren't for Water Woman's gift of the lightwand. Ammadin used it only when they came to a fork or some other ambiguity in the path, both to save the spirit's energy and to avoid attracting attention, should Sinyur Alayn's men be close enough to see it.

'I don't know what we're going to do when we reach open country,' Ammadin said to Kassidor.

'I don't either.' Kassidor paused, thinking. 'But we'll never get back to Nannes if we don't stop to sleep for a few hours.'

Yet when at last they reached the open meadows, they found that safety had come to them. The comnees had left Nannes and set up a camp about a mile east of the forest edge. When they saw the tents Kassidor nearly wept in relief, and the warparty cheered aloud, a peal of noise that woke the comnees. People streamed out to cheer at the sight of Zayn and greet the men who'd gone to the rescue. The women surged forward to take the weary horses and lead them away.

'Listen, Zayn,' Ammadin said. 'You go straight back to the tent and wait for me there.'

'Anything you say.' Zayn was looking around him in a kind of exhausted wonder. 'I never thought I'd see the comnee again, either.'

Ammadin and Kassidor went looking for the two chiefs and found them in Apanador's tent. Exhausted though they were, the two spirit riders managed to tell them about the rescue in a reasonably coherent way by taking turns at it. Sammador said nothing, deferring to the older chief, who asked questions now and again.

'Since Zayn killed a chief's son, we'd better ride back west,' Ammadin finished up. 'I don't want the zhundars coming after Zayn to hang him.'

'Yes, it's bound to cause trouble,' Apanador said. 'If the zhundars don't try to catch him, the sinyur's men will.'

'Then we'd better guard the camp tonight,' Kassidor put in. 'You're right, and tomorrow we'll get on the way early. If the sinyur's men come, we'll fight, of course, but the less blood spilled the better.'

'Zayn told us that seven men took him on the road,' Ammadin said, 'but some of them were priests. Alayn may have had more men back in his fort, of course.'

'Why did Zayn ride away like that?' Apanador said. 'Was he ensorcelled?'

'I doubt it. I intend to make him tell me right now, and then we can decide what to do next. Kasso, do me a favour, will you? Find Dallador and ask him to get another man and stand guard at my tent. If Zayn tries to run, they'll be there to stop him.'

Ammadin went back to her tent to find the saurskin panels glowing with light. On the hearth stone under the smokehole two lamps burned. Beside them Zayn was sitting on the floor cloth and looking through his saddlebags, rescued along with the sorrel gelding from the temple stable. When she came in, he began to tie them shut. Ammadin sat down opposite him.

'I've been thinking,' Zayn said. 'I've brought nothing but trouble to the comnee. You should just let me ride off alone. If they kill me, well, so what? It's better than having some of the other men die to defend me. I'll just leave the camp and ride off somewhere. Then, if anyone catches up with the comnee, I won't be there, and they'll leave you alone.'

'You know something? I'm as sick as I can be of you lying to me.'

Zayn threw his head up like a startled horse.

'You've been lying to me for months,' Ammadin went on. 'Not exactly lying, maybe, but bending the truth. Yes, of course, it would be best for the comnee if you were gone, but that's not why you're offering. It wasn't why you crept out of camp last night, either.'

Zayn winced and looked away.

'Kassidor thinks the sorcerer lured you away,' Ammadin said. 'I don't. Answer me. Did you feel him attacking your mind?'

'No.' Zayn kept staring at the tent wall.

'Then why? Who are you, Zayn? I'll bet you were never the cavalry officer you seemed to be. Why do you want to leave us? Don't you think you owe me and the comnee the truth?'

Zayn went tense, and his eyes flicked towards the tent flap.

'If you try to run,' Ammadin said, 'you won't get far. Dallador's out there on guard. Now answer me.'

Zayn took a deep breath, swallowing his anger, she assumed. He looked away, thought for a moment, then nodded, as if he had agreed with himself about something.

'You do deserve to know,' he said. 'But I really was a cavalry officer. I mean, I still am. The flogging, turning me out – that was all false. I belong to –' he hesitated briefly, 'I belong to a brotherhood called the Chosen Ones. Have you ever heard of us?'

'No.' Ammadin could smell that he was telling the truth. 'Should I have?'

'Not really. It's only the khanate that concerns us. We're the Great Khan's eyes and ears. We keep a lookout for traitors in the army, malcontents, men like that. And sometimes we investigate civilians, too, looking for anyone who's plotting against the Great Khan.'

'Ah. You're spies and informers.'

'If you want to put it that way.'

'What other way is there? You live out a lie and sneak around, spying on people, even on your fellow soldiers. Right?'

Zayn went stiff in every muscle, as if he were controlling himself only by force of will. His face went bloodless, then flushed with blood under the dark pigment of his skin.

'Interesting,' she said. 'You do these things but you're ashamed of their rightful names.'

'Goddamn it.' He was more growling than talking. 'It's done in service to the Great Khan.'

'If you say so. What are you doing for the Great Khan right now? Why did you lie and get us to take you in?'

Zayn let out his breath in a long sigh. His colour returned to normal. 'It's Soutan,' he said at last. 'Sorcerers from the Cantons don't ride to Kazrajistan without some reason. He appeared some months ago, and he got himself hooked up with a bunch of respectable men. My friend – Warkannan – was one of them. They said they were forming an investment group around some maps that Soutan brought with him.'

'Ah,' Ammadin put in. 'The blackstone.'

'Right. My superior officers were suspicious. They wanted to question the lot of them. I told them that I couldn't imagine Warkannan getting mixed up in anything wrong. So they held off, and they sent me to the Cantons to find out more about Soutan.'

'And so you needed a way across the Rift without telling anyone why you wanted one. Yes, that makes sense. Were you right about Warkannan?'

'No.' He looked away, his face twisted in something like agony. 'He – they – there's another claimant to the throne, that Kazraki officer your people found dying in the grass and then saved. Soutan ran across him somehow, and Warkannan's come to bring Jezro

Khan home and lead a rebellion. The Great Khan's got a lot of enemies.'

'Which is why he needs informers.'

'Damn you! Don't keep –' He calmed his voice, but she could see the effort it cost him. 'Yes, that's why he needs us.'

'And this Jezro, he's got a lot of friends? The rebellion could succeed?'

Zayn nodded and looked away. 'Do you know what it means if they bring Jezro back to Kazrajistan? Half the khanate goes up in civil war. A lot of men will die, a lot of farms will burn, a lot of innocent townsfolk will starve to death.'

'I know how bloody your wars are, but you're lying again. You don't care about the farmers. You're doing this for reasons of your own.'

'I'm not! It's for the Great Khan –' He stopped, and his eyes grew wide, his mouth slack as he stared at the space over her shoulder.

'What's wrong?' Ammadin made her voice gentle. 'What do you see?'

'In the Mistlands I saw ghosts,' Zayn whispered. 'And I saw –' He shook himself and spoke normally. 'But that's neither here nor there.'

'Of course it is! You know, if you keep lying to me, we could be here all night.'

'Damn it!' He rose to his knees, then sat back down again. 'Why don't you just let me ride out, and if they kill me, they kill me.'

'I won't because you're a member of my comnee. You may have been lying to us, but we weren't lying to you.'

For a moment he went so ashy-grey that she wondered if he was going to faint. He tipped his head back and stared up at the smokehole, but she could see that his eyes glistened with tears.

'I wasn't lying,' he said at last. 'I wanted to ride with you. I still do. I just can't. I've chosen my road, and there's nothing else left for me now. Some roads never fork or turn.'

'Now you're lying to yourself.'

'I'm not, damn it! What can I do? All right, suppose I decide, oh to hell with the Chosen, I'll just stay with the comnee. They'll come after me and kill me. It might take them years, but they'll find me in the end. We're good at that.'

'I see. The Great Khan you honour so much treats his servants like slaves.'

Zayn clapped his hand on the hilt of his long knife.

'If you kill me,' Ammadin said, 'I'll haunt you from the Deathworld so badly that you'll beg to die and join me.'

'Ah may the Lord forgive me!' Zayn let the knife go. 'I'd never harm you, Ammi, never.'

He had used her family name. So! she thought. There's hope for him yet.

'Look,' Zayn went on. 'I meant it when I said I don't want anyone in the comnee dying with me. I'll leave tonight. You don't know how good I am at being on the run. Once I'm alone, they'll never find me.'

'You're forgetting the sorcerer. Soutan. He's done an awfully good job of finding you so far.'

Zayn's mouth went slack.

'Think, you idiot!' Ammadin snapped. 'Someone told this Sinyur Alayn exactly what road you were travelling on, didn't he? There you were, out in the middle of nowhere on a dark night, but they knew exactly where to find you. Soutan must have got a new crystal, and he must have scanned you out.'

For a moment she thought he was going to argue; then he nodded his agreement.

'Now,' Ammadin went on, 'I want you to tell me more. Why did your officers send you after Soutan?'

'Just to find out who he was and bring the information back.'

'But now you've got this other man to worry about –'

'Jezro Khan, yes.'

'Do you know where he is?'

'Somewhere in Burgunee Canton.'

'And if you find him, what then? Do you just bring the information back?'

'No. It would be my duty to kill him. If he reaches Andjaro Province, if he crosses the border, then it's going to be too late. I know Andjaro. They've hated the throne for a hundred years. They'll raise troops for Jezro fast enough.'

'I don't understand why –'

'The khanate conquered them. It's a strange place, Andjaro, full of hills and forests, an easy place to hide in. The people that live there are mostly big landowners, who keep armed guards around. Well, they call them guards, but they're soldiers, really.'

'And the landowners will follow Jezro, right? Very well, so you want to ride off, find Jezro, and kill him.'

'I don't want to. I have to. I know my duty to the Great Khan.'

'And what about Warkannan? If he stands between you and this khan, will you try to kill him too?'

The tears were back, glistening in his dark eyes, and this time Zayn made no effort to hide them. Ammadin let out her breath in a sharp sigh. 'Well,' she said, 'you've got yourself into a really wretched mess, haven't you?'

Zayn laughed, a dark mutter under his breath. 'I like the way you put that,' he said. 'And the worst thing is, if I hadn't told my superiors how much I trusted Warkannan, I wouldn't be in it. Damn him for turning traitor!'

'Suppose you hadn't told them. This questioning you mentioned – I've heard about your Kazraki courts. They would have put these people to the torture, wouldn't they, if they didn't like their answers?'

'Yes. That's why I spoke up. Most likely they would have questioned Warkannan's nephew first. Warkannan would betray God Himself to protect him. Idres would have told us everything.'

'That's really repellent.' She paused to give her words full effect. 'Really disgusting! Zayn, how could you? How could you join a group like this? Brotherhood you called it. It sounds like a nest of firesnakes to me.'

She was expecting anger, but he merely sighed, looking away, nodding a little as if agreeing with her.

'It's because of the demon blood,' he said. 'Every member of the Chosen has some of the forbidden talents. That's why we're so good at what we do. The demon blood's damned us. Why should we care what we do?'

'But it's not demon blood, as you know perfectly well, so I don't suppose anything's damning you, either. That's a stupid excuse. I have some of those talents, too. Do you think I serve that – what is he? Prince of demons? Iblish? Something like that.'

'Iblis.' Zayn whispered the word. 'The rebel angel. Of course you don't.'

'Very good! And as I've said about fifty times before, there aren't any demons who can get women pregnant. I don't know why you and the Chosen have the talents, but I doubt if this Iblis creature has anything to do with it.'

'Ammi, you're tearing me apart. Do you realize that?'

'Of course. Now, tell me if I've got this right. You all grew up terrified, convinced you had demon blood, and that you'd die if anyone found out. What's more, the blood meant you weren't even real H'mai, but some kind of outcast to your families, who hated and feared you. So now the men in the Chosen hate everyone in return. You're getting your revenge.'

He bit his lower lip so hard it bled. With a curse he wiped the blood off on the back of his hand and glared at her.

'Ah, I'm right,' she went on. 'But there are two Kazraks you don't hate, Warkannan and this Jezro fellow. You did your best to protect Warkannan. The thought of killing Jezro makes you sick to your guts. Well, doesn't it?'

He said nothing, kept his hand pressed against his mouth, and stared at her as if he were wishing he could kill her with thoughts alone.

'So, it does.' Ammadin allowed herself a brief smile. 'You're keeping quiet so you won't have to lie to me, aren't you?'

'Damn you!' He let his hand fall into his lap.

'Tell me something, Zayn. Why are Jezro and Warkannan different? Why don't you hate them?'

'Why the hell should I answer that?'

'Because I'm a spirit rider, and the other men in your comnee risked their lives to save you.'

He started to speak, merely sighed, looked away, looked back at her. Blood trickled from the cut on his lip. She waited, afraid to speak while his soul tottered on the edge of some inward chasm deeper than the Rift itself.

'All right,' he said at last. 'I was a sergeant in Warkannan's troop, out on the border. The ChaMeech had been raiding steadily. We were out on patrol, and they made a night attack on our horses. It was dark, everything was confused. Warkannan and I got ourselves captured.'

'Oh gods! So that's why you hate them so much.'

Zayn nodded. 'They marched us for two days straight, loping along, dragging us when we fell. They'd stop to sleep for a few hours, then slap us around to wake us up, and we'd be back marching.' He looked away, his eyes bleak. 'By the time we stopped, all I wanted was to die fast, because I knew they were going to make us die slowly. I think I would have died earlier, on the run I mean, but Warkannan kept me going. I'd fall down, and he'd somehow or other talk me into getting up again.'

'I see. And then you were rescued.'

'Yes, but we never thought we would be. It's in the regulations, you see, that if men get captured, they're officially dead; the post commander isn't supposed to risk more men going after them. Jezro broke that regulation. He came after us with the whole regiment. They could have cashiered him, you know, khan or not, but he told us that it wouldn't have mattered to him if they had. Damned if he was going to leave two of his men in ChaMeech hands.'

'Are you really going to kill this man if you find him?'

Again he fell silent, staring at her. The flickering oil lamps sent shadows dancing across his face and long spears of light around the tent.

'I don't know.' Zayn's voice was a bare whisper. 'But I have to go and see if I will or not.'

'What's that supposed to mean?'

'I keep telling you: I swore I'd serve the Great Khan. If I let Jezro reach Andjaro, then I've failed, I've gone back on my oath. How could I even think of myself as a man any more?'

'How can you think of yourself as a man if you kill him?'

'Well, that's the problem, isn't it?' Zayn was whispering again. 'That's why I've got to go find him. I can't just pretend I don't know where he is. I won't know what I'll do until I see him.' He was silent for a long moment, then spoke normally. 'I don't know who I am any more. Don't you see? Ever since the Mistlands, I don't know who I am. I've got to find out if I'm the man who could kill Jezro Khan, or if I'm the man who can't. It'll be a start, anyway, on figuring things out.'

Ammadin decided that either he'd gone mad or he was sane for the first time in his life. She found herself longing for her teacher, wise old Yannador, with his eighty years of studying the human heart, but to speak to him, she'd have to journey to the gates of the Deathworld. What would Yanno have said to this man? Zayn sat watching her, his eyes full of tears that never fell.

'All right,' Ammadin said. 'That's honest. Finding Jezro Khan is like a spirit quest for you. You need to ride it.'

'Yes.' Zayn paused, gasping down a breath. 'Yes, I do.'

'Now listen. You'll be leaving the comnee to quest. While you were off getting yourself into trouble, Kassidor and I made a bargain so I could go on a quest of my own. I want to ride east with Water Woman to meet Sibyl. Sammador agreed that his comnee will ride with Apanador's for a while, so Kasso can tend my god figures and protect my people as well as his. I'll go off with Water Woman, and when I come back, I'll tell him everything I've learned.'

'A fair enough bargain, I suppose, but –'

'Just listen! To meet up with Water Woman I have to ride east into the Cantons. So I might as well ride with you – for a while, anyway. It'll be safer for both of us. I can counter Soutan's magic, and you can be my bodyguard.'

Zayn started to speak, then merely stared at her.

'But there's one thing I will not do,' Ammadin went on, 'and that's use my crystals to find Jezro. I will not join your blood hunt.'

'I wouldn't want you to. It's bad enough I have to.' He swallowed hard. 'But it's too dangerous, riding with me. I'd rather die than have you come to the slightest harm.'

'You keep talking about dying, Zayn. Is that what you were planning on doing? Riding off and making some stupid mistake so you'll die and never have to face Jezro?'

He stood up, twisted towards the tent flap, stopped, turned back. 'You really do have guards out there, damn you!'

'Yes. Sit down.'

Zayn sat.

'You must be furious at me,' Ammadin went on.

'I'm not, oddly enough. I should be, but I'm not. Maybe I'm just too damned tired to be angry. I don't know. I don't know anything any more, maybe. Nothing looks the same as it did when I left Kazrajistan.'

'Good.'

'What do you mean –'

'Judging from what you've told me, things must have looked very ugly to you for years.'

'Oh will you shut up? I –' He paused for another long breath. 'I'm sorry, Spirit Rider, but I can't take any more of your – well, whatever it is you're doing.'

'Tearing you apart, just like you said.' She smiled at him. 'I will stop, for now, but Zayn, I oversaw your vision quest. I don't think you realize what that means.'

'I didn't realize then. I'm beginning to now.'

'Good. Then it's settled. We'll ride –'

'I don't recall it being settled.'

'If you really want to die, I'll have Apanador and Dallador tie you up and turn you over to Sinyur Alayn's men, who'll be glad to oblige. Huh, I can see from the nasty look on your face that you don't want anything of the sort. All right, then, you need my magic, don't you?'

'Yes.' He sounded exhausted. 'I do. All right, it's settled. We can tell people the truth, that you're on some kind of quest for hidden knowledge, and I can go on being your servant.'

'That's not the truth. We're both riding quests, and that's what we'll say. You don't have to tell anyone what you're questing for. If anyone asks, tell them you can't discuss it because it's Bane, which it is. In the morning I'll tie you a charm for your bridle to mark the quest. And one for me, come to think of it.' Ammadin stood up. 'I'll just go tell the guards to leave. You'd better not try to sneak out while I'm asleep.'

'I won't. I promise, and I'll keep my word to you. Not to anyone else in the world, maybe, but to you I will.'

'Good. Remember that.' She picked up the tent flap and ducked outside.

Near her tent the embers of a few cooking fires still glowed. In that uncertain light she could see that Dallador and Grenidor still stood on guard, but she couldn't tell which was which. Fortunately Dallador stepped forward to talk with her. His voice was several tones darker than his cousin's.

'I couldn't help overhearing,' Dallador said. 'Or – all right, I'll be honest. I got as close as I could and listened.'

'I can't blame you. So you know the truth. What do you think of Zayn now?'

Dallador shrugged and looked away. 'Does it matter? You're both leaving tomorrow.'

She laid a hand on his arm. 'He'll come back, Dallo. He belongs with us, and he knows it.'

'I hope so.' Dallador suddenly yawned. 'It was about this time last night that we rode out, wasn't it?'

'Yes. You're exhausted, I'm exhausted, and so's Zayn. Go get some sleep. He won't be sneaking out again.'

'I heard him promise. I'll do that. Grenno, come on. You've damn near fallen asleep standing up.'

Ammadin went back inside. Zayn had extinguished one of the oil lamps. He was lying on his back on his blankets, one arm flung over his face, asleep fully dressed. She took off her boots, put out the other light, and lay down on her side of the tent. She fell asleep before she could put one coherent thought together.

Zayn woke to find the tent filled with the silver light of dawn. Ammadin had just opened the tent flap; when she saw that he was awake, she paused with a hand still upon it.

'I have to go talk with the chiefs,' she said. 'They need to know what we're going to do, and I have to scan to see if Alayn's men are on their way here. I've got to tie the charms, too, so it's going to be a while before we can ride out. Don't you have something to say to Dallador?'

Zayn winced. Had she seen –

'Well, you're having an affair with him, aren't you?' Ammadin said.

'Yes.' The word came out strangled.

'You don't have to be embarrassed. So did I, once.'

She smiled and went out, letting the flap fall shut behind her. Zayn sat up, resting his head in his hands. He found himself thinking of earthquakes, when ground that seemed solid moved and pitched, tumbling everything built upon it. The metaphor made him feel like vomiting. He got up, stretching, and went outside.

The camp was just waking. Kassidor was trotting back and forth, yelling at everyone to hurry. The women were getting up, pulling on their boots and talking about feeding the horses. Grumbling and yawning, the men moved more slowly.

'We've got to get on the road,' Kassidor was saying. 'We're not very far from Sinyur Alayn's land.' He came hurrying over to Zayn. 'Ammadin says to saddle her grey and your sorrel. Pick two pack horses, and load them with grain and food and whatever else you're taking. She's got her saddlebags all ready, and I've got the comnee's god figures, so we can strike the tent as soon as you get your things out of it.'

'All right. Tell her I'll do it right away.'

Zayn retrieved his gear from the tent, then hurried over to his comnee's wagon, where the big canvas packs sat waiting. The excellent trading had bought the comnee a good many sacks of wheatian as well as charcoal and other necessities. Zayn was just calculating how much the comnee could spare them when Dallador walked up, his hands shoved in his pockets, his face carefully expressionless.

'There you are,' Zayn said. 'I need to talk with you.'

'I've been looking for you,' Dallador said. 'Zayn, all those lies!'

'I know.' Zayn turned away. 'I thought I didn't have any choice.'

'You probably didn't.'

Zayn nodded and stared at the ground. When Dallador put his hands on Zayn's shoulders, Zayn leaned back, relaxing.

'You're coming back, aren't you?' Dallador said.

'Yes. If I live through this, and I might not.'

Dallo's hands tightened. Zayn twisted free and turned around to face him. 'Well, you don't want any more lies, do you?'

'No.' Dallador paused for a wry smile. 'Except maybe for one right then.'

'I'll never lie to you again. I'll promise you that.'

'All right. I'll hold you to it.'

'Good. I might need some help.'

They shook hands, clasped hands, stood staring into each other's eyes, while all around them the comnee hurried and bustled, packing up, saddling horses, calling back and forth.

'I'll help you load up,' Dallador said finally. 'We've all got to get on the road.'

They had just finished saddling and loading the pack horses when Ammadin came striding out to join them. She was carrying only one pair of saddlebags, slung over one shoulder. In her other hand she held a charm, a hawk feather bound to a shell, a Kazraki coin wrapped with red thread to keep it in place next to a dried and polished land-crab claw and two blue beads. She tied it to the left cheek piece of the sorrel gelding's bridle.

'There, that's one thing done,' Ammadin said. 'Now I've got to scan.'

As Zayn watched her walk away, he suddenly remembered her telling him that she'd slept with Dallador, too.

'She's not as cold as she looks.' Dallador confirmed the story with a grin. 'So good hunting.'

'You bastard!'

Dallador laughed with a toss of his head. For a moment they merely smiled at each other. 'Well,' Dallo said at length. 'What else do we have to pack?'

'Nothing. I've just got to saddle Ammi's grey and tie on her bedroll, stuff like that.'

'I'll let you do that, then.' Dallador turned solemn. 'I can't watch you ride out. All right?'

'All right.'

Dallador turned on his heel and strode off, heading back to camp. Zayn watched him till he disappeared among the other comnee men.

While the comnee finished packing up the camp, Ammadin went down to the riverbank to scan, kneeling in the purple grass. Sammador and Apanador followed her to hover nearby with their backs turned. Although the Riders hung low at the horizon, Spirit Eyes managed to get a good view of the immediate countryside. At Alayn's manor house everything seemed peaceful. In a paved courtyard, young women were laughing as they boiled laundry over open fires; in the stable yard men were grooming and watering horses, smiling and talking. Had they known their sinyur was lying dead in the forest, they would have moved and gestured in a very different way. Now that Ammadin knew where the temple compound was, she could direct Spirit Eyes to its location, and through the trees she caught glimpses of open lawn. Nothing moved.

'How much time do you think we have?' Apanador said. 'Before the chief's men come after us, I mean.'

'At least a day.' Ammadin stood up, holding her crystal. 'Zayn is pretty sure that Alayn spent a lot of time at that temple. His family probably won't miss him till late today or even tomorrow. By then you should have a good head start. Once you reach the Rift, they won't follow.'

'If they do, we have over twenty men between us,' Sammador said, 'not counting me and Apanador, and then Kassidor.'

'I just don't want any of our men to get killed.' Ammadin paused, looking at each chief in turn. 'Zayn's caused enough trouble already.'

'That's certainly true.' Sammador sounded weary. 'But men do cause trouble. It's the way the gods made us.'

'Yes, and then the women have to clean up after us,' Apanador said, 'or so my wife always tells me.'

'Gemmadin's right as usual.' Ammadin allowed herself a brief smile. 'May the gods ride with you. I'll see you at the winter campgrounds if not before.'

Zayn was waiting for her by the east-running road. He had dropped the reins of her grey and his sorrel to make them stand, but he was holding the lead ropes of the two pack horses. He stood cavalry-stiff between them, watching her as she walked across the grass. Something about him struck her as odd; with some surprise she realized that his mask, that smooth bland expression with which he'd hidden his secrets, had fallen completely away. The morning light picked out the dark circles under his eyes and the droop to his full mouth.

'Ready?' she said.

'I guess.' He shrugged. 'I don't think anyone can ever be really ready for a ride like this.'

'True enough. Here, let me explain your quest charm. The Kazraki coin represents you. The feather and shell mean that you're on a quest; every quest marker has them. The beads –'

'Idres and Jezro?'

'Right.'

'There's nothing there to represent the Chosen.'

'Oh yes there is – the red thread. A line the colour of blood, binding you.'

Zayn winced.

'The land-crab claw stands for the hold the grass has over you,' Ammadin went on, 'or the life we live out on the grass, to be more precise.'

Zayn nodded, studying the charm. 'That sums it up, all right,' he said. 'Thank you.'

'You're welcome.'

'Ammi?' He looked up. 'I've got one more thing to confess. Zayn Hassan isn't my real name.'

'I could guess that. What –'

'Zahir Benumar.' He paused for a brief smile. 'Do you know what Zahir means?'

'No. What?'

'Truth.'

'Then I'm going to keep calling you Zayn.'

'I want you to. That's why I brought it up.'

'Good. Now let's get going.'

All that morning they rode without speaking. Ammadin was more than willing to let Zayn be alone with his thoughts, which were deadly grim, judging from the play of feeling upon his face. She took the lead, and the other horses followed her grey briskly along through the sunny fields of wheatian, but she was always aware of the dark swell of the forest, angling to meet the road. When the road turned to run alongside of it, Ammadin glanced back to see Zayn grimmer than ever.

Just before noon they came to the river and the wooden bridge. Apparently the sorrel remembered what had happened there. It balked, bucked sideways twice, then tried to rear. A lesser rider than Zayn would have been thrown, but he flung his weight forward, kept the horse down and kept talking until the sorrel calmed enough to stand trembling in the road.

Ammadin dismounted, dropped her reins to make the grey stand, and ran back to pick up the lead rope of the pack horses, waiting patiently some yards behind. She walked back with the horses to find that Zayn had dismounted and was stroking the sorrel's neck.

'Did I tell you about the crane?' Zayn said. 'The one that tried to warn me about the ambush?'

'No, you didn't, but you should have.'

'Too much happened too fast. I'm sorry. But it was down in the river, fishing I guess. It called out and then flew up. But I couldn't get back in the saddle fast enough to escape.'

'Well, I never had much doubt before, but now I'm sure of it. Cranes are your spirit animal.' The thought jogged her memory. 'Wait a moment! You never learned your true name, did you? In the Mistlands, I mean.'

'No, I didn't. And I'm sorry, too.'

'Something might happen on this quest to give it to you.'

'Does it matter? If I kill Jezro Khan, if I go back to the Chosen –'

'It'll probably matter more than ever, if that happens.'

'Think so?' Zayn gave the sorrel one last pat. 'I'm going to lead him across.'

Ammadin considered pressing him to say more, then decided that she was simply too tired. She mounted up, took the lead rope for the pack horses, and rode across. Her own grey, which she'd trained herself, clopped across the bridge in sublime indifference to the hollow sound, and the pack horses followed. She hoped that the sorrel would mimic the rest of its miniature herd, but once again it balked. Getting the sorrel across took all of Zayn's patience. By the time they reached the far side, Sentry was chiming in Ammadin's saddlebags.

'Let's rest the horses here,' she said. 'I need to scan.'

It took Spirit Eyes only a few minutes to find Soutan and the Kazraks, riding along a dirt road between fields of wheatian. The sighting numbers on her crystal's equator told her that they were heading due east near the limit of her crystal's range. Long Voice could pick up nothing of their conversation, assuming they were having one. She left Soutan and sent Spirit Eyes hunting the comnee, which she found well west of the forest on their way back to the Riftgate. As for Sinyur Alayn's men, she saw no trace of them, but their horses were still at pasture, a good sign. She set the crystals out to feed, then got up, turning to speak to Zayn.

'Well, they're still ahead of us. I can't tell you much more than that.'

'For now, that's all I need to know.'

His hands shoved in his pockets, his head tipped a little back, Zayn was staring down the road to the east as if he could see nothing but horror unfolding before him. What was he thinking, she wondered, that he would look so desolate? She decided against asking him, out of the simple fear that he would start lying to her again.

'You know,' Ammadin said, 'this is the farthest east I've ever been. From now on, it's all unknown country.'

Zayn swung half-around, as startled as if she'd thrown a weapon at him.

'Oh yes,' she said, smiling. 'I won't have all the answers any more. This should be interesting.'

Warkannan and his men had spent the previous night camping near the east-running road. At about the time Ammadin was telling Zayn the meaning of his quest charm, Warkannan was taking inventory of his supplies – enough food for the men and grain for the horses to last two days. While Warkannan and Arkazo loaded the pack horses and saddled their riding mounts, Soutan walked a few yards away and sat down to mutter over his crystals. In only a few minutes he got up and came back, wide-eyed, a little pale. His hands shook as he stowed the crystals in his saddlebags.

'What's wrong?' Warkannan said.

'The worst possible thing.'

'Couldn't you find Zahir?'

'I found him, all right.' Soutan paused for effect. 'And I found the spirit rider. She's travelling with him. They've just left the comnee and are heading east. They're only about twenty miles behind us.'

'What? The spirit rider?'

'What indeed?' Soutan tried to smile and failed. 'This is ghastly. I don't dare challenge her again. If she manages to kill this set of crystals, I shan't be able to get another until we reach Burgunee. I've absolutely got to be able to scan with Gemet's trained murderer on the loose.'

'How far are we from Jezro?'

'Oh, a long ways yet. We have to ride into Dordan Canton, then head north. Now, I don't dare be seen by the authorities in Dordan, much less in Sarla. That's where my enemies are.' Soutan turned to Arkazo. 'I need to teach you a great deal more Vranz, Kaz. Let's practise as we ride.'

'Daccor,' Arkazo said. 'I'm kind of enjoying it.'

They rode hard that day, pushing the horses, who had been well rested during their stay in the forest. Every time they stopped, however, Soutan would get out his crystal and scan, and every time, he would look frightened half to death when he saw the spirit rider travelling along behind them. That night they spent beside the road in a copse of fountain trees, and in the morning they made an early start.

On the road ahead lay Leen, a city of some thousands, but before they reached it, they left the main road. Soutan scanned their way through a maze of farmers' lanes, barely wide enough for one rider, that skirted fields of wheatian or ran between scarlet hedgerows. Towards sunset they had a piece of luck when they came to a prosperous-looking farm. Out in front of the barn its owner was busy loading a wagon with foodstuffs to sell at the next day's market in Leen, and he was more than glad to turn an early bargain. As a bonus he allowed them to spend the night in a meadow near his fish pond.

While the two Kazraks set up camp, Soutan wandered out into the meadow to scan in the last of the daylight. He returned with ominous news.

'I can't find them,' Soutan said. 'The spirit rider and Zayn.'

'Zahir,' Warkannan said absently. 'Not that the name matters, I suppose. Are we too far away?'

'I doubt it. She may have figured out some way to hide from me. I wanted to see if they were gaining ground on us.'

'Why do you think they're trying to catch up with us?'

'Oh.' Soutan paused, his mouth working as he thought. 'Well, you're right. I don't know that.'

'My guess is that he's trying to reach Jezro first and kill him. Then he can deal with us later or just head back home.'

'Kill –' Soutan looked up, shocked. 'How can you be so nonchalant about –'

'I'm not. Panic won't do us any good, that's all.'

By the time they were done eating, twilight was darkening the sky. In the nearby fish pond water toads boomed; grey fish broke the surface now and then to snatch needlebuhs from the air with a 'chup' and a splash as they fell back. The little blue nightdancers whined as they called to one another, foraging for insects in the grass. Soutan rummaged in his saddlebags for a moment, then brought out a folded piece of rushi.

'Now that we're nearly there,' Soutan said, 'I have a small confession to make.'

Arkazo looked up from the fire. 'What now? Another girl who claims you raped her?'

'Kaz!' Warkannan snapped. 'That's nothing to joke about.'

'Sorry.' Arkazo ducked his head in apology.

'Here.' Soutan held out the rushi. 'You'll recognize Jezro's seal and handwriting. Read it, Captain. Aloud, why not?'

With a shrug Warkannan took the rushi. He broke the seal, which was indeed Jezro's, and angled the letter to catch the firelight. 'It's Jezro Khan's writing, all right.' He cleared his throat. 'My friends – Indan, Warkannan, whoever else is still alive to remember me – what Soutan the sorcerer is going to tell you will sound like a madman's ramblings. But it's not. I couldn't believe it at first, either, but now I've seen the proof. Listen to him. Think about it. This is the biggest thing in the world. Yours, Jezro.'

Warkannan lowered the rushi and glanced around. Arkazo was

watching him, all patience. Warkannan could remember him as a child, looking just this way while he waited for his uncle to explain where thunder came from or why he had to go to school every day. Soutan sat perfectly still except for his eyes, which flicked back and forth between the two of them.

'Well,' Warkannan said at last. 'Suppose you tell us about this marvellous thing, then.'

Soutan smiled, the first truly warm smile that Warkannan had ever seen on his face. 'Haven't you ever wondered why I want to see Jezro on the throne of Kazrajistan?'

'Often. I've always assumed you were in it for the power it would bring you. Jezro will reward you handsomely, once he's the Great Khan.'

'Ah yes, the emperor's adviser, the gold, the luxury, all the rest of it – no! I spit on all that.' Soutan illustrated his point by spitting on the ground. 'Here's why I want his help. Only you Kazraks have the men and the money I need to find the Ark of the Covenant.'

Arkazo made a choking sound deep in his throat. Warkannan's first thought was that Soutan had gone mad, completely and totally insane. His fist tightened around Jezro's letter and crumpled it; he laid the rushi on his knee and began smoothing it out. Soutan favoured Arkazo with another smile.

'This university of yours,' Soutan said, 'surely it taught you about the Ark.'

'Yes.' Arkazo's voice shook badly. 'It's part of the ship that brought us here from the homeland.'

'Do you know what part?'

'The magical pilot, like a steersman or something.'

'Very good. If we don't find it, we can never return home.'

'Now wait a minute,' Warkannan broke in. 'Who's talking about returning home?'

'I am.' Soutan went on smiling. 'The homeland isn't some country on the other side of the sea, Captain, filled with nasty infidels and demons. That's only what you've been told, what they want you to believe, your twisted little mullahs and your so-called wise men. Liars, all of them! Power-mad little liars!'

'Just what –'

'Look up!' Soutan swept one hand towards the sky. 'Look up there, Captain! What do you see?'

'The Spider, of course.'

In the velvet sky the vast silver swirl had just cleared the horizon.

'Of course,' Soutan repeated. 'Well, that's where we came from, from one world among a thousand worlds, civilized worlds, worlds where people live long lives in comfort and prosperity, worlds where the things you call magical are as common as blades of grass on the ground.'

'You're demented,' Warkannan snapped. 'What in hell do you mean?'

'If you'd let me finish! Every dot of light in the Spider is a star like our sun. Some of those stars have worlds going around them, just as our sun does. Our ancestors came from another world back in the Spider somewhere. We don't belong here. This world belongs to the ChaMeech. We need to go home and let them have it back. Our species belongs with people who can make all kinds of marvellous things, like ships that can sail between stars. That's how we got here, and if we can find that ship, we can find our way home.'

'That's stupid as well as demented.'

'No, it's not.' Soutan seemed curiously unruffled by the insults. 'It makes perfect sense, if you'd only think about it. Jezro believes me. You can tell that from the note.'

'Then exile drove him mad, too. Why didn't you tell us this back in Haz Kazrak?'

'Because you wouldn't have come back with me. You'd have called me demented then, just as you're doing now, but here we are.' Soutan gestured at the surrounding landscape with a sweep of his arm. 'Are you going to leave, Captain, without even seeing Jezro Khan?'

'No, you bastard. Of course I'm not.'

'Good.' Soutan smiled, his more usual pull of thin lips from large teeth. 'When I was perusing Indan's library, I actually came across some new evidence. The *Histories* of Hajji Ahmed contain a great many suggestive details.'

Arkazo started to speak, then choked it back. Warkannan glanced his way. 'What's wrong with you?'

Arkazo was looking back and forth between the Spider and Soutan, his eyes wide, his mouth slack. Soutan smiled at him.

'I think your nephew believes me, Captain.'

'I wouldn't say that,' Arkazo said. 'But we read the *Histories* at university.'

'So, do you remember the parts about the flying boats?' Soutan said.

'Yes.' Arkazo avoided looking at Warkannan. 'And how the Ancestors felt they'd done something wrong by coming here. The guilt's why they followed Chursavva's orders and took the land he gave them.'

'Exactly.' Soutan said. 'What else?'

'There were some quotes from an ancient sage, too, Khalifa, his name was. He talked about God creating hundreds of millions of worlds and suns. He said the universe was huge, beyond our comprehending, and that God had filled it with light and with souls. If that's true, then this can't be the only world.'

'That sounds like heresy to me,' Warkannan said. 'Heresy and a damned unlikely tale. You can write anything. Proving it's a different matter.'

'But Uncle!' Arkazo turned to him. 'It's not just the books. Some of the khans sent out ships to explore the oceans. One captain sailed south. He never saw land, but he reported that when you get far enough south, you can see smudges of light in the sky, and some points of light, too.'

'Other galaxies and stars, in other words,' Soutan put in. 'Any other sailors?'

'Yes, the ones who went west, trying to find the homeland.' Arkazo leaned forward, more intense than Warkannan had ever seen him. 'Most of them never came back. But one ship did get back. The captain said the only land they ever saw was rocky little islands.'

'So?' Warkannan snarled.

'So if no one can sail back, how come thousands and thousands of us could sail the other way, sail here from there, I mean? And there were thousands of us, maybe even a hundred thousand. There are records of the names, pages and pages of them.'

Warkannan gave the rushi back to Soutan.

'Uncle?' Arkazo said. 'Don't you believe me?'

'Of course I do.' Warkannan wiped his hands off on his shirt; he felt that he'd touched something unclean. 'If you say you read these things, then you read them.'

'There are a great many records,' Soutan said. 'I have some that are a great deal more explicit than lists of names. Or rather, Jezro has them at the moment, because I wasn't going to risk bringing them along. You'll see them for yourself, Captain, and very soon.'

'Uncle?' Arkazo said. 'I'm sorry, but a lot of us at university talked about the puzzle – of how we got here, I mean. The old stories really don't add up.'

'And I suppose this crap about worlds and the Spider does?'

'No, not really. But it doesn't make any less sense than what the mullahs tell us.'

The quiet way Arkazo spoke made Warkannan stop before he launched a tirade. 'All right,' he said instead. 'I'll keep an open mind, then.'

Arkazo smiled in profound relief.

'That's all anyone can ask, Captain,' Soutan broke in. 'I promise you, you'll see a great deal of proof when we reach Jezro. Thank god, it won't be long now at all.'

'Good.' Warkannan took a deep breath. 'This magic business, you said something –'

'Yes, about marvellous things we call magic, things like my lightwand. They aren't magic at all, Captain. There aren't any spirits, there aren't any spells. They're no different from the printing presses and spinning wheels you have back home – devices, machines, toys, tools.'

Warkannan stared, aware that he was goggling like a child.

'I'll prove it. Right now.' Soutan rummaged in his saddlebags, and came up with the lightwand. 'You can work this as well as I can. Here.' He held it out. 'Take it.'

Involuntarily Warkannan leaned back.

'Oh for god's sake!' Soutan turned to Arkazo. 'Here, you try then.'

Arkazo took it and ran eager fingers over the metal.

'You say a command word,' Soutan went on, 'but you have to say it loudly and sonorously. The word here is much like in Hirl-Onglay, when they say leet. Say lie-it, clearly and loudly.'

Arkazo took a deep breath and spoke, 'Lie it.'

In his hands the wand blazed. With a howl of laughter Arkazo raised it over his head with one hand and flung light like a spear at the sky. 'Uncle,' he crowed, 'look! It works. Just like he said.'

'Oh yes,' Warkannan said. 'It certainly does.' He could think of not one word more, could only watch, feeling like a beast, struck dumb, as Soutan took the lightwand and spoke a word that turned it dark.

'That's wonderful,' Arkazo said, grinning. 'Will it do anything else?'

'Not this piece of equipment, no, but there are other things.' Soutan turned to Warkannan. 'What do you think of this, Captain?'

'I don't know,' Warkannan said. 'I honestly don't know.'

'But do you believe him, Uncle?' Arkazo broke in. 'About the worlds back in the Spider, I mean?'

'I don't know that, either. Very well. That light stick is a machine, just like a printing press, just like a water wheel. Why does it have to come from –' He could not bring himself to say, 'the stars'. 'From so far away?'

'Well, good point.' Arkazo turned to look at Soutan.

'Yes, it is,' Soutan said. 'There's no reason at all, really, that it must. As I said, you'll see the proof when we reach Jezro.'

'I can wait.'

'No doubt you need to think about this.' Soutan was watching him. 'It must have come as a shock.'

Warkannan forced out a smile. 'I always thought you were a fake magician,' he said. 'Apparently I was right.'

'Oh yes. I can't even be offended by that, Captain.'

'But one thing I don't understand. The First Prophet, blessed be he, warns us about magic. Did he mean –'

'No, no, he meant something quite different, actual superstitions and silliness about wizards and spells and charms. We've just borrowed the names.'

'We?'

'The sorcerers of the Cantons. We're loremasters, not sorcerers at all. The pretence is for outsiders, and unfortunately, it was written into the Landfall Treaty. We've got our share of superstitious farmers and the like in the Cantons, but no one with any intelligence believes in magic here.'

'Oh? How come you're always consulting that damned oracle?'

Soutan had the decency to blush. 'Because I'm H'mai, Captain. The thing intrigues me, even though I know it's all nonsense. It's very odd how accurate it can be.' He cleared his throat several times. 'Now, on the other hand, the spirit riders believe in magic. They think they've tamed spirits, but the crystals? They're just pieces of equipment, too.'

'Well, but –' Arkazo thought for a moment. 'Why did you keep saying you had to feed your spirits?'

'That was, oddly enough, true in its own way. The people who colonized the Cantons, the Settlers as we call them, invented machines that soak up sunlight and turn it into the power that runs the crystals. This device is called an accu, a solar accu. If you don't let them recharge, they run down for good, and we don't know how to make new ones. But it's all cleverness. Nothing supernatural about it.'

'Could I use one of your crystals, then?' Arkazo said it so eagerly that Warkannan was troubled. He was even more troubled by the sly way Soutan smiled at the boy before he answered.

'The crystals present problems,' Soutan said. 'You could certainly get them to work, but you probably won't be able to use them properly. Here's another thing about the Settlers. They bred H'mai like horses, you see, to do specialized things. Anyone who wants to use the crystals has to have some of those hereditary –'

'Stop!' Warkannan snarled. 'Let's back up here. What do you mean, bred H'mai like horses?'

'Just that. Consider: the Tribes wanted to sell horses to the cavalry, so they bred their strongest mares to the largest studs. Right? And now we have horses like yours, big, heavy, almost fearless. The Ancestors wanted H'mai to have certain characteristics, too, but they didn't have to do it with ordinary breeding programmes. They could somehow change the fœtus in the womb.' Soutan frowned down at the lightwand in his hands. 'No one remembers how, exactly, they produced these talents, but they did. They called these altered H'mai the Inborn. Once the Inborn had the talents, they then passed them on to their children in the usual way, just like ordinary characteristics – curly hair or blue eyes, say.'

'Talents?' Warkannan had to steady his voice. 'What –'

'Yes, the ability to do things that aren't natural to our species, as I was trying to tell you when you interrupted me, talents such as an incredible memory, or special kinds of eyesight. I have the eyes. I can see in near-dark conditions. And when I look into this small crystal, I can make my mind magnify the images I see there. That's what you probably lack, Arkazo.'

Soutan went on talking, and Arkazo went on asking questions, but Warkannan heard neither of them. He stared into the fire and felt as if he'd seen his world split in half to reveal another world within. Demon talents, horrible impious things that would justify executing children – none of it was true. The mullahs and holy men had been lying all along, unless of course they never knew that they repeated falsehoods. His sense of fairness made Warkannan qualify his outrage. He could see how Mullah Agvar had decided that this sort of tinkering with human beings was despicable, a usurping of powers that should only belong to God. He felt the same way himself.

On the other hand, to torment children over talents they'd been born with – the First Prophet would have had a few pointed things to say about that, Warkannan figured. No wonder God had chosen to spare Zahir out of not merely His mercy and compassion, but His justice. Warkannan raised his eyes to the glowing spiral above him in the sky and marvelled at a beauty he'd never quite noticed before. God had made many things beyond H'mai comprehension, including this spiral of glowing suns. Suddenly he realized why the Second Prophet had taught men to turn towards the spiral when they prayed. That's where Mekka was, a city that belonged to another world, another star. Not over the sea at all!

'Captain?' Soutan said. 'You look grim as death. What's wrong?'

'Nothing, just thinking.' Warkannan smiled briefly. 'About doctrine. Some of it has to be changed.'

'What?' Soutan snapped. 'What do you mean?'

'Never mind.' Warkannan got up and stretched. 'You won't understand. Arkazo, come along. It's time for prayers.'

'You do that,' Soutan said. 'I'm going to risk discharging the accu in my crystal. I've got to find her.'

But when they returned from prayers, Warkannan could see by the foul look on Soutan's face that the spirit rider had managed to escape him again.

Ammadin was indeed using her crystals to hide herself and Zayn. Every time Sentry chimed to announce the presence of the Riders, Ammadin would renew the 'hide me' command she'd learned from her unwilling teacher, Soutan himself. That evening, she and Zayn were sitting at their fire by the side of the road. They'd set up camp for the night on a stretch of wild land on the banks of a river called the Loh, or so a local shepherd had told Zayn. Over the sound of the river, purling between its narrow banks, she could hear the nightdancers hunting. Above, the Herd was rising in the sky, familiar and comforting.

'I don't suppose you'll tell me,' Zayn said, 'how far Idres and his crew are ahead of us?'

'That's right, I won't,' Ammadin said. 'I meant it when I said I wouldn't join your hunt.'

'What about if they lay some kind of ambush?'

'If they do that, I'll warn you. Or at least, I'll suggest we take another road.'

'That's fair.'

'How far ahead is Leen? I'm assuming that shepherd knew.'

'Not far at all. About fifteen miles, he said.'

Their next day's ride ran through farmlands that looked little different from those Ammadin had seen before, but it ended in Leen. Double rows of red-thorn and brass-mesh walls, glittering in the slanted light, towered some twenty feet high and surrounded the town. They rode through a gate made of massive planks of true-oak, studded with brass nails. As they passed through Ammadin looked up and saw above her long iron spikes, ready to crash down and impale an enemy. The town began immediately with a crush of narrow buildings made of bundled reeds and the pale, spongy wood of the fountain trees. The cobbled streets, flecked with garbage, twisted so sharply that she could never get a clear view of where they might be going. Now and then she caught a glimpse of a river and grassy banks, but the street would snake again and she'd lose sight of it.

The citizens had built their houses close together. Out in front of each, on narrow strips of true-grass, half-naked children played with shens or chased true-hens back and forth. When Ammadin and Zayn rode by, the shens rushed to the fences and barked in a drooling frenzy till the horses had gone past. No matter where she looked, she saw people, standing in front of their shops, hurrying through the streets, sitting together on benches near public fountains. No two of them looked alike, either, or so it seemed, with their differences of hair colour and skin. Over everything hung the smells of night soil and horse manure. As the streets wound their way into town, they narrowed, forcing Ammadin and Zayn to dismount and lead their horses.

'This,' Ammadin muttered, 'is horrible. Why do people stay here, when they could move out and claim farmland?'

'What?' Zayn looked honestly surprised. 'Who would want to

farm if they didn't have to? It's a lot of hard work, and besides, there's always something to see in towns.'

'Something to smell, too.'

'It doesn't smell bad. See those holes in the street? Those are drains, and they must lead to a sewer system.'

'You don't have my nose.'

'I forgot about that. Sorry.'

Whenever they came across townspeople who looked approachable, Zayn would stop and speak briefly with them in Vranz. Ammadin could understand enough to find Zayn's fluency startling. Most of the people he spoke with assumed he came from somewhere else in the Cantons.

'They have two inns here,' Zayn told her after one of these brief conversations. 'The word for inn is hohte, by the way. Do you want to stay in town?'

'No, but I don't want to overtire the horses, either,' Ammadin said. 'So let's stop here.'

In the centre of town they found a market square similar to the one in Nannes. Announced by bright banners, various craftsmen's shops lined three of its sides. On the fourth stood a two-storey white building. In the late sun it gleamed so brilliantly white, and its surface seemed so slick, that they knew the Settlers must have built it. When Zayn asked, he was told that the white building housed the local provo – the magistrate who kept order with his men, the zhundaree – and the mayor, who presided over a town council.

Finding an inn turned out to be difficult; a clot of streets unwound from the town centre only to end against walls. Finally, several blocks west of the town square, they turned down a narrow alley and saw a long, low building with an elegant true-wood facade punctuated by panels of coloured glass. This street-front hohte looked both large and comfortable, but the maiderdee, its owner, insisted that it was already full.

'It's the Recallers,' he said, 'and you know what they're like.'

'No, actually,' Ammadin said. 'I don't.'

'Noisy. Very noisy. Children running all over. Drinking at all hours. And by God himself, these people argue all the time! They're giving me a headache.' With a long lugubrious sigh, he shut the door in their faces.

With some help from a passer-by, they found the other hohte, down by the river near a long pier where a pair of narrowboats lay docked. Around a dusty central court stood bamboid cottages, lashed together with vines, each divided into a stable for horses and a room for human travellers. A wiry little man with slicked-back brown hair, the maiderdee led them to the best of these near-shacks – a big room, reasonably clean, with stable space for four horses. By a window stood a table and chairs, furniture that Ammadin had often seen in Nannes. Up against the opposite wall stood a wide, flat piece of furniture with yellow blankets laid over it. It must be a bed, she decided. She'd heard that name for a place to sleep.

'I'm most honoured,' the maiderdee said. 'It's not often we see a spirit rider in our part of the world, and I truly hope my humble hohte will be worthy of your presence.'

'I'm surprised you even know who I am,' Ammadin said. 'Or what, I suppose I mean.'

'Oh, we're close enough to the Rift to know a little about the Tribes. And the horse-traders stay here regularly and talk about them.'

For an extra vran the maiderdee provided them with dinner, as well: fresh bread, a soup, some sort of tuber baked till soft, slices of mutton scented with herbs.

'This place doesn't look like much,' Zayn said, 'but the maiderdee's wife can cook.'

'Looks like it, yes.' Ammadin laid her saddlebags down on a wicker armchair. 'How was the stable?'

'Clean enough. I swept out the stalls again anyway. By the way, you take the bed tonight. I can sleep on the floor.'

'I'd rather have the floor.' Ammadin looked doubtfully at the bed. 'It's too high. I'd be afraid of rolling off.'

'Well, whatever you want.'

A long day on the road had left them both hungry. As they ate, barely speaking, Ammadin was remembering the other times in her life – all two of them – when she had left her people and gone out on her own: her vision quest among the sea caves of the south coast, her hunt for the slasher saur whose hide had ended up as her cloak. The quest had troubled her so little that she'd stayed out for two nights. Hunting the saur had been terrifying, every minute of it, until at last he'd lain dead and quivering, her last spear in his throat, her own blood running down her side.

Travelling to meet Sibyl would fall somewhere in between these extremes, she assumed, and of course, she'd have Water Woman and her servants for company.

From outside they heard voices, the maiderdee's chirpy tenor and then the slow, hesitant voice of someone old. A familiar voice, Ammadin thought. Zayn cocked his head to listen, then shoved his chair back and stood up.

'It's old Onree,' he said, 'from Nannes.'

Zayn flung open the door. Onree stood just outside, his usual scruffy self with his dirty patchwork smock and collection of old sacks.

'Now, you can't go disturbing my guests,' the maiderdee was saying.

'He's my friend.' Ammadin stepped forward. 'I'll vouch for him.'

Instantly the maiderdee became all bows and smiles. Ammadin brought Onree inside, settled him in a chair, and shut the door to spare the maiderdee the temptation of eavesdropping. Onree sat down with a satisfied sigh and dropped his sacks on the floor. Zayn perched on the end of the bed.

'Do you want something to eat?' Ammadin said to Onree. 'We've got plenty.'

'No, no, I just had dinner at my niece's house. I'm glad I caught up with you. It's about our friend here.' He paused to jerk his thumb in Zayn's direction. 'The provo's looking for Kazraks. He's going to make a sweep through town, they tell me.'

Zayn swore under his breath. 'They must have found Alayn.'

'Now don't go jumping to conclusions,' Onree went on. 'They may have found him, I wouldn't know, but that's not what this is all about. The provo's looking for Yarl Soutan, same as you, and they've heard he's riding with a Kazrak or Kazraks unknown.'

'They have?' Zayn said. 'How do you know all this?'

Onree smiled. 'I'm the one who laid the information against Soutan. Now, luckily, my niece's little boy told me he saw some comnee people ride in today, you see, and so I looked into it, and well! turned out to be you. So I took myself back to the provo's and told them, not the Kazrak riding with the spirit rider. Other Kazraks.'

'So Zayn should be safe enough?' Ammadin said.

'He should, yes. But I wanted you to know, just in case. You never know with the zhundars. If they give you trouble, a few coins of the right size should take care of it.'

'What?' Ammadin said. 'A bribe, you mean. I can't say I care much for Leen.'

'That's why I'm on my way back to Nannes.' Onree grinned at her. 'Tomorrow, that is. Can't let my daughter worry about me, eh?'

'Something I don't understand,' Zayn said. 'Is Soutan in trouble with the law?'

'You could say so. He's wanted for rape. Aggravated criminal assault, up Dordan way.'

Zayn whistled under his breath.

'Not a nice fellow, Soutan.' Onree stood up. 'Spirit Rider, if you'd just hand me those sacks there?'

Ammadin helped him pick up the sacks and arrange them to his satisfaction, as he passed them from hand to hand and occasionally tried shoving one into a pocket. After a few confusions he decided that the arrangement would do.

'My thanks,' Ammadin said. 'I appreciate your letting us know.'

'So do I,' Zayn said. 'But one last question: how did you get here so fast?'

'Fast? What do you mean, fast?'

'We've got horses, and you don't, but you reached Leen before us.'

Onree merely laughed and began shuffling towards the door. 'Now Zayn, if you want to know more about Soutan, go see Loy Millou in Sarla. Got that? It's a woman's name, Loy.'

'Loy Millou in Sarla,' Zayn repeated. 'All right. But who is she?'

Onree merely smiled, then turned and walked out. With a deft kick he shut the door behind him.

'I think you've heard everything he's going to tell,' Ammadin said. 'Criminal assault and rape. Your friend Warkannan's riding with some grand company.'

'If he finds out, Soutan's not going to like his reaction. I know Idres, and I can guarantee it.'

They sat back down to finish their meal, but Zayn ate very little. As the light outside began to fade, Zayn rummaged through the room, found a pair of lamps and some oil, and set them up on the table. Ammadin began thinking of the comnee, travelling fast back to the Rift. One way or the other, they could take care of themselves – she had complete faith in them. If Alayn's men wanted trouble, they would get the worst of it.

'Is something wrong?' Zayn said.

'No. I was just wondering what Maddi was doing right now. It's so strange, to be off alone like this.'

'You're not exactly alone.'

'Well, no, sorry.' She smiled at him. 'To a comnee girl like me, two people count as alone.'

'I can see that. I miss them all myself.'

'You're serious about coming back, aren't you?'

'If I can, yes. Until the Chosen find me, and it's all over.'

'What makes you think we'd let them kill you?'

Zayn shrugged and looked away. She could feel his despair, almost smell it – a cold thing, more the absence of a smell. Outside someone came tramping past, three or four men, heavy footed, laughing with one another and talking so fast she could barely understand a word.

'Barge men,' Zayn said. 'There's a tavern around here, from what they're saying.'

They walked on by, the noise died, Zayn returned to staring at nothing. Ammadin rummaged through her saddlebags and took out her comb, carved from red grassar horn. She unbraided her hair and began combing it out. All at once she could smell his arousal. She looked up to find him watching her, the smile gone, with such an intensity of longing that she felt her treacherous body respond. Soon you'll be parting ways, she reminded herself. It's not like he'll stay around to be a daily nuisance.

'You know something, Ammi?' Zayn said. 'I don't have any secrets from you any more. Do you remember what you told me once? That if I stopped lying you'd reconsider?'

'Yes, I do remember that.'

She put the comb back into the saddlebag and set it on the floor. He sat unmoving, merely watched her, but he smelled so intensely male that she wanted to rub her face on his sweaty shirt. Instead she stayed where she was and waited. The silence lengthened between them, and he began to look – not exactly frightened, she decided, more frustrated, as if he were trying to think of something clever to say and failing. She stood up and ran her hands through her hair to push it back.

'You know,' she said, 'if you were sleeping on the outside, I wouldn't have to worry about rolling off the bed.'

The smile he gave her was so open, so heart-felt that the last of her doubts vanished. He got up and walked round the table to stand in front of her. For a long moment he just smiled at her, then he laid his hands on either side of her face.

'I like your hands,' she said. 'They're warm and strong.'

'Thank you.'

He leaned forward and kissed her. She'd never taken as much pleasure from a single kiss as she did from his. Her breath seemed to catch in her throat; she turned her head away with a little gasp.

'Is something wrong?' he said.

'No. What made you think that?'

'Well, I've never been with someone like – uh, well – you're going to have to tell me what you like.'

'I'll be glad to.' She took another kiss. 'Let's go lie down.'

Later, much later, as she lay drowsy in his arms and watched the shadows thrown by the lamps flicker across the room, she wondered if she'd done something dangerous, if she had finally found a man who threatened her desire to ride alone through her life. In a few more days they'd separate, each on their own road – in that, she felt, lay her safety. And if she never saw him again? What then? The thought made her flinch so sharply that for a moment she was afraid she'd woken him, but he sighed in his sleep and fell quiet again.

She could neither foresee his death nor prevent it. Both of their fates lay with the gods, who had given them this brief moment of peace – like a tent safe and warm in the ocean of grass that made up the world. Thinking that, she could fall asleep, grateful.

In the rising light of dawn, Soutan came staggering back to camp, so exhausted that Arkazo ran to meet him and take his heavy box of crystals. Warkannan, who had been kneeling on the ground to roll up his bedroll, sat back on his heels.

'Are you all right?' Warkannan said.

'Not really.' Soutan sat down nearby. 'I can't stop worrying about that damned spirit rider. She could ruin everything.'

'Do you have any evidence that she's trying to?'

'If I could only find them!' Soutan ignored the question. 'They must be in Leen, or at least, inside some sort of building. The crystals can't see through roofs.'

'They can't?' Arkazo put the box down next to Soutan. 'Why not?'

'The crystals are only receivers. Those moving points of light in the sky? The ones you Kazraks call the Phalanx? They're actually some sort of transmitter. We think they're a type of machine called a satellite. They travel around the world above the atmosphere, and when they're visible in the sky, they capture pictures of the ground below them and transmit them to the crystals.'

'You're not sure what they are?' Arkazo knelt down beside Warkannan. 'It seems like a lot of knowledge has disappeared.'

'That's certainly true.'

'But you Cantonneurs have books, and you send your children to school. Why wasn't it all written down?'

'Therein, my dear Kaz, lies a tale. A very long one, but at root simple. The Settlers destroyed a great deal of their own knowledge to ensure we wouldn't have it. It's in the Landfall Treaty. They were trying to protect the ChaMeech on the one hand and placate your Mullah Agvar on the other. I understand the former impulse, but why they bothered with the latter, I don't know.'

Arkazo frowned and used his finger to draw in the dirt: a small circle above a long curve, and some dotted lines emanating from the circle to the ends of the curve.

'Well, well, well,' Soutan said, grinning. 'I think you're about to ask the crucial question. Sometimes you amaze me, Kaz.'

'Thanks.' Arkazo paused, smiling as if he'd been given a splendid gift. 'Why are your crystals so limited? Is that the question you mean? You can only see for a few miles in any direction, but if these satellites are in the sky, by rights –'

'I should be able to see from horizon to horizon, yes. We don't know why they don't work that way. Somehow or other, the crystals have a limited range, and that's that.'

'But it doesn't make sense.' Arkazo glanced at Warkannan.

'Yes, even I can see that,' Warkannan said. 'But we don't have time to worry about it now. Soutan, if the spirit rider's far away, then she can't be sneaking up on us, can she? Or whatever it is you're so afraid of.'

'She doesn't need to be close by to ruin my crystals,' Soutan said. 'That's what you don't understand. But it's not just her. God in heaven, I forgot – I need to – I'd better scan again.' He stood up. 'Kaz, hand me that box.'

'Damn it,' Warkannan snapped. 'We need to get on the road. That's what *you* don't understand.'

Soutan clutched his box of crystals to his chest and walked away. Warkannan got up and started after him, but Arkazo caught his arm.

'Uncle, if he scans now, it might save us time in the long run. If there's some kind of trouble brewing, I mean, and he can see how to avoid it.'

'You're pretty impressed with Soutan, aren't you?'

Arkazo shrugged and turned a little away. 'Not so much impressed with him,' he said at last, 'as with the stuff he knows. I've always liked learning how things worked.'

'That's true.' Warkannan could remember endless childhood questions, most of which he hadn't been able to answer. 'Let's get the horses saddled up and ready.'

Apparently, however, Arkazo had hidden talent as an oracle. Soutan came rushing back in just a few minutes.

'Oh my god!' Soutan stammered. 'It's a very good thing I did take a look around. Kaz, you don't dare ride into town today. It's crawling with zhundars. They're looking for Kazraks.'

'How do you know that?' Warkannan said.

'Because one of my crystals can pick up sound. I heard them talking in the outdoor market.'

'Wait,' Arkazo broke in. 'If these satellites are above the atmosphere, how can they pick up people talking?'

'I don't know. The Settlers were immensely advanced. We think that –'

'Stop worrying about the lousy Settlers!' Warkannan stepped in between them. 'We need grain for the horses and food for ourselves. How are we going to get it? That's the only problem we have time to worry about right now.'

Much to Warkannan's surprise, Soutan nodded his agreement.

'We'll have to stick to the back roads and buy from farmers,' Soutan said. 'Eventually, I suppose, the zhundars will start searching the countryside, but since I can see them coming, we should be able to avoid them. It's going to add a lot of miles to our journey, but if we all get arrested, the delay could be permanent.'

'I don't understand,' Arkazo said. 'Why are they looking for Kazraks?'

'Because of me. They know that I'm riding with a pair of them.' Soutan turned dead-white and began to sweat. 'I told you I had powerful enemies. Somehow or other, they know I'm back.'

* * *

Loy Millou, tenured professor of ancient history at the College of Sarla, swept into her office at the guildhall and slammed the door behind her. She threw the book she carried, a copy of *The Sibylline Prophecies*, onto her desk so hard that a pile of student essays slid and cascaded onto the floor. The unlit candles wobbled, but she caught the silver candelabra before it fell.

'Oh damn it all!'

She pulled her brown robe over her head and hung it on the hook beside the door. Her white shirt had ridden up, as shirts did under robes. She yanked it down over her saurskin leggings, then flopped into the swivel chair behind her desk. Late afternoon sunlight poured through the unglazed window and fell across the tiled floor. Dust motes danced in the shaft of light, and so did a swarm of yellabuhs, flying endless figure eights.

'You never get anywhere, do you?' Loy remarked. 'I'm beginning to feel the same.'

A knock on the door, which opened before she could call out – Wan Mendis stuck his timid bald head into the room.

'You must have heard the news,' Wan said.

'About Yarl Soutan? Yes, unfortunately. The fœtid stinking nerve of the man!'

Wan came in and shut the door behind him. When Loy waved in the direction of the extra chair, he sat down, glancing at the pile of rushi on the floor. He bent over and began gathering the essays.

'Thank you,' Loy said. 'What I really wonder about is the pair of Kazraks that are riding with him.'

'Me too,' Wan said. 'Old Onree's report said the older one rode like a cavalry officer.' He sat back up and laid the rushi sheets onto the corner of the desk. 'Student work?'

'Final exams in Settler history.'

Wan frowned at the top rushi. 'Their Tekspeak is very bad.'

'They're first years, that's why. They'll get you next term, and you can whip them into shape.'

Wan smiled, then let it fade. 'It must strike you particularly hard,' he said, 'Yarl's return, I mean.'

'After what he did to my daughter? Oh yes. I have fantasies about killing him, you know.'

'I can't blame you. Er, how is Rozi, these days?'

'Still lost somewhere in herself.' Loy felt her throat tighten. 'Still doesn't laugh at anything, still doesn't want to eat.'

'Still?'

'Still. She believed in his impossible scheme, you know, heart and soul. She thought he was going to save us all. That's what made it so horrible.'

'Well, it's a very attractive premise, a distant paradise that should by rights be ours.'

'And he milked it for all it was worth, the rotten bastard.'

'One reason that men go into the prophet business seems to be the women.' Wan paused for a sigh. 'Look at all those stories about Mullah Agvar and his followers' wives.'

'True. But Rozi wasn't a woman then. She was a girl.'

'Yes. I'm so sorry.' Wan arranged the pile of rushis on her desk. 'So very very sorry. But if the authorities catch him, the guild has to execute him legally, you know.'

'I told you my murderous impulses were fantasies. But when they hang him, I get to watch.'

'No one would deny you that.'

'If the authorities catch him.' Loy looked away and watched the yellabuhs, endlessly dancing. 'They did a rotten job last time.'

'Things are different this time. We know about the mask now, and Commiz Duhmars has been told what to look for.'

'No more hiding in plain sight? Well, let's hope.'

'Speaking of Duhmars, the guildmaster sent me to ask you something. He would have come himself, but there are zhundars in his office. They're taking a statement or some such thing.'

The point of this talk, at last! Loy looked back and found Wan leaning forward, his eyes solemn.

'The commiz wants to issue a trans-canton warrant for Yarl's arrest. He needs a formal complaint, of course. Master Zhoc and I thought of you immediately.'

Loy felt herself smile. 'How kind,' she said. 'How very kind of you both.'

'I thought you'd enjoy having your name on the thing.' Wan got up. 'I'll just go tell the master. The commiz will want to meet with you tomorrow.'

'Not today?'

'He needs to sound out his fellow authorities first. That's really why he's here, to get the guild to send the transmits for him.'

'Daccor, tomorrow, then. Tell him any time but noon. That's when I hand back these exams. Which I'd better start reading right now.'

By the time Loy left the guildhall, the sun hung low behind summer clouds, turning the sky as scarlet as the lace-leaf trees that decorated the central square. Students in their pale yellow robes wandered past, talking in groups or walking hand in hand in pairs. The Loremasters Guild owned most of Inner Sarla, the precinct built by the Settlers out of their mysterious flexstone. Around the square stood glossy white buildings, most three storeys high, inset with windows made of some clear substance that no one remembered how to make or even name. Unlike glass, it never shattered, never scratched, never popped out during the worst earthquakes, even when the buildings swayed and groaned and the wood partitions built by the descendants of the Settlers split and fell.

Sarla, the second-biggest city in the Cantons, stretched out around the college. Tall hedges of dark red thornbush and golden tree-ferns set the precinct apart from the rest of the town, where the buildings were mostly woven from sturdy pink hill bamboid and dark purple lake rushes. In the clear light of summer the effect was nauseatingly sweet, or so Loy found it, as if the town were a tray of petits fours baked by giants. Her destination, however, down in the centre of town, had been built by the Settlers, though for some long-forgotten purpose. Behind a reflecting pool stood a dome of white flexstone, so magnificent that it seemed a logical choice for a synagogue once the Church of the One God had established itself.

Above the door, painted directly onto the flex, was the blue six-pointed star of King David, enclosing the smaller gold cross of Joshua the Martyr. Here the rabbis taught their congregations the Torah and Dorya, the law and the gifts, the service owed to God as explicated by the prophets and the hope of Heaven as promised by Joshua. A gravelled path led around the dome to a scatter of outbuildings, some white, some pink and purple. One long, low flexstone building, Loy's destination, sat in the middle of its own garden, protected by a wall woven from brass wire and orange thorn vines. On the gate a chain held a big brass bell. Loy picked it up and rang.

In a few minutes Sister Taymah, wearing her long, white habit, her hair tucked into a blue headscarf, came out of the building. When she saw Loy she waved and jogged over to open the gate.

'Hello, Loy,' Taymah said. 'Come to see Rozi?'

'Yes. How is she today?'

'A bit better. She's in the chapel, but we're not having formal service or anything. Come in, come in.'

The main sanctuary of the temple lay under the white dome, but around the back stood a private chapel for the sisters of the Order of Judith. Chairs woven of purple rushes filled most of the sanctuary, but up on a dais stood the Ark and the bimah, both beautifully constructed of true-oak wood. When the worship of the One God had been revived, the founders had been profoundly puzzled by one rule of temple design: seating the Ark on the wall facing Jerusalem. Jerusalem, they knew, existed back on Old Earth, its precise direction impossibly lost. However, it lay somewhere in the galaxy that rose every evening in the east, and a rising star meant hope, and so the Ark now stood against the east wall in every sanctuary.

On the west wall hung a gold cross with a crown of thorns centred upon it, a memorial to the prophet Joshua bar Josef, who had died trying to free his people from the power of those priestly hypocrites known as the Fairasee. At their bidding the Romai Khanate had nailed him to a wooden cross to die; now his symbol reminded the Cantons that powerful khanates were not to be trusted. His students had gathered his sayings, and a book of them lay on the small lectern across from the bimah.

In the front row Rozi was sitting, wearing a white dress but no headscarf. Her long dark hair hung straight down to her waist, and her face – her poor little face, as Loy thought of it – was so thin that her cheekbones bulged, sharp under the skin, and there were creases at the corners of her mouth.

At the sound of footsteps coming down the aisle, Rozi turned, saw Loy, and smiled with real pleasure. In the light from the oil lamp that burned perpetually in front of the Ark, her hazel eyes looked green, deep set – entirely too deep set. 'Hullo, Mama,' she said. 'Exams must be over.'

'Yes, pretty much. I've got one last job lot of grades to post.'

When Loy sat down in the chair next to her, Rozi kept smiling but went tense. She could stand to have no one touch her, not ever her mother, and Loy had long since given up trying to hug her daughter.

'So,' Loy said. 'How are things?'

'Pretty good. I uh – well, I've made a decision.'

'Yes?'

'I want to join the order. I want to become a neophyte here.' Rozi hesitated, gulped a breath, and went on. 'I don't want to go to university.'

'Oh Rozi!' The words had spoken themselves, and Loy could hear the hurt in her own tone of voice. She forced out a smile. 'I mean, you know your own mind best. But are you sure?'

'Very sure, Mama. I knew you wouldn't like it.'

'Well, whether I like it or not, it's your decision to make.' Loy managed to get control of her voice at last. 'I mean that, darling. It's your life, and if you want to spend it here, well, then, that's the way it'll be.'

Tears welled in Rozi's eyes and spilled down her gaunt cheeks. 'Thank you,' she stammered. 'I've been so afraid to say anything, but then I realized, I was just afraid of everything, not really of you. So I decided I'd tell you as soon as I saw you.'

'And, darling, I'm not angry, no. What does Mother Superior think?'

A side door opened, and Mother Superior herself swept in, draped in white from headscarf to robe to sandals, just as if she'd been lurking there, waiting for a cue. 'Taymah told me you were here, Loy,' she said. 'I hope you don't mind me interrupting you.'

'Not at all. Rozi just told me about her decision.'

'Ah.' Mother Superior's wide grey eyes grew even wider. She had a round face, touched with pink on the cheeks, and smooth, thin, grey eyebrows that Loy suspected her of plucking in secret.

'She says it's all right.' Rozi twisted around in her chair and beamed. 'She says she's not angry.'

'Well, that's wonderful! Thank you, Loy.'

Loy smiled, shrugged, and felt like an utter hypocrite, every bit as bad as Joshua's hated Fairasee. She wanted to scream, you've stolen my daughter, you bitch! But she made small talk, chatted with both Rozi and Mother Superior, chatted with Taymah as well when the girl joined them, and smiled or looked serious as the chat demanded. At last, she felt, she'd martyred herself enough.

'I'd better be going,' Loy said. 'I know you have your evening services soon.'

Mother Superior walked Loy to the gate. For a moment Loy paused, looking back at the dome, rising white against the darkening sky.

'I'm glad for Rozi's sake that you're supporting her in this.' Mother Superior's voice was always calm, her vowels always round and full. 'But it must be a disappointment to you.'

'You've got sharp eyes. I hope I haven't been rude?'

'No, not at all. But after all, we've had these discussions before.'

'Many times. I'd just hoped for something –' Loy caught herself just in time. 'Something different for her.'

'Something better, you mean.'

Loy winced. 'Oh, who's to say what's better? You've certainly got more of God left than I do of history.'

'It's impossible to lose God entirely.' Mother Superior was smiling a calm, round smile. 'Perhaps that's what our exile here is supposed to teach us.'

'Perhaps so. I have some awful news for you, by the way. One of our retired loremasters spotted Yarl Soutan in Bredanee. Apparently he's riding north.'

'How absolutely horrible!'

'I was thinking that I shouldn't tell Rozi.'

'No, of course not. If for some reason she has to know, I'll do it. She's placed her spiritual welfare in my hands, after all.'

Mother Superior looked briefly, ever so briefly, smug; then concern reappeared in her eyes.

'I see,' Loy said. 'Well, good evening. I'd better get home. I'll be meeting with the commiz tomorrow.'

Loy walked away, waved once, kept walking until she'd left the compound behind and any chance of being heard with it.

'You sanctimonious bitch!' she muttered aloud. 'You rotten sanctimonious bitch!'

She marched on home in something of a better mood.

Master Zhoc had arranged Loy's meeting with the local Commiz duh Trib, Peer Duhmars, for late afternoon, when her classes for the day – indeed, for the entire spring session – had finished. Against the afternoon heat, the master's big office was pleasantly cool, a dark, panelled room with glass in both windows. Bookshelves lined two of the walls. Loy found Peer Duhmars there ahead of her, sitting across from the master in a stiff-backed wooden chair that matched his posture, while Zhoc, thin and almost frail, with his grey hair and huge, dark eyes, lounged in a leather chair behind his massive desk. The commiz, heavy-set, his face square and florid, nodded her way.

Loy took a chair half-way between them. Duhmars reached into his jacket pocket and pulled out a long roll of rushi.

'I have the warrant all drawn up,' the commiz said. 'All it needs is your signature, Mada Millou. Then I can file it with the Council.'

'Thank you, Mizzou Duhmars.' Loy took the proffered rushi and leaned back to read it. In the long welter of legal language certain phrases stood out as if written in blood: assault and battery, forced intercourse, sodomy, lacerations, attempted intimidation of witnesses. She read fast and tried to avoid them. Finally she found the proper place for her signature as complainant.

'Sign it with your full title,' the commiz said.

'I intended to.' Loy stood up and glanced at Zhoc's desk, normally a sea of books and rushi. An inkwell and pen stood ready in a cleared corner. As she signed, she was wishing that she were a real sorcerer like in the ancient stories, who could put a curse on Yarl, perhaps one that would make his testicles wither away with great pain. For a moment she stood waving the rushi to let the ink dry, while both Zhoc and Duhmars watched her with eyes that displayed the proper degree of concern. To them it was a serious matter; she knew that, she was grateful, but she also knew that neither shared her rage. She handed the warrant back to Duhmars.

'I'll be glad to help you in any way I can,' she said.

'Thank you.' Duhmars stood and concentrated on rolling up the warrant. 'When it comes to trial, you'll be called, of course.'

'Good.'

Loy sat back down and watched Zhoc escort the provo to the door. Duhmars paused with his hand on the jamb.

'I'll remember what you told me about that third Kazrak,' Duhmars said. 'Damned strange thing!'

'Yes, it is,' Zhoc said.

Zhoc closed the door and walked back, slowly, to his desk. He sank into his chair with a long sigh.

'You look tired,' Loy said.

'I haven't been sleeping well,' Zhoc said. 'Having Yarl around does that to me.'

'Me, too, actually. What's this about a third Kazrak?'

'It might be very good news. Onree thinks it is.' Zhoc straightened up and rummaged through the rushis on his desk. 'Ah, here we are. Yarl manages to make enemies wherever he goes, the charming fellow. There's another Kazrak – his name is Zayn Hassan – following him, and as far as Onree can tell, this Hassan might rid us of the man once and for all if he catches him. Apparently Yarl tried to have him murdered.'

'I'll wish Hassan the best of luck, then.'

'As will I.' Zhoc tossed the rushi onto the clutter, then leaned back in his chair. 'It's bad enough that Yarl's in the Cantons, but bringing Kazraks with him? I suppose they're heading to Burgunee. There's that other Kazrak there, the one Yarl was so thick with.'

'What other Kazrak? What is this with Kazraks? All of a sudden they're crawling out of the walls! Or wait – you mean that exiled leader, don't you? The khan?'

'Yes, Jezro Khan.'

'But why is Yarl bringing them?' Loy felt suddenly weary. 'I don't trust Kazraks, I really don't. I'm just glad that the Landfall Treaty set them up on one side of the Rift and us on the other.'

'So were the Settlers.' Zhoc flashed her a wry smile, then let it fade. 'I wonder what Yarl's been telling them?'

'Probably the exact same thing he told his followers here.'

'That we should be trying to go "home", as he keeps calling it? Probably so.' Zhoc leaned back in his chair and looked up as if he could see the galaxy through the ceiling. 'Return to the stars! Doesn't he realize that if it were possible the guild would have figured it out by now? How can he not have realized?'

'You told him often enough.' It was Loy's turn for the wry smile. 'If the original Shipfolk couldn't find their way back, how are we supposed to?'

'Exactly. We should have realized it early on, that he was going mad, I mean. It's generally considered madness, at any rate, when someone becomes obsessed with doing the impossible.' Zhoc shook his head. 'I feel it deeply, that I failed to reach him. Can't he see how destructive it is, offering people false hopes?'

'I don't suppose he really cares. He wants to act the part of a messiah and have a whole crowd of people telling him how wonderful he is.'

'He had something for everyone, didn't he? The young people loved the very idea of all those gadgets, all those machines. And the old people – well, I can see the appeal myself.' Zhoc sat up and swivelled his chair around to smile at her. 'A hundred and twenty years of life guaranteed, and in perfect health. Who wouldn't want it?'

'The Tribes still have it. The health part, anyway, and if they hadn't chosen such rough lives, who knows how long they'd live?'

'It's their ancestors who did the choosing. I wonder if the descendants would continue to choose it, if they knew.'

'Good question. Probably unanswerable, too.'

'Probably, yes. And not as important, ultimately, as why they stay so damned healthy. I'm envious, I'll admit it. They're just not built like us. Good God, the way they drink! One glass of that keese, and I'd have to lie down, but they knock it back all day.'

'Yes, their metabolism – you're right, they're not like us. And they're not like the other Inborn, really. If we could find the Settlers' records, we might come closer to learning why.'

'Just so.' Zhoc shook his head in irritation. '*If.* I wish they hadn't stored so much data in N'Dosha. There has to be some rational explanation, and thanks to the filthy ChaMeech we'll never learn it.'

'If the records are all lost, anyway. Everyone's afraid of going to find out, so they might as well be.'

'Yarl of course wanted to. I got so sick of him pestering me for funding.' Zhoc paused, looking grim. 'You know what my worst fear is? That Yarl isn't a charlatan, that he really believes in his grand scheme. If he does, he could cause a great deal of trouble for everyone.'

'He already has, hasn't he? What –'

'Those Kazraks.' Zhoc leaned forward, his eyes urgent. 'What if he wants to convince the Kazraks to come search for the lost ships?'

Loy felt herself turn cold. 'Trouble,' she said. 'I see what you mean.'

After she left the master's office, Loy finished posting the student grades, gave their papers to the guild clerk in case anyone wanted them back, then locked up her office for the recess. She hated holidays, when she had nothing to do but sit around her cottage and worry about Rozi. You should start a new research project, she told herself. The utter futility of the thought nearly made her weep. She had studied the Landfall Treaty for twenty years now, and what had she learned? How knowledge evaporated like water in the sun when a people, a culture, were dying, how myth sprang up like purple grass in a rose garden to strangle truth, and how well-meaning people had decided that myth was healthier than truth.

Loy left the building and went home, where a stack of books, better than any chemical anodyne, waited for her. She would lie on the couch, she decided, and lose herself in ancient works: classics of other times, other worlds, and other stars.

Before they left Leen, Ammadin insisted they take their horses to a blacksmith to have them freshly shod. Neither of them knew what the roads ahead were like. The road that ran north from Leen was bad enough, an ancient, dead-straight stripe of crumbling grey sponge through the fields and villages. No one actually travelled on it; on each side ran lanes of hard-packed dirt, where the farmers drove their wagons and travellers rode their horses or walked, pulling goods behind them in two-wheeled wicker carts.

By then the summer season had arrived, hot and parched, when the pale sun turned merciless and fended off all rain. Out in the fields water gleamed in irrigation ditches. Whenever they crossed a bridge, Zayn saw a variety of contraptions - wheels lined with buckets, wooden sluices, pumps - sucking or lifting the precious water out of the river below and delivering it to the gold and scarlet fields. Ammadin insisted on stopping often to rest and water the horses. Zayn never objected, even though he knew that Warkannan was gaining ground, that he would be pushing his men and mounts both now that he knew one of the Chosen was heading for Jezro Khan.

During that ride north Zayn took his love affair with Ammadin like a drug. His feeling for her - his honest affection, his gratitude, the sexual pleasure they shared - drowned his thoughts and changed his memories of the Chosen, of Kazrajistan, even of his days in the border cavalry, into stories he'd once heard someone tell. Those events no longer mattered, as long as he and Ammadin could ride together during the sun-drenched days and lie down together at night.

But all too soon they crossed the border into the Canton of Dordan, and another day's ride brought them to the little town of Lasko, a scatter of white houses tucked among the gaudy fields and shaded by ancient oaks. There was no hohte, but they did find a wine shop, a pleasant place with a true-wood floor, tables and chairs woven from maroon rushes, and a long bar, also of true-wood, that stood before a wall covered with pottery jars and glass bottles, all tipped onto their sides in elaborate wicker racks. The proprietor, a stout woman wearing a heavy white apron over her smock and trousers, told them that she had a small barn out in back.

'You can sleep in the hay loft for a couple of vrans,' she said. 'Not much hay up there, though, and don't you go starting any fires.'

'Don't worry,' Zayn said. 'It's too hot for that.'

'You're right, aren't you? Go get your horses in out of the sun.'

Zayn tended the horses while Ammadin disappeared round back of the barn – scanning, he assumed – and when she returned she confirmed his assumption.

'Warkannan is right at the edge of my crystal's range,' she said. 'That means he's a good long way ahead.'

'Well, not much I can do about that,' Zayn said.

'I know. You don't look particularly worried.'

'I've been learning from you. If my quest takes me to Jezro, well, then it will, and if it doesn't, it's not meant to.'

Ammadin considered this seriously. As always, she was carrying her saddlebags slung over one shoulder. Away from the comnee she never left her crystals out of arm's reach.

'I suppose that's true,' Ammadin said at last. 'But it's possible to fail a quest, you know. Usually the quester fails out of cowardice, but I can't imagine you being a coward, so if you're on the wrong path, it has to be for some other reason.'

'Such as, maybe I never should have taken the quest on. Maybe I should have just stayed with the comnee and let –'

' – the Chosen find you and kill you.'

Zayn scowled at her.

'Well, that's what you always say, isn't it? If someone would only kill you, then all your troubles would be over.'

The justice of it stung. He turned and took a step away. He heard her follow, then felt her hands on his shoulders, stroking him.

'I don't want to see you dead, Zayn.' Her voice had turned soft. 'I don't know, no one can know what the gods have in store for you, but please, try to stay alive?'

'Of course.'

'There's no of course about it.'

He shrugged, shook her hands off, and walked a few more steps away. Standing in the cool shade of the barn as he was, the sunlight outside the door looked to him like a wall of white fire, and for the briefest of moments he was afraid to walk into it. With a muttered curse he turned back to Ammadin.

'I'm sorry,' he said. 'All right, I'll do my best to stay alive. I promise. How's that?'

'That's fine.' She was smiling at him. 'If you died, I'd have to mourn you, and I don't want to cut all my hair off.'

'Heaven forbid!' He managed to smile in return. 'I've never tasted wine. Want to go try some?'

'I thought you Kazraks weren't supposed to.'

'By all the laws of my religion I'm damned already. I might as well get drunk if I feel like it.' He'd meant it as a joke, but he could hear the bitter twist in his voice. 'Sorry. I guess I'm just tired. Let's go.'

Outside, a cloud of dust like smoke drifted from the road. Big wagons were trundling past; Zayn counted six of them, each drawn by four heavy horses. Two of the wagons looked more like moving houses; their wooden sides were about eight feet high, and he could see the peaks of roofs. On this pair hung big banners, announcing 'The Recallers of Roon'. The word, Recaller, brought back the memory with it, of the small boy crouched on the cold tile floor. Caught between two times Zayn watched until the last wagon passed, and the dust began to settle with one last swirl over the grey roadway.

'Zayn?' Ammadin said. 'Are you all right?'

With a toss of his head Zayn suppressed the memory. 'Oh yes,' he said. 'Just tired.'

The wine shop stood empty of patrons. At the counter the stout woman was polishing glass goblets with a piece of white cloth.

'Something I meant to ask you,' Zayn said. 'Does this road run straight through to Burgunee?'

'Not exactly straight, no.' She held up a goblet and inspected it. 'After you leave Sarla, the road goes north, but there's a fork a few miles out of town. They both look wrong.' She smiled and set the goblet down. 'One runs north after a little detour, and that's the Burgunee road. The other heads east to where N'Dosha used to be. You better ask in town when you get there, just to make sure.'

'Thank you. I'll do that.'

Zayn ordered wine randomly, pointing at a couple of glass bottles, handing over the coins she asked for. Once she had the money, she pulled the corks out of the bottles with a spiral of metal wire protruding from a handle. Zayn glanced back and saw Ammadin sitting at a table near the open door. He took the bottles and a pair of empty glasses over, set them down, then pulled up a chair opposite her.

'I heard you asking about the roads,' Ammadin said. 'Could she tell you?'

'Yes, she sure did. Exactly where are you meeting Water Woman? Did she ever make up her mind?'

'Yesterday morning, finally. Out in what used to be N'Dosha, but not far from the Dordan border, she said, there's some kind of monument. She called it the "white cliff with pictures". She says there's an old road that will take me there. Why? Is she wrong?'

'No. It's just that your road's going to leave mine right after Sarla.'

'That's not good news.' Ammadin frowned, considering. 'You'll have a ways to travel, and I won't be able to hide you from the sorcerer. You're right to worry. You'll have to be very careful from then on.'

Zayn picked up a bottle and concentrated on filling their glasses with pale yellow wine.

'Zayn?' Ammadin said. 'Something's really wrong. Please tell me.'

'Well, hell! In a couple of days we won't be riding together. Won't you even miss me?'

Her utter surprise caught him like a slap across the face. Just lie, Ammi, he thought. Go ahead and lie, and I'll make myself believe it.

'Miss you?' Ammadin said at last. 'What do you mean by that?'

'Oh never mind! Here, have a goddamned glass of wine.'

He shoved a glass across the table towards her, but she let it sit. 'I've hurt you somehow,' she said. 'I'm sorry.'

'Well, I was hoping you liked having me around.'

'What? Of course I do. But we're both on quest.'

'Yes, I know that. But –'

'But what? Do I love you? Isn't that what you really want to know?'

'Yes, I'm afraid it is. I know it's a stupid question.'

'It's only stupid because we're both riding quests. If we were back on the grass, it wouldn't be.'

'All right. Suppose I wait till we get back there and ask it again.'

'That's fair.' She picked up her glass and saluted him with it. 'You do that.'

All those beautiful women back on the plains, Zayn thought. Beautiful, easy women – and what do I do? Fall for a spirit rider. He took his own glass, returned her salute, and drank as much as he could in one swallow.

For five days Warkannan and his men had been riding like fugitives. They followed country roads that ran like ruts between fields; when those roads threatened to take them to towns, they left them and stayed close to wild country, the rocky stream beds and remnants of the old vegetation that had once covered Dordan. No true-oaks grew here – the pale fountain trees fought for sunlight with tall scarlet lace-leafs and a welter of orange and russet herbage.

They crossed the border from Dordan to Burgunee in the middle of the night. Soutan led them straight to an abandoned barn, where they camped to hide from the dawn. What was left of the walls sagged and split, but the roof covered them enough to thwart the spirit rider's crystals, or so Soutan said.

'How do you even know if she's trying to spot us?' Warkannan said.

'I don't, but I don't care to be caught napping this time.'

'This time?'

'If she tries to kill these crystals, of course. Good God, don't you remember anything?'

'Well, if we'll reach Jezro soon, why does it matter?'

'Because we have to get him safely out of here and back across the border, don't we? Back to Andjaro, I mean. How am I supposed to do that without crystals?'

'That's true, of course. But I don't think the spirit rider cares one way or the other if we reach Andjaro.'

For an answer Soutan made a growling sound deep in his throat. Warkannan let the subject drop.

With dawn Soutan's mood improved. He rummaged through his gear and brought out a small rectangle of some substance that looked like blue quartz. When Arkazo asked him about it, he showed it round.

'This is a signal imp,' Soutan said. 'Once I charge it in the sunlight, it will send a message to Jezro, telling him we're nearly there.'

Arkazo's eyes widened. When Soutan handed him the imp, he held it up, studied it, stroked it with a forefinger as if it were a pet animal.

'We're nearly there?' Warkannan said.

'Oh yes. A day's ride – a long day, unfortunately, since we haven't come on the main roads. I'm trying to decide if we should wait till nightfall to move out. Let me scan, and then we'll know more.'

As the dawn blossomed, Soutan spent a long time out in the sun with his various devices as if he'd forgotten his fears of the spirit rider. Warkannan and Arkazo fed the horses the last of the grain and watered them at a rivulet behind the abandoned barn.

'I suppose Soutan knows what he's doing,' Warkannan said.

'Of course he does.'

A certain calm faith in Arkazo's voice caught Warkannan's attention, but he had no idea what to make of it. It's the machines he likes, he thought. Power from the sun and all that sort of thing. During their long ride, Soutan had been flooding Arkazo with so much information about the Settlers and their mechanical trinkets that Warkannan had simply stopped listening. Soutan's lectures did keep up Arkazo's morale; for that, he was grateful.

Soutan, wild-eyed and grinning, ran back to the barn. 'They've got the message,' he said. 'Jezro responded. I'd given my enemies too much credit. I assumed they'd figure out where I'd be taking you. They don't seem to have done so. The road ahead looks clear. Let's go. One last dash for safety!'

'What do you mean, looks clear?' Warkannan said. 'Is it clear or not?'

'My, and don't we have a literal mind? It is clear, Captain. It runs through fields and the like – nowhere much to hide. I saw no zhundars anywhere.'

'Good. Remember, you're the one they want to arrest.'

Warkannan had the satisfaction of seeing Soutan's smile disappear.

They saddled up and left the barn. By late afternoon, they were travelling along a straight road lined with true-oaks on one side and a canal on the other. The land here was beginning to rise, and at times the road climbed a low hill only to sink on the other side. At the top of one of these waves of earth, they saw ahead of them horsemen on the road, ten by Warkannan's hasty count, and heading their way.

'Well, Soutan,' Warkannan said, 'what do you make of this?'

'I don't know.' Soutan's face slowly drained of colour. 'The Phalanx is below the horizon. Oh my god, there's nowhere to hide!' He twisted this way and that in his saddle, then began to tremble. 'What are we going to do?'

'Be calm, for starters,' Warkannan said. 'Let's go meet them.'

Soutan squealed, but Warkannan leaned over and grabbed the reins from Soutan's hand. 'I said let's go!'

His horse set off at a brisk walk downhill, and Soutan's followed with the whining, yelping sorcerer on its back. Arkazo urged his horse up beside his uncle's.

'What are you going to do?' Arkazo said.

'If those are zhundars, I'm going to pretend we knew they were looking for Soutan, so we caught him. Then we turn him over.'

'Uncle, you can't do that! He's a friend.'

'Just watch me. We can find Jezro on our own now.'

'But –'

'Shut up,' Warkannan snapped. 'Here they are.'

With shouted greetings the horsemen spurred their mounts forward. All at once Soutan began to laugh.

'It's Marya's men,' he called out. 'We're safe!'

Warkannan tossed Soutan his reins. Laughing, shouting in Vranz, the horsemen surrounded them. Arkazo leaned forward in the saddle and listened hard. Finally he sat back. 'I can only catch a few words,' he said. 'They talk so damn fast.'

In a few minutes Soutan deigned to translate. He introduced the troop as the bodyguards of a certain Dookis Marya, who was sheltering Jezro Khan.

'Jezro himself's waiting at the house,' Soutan said. 'It's some miles on yet. Robear here –' he gestured at a burly dark-haired man on a blood bay horse, '– tells me that Marya's made sure the zhundars won't be troubling us.'

'Excellent! Give him my thanks, will you?'

Soutan spoke briefly. Robear smiled and saluted Warkannan with a casual wave of one hand, then jerked his thumb back the way his troop had come.

'Yes,' Warkannan said. 'Let's go.'

The twilight was darkening around them when they came to one last hill and saw down below a semi-circular valley, surrounded by hills on three sides. At the base of the hills a high fence surrounded an extravagant stretch of green lawns and elaborate gardens. To one side stood a stand of trees unlike any Warkannan had seen before, pale gold and shaggy with leaves as long and curved as sabre blades. In the middle of the lawn sprawled a one-storey rambling house, built mostly of true-wood and painted white. In windows lamplight glowed and sent shafts of gold out onto the green lawns. Just beyond the house, other structures stood dark in the gathering night.

'Stables and the like,' Soutan said, pointing. 'This is the manor house of Dookis Marya, where Jezro's been living.'

Warkannan was too tired to do more than smile. When he glanced at Arkazo, he found him staring wide-eyed at the distant view.

'Almost there,' Warkannan said. 'I thank God for it, too.'

Surrounded by guards, they rode downhill. When they dismounted in front of the house, shens came racing out, barking madly to greet them, but the horses were tired enough to ignore them. Soutan aimed a casual kick at the lead shen's head, caught it in the ribs instead, and smiled when it yelped and drew back. Servants came running to take the horses. One of them, a blond fellow dressed in a shirt of fine, white cloth and narrow, red trousers, spoke quickly to Soutan.

'The dookis won't be joining us tonight,' Soutan told Warkannan. 'I'm not surprised. She's something of a recluse.'

The fellow in the white shirt opened the front door and ushered them into a bright yellow room, stuffed with gilded furniture and glowing with light from tall glass lamps. More servants appeared, springing forward to take their saddlebags. In the confusion Warkannan almost overlooked the man who stood off to one side, leaning on a stout-looking walking stick; he had dark wavy hair, streaked with grey, and across his face ran a pair of brutal scars like a pucker of tan mountains, from his left jawbone to his right ear and back again. Whatever had gashed him had barely missed both throat and eyes.

It was the smile that finally made Warkannan recognize Jezro Khan, the world-weary twist of a full mouth that went so poorly with the real mirth in his dark eyes. Warkannan started to laugh, just a mutter under his breath, and strode over. Jezro laughed as well and held out his arms, but Warkannan took one step more, then knelt at his feet.

'What the hell are you doing, Idres?' Jezro said. 'Get up, for God's sake! I'm not even a khan any more.'

'That's about to change, your highness,' Warkannan said. 'There's an army waiting for you at home.'

Jezro stared, let his smile fade, took a step back and shook his head as if to say no in a prolonged tremor. Warkannan did get up, then, and held out his hand.

'We can talk about that later,' Warkannan said, and all at once he couldn't stop smiling. 'You know, it's good to see you.'

Jezro burst out laughing. 'A perfect Idres remark!'

'Oh good God! You remember that? The way you and Benumar used to tease –'

'Of course I do! I can't tell you how much I've missed you, this past ten years.'

Jezro dropped his walking stick, grabbed Warkannan's hand and pulled him close. They flung their arms around each other, laughed, nearly wept, laughed some more. Soutan hurried off, muttering about bathing, but Arkazo stood nearby with his hands in his pockets and smiled at them both.

'Kaz!' Jezro let Warkannan go and turned towards him. 'The last time I saw you, you were about this high.' He held his hand out roughly five feet from the ground. 'Do you remember? I spent the night at your family's house on my way back to Haz Kazrak, when my father was dying.'

'Yes sir,' Arkazo said. 'I'll never forget it, but I'm surprised you remember me.'

'Don't be,' Warkannan said. 'He's like that.'

Jezro shrugged, then fished in his trouser pocket and pulled out a handkerchief. He wiped his nose, then gave Warkannan a wry smile.

'These cuts?' Jezro touched a scar with one finger. 'They went right through my nose. Left me with a little problem.'

'I'm surprised you can breathe out of it at all.'

'Oh, the comnee hakeem had a rough and ready way of dealing with it. He cut a couple of pieces of hollow water reed, and – well, I'll spare you the details. I can't say I enjoyed the procedure. But the nose did heal open. It's the muscles that let you sniff that got cut.'

'Sir?' The blond fellow in the white shirt stepped forward; he spoke in heavily accented Kazraki. 'Our guests look hungry and tired.'

'And filthy,' Warkannan said. 'My apologies for that.'

'You're right, Zhil,' Jezro said. 'Guest rooms first. Talk later.'

It took Warkannan only a few minutes to realize that recluse or not, Dookis Marya was very rich. The house rambled because it held at least fifty rooms, added one to another without much plan, but all furnished with things that would have cost a fortune in Haz Kazrak. What they'd cost here in this half-settled country he couldn't even guess. Zhil followed them to translate their orders; servants stood everywhere, ready to lead them to bedrooms, set up baths, and fill them with warm water. When Warkannan asked for hot water so he could shave, a servant trained as a barber appeared to do the job for him. His own filthy clothing disappeared and clean appeared in its place. Some of Jezro's, he was told, and since he and Jezro were much of a height, it fitted well enough. During all of this Jezro hovered nearby, grinning, but they could barely say two words to each other in the confusion.

Finally, however, the servants left with a last round of bows. A clean Arkazo, freshly clothed in a shirt and trousers that Soutan had lent him, arrived in Warkannan's room, and the three of them sat down in cushioned armchairs in front of a pair of glass doors that gave out onto a little garden. Warkannan could just make out rose bushes where the light from the windows fell.

'I've got to say,' Warkannan said, 'that God seems to have provided for you.'

Jezro laughed. 'Yes, I have to admit that things took a turn for the better after I met the dookis. That was five years ago, when she still got out regularly and needed a secretary. That's what I am, by the way, at least in theory, her secretary. But before she hired me, things weren't all that bad, mind. I was surprised to learn how decent people can be to a penniless stranger.'

'But this –' Warkannan gestured at the elegant room behind them. 'It's crass of me, but I can't help asking. How do you get this rich in the Cantons?'

'You find a cache of Settler technology and know what it's worth.'

Jezro turned suddenly serious. 'Yarl did tell you about the Settlers, didn't he?'

'Oh yes. I gather he was telling the truth. I had my doubts.'

'I figured you would. But yes, it's true. They were incredibly advanced – well, when it came to machines, anyway. Here and there they left caches, sometimes of devices we can't even work, but more usually solar accus and various small things like light-wands – replacement supplies, I suppose they were. Finding one is every peasant's dream. Marya's father had his dream come true.'

'Lucky man.'

'He was, yes.' Jezro paused to pull out his handkerchief and wipe his nose and upper lip. 'You know, there's so much to tell you, I don't even know where to start. Suppose you tell me more about that army you mentioned. Are you seriously suggesting that I ride home to try for reinstatement?'

'Not in the least. I'm suggesting you ride home to overthrow your brother by force and become the new Great Khan.'

Jezro gaped at him.

'Gemet's gone mad,' Warkannan went on. 'Paranoia and greed about sum it up. If someone doesn't do something, there won't be any khanate in a few years, just a lot of impoverished provinces in a state of constant war.'

'He's quite right,' Soutan said. 'Allow me to add my voice to the captain's.'

Warkannan nearly yelped. As usual Soutan had managed to glide into the room without being noticed. Warkannan twisted round in his chair, started to speak, and felt his tongue lie frozen in his mouth. A middle-aged man, his grey hair newly cut, his wrinkled face still damp and pink from shaving, stood in the room. He had dark eyes, and a raw scabby wound, as if metal had repeatedly scraped the skin, disfigured his forehead. His thin mouth twisted in a smile, and he spoke in Yarl's voice.

'Surprised, Captain? You'll notice the headband I always wore is gone. It's a bit of old technology, of course, a hologrammatic mask. I was hoping it would help keep my enemies off my trail.'

Arkazo giggled, one high, piercing little shriek. He clapped a hand over his mouth and blushed.

'It's all right, Kaz,' Soutan went on. 'I'm afraid I gave in to my love of the overly dramatic.' He smiled at Jezro. 'I have hopes that the headband will hide our khan when we have to cross the border back into Andjaro.'

'Now wait,' Jezro snapped. 'I haven't said I'm going anywhere yet.'

'Are you really going to let your people starve in the streets?' Warkannan said. 'How about this? Anyone who speaks out against Gemet is tortured to death. Do you remember your father's councillor, Ahmed Shiraz? They stretched out his death for three days.'

'God forbid!' Jezro went pale.

'The shock killed his wife, too, though I have to admit she'd been ill for some time,' Warkannan went on. 'And his unmarried daughter – her name's Lubahva – she ended up as one of the palace girls. It's a damn good thing she's a talented musician, or she'd have been working the streets. No one dared take her in but Aiwaz.'

'Aiwaz would stand up to Iblis himself for a friend's sake,' Jezro said, 'despite his fondness for women's clothes and yellow handkerchiefs. Is he still alive, or has my brother murdered him, too?'

'He's beneath your brother's notice, just like Lubahva is. I doubt if Gemet realizes that either of them's in the palace. He knows how much people hate him. He doesn't go out of the grounds unless he absolutely has to, and even then he's surrounded by armed guards.'

'Are things really that bad?'

'Oh yes. Worse. I –'

The door behind them opened again, noisily this time, to admit Zhil. 'Dinner, sirs,' he said. 'The dookis sends her regrets.'

It was a strange meal, taken in a luxurious white room, off a long, oak table set with fine blue and white china, an abundance of food served perfectly in an atmosphere of horror. Warkannan and Soutan talked of Gemet's wide-ranging crimes. Arkazo joined them to tell Jezro about the torture-murder of a university professor who had dared criticize the Great Khan. As the meal went on, Jezro ate less and less and talked, by the end, not at all. Warkannan leaned back in his chair and waited, watching Jezro think things through, as he had so often before, back on the border when the consequences of the khan's decisions had been petty compared to the decision he was facing now.

'I don't know why I'm surprised,' Jezro said at last. 'My brother's a great one for eliminating anyone in his way.' He reached up and touched the scar across his face. 'No, I really don't know why I'm so surprised. Idres, tell me. Is there any way out of this but civil war?'

'No,' Warkannan said. 'If there was, I wouldn't be asking you to start one.'

'I certainly agree.' Soutan, this strange new Soutan whose face finally matched his old man's eyes, leaned forward to join in. 'What I saw –'

Jezro held up a hand for silence. 'Yarl, thank you, but Idres' word is all I need.' He pushed his chair back and stood up, reaching for his stick. 'Gemet's assassins cut a couple of tendons on this leg, in case you were wondering.'

'It's a miracle they didn't kill you. God must have known that the khanate would need you.'

'Well, I think that's giving me more importance than I deserve.' Jezro smiled, briefly. 'Look, I've got to think about this. Idres, for ten years I've been nothing – an exile, homeless, someone who had to work for his living for the first time in his life. I'm not the man I used to be. I've got to think about this.'

Jezro limped out of the dining room. No one spoke till the laced bamboid door closed behind him. Soutan turned, trembling a little, to Warkannan.

'Think he'll go back?' Soutan sounded half out of breath.

'I hope so,' Warkannan said and laughed, one short bark. 'We've ridden a hell of a long way to have him say no.'

'I'm stunned.' Soutan was whispering. 'I never thought he'd have doubts. I trust you believe me, Captain. To bring you all this way and then – I never thought this would happen!'

'Oh, I certainly do believe you. I can see it on your face. Yes, stunned is a good word. So am I.'

Arkazo was staring slack-mouthed at both of them. 'Uncle?' he began, then stopped himself. 'I guess we just have to wait.'

'That's right.' Warkannan wadded up his linen napkin and tossed it, hard, onto his empty plate. 'I can see his point about one thing. Ten years is a long time. A lot can happen to a man in it, and a lot's certainly happened to him.'

They returned to Warkannan's guest room to sit by the windows and wait. Every now and then someone would start to speak, then let his voice trail away. It was only an hour by Warkannan's watch before Jezro walked in unannounced and joined them, but by then

Arkazo had fallen asleep and was snoring in his chair; Soutan looked as if he might do the same at any moment. Warkannan could feel his own exhaustion, but the sheer pleasure of seeing Jezro and talking with him would, he knew, keep him awake. For a moment Jezro stood looking at the three of them, saying nothing; then he smiled and tapped Arkazo on the shoulder. The boy woke with a start.

'Go to bed, Kaz,' Jezro said. 'Your uncle and I will doubtless lapse into boring old stories.'

'Yes sir,' Arkazo said, yawning. 'But are you coming home with us?'

Jezro sighed, a long exhalation of sadness. 'I don't know yet. I'm sorry. I thought I could make a quick decision, walking in the garden like the prophet Joshua, I suppose.' His mouth twisted in a wry smile. 'Unlike the prophet, I can't seem to make up my mind.'

Arkazo bit his lip. In his exhaustion he looked close to tears, and Warkannan realized that he felt close to them himself. Jezro turned to him.

'Idres, if I go back and we start a war, I had damn well better be the answer to everyone's prayers. What if I can't be? What if I don't know how to rule the khanate? A war's going to make everything worse for everyone. It won't be worth it if all they get is a different kind of rotten bastard on the throne.'

'You know what these doubts mean?' Warkannan said. 'That you're already a better ruler than he is.'

'Better, yes. But good? I'm sorry. You're tired, and I'm not thinking straight. We can talk more tomorrow.' Jezro glanced at Arkazo. 'Go to bed, Kaz. Things will look different in the morning.'

Jezro took Warkannan and Soutan into a small parlour, lit by two big lamps with frosted glass chimneys. The pale blue walls glowed like the sky, and the furniture gleamed with gilded wood and flowered cushions. The open windows let in the cool night air. Warkannan happened to glance at one of the lamps, then swore aloud. Jezro laughed at him.

'I wondered when you'd notice,' the khan said.

Blinking against the glare Warkannan examined the lamp – no oil, no wick in the chimney, only something that looked like a twist of glowing rope. When he passed his hand above the shade, he felt no heat.

'What's it burning?'

'It's not,' Jezro said, grinning. 'It's lit by something called a luminay, powered by a solar accu, the same power source that's inside each of Yarl's crystals.'

'Only these are much larger,' Soutan added, 'and can store a great deal of power.'

Warkannan shook his head in amazement and sat back down. A servant glided in with a tray of three small glasses and a decanter of some pale brown liquor. He poured, then bowed and left the room.

Warkannan tried a sip – pleasant stuff, and strong. 'And what's this?'

'They call it brandy. The First Prophet never heard of it, so I'm assuming it's all right to drink it.' Jezro leaned back in his chair and considered Warkannan over his glass. 'All right. Suppose I do say yes. Do you really think we can win this rebellion?'

'Of course. Otherwise I'd never have asked you to lead it.'

Jezro turned to Soutan. 'I'm surprised you'd back a scheme like this. You had plans – this would ruin them.'

'Temporarily only,' Soutan said. 'Yes, Marya's rich, yes she has resources, but compared to the khanate, she's a pauper.'

'We'd better explain,' Jezro said. 'Yarl managed to talk Marya into funding an expedition east.'

'It took some doing, yes.' Yarl smiled briefly. 'Eventually, she agreed to pay for men and horses and the like, in return for a share of any technology I found. Now, however, we'll have an even better chance of success.' He glanced at Jezro. 'Once you're Great Khan, and the grateful populace is happy again, freed from the foul Gemet's misrule, well, then – oh yes, then – surely you'll have a spare regiment or two to come help me search?'

'For what?' Warkannan leaned forward. 'What are you talking about?'

'The lost ships, of course. The lost starships that brought us here, and that can, therefore, take us home again.' Soutan held his glass of brandy up to the light of the nearer lamp. 'Well, someone will have to figure out how to fly them, of course. But in the end, if we persevere, we'll succeed. My researches have made it plain that the Settlers stored all sorts of records in the ships. They must have left instructions as well.'

Soutan was smiling, his eyes wide and bright, too bright, and not quite focused. Warkannan remembered his sudden insight on the morning after they'd crossed the Rift. He's mad, Warkannan thought. As mad as Gemet in his own way. He looked at Jezro, who was busying himself with his handkerchief.

'Um, well,' Jezro said eventually. 'Let's not tempt God's wrath, gentlemen. Let's see if He wants me to have the throne before we decide what to do with it.'

'Ah yes,' Soutan drawled. 'Inshallah, or however that goes.'

'Just that,' Jezro said. 'And we're a hell of a long way from Kazrajistan at the moment.'

'That's true,' Warkannan said. 'I know I'm pushing you to make up your mind, Jezro, but we should get back on the road tomorrow.'

'What?' Soutan snapped. 'I need to rest!'

'You can rest in Andjaro.' Warkannan turned to Jezro. 'We've got to leave soon. I know the dookis has bodyguards, but it's too risky, staying here.'

'Why?' Jezro said.

'Do you remember Zahir Benumar?'

'Of course. I'm surprised he didn't come with you, frankly.'

'Oh, he's here, all right. He's probably not far away at all. He's one of the Chosen, and he's coming to murder you.'

Jezro grunted as sharply as if Warkannan had punched him in the stomach, then caught his breath with a shake of his head. 'My God, Idres! You're full of one little surprise after another.'

'Sorry, but blame the Chosen, not me. They have more power than they ever did before, and there's more of them, spying for Gemet everywhere. When Soutan arrived, Indan formed a so-called investment group, with the excuse of using those old maps to find blackstone. Apparently the Chosen got suspicious. They sent a man across to get information about Soutan here. Zahir, actually, though he's calling himself Zayn these days. And when he was asking around about Soutan, he found out about you.'

Jezro nodded slowly, but his face stayed rigid.

'He's probably not far behind us,' Soutan said. 'By the way, I asked Robear to post night guards.'

Jezro ignored the interruption. 'Benumar? One of the Chosen? It's damned hard to believe. He was a good officer. Hell, more than that! He was my friend.'

'I had trouble believing it myself,' Warkannan said. 'But it's true. I've seen him. He admitted it. By God Himself, Jezro! Why do you think we're so desperate to have you back? The khanate's rotting from the inside out.'

'I am perennially amazed,' Soutan drawled, 'by the number of clichés you've made your own.'

'Shut up!' Warkannan was on his feet before he half-realized what he was doing. 'You can shut up or –'

'Calm down!' Jezro hauled himself up and stepped between them. He laid a hand on Warkannan's shoulder. 'Yes, Yarl can be infuriating, but he has his reasons, you know.'

'No, I don't know.' Warkannan shook the hand off, but he did sit down again. 'Suppose one of you tells me.'

Soutan opened his mouth, but Jezro scowled at him. Glowering, Soutan slumped back into his chair.

'That can wait till later,' Jezro said. 'So, there's another assassin after me, is there? And you think we'd be safer on the road than sitting here like lizards in a tree, waiting to be netted and turned into supper?'

'Exactly that.'

Jezro picked up the decanter and refilled their glasses before he sat back down. He swirled the brandy and watched the liquid slide down the glass, then glanced at Soutan to explain.

'Benumar was more than an ordinary subordinate. The three of us formed a unit, once he got his commission. I could trust him, you see, like I could trust Idres here, to tell me when I was wrong. They could forget that I was a khan. It's hard to believe now, but the rest of my fellow officers thought that when Gemet got the throne, I'd end up with some nice profitable position at court. The flatterers were thick on the ground, let me tell you.'

'I see,' Soutan said. 'Well, it must be hard, then, hearing how he's changed.'

Jezro nodded. 'Why, Idres? Do you have any idea why he'd join them?'

'Oh yes, he –'

Soutan twitched in his chair, then coughed to cover his reaction. He risked looking at Warkannan with an unspoken pleading in his eyes. It took Warkannan a moment to realize why, that Soutan feared Jezro's reaction to tales of strange drugs and ritual murder. For a moment Warkannan was tempted to keep the story laid up like an extra knife in case he needed to use it against Soutan some day. But blackmail? He'd always hated the very word.

'Well?' Jezro said. 'You said you saw Benumar?'

Soutan was watching him with hopeless eyes; his hands clutched the arms of his chair.

'Yes,' Warkannan said. 'We didn't know who was following us, but we knew someone was. He was riding with a comnee. When we reached the Cantons, Soutan reported him to a local zhay pay.'

Soutan sank back into his chair and gave Jezro a watery smile. 'The captain questioned Zahir, but the comnee he was riding with – well, they must have seen him as one of their own. When we left town, they came and got him back by force.'

'I see,' Jezro said. 'But he's on his way here?'

'Yes,' Soutan said. 'He left the comnee.'

Jezro glanced at Warkannan. 'What did he tell you?'

While Warkannan explained, Jezro listened, barely moving, his brandy glass forgotten in his hand. Soutan, however, drank his straight off, then got up to pour himself more. When Warkannan finished, Jezro nodded, slowly, as if he were thinking through some difficult problem, and fished out the handkerchief again.

'That's pretty damned horrible,' Jezro said at last. 'To feel that way, to live that way! And he was only a child.'

'Yes,' Warkannan said. 'It hit me pretty hard. I keep remembering things Zahir said during our little walk with the ChaMeech warparty. He's a man with a great many strengths, but he thought of himself as some kind of shameful weakling. I couldn't understand it then, but I do now.'

'Yes, I can see it, too.' Jezro shoved the handkerchief back into his pocket. 'I can't judge him too harshly, not after my own shameful performance.'

'What? I can't believe you'd –'

'Let me finish. When I realized that Gemet was determined to murder the whole lot of us, when I knew the assassins were coming for me, I tried to hide. I took off the medallion. I hid it in my saddlebags. I was going to deny who I was to save my skin.' Jezro smiled, but there was no mirth in his eyes. 'And it didn't even work. That's maybe the worst part. As tricks went, it was a pretty crappy idea. Can't you see how I felt, when I woke up in a comnee tent, all bandaged up, still alive somehow, but the zalet – gone when my horse ran off. It was a little like drowning, that feeling. To see how cowardly I could be –' he let his voice fade, then spoke normally. 'And then the comnee found them for me, anyway, horse and zalet both. God bless the Tribes!' He saluted with his glass, then drank.

'Yes,' Warkannan said. 'Thank God they ran across you. I'll have a little more of that brandy myself, if you think the First Prophet will forgive us.'

Jezro grinned and passed him the decanter. 'But about Benumar? Idres, do you really want to just let him slide into damnation or whatever the ultimate fate of the Chosen is?'

'No, of course not. I've been praying every day that he won't.'

'I'd rather do something a little more direct. We're going to wait for him.'

'Dookis Marya's guards will make short work of him.' Soutan joined in. 'No doubt it's best to let them have their chance at this fellow.'

'You don't understand,' Jezro said. 'I'm not waiting to kill him. I want to talk with him.'

'Well, the guards can be told to take him alive, of course.'

'No, Yarl, that's not what I had in mind. Yes, of course, they could drag him in all trussed up like a true-fowl. Would he listen to me? Not if he's a man with a pair of balls. Who would? What I have in mind is a little different.'

'Like what?' Warkannan said. 'I can see your point.'

'Of course you can,' Jezro went on. 'We'll have to work out the details, but I was thinking of something like using myself as bait. Sitting outside somewhere, alone, and waiting for him to arrive.'

'What?' Soutan's voice slid upward to a squeak. 'He'll kill you!'

'I doubt it.' Jezro grinned at him. 'But I'm not leaving here till we give him his chance.'

And that, Warkannan thought, is exactly why I rode all this way, isn't it?

'Well, Idres?' Jezro said. 'What do you think?'

'That you're right. But I also think we'd better be damned careful that he doesn't get his shot at killing you before you get yours at talking to him.'

'Well, yes, I can see the logic in that.'

'And of course,' Warkannan went on, 'you can put off your decision while we wait.'

'As sharp as ever, aren't you?' Jezro saluted him with his glass.

'Now, hold on a minute!' Soutan sputtered. 'Jezro – you matter too much. How can you risk it?'

Soutan launched into a tirade, while Jezro sat, listening politely, saying nothing, but with the stubborn gleam in his eyes that Warkannan remembered from their border days. He knew why Soutan was panicking. Suppose they did manage to net Zahir – he wouldn't be likely to lie to the khan about his imprisonment.

'Yarl, Yarl!' Jezro held up both hands flat for silence. 'Everything you say is true, and I don't care. I want to talk with Benumar, and damn it, I will.'

'You're impossible!' Soutan hissed. 'Simply impossible.'

'I do my best.' Jezro grinned at him. 'What do you say, Idres? Shall we call it a night?'

'We'd better, yes.' Warkannan paused to yawn. 'Since we'll be here for a few days, we'll have plenty of time to talk. You need to hear about the men waiting for you in Andjaro. Think about Kareem Alvado, and how he's going to feel if you turn the throne down, after he's risked so much to back you.'

'Idres, you bastard!'

'Don't expect me to fight fair over this.'

'All right, I won't. I've been warned.'

The mention of Andjaro made Warkannan remember Tareev Alvado, dead in the Mistlands. As he and Soutan were leaving, Warkannan turned to him and spoke quietly.

'Not a word to Arkazo about Jezro's little talk with Zahir, all right?'

'Not one.' Soutan spoke the same way. 'I owe you more than one favour, Captain. Thank you.'

'You're welcome.' He raised his voice to a normal volume. 'I'm glad to see that headband off. Looks like you've put some salve on that sore.'

'It feels good, let me tell you. Had I known how wretchedly uncomfortable it was going to be, I would have told you the truth back in Haz Kazrak.'

Commiz Duhmars sat on the edge of his chair like a guilty schoolboy. When Loy walked into Master Zhoc's office, Duhmars greeted her with good morning, but he failed to look straight at her. When Loy turned to Zhoc, he forced out a brief smile, but his thin face, his dark, deep-set eyes – she knew them too well to miss his emotion.

'Something's gone wrong, hasn't it?' Loy said.

'Do sit down.' Zhoc began straightening the books on his desk. 'Please, Loy?'

Loy sat.

'Mada Millou,' Duhmars said. 'At my recommendation your guildmaster here contacted one of your number in Burgunee. He then put the matter of this warrant to my counterpart there, Zhospah.'

'And he won't cooperate?' Loy crossed her arms over her chest.

'No. He won't.' Duhmars sounded genuinely angry – she could take some comfort in that. 'He insists he can't honour a warrant without approval from the full Council. It's in summer recess, of course.'

'Of course. For five weeks, isn't it?'

Duhmars merely nodded.

'Soutan's found himself a patron, hasn't he?' Loy felt her voice hovering on the edge of screaming. 'The goddamned Burgunee zhundars have been bought off.'

'Loy?' Zhoc leaned forward and used Tekspeak. 'Please be calm and humour the useless little man. When he's gone, we'll talk further.'

Duhmars was glaring at them both; he doubtless could guess that he was being discussed. Loy nodded the master's way, then turned back to the commiz.

'I do not know,' Duhmars said, 'if bribery is involved or not. I can understand your frustration, Mada Millou, but those are serious charges. If you want to bring them formally –'

'No. You know as well as I do that I don't have one damned shred of evidence.'

Zhoc made a clucking noise and shook his head in a vigorous no, trying to shut her up, she assumed. Duhmars hesitated, then shrugged.

'I'll insist that it gets on the first day's agenda. Please, Mada Millou? Be reasonable?'

My only child was raped and brutalized, Loy thought, and you're telling me to be reasonable. Aloud, she said, 'I know you're doing all you can.'

'Let me assure you of that. I'm taking a personal interest in this case. We've already got all the evidence in order for the trial, just for one thing. Don't you worry. We'll get a conviction.'

If it ever comes to trial, Loy thought. If that rotten little dungworm hasn't disappeared by the time Burgunee Council meets. Zhoc escorted Duhmars out, then closed the door with a snap.

'I'm sorry,' he said in Tekspeak. 'I never dreamt this would happen, or I wouldn't have raised your hopes.'

'Thank you, but in my better moments I know that. I wonder who Yarl's found to protect him?'

'Dookis Marya.' Zhoc sat down, letting his body sag into the leather as if he were exhausted. 'That damned rich little swine! I've already alerted the Master of Burgunee. He agrees that the situation's serious, but –'

'But Marya's very powerful.'

Zhoc pursed his lips in a sour smile. 'Exactly,' he said. 'It turns out that this Kazrak khan, Jezro, is part of Marya's establishment now. Her secretary or something. Somehow she knew that Yarl and his friends were on their way and sent letters to the commiz ordering him to leave Yarl strictly alone.'

'Merde!' Loy saw him wince. 'Sorry. It's just like Marya somehow, collecting herself an exotic Kazraki secretary and a crazy loremaster.'

'The same way she collected a title?'

'Come now! She paid Burgunee Council a nice fair price for that title.'

Zhoc scowled at the joke. 'She's her father's daughter, all right. God, I hate them both!'

'Still?'

'Well, look at what they did! Hoarding the technology they found, dribbling it onto the market at high prices, not even letting us inspect the site!' Zhoc took a long breath and calmed himself. 'Anyway, Master Pool will see what he can do if Yarl tries to bolt back to Kazrajistan. Once he leaves Burgunee, he's fair game.'

'That's something, I suppose. I could go north –'

'It's too risky. Yarl would love to see you dead.'

'The feeling's mutual, and I'm smarter than he is.'

'So? He's got Kazraki soldiers with him. No, Loy, you can't go hunting Yarl. It's too dangerous, and I forbid it. As the master of your guild, not just as a friend. No. You may not.'

Loy opened her mouth to argue, then closed it. Arguing with Zhoc once he'd invoked his position in the guild would only waste her time. 'Very well,' she said instead. 'But you'll keep me informed?'

'Of course! And don't you worry. We'll get this slimy little criminal yet.'

In a grim mood Loy left the guildhall and started across the square. Students were trotting from one set of offices to another, or standing around talking about their grades. They were young, laughing, full of hope and plans – she envied them as much as Zhoc envied the Tribes. I was like that once, she thought. Once.

Outside the sheltered square a wind had come up, easing the heat. As she walked along Loy heard music, drifting from the town centre, the sound of brass trumpets and drums. Laughing and calling out, a gaggle of students rushed past her, their robes flapping behind them.

'Loremaster Millou!' a girl called out. 'It's the Recallers. They're in town!'

Loy hesitated. She could go home and brood, or she could let herself be distracted. After a brief fight, sanity won.

'Wait for me!' she called back. 'I'll join you.'

The Recallers had set up their wooden stage in their usual spot, the riverbank park across from the white dome of the synagogue. The stage rested on two open wagons with locked wheels, while one of their covered wagons stood nearby to function as a dressing room. A wooden frame rose half-way across the stage area, and upon it a pair of Recallers were hanging curtains. Around the stage a big crowd had already grabbed the best seats on the grass, while behind the lucky ones, on a slight slope up, a fair collection of people were standing, craning their necks to see. Since Loy stood just five feet two inches high, she gave up on actually seeing the performance. One of her students, however, ran off to the row of nearby shops and came back with a wooden crate.

'Thank you,' Loy said. 'Remind me next semester to give you an A.'

The girl laughed, then trotted off to join a gaggle of her friends. By standing on the crate, Loy could just see the stage, still empty of performers and props both. She turned, idly looking over the crowd. Since she'd lived in Sarla all her life, she knew most of them – students, faculty, the grocer, the wood merchant, a couple of young men who'd joined the zhundars straight out of college. Two strangers, however, stood towards the back of the crowd: a Kazrak and a tall woman, her blonde hair severely braided. Loy could just make out what seemed to be a long feather hanging from her single earring and a pair of grassar-skin saddlebags over her shoulder. A spirit rider, Loy thought. An honest-to-god spirit rider, here in Sarla! And could that be our third Kazrak with her? Loy would have jumped off her perch and gone straight over, but the performance was starting.

Dressed all in black, a stout man walked through the curtains. When the crowd clapped, he smiled, bowed, then raised the mask he was carrying and held it up in front of him. A caricature of a human face, it concealed a small megaphone in its mouth.

'In the heart of the past the secrets shine, a galaxy of buried stars,' he began. 'Where is the ship to sail between the stars of the soul? It lies in our hearts, for the past has birthed us, and we are the past and present alike. When we came to the far country, we wept. By the waters of the Rift we sat down and wept, because we remembered the stars of home.

'Eight hundred years ago it was, and the land here stretched wild. Not a house, not a ship, nothing but the saurs among the water reeds and the Chiri Michi in the hills. How could we have signed their bargain? We asked it a thousand times, but we knew that without Landfall we faced death. In the vast void twixt here and home, no stars shone to power our travelling.

'Were it not for our children we might have risked death, but they, too young to choose, deserved what life this world could give them. The wild red valley would be our home, the wild brown swamps ours, too, to do with them what we could. Yet even still, some doubted. After Admiral Raynar sealed the bargain with his death, a good many cursed him for what he'd done.'

A tattoo of drums rang out from behind the curtain. The Chief Voice stepped to one side, and the players appeared, wearing the sleek blue costumes that traditionally represented the uniforms of the interstellar fleet. What the officers from the Settlers' starships had actually worn, no one remembered, but the one-piece outfits with their multiple belts certainly looked archaic enough. Loy had heard this particular play, *Diamond Words*, so often that she knew large parts of it by heart. It wove a story around the founding of Nannes and in the process described the actual Recallers, the specially bred H'mai whose name the travelling players had taken for their guild.

Since the piece held no surprises for her, Loy spent a large part of the performance watching the Kazrak and the spirit rider. The

Kazrak she could only describe as entranced. He stood with his hands shoved into the pockets of his filthy grey trousers and his head tipped a little back to keep his gaze firmly on the stage. The spirit rider would watch for a while, then turn and look over the crowd, her face utterly expressionless. At times she rocked on her feet as if tired, bored, or both. Eventually, towards the end of the first act, she leaned close to whisper something to the Kazrak, then left him and began making her way through the crowd.

Loy jumped down and followed her. With her long legs the spirit rider walked fast, but fortunately she went only as far as the grassy bank of the river, where she sat down and hauled her saddlebags into her lap. Loy hurried up to her.

'Excuse me,' Loy said in Tekspeak. 'I couldn't help noticing that you're from the Tribes.'

The woman smiled at her. 'Since you're not blind,' she said, 'I don't suppose you could help it. You must be a sorcerer, if you know the spirit language.'

'Well, yes. That's certainly what your people would call me. My name is Loy Millou, and I was –'

'Loy Millou? Old Onree from Nannes mentioned you to me.'

'He did?' Loy sat down, facing her in the grass. 'Is that Zayn Hassan with you?'

'It is, yes. My name is Ammadin, I ride with Apanador's comnee, not that you'll know who he is. Zayn and I were going to look for you after the performance.'

'And I've been hoping to find Hassan. Onree told us about him in his report, but not about you. That's like him, though. He forgets things.'

'For a man his age, he's still pretty sharp, I'd say.'

'Yes. We should all be in such good shape at ninety, huh?' Loy smiled at her. 'I need to thank him. I'm so glad we've found each other.'

'So am I. We have a lot to talk about.'

After Ammadin left, Zayn turned around once to make sure he knew where she was going; then the performance took him over again. Since he knew so little about the history of the Cantons, the plot proved difficult to follow, but he could pick that over at his leisure, he figured. He was memorizing every word of the performance, stowing away not merely the words but images of the actors and their costumes to replay later in his mind. One thread of the play took all of his conscious attention: the Recaller herself, a woman who memorized and sorted information in exactly the same way he did.

The actress playing this Lieutenant Diamante seemed to have no real understanding of how such a mind worked. She was continually laying her hands on her forehead and rolling her eyes to indicate that she was in the process of memorizing something. That Zayn could ignore, however, in return for the sheer flood of information. The other characters took her mind for granted; they asked her questions, showed her things that she should be remembering, referred to her special training and spoke of her inborn talent.

Inborn. He had learned the word earlier, but in the players' mouths it took on a vast new significance. At first he couldn't quite understand why the characters shuddered or made some other gesture of fear when they spoke it, but a long speech from the young officer who loved Diamante finally answered his question. Her mind was no lucky accident. Somehow or other, the Settlers had managed to give children certain skills or characteristics by breeding, the same way that a gardener would produce pink roses from red and white. After those traits appeared, then the Recaller traits bred true, provided, of course, that both parents were Recallers. In the play, the young officer would never be allowed to marry the woman he loved simply because he was an ordinary human being.

Now and again the Narrator in Black, or so Zayn was thinking of the man with the mask, would appear at the side of the action and give a speech, generally concerning some obscure point of history that the rest of the audience seemed to understand. Once, however, he spoke a couple of lines that made Zayn's blood run cold.

'Did we not hate and fear the Inborn, they who knew so much more than we would ever learn? Did we not fear and hate the Inborn with other gifts, those whose minds fed upon numbers, those whose minds melded with their ships? Did we not hate and fear those as well who had created them in their mothers' wombs? Sorcery, some called it, and the work of devils, though we knew it was but knowledge applied by ruthless men.'

Some called it – Agvar and his followers. Ruthless men? The

Ancestors, Zayn supposed. What had driven the Ancestors to create the Recallers and those number feeders, whatever that meant? As the play continued, it referred to other classes of H'mai who had been altered the same way, created or engineered as the play put it, but it never gave them convenient names. The complicated plot threads began to twine together, shoving raw information aside.

All at once Zayn realized that he was beginning to feel nauseated, as badly as if he'd stuffed himself with rich food. He also realized that he now knew why, if the play was to be trusted. Recallers felt information in their bodies just as normal H'mai felt emotions. For a moment he nearly did vomit, but he caught control of himself and began to work his way out of the crowd. He could guess that he looked ill by the hurried way the audience parted to let him through.

Down by the river the air smelled clean and cool. Zayn stood for a moment, breathing deeply, letting his mind settle and his stomach with it. Overload – Diamante had called the nausea overload. Too much data too soon. Zayn filed the word away and remembered lying in Ammadin's tent, reading the Vransic dictionary, an extravagant pleasure, almost sexual, a gift from the talents – this curse of talents that had been laid upon him hundreds of years before he was born.

The crowd began streaming past; the show had ended. Loy looked over Ammadin's shoulder and saw the Kazrak striding towards them. He was a good-looking man, Loy thought, with his dark skin and curly hair, but there was something brutal about him as well. She couldn't quite place it – a hard look about the eyes, an animal wariness in the way he moved. Ammadin, who had never turned around to look, suddenly smiled.

'Here's Zayn now,' Ammadin said.

'How –'

'His scent,' Ammadin said. 'Everyone smells different, you know.'

Ammadin got up and grabbed her saddlebags just as Hassan joined them. Loy stood, too, and brushed flecks of purple grass off her leggings with the side of her hand. Ammadin and Hassan spoke in Hirl-Onglay, but Loy could follow it well enough, since Ammadin was only making a simple introduction.

'Good afternoon, Mada Millou,' Hassan said in perfect Vranz. 'I'm glad we found each other so easily. Did Ammadin tell you about old Onree's recommendation?'

'Yes, she did. What did you think of the Recallers?'

Hassan blinked several times, then looked her over with a dark stare that verged on the frightening. 'Very interesting,' he said at last. 'I enjoyed it.'

The silence hung between them like a threat. Ammadin turned to Loy and spoke in her heavily accented Vranz. 'Let's go somewhere quiet, where we can talk. What about our hohte?'

'If you don't mind, yes,' Loy said, 'that will be fine.'

They were staying in a hohte near the city gate, not a splendid place, but clean and fancy enough, Loy supposed, for people who were used to sleeping on the ground. The pale yellow room held a bed, two chairs, a table; on the back wall a window gave them a view of purple grass and a scarlet lace-leaf tree. They'd piled their saddles and other gear in one corner on the faded green rug. The room stank of horses, from the saddle blankets, Loy assumed. Ammadin laid her saddlebags on the table, then sat next to them in one of the chairs and gestured at Loy to take the other.

Hassan hovered by the door. 'Would you like some wine? I can get some from the maiderdee.'

'Yes, thank you,' Loy said. 'White for me, please.'

He nodded and left, hesitated just outside, glanced around as if for enemies, then shut the door behind him.

'Zayn can be frightening,' Ammadin remarked in Tekspeak. 'I hope he's not troubling you.'

'Oh no, no.'

'Really?' Ammadin raised one eyebrow. 'You smell terrified.'

Loy gawked.

'Don't you have the spirit powers?' Ammadin said.

'I'd forgotten about that,' Loy said. 'No, not all of them. You spirit riders are the only sorcerers who do have them all, actually. But I'll stop trying to be polite. Your man scares me half to death. I don't even know why.'

'You're more sensitive than you think, is why. Zayn can be kind of dangerous.'

'Kind of.'

Ammadin laughed. 'We're just passing through Dordan,' she went on. 'I don't want to cause trouble or have trouble caused for me. If no one bothers Zayn, he won't bother them, but I do have to warn you, he's very good at violence. Most comnee men are. All right?'

'All right. Believe me, trouble is the last thing any of us want.'

'Good. But about the spirit powers? I may have them, but I've come to realize that you sorcerers know a great deal more about the crystals than we do.'

'Um, yes.' A hell of a lot more, Loy thought, but I don't dare tell you. 'From what I've heard I'd say that's true.'

'The reason I'm asking is Zayn has to go off on his own, where I can't follow, if he's going to complete his quest. That means I won't be able to hide him from Yarl's scanning. Yarl must know that Zayn's going to kill him when he finds him. By the way, will you mind?'

'Only because I won't be there to watch.'

Ammadin's smile became a good bit warmer. Loy began to feel as if she were chatting with a longtooth saur.

'But what I was wondering,' Ammadin went on, 'is whether there's some sort of crystal that Zayn could carry, something that would keep working the Hide Me command even though I wasn't there.'

'Yes, there certainly is. It's called an interference pattern generator.'

'A what?'

'Sorry, that's a very long name for a particular kind of very small spirit. We call them imps. They do all sorts of different things.'

'Is there somewhere in Sarla where I could buy one?'

'Please, let me get it for you. I'll enjoy giving your man something that'll help him deal with Yarl.'

'Well, thank you. That's very generous.'

'No, it's not. It's vengeful, and I love it.'

Outside something bumped the door and someone cursed. When the door swung open, Loy nearly yelped, but Hassan came in, hands full of glasses, with two pottery bottles tucked one under each arm. He set them down on the table and spoke to Ammadin in Hirl-Onglay about the wine. For the first time Loy noticed that he was wearing a knife on his belt, which, judging from the sheath, had a blade nearly two feet long.

'Zayn, Loy is the mother of the girl Yarl Soutan raped,' Ammadin said. 'We were discussing it while you were watching the Recallers. I think that's why Onree gave you her name.'

'Most likely, yes.' Hassan was busy filling glasses; he handed Loy a glass of white wine with a flourish like a waiter. 'I'm very sorry to hear that.'

'So was I, yes.' Loy took a sip from her glass, a surprisingly decent wine for a hohte like this one. 'If you kill him, tell him I hope he ends up in hell, will you? While he can still hear.'

'I'll be glad to.' Hassan gave Ammadin a glass of white, took one of red for himself, then sat on the floor at Ammadin's feet.

'Well,' Loy made herself stop staring at the knife. 'What brings you to Sarla?'

'A quest,' Hassan said. 'I can't tell you for what. It's Bane. Killing Soutan's not part of it, so Onree told me to ask you about him.'

The conversation progressed in Vransic sentences kept simple enough for Ammadin to follow. Loy told them that Soutan had been a loremaster and a teacher, a good teacher at that, although there had always been unpleasant rumours about his personal life. He'd never had a long-term love affair or marriage with anyone, female or male. He preferred to visit female prostitutes who would put up with a certain level of violence, though he always travelled to other towns to do so. In fact, a street girl in Kors, a city in Burgunee, had turned up dead after one of his visits, but money had changed hands, facts had been suppressed, and no one at the college had heard of the incident until years later, during the official investigation into Rozi's rape.

After the Kors incident, however, Soutan had taken a year-long sabbatical and disappeared. Although he never told anyone where he'd been, he came back changed, obsessed with finding old magic. He was sure, he told the Loremasters Guild, that with old magic he could return everyone to the lost homeland. Most members of the guild had tried to talk him out of his obsession, but he'd won a few converts.

'My daughter Rozi, for one,' Loy said. 'He held special classes, as he called them, for his believers. He had a way of gaining the confidence of young people, you see. He'd pretend that he disliked them or looked down on them at first. Then later he'd tell them he'd been wrong; they'd proved they were really smart. The double flattery really hooked them.'

'Tell me something,' Ammadin said. 'Is Rozi the only student he attacked?'

'No. There were two others. One of them refused to testify against him after we found out about the whore in Kors. She was afraid he'd kill her, too. The other one did testify, and so did Rozi. That's when he jumped bail and ran from Sarla, two years ago now. We didn't know he'd ended up in Kazrajistan.'

Hassan's grim stare darkened further. He stood and held out his hand for her glass. 'The Three Prophets tell us that a man like that should be beheaded. More wine?'

'Yes, thank you.' Loy gave the glass over.

'Do you know where in Burgunee he's staying?' Hassan asked.

'Oh yes, just over the border, near Kors. There's a woman there, Marya her name is, and she's a dookis, very rich, owns a lot of land. She took Soutan in, because she collects magic, even though she isn't a sorcerer.'

'Isn't that against your laws?' Hassan said.

'Yes, it certainly is. When you're rich enough, the laws don't seem to apply.'

Hassan gave her back her glass, refilled. 'That's all very interesting,' he said. 'I don't suppose the dookis has taken in any other strangers.'

Ammadin snarled at him in Hirl-Onglay, furious words spoken so fast that Loy couldn't understand them. For a moment Hassan went as still as death; then he forced out a smile and answered her in the same language.

'Excuse me,' he said to Loy in Vranz. 'I shouldn't keep bothering you with questions.'

Loy was about to tell him that she didn't mind, but something about the set of Ammadin's jaw and the cold look in her eyes stopped her. 'That about sums Yarl Soutan up, anyway,' she said instead. 'He can really fool people. He keeps his nasty side for the women who attract him.'

'I've met men like that,' Hassan said. 'Good soldiers, loyal friends, as long as you're another man. Women are just prey to them, nothing more.'

'Yes. I used to wonder what Yarl's mother was like. A real horror, I bet.'

'He's not from around here?' Ammadin said.

'No. He came from down in Pegaree. People there do tend to be a little strange. It's kind of isolated.'

Hassan took his full glass in one hand and the bottle of red in the other. He sat down once more at Ammadin's feet, leaned against her chair, and proceeded to drink steadily for the rest of the conversation. Loy decided that she preferred not to know what sort of man he was when drunk, but what Ammadin had to tell kept her in the hohte room.

'I know where Soutan went when he went east,' Ammadin said in an oddly casual tone of voice. 'Chof country, where he persuaded some of their young males to present him to the full court of the Great Mother. By the way, you do know that their own name for themselves is Chof, don't you?'

'Yes, I do, but most people here just use ChaMeech, even at the college. Habit, I guess.'

'All right. Soutan's looking for something called the Covenant Ark. He told the Chof that if he had the Ark, all the H'mai would leave this world and let them have it back. Going home, he called it. The Chof didn't believe him.'

'Good, because he was lying. Well, he might want the Ark, too, but he's really after the magic ship that brought the Kazraks here.'

'So the Chof were right, then. Now they're afraid that he'll bring Kazraki soldiers with him to help him search for it.'

'Oh my god!' Loy nearly choked on her wine. 'That would be disastrous.'

'The Chof feel that way, too. Especially now that he's shown up with two Kazraks. Do you know what this Ark thing is?'

Loy debated, but if she refused to share her information, no doubt Ammadin would do the same. 'Yes, I do.' She thought for a moment – how was she going to describe an artificial intelligence unit in magical terms, when she truly didn't understand what artificial intelligence was? 'Or I sort of know. There are two things that have that name, you see. You can find an ark in every synagogue, a kind of box where they store their holy books.'

'That's not the one Soutan wants, then.'

'True. The other one is an ancient artifact. It's sort of a magical box that can answer questions. But it also steered the magic ship somehow. I don't really understand it.'

'Huh. Interesting. I wonder if it really exists?'

'None of us knows that, either. How do you – you must be able to speak with them, the Chof, I mean.'

'Not all of them, no. But I've spoken with one of the true Chiri

Michi. Her name is Water Woman, and she has spirit crystals. We've spoken through them, and I've met her as well.'

Despite the warm room and the wine, Loy felt phantom ice slide down her back. The disaster was already happening, Kazraks or no Kazraks.

'How did she get the crystals?' Loy said. 'If you don't mind telling me, that is. I don't want to break Bane.'

'Not Bane at all, but it's like you and the Ark – I don't know very much. She told me that some years ago, a great mother found a cave with a stone woman in it. The stone woman – her name is Sibyl – showed the Chof how to use the magic she had with her in her cave.' Ammadin frowned at her own words. 'I know that sounds ridiculous, but it's what Water Woman told me.'

'I wish I could meet her.'

'I can ask her about that. You must have crystals of your own, after all. Maybe she'll talk with you, too. She really does want to communicate with us, the H'mai, that is, especially about the Canton Wars.'

Loy felt as if the room had suddenly expanded, that she was sitting in the middle of an immense space with wonderful possibilities opening all around her. Frightening, yes, but exhilarating as well – her hands were shaking so badly that she set her glass down onto the table before she spilled the wine.

'It's a challenge, talking with Water Woman,' Ammadin said with a laugh. 'She says that Sibyl taught her the spirit language, but she's got her own way of using it.'

'I don't mind a little hard work. To find the truth about the Wars – that's been one of my dreams since I was a kid. But this Sibyl and her cave, with magicks in it – do you think it's true?'

'Well, Water Woman got this from somewhere.' Ammadin picked up her saddlebags from the table, unlaced one, and brought out a lightwand. 'It works. I've used it.'

'Oh my god! Do you know – no, of course you don't. That's a really old design, an ancient design, and it looks brand new. Could I –' When she held out a hand, Ammadin gave her the stick. Loy ran her fingers down it, turned it this way and that, and finally, on the very tip, found the stamp she was looking for, an embossed spiral below a capital letter R. 'It *is* old. Like, eight hundred years old.'

'Eight hundred years? Is that when we all came here?'

'Yes.' Reluctantly Loy gave the lightwand back. She would have loved to have shown it to Master Zhoc. 'Water Woman gave it to you?'

'She said it was a present from Sibyl, to be honest. She was just delivering it. She did tell me that Sibyl had a lot of magic.' Ammadin thought for a moment. 'Crates of it, I think she said. Hundreds of crystals, anyway.'

'Why did Sibyl send you a gift?'

'She wants me to come visit her, so she can persuade me to help her get rid of Soutan.'

'She sounds like my kind of woman, Sibyl. But did Water Woman say – I'm sorry. Now I'm the one asking too many questions.' Abruptly Loy remembered Hassan and turned to him. 'This must all sound very strange to you.'

'I haven't understood a word,' Hassan said. 'Do you realize that you both slipped into the spirit language?'

'Slipped?' Ammadin said in Vranz. 'I did it on purpose.'

'Damn you, Ammi!' Hassan sounded more weary than angry, much to Loy's relief.

'Well, we're discussing my quest.' Ammadin reached down and ran a hand through his hair, soothing him like a shen. 'It's not Bane to discuss a quest with another sorcerer, but you couldn't listen without breaking it.'

'In that case.' Hassan smiled at her, but Loy half-expected to see fangs when he did so. 'Still, I suppose sorcerers have a lot to talk about when they meet.'

'Especially these two sorcerers.' Loy remembered her wine, took the glass and had a soothing mouthful. 'Do you think Water Woman would talk to me?'

'I don't know,' Ammadin answered in Tekspeak. 'I'm surprised you want to talk to her. I thought the Cantonneurs hated the Chof.'

'Because of N'Dosha, you mean?'

'Yes, just that.'

'We hold grudges, yes. My people are very good at grudges, unfortunately. But we also know how to let one go when it's to our advantage. Some of us have forgotten that the Chof are the indigenous species, not us, but I try to keep it in mind.'

'Then the next time the Riders pass over, I'll see if I can reach Water Woman. Sometimes I can, sometimes I can't.' Ammadin frowned into her wine glass. 'Sometimes I can see her in the crystals, too, and sometimes I can't. I know she's not hiding from me, though.'

'That's odd. She must be inside somewhere.'

'Well, you'd think so, but where? She's travelling through the Cantons, but she can't go anywhere near H'mai settlements.'

'I see what you mean. That *is* puzzling.'

'But when we do talk, I'll ask her about you.'

'Thanks.'

For a moment they drank in silence.

'You know, I just thought of something,' Loy switched to Vranz. 'I wonder if maybe you could help me? It's about Rozi, my daughter. I think you spirit riders call it "loss of soul", the way she's been acting. It's as if she's really weary of life, and afraid all the time, and here she is, only eighteen.'

'That's horrible, and horribly sad. I don't know if I can cure it, but I could at least meet her.'

'Could you come see her this evening? She's in a sort of school during the day.' Loy paused, thinking of terms Ammadin could understand. 'She's training to be a priestess of our god.'

'Well, that's impressive. Yes, certainly. Tonight will be fine. Where shall we meet you?'

'Did you see the big white dome near the river? Near where the Recallers performed?'

'It would be hard not to see it.'

'True. Could you meet me there just before sunset? Out by the front of the dome there's a fence with a wood bench nearby. I'll be there.'

Loy was several blocks away before she remembered one particular thing Ammadin had said. *Eight hundred years ago? Was that when we all came here?* Oh my god, Loy thought. How does she know that? She suddenly realized that the Landfall Treaty stood in danger from more than the Kazraks. Technically she should report this break in the dam of myths to Master Zhoc. As she walked on, she was considering her duty to the Loremasters Guild as opposed to her duty to the truths of history.

As Ammadin was showing Loy out, Zayn hauled himself off the floor. He put his glass and the wine bottle on the table, then flopped into the other chair and stretched his legs out under the table. Ammadin came back, hands on her hips, and considered him.

'I'm sorry I snapped at you,' she said. 'But you were going to ask about your Jezro Khan, weren't you?'

'Yes.' He hesitated, then realized that he was no longer angry. 'It doesn't much matter. I bet that I'll find Jezro where Soutan is, well, if they don't leave Burgunee before I get there.'

'Did you want to leave tonight? Your horse should be rested.'

'No, no, that's not what I meant.'

'You don't really want to catch up with him, do you?'

'It's not that.' Zayn paused to finish the wine in his glass. 'I don't want to leave you.'

'You've got to.'

'I know that. For God's sake, Ammi!'

She looked at him, sadly but distantly, or so he read her expression. Continuing on in this vein, he realized, would bring him nothing but sorrow.

'I'm sorry,' he said instead.

'Don't keep apologizing for everything, will you?' She paused, then spoke more calmly. 'I've been worrying about Soutan scanning you out, but Loy tells me that there's a device you can carry that will hide you from his crystals. She's going to give you one.'

'That's good of her.'

'She really hopes you'll kill him, you know.'

'Tell her not to worry. I intend to do my best. I'll remember Aggnavvachur in my nightmares as long as I live.'

Ammadin sat down in the other chair. She picked up her wine glass and had a modest sip.

'What did you think of the Recallers?' Zayn said.

'The players, or the real ones?'

'You stayed long enough to hear about the real ones, then.'

'About the people like you, yes.'

'The people like me. How calmly you say that, Ammi! My God. Oh my God!' Zayn leaned back in the chair and contemplated the far wall. 'It makes me sick to my guts, thinking about it. I'm just like a horse from some fancy breed, right? Bred to remember everything I saw or heard, just in case the breeders needed my memories some day.'

'I don't understand why you're so upset. I'm probably the same. So? It all happened hundreds of years ago, and it's not like they meddled with us somehow, not with you and me as people. We're just throwbacks.'

'But –' He stopped, thought, considered her for a moment. 'What do you mean, you're probably the same?'

'Well, I can see in the dark. Most people can't. I hear spirit voices. Most people can't. I can smell when someone's lying or angry. How many other people can do that? Every spirit rider has silver eyes. Where do they come from?'

Zayn could barely believe that she was as calm as she looked and sounded. 'I see what you mean,' he said. 'You were lucky, though. You were born out on the grass.'

'Oh yes. My mother and father couldn't have been happier. Their child – a spirit rider! They ran around bragging to anyone who'd listen. They still do, come to think of it.' She smiled, then let the smile fade. 'For you, well, we know how different it was.'

Zayn nodded, picked up the wine bottle, and refilled his glass. 'But that's not why I feel so sick, thinking about it,' he said at length. 'Not the way my father treated me, I mean. I don't know why. Maybe I hate thinking that I am what I am because someone thought I'd come in handy.'

'Better than thinking Iblis was your grandfather, isn't it?'

At that he had to laugh. 'All right, yes, better than that. But it still gripes me. I mean, suppose the Ancestors had done this to everyone. Given everyone some kind of weird talents or strengths or something. Then it would have been –' he hesitated, found the word at last. 'It would have been fair. But the play this afternoon, it made it clear that most people were just people. And they used the rest of us like we'd use a riding horse. We were useful, Ammi. Tools. Machines.' Zayn drank half the wine straight off.

'Well, it's not quite like horses. A stud will mount any mare in heat, and a mare in heat will take any stud. Our ancestors were H'mai. They must have agreed to all of it, the long-term plan, I mean, as well as having children together.'

'You're right, yes. They must have agreed. I'm beginning to see why Mullah Agvar wanted to get away from them. The Settlers, I mean, breeding people like horses, talking people into doing it. No wonder he called them demon talents. But I wish to God his successors hadn't taken it out on us.'

'Us? Oh, you mean the men in the Chosen.'

'Yes. The legion of the damned, that's us. Through no fault of our own. How's that for justice?'

'You're not really damned, you know. The play should have made that clear if nothing else.'

'You're right.' He managed to smile. 'I don't know why I keep talking about damnation. I really don't.'

'It was something you could believe in, I suppose. Now you realize you don't really know much about yourself or what's going to happen to you. You're alone again, aren't you?'

For the briefest of moments Zayn wanted to throw his half-full glass of wine into her face. Very carefully he set it down on the table, then stood, steadying himself on the back of the chair.

'If we're going to meet Loy's daughter, and if she's a priestess in training or whatever that is, I'd better sober up. I saw a pump outside by the stables. I'll just go stick my head under it.'

Now that Soutan was no longer pretending to be a sorcerer, he had stopped running off to hide when he used his crystals. That afternoon he was sitting on the green lawn by the manor house with the box in front of him and Arkazo next to him. Warkannan saw them when he came out of the stables. On the soft grass Warkannan's footsteps made little sound, and Soutan was so absorbed in what he was saying that he never looked round. Warkannan stopped a few feet behind them and listened as Soutan muttered the strange words that he called commands.

Soutan handed Arkazo the crystal, who laughed, shook his head, and handed it back. When Soutan spoke again, he used Vranz, and Arkazo answered him in the same. Nodding in agreement every now and then, Soutan listened intently to Arkazo's every word. Warkannan disliked the way Arkazo responded to that flattering intensity by smiling and leaning a bit closer. In the cavalry he'd seen naive young officers courted this way by certain experienced sergeants – not out of sexual interest, but in the hopes of recruiting an ally against the senior officers should the sergeants need one.

'Find something interesting?' Warkannan said in Kazraki.

Soutan shrieked, startled, then twisted around and glared at him. Arkazo smothered a laugh.

'I didn't realize there was someone behind me,' Soutan said with immense dignity.

'You're not the only one who can move quietly,' Warkannan said.

Soutan muttered something under his breath and made a great show of smoothing down his shirt.

'Did you find Zahir?' Warkannan went on.

'Yes. He's in Sarla, which is the worst possible place he could be. I could only see him for a few minutes. He was washing under a pump, and the spirit rider must have been some distance away. Once he finished, he went inside a building, and I lost him.' Soutan glanced at the crystal in his hand. 'I'd better close this down. That spirit rider might be able to pick up my scan.'

'By all means,' Warkannan said. 'I'm sure she enjoys wasting her time and energy on troubling you.'

Soutan glared at him without speaking.

'Well, can't you just hide from her somehow? You used to.'

'That's what provoked her into overriding my crystals. Since we're safe here, I don't want to risk it. Once we leave, I'll have to take the chance, but it's a devil's choice.'

'Uncle?' Arkazo said. 'Why haven't we left? Everyone around here knows about Jezro Khan. It won't be hard for Benumar to find out where he is.'

'Because we can't take the dookis's bodyguards with us. We're setting a trap.'

Arkazo grinned. 'That makes sense.'

Warkannan hesitated on the edge of telling him the truth. Soutan was watching him with a bland little smile.

'Besides,' Warkannan said, 'we don't really know that Benumar's going to try to kill the khan. He may be simply searching for information about Soutan. That was his original assignment, and the Chosen tend to follow orders. As long as we reach Andjaro before he reaches his superior officers, what he does won't matter at all.'

Arkazo thought this over for a minute. 'That's true,' he said at last. 'If we even have to worry about getting Jezro Khan home.'

'Yes. If.'

Warkannan walked on, heading for the house. He was looking for Jezro and found him sitting and reading in the small blue parlour. The glass double doors led out into a rose garden; Jezro had turned his chair so that he'd see scarlet roses whenever he looked up from his book.

'There it is,' Warkannan said, 'my copy of the *Mirror*, that is.'

'I figured this was yours.' Jezro looked up. 'Do you want it back?'

'Not while you're reading it.' Warkannan sat down opposite him.

'I just wanted to look up one verse.' Jezro closed the book and handed it over. 'It goes, "And why should you not fight in the cause of God, when the weak – men, women, and children – cry out, 'Oh Lord, deliver us from this city whose leaders are oppressing us, raise up one who will protect us, and You be our Lord and Master.'"'

'That's appropriate, yes. I hope you're taking it to heart.'

'Of course I am. The question is, am I the man to do the delivering? Gemet must have sons. Can't you form a faction around one of them?'

'Here's how paranoid your brother is. Every time one of his wives gives birth to a son, he has the child smothered. The gossip is that he does it himself, but just to make sure it's done right, not because he enjoys it.'

'Lord preserve!' Jezro was whispering. 'That's really horrible.'

'Yes, it certainly is.' Warkannan laid a hand on the *Mirror*. 'Your entire family line could disappear.'

'No loss to the world, considering how Gemet's turned out.'

'It could be a loss to the khanate. When he dies, there's going to be a civil war if there's no legitimate heir. That's another reason I decided that I could stomach an armed revolt. Sooner or later, there's going to be a war in Kazrajistan. If it's sooner, the country will be worth salvaging afterwards.'

'I see your point. I might borrow the book again.'

'I can't think of anyone I'd rather lend it to.'

'Good old Idres!' Jezro paused for a grin. 'I didn't have a copy of the *Mirror* with me, and the last time I had a chance to read it was about eight years ago. I'd taken refuge in a seminary, you see, run by the Church of the One God.'

'You what?' Warkannan settled the book in his lap. 'That's the last place I would have thought you'd go.'

'Well, I had to go somewhere, didn't I? No, to be honest, I wanted to, and they were kind enough to take me in. I realized after a year or so that their way wasn't mine, so I left.' Jezro wiped his nose on his sleeve, then fished for a handkerchief in his shirt pocket. 'Sorry, the damn thing runs all the time. But go on, Idres, admit it. You're shocked, aren't you? I'm a different man from the one you used to know.'

'All right, since you've brought it up. Yes, I'm shocked at how much you've changed, but it strikes me as all on the surface. Underneath you're still the same man.'

'What? When I think back to how much I used to drink and gamble and joke around, I can hardly recognize myself.'

'That didn't matter. Underneath you were all honour and generosity. Flamboyant, yes, but so? You were young, handsome, and rich. We expected you to run wild now and then.'

'Now you're the one who's being generous.'

Warkannan shrugged the remark away. 'You've changed in a lot of little ways, but nearly dying would have changed anyone.'

'That's true. Tell me something, Idres. I was an arrogant little bastard, wasn't I?'

'Of course. You were supposed to be, a khan and the commanding officer both. The men loved you for it.'

'I've learned its limits, arrogance. I won't be able to be dashing or whatever the hell that was any more. Do you really think I'm fit to rule?'

Jezro spoke so seriously that Warkannan took his time about answering. 'Well,' Warkannan said at last. 'In the absolute best case, you'll step right into the role and do splendidly. In the absolute worst case, you'll still be better than Gemet. In the most probable case, you'll make mistakes at first, but people will overlook them because you're not Gemet, and by the time they think about grumbling, you'll have learned enough to do a good job.'

'Thank you.' Jezro was looking out the glass doors, where red roses swayed and trembled in a slow breeze. 'That's the truth, all right, the kind of truth you always could see when I couldn't.'

'If it's true you need to act on it.'

'Do I? Now, there you might be right, you might be wrong. I just don't know yet.'

Warkannan considered making another move, but he knew how stubborn Jezro could be when he felt pressured.

'It has to be your decision,' Warkannan said. 'I know that.'

'Good.'

'Tell me something though. Why did you send that letter? Just for old times' sake?'

'Mostly, yes. I wanted to see you and Benumar again or at least find out if you were still alive. I still miss Haz Kazrak. The landscape here's so damn flat, it gets on my nerves. But I also had this sentimental idea about making my old friends rich.' Jezro waved a hand at the lamps. 'How much do you think technology like this would sell for back home?'

'A fortune, yes, if the mullahs didn't confiscate and smash it first.'

'There is that. I keep thinking that it's time to open a few minds and let the truth seep in.'

'You'd have an easier time of that if you were Great Khan.'

'You bastard!' Jezro was grinning at him. 'Do you want to know what I did after I left the seminary?'

'Yes. What?'

'Washed dishes in a hohte. Then I got taken on as an apprentice vegetable seller in Kors.'

Warkannan's first reaction was laughter; then he realized, from Jezro's wry smile, that the khan was perfectly serious.

'Being a khan means nothing away from Kazrajistan,' Jezro went on. 'I had to eat, and all I knew was the army. The one here wouldn't take me, because of the leg.' He laid a hand on his right knee. 'But that's where I met the dookis, when I was selling vegetables, and she was out among the people, displaying her famous common touch. I sold her a couple of pounds of true-carrots, if I remember rightly, and then she asked about the scars. You poor man, says she, you must have had an awful accident. Oh no, Mada, says me, they did it on purpose. So she wanted to hear the whole story. But without the carrots, who knows?'

'Carrots?' Warkannan could hear how feeble he sounded, and he cleared this throat. 'Well, God works in mysterious ways. That's all I can say to that.'

After the heat and horse-stink of Ammadin's room in the hohte, Master Zhoc's dimly lit office felt cool and airy. Zhoc himself, dressed in summer whites, made a splendid contrast to Zayn Hassan as well. Loy decided that she liked her men civilized, thank you. Zhoc leaned forward in his chair, making notes on a rushi scrap as she talked.

'This could be the find we've been praying for,' Loy finished up. 'None of the usual fortune hunters could have reached a site deep in ChaMeech territory.'

'No, but it sounds like the ChaMeech have been taking things out of it,' Zhoc said.

'Maybe, but what about this Sibyl? The stone woman.'

'I'll admit that she intrigues me.' Zhoc leaned back in his chair and stared at the bookcase on the far side of his office. 'I wish the spirit rider had told you what colour of stone.'

'She may not know. Her informant's a ChaMeech, and who's to say that the ChaMeech see colour the same way we do?'

'Good point. Very good point. I wonder if they'd like to be our guests tomorrow, Ammadin and Hassan. For lunch, say, in a good restaurant.'

'Hassan's not the kind of man you take to good restaurants. He carries a long knife, and he acts like he has three balls. At least three.'

'Loy, your language sometimes –'

'So? I'm short. I've got to do something.' Loy grinned at him. 'But I'll talk to Ammadin tonight. Well, in just a little while now.' She glanced out the office window to a sky turned gold by the lowering sun. 'I have no idea when they're leaving, or what Hassan's quest is.'

'I'd like to talk with her. Huh – I'll need a refresher course in magical lingo, though. I haven't had to pretend I was a sorcerer in years.'

Here, Loy realized, was her opportunity to bring up Ammadin's remark, to tell Zhoc, as duty demanded, that at least one person among the Tribes had seen through the legal myths that defined the fragile balance of the planet's cultures. She should speak, she knew she should, but somehow she found herself answering with a smile alone.

'Well, there's probably no real rush,' Zhoc continued. 'Even if she's willing to tell us about the site, there isn't time to get funding for a proper expedition this summer. We'll have to wait till next year, anyway.'

Loy arranged a thoughtful expression and nodded. Telling him about the wild idea she was considering could wait. She still didn't know if she had the nerve to go through with it.

The sunset touched the river with scarlet and gilded the dome of the temple. The red lace-leaf trees quivered in a soft breeze. Above them, clouds of an insect Ammadin had never seen before swarmed and fluttered, caught in the shafts of evening light.

'Look at those!' Ammadin pointed at the swarm. 'Their wings.'

Zayn glanced, visibly unimpressed, but she paused, studying

the six flat blades, each about the size of a thumbnail, that made up the insect wings. When they flew, the wing-blades rippled and flashed iridescent in the sun. She wondered if they'd give that light back to the air once it grew dark.

'There's the sorcerer,' Zayn said abruptly.

Dressed in a pair of serviceable blue trousers and a grey shirt, Loy Millou was standing by a wooden bench, and to Ammadin she looked as exotic as the wingbuhs, partly because she was so petite, with delicate bones to match her short stature. She had thick, dark hair, cropped at her jawline, flat cheekbones, and eyes of a particularly luminous black.

'She's beautiful,' Ammadin remarked. 'Loy, I mean.'

'What? Oh, uh yes, she is.'

Zayn was, she assumed, still brooding about the Recallers.

'We can talk more later,' Ammadin said. 'Loy's seen us.'

Up ahead Loy waved madly, as if she thought that Ammadin would overlook her. 'There you are,' Loy sang out. 'I just got here myself.'

For a moment they stood outside the gate that led into the temple compound, as Ammadin was thinking of it. Loy chatted in Vranz, asking about their dinner, if they liked the hohte well enough, their horses, and all the while she smelled of anxiety, a smell that increased every time Zayn spoke. One anxiety, at least, Ammadin could ease.

'I did talk with Water Woman,' Ammadin said in the spirit language. 'She'd be pleased to speak with you.'

Loy beamed like a child. 'I don't know what kind of crystals you have,' Loy said, 'but I have a large one that allows you to see and speak at the same time. Maybe tomorrow morning – or wait, are you leaving first thing?'

'I don't know.' Ammadin turned to Zayn and switched to Hirl-Onglay. 'I'm thinking of staying here tomorrow, to talk with Loy and Water Woman.'

'Oh.' He looked at her for a moment, then put on his mask – she could think of no other way to conceptualize it, except as the mask, that smooth, perfect lack of any feeling or thought upon his face. 'But I'd better get on the road.'

'That's true. The longer we put off separating, the more it's going to hurt.' She hesitated, but she couldn't bear seeing him so desolate. 'Both of us.'

The mask dissolved, and he smiled in something like triumph. Loy had taken a few steps away, as if she knew that they were speaking of private things, to lean on the fence and stare up at the dome, still pale gold against the twilight sky. In the rising breeze the waters of the reflecting pool rippled, and the dome's image danced.

'Loy?' Ammadin said in the spirit language. 'I'll still be here tomorrow.'

'That's wonderful! You could come to my house for lunch, if you could spare me the time. I'll tell you how to get there after you've seen Rozi. I'd love to talk some more about Sibyl. And Soutan, too, if your man would like that.'

'He'll be leaving early in the morning on his spirit quest.'

'It's a good thing I picked this up, then.' Loy fished in a trouser pocket and brought out a small rectangle of pale blue quartz. A gold chain ran through a hole on one narrow end.

'Is that the imp?' Ammadin said.

'Yes. Zayn?' Loy held it out at arm's length in his general direction, as if she were offering food to a dangerous animal. 'You'll need to charge it in the sunlight, at least twice a day.'

'Thank you, I'll remember that.' Zayn took it and held it up to the last of the sunset. 'How does it work?'

'It's already working, and as long as you keep it charged, it'll keep working. Wear it around your neck. If you take it off to lay it in the sun to charge it, stay close to it. Really close. Now, if you're inside a building, you won't need it, but don't lose it somewhere, all right?'

Zayn laughed. 'All right.' He slipped the imp's chain over his head and settled it inside his shirt. 'Thank you. This is very good of you.'

'Anything to help you find Soutan.'

Loy led them down a narrow gravelled path to another fence, another gate, where a young woman dressed in white, her hair smoothed back under a blue scarf, stood waiting. She waved and smiled so confidently that Ammadin could guess that she wasn't the daughter.

'Hullo, Taymah,' Loy said. 'Will Rozi talk with the spirit rider?'

'Yes, she will.' Taymah hesitated, staring at Zayn. 'Uh, I don't know about –'

'He's a zhundar,' Loy said smoothly, 'working in disguise to track Yarl Soutan down.'

'Oh, how wonderful!' Taymar gave Zayn a big grin. 'But I'll run on ahead and warn her you're here. She's in the chapel, Loy, and men can go in there. Give me a head start.' She glanced at Ammadin. 'No one can be kept from the word of God, you see, but the rest of our buildings are off-limits to men.'

'That makes perfect sense to me,' Ammadin said. 'I was a girl myself once.'

Taymah giggled and ran off.

Rozi met them at the chapel door, a pretty girl, as thin and fragile as a blade of grass, Ammadin thought. Her long, dark hair fell free to the waist of her white dress, but around her neck she wore a gold Star of David on a chain. They all stood behind the last row of chairs in the back of the chapel; Rozi seemed disinclined to allow them to come further into her place of safety. From the first Ammadin could smell how completely indrawn she was, wrapped in the scent of fear, though as faint as the grass-smell of old straw. Around most young people Ammadin could see a reddish glow of heat energy, but not around Rozi.

'I wanted you to meet the spirit rider, darling,' Loy said. 'Don't mind Mr Hassan. He's a zhundar on special assignment.'

Rozi's dark eyes flicked towards Zayn, then back to Ammadin. 'Hullo,' she said.

'Will you sit down with me, Rozi?' Ammadin said. 'Just over there, say. Not far from your mother at all.'

Rozi followed in unenthused obedience. For a moment Ammadin sat with her saddlebags in her lap and considered the girl. 'Do you have bad dreams still?' Ammadin said at last.

'How did you know I had bad dreams?'

'It's part of my work to know things.'

'Yes.' Her voice dropped. 'I keep dreaming he's choking me again.' The fear-smell billowed around her, pure of any taint of lying.

'I've made you a talisman.' Ammadin unlaced one saddlebag. 'It has plains magic, magic from the Mistlands. Have you heard of those?'

This brought a brief smile to Rozi's thin face. Ammadin handed her a small vial of oil, made from the crushed leaves of a glow plant, and a piece of blue trade cloth, tied around a chip of green and white travertine.

'Keep these under your pillow,' Ammadin said. 'When you wake up from a bad dream, put a drop of oil onto the cloth. You'll see a small star of hope. Pray to your god to take the dreams away. By the time all the oil's gone, the dreams will be too.'

Rozi hesitated, sceptical, then smiled and took them. 'Thank you,' she said. 'It'll be something for me to do about them.'

'Yes, that's it exactly. You'll be able to drain all the power out of the dreams once you see that you have power, too.'

'Thank you.' She twined her long, pale fingers around the vial and the chip. 'I'll keep them with me.'

In a flood of thanks from Loy and Taymah both, they left the chapel. Ammadin glanced back before the door closed and saw Rozi walking gravely down the aisle, her eyes fixed on the golden cross on the far wall, the talisman clutched in her hands. How much good it would do her, Ammadin couldn't say, but some would be better than none.

Hand in hand Ammadin and Zayn walked back to the hohte. Neither of them spoke as they made their way through the lighted streets of the town. She was aware of him pressing closer and closer against her, of his hand tightening on hers. Will I miss him? she thought. In my blankets, certainly. But the rest of the time? He was as wounded as Loy's daughter, in his own way, and she had given him all the help she could. If he was going to heal, he would have to go among the men from his past and see if indeed, he could ever make himself whole again.

She remembered Yannador, telling her that a spirit rider could only travel so far with a person who needed healing. In the end, they would have to heal themselves with the medicines the spirit rider had given them, or it would be no true healing at all. She could only pray that she had given him all the medicine he needed for his spirit, broken so early and so repeatedly.

When they returned to the hohte, without a word he pulled her into his arms. He kissed her face, her lips, the side of her neck, and she could feel him trembling in a kind of desperate desire, as if by making love to her he could truly meld them together and never leave. Yet, although she enjoyed his lovemaking as much as always, already in her mind she had left him. Afterwards she lay wrapped tight in his arms, but she was thinking of contacting Water Woman to tell her that she'd be staying in Sarla for one more day.

* * *

Loy woke early, then spent an hour rushing around her cottage and hiding everything that looked the least bit technological, even though the effort struck her as silly. If Ammadin thought a light-wand drew its power from spirits, she would doubtless believe the same thing about a spice grinder or an electric kettle. Most of her house had sunk to the same level as the rest of the Cantons, anyway. She cooked over wood and lighted candles against the dark to spare the guild's scant supply of solar accus.

Ammadin arrived not long before the observation grid was due over the horizon. The Riders, Loy reminded herself. Call them the Riders. Ammadin wore her saurskin cloak over her shirt and leather pants, and she carried her gaudy red and white saddle-bags. When Loy showed her in to the tiny living room, Ammadin spent a moment looking around. She pointed to a picture on the mantelpiece, a head-and-shoulders drawing of a young man with straight, dark hair and pale eyes.

'Rozi's father?' Ammadin said.

'Yes, his name was Oskar. Oskar Vallohn. He drowned swimming in the river, a silly freak accident.'

'That's very sad.'

'It was, yes. It was twelve years ago, but I still miss him.'

Ammadin nodded and looked over the next set of shelves. 'You have books, a lot of books.'

'Yes, I do. Most of my salary goes for books.'

Ammadin blinked at her.

'A salary is the money the Loremasters Guild gives me for teaching.'

'Oh. The Riders will be overhead soon.'

'Yes. We can take our crystals out to the garden.'

Garden was a fancy name for Loy's patch of half-dead green grass, native species weeds, and three rows of vegetables, but it did offer a table and chairs out in the sun. Ammadin took off her cloak, folded it carefully, and placed it on the table. She brought out her crystals from the saddlebags and laid them on the cloak – to feed, she told Loy. Loy had already carried out her multi-transmit, multi-receive unit, an oval crystal about twelve inches along one axis and four on the other, flat on one side to fit into its true-wood support case. Ammadin's eyes widened at the sight.

'That's a wonderful crystal,' she said. 'Did your master give that to you?'

'Yes, in a way. It was my mother's. She was a sorcerer too, and so was my grandmother.'

'Does it bother you to have Rozi serve the temple instead?'

'Yes, it bothers me a lot. Before Yarl hurt her, she was going to go to university up in Kors. It's the most important school in the Cantons.' Loy felt like screaming in frustration. 'They were going to let her attend for free and everything.'

'And now she won't go?'

Loy nodded, not trusting her voice. It's Rozi's life, she told herself. Not mine, not mine.

'This church interests me,' Ammadin went on. 'Zayn says you worship the same god the Kazraks do, but with a different book.'

'Some of us worship that god. Not everyone.' Loy remembered that the Tribes fully believed in their own gods and worked at keeping the scorn out of her voice. 'The religion goes back a real long way, to the early days of the Cantons. The Kazraks were happy and prospering and having lots of children over in their khanate, but in the Cantons people were miserable, absolutely fixated on the country they'd come from and lost. From what I've read I'd say that the colony was in real danger of dying out. Some of the Cantonneurs even converted to Islam and went to live in the khanate.'

'That's interesting. Did they marry Kazraks and have children?'

'Yes, I'm sure they did.' The question struck Loy as odd, but she couldn't quite figure out why. 'So the rest of the colonists decided to give the Kazraki god a try. Hey, it worked for the Kazraks, didn't it?'

Ammadin laughed, nodding her agreement.

'But my ancestors wanted to worship in their own way,' Loy continued. 'So they dug out a holy book that their ancestors had believed in. It really does seem to give a lot of people comfort and the hope they need, somehow, to stop brooding about the past and the things we've lost and move on to what we have.'

'That makes me think their god must be real, then.'

'Well, I'd say it's the believing that's real.'

'Oh?' Ammadin's expression hovered on the edge of a smile. 'Not the god working for his people?'

Loy realized that they were treading on dangerous ground, should Ammadin want to discuss her own gods. Fortunately, the observation grid saved her by rising over the horizon. Two crystals chimed, hers and one of Ammadin's.

'They're up,' Loy said. 'The Riders, I mean. How shall we do this?'

'Long Voice knows how to contact Water Woman,' Ammadin said. 'Let me wake him.'

Together Loy and Ammadin fussed over the crystals until Loy's powerful unit managed to lock onto Water Woman's position. In a pale green glow the image of the female ChaMeech appeared in the centre of the oval. She was sitting haunched in purple grass, her blue and white skirt spread out around her, with two naked grey ChaMeech haunched nearby. In her pseudo-hands she held a spherical crystal. The image, this melding of alien and human, took Loy's breath for a long moment.

Ammadin Witchwoman, you are there not there? Water Woman's voice came in clearly from the receiver embedded in Loy's transmit. Loy was shocked at how clearly she formed the Tekspeak words.

'I'm here,' Ammadin said. 'But I can hear you twice.'

I understand-not, Water Woman said. *I speak only once.*

Ammadin shook her head as if something pained her. 'I hear your voice like a spirit voice, in my skull, and then I hear your voice coming out of Loy's crystal.'

Loy turned towards her in utter surprise, but Water Woman spoke before she could ask a question.

I understand-now. Ammadin Witchwoman, you know not know where the Karshaks be?

'In Burgunee Canton,' Ammadin said. 'The last I saw of them, Soutan and his Kazraks were going into a big house near the Burgunee-Dordan border. Another Kazrak lives in that house. His name is Jezro, and Soutan and his friends want to take him back to the Kazrak khanate.'

Good. I hope-now they go far away and come-not here. There be one Karshak on the road still, not far north of Sarla. He wear-now device so I see-not him, but Sibyl have power to see him. Sibyl see-always where us witchpeople see-not.

'That Kazrak's Zayn. He's my friend, my very dear friend. Is he in danger?'

No danger. The image of Water Woman frowned down at the crystal she was holding. *Sibyl ask, this third Karshak, he go not go to join the other Karshaks?*

'I don't know. He may join them, he may kill at least one of them. He may kill Soutan and not one of the Kazraks. I honestly don't know what he'll do when he gets there. Neither does he.'

This be very strange.

Loy couldn't have agreed more.

'Zayn is very strange,' Ammadin said. 'But where are you now? Are we still meeting at the white cliff?'

We meet-next-soon at the white cliff, yes. Loy Sorcerer, you are there not there?

'I'm here, Water Woman.' Loy leaned forward into the image capture range of the transmit, then realized that Water Woman could only hear, not see them with her single crystal. 'I'm honoured you would speak with me.'

That be a strange saying from a Canton woman. You hate-not us for what happen-then-long-time east of here to your fifth Canton?

It took Loy a moment to decipher her utterance. 'No, I don't hate you,' Loy said. 'You weren't born then.'

The image of Water Woman stamped a foot on the ground. *Good,* Water Woman went on. *I talk-then at early dawn this-day with Sibyl. Sibyl say-then, invite Loy Sorcerer, see if she come not come with Ammadin Witchwoman.*

'Wonderful!' Loy blurted. 'I was hoping you'd ask.'

As soon as she said it, Loy could hardly breathe. What the hell have you got yourself into? But she knew that if she backed out of this ridiculous adventure now, she would face a life of bitter regret.

So, Loy Sorcerer, Water Woman said, *you come-next-soon to meet Sibyl?*

'Oh yes,' Loy said. 'I'll come. I need to tell my guildmaster and find a horse, but I'll come.'

Part Three

The Damned

Singer: Chursavva Great Mother might have killed them all.
Chorus: The H'mai stood within reach of her servants' spears.
Singer: Chursavva Great Mother let them live.
Chorus: She showed them mercy and mild ways.
Singer: How do we sing of Chursavva Great Mother?
Chorus: We curse her name and piss on her memory.

From *Folklore of the Chof, Volume II*
ed. Yasmini Al-Norravvachiri

Before he left Sarla, Zayn asked about the road north. The maiderdee at the hohte looked weary and suggested he just buy a map in the college bookshop, a purchase that turned out to be well worth a silver vran. Where the ancient north road split into two, a few miles out of Sarla, Zayn took the Burgunee fork, which angled deceptively west to skirt a little lake, as round as a cup of water half-buried in sand, before heading north-east. That first day he travelled on the main road and spent the first night on the floor of a village wine shop without worrying about who might see him. He was assuming that Warkannan and Jezro would be long gone once he reached Burgunee and that, therefore, there was no particular reason to hide. He did make an effort, however, to keep his imp fed on sunlight. Soutan had got the better of him once; he refused to let it happen again.

At noon on the second day he stopped beside an irrigation ditch in the shade of a scant stand of pink hill-bamboid. The brown water flowed in silence and rippled around the muzzles of his horses as they drank, switching their tails to chase black midges away. When he refastened the bits of their bridles, he noticed that horse sweat and road dust had stained his quest marker, particularly the feathers. The sight bit his conscience. Riding so openly meant failing the spirit of his quest.

In the shade of the pink bamboid he ate stale bread and washed it down with wine. He could see the map on his mental screen clearly enough to study its details. From talking with people he'd met along the road, he knew that the Dookis Marya lived some five miles west of Kors, the main town in Burgunee, in something called a manor house. Apparently her wealth had single-handedly lifted the villages and farms around her out of poverty. Everyone told him how admired she was, how grateful the citizens were for her generosity, how sorry they were that she seemed to have gone mad. No one quite knew what form this madness took, but she had turned into a recluse, surrounded by bodyguards. Zayn cared nothing one way or the other about the dookis, but the bodyguards mattered.

The estate appeared on the map as a dot. Nearby he saw a triangle, marking a farming village. If a Kazrak turned up in the village, some villager or other would doubtless run right to the bodyguards to report it. He would have to circle round, avoiding the village, camping in the wild country that the map so thoughtfully marked for him, then make his final approach on foot. By then he was enough of a comnee man to worry about the horses. If he left them tethered and then never came back for them, they'd die of thirst or starve. He would turn them into some farmer's pasture at night, he decided, a gift from fortune should he die trying to honour his oath.

From that noontide on he rode as an assassin, staying on country lanes, travelling at night when the roads allowed, and avoiding other human beings as much as possible. Late on his fourth day out from Sarla, he crossed into Burgunee and arrived at a patch of wild land where an abandoned barn offered shelter. In the shade of a pair of fountain trees he dismounted and walked over to inspect it.

Someone else had camped there, and fairly recently at that. In soft ground near a tiny stream, he found hoofprints; there were horse droppings scattered in the grass. In the barn itself he could clearly see where at least two, more likely three, persons had disturbed ancient dust.

'Well, look at all this,' he said aloud. 'One of Idres' camps, I bet.'

The irony of it made him smile. He decided to camp there as well, as if by some kind of sympathetic magic he would make a link between Warkannan and himself.

After he had tended his horses, Zayn set off on foot to walk a wide circle around the campsite, just as a precaution. He was looking for nothing in particular, but he found something startling: a Settler artifact. Made of smooth-seeming flexstone, the sphere sat half-buried in the earth. About four feet in diameter, it rocked slightly when he touched it, as if it sat in a socket under the earth. When he shoved it with some force, it swivelled in a quarter-turn and squealed, as if some mechanism needed oiling.

When he was dropping off to sleep he had what might have been only a peculiar dream. He could hear footsteps and voices under him, as if he lay on the floor of a two-storey building, and something large was walking across the floor below. All at once he was wide awake; he sat up but heard nothing. He rolled off the blankets and laid his head down on the earth. Maybe footsteps, maybe the rumble of a very small earthquake, the merest tremble in the earth – the sound died away, and he never heard it again.

'Captain Warkannan?' Zhil said.

'Yes?' Warkannan put his book down.

'Dookis Marya would like to meet you, sir.'

Zhil took a few steps into the parlour. Between his white shirt and pale blond hair, his skin seemed stripped of all colour by the bright morning light. Warkannan wondered if he were unwell or if, more likely, he never left the house for more than a few minutes at a time.

'Of course.' Warkannan stood up. 'Am I presentable?'

'Oh yes, sir. Come with me, please.'

'Certainly. What about my nephew?'

'The dookis prefers to talk with only one person at a time, sir. I hope you're not offended?'

'Not in the least.'

Zhil smiled and ducked his head, as if in apology, then led the way through the maze of halls and rooms to a true-oak door at the end of a narrow, white corridor. Zhil put his palm against a depression in the door panel and said a word in Vranz. The door slid back, allowing them into a tiny room, also white, with another door opposite. As soon as they were through, the first door slid shut.

'Well, that's fancy,' Warkannan said.

'You see, sir, the dookis is very afraid of thieves. At night no one can get through these doors but her.'

Zhil cleared his throat and spoke four slow words in Vranz. The opposite door opened, and they walked into a hallway lit by a long bar of glowing crystal overhead. Glittering glass cases lined the walls from floor to ceiling. Although strong wires bound each one to the wall as a precaution against earthquakes, they leaned inward on the uneven floor, giving the impression that they might suddenly fall and bury the viewer. Things crammed every shelf of every case, so many things that Warkannan could only form an impression of their variety. He noticed books, chunks of obsidian, glass spheres, sea shells, and some shiny silver and white objects that had to be Settler work.

'This is quite a collection,' Warkannan said.

'This is only part of it,' Zhil said. 'There are four other rooms filled with cases. She spends all her time arranging and rearranging the things, you see, and cataloguing them. She has several catalogue systems, and whenever she changes the arrangement, she has to change the catalogues.'

A final door and three grey steps led up to the dookis's apartment. As far as Warkannan could figure, they were in the exact centre of the house, and indeed, when they entered, he found himself in a room without windows. Somewhere, though, there must have been ventilation, for the big room smelled fresh and clean. More glass cases, floor to ceiling, lined every wall. Cases that came only to Warkannan's waist stood back to back in the centre of the room like a barricade. Books and notebooks lay strewn about in heaps.

The only furniture, a low grey divan, sat on a grey carpet. A small white shen lounged on the divan. If it had not turned its head to eye Warkannan in evident ill-will, he might have thought it stuffed and part of the collection. The sheer weight and glitter of all those objects crammed into cabinets made it nearly impossible for him to focus on what they might be, especially the things that looked as if they could be Settler relics. In this room shelf after shelf held little boxes, metal tubes, grey twists and loops, the occasional crystal, chunks and bars of a blue quartz-like substance, and odd bits of materials odder still.

'If you'll wait here, Captain?' Zhil said. 'I'll see if Mada is –'

'Zhil?' A woman's voice called.

Talking rapidly in Vranz, Dookis Marya strode into the room, a tall woman, handsome rather than beautiful, with cropped brown hair and brown eyes. She wore narrow blue trousers and a loose white shirt, gathered at the waist by a belt made of overlapping Kazraki gold coins. Around her neck on a golden chain she wore a small oblong of blue quartz that reminded Warkannan of Soutan's signal imp, and she was clutching a bundle of Tribal arrows, each with a rushi tag. When Zhil spoke to her in Vranz, she turned to Warkannan and considered him without a trace of a smile. He got the impression that she was considering how he might be catalogued, should she wish to add him to one of the cases.

During their conversation, which Zhil translated, she never left the doorway nor invited Warkannan to sit down. At intervals the shen growled or whined, but it made no attempt to leave the divan.

'Ah, Captain Warkannan,' she began. 'I understand you're a friend of my secretary.'

'Yes, Mada, I am. I've ridden here from Kazrajistan to see him.'

As they continued, trading pleasantries through the patient Zhil, Warkannan felt more and more sorry for her. Had she seemed happy, he might not have questioned her obsession, but her eyes hinted at pain, a constant ache of longing as they peered out from deep sockets. Her gaze flicked this way and that, from him to the glass cases and back, to the shen, to Zhil, but always back to the cases. She's too young, Warkannan thought, much too young to shut herself up like a widow. Mercifully, she lost interest in him after a few minutes, turned, and strode back through the doorway into the other room, whatever it may have been. Zhil ushered him out with a long, relieved sigh.

Warkannan said nothing until they reached the blue parlour. He picked up the *Mirror of the Qur'an* he'd left behind and tucked it under his arm.

'Your poor employer,' Warkannan said. 'May God help her!'

'Yes sir, but she's been so generous to us all that we hate to – well –'

'There's nothing you can do about it, Zhil,' Warkannan said. 'I didn't mean to imply that. I'll remember her in my prayers from now on.'

'Thank you, sir.'

'When did this happen? Recently?'

'Yes sir, but she was always a nervous sort of person, always worrying if her friends truly liked her or was it her riches.'

'That's a common problem among the wealthy.'

'I didn't realize that, sir. We don't have very many wealthy people out here, I guess.' Zhil thought for a moment. 'And then she always worried about thieves, but things got really bad about two years ago.' His tone flattened. 'About the time Mizzou Soutan came here.'

'I see.' Warkannan cocked an eyebrow and waited.

Zhil glanced around as if he expected to find someone watching him.

'I see,' Warkannan said again. 'Do you know where Jezro Khan is?'

'Yes sir, I'll take you there.'

In the opposite wing of the rambling manor house Jezro Khan had his own office, a little corner room with windows on two sides. Cloth in a soothing pale green covered the walls, and a pair of blue and grey rugs decorated the true-oak floor. A desk stood against one wall, and in the middle of the room, a big oak table held books, a pair of clean handkerchiefs, and what appeared to be hundreds of scraps of rushi. Jezro was standing in front of the table, contemplating the scraps, while Soutan perched on a high stool nearby with Nehzaym's grey slate in his lap.

'My hobby.' Jezro waved his hand at the table. 'Once Marya decided to put herself into her museum, I had to do something with my time. I always thought I'd love living in idle luxury, but I was wrong. It gets boring after a while. A short while.'

Warkannan picked up a piece of rushi and frowned at it. 'Near fourth prophet second mention. One zero one.' He glanced up. 'What in hell?'

'What in heaven, actually.' Jezro was grinning at him. 'A holy book, that is, though not ours. I've been working out some puzzles. Our text for today, dearly beloved, is *The Sibylline Prophecies*. The author, whoever she was, left us clues in the form of numbers stuck in here and there. They don't seem to make any sense.'

'Later editions leave them out,' Soutan put in. 'A huge mistake.'

'Well, it's pretty obscure stuff,' Jezro said. 'You see, the numbers and the clues in the passages around them lead us to this book, the Bible. It's the other holy book that the First Prophet talks about in the ha'dith. The Church of the One God still uses it.' He laid a hand on the leather-bound volume. 'Sibyl refers to the fourth prophet a lot. The Bible's a collection of books, and they come in a definite order, organized by type. The fourth prophet on the list is a fellow named Ezekiel, and God only knows what he was drinking when he sat down to prophesy. He kept seeing things in the sky, like wheels within wheels that belched fire and spoke to him.' Jezro picked up a piece of rushi. 'Book ten, verse one – that's my interpretation of that one zero one. I quote: "Behold, on the firmament that was over the heads of the Cherubim there appeared something like a sapphire, in form resembling a throne."'

'That's supposed to be a clue?' Warkannan said. 'Clue to what?'

'The location of the Ark of the Covenant.' Soutan leaned forward, all urgency. 'If we have that, we can find the starships that brought us here. For instance, one clue leads to the line, "I lift up my eyes to the hills, where my strength comes from." So we know that it must be in some sort of hill country.'

'It would be pretty damn funny,' Warkannan said, 'if it turned out to be under Haz Kazrak.'

Jezro laughed, Soutan glared.

'That's very unlikely,' Soutan went on. 'Other clues point to the east, among an alien people. Who else but the ChaMeech?'

'Umph,' Warkannan said. 'Where did this Sibylline book come from, anyway? I'd never even heard of it till a couple of years ago.'

'Marya's father bought the original manuscript about twenty years ago,' Jezro said. 'He wouldn't tell anyone where he got it, not even her, but he had it printed up and started selling it. It made him a lot of money. I'm willing to bet, though, that Yarl's the only one who realized it contains a code.'

'And now we may have another source of information. This is called a recept-screen, Captain.' Soutan laid one hand on the slate. 'I'm trying to figure out how to use it properly. I can get it to show a series of views, but I can't make it identify what they are.'

'Views?' Warkannan said.

'Pictures of different locations, all indoors – somewhere. Some of the rooms look very much like the written descriptions we have of the inside of the ships, but I don't know if these are merely stored images from eight hundred years ago, or if they show me the interiors as they are at the present moment.'

'Why would they?'

'This thing might be a security monitor, that's why. One guard could keep track of a lot of different places if he could see them on one of these.'

'I suppose. But if the slate won't tell you where the rooms are, it won't do you much good.'

'No.' Soutan looked sublimely sour. 'It won't. Still, I persevere. Success may just be a matter of finding the right command words.'

'The slate might give us faster results than I can, putting clues together.' Jezro waved a hand at the heaps of rushi spread across the table. 'You practically need to have everything memorized before you can see the correspondences.'

'I can see why you were hoping that Benumar would come with me,' Warkannan said.

'That memory of his – yes, I need it, all right.' Jezro turned to Soutan. 'Speaking of which, is there any sign of him?'

'Not in the crystals.' Soutan slid off the stool, set the slate down carefully on the table, and began to pace back and forth. 'I've been looking everywhere, every direction – nothing. I can't find the spirit rider. I can't find Zayn. They could be up on the hill and ready to pounce for all I know.'

'Calmly, Yarl, calmly,' Jezro said. 'We still have actual eyes, you know. I asked Robear to send a couple of men down to Kors to warn people to watch for him. We've stationed other men up on top of the hills.'

'Of course.' Soutan gave him a sheepish smile. 'I forgot about that. Stupid of me!'

'Not at all,' Jezro went on. 'It would be better if we could track him, but if we can't, well, there are old-fashioned ways of dealing with assassins.'

Soutan winced and shuddered.

'I'm not dead yet, Yarl.' Jezro grinned at him. 'I'll tell Robear to order his men to leave Benumar strictly alone. They'd better be safe inside once he actually gets here.'

'Safe inside?' Soutan sneered. 'One man against ten?'

'You don't understand the Chosen.' Jezro paused for one of his twisted smiles. 'I don't want my crazy idea to cause someone's death. Huh, I'd better have Robear lock up the shens, too, come to think of it.'

'Jezro, please, don't do this!' Soutan stretched out both hands, imploring. 'It's too risky.'

'I'm sorry.' Jezro looked away. 'I've got to. It's for me as much as for Benumar, you see. I had my moment of cowardice. Before I decide what I'm going to do about the khanate, I'd better find out if I'm still a coward.' He turned to Warkannan and raised an eyebrow.

'Oh, I understand perfectly,' Warkannan said. 'But I intend to stick close to you, anyway.'

'That's some comfort, I suppose,' Soutan said.

'Something just occurred to me,' Warkannan continued. 'Suppose Zahir never returns to the khanate, for whatever reason. The Chosen will send someone else, and then someone else if that man doesn't return, and so on. Sooner or later, word is going to get back that you're alive. Even if Gemet heard you say you don't want the throne with his own ears, do you think he'd believe you? The only way you're ever going to be really safe again is to win this rebellion.'

Jezro scowled at him. 'Get out and let us get back to work, will you? I want to finish piecing together this passage.' He picked up a sheet of rushi. 'I think it must refer to the first history book about the age of kings.'

'Kings,' Warkannan said. 'Ah yes, kings.'

'Get out, you bastard!' Jezro shook a fist in mock rage.

'I'm going.' Warkannan grinned at him. 'But think about it.'

With Soutan safely occupied, Warkannan decided that the time had come for a talk with Arkazo. He found him in his guest room, a small but pleasant space with windows on one wall, a bed on the other, and an armchair and table in the middle. A scatter of shiny black tubes and wires lay on the table – some device of Yarl's, Warkannan assumed. Arkazo was sitting in the chair and reading.

'What's that?' Warkannan said. 'It must be pretty interesting stuff.'

'It is, yes.' Arkazo looked up with a grin. 'You never caught me studying like this when I was at university.'

'You took the words right out of my mouth.'

'It's a kind of maths called al zhebrah.' Arkazo held up the open book to show him pages of numbers and little symbols, interspersed with the occasional line of writing. 'Our people invented it, way back in the old days in the Homelands, but they don't teach it any more in our schools. I don't understand why.'

'I don't, either, if it's just numbers.'

'Yarl gave me this.' Arkazo shut the book and laid his hand upon it. 'It's really something, Uncle, all the things he knows.'

'That's true, yes, but what about Soutan himself?'

'What about him?' Arkazo's voice turned sharp.

Warkannan hesitated, considering words.

'I know you don't like him,' Arkazo said. 'I didn't myself at first, but we didn't know him then, really know him, I mean.'

'Well, you should never judge a man by your first impression, no, but sometimes Soutan worries me. This talk about the lost ships, going home, that sort of thing.'

'Oh, that! It's kind of demented, isn't it?'

'I thought so, yes. So does Jezro.'

'It's the other stuff I like, the things he knows, the books he has. When you live for knowledge like he does, I can see how your mind would slip over the edge now and then.'

'He lives for knowledge? What about that girl?'

'Well, he's only human.' Arkazo waved a hand in dismissal. 'And she was lying.'

'So *he* says.'

Arkazo sat up straight and glared at him. Warkannan decided to let the subject drop – for the moment. 'Well, enjoy your book. I'm going to go for a stroll around the estate.'

That same afternoon, while Jezro and Warkannan talked of prophets, Zayn was camping some ten miles from the estate. At sunset he took his horses and left them in a convenient farmer's field. His gear he hid in the tall weeds and grasses nearby, then started off on foot for the manor house. By twilight he reached the first hill, covered in high grass, and a perfect spot for a lookout. Zayn crouched down among a tangle of pink and orange shrubs at the bottom and waited, watching, until he could be sure that no one was walking or sitting up on the hill crest.

He walked part-way up, then crawled the rest of the way to avoid standing out against the dark sky and the rising silver light of the Herd. Indignant midges flew from the grass and whined around his ears. He stopped, waiting, but he heard no one moving on the crest, and when he reached the top, he found areas of flattened grass where guards had kept watch, but no guards. Why had they withdrawn? Surely Warkannan would know that the Chosen generally came by night. Maybe they'd had no reason to stay. Maybe Jezro and Warkannan were already on their way back to Andjaro Province. Zayn crawled to the edge of the slope and looked down over the long green lawn and the sprawling manor house, golden with light from open windows. To one side stood a long, shrubby line of pale yellow trees with dangling branches, thick with long reddish leaves – possible shelter when the time came. All round the edge of the lawn ran a ten-foot-high wire fence.

Someone came striding across the lawn, someone with the sort of straight back that the cavalry gave a man, but at his distance Zayn could pick out no details. The fellow stopped walking, raised his hands to his mouth, and began to shout. At first Zayn could distinguish nothing but his summoning tone of voice, but he started walking again, heading closer to the hill where Zayn lay hidden. The night breeze brought him a drift of words.

'Kaz, where are you? Kaz! Dinner!'

Idres' voice. Shit! Zayn thought. They're still here. A slender man came running from an outbuilding and called back – the nephew. Together they jogged across the lawn and hurried into the house, which, he now knew, hid in a maze of rooms Jezro Khan, Soutan, and a pack of armed guards. He was looking at the hardest job he'd ever undertaken for the Chosen.

Zayn had reached the point where magic imps meant nothing, since ordinary human eyes could see him well enough. He crawled backwards over the crest into the shelter of the hillside, made his way down, then jogged back to the farm. He thought of Ammadin, heaping scorn on his ideas about damnation and demons. Did she realize, he wondered, just how thoroughly she'd destroyed all his old excuses, his old justifications? Probably she did, but he doubted if she realized just how badly he needed them. Easy for her to say he should live without them! Her inborn talents had brought her rank, wealth, and respect, while he'd had nothing – nothing, that is, until Idres and Jezro had given him respect and rank both.

'But I never earned that, it was all lies, they never knew what I really am.'

He was shocked that he'd spoken aloud, but the words were nothing new; he'd thought them thousands of times. He wondered if he'd have joined the Chosen if he hadn't believed that the khan was dead, and if he hadn't been transferred away from Idres' regiment to the Second Bariza. What would he have done when the first hints were dropped in his hearing, when the first intimations came that he might be worthy of some special place in the Great Khan's service? He doubted if he would have listened if he'd been facing Idres every night in the officers' mess. He knew he never would have listened had Jezro Khan been alive to be disappointed in him.

'So what the hell are you doing here?' Zayn said aloud. 'He is alive.'

With that he realized that he had to act quickly or he never would. For a moment he considered taking his comnee bow, but he was too poor an archer to strike from a distance. From his saddlebags he took out a set of lock picks and a wire garotte and secreted them in his clothing. The Chosen! he thought. We're nothing but thieves. For a moment he stood hesitating, then hurried off, running on level ground, jogging on rough.

Zayn circled around the boundary of the estate to climb a different hill, the one directly behind the stand of golden trees. For some hours he lay hidden on the crest, watching the lights go out, one at time, in the various windows, waiting for the Herd to set and give him darkness. Early on he heard shens barking, but a man came out of the stables and whistled them inside. At last, under the arch of black sky, the house slept.

While Zayn couldn't see in the dark, he could remember precisely how the grounds looked and navigate by the images in his mind. He moved down the hillside slowly, crouching often, listening, waiting in utter silence. He reached the gate in the fence at last. He brought out the lock picks, but the gate swung open at his touch. He could only assume that he was walking into an ambush. He hesitated, then decided that if they killed him before he could reach Jezro, so much the better. Still, he had reflexes, he had training. He ran through the gate, dropped and rolled, used the momentum of the roll to leap to his feet, and darted into the yellow trees. He stood among the wind-driven leaves and caught his breath.

Ahead he could see the dark rise of the house, about a hundred yards away. In a lower window at the right-hand side, a light went on; on the far left, one set of curtains glowed. The rest of the windows stayed dark. Were they expecting him to come to the lighted room? Or did they think he'd see the light as a trap and thus come round the other side, where they were waiting for him? Moving carefully, one step at a time, he sidled through the long stand of trees till he reached its right-hand limit. From there he could see around to the side of the house and a little garden, set off by a low wall – too low. The outbuildings beyond the walled garden provided the only shelter between him and the house.

Zayn dropped full length into the high grass and began to crawl. Midges flew, biting, but he ignored them. A few feet, and he'd pause, wait, listen, then crawl a few feet more, then do the same again, moving in an arc that brought him at last to level ground behind the cluster of outbuildings. The longest of them had to be the stables from the smell. The shens inside would make a racket if he got too close. He set off crawling again and ended up directly behind a shed. He risked standing and sidled along the back wall until he could peer around it.

The house stood only some twenty feet away. In the glow from the window he could see the garden and the low wall. As he stood considering his next move, he heard a door open, the scrape of metal on stone, and footsteps. He drew his long knife and waited. The fellow coughed – a deep sound, probably a man's voice – and struck a match. Light bloomed behind the wall, an oil lamp from its soft gold colour.

'Hey, Benumar?' The voice sounded familiar, especially in the way it hovered on the edge of a laugh. 'Is tonight the night? Are you here? Hurry up, will you? I'm sick and tired of all these damned bugs.'

The voice – Jezro Khan, waiting for him – the best bait any ambush could have. Zayn looked around him, but he saw no one moving on the lawn, no one rising from cover off to the side, no one at all. He damned caution and stepped out of cover. Still no guards – he strode across the lawn to the garden wall.

Dressed only in a pair of loose trousers and a plain white shirt, Jezro was standing by a chair. Wingbuhs swarmed around the oil lamp burning on a nearby table. By its light Zayn could see the double welt of scars running across his face – a little gift from the Chosen. The wall stood just low enough for Zayn to swing one leg over, then the other, without having to sheathe his knife. He took a few steps, then stopped. Jezro was standing his ground. When he smiled, the scar twisted around the side of his mouth.

'You can see I'm not armed,' Jezro said. 'Are you really going to kill me, Benumar? When I can't even put up a fight?'

Hearing his real name, hearing the voice of the man he'd once honoured above all others, seeing Jezro Khan alive after thinking him dead for ten long years – Zayn realized that he was perilously close to weeping. His thumbs hooked in his belt, Jezro waited, still smiling.

'It's good to see you,' Jezro went on. 'Which is a strange thing to say to a man who wants to kill you, but it's true. You and Warkannan, you were the only real friends I ever had, you know.

No one else could ever forget my damned rank and how profitable knowing me might be one day. That's before we all learned what a murderous little turd my brother was, of course.'

Zayn felt himself trembling. It started in the hand holding the long knife, then travelled up his arm and caught the rest of him, made him quiver like trees after an earthquake. Jezro said nothing more, merely watched him solemn-eyed. With the foulest oath he could summon Zayn sheathed the knife. Jezro sighed in sharp relief.

'No,' Zayn said. 'I can't kill you.'

'I'm glad to see the Chosen don't own your soul.'

At that Zayn felt tears rise, threatening to shame him. He turned half-away, heard the gravel crackle as Jezro limped over, felt the khan's hand on his shoulder.

'You've come just in time,' Jezro said. 'It's fate, Benumar, it's got to be. Idres, you, me – I always felt that the three of us had a destiny together.' He paused for a soft laugh. 'Not that I know what it is yet, but I know there's got to be one.'

Zayn started to speak, but the tears choked him. He took one step away and covered his face with his hands, but he could feel his shoulders shaking. Jezro walked round in front of him.

'Idres told me about the talents,' Jezro went on. 'You must have been in hell, hiding all of that for all those years.'

Zayn dropped his hands and looked at him through a blur of tears. He could barely breathe from the effort of holding back tears, could not think, could not speak.

'What did they do to you, Benumar?' Jezro's voice hissed with rage. 'What did the bastards do to you to make you join them?'

'Nothing.' Zayn found words at last. 'They just told me I wasn't alone any more.'

The tears spilled and ran, shaming him, but he had no power to stop them. He heard his voice crack as if it belonged to a stranger, then sobbed, could not stop sobbing, fell to his knees and wept. He heard Jezro moving, heard the gravel crackle as the khan knelt with him, then felt arms around him, pulling him tight.

'Ah God, I'm sorry.' Zayn barely managed to force out the words. 'Forgive me.'

'It's all right.' Jezro sounded near to tears himself. 'It's all right.'

More footsteps, and light brightening around them – Zayn tipped his head back and saw Warkannan walking up, carrying a lantern in one hand. The shame of it, that Idres would see him weep – but he could only gulp for air and sob. As he knelt on the gravel, in his mind he was kneeling on cold black and white tiles and hearing a voice urge his death. I never wept then, he thought. What's wrong with me now? Warkannan set the lantern on the table, then knelt with them, sitting back on his heels as if he were readying himself for evening prayer in a mosque. Zayn gasped, choked, felt his chest aching, but the tears eased and at last let him be.

In the pool of light from Warkannan's lantern they knelt, looking back and forth at one another. Zayn had the distinct feeling that he was still in the Mistlands, seeing Idres and Jezro only in a vision, but when he looked around, he saw the rose bushes of Dookis Marya's garden, quivering in the night wind. I never would have seen those in the Mistlands. This must be real. Jezro reached into his shirt pocket, pulled out a handkerchief, and handed it over. Zayn wiped his face and blew his nose – it had been running like a child's, he realized, but he felt too much shame over the tears themselves to care about details.

'Don't be embarrassed,' Warkannan said. 'Men have to do these things, you know, every now and then.'

'A perfect Idres remark,' Jezro said. 'They never end.'

Zayn managed to smile. He wadded up the handkerchief and shoved it unthinkingly into his trouser pocket. 'One thing, though. I'm not Zahir Benumar. Benumar's dead. He's the man who would have killed you. My name is Zayn Hassan.'

'All right,' Jezro said. 'Idres?'

'Fine with me,' Warkannan said. 'I might forget occasionally, so just remind me, will you?'

Zayn nodded. Although he could breathe again, his throat ached like fire. Jezro stood up, bending over to rub his twisted right leg. 'Can't kneel for very long,' he remarked, 'thanks to my brother's loving treatment.' He straightened up, glanced at the house, and stiffened. 'Shaitan! What's wrong, Kaz?'

Zayn looked around. Warkannan's nephew was standing in the open doorway, and Zayn had never seen anyone so furious, not even his father in one of his blind rages. Arkazo was shaking with it, stammering as he stepped out into the garden. Warkannan leapt to his feet and started towards him.

'What's wrong?' Arkazo spat out each word. 'What's wrong? He killed the best friend I ever had, and you're acting like he's your long-lost soul mate.'

Zayn suddenly remembered the young Kazrak in the Mistlands. 'I'm sorry,' he said, 'but he was trying to kill me. I didn't have any choice.'

'I don't give a shit.' Arkazo took one step forward. 'You bastard, you –' His hand flicked to his belt and came away with a hunting knife.

Warkannan moved, one smooth long stride that brought him face to face with Arkazo, moved fast and grabbed his wrist. Arkazo screamed in sheer wordless rage, but Warkannan had the knife. Arkazo screamed again, shaking, then turned and rushed back into the house. Warkannan flipped the knife to land point down in the gravel where Jezro could reach it.

'You'd better take charge of that,' Warkannan said. 'And I'd better take charge of my nephew.'

As he ran into the house, Warkannan saw Arkazo dashing into the hall that led to his guest room. He pounded down the hall after him just as Arkazo disappeared into it, but he reached the door before Arkazo could lock it. He grabbed the handle and twisted. It fought him – apparently Arkazo was holding it on the other side.

'Kaz, let me in,' Warkannan said. 'Please? You've got to let me in so we can talk. Please.'

Silence, but when Warkannan tried the handle again, it turned freely. He stepped in and shut the door behind him. Arkazo was standing by the window, his arms tightly crossed over his chest, his eyes wide, his mouth a twist of fury. For a long moment Warkannan merely stood and looked at him. Eventually Arkazo turned away. He grasped the windowsill in both hands and stared out.

'I'm sorry,' Warkannan said. 'But you have to admit that when Zahir killed Tareev, we were all trying to kill him.'

'I don't care.' Arkazo's voice still shook. 'He's one of the Chosen. Why don't you just kill him?'

'Because we knew him before he joined the Chosen. Because we both think we should have done something then. We always knew that something was eating Benumar from the inside. We should have tried to find out what.'

'So? You didn't make him join the Chosen.'

'No, that's true.'

Arkazo started to speak, then choked it back. Warkannan could see over his shoulder to the lawn outside, where a bevy of night-dancers were leaping into the air, chasing the wingbuhs drawn to the lighted windows.

'I thought you might feel differently,' Warkannan said, 'after that business with the fake priests. You told me then that –'

'That I didn't want my revenge that way. I still wanted the revenge.' Arkazo spun around. 'And now you tell me I'm supposed to like the man?'

'Of course not! To be honest, I don't know what to do. It's not like you can just leave and ride home. But I can't let you kill him. He knows things we need to know.'

'Like what?'

'Like who belongs to the Chosen, and where their headquarters are.' Warkannan paused for effect. 'You can see how valuable that is.'

Arkazo nodded, staring down at the floor. 'Did the khan know about Tareev?'

'Not by name. I'll tell him.'

'Will it matter?'

Warkannan hesitated, but he knew he had to be honest. 'No,' he said. 'Not really.'

Arkazo's head snapped up, and his eyes went wide with rage. He laid a hand on the empty sheath at his belt, then winced and let his arm hang at his side.

'I'm sorry,' Warkannan repeated, 'but the simple fact is that Tareev would have killed Zayn if he'd got the chance. That's what makes all the difference, Kaz. Can't you see that? Suppose we were in a court of law. It was self-defence.'

'We're not in court.' But his voice had lost some of its certainty.

'Well, actually, we are a court in a way – you and me, judging the situation.'

'And you're asking me to forgive him.'

'No, I'm asking you to tolerate him. That's all. You can be as angry as you want. Snub him, never speak to him, refuse him common courtesy – I don't care. He won't either. Don't you think he knows how you feel?'

'I don't give a shit if he does or not.'

'Understandable. But there's one thing that the cavalry teaches a man, and that's how to work with anyone he needs to work with – someone he hates, someone he despises, someone who despises him. You need to learn that, too.'

'Oh? Well, I'm not in –' Arkazo stopped in mid-sentence.

Warkannan allowed himself a grim smile. 'You see it, don't you? If Jezro goes back with us, you'll be one of his officers.'

Arkazo nodded, his mouth slack in a kind of wonder.

'Look,' Warkannan went on. 'This is one of the beauties of army discipline. The khan will order you to work with Benumar, I mean, with Hassan. You've got to follow his orders. It's no disgrace to you, it doesn't cheapen Tareev's death, it doesn't mean you've broken your pledge of vengeance. You simply cannot disobey the khan's order.'

'The beauties of it?' Arkazo laughed, or at least, he made a sound that Warkannan assumed was a laugh. 'What's that the khan always says? A perfect Idres remark?'

Warkannan forced out a smile. Arkazo crossed the room and sat down on the edge of his bed. 'I have to think about all of this,' he whispered.

'Yes, you do. I'll leave you alone.'

'Thanks.'

Warkannan turned and opened the door.

'Uncle?' Arkazo's voice sounded thin, a little high.

'Yes?' Warkannan turned back.

'I'm glad you took my knife away. Right there in front of the khan – I just couldn't think.'

'I know. It's all right.' Warkannan decided against telling him the truth, this time, that he'd been protecting him from Zayn, not the other way around. 'You know something? No one will ever mention this again if you don't bring it up.'

'Thanks. I've got to think.'

'Of course you do. Go ahead.'

Warkannan shut the door behind him and hurried down the hall. At the other end, Soutan was standing in the middle of the blue sitting room.

'What's wrong?' Soutan said. 'What is all this?'

'I forgot how Kaz would see things,' Warkannan said. 'I made a mistake, a bad one. We should have told him when we got the idea, but for all I knew, Zahir – I mean Zayn – would never show up or would try to kill Jezro or do some other damned desperate thing.'

'Suppose he had? Tried to kill Jezro, I mean? What would you have done?'

'Stepped in, of course.'

'And killed him?'

'I would have had to, wouldn't I? You can't stop a man who's been trained like Zayn any other way. I wouldn't have liked it, but I would have had to.'

'You know, Captain, I don't think I ever realized just how hard and cold you and Jezro can be.' Soutan looked up at the ceiling and sighed dramatically. 'I don't think I ever realized just how brutal you are. You both have such civilized manners.'

Warkannan crossed his arms over his chest to control his fists. When Soutan deigned to look his way again, Warkannan noticed a thumbnail-sized flake of obsidian, or some substance much like it, pinned to Soutan's shirt collar.

'Or I should say, brutal to members of other species.' Soutan seemed to be speaking into the flake.

'What in hell do you mean by that?'

'Well, Zayn's obviously one of your own kind, and it was all quite touching, out there in the garden. But with ordinary H'mai, it's different.' Again the pause. 'Are we prey, perhaps, in your eyes?'

'What the –'

'Oh never mind!' Soutan turned away with a measured toss of his head. 'I'm going to bed. It's late, and I feel sick to my stomach.' He strode away, heading down the hallway.

Warkannan stood staring after him for a puzzled few moments, long enough for him to see Soutan knock on Arkazo's door and the door open to let him in. Was all that posturing for Kaz's benefit? Warkannan thought. But he couldn't have heard us, all the way out here. Suddenly he felt cold, wondering if perhaps Soutan, with all his talk of crystals and technology, had managed to send their conversation all the way to Arkazo's ears. Had it not been for Zayn, he would have followed Soutan right then. As it was, he realized that Jezro might well need his help in dealing with a man who'd been broken down to his very soul.

Jezro had insisted that Zayn come inside to a parlour decorated in yellows and tans, as luxurious as any Zayn had ever seen in

Kazrajistan. Dirty as he was from the road, he hated to sit on the flowered furniture, and he would have knelt at Jezro's feet like a shen if the khan had let him. Jezro however insisted he take an armchair, forced a glass of brandy into his hand, and sent a servant off to bring him food when he admitted he'd not eaten all day.

'My horses,' Zayn said. 'I've got horses and gear I left at a farm.'

'We'll send someone after them, don't worry.'

'They're at the farm to the north-west. The fenced pasture, the one that you can't see from the farmhouse. I didn't want them to starve if your bodyguards killed me.'

Jezro turned to a blond servant in a white shirt, who apparently understood Kazraki, because he nodded and hurried out of the room, leaving the door half-open. Distantly they could hear the sound of two men yelling in anger. In a few minutes the voices stopped. Warkannan strode in, poured himself brandy, and sat down nearby.

'Things are not right with Arkazo.' Jezro made a statement rather than asking a question.

'No, they're not,' Warkannan said. 'I don't know what to do. You're going to have to order him to leave Ben – I mean Hassan alone.'

'I'll talk with him later.' Jezro took a handkerchief out of his pocket and wiped his nose. 'Let's let him settle down.'

'Thanks. He never should have come with me, but I couldn't leave him behind. The Chosen would have arrested him for a certainty, if something had gone wrong.' He glanced at Zayn. 'Right?'

Zayn nodded his agreement.

'Did I tell you, Jezro?' Warkannan went on. 'We all would have been arrested, except Zayn spoke up for us.'

'How did you learn that?' Jezro said.

'He told me, that day I questioned him.'

Zayn found himself remembering the temple, Warkannan on one side of the bars, himself on the other, and Idres was saying – what had he been saying? Something about lies and God's mercy. He couldn't remember. There was something he couldn't remember. The panic caught him by surprise, that a lapse of a talent he hated could frighten him.

'Sir?' The white-shirted servant was standing in front of him, holding out a plate with bread, cheese, and some sort of pink salad on it.

'Thank you.' Zayn took the plate and put it on his lap. The thought of eating revolted him.

Jezro and Warkannan were both staring at him. The servant backed away, then turned and hurried out of the room.

'Are you all right?' Warkannan said.

'I just can't remember what you said to me that day. About mercy.'

'Oh. That. Well, I told you that I refused to believe you were damned for a trait you were born with. We'd been talking about the Chosen, actually.'

'That's right, yes.' Enough of the conversation came back to dismiss the panic, but he still could not eat.

'Speaking of the Chosen,' Jezro said, 'I suppose they made you swear some kind of oath of secrecy.'

'Of course.' Zayn felt profoundly weary. 'But the minute I refused to kill you, I turned into a deserter. What do you want, me to tell you everything?'

'Not necessarily. But if I do decide to follow out Idres' insane idea and claim the throne, it would be a great help.'

'If?' Zayn said.

'Yes, if. I haven't made up my mind.'

Zayn felt himself gawking like an idiot. Warkannan laughed under his breath.

'See?' Warkannan said. 'Hassan can't believe you'd turn the chance down.'

'Oh shut up, Idres.' Jezro sounded weary rather than angry. 'I have to admit one thing. The idea looks a lot more attractive now that Hassan can tell us who's likely to stick a knife in my ribs.' He leaned forward. 'I don't intend to kill your fellow legionnaires out of hand, not any more, not after what Idres has told me. You have my sworn word on that.'

Zayn could hear something hissing, a kettle perhaps, water boiling, but the sound kept getting louder, turned into a roar. 'I'd never doubt your word,' he managed to say.

'Then the names, if you even know them, of your officers would come in handy. And where you meet, that sort of thing. If I do become Great Khan, I have to get control of the Chosen first thing.'

Zayn tried to speak and failed. He could no longer see correctly, either. Warkannan and Jezro's faces seemed to be drifting back and forth in front of him.

'Zayn!' Warkannan's voice whispered from the other end of a long tunnel. 'Try to hold still. I'm on my way.'

Zayn felt his entire body move, felt his head snap back, felt pain as he twisted, arched, fell, heard the sound of a plate shattering. He could see nothing, then felt nothing.

Yet Zayn woke in what seemed to him an instant to find himself lying on the carpeted floor. He ached so badly that at first he thought himself a child, recovering from one of his father's beatings, but the sight of Idres kneeling beside him brought his memory back. The smell of alcohol hung in the air, strong and sickening. It took Zayn a moment to realize that his shirt was soaked with brandy and streaked with blood. His right hand throbbed.

'He's come round,' Warkannan said. 'Zhil, bring some water, and you'd better get some bandages, too.'

Zayn lifted his hand, cut and slashed in a dozen places.

'That's from the brandy glass,' Jezro said. 'You crushed it when your muscles spasmed. The strength of ten, huh?'

Zayn turned his head. The room spun, but it settled to reveal Jezro, kneeling beside him.

'You just went into convulsions,' Jezro said. 'Do you remember anything? Were you aware of anything?'

'No sir,' Zayn whispered. 'Nothing.'

Jezro let out his breath in a long troubled sigh. He laid a hand on Zayn's forehead. 'Cold as ice.'

'Convulsions?' Zayn suddenly focused on the word.

'Yes, it was quite a sight. You fell out of your chair and then twisted around and rolled on the floor. Does your back ache? It looked to me like every muscle in it had spasmed.' Jezro glanced at Warkannan. 'Let's not ask him about the Chosen again right away, shall we?'

'Was that it, do you think?' Warkannan said.

'It's a good working hypothesis.' Jezro held a hand up flat for silence. 'I'll explain later. Here comes the water.'

With Warkannan's help Zayn sat up. Warkannan propped himself against the divan and let Zayn sit between his legs and lean back against him for support. Zayn gulped water, paused to breathe, then finished the rest of it. He remembered the hissing sound, remembered hearing it in the temple as well, and knew that he had one urgent thing to say before he forgot – before he was made to forget by whatever enemy hid in his own mind.

'But I could tell Ammi everything,' he said. 'I could tell her about them.'

'Don't talk about it now,' Jezro said. 'One set of convulsions a night is enough.'

'Who's Ammi?' Warkannan said. 'Hold out that paw so Jezro can wrap it.'

'The spirit rider.' Zayn held out his hand. 'From my comnee.'

'Ah,' Warkannan said. 'How does that hand look?'

'Not too bad, by some miracle of God,' Jezro said. 'The glass only cut a lot of capillaries. It missed that big artery by the thumb. Hell – here's a splinter of glass. Hang on, Hassan. I've got to pull it out.'

Zayn leaned his head against Warkannan's shoulder in a desperate attempt to stay conscious, but the pain threw him back into the dark.

'Is there a good hakeem around here?' Warkannan said.

'Not one I'd trust with this, no,' Jezro said. 'The convulsions, I mean, not the cuts.'

In his faint Zayn was starting to crumple and slide sideways. Warkannan wrapped his arms around his chest and held on, settling him upright again.

'We'd better get him onto a bed. Zhil?' Jezro turned to him. 'Go fetch Robear, will you? Oh, by the way, did you send someone after Hassan's horses?'

'Yes sir.'

'Thanks. I appreciate your help.'

'You're welcome, sir. If I may ask, are you really going to leave us and go back to Kazrajistan?'

'I don't know yet. Why?'

'But if you do –' Zhil's eyes went wide in a kind of desperation. 'Who's going to be in charge here?'

'Hadn't thought of that. Tell you what, we'll discuss it in the morning. Go get some sleep, all right?'

'Yes sir, and thanks.'

With Robear's help Warkannan carried Zayn to his own guest room and laid him on the nearer of the pair of beds. When Robear started to pull off Zayn's boots, he woke, or partially woke, long enough to sit up and look around him.

'Just rest,' Warkannan said. 'Lie down, Hassan.'

'The blue quartz, sir.' Zayn followed orders and slumped back against the pillows. 'It had lights in it.'

Warkannan and Jezro exchanged a puzzled glance. Zayn seemed to be about to say more, then merely sighed and fell asleep.

'We could use some sleep ourselves.' Warkannan took out his watch. 'It's three in the morning.'

'Already? Wake me at first light. Robear, thanks. You can go back to bed now.'

Robear followed as Jezro limped out, leaning on his stick more heavily than usual. Warkannan took off his boots, then lay down fully dressed on the other bed. Although he was tired enough to fall straight asleep, every time Zayn made a noise, Warkannan woke. At times Zayn seemed to be talking, but the words made no sense in either Kazraki or Hirl-Onglay, nor did they sound like Vranz, but by the time dawn was turning the world beyond the window silver, Zayn was sleeping soundly, his breathing steady and normal.

Warkannan got up, stretched in every direction, then left the room to go wake Jezro. He was only half-way to the khan's bedroom, however, when Jezro came to meet him, fully dressed.

'I woke up a little while ago,' Jezro said. 'Couldn't get back to sleep, so I thought I'd just come see how you were getting along. How is he?'

'Quiet now. We had a few odd noises in the night. Do you really think the Chosen have done something to him?'

'Yes. Don't forget, I was educated in the palace. The Chosen have been around for centuries, you know. It's not just dear Gemet who's misused them, though from what you've told me, he's turned misusing them into a fine art. No one really knows the details, but I was told that they have a way of altering their men's minds to keep them loyal, of making it impossible for them to talk about the brotherhood. I never believed it till last night.'

'It sounds preposterous.'

'Yes, but consider what would have happened to Hassan if he'd been bound, tied to a chair, say, by someone trying to extract information. If he'd been unable to move freely –' Jezro shrugged. 'I'm no hakeem, but it seems to me it might have killed him. Caused a stroke or something like that.'

'Well, yes, I can see that.'

They turned down the hall that held the guest rooms. 'That's odd,' Warkannan said. 'The door's standing open. I know I closed it when I left.'

'Damn! I hope he isn't sleepwalking.'

Warkannan hurried on ahead, stepped into the room, and saw Soutan, standing by Zayn's bed. Zayn himself lay asleep, sprawled on his stomach with one arm hanging over the side of the bed. Soutan whirled around to face Warkannan, but not quickly enough. Warkannan held out his hand.

'Give it back,' he said.

'I beg your pardon!' Soutan straightened to full height. 'Just what are you implying?'

'I'm not implying anything. I'm accusing you of stealing whatever that is. The amulet thing Hassan was wearing.'

Trapped, Soutan glanced this way and that. Jezro appeared in the doorway and limped into the room just as Zayn woke, sitting up in one smooth motion.

'The imp!' Zayn laid a hand on his chest. 'Where – who are you?'

'His name is Yarl Soutan,' Jezro said. 'I thought you knew that.'

'Oh. Right.' Zayn rubbed his face with both hands. 'He's a shape-changer.'

Warkannan cleared his throat, then pointed at Soutan's closed fist. 'I said give it back.'

With a muttered curse Soutan opened his hand and tossed a gold chain and a small rectangle of bluish stone into Zayn's lap. Blue quartz, Warkannan thought. Is that what he meant last night?

'I merely wanted to examine it,' Soutan said. 'It's an imp, all right, and it's the reason I couldn't pick him up in my crystals.'

Zayn clutched the imp in one broad hand and went on staring at Soutan. 'Is this what you really look like?' he said.

'Yes, Hassan.' Soutan forced out a smile. 'This is the real me. No more shape-changing, as you called it.'

Zayn yawned and leaned back against the pillows, but he was studying Soutan narrow-eyed.

'I woke early,' Soutan went on. 'I was on my way outside for a stroll when I saw Warkannan leave, and so I thought I'd see if Hassan was recovering. The imp caught my eye.'

'It did, huh?' Warkannan glanced at Jezro to see if he believed the story, but the khan's bland expression could have meant any one of twenty things.

'I'll go see if Cook is awake,' Soutan said. 'We can discuss this over breakfast.'

Soutan swept out with dignity wrapped round him like a cloak. Warkannan shut the door behind him.

'Feel like eating?' he said to Zayn.

'Yes.' Zayn was threading the imp onto the chain, an awkward job with one hand bandaged. He slipped it over his head before he spoke again. 'I can't remember everything about last night, after we got inside, I mean. You said I went into convulsions?'

'Yes,' Jezro said. 'That's how you cut your hand. You were holding a glass at the time.'

'I remember that. I had muscle spasms, and I fell on the floor.' Zayn turned his face towards the wall, but his eyes moved as if he were looking at a picture of the event. 'Why? That's what I don't remember. Idres, do you –'

Warkannan felt suddenly cold, suddenly weary. 'Yes, I do,' he said, 'but we'll talk about it later.'

'Don't worry about it now,' Jezro said. 'Let's go eat breakfast.'

'Tell me something first, sir,' Zayn said. 'Soutan, is he a friend of yours?'

'Yes. Why?'

'Just wondered.' The expression on Zayn's face turned into a bland mask. 'Is there a place I can clean up before we eat?'

'Yes,' Warkannan said. 'I'll show you, and you can have my other clean shirt.'

Warkannan had seen Zayn's mask before, often enough to know that he was hiding some dangerous feeling. He could guess that Soutan's attempt to have him murdered lay at the heart of it. Later, if they could get a moment alone, he would sit down and talk with him about secrets and the need for them.

After a bath, dressed in clean clothes, shaved – Zayn felt like an army officer for the first time in months, ironically enough, since his actions of the night before amounted to outright mutiny and desertion. The night had also left him exhausted, and yet he couldn't bring himself to sleep and forgo the company of old friends, so long thought lost.

After breakfast the three of them rode around the estate, then sat in the blue parlour and shared stories of old times. At moments – once right in the middle of a sentence – Zayn would fall asleep only to wake just as suddenly. Any time the conversation threatened to turn towards the Chosen, he would hear the hissing begin deep in his mind and change the subject. During the entire day Soutan left them alone. At intervals Warkannan would go to his nephew's room and try to talk with him, but Arkazo never once let his uncle in. The servants told Warkannan that Soutan had brought the boy food.

Not long after sunset, Zhil the butler came into the blue parlour, where the three of them were sitting, and announced dinner. Walking into a dining room with Idres made Zayn feel that they were still the officers they once had been, serving in the same regiment, loyal to Jezro's father, a Great Khan they could admire, even though Dookis Marya's luxurious white room, gleaming with lamplight, had nothing in common with the grim, grey officers' mess of a border fort. The khan took his place at the head of the table, with Warkannan on his right, and Zayn next to Warkannan, just as they'd always seated themselves. Soutan came into the dining room, smiled pleasantly all round, and sat down opposite Warkannan. Beside his place on the table lay an empty place setting. When Jezro pointed at it, Soutan shrugged.

'He won't eat at the same table with Hassan,' Soutan said. 'I tried to talk with him, but he threw me out of his room. I'm surprised you couldn't hear him screaming at me to get out.'

'I did, actually. I'll go talk to him.' Warkannan shoved his chair back, but Jezro leaned over and caught his arm.

'Stay here and eat,' Jezro said. 'I'm the only one he can't throw out. I'll go.' He got up, then glanced Zayn's way. 'Warkannan's nephew, Arkazo.'

'Yes sir.' Zayn winced as he remembered the outburst of the night before. 'Please, tell him how much I regret –'

'If there's any fault,' Warkannan broke in, 'it's mine. I made the decision to go hunting you.'

'Not hunting me,' Zayn said. 'Hunting a threat, hunting one of the Chosen. Someone you didn't know.'

Jezro took his walking stick, which had been leaning against the wall, and limped out of the room. Soutan watched him go, then looked at Warkannan. 'That conversation,' Soutan drawled, 'was enough to terrify any sane man.'

'And just what do you mean by that?' Warkannan said.

'To hear you all busily excusing each other for that poor boy's death, that's what,' Soutan said. 'I cannot believe how calloused you all are.'

'You bastard!' Zayn said. 'After the way you tried to get me killed? In that temple?'

Soutan flinched and twisted in his chair.

'Jezro doesn't know the truth of that,' Warkannan murmured. 'Let's leave it that way, all right, Zayn?'

'If *you* say so.'

'Thanks, I do.' Warkannan turned to Soutan. 'Listen, you, have you ever been in a battle? No? I didn't think so, and that means you have no right to judge Zayn or me or any of us. Things like this happen in war. Sometimes men get killed by their own units by sheer mistake. It's hell when it happens, and it tears your heart out, but you've got to put it behind you. We all share the same risk of dying, no matter who kills us. Yes, it does make you cold and harsh. Living with death does that to a man. That's just the way it is.'

Soutan sat open-mouthed, unable to speak. Two servants came in, carrying baskets of warm bread and bowls of soup. Warkannan sat back in his chair and glared across the table. Soutan looked terrified, Zayn realized, and his contempt for the sorcerer deepened even further. He failed to understand how Jezro Khan could consider this man his friend. Unless, of course, the khan had never seen the true Soutan, a shape-changer in more ways than one.

Zayn concentrated on eating, as did the others. He had a hard time of it using only his left hand. In a few minutes Jezro returned alone. He leaned his stick against the wall, then sat down with a troubled glance and a shrug for Warkannan.

'He'll come out when he's hungry enough,' Jezro said at last. 'I decided that issuing a direct order was a good way to make things worse, so I didn't.'

'Thank you,' Warkannan said. 'I'll talk with him later.'

The servants returned with steaming pots of tay. Jezro waited till they'd poured and left again.

'Well, gentlemen,' he said. 'Here we all are.'

'Yes,' Warkannan said. 'It's time to think of heading back to Kazrajistan.'

'Like a shen with a stick, that's you, Idres,' Jezro said. 'But you're right enough that it's time I made up my mind.'

'I take it you haven't?' Zayn said.

'No. I'm sorry. I feel torn in half. But we'll have to wait here for a while, anyway. With zhundars on the prowl everywhere, hunting for Soutan, we can't just hit the road in broad daylight.'

'I have to agree, yes,' Warkannan said.

'I wonder, though,' Jezro went on, 'how long the hunt will last. Marya's put a stop to it here in Burgunee. Well, actually, I was the one who did, using her stationery – let's be honest – but then, that's what she hired me for, writing letters. Anyway, as for Dordan, I know what zhundars are like. They'll keep on a case as long as it's fresh, but after a few weeks with no progress, they ease up.'

'So what are you thinking?' Warkannan said. 'We stay here and let the hunt in Dordan tire itself out?'

'Something like that, yes. Any better ideas?'

Warkannan shrugged. In a fit of profound concentration, Soutan was chasing bits of bread around his soup with a spoon. Jezro leaned forward to speak to Zayn.

'Do you know what we're talking about?' he said. 'Yarl's political enemies had him indicted on false charges.'

'False, sir?' Zayn said. 'You mean the rape and aggravated battery of Rozi Millou?'

Soutan dropped his spoon into his bowl with a splatter. Zayn glanced over to see him pale.

'Yes,' Jezro said. 'What do you know about that?'

'Well, sir, I went to Sarla with the spirit rider from my comnee,' Zayn began. 'Ammadin and I met the girl's mother. She asked Ammadin to talk with her daughter, to try to heal her. The girl's been broken like a stick.' He swung around and stared Soutan in the face. 'Spirit riders can smell when someone's lying. I bet you know it, too. That poor child! Rozi was telling the truth, all right. She was trembling. She can't forget the way you choked her. It's still in her dreams.'

Zayn heard Jezro's chair scrape as the khan got up, heard Warkannan swear under his breath. He never looked away from Soutan, who had gone from pale to grey pallor. Big drops of sweat ran down his face and dripped onto the collar of his smock.

'How old is this girl?' Jezro said.

'Sixteen when he raped her, sir. Eighteen now. He attacked two other girls, too, but I don't know all the details there. One of them was so afraid he'd kill her that she didn't testify.'

Soutan's head swayed on the edge of a faint – whether real or feigned, Zayn didn't know or care. Soutan recovered himself, then swivelled in his chair to face Jezro, who took a few steps and towered over him.

'He's lying,' Soutan stammered. 'It's not true.'

'Oh?' Jezro said calmly. 'Why would he lie?'

Caught, Soutan looked up at Jezro and gasped for breath with an hysterical little panting sound. Jezro grabbed Soutan by the shoulders, hauled him out of the chair, and shook him.

'You lied to me,' Jezro snarled. 'God damn you. You lied to me.'

'It's not true.' Soutan twisted free and stepped back. 'It's not true.'

'Sir?' Zayn heard his own voice growling in his throat. 'If you want more evidence, there was another case in Kors. A whore who turned up dead after taking Soutan's money.'

'I remember something about that.' Jezro's eyes went wide. 'I never heard who was responsible, though, except it was someone from –' he hesitated, then sighed, 'from Dordan.'

'God damn you!' Soutan grabbed a knife from the table and heaved it at Zayn's head.

Zayn didn't bother to duck. The knife sailed wide, hit the wall, and clattered to the floor. Jezro stepped forward and shoved Soutan back into the chair.

'Besides, these infidel women!' Zayn went on. 'Why would she lie? The girl could have screwed three boys her own age, and her mother wouldn't even have cared.'

'True,' Jezro muttered. 'I wonder why I didn't think of that before?'

Warkannan stood up. 'What are we going to do with him? Should I go get my sabre?'

'No, don't behead him right here, Idres,' Jezro said. 'It'll spoil Marya's carpet.'

'I was thinking of back behind the stables, where it won't scare the horses.'

Soutan started to speak; his voice trailed off, his eyes rolled, and he sagged like an empty cloth sack. For a moment the chair held him up; then he slid off and crumpled to the floor.

'Huh,' Warkannan said. 'Guess he didn't realize that we cold-hearted bastards can joke around.'

Jezro poked him with the toe of one boot. 'I wonder if he's really out?'

Warkannan picked up a glass of ice water and dribbled it onto the sorcerer's face. Soutan moaned, opened his eyes, tried to sit up and fell back, arms and legs akimbo. 'You're going to kill me, aren't you?' he whispered.

'No,' Jezro said. 'The Canton laws are different from the ones back home. But one false step, and I turn Idres loose. Do you understand me?'

Soutan turned his head to look at Warkannan, hovering grimly with one hand at his belt as if searching for a sabre hilt. Soutan moaned again, then nodded his agreement.

'Now get up,' Jezro went on. 'I'm tempted to let you lie there like a shen, but you're a man under some definitions of the term, anyway, so get up.'

Soutan got to his knees, paused, shaking and trembling, then managed to lurch to his feet. He stared at Zayn with a hatred so intense that Zayn flung up his hand as if to block a blow.

'House arrest,' Jezro snapped. 'Idres, if you'll assist me?'

Zayn trailed along behind as they frog-marched Soutan out of the dining room and down the long hallway to his suite. Jezro opened the door, Warkannan shoved Soutan inside, and Jezro slammed the door shut and slid the bolt locked.

'Think about this,' Jezro called through the door. 'I'll be back later, and we can discuss things.'

Soutan said nothing, or at least, nothing that Zayn could hear. As they were leaving the hallway, Zayn glanced back and saw the door to another room start to open, then slam shut again. A servant, he assumed. They returned to the dining room to find a frightened Zhil hovering by the table.

'Bring the main course,' Jezro said. 'My apology for the unpleasantness, Zhil, and try to keep this to yourself, all right? Eventually it'll all have to come out, but I don't want gossip now.'

'Very good, sir,' Zhil said. 'I'll tell everyone that Mizzou Soutan's been taken ill.'

Zhil hurried out. When Jezro sat down, Zayn and Warkannan followed his lead. The khan picked up his spoon, looked at his soup, and laid the spoon down again.

'Well,' Jezro said. 'Goes to show how easily I can be fooled, doesn't it? I'm damned glad I have you two here with me. I've got to get out of the habit of trying to think the best of everybody.'

'Getting back to Haz Kazrak will break it for you,' Warkannan said. 'Soutan's small game compared to some of the bastards waiting for you there.'

'What joy awaits the returning exile, huh? Don't keep giving me reasons to turn your offer down.'

Warkannan picked up a chunk of bread and ripped it in half.

'Yarl had such a convincing story,' Jezro went on, 'and Marya trusted him. I vaguely remember thinking that if a woman believed him when he said he didn't rape the girl, then I should.' Jezro stopped, staring at the tablecloth as if he were hoping to find a written explanation there. 'Well, gentlemen, what shall we do about this? Turn him over to the zhundars? I can forge another letter, saying that Marya's changed her mind and wants him arrested.'

'How are we going to get back to Kazrajistan if you do that?' Warkannan said.

'Who says I'm going back to Kazrajistan?' Jezro tried to smile and failed. 'Damn it, I trusted the man. I thought he was my friend, I believed him when he said he'd been persecuted by his guild, and the whole time the ram-sucking little bastard was lying to me.'

'I can see why that would rankle,' Warkannan said.

Servants came in with disjointed snapper lizard en daube and bowls of vegetables, served them round, and glided out again. For a few moments they ate, but Warkannan seemed to have lost his appetite. He laid his fork down and turned to Jezro.

'You know, if you don't go back to the khanate, and soon, you'll be putting your supporters in danger. We don't want the Chosen infiltrating Andjaro when Zayn doesn't report back – or arresting Indan, for that matter. The women will be safe enough, I should think. No one's going to believe that women would risk their lives for an abstraction like justice.'

Zayn felt the roaring start, deep in his mind, but he managed to hold it back just long enough. 'Women? I never heard anything about more than one woman, no.' He gulped for breath. 'My officers figured that if you were actually up to something, you were only using the widow Nehzaym as a cover, to make your investment group look legitimate, I mean.'

The room began to distort, as if the walls were receding.

'Stop it!' Warkannan turned and laid a hand on his arm. 'Think of something else – think about Soutan. Tell me about this girl's mother. That'll do.'

'Loy. That's her name, Loy Millou.' Zayn allowed his memory to present images – Loy drinking wine, Loy talking with Ammadin. The roaring in his ears subsided. 'A sorcerer in Bredanee told me to ask her about Soutan. When I asked him about Soutan. Is this making sense?'

'Yes,' Jezro said. 'Go on.'

The room looked normal again and its proper size. Zayn took a deep breath. 'So, Ammadin rode with me when I left the grass and headed east to find you, sir. We found Loy, and she asked Ammadin to try to help her daughter. That's how I happened to meet her.' He shook his head. 'Poor little Rozi.'

Jezro muttered something under his breath, too quietly for Zayn to hear, but it must have verged on blasphemy, judging from the foul look Warkannan shot his way.

'Wait a minute,' Jezro went on. 'Why did the spirit rider ride along with you? Where is she now?'

'She had business of her own. We were riding the same way. She stayed in Sarla when I left.'

'Damned strange,' Warkannan muttered. 'I never heard of a spirit rider leaving her comnee.'

'Well, it's a long story,' Zayn said.

'We are all ears,' Jezro said. 'Divulge, Lieutenant.'

Zayn hesitated. He knew that Jezro was giving him a mock order for the joke of it. He could turn it aside by simply stating that he'd rather not discuss Ammadin's quest. Jezro misunderstood his hesitation.

'Or are you still a lieutenant?' the khan said. 'It's been ten years, come to think of it. Surely they've promoted you by now.'

'Yes sir,' Zayn said. 'They made me a company commander when Idres took over the regiment, after they told us you were dead.'

'Then about four years ago now they transferred Hassan to Bariza.' Warkannan glanced at Zayn. 'I'm beginning to think the Chosen were behind that transfer. Another man who served with us belongs, or so I heard recently – Lev Rashad, if you remember him. Or wait – sorry.'

'Let's not mention them,' Jezro said firmly. 'We don't want Hassan smashing any more crockery.'

Zayn managed to laugh. For a few moments they concentrated on eating.

'If you were commanding the regiment, Idres,' Jezro said at length, 'why didn't you retire as a colonel?'

'I accepted a demotion to get transferred to the capital,' Warkannan said. 'Arkazo was going to university there, and I figured I'd better be nearby. I was right, too. He got into enough trouble as it was.'

Zayn and Jezro both stared.

'Rank isn't the only thing in life,' Warkannan said. 'Pass me that basket of bread, will you, Zayn?'

Zayn passed it, then handed the butter after it. The tay had gone cold; he drank his in big gulps, out of sheer thirst, not a liking, and poured himself more.

'But anyway,' Jezro said, still smiling. 'Divulge, Captain Benumar, uh, Hassan that is. This story about the spirit rider will give me something to think about besides Yarl and what we're going to do about him. I'm too tired to think about Yarl right now. I've been sitting out in that damned garden every night in the hopes you'd come creeping up and try to kill me.'

That remark tipped the balance. Here Zayn was a man among men, not someone's servant, and an important man at that, Jezro Khan's trusted friend, someone that Jezro had risked his own life to save. But Ammadin – he loved her, she had saved his soul. Without the Mistlands he never could have left the Chosen behind, Jezro or no Jezro. Still, he couldn't see how it could hurt her to talk about her quest.

'Well, it all comes down to the ChaMeech,' Zayn said. 'Ammadin knows a ChaMeech woman, or female, whatever they are, named Water Woman. Water Woman came to her with a strange tale of a cave full of magical devices owned by someone named Sibyl. The ChaMeech said that this Sibyl was teaching them how to use magic, which sounds pretty ominous to me.'

Jezro made a choking sound deep in his throat and leaned onto the table. 'Sibyl who? Do you know?'

'No, sir. All I know is what Ammi told me, that this Sibyl is a stone woman – that's what the ChaMeech called her, a stone woman – who's in charge of a cave full of magicks. Ammadin was riding to join her, Water Woman I mean, and they were going to go meet Sibyl. Is this important?'

'Could be, yes.' Jezro turned to Warkannan. 'One of the leaders of the Settlers was a woman named Sibyl Davees. She was something called a xenobiologist, that is, she wanted to study the ChaMeech. Yarl thought she might be the person whom the author of *The Sibylline Prophecies* had in mind when she gave the book that title. And caves – caves loom large in her legend, judging from the clues I've put together.'

Zayn decided that he must be more tired than he'd realized. None of this talk made sense, even though Warkannan nodded in understanding.

'This Davees,' Warkannan said, 'surely she couldn't still be alive.'

'No, of course not. I'm assuming that her name took on an independent meaning, or that whoever wrote the *Prophecies* used it for some reason, probably to make it look ancient.' Jezro turned to Zayn. 'Hassan, I'm being cryptic, I know. We'll explain later. Go on.'

'There's not much more to tell, sir. Ammi was going to meet Water Woman at the Burgunee border near some kind of monument, the white cliff with pictures, I think she called it, and they were going to trek off to meet Sibyl. The Loremasters Guild in Sarla was interested in sending someone, too, probably Loy Millou. I left before that all got worked out.'

'Very interesting,' Jezro said, then glanced at Warkannan. 'What –'

Warkannan held up one hand for silence, then murmured, 'Keep talking.' Carefully he moved his chair back.

'But this Sibyl,' Jezro said hurriedly. 'Did the ChaMeech say anything else?'

Warkannan stood up and took a few quiet steps towards the door between the dining room and the hall.

'Well, sir, Ammadin didn't tell me everything. Sibyl's supposed to be rich, though. Water Woman gave Ammi a lightwand that came from Sibyl's cave. According to Loy Millou, it was an ancient one, but it looked brand new.'

'That's suggestive, all right. Unfortunately, Yarl knows a lot more than I do about suggestions like this. You see what I mean about our needing him, whether I hate his guts or not.'

Warkannan made two long strides and flung the door open. No

one stood there, no one fell into the room. 'Damn!' Warkannan muttered, then suddenly stooped and plucked something from the wall near the baseboard. 'Although I wonder.'

Warkannan brought his prize back to the table, a smooth metal ball about an inch in diameter, with a prong that allowed it to attach to surfaces such as walls. Jezro picked it up and looked at it, then tossed it back to him.

'I find those now and again,' Jezro said, 'all over the house, in fact. Zhil thinks they're part of a game Marya used to play or some such thing.'

'Um.' Warkannan set it down on the table, then picked up a heavy table knife, placed the handle on the ball, and stacked his hands on top. With a grunt he bore down with all his strength. The ball crumpled with an animal squeal.

'What?' Jezro said.

'I'm probably being overly suspicious,' Warkannan said. 'But I kept having the feeling we were being spied on. Soutan bragged to me once about how he could send spirits after people, and the spirits would report back to him. Now that I know what spirits really are, this is a good candidate for one.'

Warkannan took his hands away. Out of the crushed ball protruded a thin gold wire. 'Of course, it might be nothing.'

'Crap,' Jezro muttered. 'Once you lose faith in someone, you don't know what to believe.'

'Idres?' Zayn said. 'What do you mean, what spirits really are?'

'That's right,' Warkannan said. 'You haven't heard the truth about this magic business.'

'Let us enlighten you,' Jezro said. 'Here comes Zhil with brandy.'

That evening, in the small blue parlour, Zayn saw his entire view of the world collapse and crumble. He realized that he might not have believed Jezro alone, but Warkannan's calm agreement with the khan's talk of machines and devices, distant stars and other worlds, suns and planets, made it possible for him to accept what Jezro was saying. At first he felt staggered, as if he could no longer stand up on a world that was moving so quickly under his feet, but eventually he realized that here were the answers to the questions that he and Ammadin had asked together. He wondered what she would say when he told her the truth about her crystals, but he had the feeling that she would take it all calmly. Even as he became calm – in the end he saw that all these truths, unlike the truth about his memory, mattered very little to him. The sun would still rise in the east, no matter which sphere really moved.

'And if we can't get back there,' Zayn said at last. 'Who cares about other worlds?'

'A practical man, that's you, Captain Hassan,' Jezro said, grinning. 'I suspect that a lot of other Kazraks are going to agree with you, or would if they ever found out the truth. The mullahs are not going to want the truth out.'

'It seems to me,' Warkannan put in, 'that Soutan can talk about ships all he wants, but we're never going to be able to get back, wherever back is.'

'Oh, I agree. I let Yarl ramble on about his damned ships, but I'm actually interested in finding technical information. The Settlers must have brought books with them showing how to produce these fancy gadgets. They make life a lot easier, and I wanted to see if we could manufacture some. Everything we've found is incredibly complicated, but it can't have sprung out of the ground fully grown. There had to be a time when people invented simple versions of things like the oil-free lamps. Maybe we can figure out how to put the primitive versions together.'

'It sounds like a perfect job for the scholars back home,' Warkannan said. 'Now, if you were Great Khan, you'd have a lot of resources to draw on – men, money, the best minds at the universities.'

'A one-track mind.' Jezro shook his head in mock sadness. 'You're as bad as Yarl –' His smile disappeared. 'Damn. Speaking of Yarl, I should go talk with him, I suppose.'

Warkannan took out his pocket watch. 'It's twenty-two hundred,' he said, then yawned hugely. 'I'm too old for this. Staying up all night, I mean.'

'That's right, we pretty much did,' Jezro said. 'Last night seems so far away, but none of us slept much. Well, I think I'll let Yarl stew over his sins all night. It might make him more reasonable in the morning. Let us all go partake of the sleep of the righteous.'

'Right after evening prayers.'

'I can't –' Zayn paused in mid-sentence. That's not true any more, he thought. I'm not demon spawn. 'Yes,' he said, and he smiled. 'Right after prayers.'

The three of them slept late the next morning, a sensible enough thing to do, and the worst mistake they could have made. Before breakfast, Warkannan trotted off to the door of Arkazo's room. Zayn could hear him calling the boy's name, but in a few minutes he returned alone.

'He won't even answer me,' Warkannan began. 'If you could –'

'I will,' Jezro said. 'It's time he learned about direct orders, but I think I'll finish breakfast first. Let him stew for a while.'

They had, however, barely started their breakfast when Zhil hurried in, his perfect manners forgotten. 'Sir?' he blurted. 'Robear's got to speak with you.'

'Send him in,' Jezro said.

Robear rushed in before Zhil could leave the room; apparently he'd been waiting just beyond the door. 'Some of the horses are missing, sir,' Robear said. 'Soutan's riding horse, the captain's nephew's horse, and a couple of pack animals.'

Zayn glanced at Warkannan, who'd got up from his chair. He stood cavalry-straight, his lips a little parted, his eyes wide. 'Shaitan! He wouldn't.' Warkannan turned on his heel and strode out of the room.

Zayn and Jezro followed, Zayn a little ahead, the khan limping behind him, as Warkannan hurried down the hall to the guest rooms. He flung open the door to Arkazo's room, looked in, then took one step back.

'God help me!' Warkannan growled. 'I'll kill him for this. Soutan, I mean.'

Zayn had the morbid thought that Arkazo lay dead inside, but when he ran to the door and looked in, he saw no such thing – no Arkazo, in fact, none of his gear, either, not a blanket nor saddlebag.

'Check Soutan's room,' Jezro said.

Zayn followed Warkannan as he ran down the hall to another open door. The moment that they stepped into the suite, Zayn could see that the sorcerer was gone and his gear with him. Warkannan's face flushed a dangerous red.

'If I get my hands on Soutan,' he said, and his voice was dangerously level, 'I'm going to strangle him. Beheading's too quick.'

'Good idea,' Zayn said, 'but what is all this?'

'He's talked Arkazo into riding off with him, would be my guess.' It was Jezro, limping down the hall with Robear behind him. 'Arkazo must have opened the door and let him out. They probably smuggled their gear out a bit at a time while we were sleeping.'

'Yes sir,' Robear joined in. 'One of the guards saw Soutan crossing the lawn in the middle of the night, but Soutan told him that he was just having trouble sleeping. The guard didn't see any reason to doubt him.'

'Damn!' Jezro said. 'That's what I get for keeping the house arrest quiet.'

'But where have they gone?' Warkannan said. 'That's what we need to know. Soutan's risking more than house arrest if he goes back to Dordan. He'd hardly head for Kazrajistan without us, and there's nothing much north of here.'

'That leaves east. That metal ball you smashed?' Jezro paused to wipe his nose on his sleeve. 'If he heard what we were saying, they might have gone east to look for Sibyl. That cave could be full of old technology. Robear?'

'I'll order the men to saddle up, sir,' Robear said. 'We can make a sweep of the countryside.'

'But Soutan will be able to see you coming.' Warkannan leaned back against the wall. 'There's not a lot of hope you're going to catch them.'

'That's true.' Jezro thought for a moment. 'Robear, I've got a better idea.' He turned to Zayn. 'Keep an eye on Idres, will you? Robear and I are going to ride into town and call upon the head of the Council. We're going to have half of Burgunee out looking for the little bastard before noon.'

'I'll go saddle our horses,' Robear said.

'Fine, do that. Idres, I know what you're thinking and no, you can't go too. Stay here. Soutan might be staging this in order to get at Hassan, and I don't want him left here alone.'

Warkannan nodded, staring at the floor. Zayn tried to think of something to say, found nothing that would be any real comfort, especially since he was blaming himself. Jezro and Robear hurried out, talking together about the mayor in Kors.

'I shouldn't have exposed Soutan for what he was,' Zayn said. 'I'm sorry.'

'Never think that.' Warkannan raised his head, finally, to look at him. 'It had to come out, and sooner is better than later. I mistrusted him from the moment I met him.'

'But your nephew –'

'Has done something really stupid, and he'll have to take the consequences. When we get him back, that is. I'll pray to God we don't have to just leave him here in the Cantons when we ride back home, but if we have to, we have to.'

Zayn and Warkannan waited in the blue parlour for Jezro's return. Zhil appeared with fresh pots of tay and baskets of bread, then left. At first Idres sat silently, reading in the *Mirror*, but at length he laid the book aside, and they talked of old times and the men they'd known on the border.

'There's something you need to know,' Warkannan said at last. 'That friend of Arkazo's? He was Kareem Alvado's son.'

For a moment Zayn could neither breathe nor think. 'Oh God forgive me! I know Kareem never will.'

'You may be right about that. Let's hope he never has to know. I used to be too proud to lie, but the older I get, the more I see that lying has its uses. Life is too damn hard sometimes.'

'Maybe so. I can't tell you how sorry I am.'

'You don't need to. But you had to know.'

'Yes, that's true. I did.' Zayn got up and poured them each tay. 'Something else I have to live with.'

Zayn found himself remembering the Mistlands and the ghosts who had come to mock him. Don't you feel remorse, Zahir? He did now, especially when he thought of the reason that young Alvado had died. If only I hadn't gone back for the spirit staff. I killed him for a piece of wood with feathers and beads on it. Standing in the sunny parlour with its cushioned furniture, watching Idres with his translation of the holy book in his lap, it was impossible to believe that the staff could have been worth a man's life.

But his memory took him back to that afternoon, when he'd been wading through the warm water with Palindor's bow held above his head. It seemed to him that he could smell the mineral brine and feel once more the shock and its concomitant despair when he realized he'd left the staff behind. His comnee's spirit rider had given him that staff and told him not to lose it. He had lost it, and if he'd not gone back, his cowardice would have damned him in the eyes of a second set of gods. In the memory he could hear the spirit crane, shrieking at him. I did have to go back. I really did have to.

'Zayn?' Warkannan said. 'Did you hear me?'

Zayn looked around gape-mouthed at the sunny parlour, the

flowered furniture. 'Sorry, Idres. No, I didn't. Just thinking about something.' He handed Warkannan his cup of tay, then took his own back to his chair and sat down.

'I'll repeat it,' Warkannan said. 'If we hadn't been hunting you, it never would have happened.'

'I know that, but – you know, sometimes I wonder if I'll ever be able to go back to Kazrajistan after the things I've done. You don't know all of them. I don't want to tell you any of them.'

Warkannan considered him over the rim of his cup. 'After you got your commission, Jezro and I had a long talk about you. We knew something was wrong then. We did nothing about it. We were embarrassed, may God forgive us both! Embarrassed to ask a brother officer what was tormenting him. So we did nothing, said nothing. I keep thinking, if we'd had the guts to sit you down and ask you why you were so – so, well what? Unhappy, I suppose I mean. If we'd asked, I wonder if you ever would have joined the Chosen.'

'What made you think something was wrong?'

'The way you drank, for one thing. Out on the border most men drink for one of two reasons, to have a good time on leave or because they're bored sick. You drank to drown something.'

'Did I?' Zayn hesitated, but only briefly. 'I still do, I suppose.'

'I was afraid of that, but the drinking's secondary. The way you'd suddenly go off somewhere in your own mind was the primary thing, like you did just now, standing up to pour tay and then all of a sudden, you were gone.'

'I didn't realize it was so obvious.'

'It was.'

'It comes from being one of the Inborn. It's another thing my memory does, takes me back places until I think I'm there.'

'Well, that's alarming.' Warkannan shook his head. 'But what I'm really trying to say is, don't blame yourself for what happened in the Mistlands. We could talk for hours, assigning blame here, taking it away there, but you know what the truth is? Sometimes we can't control what we do. Sometimes life's like a net that tangles us up, and we don't even know who threw it over us. Don't keep brooding about Tareev. Who knows what God has in store for any of us?'

'That's true. Inshallah.'

'Yes, exactly. Inshallah.'

Jezro returned not long after, with the optimistic news that the town council would take the matter up immediately. To start things moving, they had accepted the outstanding warrant for Soutan's arrest; they would send messages to the various zhundarees of the canton. The mayor had assured Jezro that he personally would go to the Loremasters Guild and get the messages transmitted immediately.

'That's all going to take time,' Warkannan growled. 'A lot of time.'

'Oh yes, and it's probably useless.' Jezro poured himself cold tay and sat down. 'Soutan has his crystals.'

Warkannan pulled his pocket watch out and frowned at it. 'Eleven hundred,' he announced. 'We can assume they left right after the guard saw Soutan, oh three hundred, say. They've got quite a head start.'

Both Zayn and Jezro studied him while he put the watch away. He looked steadily back, in control of himself, but his eyes seemed to see beyond the room to something not horrible but bleak, an outcome that was sour rather than tragic. 'He's a grown man now.' Warkannan answered their unspoken question. 'Has to make his own choices.'

'I'm sorry, Idres,' Zayn said. 'I shouldn't have –'

'Hassan, shut up!' Jezro said. 'It's not your fault. You've probably saved my arse by getting rid of Soutan before he corrupted everything around him. Like a fart in the mosque, our Soutan. What matters is what we're going to do now, and what we're going to do is hunt the bastard down.'

'What?' Warkannan said. 'He could be riding for ChaMeech country.'

'He probably is, yes. If we find him before he gets there, it won't matter, will it?'

'If. He's found himself allies among the ChaMeech. At least six of them, all armed.'

'Then we'll be careful. I've already got the servants putting together provisions. It's time for you gentlemen to start packing. We're leaving as soon as possible.'

'It's too damn dangerous.' Warkannan got up and turned to face the khan. 'You're the last heir, the only hope we have of deposing Gemet.'

'So? I still haven't agreed to go back, have I?' Jezro held up a hand flat for silence. 'And suppose I do decide to go back. Shut up, Idres, and let me finish. It's not safe leaving Soutan loose behind us. He's got good reason to hate all of us now, not just Hassan. I wouldn't put it past him to come back here and loot the house. Marya treated me too well for me to let that happen.'

'Yes, but –'

'I said let me finish.' Jezro got up to face Warkannan. 'I've got a few things I want to say to Soutan, and I'm going to say them, even if it means spending all summer riding after him.'

'But –'

'Listen, Idres, who's the commanding officer here, me or you?'

Warkannan sighed and turned his hands palm upward, as if invoking God. 'Very well, you are. I won't say one thing more.'

'What about you, Hassan?'

'I think Idres is right, sir,' Zayn said, 'but I'll follow your orders.'

'Good.' Jezro paused, his hands on his hips, and in his grin Zayn saw the arrogant young officer he had known so long ago. 'Idres, you came all this way to offer me a throne, and here I don't even know if I want it or not. It's ungrateful of me, isn't it? The least I can do is get your nephew back for you. As long as we're in Burgunee, we'll be perfectly safe. Besides, if some fluke happens, and I'm killed, well, then, you'll know that God doesn't want me to be the new Great Khan.'

'I appreciate your concern for Arkazo,' Warkannan said. 'Don't get me wrong about that. But your theology is pretty damn weak.'

Jezro laughed. 'Go pack up your gear,' he said. 'Hassan, Zhil piled your gear up in my office. I'll take you there, and then I have to tell Robear how to handle things here while we're gone. I'm leaving him in charge.'

Something came clear to Zayn. 'You pretty much run this estate,' he said, 'don't you, sir?'

'Yes, unfortunately, because of the way Marya's installed herself in her own collection.' Jezro glanced at Warkannan. 'You see, I've got something to lose here.'

'I noticed,' Warkannan said. 'But it's not a khanate.'

'No, and that's one reason I hate to leave it. I'm not an ambitious man. I never was. It was so damn stupid of Gemet to try to have me killed! But we'll worry about all that later. What counts now is hunting Soutan down before he gets into wild country.'

* * *

While he packed, Warkannan was trying to imagine what had induced Arkazo to run off. Yes, he hated Zayn Hassan, and the new-found glamour of all those machines had certainly snared him. But to betray his family for such things? Warkannan saw Arkazo's actions not merely as a betrayal of him personally, but as a failure of the loyalty Arkazo owed to all his kin, the two great families of Warkannan and Benjamil that joined in him.

'You're brooding,' Jezro said.

Warkannan nearly yelped in surprise. He looked up to find Jezro standing in the doorway, dressed in boots and riding clothes, holding a riding hat in one hand and his walking stick in the other.

'Of course I am,' Warkannan said. 'Do you blame me?'

'Not in the least.'

'Thanks.'

'You're going to brood all day, aren't you?'

'Probably.' Warkannan felt the anger rising, burning just the edges of his soul. He took a deep breath and put it out.

He knew that Jezro was waiting for some outburst on his part – a fit of rage, a spasm of sorrow or fear for Arkazo's safety. He felt all those things, but he'd not spent his life sculpting his personality into the perfect officer for nothing. Rage could be useful, provided you didn't let it take you over; fear and sorrow had their place as well, prompting the kind of caution that wins campaigns. But to give in to them generally meant defeat, and he had no intention of losing this fight with Yarl Soutan over his nephew's soul.

'Is Hassan ready to ride?' Warkannan said.

'Oh yes. I helped him pack, thanks to that cut hand of his, and he showed me some of the equipment he brought with him. I'm damned glad he's come over to our side, let me tell you.' Jezro shuddered, but it was a mock-gesture, and he grinned. 'I've never seen some of those weapons before.'

'Oh? Like what?'

'Well, for one, this tricky little set of brass balls on cords. You apparently throw it at something's legs to tangle them and bring it down. And then a wire garotte, which he admitted he'd been thinking of using on me.' Jezro's grin disappeared. 'He wanted to bring it all with us – in case we suddenly needed someone assassinated, I suppose – but I got him to leave his comnee bow and arrows behind at least.'

Warkannan made a sour face.

'Not nice people, the Chosen,' Jezro went on. 'If I do decide to ride home, it'll be for the pleasure of wiping their officers up like so much spilled piss. Some of the men we can probably save.'

'That's the only reason you'd go back?'

'No, of course not.' Jezro paused to tuck the hat under one arm, then fish for a handkerchief in his shirt pocket. 'Look, Idres, I haven't made up my mind not to go back, either. Do you realize that? I want to stay here, but I know I have a duty to the people back home. That's why I'm torn. I'm not like you. No matter how badly you wanted to stay, you'd go.'

'That's true. I would.'

Jezro looked away. 'I might be a pretty weak reed for the khanate to lean on,' he said. 'It's too bad God didn't make you the heir.'

'He knows His own business best, and He didn't. I don't have enough imagination for the job.'

Jezro wiped his nose and shoved the handkerchief away before he answered. 'I suppose that's true. But what if I have too much?'

Warkannan had no answer to that. He finished cramming clothing into his duffel bag while he tried to forget that Arkazo had packed it the last time. On the way out they passed Zhil, hovering in the hallway.

'Sir?' Zhil said to Warkannan. 'A word with you?'

'Certainly.' Warkannan paused and let Jezro hurry on ahead. 'What is it?'

'Do you remember when you asked me about the dookis's madness?'

'Yes.'

'I didn't say anything then because of Soutan. He always seemed to know everything that anyone said about him, and he could be really nasty if he didn't like it. But he's gone now. Sir, I'm sure as I can be that he had something to do with the dookis's illness. I don't know what, but she changed when he came to live here.'

'I thought that might be the case.'

'She decorated her rooms that way years ago, long before he came, crammed all those cases with things, I mean, but she did it because she enjoyed looking at them, and if a friend of hers admired something, she'd insist on giving it to them. Not now. All this business of being afraid to leave her rooms, afraid of thieves, and all the time she spends moving things around – that's all new.'

'Did she get any better while he was gone, off in Kazrajistan?'

'No sir.' Zhil sounded miserable. 'Maybe what he did was permanent. I don't know, sir.'

'Well, I'm glad you told me. Let me see what I can find out when we catch up to him. There may be something we can do.'

'Thank you, sir. I can't tell you how much we'd all appreciate it.'

What with packing their gear, giving Zhil orders, leaving Robear in charge with more orders, and other such business of the day, it was the middle of the afternoon before they were finished at the estate. By then Warkannan's rage had soured into simple frustration. He had to stop himself from yelling at the grooms to hurry and barking orders at Robear, who wasn't his man to command.

Getting on the road did soothe Warkannan's nerves, but that first day they travelled only some ten miles. First they stopped in Kors. Watching the mayor defer to Jezro, watching the town council, too, scurry to do everything he asked, made it more than clear why the khan hated to leave. Once they left the city, they travelled only as far as the next great estate, where Jezro was treated as an equal, a landowner in his own right rather than a mere secretary.

The owner of the estate, one Mor Gairmahn, insisted that Jezro and his men stay the night rather than camping out. At dinner the eldest Gairmahn daughter flirted shamelessly with the khan while her mother smiled at the daughter's efforts and Jezro seemed to find them welcome enough. Warkannan began to feel defeated. With the tay and dessert the servants brought news – a messenger had ridden in from Kors with a letter from the mayor. Jezro read over the rushi fast, then slowly, then looked up with a sigh.

'No sign of Soutan,' he said, first in Kazraki, then in Vranz. 'No one's seen him. Anywhere. It's like he's vanished.'

When Gairmahn spoke and Jezro answered, Zayn translated for Warkannan without being asked.

'He'll have to turn up sooner or later,' Gairmahn said. 'Horses can't fly.'

'He's good at hiding,' Warkannan put in. 'I know that from personal experience.'

The others nodded, shrugged. Jezro stuffed the letter into his pocket and returned to making conversation with their host and his family.

After the meal, Warkannan stood in the corner of the towering great room and watched Jezro talking with Gairmahn, heads together over a long narrow map, as they sat side by side on a red velvet divan. The glow from one of those mysterious lamps that burned nothing caught them in a pool of gold and sent light like a fountain up to the beamed ceiling. Warkannan had no idea, of course, what they were discussing. Eventually Zayn joined him and told him.

'Water rights,' Zayn said. 'Jezro's trying to get support for some kind of long-term irrigation project.'

'Long term, huh?' Warkannan said. 'Tell me something, Zayn. Do you think he'll ever leave here?'

'I don't know. You must be worried sick.'

'I am, yes. Well, if he won't go back, there's only one thing to do about Gemet, and that's assassinate him. I probably won't live through the attempt, but as God is my witness, I'll have to try.'

Zayn started to speak, then merely shook his head.

'You can give me some pointers,' Warkannan went on. 'I have a feeling that you know a lot more about palace security than I do.'

'I do, yes, and that's why I'd rather talk you out of trying. You'd never even get close to him.'

'Well, maybe it won't come to that.' Warkannan fell back on the one person who had never disappointed him. 'Inshallah.'

'Inshallah,' Zayn agreed. 'I'm more worried now about Soutan. I never should have talked about Ammadin's plans. He's probably going to try to follow her. If something happens to her, I'll never forgive myself.'

'I've never known a comnee woman who couldn't take care of herself, especially a spirit rider.'

'Yes, but –' Zayn hesitated for a long moment. 'It's Bane, what I did. Talking about her quest with an outsider, I mean. I broke Bane.'

'That's serious, all right, or it would be if you were a comnee man.'

'What makes you think I'm not?'

Warkannan laughed. 'Still,' he went on, 'I'm just as glad that we're going after the slimy bastard.'

In the morning they left the Gairmahn estate early, but not before a second letter came from Kors. Soutan and Arkazo had been spotted once, at sunset the day before, heading east on a back road, about forty miles from Kors.

'They've covered a lot of ground,' Jezro remarked. 'They must have stayed in the saddle all day yesterday.'

'They'd better be careful,' Warkannan said. 'If they founder or lame those horses, they won't be going anywhere, fast or slow.'

'Let's hope we're that lucky.'

In the event, luck was the one thing they lacked. Over the next several days they rode east steadily but slowly. The entire canton knew Jezro, it seemed, and everywhere they stopped they found the zhundars, the landowners, and the local priests of the One God willing to offer information and advice, but always at the cost of delay. None of them, however, had seen Soutan and Arkazo. Occasionally, very occasionally, a zhundar did have a second-hand sighting to offer, usually from an isolated farmer who had sold two mysterious strangers food and grain.

After three days of this futile searching, Warkannan was ready to give up, but Jezro refused. That night, by the light of an oil lamp, they sat in their room in a shabby country hohte and studied the map Zayn had brought from Sarla.

'We're only about ten miles from Shairb,' Jezro said. 'That's right here on the border between Burgunee and what used to be N'Dosha. The last time anyone saw Soutan, they seemed to be heading that way.'

'We might as well go there,' Warkannan said. 'But let's face it, they're long gone by now, out in wild country.' He felt as if someone had reached into his chest and squeezed his heart, just for the briefest of moments. The strength of the grief surprised him. Jezro laid a hand on his shoulder.

'Idres, I'm sorry.'

'Don't be. We've got to get back home. Arkazo's only one man, and the khanate –'

'Can wait for another couple of days, damn it. I told you, I've got things to say to Soutan. No, don't bother to argue.'

Zayn had been studying the map. He laid a finger on a straight line that ran from Sarla east to the hills at the map's edge.

'The old N'Dosha road,' Zayn said. 'There's a feeder road that starts near Shairb and leads straight there.'

'I see it.' Jezro nodded agreement. 'Shairb it is, gentlemen. It's a trade town, by the way.'

'Trade?' Warkannan said. 'Trade with whom?'

'The ChaMeech.' Jezro glanced back and forth between Zayn and Warkannan.

For a moment Warkannan was too angry to speak. Zayn's face had lost all expression.

'People out here have a different view of the ChaMeech,' Jezro said at last. 'Despite what happened in N'Dosha. Huh. I wonder if Soutan's planning on meeting those allies you told me about. Shairb would be a logical place to do it.'

'Maybe so,' Warkannan said. 'Let's hope there's only six of them.'

Zayn looked up with his mask firmly in place.

'What's wrong?' Warkannan said.

'Nothing.'

'When you get that look there's always something wrong.'

'Damn you!' Zayn's voice lacked real anger. 'I'm worried about Ammadin. If that bastard hurts her, I'll skin him alive.'

'We'll help,' Jezro said. 'It'll give us all something pleasant to look forward to.'

Like most citizens of the Cantons, Loy had taken riding lessons as a child, but neither her family background nor her personal taste ran to keeping large expensive beasts in her garden. While the Loremasters Guild did eventually give her a horse, along with the necessary equipment and provisions for her trip, getting these things took time. She ran from office to office in the guild precinct, talked Wan Mendis into assuming her one crucial autumn class, cancelled the others, argued with Zhoc over funding, and eventually hauled a sheaf of rushis around for signatures. Ammadin watched all of this frantic activity with amusement at first but ultimately, exasperation. They finally left Sarla a full five days after Zayn.

On the road a new problem presented itself. Loy hadn't been on a horse in years, as she'd ruefully admitted to Ammadin.

'Oh, you'll remember fast enough,' Ammadin had said.

What would never occur to a comnee woman was that remembering might be painful in the extreme. After one day in the saddle, Loy could barely walk, and after a night of sleeping on the ground, she could barely get back on the horse again. Day followed painful day until, on the morning that Jezro Khan and his men set out for Shairb, Loy was ready to break down and weep at the very thought of riding.

She and Ammadin had camped the night before near the Dordan border on the grassy bank of a river, or to be precise, Ammadin had made the camp while Loy sat miserably on the ground and watched. Seeing Ammadin so calm and competent humiliated Loy further. She'd gone to bed that night determined to tell Ammadin in the morning that she would simply have to turn around and walk home. When dawn woke her, at first she couldn't move. By rocking back and forth like a baby in a crib, she managed to sit up and look around.

Nearby, the horses – Ammadin's grey, the chestnut pack horse, and the black gelding Loy had borrowed from the college stables – were tethered and grazing. Ammadin had already rolled up her bedroll and left the camp. Loy rocked some more, got to her knees, stretched every way she could think of, and then, slowly, with some trepidation, got to her feet. In the warm morning sun her muscles began to relax; the pain, she realized, wasn't as bad as it had been the day before. When she turned and looked upstream she saw Ammadin kneeling near a brushy red and gold Midas tree, her crystals spread out in front of her. Barefoot, Loy limped over to join her.

'Good, you're awake,' Ammadin said. 'I've just spoken with Water Woman, and she had some strange news for us. Soutan's riding east.'

'East? What's bringing them all east?'

'It's not all of them. It's just Soutan and Warkannan's nephew – oh, what's his name – Arkazo, that's it.'

'Not Zayn?'

'No, just the two of them and a couple of pack horses.' Ammadin sat back on her heels. 'I tried to spot them, but Soutan must have used his crystals to hide them.'

'Then how did Water Woman see them?'

'She didn't. Here's the odd thing – Water Woman told me that Sibyl heard they were coming. Not that she saw them, but that she heard them. Sibyl has incredibly powerful magic at her disposal, powers that are way beyond anything you or I can do. Water Woman calls this one the spell of a thousand ears.'

Sibyl may be able to tap directly into the observation grid, Loy thought, then sighed in sudden misery. Hearing about Sibyl's technical prowess had just made it impossible to give up and go home. Ammadin began to wrap up her crystals.

'Are the Riders down?' Loy said.

'Yes.' Ammadin sat back on her heels. 'We need to get on the road. How are you feeling?'

'Abysmal, actually, but it doesn't matter. If I can get my boots on, I can ride. Ammi, have you thought of asking Sibyl to scan for Zayn? She saw him before we left Sarla, so we know she can pick him up again.'

'Why would I want to do that?' Ammadin's eyes became expressionless. 'If something's gone wrong, there's nothing I can do about it way out here.'

'But don't you want to know?'

Ammadin shrugged and concentrated on wrapping the crystals.

When it came time to ride, Loy's muscles screamed, but they weren't quite as loud as they'd been the day before. The old N'Dosha road headed due east through land gone wild with second growth. The pink hill-bamboid grew up through patches of wheatian; old oaks branched above golden stands of Midas trees. At times crumbling fences paralleled the road, and now and again they saw the remains of farmhouses and barns, roofless and tilting. Purple grass grew as high as the horses' bellies in a tangled thatchy mass, bleaching out blue in the arid summer weather. Darker stripes of purple followed the courses of ancient irrigation ditches down to the streams, where trees and waist-high ferns crowded close to the water. Insects swarmed and droned over the fields.

Not long before noon the land began to rise. At the horizon, dead east of them, hung a dark mass that at first Loy thought clouds. In a few miles, however, she could just discern that the mass made a sharp edge against the clear sky. She caught Ammadin's attention and pointed.

'The hills,' Loy said. 'Chof country.'

Ammadin nodded, staring at the distant hills. 'That's where Sibyl must live. You don't find caves in flat country.'

'That's true. Oh God! they're so far away!'

Ammadin laughed, but in a friendly sort of way. 'Another thing Water Woman told me? We need to be careful about yap-packs.'

'What are those?'

'Some kind of reptile. They're not very big, but they hunt in packs. They're noisy, so we should be able to hear them coming. She says that they're pretty cowardly. When we camp, we should gather throwing stones.'

'Oh great, just what we need! Hungry wildlife! It's a good thing I brought the family legacy. I'd better wear the power pack from now on to keep it charged.'

'The family legacy?'

Loy had to do some fast thinking. 'Death spirits,' she said. 'They throw a particular kind of fire on command. They're powerful, but they need a lot of feeding.'

'I've never heard of such a thing.'

'Well, they're very very rare. I'll show you when we camp. But I inherited it from my mother, who got it from hers, and so on, all the way back to the Chof Wars. The Loremasters Guild issued them, because of course everyone was terrified, thinking the Chof were out to kill us all. That's why I call it the family legacy.'

'I see. I'll tell Water Woman we've got a weapon, then, when I talk to her next.'

'How long before we meet up with her?'

'I don't know. She had to come from the Rift by some roundabout way.'

A few miles on, a white pillar stood beside the remains of the road. It gleamed, so slick and bright that it had to be flexstone, rising tall out of the grass and debris that had collected around its base. Loy dismounted and led the black over; she let him crop the high grass while she searched for inscriptions. Beneath the galactic spiral she found writing in Old Vranz.

'I need to get out my notebooks,' Loy said. 'I want to copy this down.'

'Well, let's camp here,' Ammadin said. 'The horses are going to need some rest time, and it looks like a good spot.'

Loy glanced around and saw that they stood at the edge of a grassy field, thick with purple grass. A stand of Midas trees marked a stream running at the far side.

'Let me help set up the camp,' Loy said. 'I can scrounge dead wood and dig our latrine.'

'I won't say no.' Ammadin grinned at her. 'You must be feeling better.'

The stream turned out to be broad enough to be called a shallow river. Once they had a camp laid out near the trees, and the horses were tethered and grazing, Loy took a notebook and a pencil out of her saddlebags and hurried back to the pillar. She had brought a good many pounds of bound rushi notebooks and pencils with her to gather the data she'd need for her reports.

There were two separate inscriptions on the pillar. Words engraved with artistic precision declared that it marked the border between Dordan and N'Dosha cantons. Words hacked out with some inappropriate tool memorialized all those who had died in the Chof Wars. 'Too many to list in their hundreds,' the inscription finished, 'slaughtered defending their farms and their children.' Loy turned cold. What was she doing, riding off to Chof country with only a spirit rider, a woman she hardly knew, for company?

The spell of a thousand ears, she thought. But it's more than the tech that's bringing you. The truth. An abstract thing to many, maybe, but it had drawn her east more strongly than any Settler gadgets could have. Water Woman would know Chof lore about the wars, she would see them as her species saw them, and she might be willing to share that knowledge. Sibyl's cave might hold other truths about the Settlers as well.

Ammadin strolled over to join her. 'What's this white stuff made of? Do you know?'

'In a very general way. It's a ceramic – baked like pottery, but it's not made out of clay, obviously, and it's much stronger. You can't drive nails through it, so the Settlers must have had some way of glueing it together. They left big sheets of it all over the Cantons, I guess where they were planning on building more things, but we don't know why they never finished them.'

'I'm beginning to understand why you study the Settlers. They left you all kinds of puzzles.'

'Yes, they did. May they rot in hell for it, too.'

Not long after, the observation grid rose over the horizon. Loy had brought crystals with her, but not her multi-unit, an irreplaceable piece of equipment. While Ammadin scanned for Water Woman, Loy carried her own saddlebags to the other side of the campsite. She had a crystal for sending and receiving sound that would soon be useless; she'd brought it to keep in touch with Master Zhoc, who was now at the very limit of its range. Unlike Ammadin, she lacked the power to hear without a crystal, and talking was an awkward process, requiring her to constantly switch modes between receive and send.

When she managed to connect with Zhoc, she could barely hear him. Her end of the conversation seemed to consist mostly of 'what what what?' Finally they agreed to break the link and try again at the sunset segment of the grid. Thinking about the grid made her frustration double. Like Yarl, she was aware of the paradox that short distances between surface units quite simply should not have mattered. Goddamn the Settlers! she thought. They had trusted their descendants about as much as a sane person would trust a longtooth saur.

After she gave up on the conversation, Loy retrieved the rifle stowed in the horse packs. It was an unprepossessing object, at first glance no more than a squat cylinder of silver metal with a handle near the base and a pop-up sighting lens near the tip. The cylinder telescoped out to form a long, frail-appearing rod. A spiral of black tubing attached it to a cubical power pack. Like all Settler technology, it had been engineered to function with voice commands in Tekspeak. When Loy said 'charge pack', a glowing red strip appeared on one face of the cube. It would stop pulsing when fully charged, a long process, since the pack had been designed as an emergency backup and nothing more. The Settlers had had some other way of supplying energy to these weapons, but they had carefully destroyed all traces of that knowledge to protect the Chof. Probably they'd thought they'd destroyed all the weapons as well. In a few minutes Ammadin joined her, hunkering down in the grass. She looked at the rifle with narrowed eyes.

'Death spirits?' Ammadin's voice dripped scepticism. 'It looks like some kind of fancy tool to me.'

'Well, you're right, of course,' Loy said hurriedly. 'The spirits only supply the power.'

'Oh.' Ammadin looked unconvinced, but she let the matter drop. 'I spoke with Water Woman again. We should get to the white cliff tomorrow well before sunset. She and her servants should arrive the next day.'

'Excellent! I'm really looking forward to meeting her.'

'Will you be able to hear her?'

'Yes. That's one of the spirit powers I do have, hearing beyond the normal register. It's one reason I chose Settler history for my field – I can interview Chof.'

Ammadin sat down cross-legged with a nod at the pack. 'Those spirits are the hungry kind, I'd say.'

'You bet, very hungry.' Loy took off her riding hat and wiped the sweat from her forehead on her filthy sleeve. 'What about those yap-pack things? Did Water Woman have anything more to say about them?'

'Only to keep the horses tethered in near us at night.'

'That sounds ominous.'

'Yes, it does. We should sleep this afternoon, because we might be up all night. I'm glad you've got a weapon.' Ammadin smiled, then looked away. 'I asked Water Woman if Sibyl could find Zayn for me.'

'Well, I'm glad. You seemed worried about him.'

'The quest he's on could kill him, yes.'

'You must be worried.'

Ammadin nodded. Loy waited. In the past few days, she'd learned that Ammadin never chatted or, for that matter, talked much at all about anything that she considered unimportant in the present moment. Eventually, though, she stopped contemplating the distant hills.

'I was wondering if you could tell me something about the Inborn,' Ammadin said. 'I know about the spirit powers, of course, but Zayn's a Recaller. A real Recaller, I mean, not a player on the stage. Like in the old days.'

'Really?'

'Really. It's made his life very painful. The Kazraks call that kind of mind a demon talent.'

'Yes, they would.' Loy could feel her own mind racing. 'Do you know, I mean do you mind telling me, just how extensive his talents are?'

'Very, from what he's told me and what I've seen him do. He read a Vransic dictionary once through and knew every word in it. He can look at a picture and then draw it months later. When you ask him to remember something he read in a book, you can tell he's seeing the pages in his mind and reading the information off.'

'That's staggering. I didn't know it was still possible. I mean, some of the old talents have survived, but mostly among your people, because you keep marrying each other rather than marrying out of the Tribes.'

'Ah. They are inherited then, just like that play said. You told me some Cantonneurs went to live with the Kazraks, right? They must have brought the talents with them.'

'That's the most likely explanation, yes.'

'What other spirit powers do you have?'

'I can magnify the images in crystals. But that's all, just a fragment of what a spirit rider can do.'

Ammadin was watching her with the barest trace of a smile. Loy had the unpleasant feeling that Ammadin knew she was talking around the truth. Merde! Loy thought. I'll bet she can smell the difference.

'Well,' Ammadin said at last. 'Zayn's told me that there are a number of Kazraks who have some of what we'd call spirit powers. Or at least, I'd call them that.'

Her emphasis on the 'I' was unmistakable. Loy arranged a sickly smile and kept quiet. Ammadin stood up, stretching.

'I'm going to go bathe in the stream,' Ammadin said.

'When I'm done feeding these spirits, I will too. I want to wash out my clothes. They should dry fast enough in this sun.'

'Good idea. And then we should get some sleep.'

'Yes.' Loy paused for a long sigh. 'We should. I should have known better, but I forgot all about predators. Uh, there aren't any longtooths or slashers in this part of the world, are there?'

'Water Woman said no. Don't worry, I asked her.'

Warkannan may have been frustrated by how slowly they were travelling, but Zayn hovered on the edge of fury. Ammi was on her own in the ruins of N'Dosha, Soutan was chasing after her, while during the past few days, he'd been forced to stand around and listen while Jezro Khan talked with one official or farmer after another. Jezro must have noticed his black mood, because the khan led them straight to Shairb without a single stop.

They reached it by mid-morning, an ugly little town, about three hundred dirty-pink buildings with slanted grey roofs. Its circular streets centred upon the militia armoury and huddled inside thornvine walls. The armoury, made of brilliant white flexstone, also housed the mayor's office and served as a station for the town's two zhundars as well – a convenience in vain, since none of them had seen Soutan and Arkazo. The mayor, a stout man with thinning grey hair, apologized repeatedly to the important Jezro Khan. Since the mayor knew only Vranz, Zayn acted as Warkannan's translator.

The mayor finished his apologies at last. 'Allow me to show you around my humble town,' he said. 'It would be an honour, Jezro Khan.'

'We should get on the road now,' Warkannan muttered in Kazraki.

Zayn agreed, but Jezro wavered.

'Besides,' the mayor continued. 'It's possible that one of the citizens did see something or hear about these fellows. We held a farmers' market yesterday.'

'All right,' Jezro said. 'Let's have the tour.'

The mayor smiled in honest delight. 'Let me just get my hat,' he said. 'Won't take a minute.' He rushed into an inner office before Warkannan could argue further. They heard him speak to someone; then he popped out again before the minute was up, hat in hand.

The town itself continued as dull as it looked. Outside the walls, about a quarter of a mile to the east, stood a pair of long, rambling buildings with oddly tall doorways, a permanent market for trading with the ChaMeech. The mayor himself owned a stall there, he told them, and he made a nice profit, too, trading cloth and finished leather goods for the carcasses of game animals, gold panned from the streams in the hills, little figurines and beads made from obsidian, or even, on rare occasions, items of the old technology.

'They won't say where they get them,' the mayor said. 'Can't blame them, I guess. They don't want us just going out and digging the stuff up ourselves.'

'There can't be too many objects left anyway,' Jezro said. 'I don't suppose the farmers out there ever had much.'

In the hot, muggy morning everyone was sweating by the time that they headed back to the armoury, where a zhundar waited with their horses. On the way, Zayn noticed another white sphere such as he'd seen when he first crossed into Burgunee. The town had erected a fence, woven of pink bamboid and vines, to set it off from the town plaza.

'Children kept sitting on it,' the mayor said. 'I don't have the slightest idea what it is, but it's old, and it could be dangerous.'

'Dangerous?' Jezro said. 'Has anyone ever dug one up?'

'No.' The mayor looked startled. 'Why? You never know what could happen to you if you fool around with this old stuff. It could blow up in your face.'

'Has that ever actually happened?'

'Well, not that I know of, but it could. You can't be too careful.'

'Actually you can,' Jezro muttered this in Kazraki, then returned to Vranz. 'Well, maybe so. Thank you so much for showing us around. We've got to get on the road.'

'You're going home, eh?'

'Eventually. We wanted to take a look at the old N'Dosha road.'

The mayor smiled as broadly as if he'd been given a compliment. 'Just about half a mile west of here you'll see a feeder road south. Follow that, it's not far.' With a cheery wave, he turned and hurried back inside his office - oddly fast, Zayn thought, for someone who had just insisted on wasting their time.

Just outside of town they found the narrow dirt road. Marked by a wooden signpost, it ran straight south between two fenced fields of gold wheatian.

'Well, gentlemen,' Jezro said. 'The N'dosha road isn't far, just a couple of miles according to Hassan's map. Want to take a look?'

'Yes, sir,' Zayn said.

'No,' Warkannan said. 'We're too close to ChaMeech country. Yes, I'm worried about my nephew, but –'

'The khanate comes first,' Jezro said. 'I know, I know. But if we pick up Soutan's trail, and if his tracks head east out into the great and perilous unknown, then we'll turn back.'

'All right,' Warkannan said. 'That sounds reasonable.'

Right around noon they reached the N'Dosha road, a wide strip of crumbling grey edged with the usual hard dirt, heading east through abandoned farmland. Here and there a decaying house broke the long flat view of bluish-purple grass and weeds that stretched to the jagged horizon of the hills. Only a stand of Midas trees, clinging to a riverbank, disrupted the flatness of the landscape, and only the trees moved, rustling in the warm wind.

'God in heaven!' Warkannan said. 'It's desolate out here. You'd think we were a hundred miles from Shairb, not five.'

'Yes,' Jezro said. 'I've been told that this farmland was all as prosperous as Kazrajistan once. Long time ago now.'

Zayn, however, had no time to waste on either the view or ancient history. He dismounted, crouched down on the dirt road, and found a muddle of hoofprints. He walked on, crouching often, until he could break them down into two sets, the one overlying the other, and all of them headed east. As far as he could tell, none came back west.

'The older set was made by three horses, which says to me Ammadin, a pack horse, and another rider,' Zayn said. 'We had our horses re-shod in Leen, and two of these horses have left hoof-prints that don't show much wear. The third horse has old shoes. The Loremasters Guild must have sent someone with her, maybe Mada Millou. That third horse is carrying a light burden, and Loy's short and thin. The second set – four horses left those, two carrying heavier loads than the others.'

'Soutan, Arkazo, and the two pack horses?' Jezro said.

'Most likely, sir.' Zayn stood up. 'There's old horseshit in the road, too. Judging from how dry it is, Soutan must have a good three days' lead on us. We spent a lot of time socializing.'

'Yes. Sorry.' Jezro smiled, utterly unrepentant. 'It'll pay off in the end. Soutan can't stay in ChaMeech territory forever. When he comes back, everyone will be looking for him, especially the zhundars.'

'That's true.' Warkannan was staring at the thin line of distant hills as if he were memorizing the view.

Zayn took the reins of his gelding and mounted again, guiding the horse around to face Warkannan and Jezro. 'Idres? My turn to ask you what's wrong.'

'Just thinking about my nephew, of course. He's out there somewhere with a renegade and a criminal. How in hell did Soutan manage to get his confidence? That's what really hurts. Kaz respects the little bastard.'

'Soutan can be oddly persuasive,' Jezro said. 'Don't blame the boy too much. Look at me. I believed his sheepshit story, didn't I?'

Warkannan nodded. With a sigh he turned his head away from the eastward view. 'We should head back.'

'There's a stream over there,' Jezro said, 'and the horses need water. It's too damn muggy today. I'm hungry myself. We might as well stop here and eat.'

They slacked the horses' bits to let them drink, then unsaddled them to let them roll and rest while they brought out the food they'd bought in Shairb. Zayn took his chunk of bread and cold meat and walked back to the road, where he stood eating and looking east at the rise of hills. Somewhere out there Soutan was searching for Ammadin. If you'd only kept your mouth shut, Zayn told himself. If you hadn't gone and told the khan everything, Ammi wouldn't be in danger now.

Why had he spoken, why had he forgotten that discussing another's quest was Bane? Because he'd forgotten all about Bane in that moment, sitting in a dining room with brother officers. He now understood something about himself, that he became different men at different times. It wasn't a question of merely changing certain actions or obeying social mannerisms. Whole personalities rose and fell, embedded in memories like sea-wrack rising and falling with the waves in Haz Kazrak's harbour. Zahir Benumar, faithful member of the Chosen, had died when he'd failed to assassinate Jezro Khan. But who was he now? Captain Hassan of Jezro Khan's new revolutionary cavalry? Zayn the comnee man who needed to return to the Mistlands to find his true name? Someone else entirely? That question had still to be answered. He was beginning to wonder if it ever would be.

Zayn had just finished eating when the wind brought him an all-too-familiar scent. He tossed his head back and breathed deeply – ChaMeech, all right, and close at hand from the strength of the smell. He whirled around and ran back, yelling to the others.

'ChaMeech coming!'

Swearing and shouting, Warkannan and Jezro leapt to their feet. Jezro was unarmed except for his walking stick; Zayn had his long knife, useless against ChaMeech. Warkannan had the only sabre among them, not that it would do him much good on the ground.. The horses picked up their alarm and tossed their heads, pulling at tether ropes. With years of long practice behind them, the men rushed over, scooping up their saddles on the run, and reached the horses before they could pull free. They had the bits in place and the saddles on and cinched before the stink of male ChaMeech grew much stronger.

Zayn laced his hands together and gave Jezro a boost up, then turned to his own horse and swung himself into the saddle. Warkannan was already mounted; he drew his sabre and made the long blade flash in the sunlight.

'Get going,' Warkannan snapped. 'I'll take the rear guard.'

'It's too late,' Jezro said calmly. 'We'll never outrun them now. Besides, there's a female with them. We may not be doomed after all.'

Across the road, in the tall blue grass, six big grey males, all carrying spears and wearing yellow kilts, were trotting straight for them, led by one small ChaMeech with lavender skin. 'Shaitan!' Warkannan kept the sabre up and ready. 'What's a female doing out here? She's not much more than a filly.'

Zayn could barely focus his eyes. His mind was drowned by those other memories, as vivid as hallucinations, of running at the end of a rope, his whole body cramped in agony, his lungs burning, his hands covered in the blood from his wrists. He was choking on fear, he realized, could barely breathe, could barely think, caught and suffocating in sheer ugly panic. Jezro and Warkannan were talking, but he could understand nothing of what they said. The ChaMeech came closer, they reached the road. Zayn could only stare, clutching his useless knife.

The males spread out, spears at the ready, then stopped in a half-circle that corralled the men on horseback against the stream. The lavender female, naked except for a necklace of trade beads, paused some ten feet in front of the three riders. Up close Zayn could see how young she was, a bit smaller than his horse. She held up both pseudo-hands in a gesture of peace.

'Jezro,' she said. 'Jezro Khan.'

Zayn stared, shaking in shame as much as fear. She couldn't possibly have said the khan's name, or so he thought until she repeated it. Her voice rumbled like thunder, but it fell well within the ranges of human hearing. Jezro seemed perfectly calm as he urged his trembling horse a few paces towards her.

'I'm Jezro Khan.'

'Khan. Come with.' She was speaking in Hirl-Onglay, Zayn realized, though with an odd accent.

'Why?' Jezro said. 'Come with where?'

She hesitated, then swung her long neck down to bow her head, a gesture that, Zayn knew, meant submission. She was trying to convince them that she was harmless, and he realized that had the males wanted to kill them, they would have already attacked. She bent her forelegs to lower her head further. 'Please,' she rumbled. 'Come with.'

Zayn wanted to turn his horse and run. He could feel every muscle in his body aching with that desire, even with Idres and Jezro there to see his cowardice. If he did run, he knew that he would despise himself for the rest of a life that he'd make as short as possible.

'Come with you?' Jezro said. 'Why? Are you friends?'

She stamped a massive foot on the ground and bobbed her head, then straightened her neck to look at him normally. Her eyes gleamed, both pairs as blue as the sky.

'Not friend,' she said. 'Bigger. Many us. Come with. Not hurt.'

Sitting easy in the saddle Jezro considered her for a moment. 'You want us to come with you.'

'Yes.'

'We have no choice. You are bigger, there's more of you.'

'Yes. Come with, no hurt.'

One of the males turned towards her; his throat sac swelled, his lips moved, but Zayn heard nothing. The female, however, stamped her foot again in the equivalent of a smile.

'Hostages,' the female said. 'Be hostages. We bargain-next-soon. No hurt.'

'Hostages for what?' Jezro said. 'What do you want to bargain over?'

'No say.' She lowered her head again. 'Come with. Us bigger.'

'Is it Soutan? Will you take us to Soutan?'

'Soutan madman! No Soutan.' She made a dipping motion with her pelvis, as if she might squat on Soutan's name. 'Come with now!'

Once more Zayn had to force himself to breathe. He turned and looked at the khan, who was leaning forward in his saddle, watching with no trace of emotion. Warkannan sat like a ceremonial statue, motionless on horseback, his sabre raised. Jezro reached into his shirt pocket, took out a handkerchief, and wiped his nose.

'Well, gentlemen,' Jezro said. 'We can't outrun them and we can't outfight them, so we don't have a lot of choice in the matter. Idres, you may now say "I told you so". We should have stayed in Burgunee.'

Warkannan growled like a shen and sheathed the sabre. Zayn did the same with his long knife. At the gestures the female stamped both forefeet in delight.

'Hostages,' she repeated. 'Come with.'

'All right,' Jezro said. 'We'll come with you, but it's under duress. Don't try to take that sword away from my friend. He'll kill you before you can get it, and then one of your men will kill him, and you'll only have two hostages, not three.'

Zayn doubted that they could understand, but no ChaMeech made an attempt on their weapons, not then nor during the rest of their captivity. The female gestured at the riders to follow her, then led the way back across the road. As the men fell in behind, the ChaMeech males closed their circle, but they stayed a good ten feet away. The familiar rhythm of riding eased Zayn's panic. No one tortures hostages to death, he reminded himself. We're valuable alive.

'This should be interesting,' Jezro said, grinning. 'I'm glad we loaded up on food in Shairb.'

'Interesting!' Warkannan snarled. 'Shaitan!'

'What I wonder,' Jezro went on, 'is how they knew who I am and where I was.'

'The mayor back in Shairb,' Warkannan said. 'Who else? I'll bet he had some sort of signalling device, like the one Soutan had.'

'No wonder he wanted to show us around,' Zayn said. 'The little bastard was stalling for time. Remember how he rushed back inside when we were leaving?'

'Yes,' Jezro said. 'If we get out of this, he's going to regret it, I can promise you that.'

Ahead, one pair of ChaMeech males were busily trampling down the high thatchy grass to clear a path for the horses. Chirring and shrieking, blue-winged lizards burst into the air and circled overhead to scold them. Every now and then the female ChaMeech would snake her head around and make sure that the H'mai were still following. Soon they came to a white sphere, surrounded by faded grass, once high, now trampled down and broken. The ChaMeech drew up in a rough circle around it, and the female gestured at the men to dismount. Once they had, she gestured again, pointing first to their hands and then to the horses' heads.

'I understand,' Jezro said abruptly. 'She wants us to hold the bridles. She's afraid of scaring the horses.'

Jezro followed her orders. Zayn caught the sorrel gelding's bridle and murmured the meaningless Hirl-Onglay syllables that comnee men used to calm their mounts. Warkannan's cavalry-trained horse cocked one ear forward and one back, as sceptical as its owner, but it never showed the slightest trace of fear, not once in all that followed – and a good thing, too, since the other two mounts gave the men more than enough trouble.

Two of the males laid down their spears, then stood waiting, pseudo-hands at the ready. The female tossed back her head and thrummed. Her throat sac swelled out golden, and she let out a sound just barely audible to the human men, a rumble like distant thunder, a pressure in the air like a blast of wind. The white sphere squealed in answer and began to turn in its hidden socket.

'What in hell?' Warkannan muttered.

She thrummed again. The sphere emerged spinning from the ground. At first Zayn thought it was floating; then he saw that it spun on top of a slender, transparent rod. The rod in turn was connected to an enormous plate of white flexstone, at least fifteen feet across, that slowly rose to the surface. When the sphere stopped turning, two males rushed forward and caught the rod in their pseudo-hands. Grunting and booming, they pushed it down, proving it to be a lever. The white plate tipped up on edge, then settled into some sort of slot to expose a round opening in the earth. Zayn could just see the head of a ramp that led down into darkness.

'Come!' the lavender female said. 'Down.'

The males retrieved their spears, tucked them under their pseudo-arms, then one at a time stepped onto the ramp and started down. The remaining four ChaMeech moved in close and waved spears to urge the H'mai on. Some twenty feet down, a light gleamed, and a tunnel opened out at the bottom of the ramp.

'Down!' the female repeated. 'No harm.'

Grinning like a maniac, Jezro saluted her, then clucked to his horse and led it forward to the top of the ramp. The horse predictably balked, and it was only after Warkannan coaxed his mount down that they could convince the other horses to step onto the ramp. Behind them the sunlight streamed in, and ahead a lightwand glowed, held aloft in the pseudo-hand of a ChaMeech. The males were standing on a stone platform at one side of what proved to be a white flexstone tunnel, heading off into darkness in both directions. Two sets of tracks, moulded as an integral part of the flexstone, ran along the tunnel floor. Sitting on the tracks beside the platform was one of the most peculiar contraptions Zayn had ever come across.

Whoever had constructed it must have seen canal boats. The barge stretched about thirty feet from bulbous nose to irregular stern and about half that from side to side. Its flat wooden bottom must have concealed many sets of little wheels under it somewhere, for eventually it rolled along the tracks with some stability. The sides, made of bundled bamboid and vines, ranged in height between three feet at the lowest and five at highest; they sloped, bulged, dipped, and in places looked as if someone had absent-mindedly chewed on them. From the nose hung harnesses made of magenta saurskin. Three of the males trotted to the front and strapped themselves in. They adjusted a welter of buckles, then folded their arms across their chests.

The female ChaMeech took the lightwand. With gestures she told the H'mai men to get themselves and their horses aboard – a shaky process that nearly tipped the cart-barge over. Once they were settled, the remaining three males positioned themselves behind the cart. The female turned and thrummed. At the top of the ramp the circular plate slowly lowered itself, then fell into place with a boom that echoed and died along the tunnel. The air, however, stayed fresh, hinting at hidden vents. The female stepped into the cart and hunkered down at the front.

Zayn started to tremble; no matter how hard he tried, he could not stop shaking in terror at being shut up underground with ChaMeech. Warkannan flung an arm around his shoulders. 'Steady on,' he said. 'We'll get through it together.' Zayn managed to force a 'thank you' through parched lips.

Ahead the harnessed males started walking; the cart lurched forward. Those behind grabbed a twisted bamboid rail and pushed, slowly at first, then faster, and faster still as the males in front broke into a trot, until all six were loping along more or less in unison. The cart squealed and tilted, shook and veered back and forth as it plummeted through the darkness. Now and then a chunk of bamboid fell off, but none of the ChaMeech seemed to notice or care.

The tunnel stretched on and on, as straight as a piece of string pulled tight between two hands. The ChaMeech males loped along, never slacking nor speeding up. Now and again they would thrum; they filled their throat sacs and let the air out in great gusts that sang at a high enough pitch for the men to hear. The female never spoke, merely switched the lightwand from one pseudo-hand to the other at intervals.

Warkannan and Jezro turned all their attention to keeping the horses calm. Zayn fought with his memory. In the play performed in Sarla, the Recaller character had wrestled with bad memories of her own. Zayn repeated her line silently, over and over, 'you are not there then – you are here now'. Eventually he began to believe it, and the memories receded, though they never quite left his consciousness – rather they lurked at its edge, like wild animals at the edge of firelight. As soon as he stopped concentrating on keeping them away, they crept back, and he would return to the plains, the burning in his wrists and lungs, the cold terror not so much of dying itself, but of the inevitable damnation that lay waiting for him on the other side of Death's gate. He had known that he was damned with a certainty more painful than any torture the ChaMeech might have worked upon him. The torture would have had its inevitable end, but damnation would last forever.

Now at least he no longer feared eternity. Zayn desperately wanted to talk with Warkannan, but the clatter of wheels on track was so loud that they had to shout at each other to be heard. Jezro tried to start a conversation, only to give up the effort after a few exchanges.

'I think we know how Yarl managed to stay out of sight,' Jezro shouted. 'These tunnels must run under parts of Burgunee, too.'

'It's a good guess,' Warkannan said. 'His tame ChaMeech would have let him in on the secret, I suppose.' Warkannan laid a hand on Zayn's shoulder and leaned close to speak normally. 'How are you doing?'

'I'll live,' Zayn said, then raised his voice. 'Just wondering how long this tunnel is.'

'So am I,' Jezro said. 'I suspect we're going to find out.'

Shortly before sunset Sentry's chimes woke Ammadin. The sun was just touching the horizon, and Loy still lay asleep with her hat over her eyes to block the light. Ammadin picked up Sentry and quieted him. For a moment she wondered why she was even bothering to scan. The one person she wanted most to see had become invisible, thanks to the imp he was wearing. At that moment, caught by cold anxiety, Ammadin was forced to admit that she cared more about Zayn than she had ever wanted to care about anyone.

With an animal growl for her own weakness, she activated the crystal. In the late hush of the golden day, the dry, blue grass stood unbending, unmoving for mile after mile. She did see animals similar to grassars, mottled white and violet beasts with six sturdy legs, drinking warily at a stream under the watchful eye of a bull with three big, twisted horns.

'Spot anything?' Loy said from behind her. 'Anything that wants to have us for dinner, I mean?'

'No,' Ammadin said, turning. 'You're up?'

'Oh yes, and god, I feel almost human.' Loy was actually smiling. 'Clean shirt, nap, no saddle beating my behind – this is really living, I tell you.'

Ammadin had to laugh.

'When you finish,' Loy went on, 'we can chomp our way through some more of these ghastly trail rations. I wonder if these yap-pack lizards are tasty? I wouldn't mind a little fresh meat.'

'Neither would I, but do you know how to cook? The men take care of all that back on the grass.'

'They do? Maybe I should seduce a comnee man one of these days. I know how to cook, but I get very tired of it.'

Ammadin returned to Spirit Eyes. About half-way between the camp and the eastern end of the crystal's reach she had a piece of real luck. Apparently Arkazo had wandered beyond the range of Soutan's 'hide me' command; she saw him clearly, standing out in the grass and taking the nosebag off one of four horses. The other three were already grazing peacefully at tether. Ammadin watched as he tethered out the fourth horse, then stooped and picked up the nosebags from the ground. For a moment he stood wiping the sweat from his face onto his sleeve. Ammadin focused in close. She could see that he was wearing something on a chain around his neck – an imp, maybe? He ran both hands through his hair to shove it back, then unbuttoned the top button of his shirt. As he did so, she got a glimpse of the object on the chain – made of blue quartz, all right. She wondered what spell it carried – obviously not 'hide me'.

Arkazo walked off towards the east and disappeared under the cover provided by Soutan's crystal. What had Loy called the imp she'd given Zayn? An interference pattern something-or-other. Ammadin studied the place where Arkazo had disappeared; she noticed an odd edge or join, as if the grass beyond that point had been somehow pasted onto the real view. As she studied the image, she realized that she was seeing a portion of the ground by the horses, as if it had been copied and put in place of Soutan's camp.

I never thought to look that closely before, she thought. Well, now I know.

Just as the sun touched the western horizon, she took her crystals back to camp. By the twilight glow in the sky she hobbled the horses as well as tethered them on short ropes between the circle of fire stones and the river. Water Woman had assured her that the yap-packers couldn't swim. Loy was already splitting spongy yellow wood with a hatchet.

'I was lucky,' Loy said. 'I found a whole downed tree.' She gestured at a stack of wood. 'We'll probably need to keep the fire going all night.'

'Maybe,' Ammadin said. 'Predators usually have a territory that they defend from other predators. I'm hoping that there's only one pack of these creatures around. If so, and if we scare them off a couple of times, they'll give up.'

'We should be so lucky. Hope is lovely, but let's not douse the fire too soon.'

Ammadin went down to the stream and gathered an armload of stones, which she stacked near the fire-pit. Loy had finished laying the fire. She took a metal box of matches out of her pocket, knelt down, and lit the tinder while Ammadin watched. The tinder took, the kindling glowed, the fire caught, all on one match.

'Good job,' Ammadin said.

'Thanks,' Loy said. 'My family used to go camping when I was a kid. My father was a great one for hiking, the bastard. Tramp tramp tramp, no matter how much our feet hurt. My poor mother's idea of a vacation was lounging around reading, not that he ever listened to her. But anyway, let's have dinner, such as it is.'

Loy's guild had given them packs of dried flatbread and cheese, little bags of a dried fruit that Loy called grapes, oil beans, jerky, and the like – all of it edible and to Ammadin's taste, not bad at all. Loy, however, complained. Apparently, like so many people in the Cantons, she had high standards when it came to food. By the time they'd finished eating, the Herd had risen, and a faint silver light lay over the wild pasture. Ammadin got up and walked a few steps, turning her back on the firelight. Nothing moved beyond the camp but a breeze, rustling the leaves of the Midas trees by the stream.

'If they've got a name like yap-packers,' Loy said, 'we should be able to hear them coming.'

'The horses will warn us long before then,' Ammadin said. 'They can smell things that are too far away for me to pick up.'

'All right. That's reassuring.'

'Here's something that isn't. I spotted Soutan's camp.'

Loy said something so foul that Ammadin was honestly startled.

'Well, sorry,' Loy went on. 'He affects me that way.'

'I can understand. I'm surprised Warkannan let his nephew go off with him.'

'I don't know who Warkannan is, but he may not have had any choice. Soutan's particularly good at getting young men to follow him. He needs someone to wait on him, after all. He's not the kind to take care of his own horses or split his own firewood.'

'Well, that's what I saw Arkazo doing, all right, taking care of the horses. I wonder why they're riding east? I hope it doesn't mean that Zayn's dead. It might.'

'You must be worried sick.'

'No. It might also mean that Zayn's alive, but the man he was hunting is dead.'

'He was what?'

'It's too complicated to explain. I *am* worried, I guess.'

'I'd be, in your position. Though I'll bet you won't go all to pieces like I did, if something's happened to him. When Oskar drowned, I mean, I hardly knew where I was for months.'

'And Rozi?'

'What energy I had went to her, of course. There wasn't much left over. She was really devastated. I wonder if that's why Soutan meant so much to her? Sort of a substitute father.'

Ammadin's grey suddenly tossed up its head and snuffled at the evening breeze. All three horses moved with a little hop of hobbled forelegs; the chestnut stamped a hind leg and snorted. Loy scrambled to her feet.

'You'd better get that weapon,' Ammadin said. 'I'll put another log on the fire.'

In a few minutes they understood why the ChaMeech had named these predators yap-packers. Yap they did, and loudly, continually, a stutter of sound against the quiet night like the clapping of a dozen pairs of hands. Most likely they deliberately panicked their prey, as the sabre lizards did, in order to cut the weak and aged members out of a herd. Ammadin stood by the blazing fire with a stone in each hand, Loy stood on the other side with her weapon at the ready and the pack slung from her back. The silver tube looked so flimsy that Ammadin doubted if it would do much good. Death spirits! she thought. As if I'd believe that!

The yapping came closer, louder. The black gelding whinnied and tried to dance, pulling at the tether rope, but the hobbles kept him in place. Her grey snorted; the chestnut merely trembled in abject terror.

'A dozen of them, maybe,' Loy said.

'That sounds about right, yes.'

The yapping sounded again, quite close; then suddenly the pack fell silent. Ammadin could hear them rustling through the grass; they were coming straight for camp. She could smell them now, a sour beast-stink like spoiled keese. All at once something gleamed at the edge of the circle of firelight. Eyes appeared, gleaming red, and the glistening blue-grey skin of an animal's head. It yapped, the mouth opened to reveal teeth, a lot of teeth. The horses whinnied, danced, huddled as close together as they could get. Other eyes appeared, gleaming; other skins glistened. One bold reptile stepped forward, fully in the light.

'Small?' Loy whispered. 'Maybe to a ChaMeech.'

Ammadin nodded and hefted stones that suddenly seemed useless. The creatures stood a good three feet at the shoulder on six agile-looking legs. The yap-packer snuffled open-mouthed and took a step forward, its flat tail lashing. The others followed with one cautious step, a pause, a glance at the creature in the lead.

'Lock,' Loy said. 'Fire.'

Something slithered like a noiseless rope, a flash, a gleam, light that was not firelight. The leader's head exploded before it could even scream. The force knocked it back, jerked it around. Blood and grey matter spewed everywhere. Legs scrabbled, and it fell. The rest of the creatures squealed and cowered, shoving one another as they burst out yapping.

'Lock,' Loy said. 'Fire.'

Another head burst, spattering blood and bone over the pack members nearest by. The beasts reared up, leapt back, turned on their middle legs with a kick of the back pair. The yapping turned to howls as they fled, screeching and scrabbling through the grass. Ammadin suddenly remembered the stones she held and let them fall to the ground. For a long time the two women could hear the pack, howling in terror, farther and farther away, until at last they heard nothing but the wind in high grass. The horses quieted as the howls died, and the wind scoured the last of the stink.

'I owe you an apology,' Ammadin said. 'Those really are death spirits, aren't they?'

'To tell you the truth,' Loy said, 'I honestly don't know how this thing works. But it does. Think they'll be back?'

'I doubt it. They acted like they had some intelligence, not much, maybe, but enough to follow a leader. They're probably thinking, oh well, I bet they weren't tasty anyway.'

Loy laughed, but it was an odd sound that hovered on the edge of a sob. 'I've never killed anything before but bugs,' she said. 'And it's disgusting. Really fucking disgusting.'

Ammadin turned to look at her face and saw firelight dancing across dead-pale skin. The hand holding the weapon hung at her side; Loy suddenly raised the other one to her mouth.

'Are you going to throw up?' Ammadin said.

She shook her head in a violent no, then turned and rushed for the latrine ditch beyond the camp. Ammadin could hear her vomiting. Ammadin walked over to the first dead yap-packer and squatted down next to it. It looked meaty, tough most likely, but meaty. As the leader it would have had first feed on all the kills. Beyond that, she had no idea what to do with it. She'd never cooked an animal in her life, and the only one she'd ever skinned was the saur for her cloak. She'd done a messy enough job on that, too.

In a few minutes Loy came back in full control of herself. She joined Ammadin, took her knife from her belt, and poked it experimentally into the dead yap-packer's middle shoulder.

'We'll have to stew this to eat it,' Loy said. 'If I gut and clean it, though, we can take at least part of the carcass with us and cook it while we wait for Water Woman. We might as well use that kettle the guild bursar foisted off on me. Or will the pack horse rebel if we make it carry a dead animal?'

'If you drain the carcass and wrap it in grass, I don't see why it would. But can you do that?'

'Yes. It's done dying. I've cleaned plenty of game. It was seeing the heads – oh merde –' Her voice trailed off.

'Don't think about it! Should I go haul in the other one?'

'Let's see how smart they are. Leave it out there as a warning. We won't even be able to eat all of this one.' She snorted like a horse. 'Small! You better tell Water Woman about that.'

* * *

Had it not been for his watch, Warkannan would have lost not merely track of time but Time itself, or so he felt. The constant clatter of wheels on tracks made it impossible to speak and hard to think, and while it was loud, it was also oddly soothing. In a little pool of dim light the cart kept hurtling through the tunnel. The ChaMeech kept loping and booming, sending waves of thunder ahead of them into the darkness. The H'mai men took turns standing with the horses and sitting to rest. Standing in the jouncing cart pained Jezro's twisted leg so badly that eventually Warkannan and Zayn insisted he stay sitting. On and on, rattling and lurching – Warkannan had no idea of how fast they were going or how many miles they'd travelled. From bitter experience he knew that ChaMeech males could keep up this pace for an entire day.

Every now and then Warkannan would take out his watch and call out the hours like a sentry on fort duty. Thirteen hundred came and went; fourteen hundred, fifteen, eighteen followed. Up on the surface the sun would be hanging low in the sky, but still the ChaMeech ran in their easy lope. Although Zayn seemed calm, Warkannan dismissed the appearance. Discipline would keep a man together on the outside even when his mind was half-torn to pieces. He could remember the ordeal they had shared, and how, at the very end, when they were safe with the regiment around them, he had suddenly realized how young Sergeant Benumar was, from a joke Zahir made, and the look in his eyes when he'd made it. He was no more than twenty then, Warkannan thought. He must have lied about his age to enlist.

Warkannan was just taking out his watch again when the ChaMeech in harness suddenly let out a burst of high-pitched sounds, clearly audible as words. All six began to slow down, and the cart jerked and swung until at last they walked in unison. The lavender female got to her feet and pointed down the tunnel, where another stone platform was emerging from the darkness. With one last jerk and wrench, the barge stopped.

'Up!' the female said. 'Food. Rest.'

She climbed out of the cart and onto the platform, then gestured at the H'mai to follow her. The ChaMeech males in front began unharnessing themselves. She tossed her head back, filled her throat sac, and thrummed long and hard. From somewhere above Warkannan heard creaks and scrapes. A thin crescent of sunlight appeared and slowly waxed, revealing a ramp leading up to a circle of light and air.

'Thank God,' Zayn muttered.

This time the horses showed no fear of the ramp. They walked up quickly, switching their tails, as if they knew that real ground and grass waited ahead of them. Getting them off the ramp and onto solid ground took some manoeuvring, but at last all the H'mai, horses, and ChaMeech stood in a wild meadow. While the female thrummed the entrance shut, the H'mai led their horses a few paces away. The spear-carrying males followed, scowling. Warkannan turned slowly around, scanning their location – bluish grass and sunset sky as far as he could see. The jagged horizon of hills seemed a little closer, a little darker.

'What's that, I wonder?' Jezro was pointing off to the west.

Warkannan could just make out something tall glittering in the sunset. 'Flexstone, I suppose. I wonder where we are?'

The female came up beside them and pointed at the gleam.

'Pillars,' she said. 'We meet there.'

'Meet whom?' Jezro said.

'More us. Rest, food, all. Horses need-now eat lots. New Chur pull-next, push-next.'

'I think I understand her,' Jezro said. 'We all get to eat and rest, and they'll let the horses graze. Then it's back in the cart.'

Two white pillars stood close together, and at their bases over a dozen ChaMeech males stood waiting, some wearing yellow kilts, others naked except for yellow scarves around their necks. Behind them a meadow stretched to a shallow river, running east and west, bordered by Midas trees. The little female allowed the H'mai to tend their horses and take food from their saddlebags, then made them sit between two armed guards while she talked with the largest male present. Warkannan could hear only the occasional burst of their conversation, not that he understood any of it. Warkannan laid a hand on Zayn's shoulder and found he'd stopped trembling.

'Things are different now,' Warkannan said. 'Dead hostages won't do them any good.'

'Yes, I figured that out.' Zayn managed a smile. 'I'm sorry. I feel like the biggest coward in the world.'

'Don't! It's that memory of yours, isn't it?'

One of their guards made an audible thrumming noise and poked his spear in their direction.

'No talking in Kazraki,' Jezro said in Hirl-Onglay. 'It upsets our hosts.'

'Apparently so,' Warkannan said, also in Hirl-Onglay. 'They seem to understand this language well enough.'

'Better than they can speak it, much better. Huh. I wonder why?'

Neither of their guards deigned to answer.

The Spider was just rising when the female chose a new set of males to propel the cart. By the glow of two lightwands she herded everyone onto the road and started moving them back to the white sphere marking the tunnel entrance. The men walked, leading their horses, and decided to risk some conversation.

'Idres?' Zayn said in Hirl-Onglay. 'For a while there I couldn't make my mind stop remembering. From something I heard in Sarla, I'd guess that the Inborn got some kind of special training. I've never had it.'

'Stands to reason you wouldn't, yes.' Warkannan switched to Kazraki and dropped his voice. 'Wait a minute. I've got an idea. Can you frighten yourself again?'

'What?'

'Can you work up that cold sweat kind of terror? Maybe we can get –'

One of the males grunted and waved a spear in Warkannan's face, a bare few inches from his skin. Warkannan stopped talking, but he'd said enough. Zayn nodded to show he'd understood, then took a deep breath. Warkannan could see Zayn's eyes move as if he were studying a picture until he caught his breath with a choking sound. He began to shiver, but sweat ran down his face as well. In a few seconds the sweat began soaking through his shirt.

Up ahead the female stood ready to thrum and open the way down. Warkannan handed a startled Jezro the reins of his horse, then strode up to her. When he tapped her on the shoulder, she swung her head around, and the males moved closer, raising spears.

'My friend is sick,' Warkannan said, pointing to Zayn. 'Two hostages are enough. Let him go. He is sick. Maybe we all get sick if he is here.'

The female lowered her head to look him in the face with her doubled blue eyes. Warkannan cleared his throat and repeated everything a good bit louder. 'Two hostages good,' he finished, bellowing. 'Three sick hostages no good.'

She raised her head and glanced at a male who wore a twist of yellow trade cloth around his middle. He inflated his throat sac, his long mobile lips moved, but Warkannan heard nothing. She walked over to Zayn, then swung her head close and seemed to be sniffing his clothing. For a moment Zayn staggered as if he would faint, then recovered himself.

'Yes,' she said. 'Very sick.'

The same male stepped closer and spoke, again far too low for Warkannan to hear.

'Yes,' the female said. 'Know-now us hurt-not.' She pointed at Zayn with a lightwand. 'No down. Go home.'

Zayn turned to Warkannan. 'I can't desert you,' he stammered in Hirl-Onglay. 'It's bad enough that I'm a coward –'

'Shut up!' Warkannan barked. 'It's not cowardice. You're ill.'

'Captain Hassan, I'm giving you a direct order,' Jezro said in Hirl-Onglay. 'The border fever you've got is dangerous. Why, it could even infect the ChaMeech.'

The female turned sharply to her group of males; throat sacs fluttered as they all spoke at once, though silently to Warkannan's ears.

Jezro switched to Kazraki. 'Get back to Burgunee and bring help. You idiot, this is our chance. Now go!'

'Yes sir.' Zayn saluted him. 'At your orders, sir.'

The female escorted Zayn part of the way back to the pillars. Warkannan could just barely hear her calling to the other ChaMeech – telling them that Zayn was being released, he supposed, because when Zayn mounted up and rode back west, none of them did a thing but watch him go. The female stayed out in the road, waiting until Zayn had ridden a fair ways off; then she turned and trotted back to the white sphere.

'There,' she said. 'Hurt-not sick friend.'

'You're a good little ChaMeech,' Warkannan said. 'Thank you.'

By the glow from the female's lightwands, Warkannan could see Jezro, smiling at him.

'Not bad,' Jezro muttered in Kazraki. 'You always could think on your feet.'

'I'm surprised it worked, frankly.' Warkannan returned to speaking Hirl-Onglay. 'Now, we'd best follow our lady friend. I don't like the look of those spears her escort is shoving at us.'

* * *

Zayn's sorrel gelding had rested, in a way, during their ride through the tunnel, but only in a way. Standing on an unstable moving surface, surrounded by meat-eaters, enclosed in a dark space with no long view nor room to run – the sorrel had experienced an equine version of Hell. As soon as he was well out of sight of the ChaMeech, Zayn dismounted. He unlaced his saddlebags and slung them around his own neck to spare the horse the weight, then walked on west, leading the gelding. He felt as exhausted as the horse, and for similar reasons, but he could push himself to keep walking, he figured, for a couple of hours at least.

Leave it to Idres, Zayn thought. He's like Mullah Nasrudin in those old stories, always something up his sleeve. Still, he wondered how he was going to make Idres' trick pay off. Get help, the khan had said. Where, and from whom? Certainly not from the mayor back in Shairb. And how far away was the Burgunee border? They might have travelled fifty miles or a hundred while underground, for all he knew. Fortunately, he could call up his memory of the map. Sarla lay closer than Kors, and there he could count on help from people who didn't turn a profit trading with ChaMeech.

Zayn kept walking until the galaxy began to set and take its pale light away. Down by the river that ran parallel to the road, he saw a faint glow of phosphorescence from among the Midas trees. When he led his horse over to investigate, he found glowing mosses and algae floating in a backwater near shore. Fumbling in that scant light he got his horse tethered and his bedroll down from behind his saddle. He spread out the blankets, knelt down, and felt the imp hit against his chest. The imp. All afternoon they'd travelled in darkness. He'd not exposed it to the sunlight for a long time, not since their walk around Shairb.

'Shit,' he muttered. 'What'll you bet it's stopped working?'

He lay down, wrapped himself in a blanket, and fell asleep before he could worry more.

At dawn Ammadin inspected the remains of their night visitors. A roiling mass of tiny worms, striped red and purple, covered the second dead yap-packer and the skin and offal from the first. As the light brightened, long-beaked birds flew shrieking to the carrion. Wings of pale blue skin slapped the air as they dropped to the feast, then wrapped around their owners with a last flutter. The largest birds tore at the flesh with ivory bills and gobbled it down, worms and all, while the smaller, wings still akimbo, dragged themselves on four tiny legs around the circle, pecking and shrieking as they tried to fight their way in.

Loy got out a notebook to write down a description of the scavengers – for old Onree, she said. Ammadin left her to it and brought out her crystals. Water Woman answered her signal immediately.

Much news, Water Woman said. *Sibyl tell-then-just-now me much. All bad.*

'Could she find Zayn?'

Yes, she see-many-times Zayn. I writhe-now in shame, I hide-then too much, I be bad bad person, soul of Chur not Chiri Michi be in my heart, I writhe and grovel with my neck bent. I piss on my own feet.

'Water Woman, please, what's happened?'

I start-now at the beginning. Three Karshaks Sibyl see-many-day-past riding on Burgunee road. They head-then east, turn-now south. One Karshak ride-then-before with Soutan. Two Karshak, Zayn. Three Karshak, not ride-then-before.

'Three Kazraks. Warkannan, Zayn, and Jezro Khan – it could be. Did Sibyl say that one of them looked like a prisoner?'

No, Sibyl say-then that they laugh-then-day-past all together, talk-then together when they ride. Sibyl say-then that one wear-always imp. She jam-then imp, see-then him. Zayn wear-always imp, not wear?

'Yes, that's Zayn.'

So, all well-then. Then not now. They ride-then east to Shairb. They leave-then Shairb, go-next to old road. On the old road many Chof come-then, surround-then them and take-next away.

'They did what? What happened?'

Many us – Chof – six Chur and one Chiri Van – capture-then the three Karshaks. Take-then them as hostages. Carry-then-next them on secret roads east.

'Six Chur? Soutan's spear servants?'

No, not Soutan, he be too stupid to think up something like this. I grovel-next-soon, I writhe-always in shame. I tell-not you enough, I warn-not your friend Zayn. She began to moan into her transmit crystal.

Ammadin's heart started pounding. 'Water Woman, it's that

other group, isn't it? The faction you told me about once, the ones who want Sibyl to give them weapons.'

Yes, yes, that be the truth. I think-never they grow-never so brave. They take-then on lastday the three Karshaks. I know-not what they do-next-soon, but I think-maybe they try trade Karshaks for the location of Sibyl's cave.

'Trade them to who, though? You?'

Maybe me, maybe the Great Mother, I know-not.

'That doesn't make any sense. Your people aren't going to care if this faction kills their hostages.'

I care. No more death, Ammadin Witchwoman. I want-never no more death, not Chof not you not even Karshaks. Especially not this important male Karshak, Jezro Khan. I ask-then Sibyl about khan, what it mean, this word. She tell me, very important, very holy, marked by Karshak god. If a khan die, his people come-next with an army and kill-next-soon us all.

Ammadin decided that Water Woman didn't need to know that Jezro was a powerless exile. 'All right, so this faction wants to trade the Kazraks for the location of Sibyl's cave.'

I think-only this be true. I know-not. They send-maybe soon message to me or to Great Mother. We know-next if they send. If I know I tell-next you about Zayn.

Ammadin squelched a brief impulse towards tears. 'What about Soutan? Has Sibyl seen him?'

Sibyl tell-then me – yes, I be foolish and forget-now to tell you. Here be bad more news. Soutan and that young Karshak, they ride-still east on the old N'Dosha road. Six of our men walk-now with them, the renegade men that I tell-then-long-time-ago you about. Sibyl fear-now that Soutan make-next ambush.

'You know, if Soutan has an ounce of sense, he won't come near Loy. She's a very powerful sorcerer, she hates him, and I think he knows it.'

Good. Let him fear. You keep-now travelling and get to the white cliff. We come-soon. I call-next my men, my servant spears. We reach-soon you.

Abruptly she closed down, leaving only the sound of the illusory sea whispering on the non-existent beach. Ammadin came back to camp to find that Loy had finished with her writing. She'd taken out her own crystals and had some news of her own.

'My spirits did finally manage to reach Master Zhoc,' Loy told her. 'It sounds like the zhundars in Burgunee have finally seen reason. They're honouring that warrant for Soutan's arrest.'

'Too bad he's not still in the Cantons, then.'

'Yes. How I hate him, the wormy little sheep cunt!' Loy hesitated. 'Happier thoughts: was there news of Zayn?'

'Oh yes. He's probably still alive. He was yesterday. He rode across the Burgunee border with Warkannan and Jezro Khan. Come to think of it, they were probably trying to find Warkannan's nephew, but anyway, they've been kidnapped by a rival faction of ChaMeech.'

Loy opened her mouth, but no sound came.

'Yes,' Ammadin said. 'Not the kind of news I was hoping for.'

'Rival faction?' Loy sounded briefly feeble. 'Don't tell me they have politics?'

'Let's pack up the camp. I'll tell you what I know while we work.'

By the time they rode out, the sun had climbed high in the sky. With the pack horse they could ride at no faster than a jog, and that only at intervals, but Ammadin kept her little caravan moving. They did pause once, long after the sun had passed zenith, to scan. Ammadin found no trace of Soutan, and Water Woman never answered Long Voice's call.

All night Warkannan, Jezro, and their horses had struggled to find some degree of comfort in the bamboid cart, plunging onward through the darkness. Sleep avoided them, though they did at odd moments manage to drowse. It was 08.30 by Warkannan's watch when the ChaMeech finally halted beside another underground platform. Once again the lavender female, backed by the armed males, herded them onto a ramp, but one at least twice as long and steeper than the others they'd seen, or so it seemed as they dragged themselves along.

At last they reached solid ground and sunlight. Behind them stretched the grassy valley, sloping down at a considerable angle to the western horizon. To the east – for some minutes Warkannan stood speechless, staring at the view. They had reached the hills, and they were so bizarrely different from any hills he'd ever seen that he could form no clear idea of their height. At first, in fact, he thought he was looking at fortifications.

A forest of stone columns and pillars stood at their base, eroded into fantastic shapes and tufted here and there with red and gold vegetation. Some looked like misshapen H'mai, some like spindles of wool, others like sagging cones topped with odd black hats. Behind them great chunks of hill rose in flat cliffs of a reddish-tan stone striped here and there with black. Sporadic vegetation stippled cracks and ledges with maroon and gold. More pillars, eroded into lacy shapes, and great arches of stone clung to the cliff faces. Behind some of the arches, dark shadows marked cave mouths.

In between each massive chunk of hill ran deep canyons, guarded by what appeared to be striped watchtowers, looming in the shadows. The hill crests made a staggered, tilting line in relation to the horizon, as if God had carved the hills out of a high plain, then pushed on them to make an artistic arrangement. At their rims stood more columns and clumps of stone, marching back beyond the line of sight, turning crimson as the sun rose high enough to top the cliffs.

'Shaitan!' Warkannan whispered.

Jezro nodded his agreement, open-mouthed.

Their immediate surroundings were far less impressive than the hills. Just north of the white sphere a stand of Midas trees stood dripping with red leaves. Off to the south, in the midst of purple grass, stood a white flexstone building, a mere cube about fifteen feet on a side. The wall facing them sported a pair of unglazed windows and a stout true-oak door. Below each window a narrow ledge jutted out.

'I wonder what that is?' Warkannan said.

Their holding cell, as it turned out. With spears and grunts the males marched them over to the building. Warkannan pointed out some Vransic words moulded into the flexstone over the doors and windows.

'It says luh metroh and billay,' Jezro said. 'I don't have the slightest idea what that means.'

Before the little female opened the door, she pointed to their saddlebags, back to them, to the horses, and back to them. When she pantomimed lifting something, they realized that she wanted them to unsaddle the horses and carry their gear inside.

'Now listen you,' Warkannan said. 'Don't you dare eat our horses.'

She stamped her foot several times. 'Eat-not,' she said. 'Promise. In.'

She raised her head and inflated her throat sac. Although Warkannan heard nothing, this close he could feel air vibrating when she spoke. The door, however, heard her and slid back into a channel in the wall. Loaded with gear, they staggered inside. Their footsteps echoed under the high ceiling of a stark, white room, empty except for one long bench, moulded seamlessly into the flexstone floor, running down the middle. The female pointed at a door on the wall.

'Water,' she said. 'Yours. Food soon.'

With that she turned and left. They could hear the door slide shut and lock behind her. Jezro dumped his gear at one end of the bench. Warkannan followed his lead, then walked from window to window; he found a pair of ChaMeech males haunched beyond each. Still, by craning his neck he could look around their broad backs and see the little female tethering the horses out in the high grass.

'Well, here we are,' Jezro said. 'Home. For now, anyway.'

'Yes, apparently so. All we can do is pray that Zayn can get back to Burgunee.'

'Well, if nothing else, Robear and Zhil will start worrying when we don't come home in a couple of days. What they'll do about it, I don't know. You can say I told you so if you want.'

'Don't tempt me.'

Jezro limped across the room and pushed on the side door, which opened to a narrow room, as white and loud as the first. In one corner water gushed up into a flexstone basin, overflowed, and ran across the floor to the far corner, where it drained through a hole about a foot across.

'Sanitation of a sort.' Jezro shut the door again. 'Hostages have been treated worse.' He paused to wipe his nose on his sleeve. 'Well, hell, I am now a captive audience in every sense of that term. I suppose appealing to your better nature isn't going to work.'

'Work for what? Oh, wait: you mean, make me stop haranguing you about going back to Kazrajistan. When it comes to that, I don't have a better nature.'

'Exactly. We have a few other things to mull over, too. For instance, who in hell is going to be interested in ransoming us, way out here? I wonder what this bunch really wants us for? The main course at a banquet? Or appetizers?'

'That thought had occurred to me.' Warkannan yawned with a

shake of his head. 'But what I really wonder is if I'm tired enough to fall asleep on the floor. Damn good thing we brought bedrolls. I think I'll try it and see.'

When Zayn had woken that same morning, the first thing he'd remembered was the imp. He pulled it out of his shirt to let it soak up the sun; he could only pray that it would recover from its long time in darkness. When he inspected the road for tracks, he found none, but now that he knew about the tunnels, the lack of tracks told him nothing. Soutan might be near, far, still ahead of him to the west or long past him to the east. He had no desire to round a turn in the road and see the sorcerer waiting for him. He could take some comfort from the desolation of the countryside; in this flat, empty landscape, where the only cover stood far from the actual road, laying an ambush would be difficult.

After a long graze, the sorrel gelding had recovered from its nightmare journey. For the sake of speed, Zayn mounted and rode at a brisk walk, but always he stayed aware of the horse. He had no intention of being caught in ruined N'Dosha with a lame mount. At intervals he stopped, dismounted, and checked the road for tracks. He never found any hoofprints, but late in the afternoon he ran across a profusion of very different tracks, scrambled and messy, as if a pack of animals had rushed across the road. Off to one side he discovered a few clear prints. A mid-size animal, with thick round feet, tipped with claws – he didn't like the look of them. Leading his horse, he followed the trail to the side of the dirt road and saw trampled, broken grass where the pack had charged through. He also found excrement, tubular, dark in colour, and still stinking though nearly dry.

'A meat-eater,' he said aloud. 'A meat-eater that hunts in packs.'

And there he was, one man with no sabre or bow, nothing but a long knife that would do him no good at any sort of distance. He'd been lucky the night before, blind lucky, and he muttered a prayer of thanks to God. But if they smelled him out and attacked during the coming night, he suspected that his luck would run out and God would be busy elsewhere. He could, he supposed, climb a tree, but that would mean abandoning the sorrel.

'I think we'll stop here,' he said. 'There's some wild wheatian growing in this field. You eat that, and then when it's dark, we'll keep moving.'

As he tethered the horse out in the patch of wild grain, Zayn was thinking of his comnee bow and quiver of arrows, lying on the bed in the guest room back at Marya's manor house - not, he supposed, that he could have hit anything with them anyway. He'd never hit anything except for that one lucky shot in the Mistlands. But had it really been luck, or did the difference lie in the drug that Ammadin had given him? The drug had wiped away his old mind set to make him see things anew, and perhaps it had done the same for his physical reflexes. In that moment he finally identified the problem. Undrugged, his fingers, his arms, the muscles and tendons - they all remembered his old bowcraft with that vertically held Kazraki weapon he'd learned at such a young age, and he'd not made the properly conscious effort to teach them the new.

Every inch of him was a Recaller.

Had it been night and the galaxy risen, Zayn might have turned towards the stars and screamed curses at the ancestors who had made him what he was. Instead, he lay down to sleep with his saddle for a pillow and dreamt that he was lying in a comnee tent with Dallador's arms around him.

Through a sweltering day, Ammadin and Loy followed the dead-straight road. Far off in the east they could see the dark line of hills, dancing in the heat haze.

'I don't understand,' Ammadin said to Loy. 'How are we supposed to find a white cliff before we reach the hills?'

'Good question. It's probably artificial, made of the same stuff as the border pillar.'

Loy's guess was proved right in mid-afternoon, when they saw, ahead and beside the road, some wide, tall thing gleaming in the angled sunlight. As they rode closer, it resolved itself into a wall of white flexstone, curved in a gentle arc, ten feet high and about fifty yards long. Carvings revealed by pale grey shadow covered the surface.

'Merde!' Loy said. 'I wonder just what those bas-reliefs show.' She was leaning forward in the saddle, unsmiling, staring ahead at the wall.

'Something you don't want me to see?' Ammadin said.

Loy winced. 'Not me, Ammi. The Landfall Treaty. Ever heard of that?'

'Yes, of course. It keeps the Kazraks from moving out onto the plains.'

'It was also supposed to keep everyone from killing off the Chof, and the Chof from killing off us. Neither of those parts of it have worked so well.'

Behind the wall a blue and purple meadow stretched out to a stream, the same river that they had camped beside the night before. Midas trees grew along it, tangled here with pink bamboid and tall maroon ferns. Neither Ammadin nor Loy wanted to wait to look at the wall until after they made camp. They did tend the horses first, and out of prudence wrapped the dead yap-packer with fresh leaves, then sank it in the cold river with stones. They left the rest of their gear in a heap and headed for the flexstone.

Ammadin felt her heart pounding. Here there could be answers, here there could be truth. The first panel, at the end of the wall on the side facing the road, displayed just that, not that she could grasp it at that moment. The carving showed the Herd as she had always seen it, but near the spiral floated a lone dot with an arrow connecting it to a square. Inside the square was a big dot with circles around it. Another arrow pointed to the small dot on the fourth circle.

Ammadin shrugged and moved on to the next panel, which told her even less. A round ball, marked with a row of little squares and some wavy lines, supported a long cluster of what might have been tubes wound round with ropes and decorated with dots and arrowheads. At the far end of the tubes dangled another ball, much smaller, decorated with three arrowheads, point to point to form a circular symbol. At the third picture, however, she felt her breath catch in her throat. Flying things were sailing over the plains, flying things were landing among hills, long sleek tubular machines with pointed noses and swept-back wings.

'Merde!' Loy muttered. 'Well, so much for that.'

'What do you mean?' Ammadin said.

'So much for the Landfall Treaty and you. The Tribes aren't supposed to know all this.'

'Why?'

'Because your ancestors didn't want you to know.'

'That doesn't make any sense. Why the lies?' Ammadin turned to look at her. 'I'm sick to death of hearing one lie after another.'

Loy took a frightened step back. Ammadin followed.

'Why tell the Kazraks they came from over the seas, why tell us we've always been here? Water Woman told me that the Tribes came with the rest of you, in those ships.' Ammadin pointed to the carvings. 'She was right, wasn't she? Why have you people been lying to us?'

'Because that's what we promised to do. It's all in the Landfall Treaty.'

'Oh is it? How come I've never heard all of it, then?'

'Hey!' Loy snarled right back. 'Do you think I like to lie? My business is finding out the truth of things.'

Ammadin took a deep breath and spoke more calmly. 'No, I don't suppose you do like it. Sorry. I'm just so sick of being frustrated by half-told stories.'

'So am I. Look, I've studied the Landfall Treaty for years. I've picked it clean of every scrap of historical information I could, and I've spent more years hunting down surviving letters and other records from that period. Even so, I can't tell you everything because I don't know everything. But I'll tell you what I know. Fair?'

'Fair. After all, it's the only bargain we can strike.'

'That's true, isn't it? Unfortunately.' Loy paused for a smile. 'But anyway, your ancestors left their home planet to live an entirely new way. Now, I don't know what they left behind. That's an answer that's eluded me for my entire career. We know the Kazraks wanted a place where they could be pure and live simple religious lives without a lot of machines around. No secrets there. But your people – they're the mystery, because after that first generation, no one knew the truth.'

'Wait! You mean my ancestors lied to their own children.'

'As far as I know they did, yes. Let's see if I can remember how the clause in the Treaty goes. Something like, the people of the Tribes shall belong to the grass and believe they have always belonged to the grass.'

'But who wrote that in?'

'A woman named Lisa Barlamew. You may have heard of her under her comnee name. Lisa adin Bar, Mother of Horses.'

'Yes, yes of course I have.'

'She's one of the signatories to the Treaty. So is Dallas ador Jenz, Father of Arrows.'

'Gods!' Ammadin shook her head as if she could physically throw off her confusion. 'I don't even know what to say to that. It's the opposite of what I've been thinking.'

'Which was?'

'That you Cantonneurs were lying for reasons of your own, of course. Why do you think I got so angry?'

'Huh, wait till I tell you the big truths.' Loy grinned at her. 'Things are very very different, Ammi, than you were taught.'

'I'm beginning to see that, all right. Go on.'

Loy moved back to the first panel. 'See that spiral? That's the galaxy, the Herd. It's made up of suns just like the one hanging in the sky over there. A lot of them have planets just like the one we're standing on circling around them. This is the world, Ammi.' Loy pointed to the dot on the fourth circle. 'It's round.'

'Everyone knows that. The world's round, it circles the sun, that's what makes the seasons.'

'Oh.' Loy glanced away and blushed. 'I'm afraid I've been thinking that the Tribes know a lot less than they do.'

'A lot of people seem to think that. Go on.'

'All right. We H'mai started life on one planet near the edge of the Herd, but we invented ships to take us to other worlds, and we settled those, too. Do you believe me?'

'I don't see any reason why you'd lie.'

'That'll do to get on with, yes. We'll come back to the galaxy later. This next panel –' She stopped in front of the balls and tubes. 'What in hell is this thing? Something else I don't know. Okay, we move on to panel three. You've heard legends of flying ships, right? They're all true. Look at the next one. There are the Settlers getting out of the ships, our ancestors, bless 'em. There's Chursavva the King –'

'Not a king. Chursavva Great Mother. She. A true Chiri Michi.'

'She was female? Then Chiri Michi must mean –'

'That she's a mother, that she lays fertile eggs. We're finally getting somewhere.' Ammadin crossed her arms over her chest. 'Keep talking.'

In the golden light of a summer day they moved along the wall, while Loy talked and pointed, laughed even, at the pleasure of explaining what she knew. Ammadin realized that her students back at the Loremasters Guild were learning from a true master indeed. Her story swept Ammadin into a grander world than any she could possibly have imagined: ancestors who sailed between the stars, who had settled many planets with many forms of sapient life, who had evolved a society to deal with all these peoples as equals and without endless wars.

But their starships, those marvels in themselves, did make at times, somehow or other, enormous mistakes. No one alive now knew how or why the mistake had happened, but these particular ships ended up so far from the settled planets that they could find no way back.

'But my ancestors were a lucky bunch of bastards,' Loy said at last. 'The odds against finding a habitable planet out here, so far beyond the central cluster of the galaxy – God in Heaven, they must have been enormous! The Chof were the ones with the bad luck. The planet belonged to them, and all of a sudden they were sharing it with another sapient species, one that had the weapons to wipe out every last one of them.'

'I'm surprised the Ancestors didn't,' Ammadin said. 'I'm glad, but I'm surprised.'

'That's why the Treaty exists. H'mai history is full of ugly things, such as our ancient habit of exterminating whole nations of people we didn't like. We all fear the Kazraks now, but as H'mai go, they're not really that bad. Other groups of H'mai did much worse in the past. So we knew better than to trust our own kind here.'

'There's something I still don't understand. You say they kept knowledge from us, but they didn't hide it all. You have that gun. Spirit riders and sorcerers have crystals. They left flexstone buildings behind them and all kinds of other things.'

'I don't understand that, either. The Treaty pretty much forbids anything technological. One thing that's pretty clear, though, from some other records, is that my ancestors weren't thinking real clearly. They were panicked, actually, when you come right down to it.'

'That play we saw in Sarla – the man in black talked about this, right?'

'Yes. "By the waters of the Rift we sat down and wept, because we remembered the stars of home." That line always gets me, because the "we" are my people, the Cantonneurs. They didn't want to settle here or anywhere. They were running a ferry service. They were supposed to take the religious fanatics and the comnees to two different planets, but somehow or other they failed. That's why they panicked. We know that the fleet was huge, and that the ships were huge, too, so there were thousands of crew members, enough to found colonies. When they were stranded here against their will, they named the planet Snare.'

'Snare? This language we're speaking, the spirit language. Is that what they spoke on the ships?'

'Yes. It was a kind of common tongue, called Tekspeak.' Loy stared at the tubular ships for a long moment. 'They're way too small. I guess if they showed them as large as they were, it wouldn't fit onto the panel.' She glanced at the next. 'Here, look! They're unloading the horses.'

Down a ramp from the side of one of the flying ships horses were walking in a long line. Assorted people stood around, Chof as well as human. Loy peered at letters written above the carving.

'Chursavva and Lisa adin Bar watch the creation of horses,' she read. 'What? That's not true! What do they think they mean, creation of horses? They had horses back on the home planet.'

'Are you saying that these pictures are false, then?'

'Only this one so far. The rest agree with what we know from other sources.'

By the time they had worked their way along both sides of the wall, the sun hovered on the horizon. In the fading twilight they culled firewood from the stand of trees bordering the river, and Loy put the pieces of her rifle together. With the rifle in her lap Loy ate her dinner, then sat with a notebook and wrote a description of what they'd seen, a very detailed one, Ammadin figured, because it took her a very long time to write down. Ammadin brought the horses in, hobbled them twixt fire and stream, and gave them each a nosebag of grain. Out in the fields the wild wheatian would be getting ripe. She could let the horses graze it when their stock of grain ran out.

Loy was still writing, stopping occasionally to stare into space and chew on her pencil. Ammadin stood near the fire and kept watch, waiting for the first smell of yap-packers. Across the meadow she could see the wall, glimmering in the light from the rising Herd. From the galaxy, she thought. From the stars of home. Yet the phrase lacked for her the magic Loy seemed to feel. Snare's my home, she thought, and the comnees are my people.

The horses turned restless, stamping, flinging up their heads. The night wind brought the sour smell of beasts.

'Loy?' Ammadin said. 'Here they come.'

Loy tossed notebook and pencil onto her bedroll, then stood up, rifle at the ready. Distantly the hunting pack yapped. Loy muttered something under her breath; Ammadin put another golden log on the fire, which leapt up high and smoky. The yaps sounded louder, then louder still, until they could hear the pack rustling through the grass. Once again, at the edge of the firelight eyes gleamed. A bold creature stepped forward, raised its head, sniffed the air, and squealed. It wrenched itself back, howling, then turned and raced off. The rest of the pack followed, shrieking and yapping as they ran. In a few minutes the sound faded, merging with the wind in the grass.

'They have memories,' Loy said. 'Merde! I hope I didn't kill a pair of sapients!'

'Horses have memories, too,' Ammadin said. 'And as much as I love them, I'd never call them smart.'

'That's a comfort. You know, I think we'd better sleep in shifts anyway. I don't trust those blue bastards, and you know how to use this gun now.'

'Yes.' Ammadin paused for a laugh. 'You've taught me a lot of things, as a matter of fact.'

'Well, the wall did most of the teaching. God damn, Ammi! I can't believe how calm you are. What I've told you must have blown your worldview apart, but you can laugh about it.'

'I might be in shock.' Ammadin paused, thinking. 'I doubt it, though. But the thing is, I've had doubts for years about a lot of things we – the spirit riders, I mean – take for granted. Talking with Zayn gave me more questions, and Water Woman's given me some answers. Your talk was only more of the same.'

'I can understand that.'

They sat down together and watched the fire, leaping from the dry spongy wood of the Midas trees. It would take a long time, Ammadin realized, to truly understand everything Loy had told her, simply because there was so much of it. There remained the largest question of all: who were the gods that the comnees carried with them? She felt peculiarly unready to ask it. The gods and their Banes lay at the core of comnee life. If they were – she shook her head and shuddered, shoving the question away. The gesture caught Loy's attention; she studied Ammadin's face so intently that Ammadin laughed again.

'I'm not going to burst into tears or fall apart,' Ammadin said. 'Or curse you, either.'

'Oh good!' Loy grinned at her. 'But you do understand about the Treaty now, don't you? Your ancestors and the ancestors of the Kazraks made my ancestors promise to lie. And for some bizarre reason, we've honoured those promises for eight hundred years.'

'Not bizarre at all, if it was a promise. Honourable.'

'Think so? Maybe.' Loy paused, watching the flames leap. 'When you get back to the plains, what are you going to tell your people?'

'I don't know yet. I have to think about it, and it might depend on what Sibyl has to say. I see why your people decided to live on the other side of the Rift. You could keep things to yourselves that way.'

'Yes, there used to be a law in the Cantons about travellers from either the Kazraks or the Tribes.'

'I've heard of that. You killed anyone who rode beyond Nannes.'

'That's right. A stupid law, and I'm glad everyone stopped obeying it. God, we've kept each other ignorant, haven't we? How would I have learned about Chursavva being a Great Mother if you hadn't told me?'

'You could have asked the Chof.'

'None of the Chof I've met would have told me that. When they found out I could hear them, they were willing to chat, but they set up definite limits and boundaries.'

'Where did you meet them, anyway?'

'In this awful little town called Shairb on the Burgunee border. That's where they come to trade for cloth. When I was a graduate student, I spent time working in the mart to learn what I could about them.'

'But you never went across the border?'

'No one wanted to risk coming out here uninvited. They wiped the N'Dosha settlement off the face of the planet, didn't they? We didn't want to be next. It's the Treaty again, set up to keep the cultures apart. Stupidly!'

'Stupid? The Kazraks didn't want to know the truth. You said yourself that they were happier than the Cantonneurs were, knowing what you'd lost.'

'What's more important? Being happy or knowing the truth?'

'I don't know.' Ammadin considered for a long moment. 'But it's a question I'm going to have to answer before I go back to the grass.'

Just at sunset Zayn had saddled up and headed west, but although he left his gear tied to the saddle, he walked and led the sorrel to spare its strength. If they ran across that pack of meat-eaters, their best hope would lie in outrunning them, and for that, his horse needed to be fresh. He wished he knew how they hunted, by smell or sight, because if they tracked by smell, he could perhaps throw them off by taking the gelding into the shallow river and wading through the water.

The Herd was just cresting the eastern hills when he realized that the land was beginning to slope downhill, just a gradual descent, but one that would spare his legs and the sorrel's, a piece of luck when he needed every piece he could scrounge. As they picked their way along through the ruts and stones in the road, Zayn found himself thinking about Idres and Jezro. How far had they been taken, he wondered, and where had they ended up? Somewhere among the hills of N'Dosha, most likely. At least these ChaMeech seemed determined to treat their prisoners decently, unlike – he shoved the memories down fast.

At that moment he realized that he was picking up some sound at the threshold of his hearing. Animals, a lot of them, howled and yapped. The sorrel tossed up its head, sniffed the wind, and pulled at the reins with a nervous toss of mane.

'Steady on!' Zayn patted its neck. 'They're ahead of us.'

He hesitated, considering the river. The yaps and howls neither diminished nor grew louder; they apparently were moving at right angles to the road, some way away still. Zayn mounted, then rose in the stirrups, scanning for the threat, and saw, far down the road at the end of the view, a bright dot of gold, glimmering. A fire, a campfire – Soutan? That it might be Ammadin crossed his mind, but he doubted if he could ever be as lucky as that. The sorrel snorted and danced under him.

'Wait, just wait, old boy,' Zayn murmured. 'Let's see which way they're going.'

The howling changed to a steady, distant yap, a sound like clapping hands on the night air. It seemed to be moving off, then suddenly grew louder, as if the pack was running a zig-zag route, crossing the road, coursing a long way out, then turning and coming back again. Zayn dismounted.

'Well, if they hunt by sight, nothing's going to save us.' He spoke aloud to keep the horse calm. 'But if they hunt by smell, the river might do the job, so what the hell, let's head for the river.'

At a jog he led the horse across the grassy field towards the trees that marked the river course. The dry grass stood high and thatchy; pushing their way took effort, and all the while he could hear the yaps coming closer. The trees at last! Zayn kicked dead wood out of the way and led the horse down to the riverbank. By then the yapping was so loud that the sorrel stepped into the river without any need for coaxing.

The Herd had risen into the sky, and by glittering starlight they could pick their way through the shallows to the centre of the river. The water, cold but not unbearable, came up to Zayn's knees. Where they stood, gravel and firm sand carpeted the river bottom, decent footing assuming it didn't turn muddy farther west. Zayn muttered a few soothing words to the sorrel and walked on, one foot at a time, testing the bottom at every step. The yapping of the hunting pack suddenly stopped. In its place he could hear the brushy scraping sound of animals, a lot of animals, pushing their way through dry grass. He glanced back, but trees obstructed his view.

Zayn walked faster, sloshed through the water with the horse coming along right behind. The thrashing, scratchy sound behind them seemed to be keeping pace. Zayn glanced back and saw in between the trees things moving, things with eyes that caught the dim light and gleamed, things that pushed their way through the trees and stood on the riverbank.

'Shit!'

He counted ten of them. The sorrel threw up its head, then pulled at the reins. Zayn shortened his grip on the reins with his left hand and with his right caught the bridle itself.

'Steady on, old boy, steady on.'

When they started walking again, the predators walked with them, but they kept to the riverbank. Now and then one would strain forward and whine, take a step into water, and draw back fast.

'As long as we keep to the water, we might be safe. Steady on, old boy. Let's just keep moving and maybe they'll decide to look for something easier to kill.'

The horse tried to toss its head, then suddenly whickered, thrashed its tail, and neighed, a good long call. Other horses answered from some distance. That campfire, Zayn thought. Well, if it's Soutan, I'll end up in a hell of a mess. Or if Arkazo's got a bow, I might just end up in Hell. On the riverbank the animals began to whine and cluster, as if they were preparing to charge. The distant horses whickered again. Three of them, Zayn suddenly realized, only three horses. He had never trusted to luck before in his life, but luck was all he had left.

'Ammadin!' Zayn yelled as loud as he could. 'Ammi! Help!'

When their horses neighed in answer to the distant horse's call, Ammadin and Loy both jumped to their feet. Ammadin walked away from the fire to peer into the eastern darkness.

'Maybe it's Soutan?'

'Oh please, God!' Loy patted her rifle.

Their horses neighed again, and distantly the strange horse answered. Ammadin took a deep breath of the night wind.

'Yap-packers!' Ammadin said. 'I wonder if they've got the poor beast trapped? I'll get the lightwand.'

'Do you think it's safe to go out there?'

Before Ammadin could answer, they both heard the voice – a H'mai, male, calling for help.

'That's Zayn!' Ammadin snapped. 'Come on!'

Ammadin scooped up her saddlebags and slung them over one shoulder, then ran for the road. As she ran she fumbled in one bag, found the lightwand, and pulled it out.

'Light!' she said. 'High!'

A fountain of light rose up and illuminated the road, the fields, the Midas trees. When she glanced back, she realized that Loy was struggling to keep up. She slowed down to a jog and brought the stick down level with her waist. With the motion the light turned to a wide beam, leaping down the road ahead. Ammadin swung the stick back and forth, raking the fields on either side with light.

'Zayn!' she yelled. 'Hang on!'

It struck her as a stupid thing to say, but she could think of no better. The dazzling light was already beginning the rescue. The yap-packers began whining and yowling in sudden fear just as a panting Loy caught up with her.

'There they are!' Loy gasped, pointing.

A cluster of blue beasts came slinking out of the Midas trees, yapped, howled, and began milling around. Ammadin swung the lightwand around and pinned them in its glare. She heard Loy's calm voice behind her.

'Lock. Fire.'

The ripple of light flashed to the nearest yap-packer. Light exploded along with the creature's head, a ghastly display of white fire and maroon blood bursting into a split-second blossom. The glare died, leaving Ammadin half-blind. The yap-packers raced back and forth, ramming into trees, alternately yapping and screaming in hideous counterpoint. Finally they collected themselves and as a pack raced off north, howling surrender. In the dimmer glow from the lightwand Ammadin could finally see. Something else moved among the Midas trees.

'Ammi!' Zayn was shouting. 'Ammi, do you hear me?'

'Yes.' She shouted in answer. 'What's wrong?'

'Nothing. I'm bringing my horse through the trees. I don't know what that was, but don't use it on us.'

'It's safe. And I thank the gods you are.'

Although she wanted to run and throw herself into his arms, Ammadin stood waiting on the road, watching as he led the sorrel out of the trees and across the field. When he reached the roadside he dropped the horse's reins, strode over, and threw his arms around her. She kissed him once, then pulled away.

'How did you get away from the ChaMeech?' she said.

'It's a long story.' Zayn sounded exhausted. 'How did you know I – wait, Water Woman must have told you.'

'Yes, she did. Let's get back to camp. We've got a lot to talk about. I want to know what happened in Burgunee.'

'A lot.' Zayn managed a smile. 'And I see you've brought the loremaster with you. Good. I need to ask her a lot of questions.'

The three of them stayed up talking till long after the Herd set. Even so, Ammadin roused herself at Sentry's dawn chime. She sat up, yawning, then grabbed her saddlebags without disturbing Zayn, lying sprawled and snoring next to her. When she stood up, he muttered a few incomprehensible words and flopped over onto his stomach. On the other side of the campfire Loy's blankets sat already rolled and tied for the day. Out in the field, three of the horses were grazing at tether, and as she watched, the sorrel, which had been tired enough to sleep lying down, heaved itself to its feet and joined them.

Ammadin walked out into the grass, then knelt and brought out Spirit Eyes – or was she really holding a spirit in her hand? She laid them in a row to feed, Sentry, Long Voice, Spirit Eyes, Earth Prince, Rain Child, even Death Chanter. She had thought them living things, wild spirits that she had tamed and trained. And what if it weren't true, she asked herself? What if her crystals were dead things, no different in kind from the machines that carried water from the rivers to the ditches in the Cantons, or those printing presses Zayn had spoken of? She would feel no lonelier; she had never thought of them as persons, merely as spirits, each with a very narrow range of skill and no character to speak of. They were servants, not friends.

What did matter was the chain of lies. Someone, those Settlers Loy spoke of, had lied to the first spirit riders. They in turn had taught their apprentices those lies in good faith. Down through the long years, eight hundred years, as she now knew, the lies had travelled, and each year they had expanded, eating up the truth. With time the teachers had known less to teach. That mattered to the point of fury.

As Ammadin expected, Water Woman never contacted her, nor could she find the Chiri Michi in her scan. In some minutes Loy joined her, carrying her own saddlebags.

'Nothing,' Loy said without being asked. 'Did you have any luck?'

'None, no. Not a trace of Soutan. You do know that he has his own ChaMeech allies, don't you?'

'He bragged about that once, yes. He claimed he'd dominated an alpha male and won his submission. My theory is that the male decided Yarl was useful.'

'That's what Water Woman told me.'

They shared a laugh.

'But anyway,' Ammadin went on. 'At least now we know why we can't find them.'

'Yes, we certainly do.' Loy shook her head in amazement. 'Tunnels. An entire network of tunnels under the Cantons! Now, we did know that a few short tunnels run under Dordan and Bredanee. Old Onree found those. But no one had the slightest idea that there was another network out here. How in hell does that kind of information just disappear?'

'Eight hundred years is a long time.'

'Not that long! Damn the Ancestors! Everything I know about the first hundred years on Snare I've had to piece together and fill in with guesswork.' Loy stood up, stretching. 'Merde, I'm tired! I'm glad we're not travelling today, let me tell you.'

'Yes, nothing to do now but wait for Water Woman.'

'And I've got to cook that yap-packer. It's aged enough, and it'll start to turn pretty fast in this weather.'

They returned to camp to find Zayn awake, stripped to the waist, and wet – he'd been bathing in the stream, he told them. Loy glanced at the scars on his back, winced, but said nothing.

'Look, Ammi,' Zayn said. 'You really think I should wait for your ChaMeech friends to get here?'

'Do you really think you'll get back to Dordan alive with the yap-packs roaming around?'

'You win. I'll wait.'

'From what Water Woman told me,' Ammadin went on, 'it's likely that the kidnappers want hostages to bargain with her. If so, they'll have to keep your friends safe, won't they?'

'That's true, yes. I just – well, hell, I'm worried, I guess. I don't want anything happening to the khan.'

'He really is the khan to you, isn't he? I can hear it in your voice.'

'I'm not surprised. After what he did for me –' Zayn paused for a long moment.

'I'll admit to being impressed, yes. That reminds me. Bring me your bridle. It's time to take the quest marker off.'

Zayn turned solemn, hesitated, his eyes so troubled that she thought he was about to divulge some painful story, but he turned and jogged off to bring her the marker.

After the camp fed, Loy rummaged through one of the pack saddles and brought out a flat circle of strangely pale and lightweight metal. The disc seemed to be constructed of a number of overlapping flat rings, but when Loy laid a hand in the centre and pushed hard, it unfolded into an enormous stew pot.

'Clever, huh?' Loy said. 'I thought the bursar was crazy when he insisted we take this, but we can use it after all.'

'Do you have a spit to hang it on?'

'Sure do. I'll have to cut some branches to hold the spit up, though.'

Zayn hauled the dead yap-packer, still wrapped in its layer of leaves and rope, out of the river and carried it back to camp. Loy cut it into big chunks with the hatchet, boned them with a knife, then put the meat, a handful of salt, and stream water into the kettle to stew over a slow fire. She scrounged around in the shrubby brush along the stream bank and came back with handfuls of pale yellow plants, which she threw into the kettle as well.

'There,' Loy said. 'I'll add some dried grapes towards the end, too.'

'While you're doing that,' Zayn said, 'could I have a look at that – well, whatever it was you used last night. The thing that killed the yap-packer.'

'A look at it?' Loy raised a sceptical eyebrow.

'Well, I want to know how it works. Could you show me?'

Loy glanced Ammadin's way. 'It's your rifle, not mine,' Ammadin said.

Loy considered for a few minutes while Zayn watched her like a hungry child hoping for a treat. 'Men and weapons,' Loy said. 'What is it with men and weapons?'

'I don't know about other men,' Zayn said, 'but weapons are my job, after all.'

'As a comnee man or a cavalry officer?'

'Both, really.'

Loy frowned down at the stew pot; the water was beginning to simmer. She took a long stick of whittled firewood and poked at the chunks of meat, shoving them under the surface.

'No,' she said at last. 'You can't. Neither of your jobs were meant to have that kind of rifle. The thought of a lot of Kazraks with rifles makes my blood run cold.'

'Well, hell,' Zayn snapped. 'What do you think we could do? Just sit right down and manufacture them by the hundreds?'

'You've got a point. The answer's still no.'

When Zayn started to argue, Ammadin laid a firm hand on his arm. 'There's something I want to show you,' she said.

Zayn looked at her, and she could smell anger, simmering like the water in the pot. 'Come on,' she said. 'Now.'

He hesitated, still angry, then suddenly shrugged. 'You're right,' he said. 'Loy, I'm sorry. It's your rifle, so you do what you want with it.'

'That's right,' Loy said cheerfully. 'I do.'

Ammadin hurried Zayn along to the white wall. She was expecting him to find the bas-reliefs fascinating, and he commented that they were, but he glanced briefly at each panel and moved fast to the next.

'Don't you want to study them?' she said.

'Of course. I'm memorizing them for later.'

'You know, it's such a waste, your talents. They're splendid, really amazing, but your people had to go and torment you for them.'

'It's not like they had much of a choice. It always seemed inevitable to me, I mean, if you consider who Agvar was, and the people who followed him.'

'Maybe so, but that doesn't make me hate them less.'

They sat down together in the shade of the wall. He caught her hand, kissed the palm, smiled and tried to draw her close, but she jerked her hand free.

'Don't start,' she said. 'Loy's right over there, and Water Woman and her entourage could show up at any time.'

'You're right. I wish we had a tent.'

'So do I. But we don't.'

He started to say more, then let his smile fade as he thought something through. 'While we've got this chance alone,' he said finally, 'there's something I need to talk with you about. The Chosen.'

'Let me guess. You're sure they're going to come after you and kill you.'

'All right, I deserved that, but no, that's not it. Let me see if I can tell you things about them.'

'Uh, I don't understand –'

'The Chosen did something to my mind, I guess. When I tried to tell Jezro Khan about them, I went into convulsions.'

'You what?' She leaned forward.

'Convulsions. First I heard a hissing sound, and then it got loud, like water boiling, and then I blacked out. I don't remember what happened next.' He held up his right hand, flecked with new scars. 'I was holding a glass, and I crushed it.'

'Your muscles must have gone completely rigid. It's no wonder you don't remember anything, after a fit like that.'

'But what I don't understand is, I could tell you about the Chosen.'

'That's true. So what do you want to do now? Try to tell me more and see how you react?'

'Just that.' Zayn took a deep breath. 'All right?'

'All right. Go ahead.'

'It was an officer named Lev Rashad who figured out I had some of the demon talents. We ended up in the same regiment after we'd both been transferred off the border. He dropped a few hints, I made the right responses, and so he took me to meet a certain Colonel Shah, infantry, retired. That's not his real name, you can bet on that. But in Bariza he was the chief recruiter for the Chosen.' He paused, looking her way.

'How do you feel now?'

'Same as always. Let's try some more details. I made up an excuse and applied for two weeks' leave from my regiment. Then they took me up to Haz Kazrak where I was initiated. Well, actually, the headquarters of the Chosen are a couple of miles north of town, cut out of the side of a hill. The entrance is hidden in a stand of fern trees, about two miles from the main road. I realize now that it has to be an old supply depot or bunker or some such thing, dating from the colonist days, I mean, because it was made of flexstone. At the time, it looked pretty damn impressive. It had a light strip running around the base of the wall, so everything turned gold and glittered.' Zayn smiled, his eyes wide, as relieved as a man who finds out that his battle wounds aren't fatal after all. 'I don't hear the hiss. I don't feel disorientated.'

'Good. Do you have any idea of what they might have done to you?'

'It must have happened in the initiation ceremony. They tie you to a pillar of blue quartz.' Zayn reached into his shirt and pulled out the imp. 'Just like this stuff. And then the officer in charge has a knife made out of some kind of clear crystal. Or I thought it was a knife at the time. It didn't have a sharp edge.' His eyes seemed to be tracking some moving object.

'That's really odd. Are you seeing this in your mind now?'

Zayn nodded. 'They laid it on my throat, then across my eyes, as a death threat if I ever betrayed the guild.' He cocked his head as if he were listening to distant voices. 'It's hard to make sense of the memory. They drug you before the ceremony starts.'

'What with?'

'I don't know. Something that made me puke a couple of times, and then everything got, well, strange. It was different from that pink drug you gave me in the Mistlands. That just made me feel more alive.'

'It's supposed to, yes. How did they give you the drug?'

'In some sort of liquid, in a glass.' He swallowed heavily. 'It's bitter, and they're telling me that I should always remember the bitterness, because our lot in life's so bitter, too.' He paused, his eyes wide, his mouth slack, and at that point she realized that he'd slipped into a trance much like that of a spirit rider seeking a vision. 'Walking into the room is like walking into a fire. The gold walls are moving. It's like there isn't any floor, just fire.'

'Is the pillar made out of fire?'

'No, it's cold.' He leaned his head back, and his arms twitched, as if someone were pulling his hands behind him. 'So are the hand-cuffs.'

'What are they saying to you?' Ammadin deliberately softened her voice. 'The knife touches your throat. What are they saying to you?'

Zayn spoke in Kazraki – several sentences as far as she could tell.

'Remember that,' she whispered. 'Remember what you just said.'

He nodded so slowly that for a moment she thought he was about to faint, but he sat unmoving. She leaned close to him, paused, then, when he didn't respond, laid her hand on the side of his face. In the heat of the day he felt cold, and she could feel his pulse beating fast in his throat. He's not a spirit rider, she thought. This could be dangerous.

'Zayn?' She ran her hand through his hair. 'Zayn, come back. You've gone off somewhere.'

He twisted away from her touch, then stared, dazed, at her face.

'Zayn? It's me, Ammi.'

Suddenly he shook his head like a fly-stung horse. She rose to a kneel and reached for him, but he smiled normally and turned to look at her.

'What was all that?' he said.

'You were reliving something.' Ammadin sat back down. 'Do you remember what I asked you to remember?'

'Yes, from the initiation ceremony. They laid the knife on my throat and told me, one word to any man about our secrets means your death.' He frowned, thinking. 'Your death lies within you –

that's when they put it over my eyes – like a snake coiled within your soul. And then they put the knife on the back of my neck, and it hurt like hell, I could feel the pain all up and down my spine, but you know something? At the same time it felt like sex. It got me off, anyway.'

'Oh, did it? I'd be willing to bet that's when they put the snake in your soul, whatever they meant by that.'

'Maybe so. There were lights in the blue quartz. For some reason that matters.' Zayn began rubbing the back of his head as if it still ached. 'I told Idres about them, too, the lights, but I don't know why.'

'Neither do I. Can I see that imp?'

'Sure.' He slipped it over his head and handed it to her.

When Ammadin held it up to the sunlight, it glowed like a feeding crystal. 'Did the lights look like this?'

'No. There were points of light moving inside the pillar, going up and down.'

'How could you see them if you were tied with your back against it?'

Zayn stared at her so blankly that she feared he'd slipped back into trance. 'I don't know,' he said at last. 'I just did. I could see myself and the pillar, and the lights were moving inside it.'

'You could see yourself? Did you feel like you were floating up by the ceiling?'

'No, because I could see everything in front of me, too. The officers, I mean, and the room itself. I –' He hesitated, eyes narrowed. 'Shit! I don't know. I just could.'

'Huh.' Ammadin handed the imp back. 'I don't understand this at all.'

She could smell his sudden fear. He took a deep breath and with it slapped his mask over his face.

'You were hoping I'd understand it,' Ammadin said.

'Hell yes. I don't know anyone else who would.'

'Neither do I. Unless maybe Sibyl. To hear Water Woman talk, anyway, she knows everything worth knowing, more than any spirit rider ever did.'

'Do you think she'll let me talk to her?'

'Maybe. You can ask Water Woman when she gets here.'

The mask turned rigid around his eyes.

'Well, if you can,' she said.

'I'm sorry, Ammi. After this last go-round with the ChaMeech –'

'Wounds on top of wounds?'

'Yes, 'fraid so. I'm not proud of it, you know, panicking every time I get close to them.' His voice ached with shame. 'Do you think I like feeling like a goddamned coward?'

'Oh shut up!' She laid a hand on his arm. 'You're not a coward.'

'Well, who else would be so frightened of something that happened eight years ago?'

'Another Recaller. I'm beginning to get an idea of what it means, being one of the Inborn.'

'Well, maybe that's it, but –'

'Do you think I'd sleep with a coward?'

At that he smiled and laid a hand on top of hers. 'Thanks,' he said. 'You're a comnee girl, and I know you wouldn't.'

He leaned forward and kissed her. Reflexively she freed her hand and ran it through his hair, ran it down the back of his head – and pulled away from him.

'What's wrong?' Zayn said.

'Hold still.' Ammadin rose to a kneel and ran her fingers along the back of his skull where it joined the spine. 'Whatever they did to you left a scar.'

'It did?' He raised his own hand, let her fingers guide his to the ridged circular depression in his skin, then smiled. 'Oh, that! I've always had that.'

'Always?'

'As long as I can remember, anyway. Since I was a baby.' The mask cracked, and he looked on the edge of tears. 'One of the healers my father took me to called it a demon mark. He thought that the demons claimed their own by biting them or something like that.'

'Gods, they were so stupid! It's not a demon mark or a gennie bite or anything else they might have called it.'

'You're sure?' He managed a smile.

'Very sure. I don't know what it is, but demons don't have real teeth.'

In between bouts of poking at the stew, such as it was, Loy spent the morning writing. She finished the first notebook and started a second, filling the pages with data on the tunnel system, Zayn and his Inborn talents, the wildlife, the Chof, the Settler artifacts. When she finished, each notebook went into a waterproof, fireproof, double-sealed pouch. Already she had information worth the cost of her expedition, and she had no intention of losing a word of it.

Loy was just putting away the second notebook when she heard, or perhaps felt, the sound of Chof thrumming. She stood up, turning to the south to listen. The thrum came again, and this time, thanks to her own Inborn talent, she could pick up actual sound. A pack of Chof were calling back and forth to each other, off to the south but fairly close by.

'Ammi!' Loy yelled at the top of her lungs. 'Do you think that's Water Woman?'

'I hope so,' Ammadin called back. 'But get out that gun. Zayn, bring in the horses!'

Zayn had just finished tethering the horses on short ropes between the fire and the stream when the wind brought a waft of Chof scent. Even Loy could smell it, and the horses turned nervous. Ammadin tipped her head back and sniffed the air like a shen.

'Three females,' she announced, 'and maybe four males. It has to be Water Woman.'

Not long after, the Chof appeared, tramping through the high grass on the far side of the road. Their long necks swayed and their bulbous heads bobbed as they strode along, and Loy was struck once again by how inherently graceful they were, with their slender pseudo-arms neatly folded across their chests as they marched in step with one another. Water Woman, her skin oiled to a brilliant purple, her blue and white skirt hiked up and tied around her middle, led the way. Her smaller grey servants came directly after, loaded down with bundles and sacks. Behind them marched the four males, spears tucked under their pseudo-arms. They wore kilts of blue trade cloth and carried an assortment of strangely lumpy packs lashed to their backs. When they reached the road, Water Woman boomed once and waved both her pseudo-hands.

'Ammadin, Loy!' she called. 'At last at last we meet-now.'

Loy collapsed the focus rod of the rifle and slipped off the heavy power pack. She happened to glance at Zayn and nearly dropped the gun in surprise. Under the heavy pigmentation of his skin his face had turned bloodless, and he was sweating far beyond the heat of the day. He's afraid, Loy thought. My god, I never thought anything would scare a man like him! When he realized that she was staring at him, he flinched, then strode back among the horses.

As Water Woman hurried across the field, her two female servants kept pace, but the males fanned out. They stopped some twenty yards from the camp and arranged themselves in a semi-circle, facing the road, and lifted their spears to the ready. Loy and Ammadin exchanged a troubled glance. Water Woman confirmed the trouble when she arrived.

'Danger,' Water Woman said in Hirl-Onglay. 'Trouble among us Chof, and Yarl be somewhere. Everything be-now all wrong.' She waved her pseudo-hands in vague circles. 'I apologize-now to you, Ammadin Witchwoman and Loy Sorcerer. Our gods be-must dead I know-now. Everything fall apart, and our Chof ways fray-now like an old cloth.'

The two servants threw back their heads and moaned.

'What's happened?' Ammadin said. 'Who's chasing you?'

'I know-not. Maybe they chase or not chase.' Water Woman bent her long neck to bring her head low. 'I have-not the power to think-now clearly. Awful awful awful.'

'It's that other faction, isn't it?' Ammadin said. 'The one who took Zayn's friends hostage.'

'Yes. Faction.' Water Woman's voice cracked, possibly from anger, more likely from the effort she was making to speak high enough for H'mai ears to hear. 'You know-not, Loy, Ammadin, what this mean to us Chof. We agree-always not on the little questions, no, but on the big issues Chof agree-always. We argue, we scream, we raise our heads high, but agree-next-soon. Now no agree-not never. Awful awful awful!'

Water Woman abruptly haunched. One of the servants hurried forward to untie her mistress's skirt and arrange it over her hindquarters.

'Come have some food.' Loy pointed to the stew pot. 'Please share our food.'

'Thank you, Loy Sorcerer.' Water Woman bobbed her head. 'You know something of our Chof ways, I see-now. Food, yes. We all share-next some food.'

With a meal to supervise Water Woman became much calmer. Loy herded Ammadin and Zayn away from the stew pot.

'Let her do it her way,' Loy whispered. 'It would be rude not to. She's the highest-ranked female here, in her eyes anyway.'

First Water Woman had her servants unpack their collection of sacks, most of which contained foodstuffs. When they'd unloaded each other's burdens, the females trotted out and fetched those carried by the males. The males haunched, but they kept their spears raised and ready. With one thrust of their powerful hind legs, they would be up and facing any enemy who might appear.

Water Woman joined the H'mai and haunched with a long sigh. At this signal, Loy sat herself and gestured at Ammadin and Zayn to do the same. After rummaging through everything, the two servants brought out oily rounds of a rough-milled wheatian bread and big wooden bowls for the chunks of yap-packer; they served first Water Woman, then the two H'mai women. They stopped in front of Zayn, however, and stared in confusion.

'He eats with us.' Loy reinforced her words with gestures.

The servants each stamped a foot in thanks, then trotted back to the fire for more food. After they'd served Zayn, they took food for themselves and sat behind their mistress. The Chof women ate steadily and silently; Loy, Zayn, and Ammadin followed their lead.

After the females of both species and Zayn had taken what they wanted, Water Woman led them away from the place where they'd eaten. They sat in the shade of the Midas trees with the two servants haunched behind their mistress. At that point the males got up and went to eat the remaining meat straight out of the stew pot; they used the remaining bread to sop up the yap-packer broth. When they finished, they grabbed their spears and returned to their position between the females and the road.

'Maybe I should have eaten with them,' Zayn said in Vranz. 'Should I go help guard?'

'No,' Loy said. 'If you're marked as having a higher rank, it'll be easier to rescue your friends.'

'Good. Would it be rude if I got up and put the horses on full tether again?'

'No. Everyone's finished now.'

Zayn got up, nodded pleasantly at the Chof women, then trotted off to take care of the horses. As soon as he was well away, Water Woman swung her head around close to Loy and Ammadin.

'I speak-then with Sibyl this morning. She tell-then me that the other faction hide-then the Karshaks in an old building made of white curse stone. They be-now all near the hills.'

'Curse stone?' Ammadin said.

'Your people make-then-long-time-ago this white stuff, like the picture cliff here. Chof have-not the power to destroy-then-now-next-soon, so we call it cursed. But tell-not Zayn. He want-maybe to rush off and try to rescue the other Karshaks. We have-not the power to rescue his friends.'

'Is it too dangerous?' Loy joined in.

'Not dangerous, no. I explain-now our Chof ways. The faction go-then to find the Great Mother. They make-soon an appeal to her. We have-not power do-now more. Only Great Mother have the power to decide who be right, who be wrong.'

'They've gone to the Great Mother already?' Ammadin said.

'No, but they be-now closer than us. They get-first there. And we Chof have-always a law. No one have the power to stop anyone who want to appeal to Great Mother.'

'So,' Loy said, 'did Sibyl tell you they were going?'

'No, they tell me. You learn-then about our secret roads from Zayn?'

'The tunnels, you mean? Yes.'

'I tell-next another secret. Chof talk-easy when we be in the roads. Listen.' Water Woman raised her head, inflated her throat sac, and let out a deep note, so deep that Loy felt more than heard it. 'When we do that, it travel-next long long way in the roads.'

'Yes,' Loy said. 'I just bet it does.'

'So what are we going to do, then?' Ammadin leaned forward. 'Will the Great Mother listen to us, too?'

'Yes. Great Mother listen-always to all. I call-then-yesterday my other spear servants. When they come-next, we all go-soon.'

'Are we going to travel in the tunnels?' Loy said. 'I'd like to see them.'

'I know-not. We wait-next, spears come-soon, tell-next-soon. Maybe safe, not safe. The others be-now on the secret road. I want-not fighting, my spears her spears.'

'Who is this other her?' Loy said. 'The leader of the faction?'

'Yes.' Water Woman raised her hindquarters a couple of feet off the ground and made a dipping motion before she sat back down. 'Lastunnabrilchiri, Herbgather Woman. I wish-now that her eggs dry to a nasty dust. She put-then-now-next many spear servants on the secret road. I want no dead males, Loy Sorcerer, no dead females either, not even Karshaks.'

'Good,' Loy said. 'How long will it take us to reach the Great Mother if we ride our horses?'

'Days.' Water Woman raised her head and moaned. 'And Herbgather Woman, she have those days to talk talk talk in Great Mother's ears.'

'How close is Sibyl to this flexstone building?' Ammadin put in. 'More days' ride?'

'Many days' ride, yes. The secret road run-not there. All must walk to Veeduhn Dosha.'

Loy felt a thin, cold line of excitement run down her back. Sibyl lived in N'Dosha Town, where the archives had been kept.

Although Loy had enough questions to fill fifty notebooks, she had few of them answered that afternoon. The rest of Water Woman's loyal males – a contingent of some thirty spear servants, as she called them – arrived far earlier than the Chiri Michi had expected. Water Woman heard them first; she scrambled to her feet and stood looking across the road to the open field.

'There they be!' she said. 'A good sign, a good omen! They get here so fast, no time for fighting.'

Thrumming and booming, the blue-kilted males came stalking across the dried grass. Water Woman thrummed in answer, then hurried off to meet them. The two servants calmly began packing the various boxes and sacks. Ammadin and Loy walked over to join Zayn, who looked merely frightened, not terrified.

'Are you going to be all right?' Ammadin said to him.

'Yes.' His voice sounded reasonably steady. 'Having you along's going to make a hell of a difference.' He took a deep breath, then managed to smile. 'It's going to be interesting, anyway.'

'That's certainly true. And with all those spears along, it should be safe enough. There's not much Soutan's supporters can do against so many.'

'Ah yes,' Loy said. 'Yarl. I don't suppose you've seen him in your crystals.'

'No, I haven't.' Ammadin thought for a moment, then turned to Zayn. 'Another mystery – do you know what Soutan and Arkazo are doing out here?'

Zayn's face became a mask. Even though Loy had seen him suppress his feelings before, she found it profoundly unsettling.

'I'll get the horses saddled and loaded,' Zayn said, and his voice carried not one trace of what he might have been feeling. 'Either way, we'll be getting on the road.'

Zayn hurried off to fetch the horses in from pasture. Ammadin stood looking after him, and Loy had no trouble understanding her feelings: raw fury.

'Does he do that often?' Loy said.

'Yes. It's his way of lying without saying a single word.' Ammadin made a visible effort to calm herself. 'Well, there's no time to deal with him right now. Water Woman's dithering is all I can handle anyway.'

'I'm surprised at how badly conflict upsets her.'

'It makes sense to me. Factions are like comnees, aren't they? Being part of a comnee teaches us how to get along with other comnees in the Tribes, and in the Cantons, you've got families that do the same thing. Chof don't have families like we do, because of the way their children grow.'

'Of course! By the time they get back to land, the adult Chof can't tell whose child is which, and the children belong to everyone.'

Water Woman and her male servants were all milling about in the field. Loy could just hear her booming voice, and now and then the males inflated their sacs; if they were speaking, they were doing so at too low a pitch for even her genetically enhanced hearing. Eventually Water Woman strode across the road and headed for the camp. Her spear males followed, some bunched together, others straggling behind. She waved both pseudo-hands and boomed as well.

'Good news!' Water Woman called out. 'The tunnel roads be-now safe. We travel-next-fast to meet the Great Mother.'

Warkannan had his copy of the *Mirror*, and Jezro had brought a thick pad of rushi and some pens to make notes as they hunted for Soutan. Otherwise, Warkannan decided, they might have gone half-demented shut up in that white room, and mostly because of the noise. The shiny flexstone surface absorbed so little sound that they were forced to whisper. During the day they left their blankets spread out in a corner and sat on them, but even the thick wool muffled few of the reverberations. Every time they spoke in a normal voice, their words echoed and boomed under the glittering ceiling.

The first day after their arrival, they'd mostly slept; when they woke, in mid-afternoon, they'd inspected their prison carefully only to arrive at the conclusion that they'd never be able to dig or climb their way out. The floor met the walls in a smooth curve of material rather than any sort of seam or join, giving the impression that a single sheet of flexstone had been folded and fused to form the cube.

At twilight, the lavender female appeared with a crude basket filled with greasy rounds of some grain-based baked thing and a chunk of roasted meat. When Jezro asked her for a lamp, she obligingly handed over a light stick. After a few false commands, Jezro succeeded in making it work, but its high setting made the walls glare like the heart of a fire. He spoke fast and returned it to a dim glow.

'Not enough to read by,' Warkannan said, 'but that's all right, I'm not complaining. How did the Settlers live in rooms like this?'

'They hung the walls with panels and tapestries, I suppose,' Jezro said. 'And put rugs on the floors.'

'That makes sense. Well, if we can't read the *Mirror*, we've got to figure out something to do besides sit here and worry about Zayn and Arkazo. Too bad we don't have a chess set.'

'Yes, it is; or wait, we could make one out of rushi. You know, draw a board and write the names of the pieces on scraps.'

'Sounds good to me.'

With their improvised game they picked up a tournament that had ended abruptly at Jezro's supposed death. Warkannan was amused to realize that even after ten years, they each remembered the exact number of their wins and losses, a hundred thirty to a hundred twenty-eight, with Jezro in the lead. On the border all the officers had played for money, and the side betting had grown fierce, but considering the circumstances, they decided that this time, the winning itself would be enough of a reward.

'I'll never play with Benu – I mean, Hassan again, though,' Jezro said. 'It was humiliating how fast he beat me, and every damn time, too.'

'It's not like you were his only victim,' Warkannan said. 'Did he ever lose a game to anyone?'

'Not that I ever saw. He must have won enough to double his salary. Well, now we know why, don't we? It's that memory of his. Between turns he could probably refer to every book he'd ever read about the game.' Jezro paused, laughing. 'And I'm going to give him hell about that, too, if I ever see him again, anyway. An officer and a gentleman, cheating at chess!'

'Well, you could make a case that way, but it's not like he could help it.'

'True. It's a funny thing, memory. I haven't thought about those games for years, but seeing the pair of you again has brought it all back. I keep remembering Haz Kazrak, too, and how much I used to love it.'

'I don't see why you're surprised. It's your home.'

Jezro started to speak, then hesitated, his eyes abruptly sad. 'Yes,' he said at last. 'Home. A powerful little word, home.'

Warkannan waited, smiling.

'Damn you, Idres,' Jezro said. 'Let's play. You can take white, just out of the goodness of my heart.'

They played chess all that evening by the dim glow of the light-wand. The next morning, when sunlight came through the windows, they laid the stick in one patch of light to recharge and continued playing near the other. The difficulty of moving one rushi piece without brushing others off the board was irritating, but nowhere near as irritating as sitting around trying to speak in whispers. Twice the lavender female appeared with food, some of which they simply could not eat because of the grease and the foul taste. The guards at the windows, however, were glad to take it off their hands.

The patches of light moved across the glittering floor and eventually disappeared. They sprawled on the floor at either side of their game board like children, talked little, and studied every move. Warkannan was considering castling when the floor suddenly lurched, fluttering the rushi pieces on the board.

'Shaitan!' Jezro muttered. 'A quake!'

They managed to get to their knees, but by then the building was swaying too hard for them to stand. The walls groaned like a drunken cavalryman about to vomit. Warkannan mentally counted the seconds; at forty-one, the noise stopped, the sway turned to a tremble, and slowly, all too slowly, the building and the earth settled down.

'The horses!' Warkannan clambered to his feet and ran for the window.

Jezro followed, swearing under his breath. The guards had run off, but Warkannan could only get his head and one shoulder out of the narrow unglazed window. Jezro did the same at the other. They could see a long stretch of purple grass and the distant hills, but no sign of horse or ChaMeech. Jezro pulled his head back inside and trotted over to the front door. He pushed it, pulled it, slammed against it with his shoulder, but it stayed shut.

'Try talking to it,' Warkannan said.

'Right you are.' Jezro cleared his throat and spoke in Vranz several different words, pausing between each, then tried Hirl-Onglay. 'Open. Slide back. Open up. Exit.'

Nothing happened.

'So much for that,' Jezro said. 'It must respond to some command in ChaMeech. But then how come we never hear Miss Lavender opening it?'

'She keeps her voice pitched too low for our hearing,' Warkannan said. 'I was hoping it would work in more than one language.'

'Damn!' Jezro returned to his window. 'Here they come, anyway.'

The four ChaMeech guards were loping across the grass, leading the trotting horses back to pasture. The little female came hurrying around the corner of the building, then stopped to boom at them. From the way she raised her head up high and waved her pseudo-hands, Warkannan could tell that she was furious. The guards stopped and lowered their heads almost to the ground. Finally she ended her harangue and took over the horses. Warkannan hung part-way out the window and watched her tethering them until one of the guards trotted up, shaking his spear, and chased him back inside. Jezro was already sitting down by the chessboard.

'Well, that was a nice break in the routine,' Jezro said. 'What next? Another game? You do know you were going to win that last one, don't you?'

'I had hopes that way, yes.' With a sigh Warkannan joined him. 'I wonder when they're going to take us out of here?'

Jezro turned his hands palm up. 'Inshallah.'

The sorrel gelding seemed resigned to its fate, this time, and gave Zayn no trouble as the carts trundled and clacked through the tunnels. He could give his full attention to thwarting his memory. If he studied both the territory and the ChaMeech – or the Chof, as he reminded himself – and memorized every detail he learned, then perhaps his accursed mind would be too busy in the present to keep taking him back to the past. He forced himself to memorize the shape of the carts, to organize his muddled information about the tunnels. Since he'd ridden back west after leaving the khan and Warkannan, he was retracing part of the route they'd all taken, but now he could notice details that had escaped him when panic had filled his mind.

At times they passed the mouths of what seemed to be cross-tunnels, though in the darkness he couldn't even estimate how far they ran. He kept track of the air quality and noticed that it freshened considerably whenever they approached one of these openings. At other times they passed Vransic messages, moulded directly into the flexstone. None of them made much sense, and they might have been construction marks. They took the general form of a letter followed by a number or some directional word, such as 'A27 Up', nothing evocative, but he memorized them as possible clues to a general plan.

Soon, though, the tunnels stopped holding his interest. He wished he could hear what the Chof were saying; he would have liked to have learned their language, assuming of course that his throat and mouth could make the full set of their sounds. Now and then the males called out in a high enough register for him to hear their thrumming, which seemed to be patterned like speech. Maybe they were relaying messages to other Chof farther up the line, or perhaps warning Water Woman's rivals to stay away. At other times, he could see their throat sacs inflate, then empty in puffs and bursts that seemed to measure out words and phrases.

Water Woman confirmed Zayn's guess when they stopped at sunset to rest and eat. They climbed out of the tunnel to find themselves back beside the N'Dosha road. Not far away a pair of pillars gleamed in the red-stained light.

'I've been here before,' Zayn told Ammadin. 'This is where Warkannan got his bright idea, and I played sick.'

Before Ammadin could answer, Water Woman came hurrying up, waving her pseudo-arms in excitement. When she first began to speak, Zayn could barely hear her, but she glanced his way and saw his confusion.

'I speak-now in high voice,' Water Woman did so. 'You hear not hear, Zayn?'

'I can hear you, yes,' Zayn said. 'Thank you.'

'Friends tell-now me that Great Mother come-soon-next to meet us. We have need-not travel in hills. She bring-now her spear males, her servants, her people all of them, they come-soon to curse-stone station.'

'Where's that?' Ammadin said.

'At end of secret road tunnels. Where Zayn friends be-now.' Water Woman glanced Zayn's way. 'So, you see-soon them. See-tomorrow most likely.'

'Good,' Zayn said. 'How do you say thank you in your own language? Could I learn how?'

'I see-not why not. Watch.'

Water Woman lowered her head and swung her pseudo-arms behind her. At the same time, she let out a hissing sound. When Zayn imitated her, she stamped a forefoot.

'Very good,' she said. 'We make-soon you into real Chur.'

'Well, I'd really like to learn your language, but I don't think I can. I can't hear any of your men.'

'Ah. You be-not a witchman.'

'No, I'm a Recaller.' The moment he spoke Zayn wondered why he'd used the word, but Water Woman seemed to understand.

'Very good,' she said. 'We find you Chiri Van or Chur An, because you have power to hear a squeaky young voice, and you learn-soon.'

In that moment Zayn realized two disparate things. The Chof language was heavily gendered; and he was no longer afraid. He also realized that while other men would consider the lack of fear the more important of the two, to him they held equal weight.

Just at sunset, the little lavender female brought Warkannan and Jezro greasy rounds of cracker bread and chunks of fatty meat on sticks. They picked at the meat for a few minutes, then handed it through the window to the grateful guards. Wiping their hands on their trousers, they came back to their chess game and sat down.

'I get the general impression,' Jezro said, 'that the ChaMeech fry everything in old grease.'

'At least it wasn't raw,' Warkannan said. 'And there's the bread. They must have learned how to grow wheatian from the settlers out here.'

'Sounds likely, yes. Hmm, I wonder if we'll end up deep fried or just tossed with a little oil in a shallow pan?'

'You've learned too much about cooking lately, haven't you?'

'Living in the Cantons will do that to you. We might as well get back to playing chess. Only the Lord knows what recipe will mark our passing.'

They were just finishing the second game when they heard some sort of commotion beyond the door.

'Sounds like our gracious hosts,' Jezro remarked. 'Let's see what's up. Maybe the banquet guests have arrived.'

'I wish you'd stop talking about cannibalism,' Warkannan said.

'It isn't cannibalism. They're a different species. So if they eat us, at least they won't be breaking any moral laws.'

'How very reassuring.'

'I thought moral questions mattered to you.'

'Not when they concern what someone's going to do with my corpse.'

From the windows they saw the lavender female standing in the midst of some twenty armed males, who were also carrying an assortment of sacks and bundles tied to their wide backs. The female, unburdened, was leading the horses. Warkannan watched her throat inflate and her lips move; sure enough, the door slid open.

'Out,' she said. 'Ride.' She pointed to their scatter of gear on the floor. 'Bring.'

By the time they got everything into their saddlebags and bedrolls, and their horses saddled and bridled, the sun hung low in the sky. Warkannan took one last look around their temporary quarters and noticed a piece of rushi lying in a corner.

'Leave it,' Jezro whispered in Kazraki.

Warkannan could guess that it would indicate their presence, should anyone come looking for them. 'Very well, young lady. We're ready.'

'Good,' the ChaMeech said. 'Ride.'

'Where are we going?' Jezro said. 'If you don't mind telling us, of course.'

She stamped a foot in amusement. 'Lastunnabrilchiri next.'

'Is that a place?'

'No. It be her, big power woman. I be-only messenger.'

'A power woman? You mean a leader of some sort?'

She turned away without answering and pointed to the horses.

They mounted up and rode out at a walk, surrounded by ChaMeech warriors, spears at the ready. With their long shadows leading the way, they headed east, but once they reached the cliffs, the lavender female turned north. She raised her pseudo-arms and boomed a signal to the males, who turned to follow, menacing the two H'mai with their spears to ensure they did the same.

The level ground of the valley gave way to a trail that threaded its way through tan boulders and broken, rust-coloured pillars, tumbled this way and that on the ground. Some long time past they must have eroded free of the cliff and fallen, most likely in an earthquake. Above them loomed the cliffs, gashed with fissures and pitted with caves, the slits and punctures so black with shadows in the sunset light that they looked like writing in some alien script. Along the rim stood tall striped pillars and piles of rock, carved by wind and water until they looked like sentries turned to stone by evil magic.

Up close Warkannan could at last grasp the scale of the hills. They stood a good thousand feet at the high points and stretched north and south as far as he could see. It was going to be impossible to take the horses up their jagged sides. He considered trying to tell this to the female, but she strode along fast and steadily at the head of the line.

Night had fallen by the time she turned east again, leading her men into a long narrow cul-de-sac between two slab-sided cliffs. Once the last ChaMeech had entered, she thrummed for the halt. Everyone rested while she rummaged through a pair of sacks tied to a male's back and brought out lightwands, two for her, one for Jezro. By their light Warkannan could see their destination, a series of broad switchbacks much like the ones in the Rift, cut deep into the living rock.

Ahead, Jezro turned in the saddle to call back to him. 'This road has to be Settlers' work.'

'Oh, definitely,' Warkannan said. 'I just hope it's in better shape than the cliffs are.'

Riding at night on a road that hugs a steep cliff is not the most pleasant of experiences, even with lightwands for guidance. Jezro, riding directly ahead of Warkannan, let his dangle from his hand, pointing down to illuminate the trail on a setting low enough to avoid blinding those coming after. At the front of the line, the little female turned the pair she carried to high. She tended to keep hers aimed uselessly at the cliff face above, except for the times when she'd turn and send the beams straight back. No doubt she was making sure that her hostages hadn't escaped, but by blinding everyone she very nearly killed the pair of them and some of her men as well. Every time, the males would boom at a high pitch, and Jezro would yell and swear, but she paid attention to none of them, apparently, since in another few minutes she'd do it again.

Just as the galaxy was rising, they reached a cave mouth, such a perfect half-circle that only Settler tools could have cut it out of the living rock. With the wave of one pseudo-arm and a chirp of 'careful, careful!' the female navigated a tricky corner and led her expedition inside. They found themselves in a domed room whose walls and floor were as smooth and level as those underground but constructed of a pale grey substance that lacked the slickness of flexstone. On the opposite side, a tunnel ran into the cliff farther than the light from the wands could follow. Near the entrance, arcs of grey metal loomed, far taller than a ChaMeech, and beside them on the ground lay huge gears, half-covered with dirt but still in places gleaming white.

By then the horses were tiring, but when Jezro called to the little female, she ignored him. By shouting and swearing loudly enough Jezro and Warkannan did manage to stop the males behind them. The pause allowed them to dismount and sling their saddlebags over their own shoulders to spare the horses their weight. Up ahead the little female suddenly thrummed in alarm. The males behind them gestured with their spears, and the two H'mai started walking, leading their horses and hurrying to catch up. In only a few yards the khan began limping badly, despite his walking stick.

'Jezro!' Warkannan called. 'Let me take those saddlebags for you.'

'No. You're as tired as I am.'

Stubborn bastard! Warkannan thought. Arguing would be useless, but he could feel rather than hear one of the males behind him booming. He must have been speaking to the female about Jezro's bad leg, because she called a halt, then came trotting back along the line, swinging her lightwands into everyone's cursing faces. She considered Jezro for a moment, then filled her throat sac and – as far as Warkannan could tell – began giving orders. One of the males first haunched, then bent his front legs and knelt.

'Sit,' the female said, pointing to the khan. 'Ride.'

'Daccor,' Jezro said. 'I'm tired enough to take you up on that.'

Jezro handed Warkannan the reins of his horse, then studied the ChaMeech's ample back. Once he found some sort of seat among the sacks and bundles, the male lumbered to his feet, and their strange caravan travelled on. The tunnel was leading them north-east, as closely as Warkannan could reckon, but he soon lost track of distances. He only knew that he was stumbling weary from walking on rock and determined not to show it.

After some hours the view ahead brightened. Dawn was breaking, and the tunnel suddenly debouched onto a long slope down. Loose gravel marked a path, but to either side maroon shrubs and brushy red grasses covered the hill. As the light turned silver, Warkannan could see what lay at the bottom of the gentle slope. A vast uneven plateau stretched north and south beyond the limits of his sight. To the east, however, the mesa seemed to drop away after a few miles. Beyond, at the eastern horizon, mountains rose, capped with white, shadowy in the dawn haze.

Up at the head of the line, the lavender female waved, pointed, and called back. 'Not long now! Water here soon.'

They made their way down the gravelled slope to the flat, where scrub plants gave way to lush purple grass on a plain dotted with boulders and broken rock. Water gleamed in a precisely straight canal, running west to east across the plateau. At first Warkannan thought the water filthy and spoiled, because it appeared black; then he realized that the canal had been lined with aggregate, pebbles bound together by some black material. After everyone had drunk their fill, the lavender female trotted up to them.

'See.' She pointed straight east. 'Village. We go-now.'

About half a mile away stood irregular domes of grey and reddish brown. From his distance Warkannan thought them boulders, but as they came closer, he realized that they were structures made out of sticks, rushes, and vines, about twenty of them arranged in a rough circle.

Once they reached the village, Warkannan could get a good look at them. They were about forty feet in diameter, roughly so thanks to their irregular shapes. The builders had stuffed the cracks between their various components with leaves and dead grass, which hung loose by the handful where they weren't plastered over with a strange greyish substance – either paint or mud, Warkannan wasn't sure which. As they passed the domes, heading for another canal, other ChaMeech came hurrying out to take a look at them. Their throat sacs pulsed, and their lips moved in seeming silence – everyone's talking at once, Warkannan thought. We're the latest nine days' wonder around here.

Yet no one followed them as they left the village behind. Down near the canal stood one last dome, about half the size of those in the village. When they reached it, the female called for the halt. She walked back to Warkannan and Jezro, then pointed at the door.

'Home,' she said. 'Rest now.'

Warkannan and Jezro unloaded their horses. The female refused to let them take the horses to water or tether them out, but with gestures she let them know that she'd do both. Two of the males came forward with spears and herded them into the doorway.

'Oh God!' Jezro muttered. 'The stink in here!'

Warkannan nodded; he was too close to choking to speak. The air smelled of mildew and mould, spoiled food, rancid grease, and urine. The only flooring was soft dirt, scattered with things that he decided not to identify. The faintness of the light coming through narrow slits of windows made them easier to ignore. As they stepped inside, their feet sank into the floor.

'This is no way to treat prisoners,' Jezro said. 'This is a bad place.'

'Bad?' the female said.

'It stinks. Smells bad. Disgusting.'

'Ah. I see-now. You want make own marks. All right to do that.'

'No!' Jezro snapped. 'I do not want to add my own piss to the ground. I want a place that doesn't stink at all.'

'None. Inside.' She waved a pseudo-hand, and the males stepped forward, brandishing spears.

Fortunately the worst stink hung like a curtain right inside the door. By going all the way across to a rank of window-slits, they found breathable air and bare ground that seemed clean enough to lay their gear upon. With a weary sigh Jezro sat down on his saddle.

'I am sorely tempted,' the khan said, 'to do as the male

ChaMeech do here in their lovely accommodations. Pissing all over the door just seems polite, somehow.'

'Go ahead,' Warkannan said, grinning. 'You're the commanding officer, so it's your job.'

Jezro made an obscene gesture in his direction.

'Well,' Warkannan said, 'we'll have to make some provision for a latrine. Dig one, I guess.'

'Hah! Since I'm in command, that's your job, soldier! I just hope that Hassan makes it back to civilization safely, and that he gets his narrow arse back out here fast. Along with a couple of cavalry companies, preferably.'

By standing on his toes Warkannan could see out of the window. Beyond the hut lay a field of purple grass that stretched to a stand of trees, apparently planted by design, as each maroon trunk stood at the same distance from its neighbours. Beyond them a broad canal ran dead straight from the north to the south. As he watched, a pair of ChaMeech males, wearing dirty yellow kilts and armed with spears, walked into his field of vision, turned to face the hut, and haunched.

'Guards,' Warkannan said. 'I don't think we'll be able to escape.'

'I figured that,' Jezro said. 'Well, at least we can talk at a normal level in here.'

'True. We can start planning our strategy.'

'Strategy?'

'For the civil war. The one we're going to fight once we get back home.'

'Like a shen with a bone, that's you.' Jezro shook his head in mock despair. 'But before you start in on me, let's get some sleep. Last night was just a little too eventful for my tastes.'

Warkannan and Jezro had just reached their new prison when Zayn arrived at the old. After he brought the horses up to the surface, he paused and let the red hills catch his gaze. He and Ammadin stood staring at the tip-tilted layers of stone, the arches, the caves, the vast cliff faces rising among the sculpted pillars and lacy columns to their strangely flat crests. Loy led her horse up to join them, then pointed at the hills.

'They're called traps,' Loy said. 'The N'Dosha Traps.'

'I've never seen hills like that,' Zayn said.

'They're not exactly hills, is why. A long time ago this region was flooded with lava, and as it cooled, the flood cracked into chunks. Wind and water have done the rest. The Settlers left us their analysis of the terrain, which is how I know.'

'A volcano, you mean?' Ammadin put in.

'Not exactly. The explosion was supposed to have been so violent that it never formed a mountain, just some enormous crack or crater in the ground. The pale reddish stone is something called tufa, and those black streaks are basalt. They've formed layers because there was more than one eruption. But the last one was something like thirty million years ago.'

'In that case,' Zayn said, 'I won't worry about another one. I'm going to take a look around and see if I can find out what happened to the khan and Idres.'

The trampled grass, beaten down to bare soil in places, told him that until recently a fairly large number of sapients had camped outside the white building, along with two horses, who had left reasonably fresh evidence behind them. He found as well tracks heading east, Chof feet and the occasional hoofprint, indicating that Chof guards had walked before and behind the two horses. Ammadin followed him when he jogged over to the white cube of a building. He leaned into a window and looked through the shadows inside.

'The place is empty,' Zayn said. 'I can see a piece of rushi in the corner, though. I wonder if they left us a note?'

'It's worth checking.'

At the closed door Ammadin said one word in Tekspeak – it sounded enough like Hirl-Onglay that Zayn could guess that she was saying 'open', especially when the door slid back into a channel in the wall. Zayn hurried in, retrieved the rushi, and trotted back out again.

'Jezro's handwriting, all right,' he told Ammadin. 'They were here until last night.' He read on further, then laughed aloud before he could stop himself.

'What?' Ammadin said.

'Sorry. It says, "All right, Hassan, I want my money back. I've been thinking about all those bets you won. What did you do? Have every book on chess ever written crammed into your damned memory?"' Zayn glanced at Ammadin. 'We used to bet on chess, you see, back in the officers' common room, and I always won. Jezro's right, of course. I did memorize books, and I could remember every move my opponents had made in other matches, too, so I could predict how they were likely to move.'

Ammadin was looking at him as if she thought he'd gone mad.

'Well,' Zayn went on, 'no one but Jezro could have written this, except maybe Idres, but either way, it has to be genuine.'

'All right, fine. But this chess – it's some kind of a game?'

'Yes. I'm sorry. I forgot you wouldn't know.'

Near the entrance to the tunnel system, Water Woman stood talking with Loy and the male, a large fellow, so dark a grey that at times he seemed ebony-black, who led the spear servants. The two Chof were waving their pseudo-hands and booming at one another while Loy mostly listened. Eventually Loy left them with a shake of her head and joined the other two H'mai.

'Could you understand any of that?' Ammadin said.

'No, but Water Woman translated now and then. Stronghunter Man – he's the leader of the Chur – wants to march over the hills and burn down Herbgather Woman's village. I guess it's not all that far away, and he suspects that the hostages have been taken there.'

'Who's winning?' Zayn said.

'Water Woman, of course. She's allowing Stronghunter Man to argue for the sake of his morale, but he'll follow her orders. He has to. She's true Chiri Michi, and he pledged his loyalty to her.'

'Is Stronghunter Man a Chur Vocho?' Zayn said.

'He must be,' Loy said. 'He's obviously her second in command.'

Once she'd won the argument, Water Woman rounded up H'mai and Chof alike. She appeared to be looking for some particular quality in a campsite, because she led her entire retinue to the white building, glanced in, led them away again, walked round the grassy field in front of it, then set out back west. Some hundred yards away she found a stream, thrummed once, and sat down, haunching.

'Loy Sorcerer, Ammadin Witchwoman, Zayn Recaller,' she called out. 'Come sit with me. My servants bring-next your horses to water.'

Stronghunter Man himself took their horses, unsaddled the riding mounts, unloaded the pack horse, then led them behind the white building, where a stream ran. Zayn was impressed with how easily he managed the buckles despite having only two fingers and two thumbs to work with. The other males and the grey servants made camp by unloading their assorted bags and packs and strewing them across the grass.

'I bc sorry, Zayn,' Water Woman said. 'I hope-then your friends, they be-now here, but Herbgather Woman take-then them somewhere, maybe her village maybe not.'

'She was probably afraid we'd rescue them by force.'

'Yes, that be true. Stronghunter Man say-just-then the same thing. There be more of us, we have better weapons, especially Loy Sorcerer. That gun be the kind of weapon Herbgather Woman want us to get from Sibyl, but Sibyl say-over-and-over that she have no weapons to give anyone.'

'Those guns would defend you against the Kazraks, all right,' Zayn said. 'Our cavalry couldn't stand against them.'

'No, no, no, not for Karshaks. Herbgather Woman fear Karshaks, yes, we all fear Karshaks, but she want-not weapons for killing them.'

'What?' Loy broke in. 'Then what does she want them for?'

'Birds. I tell-not you? I be sorry. Everything be awful, all this argue argue argue! I have-not power to think clearly. But she want-now to kill all the birds, because she think that then more of our children be safe, the children who come up on shores where we be-not, that is. If they live to cross the beaches, maybe they find us. This be what she say, anyway.'

'Oh good god!' Loy rolled her eyes heavenward. 'She wants to kill every bird on this land mass?'

'No, not every bird, just kri altri. They be the kind of bird who eat our children.'

'And you don't want to kill them?'

'I be torn. I want-always the children to be safe. But if our men, they get-soon those guns, who be safe then? They argue, they use guns on each other. Evil evil thing. Bad enough they fight-all-time with spears. And then, I think, the birds, they have the right to live. They eat many nasty things, like poison squeakers that attack-sometimes Chof. I want-not destroy all of them. If the coasts be-still-now ours, we have power to defend the children, we need-not guns. Our men wave spears, kill maybe one or two birds, and the rest stay-then up high and kill-not our children.'

'But you don't have the coasts,' Ammadin said.

'No, we have not the coasts. So, Herbgather Woman speak-then about killing birds, but I wonder-then and I wonder-now, too. If her men they get those guns, what they do-next? My men, they have-not guns. She talk-always of children. All Chof, both Chur and Chiri, talk-always of children. We do-must this, do-must that, all for the children. But we talk-sometimes of children and do-next things for another reason. You see?'

'Oh yes,' Loy said. 'My people have been known to use exactly the same tactic.'

'So, Herbgather Woman claim they smash-already all the eggs they find, but kri altri, they make-always their nests up high in rocks, where Chof go-not easily. How many she smash-really, I wonder?' Water Woman lowered her head and looked round the circle of H'mai, inviting comment.

'Those aren't the birds we call cranes, are they?' Zayn said. 'The grey birds who fish in the Mistlands?'

'No, those be kri ashkamik.'

'Good. Cranes are my spirit animal.'

Ammadin suddenly laughed. 'You really are a comnee man now, aren't you?'

Zayn started to make some joke, then remembered that he'd broken Bane. He forced out a smile and paid strict attention to the conversation around him.

'I don't understand,' Loy was saying. 'If Sibyl really doesn't have any guns, then why not take Herbgather Woman there and let her see for herself?'

Water Woman's throat sac swelled and turned not gold but a pale grey. She made a small rumbling sound, looked at the ground, then at the sky, rumbled again.

'Something else is going on, isn't it?' Loy, ruthless, continued. 'You don't want her to have access to Sibyl.'

Water Woman deflated her throat sac with a long, sad-sounding hiss. 'You be too smart, Loy Sorcerer,' she said at last. 'Our Great Mother, she be-now old. I want to be the next Great Mother. Herbgather Woman want-also this. We both try-now get supporters for later.'

'And knowing Sibyl gives you prestige and more support?'

Water Woman caught the edge of her red scarf twixt thumb and forefinger and twisted the cloth back and forth. The blue spiral pin caught the light and shimmered. 'Yes,' she said at last. 'This be the other reason Herbgather Woman take hostages. I owe-now you apology, Zayn Recaller. I think-never she take anyone hostage, whether that be your friends or someone else. She be a violent woman. She want-now kill all birds, she steal people on roads, she make a very bad Great Mother.'

'It sounds like it,' Loy said. 'Can't you convince the other Chof of that without using your friendship with Sibyl?'

'Maybe so, maybe not.' Water Woman let go the scarf. 'There be-also the question of magic things. Sibyl want-not to give them to anyone who ask.'

'Meaning, you get to dole them out and get more support that way?'

Water Woman raised her massive head up high and rumbled, loudly this time. Petite Loy scrambled up to stand on tip-toe and rumble right back. All at once Water Woman stamped a forefoot and lowered her head; Loy laughed pleasantly and sat back down.

'Much too smart,' Water Woman said.

'No, just reasoning from past experience,' Loy said. 'We have something called elections in the Cantons.'

'But Herbgather Woman, she dig-always for things to trade. She make-always her servants dig, too. She get-often many things in Shairb, but she give none away, give-not even to her servants, they who dig with her. She keep everything for herself. This be-not the Chof way. We true Chiri Michi, when we get treasures or trade goods, we give most of them away. If we give-not, the true Chur, they have-never anything to give to their followers, our spear servants.'

'Do you think she's saving them up?'

'Till the Great Mother die, yes.'

'While you distribute gifts to your followers now.'

'It pay to be prudent. Though I pray-always to all our gods that our beloved Great Mother live a long long life, of course.'

'Of course,' Loy said. 'I think I'm beginning to understand a number of things now.'

Events were beginning to make sense for Zayn as well. The mayor in Shairb must have had some business arrangement with Herbgather Woman, profitable enough for him to help her with her long-term politicking. When an important possible hostage like Jezro Khan had ridden his way, the mayor had notified her somehow. Some of her supporters must have been waiting nearby for just such a chance.

'Zayn Recaller,' Water Woman said. 'You be be-not angry with me?'

'No, I'm not,' Zayn said. 'You had no way of knowing what was going to happen.'

'I thank you.'

Zayn, of course, could never admit the real reason he was so forgiving. If he hadn't broken Bane and tipped Soutan off, Jezro Khan would never have ridden near Shairb. Ammadin gave him a sharp look and laid a hand on his arm.

'What's wrong?' she said.

'I was just thinking about Soutan.'

His statement was close enough to the truth that she accepted it. 'We can't forget him, no,' Ammadin said. 'From what you told me, he's crazy enough to be really dangerous, and he might be close by. I can't find him in my crystals.'

'Your crystals,' Water Woman said. 'They be dead not dead?'

'Not,' Ammadin said. 'But Soutan can use his crystals to hide himself. He does something that interferes with the images. It's a command called "Hide Me".'

'I know-not this before. So! I think-long-time he hide in the secret roads, but I see-now he know something I know-not. I ask-soon Sibyl to kill his crystals. Then we all have power to see him.'

'Can she do that?' Loy said. 'Kill a crystal, I mean?'

'Yes. Sibyl have power to do many things none of us have power to do. She tell-once me that she talk to the Deathbringers, or the Riders like Ammadin call them. The Riders give orders to the crystals, she say-then. Sibyl call-then the orders settings.'

'Settings?' Loy said. 'Do they control how far a crystal can see or hear?'

'Just that. Sibyl say-then that the Riders control all crystals, make them strong or weak, and decide what they have power to do.'

'Well, I'll be damned! That answers a big question. Now where did I put my notebooks?'

'You write, Loy Sorcerer. I get-now my servants to hunt, and we all share-soon lots of food.'

Water Woman followed through on her promise about the crystals. When in late afternoon the Riders returned to the sky, Ammadin took Zayn with her and walked some way away from the noisy camp. They found a copse of strangely twisted trees, whose dark maroon trunks curled around themselves like a piece of clothing wrung out in strong hands. Instead of leaves, scarlet needles bristled from every branch, thick or fine, and at the branch tips hung yellow domes. When Zayn touched a dome, it shattered and released a cloud of spores. He sneezed and wiped his nose on his sleeve.

'What are these things?' Zayn said.

'I don't know. Do they smell bad or poisonous?'

'No, just itchy. Can't you smell them?'

'It's being surrounded by all the Chof. I can't smell anything else.'

Zayn's expression froze on the edge of a smile.

'Damn you,' Ammadin said. 'I can guess why you're smirking like that.'

'Smirking? Who's smirking?'

'Oh shut up and let me scan.'

With Zayn standing nearby on guard, Ammadin brought out her crystals and activated Spirit Eyes. She began moving the crystal's focal point, spiralling out from their camp to hunt for Soutan. The spiral grew wider and wider; she was expecting to hear the angry chirp that marked the limit of the crystal's range, but it never came. Finally, on the western edge of the traps, Ammadin found her prey and realized that indeed, Sibyl had overridden Soutan's crystals.

She could see Soutan crouched in the high grass, studying crystals of his own, his face bright red, his eyes narrow and his mouth twisted with rage. Some yards away, Arkazo was leading two of their horses to drink at a stream. Something about the boy's appearance struck Ammadin as odd. She focused Spirit Eyes down to study him and realized that he seemed half-asleep, moving slowly, glancing languidly around him with half-closed eyes. At the open throat of his shirt, the imp glittered on its golden chain. Out in the grass something moved – a Chof warrior got to his feet, stretching his pseudo-arms and both pairs of legs. Others joined him, six Chur in all.

Where, exactly, was Soutan and how far away? Ammadin moved the focus point of the crystals south, keeping to the west side of the hills, until she saw her own camp, the white flexstone building, Loy sitting on the ground and writing in a notebook, Water Woman haranguing her servants.

'He's north and no more than ten miles away,' she said to Zayn. 'Arkazo looks like he's either exhausted or ill.'

'He's probably both,' Zayn said. 'You know, if Water Woman agrees, I could just take some of her men and go after Soutan tonight.'

'It's not that simple. Soutan's got his own Chof with him, six of them. Water Woman's made it very clear that she doesn't want any bloodshed.'

'She may have to change her mind.'

'Maybe, yes, if things get bad enough. But what about Arkazo? Do you want to risk him dying in a night fight?'

Zayn winced. 'That would break Idres' heart.'

'Arkazo must mean a lot to him.'

'Well, his sister's husband has two older sons by his first wife, and they get all his attention. Idres has pretty much been the only father Arkazo's had.'

'His sister's a second wife? I thought you said Warkannan came from a powerful family.'

'He does. But unfortunately Kaz inherited that nose from his mother.' Zayn smiled as if he'd made some point.

'So?' Ammadin said.

'She's not pretty, just the opposite, not that I'd dare say that around Idres.'

'What does that have to do with her family?'

'It means they couldn't make her a better marriage.'

Ammadin rolled her eyes in disgust, then got back to work. She swept the scanning focus back to Soutan, then brought out Long Voice and locked it onto Soutan's image. At first she heard nothing except the occasional burst of Vransic profanity, but when Arkazo returned, Soutan had more of interest to say.

It's that witchwoman. She's killed my crystals again, and I don't have the slightest idea how she could have done it.

Oh? Arkazo said. *Does it really matter? We've got the slate, and if we get to Sibyl first, we can get new ones.*

That's very true. I'm not going to use it now, though, with the Phalanx up, just in case she's watching us. If you are, bitch, I hope you choke to death on rancid saur jerky!

Ammadin burst out laughing; she was still smiling as she set the crystals out to recharge.

'What's so funny?' Zayn said.

'Soutan. He's blaming me for the death of his crystals, and he figured out I might be watching him, so he threw a few insults my way – really childish insults. He's furious, which is all to the good.'

'You bet. Angry men make mistakes.' Zayn knelt down in front of her. 'You know, I keep thinking about tonight. Do you think anyone else is going to want to sleep inside that building?'

'Probably not, because there's a latrine in there, and everyone will be tramping through to use it.'

'Damn!'

'We can just come back to these trees. The dark's as good as a tent.'

He caught her by the shoulders, pulled her close, and kissed her. In answer she twined her hands behind his neck and let him pull her close, but as he kissed her again, she could hear the Chof, booming and thrumming back in camp. She pulled away and stood, grabbing her saddlebags, just as Loy came running, calling their names.

'News,' Loy said. 'Several kinds, in fact. Did you realize that Sibyl's reset our crystals?'

'I knew something had changed,' Ammadin said. 'There doesn't seem to be any limit to my scanner's range.'

'Not on mine, either, and the sound pick-up is just as powerful. Water Woman helped me set up a relay, too.' Loy paused for a smile. 'I reached the Loremasters Guild, and I managed to talk with my daughter.'

'That's wonderful. How is Rozi?'

'Better. Not completely well, but better. The dreams are fading. She's eating more, not a lot yet, but more. She says to thank you for the bottle of oil.'

'I'm glad I could help. What was all that noise in camp?'

'Excitement. I'm not sure how Water Woman got the message, but the Great Mother's on her way here. She should reach us tomorrow, Water Woman says.'

'That's good, because Soutan knows where Sibyl is. He's talking about getting there ahead of us.'

'That butt-faced bastard! How could he?'

'He's got something Arkazo called a slate. I saw it once before when I was scanning back on the grass. It's flat and thin and grey.' Ammadin held up her hands to indicate its size. 'About so, and I saw blue lights dancing on it. Zayn, what did you call that mask thing again? The one Soutan was wearing?'

'A hologram.'

'That's it, yes,' Ammadin said. 'When I was using the crystals, I could see right through Soutan's mask, but it did show up as blue light, dancing around him. The light on the slate's surface looked the same.'

'I've never seen anything like that.' Loy paused, thinking. 'But I've read about it. The Settlers had a device called a recept-screen. It did something called accessing a cache and then displayed the information it found, and the display probably was hologrammatic.'

'Do you think those caches might hold maps?' Zayn said.

'It would be a logical choice, wouldn't it?'

'I suppose so,' Ammadin said. 'I've never used a map, so I wouldn't know.'

'Doesn't matter,' Loy said. 'We need to tell Water Woman about this. Not, I suppose, that she can do anything about it tonight. She made it clear that she absolutely has to wait for the Great Mother, Yarl or no Yarl.'

'Well, we can't go breaking their laws if we're going to get Zayn's friends back. Which reminds me. Loy, these imps – you said once there were a lot of different kinds.'

'Yes, there are. Oddly enough, I learned about them from Yarl. He did a lot of research on them at one time.'

'Arkazo's wearing one, and it can't be one like Zayn's. I had no trouble seeing him.'

'Huh.' Loy thought for a moment. 'Unless Sibyl can override imps, too. We don't know what she can or can't do.'

'Well, remember when I saw Arkazo a couple of days ago? Sibyl hadn't overridden anything then.'

'That's true. His imp must have a different function.'

'I don't suppose,' Ammadin went on, 'that there's an imp that can influence what a person thinks or feels.'

'Oh yes, several. The Settlers used one kind to keep prisoners from causing trouble, but I don't know how they worked, exactly. Yarl's paper on the subject said that they send out energy pulses or waves of some kind. The wearer's brain can sense them, and eventually the brain activity changes as it synchronizes to the pulse.'

Ammadin understood this explanation only in the most general way, but the general way sufficed. 'Arkazo's acting like he's half-asleep. Could an imp affect him that way?'

'Most likely, yes. They called that function "tranquillise".' Loy glanced away, scowling. 'It would be just like Yarl, too, to use a dirty trick to dominate someone who trusts him.'

After the evening meal, Loy noticed Ammadin and Zayn surreptitiously grabbing bedrolls and saddlebags. In the gauzy twilight they slipped away, heading off for a little privacy, Loy figured. Although she had long subscribed to the principle of 'to each their own', she still found Ammadin's taste in men appalling. Better her than me! With a shrug she got out her latest notebook.

Loy sat by the fire and wrote up the day's log while she kept an unobtrusive eye on the Chof. The two servant females wandered around, picking up bags and bundles, setting them down elsewhere, then picking some of them up later to move them again. Loy could see no pattern in what they were doing, but she was willing to bet there was one. With the exception of Stronghunter Man, the male Chof withdrew to the edges of the camp. As far as Loy could discern in the darkness, they were disposing themselves in a rough guard circle.

Stronghunter Man and Water Woman stood near the door of the white building and argued. While Loy could hear Water Woman's voice, the Chur Vocho's lay beyond the range of her hearing, but she could see his throat sac filling and pulsing. Water Woman began stretching her neck higher; he stretched his to match; she waved her hands; he leaned his spear against the wall and waved his. After some minutes he let out the series of high-pitched yips on a single note that meant surrender, but he never lowered his head or bent his neck. He grabbed his spear and, thrumming on a deeper note, stomped off into the darkness to join his subordinates. Water Woman came to the fire and haunched a few feet away from Loy.

'H'mai men,' Water Woman said, 'they be or be-not as stubborn as Chof men?'

'Every bit as stubborn,' Loy said. 'Does he still want to try rescuing the hostages?'

'No, he want-now to go and make a night raid on Yarl's camp. I say no. Zayn Recaller have-now a friend in that camp. We have-now six Chof men there, too. No deaths. No fighting. I want-next none none none.'

'I agree with you, for what it's worth. Things are too complicated already.'

For a few minutes they sat staring into the fire. Loy had a long list of questions that she was eager to ask, but she felt that grilling Water Woman about her people would be rude. One subject, however, logically seemed open to discussion.

'Now, when the Great Mother arrives, what exactly are the protocols?' Loy said. 'Do we all line up in front of her and just start arguing?'

'No.' Water Woman raised a forefoot and tapped it on the ground. 'We observe-first some courtesies. This time, we need-also decide what language we all use. Great Mother be the one who decide.'

'Do you mind if I make notes on the things you tell me?'

'Not mind. I make-always an effort to remember everything I learn about H'mai. It be the same thing, though I be no Recaller like Zayn.'

'Your people remember what a Recaller is, then.'

'We remember everything we have power to remember. We learn things as children and recite them over and over. Lost lore be a sad thing.'

'Very sad, yes. Our people have lost so much, over the years. A lot of our lore was stored in N'Dosha.'

'Most likely it be-still there.'

'I heard that the Chof burned the city.'

'Not true. You wait till you see N'Dosha. You see-soon that it be impossible to burn.' Water Woman put her pseudo-hands over her eyes, then lowered them and stamped a forefoot. 'And wait-also till you see Sibyl. She tell-soon you many interesting things.'

'Like what?'

'Wait. You see-soon. I give-not-away the surprise.'

Loy tried wheedling, but Water Woman only stamped a foot and repeated that she should wait. Finally Loy decided that she'd have to do just that and went to her blankets. As she was falling asleep, she heard the Chof booming and thrumming to each other, a comforting sort of sound, as they too settled down to sleep.

The Great Mother and her retinue had set up her justice court just a few miles away from the old Metro station. In the morning Water Woman appointed guards to stay behind in the camp, then led her dependants, H'mai and Chof both, to the appointed place.

The Great Mother was waiting beside a shallow lake, where the red-leaved Midas trees and pale yellow ferns grew thick around the water. A whole squad of servants and the usual heaps of bundles and sacks were sitting among the trees, but the Great Mother herself had taken up a position out in the open. She sat haunched in the middle of a huge expanse of green and white trade cloth, pegged down at intervals to keep it taut.

She was enormous, easily twice the size of Water Woman, and her skin had turned a rich blue with age. With age as well the cartilage that shaped her face had grown long and thick, so that she seemed to have a ridged beak extending beyond her lips. She wore a cloak of green cloth, falling in folds down her back, and an apron or long bib of sorts, an expanse of green fabric, fastened at the back of her neck with a huge silver brooch and pulled between her front legs to tuck into her skirt and cover her stomach. Behind her stood three long rows of spear Chur, kilted in green, and to either side stood grey females, each of whom wore a green skirt around her mid-section.

Off to her left sat another Chiri Michi, as large as Water Woman and the same rich purple colour. Herbgather Woman, Ammadin assumed, and the hissing sound Water Woman made when she saw her confirmed the assumption. Herbgather Woman wore yellow and white striped trade cloth, and her five spear males had yellow kilts. Water Woman arranged her retinue to the right of the Great Mother, herself in front, the H'mai behind and a bit to her right, and behind them her complement of twenty guards.

Ammadin had expected Zayn to keep close to her and Loy, but he stepped back to join the Chur. She was about to ask him why when the Great Mother filled her golden throat sac and boomed, such a low, strong note that Ammadin felt as if her entire body were vibrating in sympathy. Loy shuddered and whistled under her breath; she'd felt it too. Water Woman and her rival both stepped forward and boomed in answer.

'We be here,' the Great Mother said in Vranz. 'We listen-now to each other, and I decide-next what we do-soon.'

Both Chiri Michi lowered their heads to show that they agreed, then walked forward. When they stepped onto the striped cloth, they lowered their heads again, then took a few more steps to stand facing each other in her presence.

'We speak-now in the language of the H'mai,' the Great Mother went on, 'so they have power to understand what we say here.'

The Chiri Michi lowered their heads and agreed, but in actuality, the proceedings went forward in a strange mix of languages and gestures. The rival females tended to forget about the H'mai and lapse into their own language. At times Water Woman would remember and call for a pause, then hurriedly translate the portions they'd missed, but at others she seemed too angry or troubled to think of Ammadin and Loy. Every now and then the Great Mother would stop the proceedings and with her deep soothing voice summarize in Vranz.

To a large extent, Ammadin realized, Water Woman had been telling the truth. Herbgather Woman had indeed taken hostages because she wished to trade them for the location of Sibyl's cave. While they both referred to other Chiri Michi scattered throughout Chof territory, apparently Herbgather Woman and Water Woman were the only serious contenders for the role of next great mother. When she remembered to speak Vranz, Herbgather Woman sounded aggrieved, harping on the way she and her people had been excluded from Sibyl's bounty. She clearly saw herself as a victim of unfair tactics and tried to paint Water Woman as a miser and hoarder, words that made Water Woman stretch her neck to the sky and rumble like a winter storm.

'I be miser?' Water Woman snarled. 'You be the one who get trade goods and share-never. You keep your people in poverty.'

At this point the Great Mother spoke in their own language, but Ammadin could tell from the tone of voice, and the way that both complainants flinched, that she had said something sharp. Through the long arguments, the Great Mother barely moved. At times she seemed to be some natural object, a great outcropping of veined blue rock, rather than a sapient being, until some statement would make her swing her massive head around to look at one or another of the speakers. Each Chiri Michi had a long list of grievances to air, some dating from twenty years back. Finally, however, the Great Mother had heard enough complaining.

'Stop!' she said in Vranz. 'I want-now short answers. Herbgather Woman, what want-now you from Sibyl?'

'Guns, Great Mother, magic guns to kill kri altri and save our children.'

'We need-not guns for this. Spears frighten the kri altri.'

Water Woman could not contain herself. She stepped forward

with a swing of her head. 'She want to kill all the kri altri, Great Mother. She and her people, they smash the eggs when they find them.'

'I kill-only for our children, our lost children,' Herbgather Woman said, then lapsed back into her own language.

The debate continued on, breaking now and then into Vranz or Hirl-Onglay with no particular reason or stimulus. Ammadin eventually pieced together that the presence of Jezro Khan deep in Chof lands alarmed the Great Mother.

'You think to save us, Lastunnabrilchiri,' the Great Mother said, 'but you put-then us in worse danger when you steal-then this man on the road. He know-now too much about the Chof.'

'Then we kill-must him,' Herbgather Woman said, 'and all the H'mai who see-now us here.'

'Kill-never!' Water Woman turned on her rival and thrummed. 'I give-them my word, they be safe here. You try kill-now them, my spear servants have power to stop you.'

'You give-then *your* word. I give-never mine.'

Water Woman raised her head high and boomed so loudly that Ammadin's ears overloaded with sound and crackled. Beside her Loy clapped her hands over her own ears.

'Stop!' the Great Mother said. 'Stop-now!'

The Great Mother hissed long and hard first at Water Woman, then at Herbgather Woman. She spread her pseudo-arms, then lurched to her feet. Water Woman backed away fast, and Herbgather Woman lowered her head. For some minutes the Great Mother spoke; Ammadin could hear most of her words, though she could decipher none of them. Herbgather Woman lowered her head and whined an answer – a high-pitched wavering sort of sound, at any rate, that to Ammadin sounded like miserable pleading. The Great Mother grunted a few words, and Herbgather Woman knelt to lay her head directly onto the ground cloth. When the Great Mother placed one huge foot on Herbgather Woman's neck, the younger Chiri's whines grew louder still, and she slapped her pseudo-hands onto the cloth. With a grunt the Great Mother removed her foot.

'This looks promising,' Loy whispered.

Ammadin nodded her agreement. With a toss of her magnificent head, the Great Mother stepped back, and as she did so, her bib pulled free of her skirt and slipped to one side. Ammadin's first thought was that the Chiri Michi was carrying something under her body; then she realized that the something was flesh and blood, a tubular protrusion, bright blue, as long as a H'mai man's arm, that hung parallel to her stomach in a sling of dark blue skin. The servants rushed forward and tucked the errant bib back into the skirt as the Great Mother haunched.

'Ovipositor,' Loy whispered. 'And now we know why my dear ancestors thought Chursavva was male.'

Herbgather Woman stayed kneeling where the Great Mother had left her. Water Woman took the opportunity to step forward again, though she lowered her own head to show respect. For some minutes they talked back and forth in such level voices that Ammadin had no idea of the emotional tone of the conversation. At last, however, Water Woman turned and pointed at the H'mai.

'Ammadin Witchwoman,' Water Woman said. 'You come-now and tell-next what you know about Jezro Khan.'

'Very well,' Ammadin said. 'I'll be honoured to speak in front of the Great Mother.'

Ammadin adjusted her saurskin cloak to ensure it hung smoothly from her shoulders, then walked forward. At the edge of the green cloth she stopped and bowed, swinging her head low, then straightened up to stand in front of the enormous Chof. The Great Mother inclined her own head a few bare inches to acknowledge her presence.

'Ammadin Witchwoman!' She seemed to be pitching her voice as high as she could, but still it rumbled like thunder. 'I ask-now you to tell us always the truth. I want-not to hear lies in my justice court.'

'Great Mother.' Ammadin bowed again. 'I promise you that I will never lie to you. I'll tell you the truth as I know it.'

'Very good, and I thank you. Now. Water Woman say Jezro be a very important man among the Karshaks. This be true or not true?'

'True, very true. He's a khan, which means he's one of the sons of the Kazraks' last supreme ruler, their king, the Great Khan. His brother is Great Khan now, but he is a terrible ruler. He is cruel, and he steals from his people, then kills them if they object. You can see why they want Jezro to come home and replace him.'

'Yes. I see-indeed why they want to be rid of this brother,' the

Great Mother said. 'So, then, if Jezro die-next, these Karshaks gather an army and march-soon here?'

'They might. I can't lie and say that I know they will. But here's something to think about. If Jezro Khan returns home, he'll lead a rebellion against his brother. I've been told that he has a large army waiting for him. This means the Kazraks will be killing each other. If the war goes on for a long time, then they won't have the men or the will to cross the plains and come bothering you.'

Herbgather Woman lurched to her feet. 'We know-not if you lie not lie, Witchwoman.'

'That's true.' Ammadin turned to face her. 'It's too bad you didn't bring Jezro with you. He could tell you himself.'

Herbgather Woman inflated her throat sac and spoke one burst of words, but the Great Mother boomed and stopped her.

'Speak now so Ammadin Witchwoman has the power to understand you,' the Great Mother said.

'I obey,' Herbgather Woman said. 'I want-not bring Jezro here. Water Woman have-now many spear Chur with her. What if they start-next a fight and take my hostages away? I have-now only a few of my Chur with me.'

'Where be the rest?' the Great Mother said.

Herbgather Woman stared at the ground between them.

'They guard not guard your hostages?' the Great Mother went on. 'In or not in your village?'

Herbgather Woman lowered her head almost to the ground. 'They guard in the village.'

'So I think-then,' the Great Mother said.

Herbgather Woman haunched and stared at the ground. The Great Mother boomed out something in their own language that made Herbgather Woman bend her forelegs and kneel as well.

'I want-next to speak with Jezro Khan,' the Great Mother said. 'Lastunnabrilchiri, I come-next-soon to your village. You keep me out or let me in?'

Herbgather Woman lowered her head to the dirt and whined an answer so miserable that it was easy to understand without knowing a word of her language. No, Ammadin thought, you wouldn't dare keep her out, and you know it, don't you? When she glanced at Water Woman, she noticed that the Chiri Michi's front legs were quivering – she was evidently restraining herself from stamping her feet in joy.

'We all go-next-soon to Lastunnabrilchiri's village,' the Great Mother said. 'First we rest the night, each in her own camp. Dawn come, we all meet-next-again by this lake. We all go-soon to meet Jezro Khan. I hear-next-soon his answers; I decide-after what to do.'

During the long deliberations in front of the Great Mother, Zayn had stayed back among the Chur. Stronghunter Man had used gestures to indicate that Zayn should stand next to him, at the head of the contingent. Zayn didn't need to be told that this positioning meant he'd been given the status of a Chur Vocho. Stronghunter Man planted his spear, obsidian edge up, in front of him and kept his pseudo-hands wrapped around the haft. The other spear Chur followed his example. Zayn drew his long knife and held it one-handed, point down but ready. On the far side of the Great Mother's cloth, the spear Chur belonging to Herbgather Woman planted their spears as well.

While he watched, Zayn was storing every action, every gesture, every word of the scene in his memory. He was shocked at how little he'd understood the enemy he had fought on the border, how easy it had been to dismiss them as animals and little more – not that he felt any deep sympathy for them now or any guilt about the skirmishes he'd fought and the kills he'd made. He did, however, see a certain hope for negotiations, for discussions about territory taken or relinquished, that might replace the endless bloody game of raid and counter-raid.

Stronghunter Man watched without moving, braced on his spear, during all the long discussions, though occasionally he would shift his weight from back legs to front. Zayn began to envy him for having four legs. With just two he had to readjust his balance and take a step now and then, but the feel of possible danger was so strong that he never once considered sitting down. Sure enough, the moment came when he realized why they stood on guard.

'Then we kill-must him,' Herbgather Woman said, 'and all the H'mai who see-now us here.'

'Kill-never!' Water Woman turned on her rival and boomed.

At that Stronghunter Man swelled his throat sac and thrummed, a sound that Zayn felt rather than heard, a tremor like that of an earthquake. The Chur Vocho raised his spear and took one step forward. His men, Zayn among them, did the same. On the other side of the meeting Herbgather Woman's spear Chur thrummed and raised their spears, but they never moved. Zayn assumed that they could tally up five of them to the twenty on his side.

Before violence became more than a possibility, the Great Mother took charge, hissing the two rival Chiri Michi into silence. Stronghunter Man lowered his spear and took a step back; so did his men. Zayn realized that he was seeing in the Great Mother a person, a sapient, who understood how to rule. He had never thought it possible, never even thought that the ChaMeech, his hated ChaMeech, would have rulers and chains of command. He understood something else, as well, that his realizations, all this new information and insight, had made his long journey here, even the flogging back in Blosk, worthwhile.

At the end of the proceedings, Herbgather Woman rushed off as fast as she could gallop, and her spear Chur and servants fell into line behind her. At a more leisurely pace Water Woman gathered up her retinue and, with one last lowering of her head to the Great Mother, led them away. Zayn retrieved the three horses from the Chur servant who'd been guarding them and brought them over to Ammadin and Loy.

'Goddamn!' Loy said. 'This has been wonderful! I can't wait to get back to camp and my notebooks. I hope I don't forget anything.'

'Ask Zayn for help if you think you have,' Ammadin said.

'Oh, why not?' Zayn said. 'I might as well do what I was bred for, I guess.'

'They bother you, your talents?' Loy said. 'I mean, I know about the way you were treated when you were a child, and that would bother anyone. But the talents themselves –'

'Are something I never asked for and never had a chance to turn down. I don't like thinking I'm just some kind of gadget.'

'That's too bad. I'd give my left arm to have your memory.'

That someone might envy his talents shocked Zayn into silence.

As soon as they returned to their camp, Ammadin and Loy hurried away from the general confusion in order to scan. Zayn tended the horses, then joined them. They were sitting cross-legged on the ground near the twisted trees, each frowning into crystals, or passing them back and forth while they talked in low whispers. Finally Ammadin looked up and saw him.

'We've found Soutan, all right,' she said. 'He's on the eastern side of the traps.'

'And he's turned north,' Loy said. 'Just like he knows where he's going.'

Zayn braced himself for the logical next question: I wonder why he's out here? Fortunately for him, the two women returned to their crystals without voicing it. You've got to tell Ammi, he reminded himself. And yet a traitor thought sounded in his mind: why? Maybe she'll never have to know.

'How long have we been here?' Jezro said. 'Is it really only four days?'

'Yes,' Warkannan said. 'Feels like a lot longer.'

'Feels is the right word.' Jezro paused to scratch the back of his neck. 'As scabby as a shit-stained beggar, that's me. There's got to be some kind of parasite living in this dirt.'

'More than one kind, I'd say.'

Jezro groaned and slumped back against the rough woven wall of their prison. Through the window slits the afternoon sunlight streamed in, thick with dust, and fell upon their gear, thick with dirt. They'd been given enough water to drink but little more, and what extra they had went to keeping Jezro's handkerchiefs clean enough to use. The soft dirt floor kicked up whenever they walked upon it. Dirt crusted their blankets whenever they sat on them. In the summer's heat they'd been sweating, as well, and the food they'd been given was universally greasy. Their attempt to play chess had ended when the rushi pieces became too filthy to read. Warkannan had refused to touch his copy of the *Mirror*.

'Last night I dreamt about the bath houses in Haz Kazrak,' Warkannan said. 'The ones on the palace hill, but I'd settle for a swim in the harbour if I could get it.'

'What really gripes me is that canal out back. I can look out at the water, I can smell it, and a fat lot of good it does us.'

'What I wonder is how they get running water up here. The canal must carry run-off from the rains, but by now it should be dry.'

'I'll bet you vrans to breadmoss that the Settlers dug it, and there's a pump somewhere underground.'

'That makes sense, yes.'

The khan went back to scratching under his filthy collar. Warkannan walked over to the window slits near the door. He'd found that by grasping the rough sill and finding toe-holds in the wall, he could climb up a few feet and steady himself for some minutes of watching the village beyond.

At this time of day, when the sun was just moving past zenith, the ChaMeech were normally out and about, going into each other's huts, meeting out in the middle of the village, or fetching water in big, round jars, covered with scarlet saurskin, from the canal. Today more ChaMeech than usual had come out for what appeared to be some kind of meeting. The females stood out in the open space and waved their pseudo-arms. Their throat sacs inflated and deflated, and now and then Warkannan could hear some particularly high-voiced speaker, probably the little lavender female who had brought them here. The males, spears in hand, stood at the outside of the group and merely listened.

'Something's going on,' Warkannan said. 'We have quite a gathering.'

'Yes?' Jezro walked over to join him. 'Maybe they're having a banquet, and we're on the menu.'

Warkannan said nothing. He was getting sick of Jezro's culinary jokes.

'I thought H'mai noses were supposed to stop noticing constant stinks after a while,' Jezro went on. 'Mine hasn't.'

'Well, it's worse here near the door.' Warkannan shifted his weight and inched up a little higher. 'Huh. Now they're all walking away, out of the village, I mean, and towards the road down from the tunnel.'

As they walked, the ChaMeech sorted themselves out: the largest females at the head, the largest males at the rear, but they all used their pseudo-hands to straighten their yellow kilts and skirts. Two males came hurrying around from behind their prison and broke into a trot to catch up.

'Wait a minute,' Warkannan said. 'Some of our guards are joining the pack.'

'Think they'll keep away long enough for us to get out of here?' Jezro said.

'No, unfortunately. The two out front are staying at their posts. The whole damn village has settled down by the road. It looks to me like they're waiting for something. Or somebody. I can see ChaMeech moving down the hill road.'

'The guests of honour, no doubt. I wonder if they'll stuff us with herbs first or just roast us whole?'

'Will you shut up?' Warkannan snarled. 'Sir.'

Jezro laughed at much too high a pitch.

About a hundred yards away from the village, the ChaMeech formed two rough lines. At his distance it was hard to be certain, but Warkannan thought he could hear, and feel more than hear, the deep notes of ChaMeech shouting some sort of welcome. Dust clouds drifted down the road, kicked up by a lot of feet.

'Someone's coming, all right,' Warkannan said. 'Shaitan, she's huge!'

Four males carrying spears marched at the head of the column, but right behind them, moving with a calm and even step, came an enormous ChaMeech, a deep royal blue in colour, draped in green cloths. At her approach the villagers raised their pseudo-arms high and began to chant – a high-pitched yodelling sound that Warkannan could hear clearly. Behind her came more males with spears, and following right behind came horses – H'mai on horseback, he realized – three riders and a pack horse, with yet more ChaMeech bringing up the rear.

'It's Hassan,' Warkannan said. 'Zayn and two women.'

'Two?' Jezro said. 'Greedy bastard! Are they prisoners?'

'I can't tell.'

Their guards, who had been standing near the hut door, suddenly boomed and took a few steps forward. From the crowd in the village someone must have answered, because the guards went trotting off to join the welcoming committee.

'The guards are gone,' Warkannan said, and he let himself drop back to the floor. 'And they never lock the door.'

Jezro strode over to the door and pushed it open. 'Right you are. We can get some fresh air at least.'

Outside the air smelled no cleaner, thanks to the proximity of the village, but it was, at least, different air, stirred by a warm summer wind. Warkannan and Jezro walked a few yards away from the hut, then stopped to watch as the procession filed into the village. The enormous blue female swung her head from side to side as she walked, apparently looking over the territory, because in the central round of the village, she stopped and raised a pseudo-hand to signal her followers to do the same. Other females hurried up to flock around her. The contingent of green-kilted spear males spread out around the perimeter of the village to secure it.

'So much for our chance at escaping,' Warkannan said.

'We wouldn't have got far on foot anyway,' Jezro said. 'Besides, with Hassan come to rescue us, escaping would have been rude.'

The H'mai had dismounted and were leading their horses up to the enormous blue female. Warkannan watched the two women, one tall and blonde, obviously a comnee woman from her clothing, and the other short and dark, wearing khakis like a Canton soldier. The comnee woman gave a shout and pointed at the two Kazraks. Warkannan noticed that she was carrying a pair of red and white saddlebags over one shoulder – the spirit rider, most likely. Zayn shouted in answer, tossed her the reins to his horse, and came running, grinning like a maniac. A pair of blue-kilted ChaMeech males lumbered after him, but they held their spears carelessly, point down.

'Well, Hassan.' Jezro glanced at Zayn's escort and spoke in Hirl-Onglay. 'Good to see you and all that, but what in hell is going on?'

'You ordered me to bring help, sir.' Zayn snapped off a salute. 'Here it is.'

'Very good, Captain.' Jezro returned it. 'But who is that? The blue female, I mean.'

'The Great Mother, sir. The Great Mother herself.'

The servants were swarming around her, the other females lowered their necks before her, while the males kept a respectful distance.

'It's true, then?' Jezro said. 'The ChaMeech have a female ruler?'

'They do, sir, yes.' Zayn glanced at Warkannan. 'It's a shock, isn't it?'

'Yes and no,' Warkannan said. 'If I'd never served on the border I'd be shocked, but not after getting to know the comnees.'

Apparently the two males with spears found this opinion amusing. They each stamped a foreleg, then inflated their throat sacs and thrummed.

'I've got to talk fast,' Zayn said in Kazraki. 'When she asks you if you're going back home, your life depends on saying yes.'

The nearest ChaMeech male swung his head around and glared over the obsidian blades on his spear.

'Sorry,' Zayn said in Hirl-Onglay. 'Allow me to introduce you. Jezro Khan, this is Stronghunter Man. Stronghunter Man, Jezro Khan and Captain Warkannan.'

When the ChaMeech held out a pseudo-hand, Jezro shook it solemnly. Warkannan followed his lead. Since the ChaMeech's finger and thumb were, after all, a good deal cleaner than his own, he saw no reason to give himself airs. Stronghunter Man swung his head around to look back over his shoulder, then inflated his throat sac and boomed. One of the female ChaMeech near the Great Mother answered with a booming sound of her own. The other ChaMeech were milling around and trotting back and forth in their usual chaotic way. The H'mai women were standing off to one side. A young ChaMeech had taken their horses and was keeping them clear of the confusion.

'The short woman? That's Loy Millou,' Zayn said. 'I was right. She did go with Ammi.' He smiled, a bare twitch of his mouth. 'And that's Ammi with her. I mean, Ammadin, the spirit rider from my comnee.'

'I see.' Warkannan could indeed see a number of things, all of a sudden, just from Zayn's smile and the way he coupled it with the family usage of her name.

'Hassan, what should we do now?' Jezro said. 'The last thing I want to do is insult the powers that be.'

Stronghunter Man tapped the khan on the shoulder, then pointed towards the gathering.

'We need to join them,' Zayn said. 'The Great Mother wants to talk with you.'

'I'm honoured,' Jezro said, 'but can we wash off some of this muck first?'

Stronghunter Man looked them over, then rumbled a barely audible 'yes'.

'How come you can understand everything we say,' Jezro said, 'but you only speak a few words of our languages?'

Stronghunter Man stamped a forefoot. 'Hurts.' He laid a pseudo-hand on his long throat just above the sac. 'Squeaky high talk hurts.' He turned and gestured to the other blue-kilted males. Four came trotting over at the summons.

'They'll keep you safe,' Zayn said in Hirl-Onglay. 'Don't trust anyone wearing yellow. That's the faction that wants to kill you.'

'I see,' Warkannan said. 'It's a bit premature, then, to assume we've been rescued.'

'A perfect Idres remark,' Jezro said, grinning. 'Now let's go. I want to get clean. Or wait. Hassan, do you have any news of Soutan?'

'Yes sir. He's not far away, and he knows where Sibyl is.' Zayn turned to Warkannan. 'Ammadin's seen your nephew a couple of times in her crystals. He looks healthy, if not exactly safe at the moment.'

'Ah.' Warkannan managed to keep his voice steady. 'Glad to hear it.'

'Ammi can tell you more. I'd better get back to the others. Water Woman needs to know what you're doing.'

As he walked back to the village, Zayn was arguing with himself. He should tell Ammi about his broken Bane. He should keep his mouth shut and hope she never found out. He'd promised her that he'd never lie to her again, and while simply avoiding any mention of his transgression might not count as actual lying in a court of law, in the court of his own conscience he knew himself convicted. Seeing Jezro Khan had reminded him, somehow, that he had a conscience. For that matter, what if Jezro or Idres casually mentioned the truth? In his mind he could imagine Ammadin's face, stricken with profound disappointment. The image helped him find the courage to confront her.

In the centre of the village, the Great Mother's servants were unrolling her green and white ground cloth. Her spear Chur had taken up positions among the houses as well as at the village perimeter. Herbgather Woman trotted this way and that, booming out instructions, waving her pseudo-hands, alternately raising and lowering her neck as if she felt unjustly treated. Her servants and yellow-kilted Chur loped back and forth, following her orders. Water Woman had gathered her people out in the grass off to one side. Carrying her saddlebags, Ammadin and Loy were standing next to her, and a young Chur had taken charge of the horses.

'Zayn Recaller!' Water Woman said. 'Where be Jezro Khan?'

'Bathing,' Zayn said. 'They were kept prisoner in a filthy hut, and they didn't want to insult the Great Mother.'

'Good, good, this be smart of them. I go-now tell-next Stronghunter Man some things.'

Water Woman hurried off towards the canal, booming and thrumming. Zayn watched until he saw Stronghunter Man coming to meet her; then he gathered his courage and strode over to Ammadin.

'Ammi?' he said. 'I've got to talk with you.'

'All right,' Ammadin said. 'Here?'

'No. Privately.'

They glanced at Loy, who smiled as if to say she understood.

'Ammi,' Loy said, 'I'm going to get my horse and mount up, so I can see what's going on. Should I fetch yours?'

'Yes, good idea.'

Loy hurried off, and together Zayn and Ammadin walked through the mob of spear Chur to the grassy meadow beyond. She slung her saddlebags over one shoulder and laid her free hand on his arm.

'You look terrified,' she said. 'What's wrong?'

'I've broken Bane.'

Ammadin took her hand off his arm and stepped back. 'How?'

'I told Jezro Khan about your quest to meet Sibyl. Soutan heard me, and that's why he's out here. He was following you.'

'Gods, that was stupid!'

He winced. 'I know. I'm sorry, oh God I can't tell you how sorry. It's been hell, this past few days. I knew I should tell you, but I was – well, hell, I was afraid of what you'd think of me. I was afraid you'd just send me into exile.'

Ammadin crossed her arms over her chest and looked at him for an agonizing span of moments. The noise and bustle around them was quieting, he realized. He glanced back and saw that Water Woman had returned. The Chiri Michi was both talking and thrumming, pointing this way and that with her pseudo-hands as she gave orders to her servants.

'I might have done just that, once.' Ammadin spoke at last. 'I might have spat in your face and turned you out of the comnee to live or die alone.'

'I was afraid of –'

'Let me finish! I've learned too much, these past few weeks. I've lost something, Zayn. I used to feel so sure of the laws of the gods. Now I don't.'

'You must think I'm contemptible anyway.'

'No, I think you were really stupid. Why did you tell him?'

'I'd mentioned you were with me in Sarla.' Zayn could no longer look her in the face; he stared at the ground between them. 'So the khan asked me why you were there. And I forgot who I was. Can you understand, Ammi? Just being with Jezro and Idres, I turned back into the man I used to be. And that man was a Kazraki officer, not a comnee man, and the idea of Bane – I forgot it, because Kazraki officers don't give a shit about it.' He forced himself to look up. 'But later I remembered. It was like waking up from a dream. And I knew I'd done something wrong. It's been eating me alive.'

'It should. You're ritually unclean. You will be until I give you some kind of penance, and you do it. Until then, you're going to have to eat by yourself and ride at the rear of the herd – well, behind us all, I mean – and you can't speak to anyone but me unless there's some kind of danger threatening. I'll explain the ritual to your friends.'

'I'm sorry.'

'So am I. Very sorry.'

Ammadin turned on her heel and strode off, leaving him heart-sick behind her.

Out in the centre of the village the Great Mother was sitting haunched on her striped cloth. Herbgather Woman and Water Woman had taken up positions in front of her with their spear Chur behind them. Loy had retrieved her black horse and was sitting on horseback some yards off to the side with the grey gelding in tow. Ammadin trotted over, took the reins, and mounted.

'I couldn't see a damn thing otherwise,' Loy said, 'not in all this confusion. God, I hate being short!'

Chof, both male and female, were bustling around, approaching the Great Mother, backing away again, rushing from house to house or standing talking in little groups. Both horses, Loy's black and Ammadin's grey, snorted and pulled at their bits. At times when the Chof came too close, the horses danced and tossed their heads, but they never made a serious effort to bolt. Neither Water Woman nor Herbgather Woman seemed to be in any hurry to have the formal proceedings start – if indeed there would be a formal proceeding.

Ammadin was just as glad of the delay. Zayn's confession had caught her completely off-guard, to the point where she hardly knew what she felt, except a certain dull anger that she'd been sleeping with a man who was ritually unclean. Had they been back on the grass, she could have consulted another spirit rider and come up with a purification for both of them. As it was –

'What's wrong?' Loy said suddenly. 'Something is.'

'It shows?' Ammadin said. 'I was just wishing I'd never left the plains. I used to know exactly what to do about almost everything.'

'What?' Loy turned in her saddle to look at her.

'Oh never mind! Here come Jezro Khan and Warkannan, anyway.'

Stronghunter Man and a cluster of his spear Chur were striding through the village. In their midst walked the two Kazraks, dripping from wet clothes, bearded and shaggy-haired, but clean. When Stronghunter Man filled his throat sac and boomed, the yellow-clad Chof scrambled out of his way. Stronghunter Man and the Kazraks stopped at the edge of the striped cloth, and even though Jezro carried his walking stick, they both stood straight-backed and proud, officers still, at attention before an authority, but an authority over equals, not superiors. The Chur Vocho gestured at his two charges to stay, then led the rest of his men away to take up a position behind Water Woman. Loy leaned in the saddle to speak with Ammadin.

'Where's Zayn?'

'I don't know, and at the moment I don't care.'

Loy's eyes widened.

'We'd better be quiet,' Ammadin said. 'It's starting.'

The Great Mother boomed several times, and gradually the other Chof fell silent and stood still. She folded her pseudo-hands across her chest, stretched out her long neck, and studied Jezro and Warkannan with her pairs of golden eyes. The two Kazraks held their ground. Jezro was even smiling in a pleasant sort of way. Through his dark beard welts of scar tissue glistened with damp.

'So now,' the Great Mother said in Hirl-Onglay. 'You be Jezro Khan, son of the former Great Father of Kazrajistan?'

'I am, your highness,' Jezro said. 'I'm honoured to be in your presence.'

'You speak-now nicely for a Karshak. I hear-two-day-past about your brother. I think-then, this brother be a foul sort of H'mai, stealing from his own people.'

'Yes, foul's a good word for it. I have a personal reason to hate him, too.' Jezro raised a hand and pointed to the scars across his face. 'He had this done to me. He was trying to kill me, you see, so I wouldn't pose a threat to his rule.'

'I hear-then he kill any person who speak-dare to argue with him.'

'That too, and he's demanded so much money from his people that many of them don't have enough to eat.'

The Great Mother made a trilling sound through both nostrils. 'He be-very a bad ruler.'

'Very bad, yes.'

The Great Mother considered him for several moments. 'So then,' she said at last, 'you go home not go home to fight this brother?'

Jezro took a deep breath. 'I am going home, or I should say, I'll go home if your people allow me to. At the moment we seem to be your prisoners.'

'Not my prisoners, no. So, you go-soon home if you have power to go home. What you do-next there?'

'Try to take the throne away from my brother. My friends tell me that I've got an army waiting for me.'

'I hear-then this, too.' She lowered her head a scant foot and peered into his face. 'So, you swear not-swear upon your god's name that all this be true?'

Jezro Khan stood silently, staring at her, his face a little pale, his mouth half-open in mute surprise. Warkannan made an odd sound, rather like a whoop of triumph suddenly cut off, then raised a hand to cover his mouth and pretended to cough. The Great Mother swung her head and contemplated him.

'You be wet and cold,' she said, then returned to studying Jezro. 'I ask-then you a question. Jezro Khan, you swear not swear?'

Jezro took a long deep breath. 'I swear to you, Great Mother. By my god the Lord, the merciful and compassionate, I'm going to go home and try to free my people from my brother's misrule.'

'Good. This please-now me, and it please-next your people even more.' The Great Mother turned her head and looked at Herbgather Woman. 'Lastunnabrilchiri, you hurt-not this man. You set-now him and his friend free. You give back their horses. You give back all their goods. You let him and his friends go free from your village.'

Herbgather Woman whined, but she lowered her head almost to the ground. 'I obey-now and next and soon you, Great Mother.'

'Good. Tomorrow Jezro Khan leave-next your camp with all the H'mai. I stay here with my people. I visit-not you in too long. It be time-many-days for a nice visit, and we share much food.'

'Yes, Great Mother,' Herbgather Woman said. 'I be-now so glad you visit me.' Her words dripped misery, but she stamped a flaccid foreleg anyway. 'We share much good food.'

The spear Chur on both sides boomed and pounded the hafts of their spears on the ground. Water Woman could no longer contain herself; she stamped her forefeet in such a rapid flurry that she seemed to be dancing. Herbgather Woman turned and strode off, thrumming to her servants, while the Great Mother's servants rushed to tend their mistress.

In a few brief moments the Chof villagers changed from participants in an orderly court of law to a random sort of mob, with individuals wandering this way and that, booming and chattering among themselves, picking up sacks and bundles only to lay them down again elsewhere, over and over. Loy and Ammadin dismounted and led their horses through the confusion to join the khan. Jezro hurried forward to meet them with Warkannan right behind. The captain's height and the strength his body displayed surprised Ammadin. She'd seen him so often as a tiny image that she'd been thinking of him as short and slender.

'Spirit Rider,' Jezro said, and he bobbed his head in respect. 'I'm willing to bet that you've got something to do with this.'

'You'd win the bet,' Loy said, smiling. 'I'm impressed, Ammi, I'll admit it.'

'I'm glad you said yes, is all,' Ammadin said to Jezro. 'They might have killed you otherwise.'

'So Hassan told me.'

During this conversation in Vranz, Warkannan had merely listened, his expression so blank that Ammadin suddenly realized he'd not been understanding a word.

'Do you speak Hirl-Onglay, Captain?' Ammadin said in that language.

'I do, but not Vranz.' Warkannan was struggling to keep from laughing. 'Was it you who told the Great Mother that Jezro should go back to Kazrajistan?'

'Yes. I didn't want to see you both killed.'

'Then I need to thank you, too, but for more than you probably realize. Our khan was trying to avoid going home, you see, and I was beginning to run out of ways to persuade him.'

'You bastard, Idres,' Jezro said. 'Gloating over the way I've been trapped. I suppose you think I'll go through with this now.'

'Of course.' Warkannan turned solemn. 'I know you'll never break any oath you swear before God.'

'And you're right, damn you.' Jezro growled like a shen and turned back to Ammadin. 'What can I do to repay you?'

'Repay?'

'Well, I want to do something, and something large, at that. You did save my life.'

'I suppose that's true.' Ammadin considered his offer, too generous to dismiss with a few polite words. 'Someday I might take you up on that. There's nothing important that I can ask you for now, although I could use your help in dealing with Yarl Soutan.'

'There's nothing I'd like more.' Jezro suddenly smiled. 'You can count on us to help you hunt. I wouldn't mind meeting this Sibyl person, either. Hassan told us about your quest –'

'I know.' Ammadin interrupted him. 'He admitted it to me earlier.'

'Merde!' Loy whispered. 'Now I understand!'

Utterly puzzled, Jezro glanced back and forth between the two women.

'I know he told you,' Ammadin said. 'Do you realize he broke Bane when he did? He's ritually unclean now, and I've ordered him to stay away from everyone.'

Jezro winced. 'That's my fault, Holy One. I ordered him to tell us. By rights I'm the one who should pay for it. Set me a penance and I'll do it.'

Ammadin considered him as he stood with his head bowed, his eyes lowered. Even without her hypernormal sense of smell she could intuit that this man was incapable of lying. 'You're the heir to your country's throne. I'm surprised that a man of your rank would take the blame for something like this.'

'My rank? I don't have any rank, not out here.'

'But Zayn obeyed your order.'

'Yes.' Jezro winced again. 'I owe him and you a thousand apologies. I didn't realize what it meant.'

'You're not a comnee man. Bane doesn't concern you, any more than your Kazraki sins concern me.' Ammadin turned to Warkannan. 'Did you witness this, Captain?'

'I did, Spirit Rider. The khan had to order Zayn twice before he told us anything.'

'Well, that makes an enormous difference, yes. All right, he's forgiven. I'll go tell him.'

'Thank you,' Jezro said. 'Do you want me to do some kind of penance?'

'No, of course not. You have your own god. Mine won't care what you do.'

'I see.' Jezro allowed himself a slight smile. 'That's one way to keep the theology simple.'

Zayn had lingered at the edge of the proceedings until the Great Mother pronounced her verdict. Once he knew that the khan was safe, he retrieved his sorrel gelding and the pack horse from the young Chur and led them from the village. Down by the canal and its guardian twistrees, Warkannan's mount and the khan's were grazing at tether. Zayn unsaddled his pair, put them on the halter and tether ropes, and coiled the surplus ropes over his shoulder so he could take them on a short lead to drink at the canal.

Out in the middle of the canal, the moving water had scoured the underlying black aggregate clean, but soil had drifted in and piled up along the edges, providing beds for rushes and fronded stream weeds. The shallow water lay like liquid gold against the black in the afternoon sunlight. When the horses waded a few paces out, the ripples around their legs broke into rainbows. Already in the shallows the frogs were croaking; needlebuhs hummed and darted through the maroon water reeds. An auburn glow washed the distant mountains of the east. Faced with all this beauty the only thing Zayn could feel was his shame: a physical, cold exhaustion, a twist in his stomach.

He had offended the most important person in his world. Quite possibly she would forbid him to return to the comnee. If she did, he would go back to Kazrajistan with Jezro Khan and throw himself into the first charge they had to ride. With luck, an enemy's sabre would end the shame for him permanently, and if not in that charge, then in the next. From somewhere upstream among maroon reeds a crane called, its cry a harsh shriek. Zayn turned towards the sound.

'Little brother!' he called in answer.

With a flap of naked grey wings, the crane rose and flew, shrieking again as it headed off west, its pink legs and tail dangling.

With a snort the sorrel gelding raised its head as if to watch the crane's flight. I don't want to die, Zayn thought. What in hell was I doing, brooding like that?

'Zayn?' Ammadin was calling him. 'Zayn, where are you?'

'Over here.' He felt his stomach clench cold. 'Through the trees. By the canal.'

He heard dead tree-needles rustle and fallen twigs snap as she made her way over to him. He was afraid to turn and look at her.

'I just spoke with Jezro,' Ammadin said. 'He told me he ordered you to discuss my quest. Warkannan said he ordered you twice before you told him. That changes everything.'

Zayn caught his breath. It would be so easy to let her believe him blameless, so easy, so tempting, so wrong.

'That's true,' he said, 'but if I'd explained it was Bane, he would have let me out of the net.'

'Oh.' She paused. 'You didn't have to tell me that, did you? You could have just let Jezro's excuse stand.'

'Ammi, I promised you and Dallo both: no more lies.' He turned to face her. 'I'm sick of lies. I'm only sorry it took me so long to tell you the truth.'

She studied him, her expression solemn, unsmiling while he felt his heart pounding in something much like fear. 'You're forgiven anyway,' she said at last. 'You've just earned it.'

Zayn started to speak and found himself near tears. Ammadin put her saddlebags on the ground and reached up to lay her hands on either side of his face. He flung one arm around her waist and kissed her, but he was comnee man enough to keep hold of the lead ropes with his free hand.

'Uh,' he said. 'What about tonight?'

Ammadin burst out laughing and pushed him away.

'What's so damn funny?'

'One minute you look like you're going to grovel at my feet, and then the next all you can think about is getting me onto a blanket somewhere.'

'It's your own fault. You're the one who's so beautiful.'

'There's a proverb among the comnees – never trust a flattering Kazrak.' Ammadin stooped and retrieved her saddlebags. 'But once it's dark, we can come back to these trees.'

* * *

After a brief consultation with Water Woman, Loy decided that the H'mai should make a separate camp with Water Woman's people between them and the village. Water Woman agreed and designated one of the servants to take care of them and five spear Chur to guard them and the horses.

'Go-not too far,' Water Woman said. 'We want-not to be rude, but we want-not either to rub the shame like sand in Herbgather Woman's eyes.'

'My thought exactly.'

'My Chur bring-next you wood for a fire and food, of course. You and Ammadin have food, I see, but Zayn, the khan, his friend – they have none, and so I send-next some. When we travel-soon to Sibyl, my Chur hunt and get more food.'

'Are we going to go to Sibyl's right away? I hope so.'

'Yes.' Water Woman stamped her forefeet. 'Since the Great Mother stay here, Herbgather Woman stay-must too. She follow-not us.'

'Victory!'

'Just that, Loy Sorcerer. Victory!'

By the time they got the two camps sorted out and set up, the sun had sunk below the traps. Although the sky above shone blue, shadows fell across the plateau and filled the valley. When Loy and Ammadin tried to scan, they found that the rise of stone at the traps' western edge cut them off from the observation grid as well.

'That's worrisome,' Ammadin said. 'I wanted to get another look at Soutan before nightfall.'

'So did I,' Loy said. 'We're going to have to remember this. The grid's not going to be overhead for very long at each pass.'

'We'll try again in the morning.' Ammadin stood up, glancing around. 'Zayn and I will be down near the river if you need us. In the trees not far from the horses.'

Loy returned to camp. When the wood arrived, she made a fire for the light, then got out her notebook; she had pages of important material to record and expand from her hasty notes. The two Kazraki men sat on the other side of the fire and talked between themselves, at least at first. After some while Loy became aware that they'd fallen silent. She looked up to see Warkannan reading a book, and Jezro studying her.

'I don't mean to be rude,' Loy said in Vranz. 'I'm almost done.'

'That's quite all right,' Jezro said. 'And I didn't mean to be rude, either, by staring at you. Once Idres here gets to reading he can be pretty dull company.'

Warkannan looked up at his name, smiled, and went back to his book. Loy finished off her notes, then got up and put the notebook and pen away. All her life she'd heard about Kazraks, but she had never actually met one before. She was tempted to take notes on them, too. Jezro of course was half a Cantonneur, but Warkannan struck her as very foreign indeed. She came back and sat down some feet away from the fire itself to avoid the heat. Jezro moved round to join her, but Warkannan never looked up.

'That's your holy book, isn't it?' Loy said. 'The Qur'an, I mean.'

'Yes, though what he has is a translation,' Jezro said. 'The original's in an Old Earth language, Arabic.'

'That's right – you've lived on this side of the Rift long enough to learn some things.'

'I know the truth, more or less, yes,' Jezro continued, smiling. 'About where we came from, how we got here, and the mess we're stuck in now. So do Hassan and Warkannan. Tell me something, Loremaster Millou. How long do you think we can all keep up this charade?'

'Not very much longer at all. The Landfall Treaty's outlived its reasons for existing.'

'I've had thoughts that way myself. It seems to be putting the Chof in more danger, not less.'

'I agree with you. And I think the Chof want to end it, too. I had some good long talks with Water Woman on the way here. The Great Mother seems to feel that change is going to happen whether they want it or not, and so she'd rather be the one to initiate it.'

'She'll have more control that way, certainly. Where does Sibyl fit into this?'

'I don't have the slightest idea yet. I suspect that Sibyl herself will tell us when we get there. Water Woman won't say who or what she is, beyond calling her the stone woman.'

'All right.' Jezro considered this for a moment. 'You know, I owe you a profound apology.'

'What for?'

'Yarl Soutan. I should have turned him over to the zhundars the minute Hassan told me the truth about what happened to your daughter. I was arrogant enough to think I could handle the situation on my own, and he escaped. I'm sorry. I can't tell you how sorry I am.'

Loy shrugged and stared into the fire. She was remembering sitting in the Sarla courthouse, waiting for Soutan's trial, only to have a furious bailiff tell her that he'd forfeited his bail and fled the canton.

'We'll get him yet,' Jezro went on. 'Sibyl's the best bait in the world to draw him.'

'That's true, isn't it?' Loy said. 'I'm sorry he managed to get his claws into the captain's nephew.'

'So am I. You know, when Hassan told us that Soutan was lying, Idres wanted to enforce the laws of the Three Prophets right then and there. I should have let him.'

'What kind of punishment do they provide for rape?'

'Beheading.'

'Sounds good to me. If you catch him, I get to watch.'

Jezro smiled, then fished in his shirt pocket for a handkerchief.

'You know,' Loy said, 'I hope this isn't insulting, but when I think of someone who's heir to a throne, I don't think of someone like you.'

'Insulting? Actually, I'd call it a compliment.'

They shared a laugh. When Warkannan looked up from his book, Jezro spoke in Kazraki. Warkannan grinned and nodded Loy's way, as if to agree.

Just as the sun was clearing the eastern mountains, Sentry chimed, and Ammadin woke. Still naked, she knelt on the blanket and brought out her crystals. She could hear Zayn moving around and yawning behind her, but she ignored him and concentrated on Spirit Eyes. First she scanned from side to side to gauge the plateau's width, which turned out to vary considerably from narrow necks of about a mile in some spots to a wide plain of at least thirty miles in others. She decided to assume that Yarl had travelled north from his last position and gained the plateau. She sent the focus scanning to the north, following the canal.

Some twenty miles north her focal point reached a canyon between two plateaus, a break in the traps. Lacy pillars and arches lined the pale walls, and dark flecks on the cliff faces turned out to be caves. As she examined the canyon, she came across a place where the stone walls twisted. A stretch of cliff faced due east. The rising sun picked out an arch and illuminated the cave behind it. Something stood there, and she thought it at first a giant Chof until its glittering green surface made her realize that it was a sculpture, and most likely that of a god, since it was large enough to be visible through a crystal.

She followed the canyon east. It cut all the way through the plateau and debouched into a narrow valley. Here and there in the tall grass she saw things moving, but every time she focused down she found only animals, mostly the small blue and white browzars, occasionally a yap-pack. In the sky birds flew, tiny dots within the crystal, perhaps the kri˙altri that the Chof so hated. She was about to close down when at last she saw Soutan's little gang of H'mai and Chof, travelling north. Just before the image dissolved, Ammadin saw Soutan dismount and turn to rummage in the saddlebags slung over his saddle's horn.

'Ammi?' Zayn's voice cut into her concentration. 'Here's your shirt. Someone's coming.'

She looked up and saw Loy heading their way. Zayn was holding out the shirt at arm's length.

'It's only Loy,' Ammadin said.

'Ammi!' He sounded so distressed that she took the shirt and slipped it over her head.

'Ammi?' Loy called out. 'Water Woman says we should get on the road soon.'

'Good. I just need to let my crystals recharge.' Ammadin pulled the shirt's hem down to her hips. 'I've found Soutan. He's a good long way ahead of us.'

'Soon' in a Chof context turned out to mean 'in several hours or at least by noon'. Water Woman had several elaborate farewells to make. First, while the Great Mother watched, she and Herbgather Woman bowed repeatedly to one another. They clasped pseudo-hands, then briefly – perhaps as briefly as the Great Mother would allow – and twined their long necks together. After a last bow, Herbgather Woman rounded up her people and disappeared with them inside the houses.

The H'mai, their horses, and the Chur all stood in a long line at the edge of the village and waited for the most important farewell. Water Woman stood at the edge of the Great Mother's ground cloth and alternately lowered her head and spoke at some length. At last the Great Mother thrummed; Water Woman made one last bob of her head and turned away.

'We go-now.' Water Woman strode over to take her place at the head of the line. 'We see-soon Sibyl. At last!'

'At last, yes,' Ammadin said. 'Did Loy tell you that Soutan's way ahead of us?'

'She tell-then, yes. I worry-not. He have power to reach Sibyl's cave, but she have power to keep him out of it. She have doors, and she know how to lock them. So now, we go-onward!' Water Woman thrummed, and her odd little caravan set off.

They followed the canal north. Away from the secret roads, the Chof travelled slowly, plodding along, talking with each other, booming and thrumming, pausing often to drink or to splash around in the water to cool themselves. Late in the afternoon Stronghunter Man took five of his spear Chur and set off to hunt, and at that point travel slowed further. Water Woman began to look for a suitable campsite.

'We're going to crawl the whole fucking way, aren't we?' Loy said in Tekspeak. 'I can't believe this.'

'You Cantonneurs are always in a hurry,' Ammadin said.

'Well, it's because of Yarl. This is my chance to catch the bastard.'

While Water Woman's servants were setting up camp, Ammadin and Loy hunted for Soutan. Ammadin found the canyon and the valley easily enough, but Yarl and his Chof proved more elusive. Slowly and carefully she moved the crystal's focus along the base of the cliffs.

'Damn him!' Ammadin said. 'He might be hiding inside one of the caves.'

'I wonder if Sibyl's put a trace on him,' Loy said. 'She could possibly use that imp of Arkazo's. Try it.'

'Try what?'

'The trace command. Sorry, I see you don't know that one. Say, "jump to tracking crystal".'

When Ammadin did so, Spirit Eyes chimed twice. The view inside changed so fast that she felt briefly nauseated. When her vision settled down, she could see Arkazo in the exact centre of the crystal's view.

'Yes,' Ammadin said. 'There he is.'

'And that bastard Soutan is still with him?'

'Yes, and his Chof, too.'

The two H'mai were sitting on purple grass, one on either side of the slate, which Soutan had placed on a flat rock. When Ammadin locked Long Voice onto their position, she could hear, through the bone behind her ear, Soutan's voice, heavy with despair. She handed Long Voice to Loy so that she could hear as well.

It has to be right here somewhere, Soutan was saying. *I just don't understand, Kaz. According to the map cache, the installation absolutely has to be somewhere in this stretch of cliff.*

Maybe it was moved after this map was made. Arkazo sounded merely weary, and he stifled a yawn. *Can't think of anything else.*

Maybe so. Ah God! we'll never find it in all of this mess!

Both Arkazo and Soutan turned to look back at the traps rising behind them. Pillars and vents, caves, arches, deep gouges in the rock – millennia of rain storms had dug architecture into the pale cliff face. From the ground a sloping path led up to a flat lip of stone under an arch of black rock. Set back from the edge were two black pillars that resembled stacks of beads. Between and around them strands of blue light sparkled and danced. When Ammadin focused in, she could see the entrance to what seemed to be a sizeable cave behind the crackling light. She could make out a barrier, perhaps a solid metal door, first hidden, then revealed, as the blue light flickered.

'Loy, it's right there behind them. They just can't see it. It must have one of those hologram things hiding it.'

Loy took the crystal, stared into it, then howled with laughter. 'I love it!' she said at last. 'The poor little bastard! Oh, suffer till your balls fall off, Yarl!'

Arkazo was speaking again, and Loy stopped in mid-diatribe to listen.

Well, if we keep going, we're bound to come to it sooner or later. It's got to be here somewhere, or Water Woman wouldn't have told that spirit rider about it.

That's true. Soutan took a deep breath. *You know, that gives me an idea. Why don't we find somewhere to hide and wait for her to catch up to us? Chiri Michi never go anywhere alone. This Water Woman person must have a retinue with her, and that means dust, a lot of it, rising into the air. We'll be able to see them coming and follow.*

They'll be able to see our dust, too. It's so barren out here.

That's true. Well, let me think. There has to be a way. We've come this far, and damned if I'll give up now.

'Isn't this interesting?' Loy said. 'We're both the bait and the hunters.'

'If they do what Arkazo suggested.'

'True. If. But I'll bet you silver vrans to horseshit that they can't come up with anything better.'

When they told Water Woman about Soutan's predicament, she stamped both forefeet. 'I tell not-tell you? Sibyl know how to shut her door.'

'You were right, yes,' Ammadin said. 'But there's something I don't understand. You told us that the way to Sibyl lies through the town of N'Dosha.'

'This be true.'

'But when I used my crystals, I didn't see any town.'

Water Woman raised her pseudo-hands and peered between them, then stamped her forefeet. 'Oh, I think-now, Ammadin Witchwoman, that you see-then the town. I think-now, however, that you know-not you see the town.'

'And what is that supposed to mean?'

'You see-next-soon. We get there short while now.'

And that was all she'd say, no matter how Ammadin and Loy prodded her.

Loy wasn't the only impatient member of the caravan. After the evening meal, Zayn sat with Warkannan and Jezro Khan while the two H'mai women went off to scan. With the last of the sunset, a young Chur brought the H'mai men food, stacked wood for an eventual campfire, then bobbed his head to each of them before he left. The other Chof seemed to be holding some sort of meeting. They stood in a rough circle around Water Woman and Stronghunter Man, who were sitting haunched face to face. Their throat sacs pulsed and fluttered; every now and then the Kazraks could hear a high-pitched thrum or a few bursts of words. Stronghunter Man waved his pseudo-hands in the air, while Water Woman had folded her arms across her chest to listen.

'What's that about, I wonder?' Jezro said.

'I have no idea, sir,' Zayn said. 'Maybe it's got something to do with Soutan. Ammadin tells me he's nearby.'

'Oh, does she?' Jezro leaned forward. 'How near?'

'Maybe twenty miles away, maybe thirty,' Zayn said. 'Apparently he's waiting for our line of march to reach his hiding place, so he can follow us to Sibyl's cave.'

'Good,' Warkannan said. 'That means Arkazo will be within reach.' He glanced at the other two men in turn. 'Yes, I'm admitting I'm worried – worried sick, in fact. I don't want to leave the boy with Soutan when we ride back home. Who knows what that would do to his mind?'

'It's a worrisome thought, yes,' Jezro said. 'I hope these Chof move a little faster tomorrow. Now that I know I'm going back, I'm getting impatient.'

'Well, maybe we should just leave,' Warkannan began.

'Idres, you don't need to martyr yourself. I promised the spirit rider our help. And we're going to need hers to get back across the Rift.'

'Hadn't thought of that.'

'It's too bad that I don't know this territory,' Zayn said. 'I've been trained to remove annoyances like Soutan, and with his crystals dead, he'd never see me coming.'

Jezro considered him with weary eyes. 'Ah, the temptations of power!' he said at last. 'I begin to see why my brother grew so fond of the Chosen.'

'They can be convenient, yes,' Warkannan put in. 'But it's a dangerous convenience.'

'Yes.' Jezro turned to Zayn. 'I've been thinking about your guild. I'm going to have to take some kind of steps when I get home. Look, Hassan, if you start feeling like convulsions are coming on, please tell me, and I'll shut up.'

'Don't worry, sir. I will.'

'Good. Do you think they'll try to assassinate me first chance they get?'

'Maybe, if it looks like their side is losing.'

'What about if we win, and we take Haz Kazrak?'

'Someone might try to get at you, but most of the men that loyal will have made a point of dying with your brother.'

'Shaitan!' Warkannan said. 'Why?'

'We were always told that it was our one chance to escape damnation, if the Great Khan spoke for us before God.'

Every muscle in Warkannan's face turned tight with rage. He

tried to speak, could only make a growling sort of noise, took a deep breath instead.

'Calmly, Idres, calmly,' Jezro said. 'Yes, I know that's blasphemy, but don't have a stroke over it. We're going home and we'll fix it, all right?'

Warkannan forced out a smile, but he didn't even try to speak.

'Hassan, what about the less loyal ones?' Jezro said.

'If you offer them the right bait, they'll switch sides and protect you.'

'And what's this bait?'

'The same thing you offered me. The chance to feel like a man instead of an abomination.'

'Which means stopping the persecution of the – what's the name again?' Warkannan had regained his voice. 'The Inborn, that's right. Anyway, you'll have to do something about that, Jezro. We can't have children burnt alive for talents they can't help.'

'I'd prefer not to have children burnt alive for any reason whatsoever.' Jezro paused for a wry grin. 'Although – hang on a minute here. I've never heard of any children actually being burnt. Have you, Idres? Hassan?'

'No, I haven't,' Warkannan said. 'But I have heard of children being taken from their mothers and smothered because of the talents.'

'So have I,' Jezro said. 'But not being burnt.'

'All I know is what my father used to tell me,' Zayn said. 'He told me they'd burn me alive if they found out.'

'I wonder.' Jezro glanced at him. 'I'll bet he was as frightened of the mullahs as you were. He may have invented the death by fire to scare the shit out of you, so you'd keep your mouth shut, although you'd think being smothered would be threat enough.'

'Smothering's relatively painless,' Warkannan said. 'As those things go, of course.'

In unison Jezro and Zayn blurted, 'A perfect Idres remark!' Warkannan favoured them both with a sour smile.

'Doesn't matter anyway,' Jezro went on. 'If the Lord wills that I become Great Khan, there will be new laws and proclamations about those talents. No one is going to suffer because of them again. I promise you that.'

'Thank you, sir.' Zayn suddenly found it hard to speak.

Warkannan leaned forward and laid a hand on Zayn's arm. 'Are you going to be all right?'

'Oh yes.' Zayn swallowed heavily. 'It's not convulsions. Just gratitude.' He stood up, desperate to keep control of himself. 'Sir, if you'll excuse –'

'Of course, Hassan.'

Zayn turned on his heel and strode away before he wept and disgraced himself – again – in front of Idres and the khan. He was remembering his father and his father's threats of death by fire. What if Jezro were right, and it was only fear that had made the old man threaten such a horrible punishment? What would he have been afraid of, except losing his son? And that would mean – Zayn found himself unable to finish the thought.

Walking soothed him. He decided that Loy and Ammadin shouldn't be off alone and left the camp, heading for the twistrees. Due east the young mountains rose like the heads of giant birds, pointing their beaks at the fading light in the sky. Out in the river frogs croaked; little greenbuhs rose from the thatchy grass and sang their one faint note. At the riverside beyond the trees, Loy and Ammadin were just packing their crystals away.

'Any sign of Soutan?' Zayn said.

'No,' Ammadin said, 'but he has to be nearby. The traps are riddled with caves. There's plenty of places to hide.'

They returned to camp to find that the Chof meeting had broken up. The spear Chur had resumed their guard of the campsite. Water Woman's servants were rubbing their mistress's skin with oil from a leather bottle. Stronghunter Man, spear in pseudohand, saw the returning H'mai and boomed a greeting. He strode over, nodded to the two women, then spoke to Zayn, pitching his voice as high as a human basso. He coughed as the effort pained him.

'Idea,' Stronghunter Man said. 'We go, you, me, some Chur, find Soutan and kill him.'

'I'd like nothing better,' Zayn said, 'but what does Water Woman say?'

'She let-now us go. I talk-just-now her round.' He stamped a heavy forefoot. 'We leave-next morning, travel-soon ahead.'

'Sounds good to me. But we'll have to be careful. My friend Warkannan's nephew is Soutan's prisoner.' Zayn decided that this small exaggeration would do no harm – it wasn't as if Arkazo had really understood the situation when he'd gone with Soutan. 'We can't kill him.'

'Kill-not boy, then. You agree-now?'

Zayn was about to say yes when he remembered Jezro Khan calling the Chosen a temptation. 'I don't know. I have to talk with the khan.' He glanced at Ammadin. 'What do you think?'

'I'm still worried about Arkazo, but Warkannan's here now. Why not ask him what he wants you to do?'

'Good idea,' Stronghunter Man said. 'We go-now, talk with the khan and Warkannan.'

The night sky was darkening, except for the faint silver glow that the galaxy, rising beyond the mountains, sent ahead of itself like the promise of salvation. A servant Chur was just lighting the fire previously laid; once the tinder caught she bowed her head and scuttled away. Jezro and Warkannan rose to greet Stronghunter Man, Idres warily, Jezro with an open smile.

'Stronghunter Man's come up with an idea,' Zayn said. 'He wants to go hunt Soutan down, and he's asked me to go along with him. He knows the territory.'

'You know H'mai mind.' Stronghunter Man pointed at Zayn. 'Easier if I go-not alone.'

'I see.' Jezro hesitated and looked at first Zayn, then the Chur Vocho, in the flaring light of the fire.

'You talk-next Karshak speak.' Stronghunter Man haunched and sat. 'I wait.'

The three H'mai walked a few paces away from the Chur Vocho.

'Soutan's a criminal, sir,' Zayn said. 'Any court at home would have him executed for raping that poor girl.'

'There's that, yes.' Jezro glanced at Warkannan. 'But a Canton court would only send him to prison.'

'Well, true,' Warkannan said, 'but we're not in the Cantons any more.'

'Not technically, anyway.' Jezro turned to Zayn. 'Think you could take him alive?'

'We could try, sir.' Zayn shrugged and turned his hands palm up. 'But it's going to be hard enough to keep Arkazo safe if we get into a fight with his spear Chur. I don't understand why you care what happens to Soutan. Back at the dookis's manor, you told me you were afraid he'd show up there after you were gone, maybe try to hurt Marya somehow, steal from her at the very least. That's the kind of scum he is.'

'That's true, Jezro,' Warkannan joined in. 'We won't want to leave Soutan on the loose behind us when we head back home.'

'So,' Zayn said, 'why don't I just solve the problem once and for all?'

Jezro considered with a sharp sigh. 'For some strange reason the idea of sending a man out to murder someone for me isn't sitting well.' He glanced at Warkannan. 'Maybe because I've been at the other end of this proposition.'

'Are you asking me to pardon you for it in advance?' Warkannan said.

Jezro winced. 'Not any more.'

'Sir?' Zayn said. 'What's the difference between sending me out after Soutan and sending an army out after a regiment?'

'Well, I probably never considered this hypothetical regiment to be a friend of mine.' Jezro paused for a wry smile. 'Maybe that's what my scruples come down to. I don't know, Hassan. I don't know what I want you to do.'

'Well, sir, Stronghunter Man's going after him whether I go or not. I might as well ride along and see what I can do about rescuing Arkazo. But I can't vouch for Soutan's safety.'

Jezro looked at the empty air when he spoke again. 'Isn't this handy? Now I can pretend that you're only going to fetch Kaz back, and if something should happen to Soutan, I won't even need to know. Unfortunately, that's so much sheepshit.' He turned to look Zayn straight in the face. 'If you can, kill him, Hassan. And may God forgive me!'

The camp woke before dawn, and the warparty – one Chur Vocho, ten Chur, and one H'mai – assembled out down by the river to wolf down breakfast. Ammadin and Loy sat nearby, backs to the men, and searched for Soutan in their crystals. While they never actually saw him, they did spot a tendril of smoke; it seemed to come from a cave mouth on a cliff perhaps two miles north of Sibyl's location.

'That's as good a place to start as any,' Zayn said. 'But don't worry, we'll find him, sooner or later.'

'I hope so.' Loy looked and sounded weary. 'I keep thinking that maybe Rozi can be healthy again, someday anyway, if she knows he's dead or at least in prison.'

'Maybe so.' Zayn glanced at Stronghunter Man. 'I'd better go get my horse.'

'No horse,' Stronghunter Man said. 'Keep-never up with Chur. We move-next fast, steady.' He pointed to a young Chur whom Zayn had assumed to be a servant. 'Ride.'

The Chur lowered his head submissively. 'I speak some Comnee speak.' His voice, a deep baritone, was high enough to be easily heard. 'When Stronghunter Man speak, I repeat.'

'All right,' Zayn said. 'But a saddle's not going to fit you. Can you stand wearing a halter? I'll sling my saddlebags over my head. The bedroll – I can tie that on somehow.'

The Chur looked at Stronghunter Man and whined.

'Halter, yes,' Stronghunter Man said firmly. He dropped his voice to a pitch that fell below Zayn's ability to hear, but the young Chur repeated his words. 'H'mai need hang on. Zayn, get-now your gear. One other of us carry bedroll. All carry things but not Stronghunter Man.'

'All right. What's your name?'

The young Chur thought for a moment, then answered in Hirl-Onglay. 'Fifth Out.'

'Fifth Out? Out of what?'

'The ocean, when the change come-then and some of us, we leave-then the ocean for land. Young Chur get real names later, when we see if we be michi or vocho.'

Zayn nearly blurted, 'You mean you don't know yet?' He managed to turn the blurt into a cough. None of the strange revelations he'd heard lately had surprised him as much as this, that a sapient being might not have the slightest idea whether it was male or female.

Zayn had left his gear at Warkannan and Jezro's fire, and Warkannan stood nearby, waiting for him. The khan and Water Woman were walking back and forth nearby and talking about the journey ahead. When Zayn knelt by his saddlebags, Warkannan joined him.

'I'll do my best to keep Arkazo safe,' Zayn said.

'I know you will,' Warkannan said. 'But it's in God's hands.'

'Be glad. He has better hands than mine.'

Warkannan managed to smile at that. Zayn opened his saddlebags and looked over the contents. He could lighten them by leaving things with Warkannan, but you never knew when some piece of equipment or weapon would save your life or make your kill. He still regretted leaving his bow behind at the dookis's manor. He closed them up, tied them loosely together, and pulled them over his head to hang over his chest and back. The two men stood up, turning to look at the khan, still deep in his conversation with the Chiri Michi.

'Jezro's already learning how to rule,' Warkannan said, 'or what it's going to cost him, anyway.'

'What it's going to cost all of us,' Zayn said. 'If I do manage to kill Soutan, do you think Jezro's going to see me the same way as he always did? I'll always have a smear of his guilt on my face.'

Warkannan winced with a little shake of his head.

'Doesn't matter much,' Zayn went on. 'I won't be going back to Kazrajistan.'

'I was beginning to get that impression. Because of Ammadin, I suppose.'

'She's part of it, yes.'

'Only part?'

'Yes. I learned something this summer. I don't really know how to explain, but I belong in the comnees.'

'What? Why? They worship those false idols. They're not even civilized.'

'No, they're not, but neither am I, not any more. The Chosen saw to that.'

After the warparty left camp, the rest of the expedition lingered to let them get a head start on the trail north. Warkannan realized that if he didn't get control of himself, he would plunge over some inner cliff of worry and break at the bottom of it. Only God knew what would happen to Arkazo, he reminded himself, or to Zayn, for that matter. The remaining Chur and the two female servants were wandering around the campsite, picking up bundles, putting some down, loading others onto each other's backs. Warkannan carried his gear down to the shade of the twistrees, where the murmur and splash of water in the canal soothed his nerves. With his back comfortably against a tree trunk, he got out the *Mirror* and began leafing through the pages, glancing at a passage here and there. The simple sight of the holy words offered comfort.

Warkannan had just begun to read in earnest when Water

Woman came lumbering down to join him. She waved a pseudo-hand in greeting, then haunched opposite. She lowered her head and looked over her wedge of cartilage with her double eyes.

'I interrupt, I know. But that book you read-always, Warkannan Captain. Ammadin Witchwoman tell-just-now me it be a holy book. Your god write-then it?'

'Not precisely,' Warkannan said. 'He dictated it to the First Prophet, and the First Prophet spoke it aloud to his followers, who wrote it down.'

'Ah. Your people say there be one god, not many. Right not right?'

'Right.'

'Our gods be many. I think. I know-not-no-more. We Chof, we believe-long-time-then the gods live up in the Silverlands. We know-now the Silverlands be a group of suns like that sun.' She pointed vaguely at the sky. 'We make-long-time beautiful statues of our gods. We tell-always beautiful stories about them, too. They still do-never nothing for us. We pray, they answer-not. We argue argue argue but they give-not us a sign.'

'Well, they're not real gods, that's why. They're just idols. I mean – sorry, I don't want to insult you.'

'It be all right.' She heaved an enormous sigh that made her throat sac flutter. 'I think-many-times now same thing. So do Great Mother, so do we all.'

Warkannan felt a rising panic that had nothing to do with Arkazo. It was his duty as a believer to tell these receptive infidels about the one true god, but he had no training, no skill with words – what if he, out of simple clumsiness, turned her against the faith? He swallowed heavily and took a deep breath.

'I could read to you from our book,' he said. 'If you'd like to hear some of it.'

'Your god be-only a god of the H'mai, not the Chof.'

'I don't see why.' He could only pray that he wasn't wandering into heresy. 'I've learned something new about your people, just lately. You're as much H'mai as we are. Well, no, I don't mean that exactly.'

Water Woman raised a forefoot and stamped. 'I think I understand-now you, Warkannan Captain. I say, you be as Chof as we be. But I hear-many-times, you Karshaks think men lead-must women. We think opposite. Your god, he like-not like that?'

'I honestly don't think that would matter to the Lord.' A new thought struck him with the force of a blow. 'After all, He must have created you to be the way you are just like He created us to be what we are. And the same would go for all the other peoples in the universe, too, now that we know there are some. I'm sorry, I'm not being very coherent, am I?'

'You make-now sense, Captain. But I think of the comnees. Their women be-not led by males. In Cantons, both males and females lead. But they all be H'mai.'

'Well, those are their ways, not Kazraki ways. I suppose it comes down to that, at any rate. Some of our women would like to be more like the Canton women.'

'And your god, he get angry at them?'

'I honestly don't know. In fact, I've never much thought about it before.' He found himself remembering Lubahva, and her occasional pointed remark about such matters. 'If I live to get home, maybe I should talk about it with my woman.'

'Maybe? *Maybe*? What sort woman she be? Beautiful?'

'Very.' Warkannan smiled at the memory. 'And strong-minded. Brave, too, really. Without her, I'd never have been able to bring the khan home.'

'A good match for you, then?'

'Yes, yes she is.' Warkannan found himself remembering Lubahva's tears when they'd parted. He was shocked at how deeply the memory affected him. He would have given a year off his life to be able to soothe her fears. 'You know, I love her, now that I think about it.'

'H'mai men, you be very strange.' Water Woman raised a coy pseudo-hand. 'Ah but it be-not my business, as H'mai say. This all be very interesting.' Water Woman raised her head and looked back towards camp. 'It be time we leave-now here and start-next going to Sibyl. But tonight, we stop, and you tell-next me more about this god. Yes?'

'Yes, certainly. I'll be glad to.'

The warparty set out at a steady lope, heading north-west across the plateau. Meadows of wild grass gave way to wheatian fields, some roughly square, others rambling and amorphous. Low fences made of sticks and ropes of braided grass marked them off one from another, and naked Chur sat beside them or wandered back and forth on the wild grass between. At the sight of the warparty these Chur would boom or thrum, then turn and run in the opposite direction. If they were guards, Zayn thought, they were doing one hell of a bad job.

At noon the warparty stopped to eat on the shores of a small circular lake, framed by two curved stands of Midas trees. Out in the water, on a circular island, sat a small structure made of white flexstone pillars topped with a black dome. When Zayn walked down to the water's edge, he heard a high-pitched whine and a rhythmic throb coming from inside the structure – a pump, he figured. Stronghunter Man, through Fifth Out, confirmed his guess.

'The Settlers must have built this,' Zayn said.

'They start-then it, build-then lake and house. Chof finish-then canal, when the Settlers stop building.'

'Why did they stop?'

'I know-not.' Stronghunter Man bobbed his round head twice, and the young Chur did the same. 'No one know. Settlers build-then the way down, too.'

'The way down?'

'From this tableland, yes. You see-soon-very.' Stronghunter Man pointed to the north-west, and again, Fifth Out mimicked him as he passed the message along. 'Or maybe you see-now. H'mai eyes be better than Chof eyes for things far off.'

Zayn shaded his eyes with his hand and followed the point. At some distance a glittering structure, white and round, rose from purple grass.

'I can see something, all right. It looks like a dome.'

'Half of one,' Stronghunter Man said. 'It stand over the way down. Or the way up, depending, of course.'

Whether up or down, the way turned out to be a spiral ramp, constructed from flexstone but coated in some black substance that allowed for traction. Zayn insisted on walking down, partly to spare Fifth Out's back, but mostly because the ramp lacked any kind of safety railing, and he preferred his own feet for the trip. In the dim light filtering down from the domed entrance, and up from what appeared to be a similar exit below, they spiralled down and around until Zayn lost track of distance and direction both.

They came out into bright sun that had him blinking until he shaded his eyes. A quick look around confirmed that they were back in the farmlands of N'Dosha, on the western side of the traps.

'Ammadin told us that Soutan was in the east valley,' Zayn said.

'I know.' Fifth Out relayed Stronghunter Man's words. 'There be-not a way east from that tableland back up there. We go-must through N'Dosha.'

The Chur Vocho swung his pseudo-arm around in a half-circle and pointed to a break between two of the traps, about a mile away.

'N'Dosha's on the other side of that canyon?' Zayn said.

'No. N'Dosha – it be the canyon. Get on and ride again. We show-now you.'

Zayn settled himself on Fifth Out's back, and the warparty set off at a steady walk. As they approached the entrance, a river of green poured out to meet them. For several miles from the canyon's wide mouth green life predominated, not merely green grass, but green shrubs and bushes, green vines twining over green-leafed trees, little green plants with yellow and white flowers, taller florals with dark green leaves, and green mounds made of thorny canes, dotted with tiny red spheres.

'Grapes?' Zayn said.

'No. Fwambah.' Stronghunter Man spoke these words himself. 'Good to eat.'

A path, paved once, crumbling now, led into the canyon itself. As the Chur strode along, Zayn had the sudden feeling that the Settlers had transplanted here a little bit of Old Earth, green, cool in the hot sun, perfumed with the fresh smell of growing things. The canyon seemed a road through a wild garden that would magically lead into that lost world. Here and there water welled up in white basins and spilled over into thick carpets woven of green life – grasses and leaves, stems and branches, all green except for a scatter in the grass of tiny white flowers. Back by the shaded canyon walls, green moss, as soft as velvet, covered rocks; green ferns clustered between. Zayn was so entranced by the verdure that he never looked up to see the canyon walls until Stronghunter Man told him to do so.

'My God!' Zayn whispered.

Above and around him towered the pale soft tufa cliffs, their surface transformed into something as intricate as the lace on a court official's robes, with caves for openwork and stone pillars and arches for threads. Cut into the living rock, stairways rose to ledges and landings where the mouths of caves yawned, hundreds of them, leading back into darkness. Some of the caves were large enough to contain the porches and facades of what appeared to be entire houses carved right out of the stone. Others were mere square holes, perhaps ventilation, perhaps windows for hidden dwellings. On both sides the cliff faces displayed this elaborate architecture, chipped and dug from the soft rock.

'The H'mai,' Zayn said. 'Did they make this place?'

'No and yes,' Stronghunter Man said through the young Chur. 'They improve-then it, but many caves, they be-already here.'

'Do you think Soutan and his Chur are hiding in here?'

'Yarl, maybe.' Stronghunter Man stamped a forefoot. 'Chof, we get-never up those stairs. We fit-not in those caves, not in the tunnels, either.'

'There are tunnels?'

'So I hear-always. Miles of tunnels connect the caves, lead to secret ways out. But I know-not for certain. I fit-not in any of them to see for myself.'

Zayn looked back to judge how far they'd come and noticed a twist of cliff, facing east. In its high cave something stone glimmered.

'Who put that statue up there? The green one.' Zayn pointed out the cave mouth far above them. 'It's one of your gods.'

'The H'mai, of course. Who else have power to get it there? Why they do-then it, I know-not, maybe to remember that all things die-soon-next. That be Aggnavvachur.'

'I should have known.' Zayn felt his stomach twist with remembered fear. 'I nearly met him face to face, and not all that long ago. Soutan tried to have me sacrificed on his altar.'

'Then you go-never up to that cave. He let-not anyone escape twice, not Chof or H'mai.'

As if they felt the death god watching them, the Chur strode fast along the broad path. Zayn could have lingered in the green canyon for hours, even though he could find no logical reason for his desire. Oaks, grass, and roses were the only green plants he'd ever known until he'd come to the Cantons and added grapes to the list. The canyon must have sheltered several dozen species more. The N'Dosha colonists had established far more species than the Landfall Treaty allowed, and he wondered why they'd done it and even more, how they'd got away with it.

When they emerged into a valley of purple grass and Midas

trees, Zayn nearly wept, feeling that he'd woken from a dream of Paradise. The Chof, however, thrummed and boomed at one another in relief.

The rest of Water Woman's people left late in the morning and stopped travelling early. When they reached the circular lake, Water Woman announced that she was tired of walking, marched over to the shade of the Midas trees, and sat down without further comment. One of her female servants rushed over to arrange her skirt. While the Chur unloaded each other and strewed their burdens across the grass, the Kazraki men insisted on taking care of the horses.

'We can't help it,' Jezro said. 'Old cavalry officers, you know. Horses count for more than men, out on the border.'

Ammadin and Loy sat down with Water Woman. A servant hurried to the lake with the metal cups from Loy's kit and brought back fresh water.

'I must admit,' Loy said, 'that I could get used to having servants wait on me.'

'I'm surprised you don't have them already,' Ammadin said. 'Since you're a loremaster, you should be treated with respect.'

'That's not the Canton way, or I should say, the Shipfolk way. The ships had ranks and officers, but everyone had inherent rights, and no one thought they were better than anyone else just by existing. We hold to those principles.' Loy finished her water and handed the cup to the servant. 'Well, most of us. There are those that think titles like dookis mean something.'

'Old ways, they change-sometimes, Loy Sorcerer,' Water Woman said. 'We want or want-not, it matter-not.'

'That's true. And things seem to be changing now.'

'Yes, and better to be in charge of change,' Water Woman continued, 'if change come-must. Better to walk in front of the people, not running along behind and breathing dust from feet of those in front.'

In Ammadin's saddlebags Sentry began to hum and chime. 'I'm going to scan,' Ammadin said. 'Soutan might be getting careless.'

Unfortunately, Soutan was doing nothing of the sort. She could pick up no trace of him, Arkazo, or even his six Chof, who should have been hard to hide. When she widened her focus, she did see Zayn and the warparty. In a grassy valley the spear Chur were standing in a circle around Stronghunter Man, whose throat sac fluttered and pulsed. Now and then he would emphasize some point with his pseudo-hands. Zayn stood next to the young Chur who'd been carrying him, one hand on the hilt of his long knife. Although she considered listening, the Riders were sinking, and the signal faded away.

After the evening meal, Ammadin noticed that Water Woman had settled herself next to Warkannan. The Chiri Michi was holding a lightwand to allow the captain to read aloud from his translation of the Qur'an, and Ammadin could tell that she was listening intently. Loy had noticed as well.

'Would you look at that?' Loy said. 'Well, Water Woman keeps whining that the Chof gods are dead. I guess she's looking for a new great big spirit to pray to.'

'You sound disgusted.'

'I am. That's all we need in the Cantons, Kazraks in our back yard.'

'Do you really think the Chof are all going to turn into Kazraks? For one thing, I'll bet the Great Mother isn't going to take the veil and let the Chur Vocho make her decisions for her.'

Loy laughed. 'Good point,' she said. 'I don't know why it rubs me wrong, but it does. It's the superstitions, I guess, all that merde about Iblis and angels and paradises.'

'I take it you don't believe that gods exist.'

'No, I don't. The whole thing, the whole idea of some good father god that loves us but lets us suffer – it doesn't make one fucking bit of sense. I'm sorry, Ammi, I don't mean to offend you, because I know the comnees are believers.'

'Not in the kind of god you mean. In gods that rule different parts of the world, specific places, yes, but forces, too – the wind, the fire, things like that. None of them have the power your kind of god does.'

'You know, those sound a lot more possible.'

'You don't need to be polite.'

Loy hesitated, then shrugged. 'Well then, I don't believe in those, either.'

'I didn't think you did. Is religion just another lie, then?'

'I'd say so. Yes, I know that people seem to need it. Death is a hard thing to face, and here we are – we being the Cantonneurs, I mean – a remnant stuck out here, always brooding about what we've lost. A lot of people desperately need to believe that some god had plans for us. But just because they need it, doesn't mean they're not lying to themselves.'

'And so if the Kazraks try to convert the Chof, they'll be lying to them. Is that how you see it?'

'Exactly. Why should we saddle the Chof with our ancient wish-fulfilment fantasies?'

'Maybe they need them, too.'

'I suppose they do, or Water Woman wouldn't be hanging on the captain's every word. But it's still lies and superstitions.'

'Which would you rather be? Superstitious or dead?'

'What?'

'What's going to happen if the Kazraks come here to hunt for old machines and books?'

'That's probably *when* they come, and it's my worst fear. They'll slaughter any Chof who stand in their way.'

'Not if the Chof share their religion. Zayn's told me a lot about his beliefs. If the Chof convert, the Kazraks will have to respect them as part of the ummah, I think the word is. The community of believers.'

'I've heard about that.' Loy smiled, but wryly. 'All right, so religion might have its compensations. Daccor. I don't think I've ever met anyone as hard-headed practical as you.'

'Probably not. Out on the grass you have to be.'

'Still, when we get home I'm going to consult with the people down at the synagogue. Their church should have a chance to convert the Chof, too, just to keep things fair.'

'And that would be just as good. You're people of the book, Zayn tells me, so the Kazraks will still have to respect the Chof if they join you.'

Loy's mouth suddenly slackened, and she looked away, staring at the empty air.

'What's wrong?' Ammadin said.

'I just had this horrible thought, well not horrible, I suppose, but I've got the strangest feeling that Rozi's going to end up out here, preaching to the Chof. She'd be perfect for the job because she can hear them. She gets that talent from me.' Loy sighed and shook her head. 'I wonder what Oskar would say if he knew. It's probably better he doesn't.'

* * *

The warparty had camped among Midas trees near another canal, this one narrow and silt-choked. After a restless night, they woke early. The valley still lay in shadow, but dawn had turned the sky pale when Stronghunter Man led his men back out to the open grass.

'Soutan, the boy, six Chof, horses.' Stronghunter Man pointed his spear at the cliff face. 'There be few-many caves big enough to hide them.'

The other spear Chur thrummed their agreement. In the silver light they clustered around their leader, who paused often to allow Fifth Out to translate for Zayn.

'Tracks, they show they go-must north,' Stronghunter Man continued. 'North lie many trees and the big gate into N'Dosha, where he have power to hide. We go north, too, but carefully. I trust-not Yarl Sorcerer and his spirits.'

Zayn remembered Loy's rifle and the headless yap-packers. 'I don't trust him, either,' he said. 'He might have magic weapons with him, ones that can kill you from a long distance away.'

Stronghunter Man made a sharp noise, a whuff! of air from his throat sac, and spoke directly. 'We go-must carefully,' he said. 'Maybe circle round to reach the North Gate. I decide-soon, when we arrive-next there.'

'I take it that the North Gate's more than just a cave or tunnel,' Zayn said.

'Much more. You see-soon when we get there.'

They set off again, heading north. Zayn made a quick mental inventory of his saddlebags and realized that he had only one weapon that could strike from a distance, the bolas, and those had never been designed to stand up to guns that could spit fire and explode a target from several hundred feet away. He rummaged through the bags, found the bolas, and laid them right at the top. Something was better than nothing, but he wished he'd thought to beg Loy to let him borrow her rifle.

Loy had never thought of herself as afraid of heights, but travelling down the spiral ramp in semi-darkness proved an ordeal. For a change Water Woman had got her people on the road early, and they arrived at the way down at noon, when the sun stood directly over the sheltering dome and covered the ramp below with shadow. All the H'mai decided to dismount and walk, but it still took the combined efforts of Ammadin and the two Kazraks to get the horses onto the ramp and down.

Loy had no attention or energy to spare for the stock. As soon as she walked under the dome and looked down at the ramp, spiralling into darkness without guide rail or wall, she broke out in a cold sweat. The Chof all charged right onto the thing and dashed down, booming and thrumming, but Loy held back until the horses and H'mai had begun their descent. Finally she forced herself to step onto the ramp by promising her anxieties that she'd only take a few steps, then return to solid ground. Once she'd got on, she told herself that she'd only take four steps more, then four after that, and so on all the way to the midpoint, when going down would bring her to ground faster than going back. By the time she trotted out into the sunlight to join the others, her shirt was soaked through.

Ammadin turned to her and sniffed the air. 'You were frightened,' she said. 'I can smell it even with all the Chof around.'

'Frightened? Heavens, no. Scared shitless.'

'If you'd said something I would have walked with you.'

'I made it, didn't I?'

'Yes, you sure did. And from what Water Woman tells me, we're not all that far from the cave.'

Sibyl better be worth it, Loy thought to herself, but long before they reached Sibyl she had her recompense for her time on the ramp. Despite the war with the Chof, a fair amount of information about N'Dosha had survived in the Cantons. When they rode up to the river of green spreading from the canyon's mouth, Loy's only surprise lay in finding the gardens still alive.

'They broke the Treaty about fifty times over,' Loy said to Ammadin. 'I guess they must have smuggled seeds and starts down from one of the ships to grow all this.'

'These are all Old Earth plants?' Ammadin said.

'Well, I don't know about that. The colonists came from a variety of worlds, after all, and I gather that plant life tended to be green on most of the planets where it grew at all.'

'That's odd. Why?'

'I don't have the slightest idea. The Settlers didn't bother to tell us that, the bastards.'

Still, the canyon itself came as more than a surprise. Surviving lore had told Loy that the research facilities had been built underground, but no one had mentioned that here 'underground' also meant 'up in the air'. The H'mai all slowed their horses and lingered, riding with their heads tipped back to stare at the handiwork of their ancestors. A few at a time, impatient Chof passed them and trotted on ahead, but Water Woman lingered as well.

'So this is N'Dosha,' Jezro remarked. 'I can see why it's legendary.' He glanced at Loy. 'More tunnels, right?'

'Miles of them,' Loy said.

'Shaitan!' Warkannan shook his head in disbelief. 'I don't see how the Chof managed to drive the Settlers out of here.'

'My people manage-not,' Water Woman said. 'Our lore say some H'mai continue-then to live in there for years and years. They sneak-then in and out through secret tunnels, get-then food somehow. This be-may silly of me, but I be-not surprised to learn some live-still there.'

Here was the opening Loy had been hoping for. 'One of these days, I would love to sit down with you and discuss the war.'

Water Woman's throat sac turned grey, and she lowered her head. 'We talk-must, yes, but it be such sad lore, even now. Our children they die-then, but our Chur – they kill-then children of the H'mai. Not good, this, horrible it be.' She shook her massive head hard, then strode off to hurry on ahead.

'Merde!' Loy said. 'I've just made a faux pas.'

'That's strange,' Ammadin said. 'She was willing to talk about the war with me.'

'That's because you're comnee.' Jezro turned in the saddle to look at Ammadin. 'It wasn't your children they killed.'

'That must be it, yes.'

'Fascinating!' Warkannan said. 'They really do have true consciences. No wonder she wants to hear about the Lord.'

'Idres, my dear old friend!' Jezro paused for a sigh. 'There's something going on here that you're not seeing. We've had a double dose of Chof politics just lately, and I'll bet you vrans to breadmoss that it isn't piety blooming in Water Woman's six-chambered heart. If she brings a new religion to her people, she'll be way ahead of her rivals when the Great Mother dies.'

'What a damned cynical remark!' Warkannan looked genuinely distressed, so much so that Jezro winced.

'Well, I could be wrong,' the khan said.

As they rode free of the canyon, Warkannan and Jezro urged their horses forward and pulled ahead of the two women to continue their talk in Kazraki. Loy turned to Ammadin.

'Think Jezro's right?' Loy said.

'Of course,' Ammadin said. 'And I think he's going to make a fine ruler, assuming he can fight his way to the throne.'

After N'Dosha, the eastern valley appeared profoundly ordinary – another stretch of drying grass, dotted here and there with Midas trees. Small maroon birds broke cover and rose shrieking with a flap of naked wings as the Chof loped through, hurrying east. Booming in excitement, Water Woman came trotting back to meet the H'mai.

'Ride faster!' she said. 'We camp by water, and then we be at Sibyl's cave.'

The water, another canal, lay only a few miles from the canyon's mouth. While the servants made camp, Water Woman led Ammadin and Loy back to the traps. Out of a scatter of rocks, the cliff here rose sheer and high. Although pitted with caves in its upper reaches, from the valley floor up to some hundred yards it presented a smooth pale face, stippled here and there with black stone. Water Woman stamped both feet in a brief jig.

'There be Sibyl's cave. You see not see it?'

'We don't,' Loy said, smiling. 'That's a pretty convincing holo.'

'Yes.' Water Woman tipped back her head and thrummed a command.

A long, low stripe of cliff shimmered once and vanished. About twenty feet up, a dark slit appeared, flanked by two black pillars, shaped like stacks of flattened spheres. This close Loy could see that they were not rock but some artificial substance, gleaming and perfectly smooth. She swore under her breath in sheer awe. Ammadin's carefully composed face revealed no feeling at all.

'That's clever,' Ammadin said. 'Can I go in now?'

'You want-not eat first?' Water Woman said.

'I can wait for food, if it won't offend you.'

'You come-now many long miles. I see why you want to enter right away. Loy Sorcerer, Sibyl like-always to see new persons one at a time. It be best that Ammadin go first.'

'Fine with me,' Loy said. 'I've got to write up our trip through N'Dosha.'

Water Woman led Ammadin up the path, cut shallow into the side of the hill, to a landing directly in front of the overhang of rock protecting the entrance. In the shadows Ammadin could see a pair of metal doors. Water Woman inflated her throat sac and thrummed one long high note. The doors clanked, groaned, and slid open.

'They stay open-next-soon till I command-again. It be safe to enter.'

The sunlight illuminated the beginnings of a narrow hallway leading deeper into the cliff. At the moment Ammadin walked in, ceiling panels began to glow with a pale silver light. Down at the far end of the hallway, other lights turned themselves on in a circular room, some twenty feet in diameter. Floors, walls, free-standing metal screens propped between flexstone pillars, a collection of sleek blue boxes the height of a man, a square dais sitting in the centre of the room – they all glittered silver in the light from above.

Ammadin hesitated at the door to the circular room. She was afraid, she realized, and the fear stretched the hallway behind her until the exit seemed to stand miles away. Outside lay everything she knew. In the room ahead of her she would learn new truths, perhaps even more dangerous than the ones she'd already faced. She took a deep breath and walked in.

At each corner of the dais stood an oblong blue box, and in the centre sat a chair made of the same blue crystalline substance as Zayn's imp. Sitting in the chair was a woman, dressed in a pair of narrow blue trousers and a loose shirt of the same material, decorated with squares of coloured metal on the pocket and gold leaves clipped to the collar points. She looked no more than thirty, with her smooth, pale skin and long, brown hair, but her haunted dark eyes marked her as old, so weary that one could think her as old as the cliffs themselves. She looked Ammadin over with a bitter smile.

'Well, Lisa adin, I suppose you've come to gloat over your damned horses.' She spoke Tekspeak, and her words crackled with anger. 'I never thought Chursavva would be stupid enough to let you have them.'

'What? I'm not Lisadin. My name is Ammadin, the spirit rider of Apanador's comnee, and I'm here because you wanted my help.'

The woman vanished. Ammadin stood gaping until, just as suddenly, she reappeared.

'I malfunctioned,' Sibyl said. 'My memory banks at times make incorrect connections. I beg your pardon. You look almost exactly like Lisa adin Bar, Mother of Horses. Considering the small size of the Tribal gene pool, this is not surprising.'

Faced with greater marvels Ammadin had no interest in whom she resembled. 'How did you disappear like that?'

'I'm not really here. I am what is called a REV, a name that comes from the Old Vranz phrase retrouver et voir, a databank made up of electronic circuits housed in a variety of devices. Part of me exists here, in the Analysis Lab. The rest exists in some of those objects you call the Riders. If I have any body at all, it exists only as polyquartzine and other such materials. This is why the indigenes call me the stone woman.'

'But you look so solid.'

'What you are seeing is a hologram that preserves the appearance of the flesh-and-blood woman I once was. All organics have been stripped away. I exist only as a collection of data. Never make the mistake of thinking of me as a living H'mai. The hologram exists only to make my functions easier to access.'

'Did they take pictures of you, you mean, before you died?'

'No, I died in order to become a REV. You will not be able to understand how this was achieved. My ancestors developed the process of transferring a H'mai mind into what were known as artificial intelligence units. It was not widely used, as the actual person died once its flesh-and-blood neurons were catalogued and replicated. I remember the process as very painful, but fortunately I have no physical nervous system left to actualize that memory.' Sibyl leaned forward and held out one arm. 'Try to touch me.'

When Ammadin laid her fingers on what appeared to be Sibyl's wrist, they felt nothing. She waved her hand back and forth, passing it through the apparently solid flesh.

'Very well,' Ammadin said. 'So you're a ghost. I believe you now.'

'Good, but the accurate term is REV. Let me remind you that I am fully interactive. I will answer questions if you have any. My prime functions are to act as a repository of knowledge and to answer questions.'

'You brought me here to stop Yarl Soutan from finding the Ark of the Covenant. Is that right?'

'Not precisely. When I sent Water Woman to the grass, I wanted to stop him from trying to find it. The Ark as he has conceptualized it no longer exists. As you now know, I have no true physical existence. Thus, I could not stop him personally. Water Woman is enmeshed in the politics of her kind. Thus I thought it wise to ask for human help.'

'All right. You know about Zayn Hassan. He's a highly trained soldier, and at the moment he and some of the Chur are hunting Soutan down.'

'I am pleased to hear that, but it is too late to prevent all negative consequences. Yarl has already told other H'mai about the items and lore that may be found here. I have reformulated what I want thusly: help me minimize the damage Yarl has caused.'

'I'll do what I can, certainly.' Ammadin hesitated, debating where to start. 'You'll answer my questions?'

'One of my functions is to answer questions provided the answers are stored in my memory banks.'

'What if the questions are about things the Landfall Treaty says we shouldn't know?'

'I will answer. The time has come for the truth. The Treaty is now eight hundred years old. The concerns it was meant to address have changed since that time.'

'Good. I know that we're all on Snare because of some kind of mistake. What was it?'

'A jumpshunt accident that damaged the astrogation unit, which Soutan calls the Ark. I see that you don't understand. Travel between stars is difficult. Given the state of your general knowledge, I cannot possibly explain how ships manage to cover vast distances in small amounts of time. You will have to take it as a given in this discussion that there are places in space that make such travel possible. These locations are called jumpshunts. Travelling through them is dangerous. Something happened while our fleet was in the shunt. No one ever discovered the cause, and thus that answer is not in my databanks. But it resulted in our being thrown off-course.'

'So we fetched up here, and you decided to come to terms with the Chof.'

'This is correct.'

'So your people drew up the Landfall Treaty.'

'Correct.'

'And one of the terms was that we'd all lie to each other, the

Cantonneurs, the comnees, and the Kazraks. You set up lies right in the Treaty.'

'We did so in an attempt to protect the indigenes. We wished them to develop in their own way in their own time. Sibyl Davees, the person from whom I was created, was a xenobiologist. I was trained to protect sapient species wherever she found them. Our species, the H'mai, in its early days interacted very poorly with other species. We learned to defend against such self-centred actions with time.'

'But why the lies? I've been told that my ancestors wanted them.'

'Yes, precisely.' Sibyl leaned forward, and suddenly her eyes, her voice, took on life. 'Your ancestors signed on to the migration because they wanted to live simple lives as wandering nomads. They needed myths for their new culture, and so they created some. The Treaty protects those myths.'

'Like, the Tribes shall believe they have always belonged to the grass?'

'Exactly. Hypothesis: Loremaster Millou has already told you things forbidden under the Treaty.'

'Yes, but she had no choice. We found the wall with the sculptures on it. Your ancestors must have made it.'

'They were not my ancestors. I co-existed with them.'

'Sorry. I should call them the Settlers, Loy says.'

'Loremaster Millou is correct. Yes, the Settlers created long-lasting records of their circumstances.'

'Loy told me that the world is huge. If you were so worried about the Chof, why did you settle down right on top of them?'

'The world is indeed very large, but it is mostly water. There is only one land mass, a pangea as such are called. It would have been possible to settle on the opposite coast from the Chof, yes, but in the past, H'mai colonies have always spread across any land mass upon which they found themselves. Inevitably the descendants of the Karashiki and the Companies would have made contact with the Chof at a time when none of the original Settlers were alive to guide the meeting. We – I mean they, including the woman upon whom I am modelled – the fleet council decided after much debate that it would be better to supervise the process and set up laws and procedures to protect the indigenes, to teach the colonists from the beginning that the Chof are sapient beings like ourselves. Further questions?'

'Yes. Who were my ancestors and where did they come from?'

Sibyl leaned back in her armchair; her illusion of a face turned pale and for a moment seemed to dissolve into a stack of tiny cubes. When she spoke, however, the illusion came back strong. She twined her fingers together, glanced away, her eyes narrowed in thought. 'I will explain with basic definitions. Your ancestors were soldiers. They were also victims of a great crime. The crime was necessary to save billions upon billions of lives. There was an enemy that our ordinary soldiers could not defeat. This enemy wished to feed upon other sapient races as you feed upon saurs. Your ancestors were created to kill this enemy.'

'Wait! What do you mean, created?'

'I cannot answer that question with any precision in terms you can understand. Giving you the correct terms will take –' here Sibyl paused '– twelve to fifteen standard hours, and even then there is no guarantee you will understand me.'

'Sibyl, I've got to have some sort of answer. It doesn't need to be precise.'

'Very well. You have released me from a constraint. I will answer in terms that are not precise. Do your people still remember the role of the female in human reproduction?'

'If you mean producing eggs in her womb, of course we do.'

'Very good. The word you need to know is clone. They recruited the best soldiers they could find to supply them with reproductive materials, eggs and sperm both. They changed the nature of these materials in the fertilized egg. Then they treated the earliest stage of each embryo with a substance so that it divided into many embryos, identical and healthy. They grew them in vitrinuters –' another pause '– think of glass bottles, very large. In less than a year they had thousands of infants. They placed these infants in other mechanisms and raised them to adulthood in four more years. They continued growing infants for some years more.'

'What? How could –'

'Please.' Sibyl held up a hand for silence. 'Think: magic. They used magic to speed up the growth process for their altered H'mai. These men and women could see, hear, smell, and do things no other H'mai could. Each possessed special talents in the areas of memory, perception, and warfare.'

'Oh gods!'

'No, they were not gods. They were specially created H'mai.'

'Yes, yes, I know. I was saying those words because I suddenly understood something.'

'Very good. What do you understand?'

'The Kazraks say that all those talents came from demons. They must have meant the people who made those – what was that word?'

'Clones.' Sibyl deigned to smile. 'You have guessed correctly. The ancestors of the Kazraks – the Karashiki – had a very low opinion of my people. They expressed this contempt by using words such as demon, jinni, and the Great Shaitan to describe us.'

'Did they really think you were demons?'

'Of course not! They were using what is called a figure of speech. The person from whom I was created did not like Mullah Agvar, and he did not like her, but I never made the mistake of considering him stupid or superstitious.'

'His descendants aren't using a figure of speech. They think you really were demons.'

Sibyl's illusionary eyes blinked several times. 'This is distressing. They have lived too long in isolation.'

'You could say that about all of us.'

'Very true.'

'Were these soldiers the same as the Inborn?'

'They were a new kind of Inborn. The Inborn who existed before them were civilians given special talents but who were born in the ordinary way. They were not raised in glass bottles. They had parents who raised them in homes.'

'I see. Go on.'

'These soldiers were created, cloned, grown in tube-wombs and in the process conditioned to be human by psycho-formative imprint technology. They were trained to be soldiers in special hidden camps. They were then released upon the enemy's home planet. They were told to destroy the core-mind of the alien race. They did. We committed two great crimes: one to breed soldiers like horses, the other to exterminate another sapient species. But without those crimes, billions would have perished. The situation was so desperate that some members of the governing Council thought that the soldiers might be the only H'mai to survive the war. It fell to them to save the H'mai race if they could or to continue it on some hidden world if they could not.'

'But the soldiers – we – won the war.'

'Yes, you won, but at great cost. Most died. Some thousands however survived, a body of soldiers who could kill anything, hide anywhere, soldiers trained to have no mercy, who had reason to hate the Council for their creation.'

'I think I see. You had to get rid of us.'

Sibyl winced. 'I apologize for the behaviour of my people, but yes, we had to get rid of you. The Council settled your people on a continent of your own on a planet named Ruby. There were problems there with another race, the Hirrel, who occupied the other continent. Your language - you speak Hirl-Onglay. This name means Anglis as spoken in the territories of the Hirrel.'

'But what happened? Why did we come here?'

'Your ancestors had studied databanks concerning the ancient ways of H'mai upon Old Earth, the home planet, because they wanted to be free of the Council and live the way humans lived in primitive times. They decided that they would live like a group of ancient H'mai called variously the Soo or the Skithyans. The government agreed to send them to a planet where they could live as they wished.'

'The accident must not have mattered to them, then. They got what they wanted anyway.'

'They received some of what they wanted, not all. So did the Karashiki. Each group wished to live in isolation from all other groups. After the accident, that was not possible.'

'So you all worked out a system of separation, and everyone agreed to lie to their children.'

'Yes, but lie is a harsh usage.' Sibyl leaned forward in her chair. 'We did it because we thought it was best.'

'You still lied.'

'Oh very well then! We did lie. That is why I decided to keep living in this form. Someday, I knew, someone would want the truth.'

'But you hid the complex away?'

'No. When Sibyl became a REV N'Dosha was a flourishing community. Everyone knew about this cave.'

'Did the Settlers hide it during the Chof Wars?'

'No. Just before the wars started, a volcanic eruption further down the N'Dosha fault caused massive earthquakes. The side of the trap above this installation gave way and buried the entrance. The Settlers would have dug it out again, but the war intervened.'

'You were cut off, then.'

'Completely.' Sibyl's voice suddenly shook, and her eyes widened. 'For two hundred and fifty years I was isolated. Fortunately, as a REV I access no emotions, so the isolation did not –' Her illusory face suddenly froze and became as flat as a drawing on a piece of rushi. When she spoke, only her lips moved. 'The isolation was burdensome, yes.' Somewhere behind her a high-pitched bell chimed. Sibyl's image inflated into three dimensions and began to move, stiffly for a few moments, then with a natural fluidity. She sat back in her chair and smiled. 'Fortunately, the Settlers had got as far as digging out and repairing the two solar pillars, and I had power with which to operate. To keep myself occupied I ran long data chains and analyses that resulted in the book of predictions called *The Sibylline Prophecies*. From my analyses I saw that eventually someone would find the complex again. I just never thought that the Chof would find it first.'

'And when they did, you helped them. So much for letting them develop in their own way in their own time.'

Sibyl vanished. The illusionary chair and the blue quartz platform remained. Ammadin waited until Sibyl reappeared.

'In this form,' Sibyl said, 'I cannot handle contradictions.'

'But you did things that were contradictions.'

Once again the image vanished, and once again, after a wait, it reappeared.

'In this form,' Sibyl said, 'I cannot handle contradictions.'

'I'm sorry,' Ammadin said. 'I keep forgetting what you are.'

'I am not surprised that this is so.'

'Now, let me make sure I understand. Your people created mine to fight and die for them. Then, once most of us were dead, you decided that you were too good for the survivors. You had to get rid of your own creation, but we were too dangerous to just kill off.'

'I never relayed any such information to you.'

'No, but it's obvious.' Ammadin crossed her arms over her chest. 'Am I right?'

'Yes, you were too dangerous to attack. No, we did not decide that we were too good for you. We were afraid. You were fearsome.'

'Are we still?'

'In your present situation, armed with spears and knives, no, you are not fearsome.'

'Let me rephrase my question. Do these traits, the ones you just told me about, the traits that made us like the Inborn, do they breed true?'

Sibyl's image froze. When at last she spoke, only her mouth moved.

'Yes.' Her voice sounded hollow. 'They breed true.'

'Then we're still dangerous. You should have made us marry into the Cantons or Kazrajistan.' Ammadin uncrossed her arms and shook them; her muscles had tensed to the point of aching. 'That would have thinned our bloodlines.'

The image moved and became three-dimensional again.

'Perhaps so.' Sibyl's voice sounded alive again as well. 'But let me clarify. This decision to treat your ancestors so badly was not my decision. It was made by the ruling government, the Rim Council, as it was termed and may indeed still be termed. I have no information as to its continued existence.'

'Suppose they'd asked you? Would you have agreed with them?'

'No, I would not have agreed. But I would have had no other idea of how to solve the problem your ancestors presented.'

'That's fair.' Ammadin considered her next question. Those that she'd so carefully prepared were beginning to seem oddly trivial. 'You talked about the Hirrel. One of our gods is named Hirrel.'

'This is true. Each of your gods is named for one of the sapient species that made up our interstellar culture. The figurines you carry each represent one of these species. This was done in case a rescue unit managed to reach Snare. The Settlers wanted your people to treat this unit with respect rather than destroying them as invaders.'

Ammadin stared at her for a long moment. She could not speak; she could barely breathe.

'You are distressed,' Sibyl said.

'Distressed? Not exactly. I'm furious.'

'I do not understand the cause of this emotion.'

'You're telling me that my gods – you're telling me that there are no gods.'

'I am not competent to judge the question of whether any power that might be termed god or gods exists or does not exist. The figurines that you call gods, however, are not gods in any sense of the word. They are representations of the sapient species that together instituted the Rim Council.'

'You – your people – they tricked us into worshipping something that doesn't exist.'

'Most sapients who worship a god or gods worship something that does not exist. If such a thing as a god does exist, it would not equate to the representations they make of it.'

'That's not what I'm talking about. The gods lie at the root of who the comnees are. Bane, for instance.' Ammadin felt her hands tighten into fists beyond her power to stop them. 'What happens to Bane without gods?'

'Your Banes were instituted as a logical set of instructions to preserve the native environment and the indigenes. I will admit to having a hand in their creation.'

'You are not a god.'

'No, I am a REV image produced by electronic fields in an arrangement of devices.'

'You're not understanding me. You had no right to make up Banes and then tell us they came from the gods.'

'This is true. I remember feeling doubts, but the step seemed to be necessary to protect the indigenes. Still, I fail to see how those twenty rules could be so important to you.'

'Twenty? There are hundreds of them.'

Sibyl's image briefly froze. 'I can only conclude that the Companies have elaborated upon those twenty and created entirely new ones as well.' She thawed and smiled, entirely too smugly for the dead thing she claimed to be. 'You spirit riders are as much to blame as Sibyl is, therefore.'

'Blame? No. That makes it better, somehow. It means that at least part of them belongs to us. And what about the quests? What about going into the sea caves or the Mistlands for visions? Did you make that up, too?'

'No. Dallas ador Jenz, Father of Arrows, found such rituals to be a part of the Soo-Skithyan culture. He considered them an essential part of true humanity.'

'All right, good. Then those belong to us, too.'

'In fact, Sibyl objected to the choice of the Mistlands as a site for questing. I feared that the indigenous life cycle might suffer from human presence there.'

'Oh did you?' Anger began to pound in Ammadin's blood like

a drug. 'What about your own people? The H'mai. Remember them? What about us?'

'I drew up the Banes to protect you, too. If the Chof had been given unlimited access to technology –'

'It would have damaged their culture, yes, I know.'

'Let me finish!' Sibyl leaned forward, raising a hand palm out. 'If the Chof had been given unlimited access to technology, the outcome had a high probability for being disastrous to the H'mai, given the complexity of the Chof brain and the potential of their intellects.'

'I don't understand.'

'They are much much smarter than we are. I don't know how to make it any clearer. Consider how quickly and well they learned all our various languages, how easily they switch back and forth between them.' Sibyl sat back in her chair and folded her hands in her lap. 'I did not want the Chof to absorb the H'mai any more than I wanted the H'mai to absorb the Chof. I see by your facial expressions that you are still angry.'

'Yes, but I'll grant that you meant well. It's the way you did it! Having us worship something that doesn't exist, and then –' Ammadin paused, gulping for breath. 'And then bringing me here. Damn you, Sibyl! You brought me here to destroy my people, didn't you?'

'What?' The image froze. 'I had no such intention. I brought you here to help me deal with Yarl Soutan. You are the one who has asked other questions.'

'Oh? It's pretty damn obvious that you're still angry with Lisadin for giving us horses. And how come you told me that it was time for us to know the truth?'

Sibyl faded to the edge of vanishing, then suddenly solidified and moved. 'You have detected an error in my functioning,' she said. 'I behaved in a contradictory manner.'

'I know that. Why?'

'I thought that it would aid in the survival of the indigenes if spirit riders knew certain basic truths. So I tempted you to ask the questions so I might supply the answers.'

'Eight hundred years too late! We've woven your lies into our lives. Can't you see that? We believed them all, we depended on them, we've lived them. You can't take that all away from people and expect them to go right on the way they did before. Why should anyone follow Bane if a bunch of H'mai just made it all up?'

'Attitude adjustments will need to be made, yes, among the spirit riders.'

'Is that all you have to say? How can we trust our laws any more? We followed them because we thought the gods gave them to us, but the gods are just a bunch of figurines. And you've got your filthy nerve, saying you're cutting the cinch but the saddle won't fall.'

The image blinked its eyes. 'I do not foresee the consequences you imply with that metaphor.'

'No? Then your information about us is all wrong. Once my people know the truth –'

'Do not tell them the truth! This information should be kept to a small group, a council of spirit riders. You may then make decisions based upon it in private. The technology will remain magical to the uninitiated.'

'We should become a lot of stinking mullahs and priests, you mean? Lie to our own people? No! We *will* know the truth. All of us.'

'The consequences of that will, as you have surmised, be unfortunate for your people and dangerous for all other sapient societies on this planet.'

'Right now, right here, I can't care about that.'

'Your ancestors had little grasp of consequences as well. That's what made them so dangerous.'

'Well, whose fault is that? We were bred to destroy other species, weren't we?'

'You are being illogical by seeing this information as reflecting upon you and your contemporaries in such a personal manner. The actions of which you speak took place over eight hundred years ago.'

Ammadin took a deep breath, then another. Slowly the rage left her.

'I cannot be your enemy,' Sibyl continued. 'If the actual Sibyl Davees still lived, then your anger at my decisions would be justified, because in fact she did not take the feelings of the Companies into account during the debates over Bane. Still, I was merely someone who feared you.'

'All right, fair enough. Another question. What about Loremaster Millou? Why did you bring her here?'

'In the service of my most important function, protecting the indigenes. Thanks to Yarl Soutan, the Karashiki now know that in N'Dosha lie many things of value. If they come here to confiscate those things, the indigenes will suffer. Loremaster Millou will take the news of this threat back to the Cantons, where she and her kind will devise a plan to deal with the inevitable consequences.'

'That makes sense. And now Jezro Khan is here too.'

'Yes. Herbgather Woman's actions have produced a serious problem. She meant to protect her people, but she has increased their danger.'

'Jezro's a decent man. Have you thought of talking with him?'

'I had not. Please input more data.'

'He's quite reasonable, he doesn't take himself seriously, and while he believes in his god, he's not a fanatic like some of the other Kazraks. He doesn't want to hurt the Chof, and he doesn't want a huge empire. He doesn't even want the one he's heir to.'

'This is extremely valuable data. I require more information about the current state of the Karashikis' thinking. If I can find some suitable reward, perhaps Jezro Khan will supply what I need.'

'Oh, I know what Jezro wants. He's looking for information on how to build simple machines. He wants lamps that give light without burning anything, a way to talk with someone over a long distance, better medicines and tools, that kind of thing.'

'Some of these objects may lie within the parameters defined by Karashiki resources. Thank you for telling me. I repeat: I brought you here to help deal with Yarl Soutan. That was my primary motive. But my nature is such that I must answer questions when they are asked.'

'But you used the word tempted,' Ammadin said. 'You tempted me to ask questions.'

'Yes. It was not a logical usage.'

'Are you really only a machine? You say she, you say I, back and forth, when you talk about Sibyl Davees. I think there's more of the H'mai left in you than you want to admit.'

Sibyl disappeared, chair and all. Ammadin waited. The silver light glowed steadily, and the room seemed to be humming under its breath. She suddenly felt that the entire complex was alive in some way that she couldn't comprehend.

'Sibyl,' Ammadin called out. 'Your primary function is to answer questions. I have a question that needs answering.'

With a glimmer of bluish light, Sibyl reappeared, but only as a flat, frozen image.

'What is your question?' Only her lips moved when she spoke.

'I said, more of the H'mai's left in you than you want to admit. Is that true?'

Sibyl became three-dimensional, slowly, starting with her feet; the effect worked its way upward much as dried breadmoss expanded when dipped in water. 'Yes, it is true. You are very perceptive.'

'I'm a spirit rider. Helping people understand themselves is part of my work.'

'I had not realized. Your work has changed since the original formulation of the Tribes.'

'Good. That's something else that's ours.'

Sibyl leaned back in her chair and looked at the ceiling. 'There has been a considerable drain on my power banks. May we end this session?'

'Yes. I'm tired, too.'

Sibyl disappeared. Ammadin took a deep breath and walked out of the room. She wanted to run for the outer door, but she forced herself to move slowly, with the dignity befitting a spirit rider. When she stepped outside, she found it was night, and the Herd was rising over the mountains to the east.

Ammadin paused, staring at the stars. Did they still live in the Herd, the ancestors who had created her and the other Inborn? She wondered if they'd ever manage to find their lost children, and if she hoped or feared that they would.

'Ammi!' Loy was puffing up the path towards her. 'I'm dying to know what she said.'

'Are you?' Ammadin said. 'Well, it's a good thing you brought all those notebooks.'

At about the time that Ammadin was walking into Sibyl's cave, Stronghunter Man was leading the warparty due east, across the valley and away from the traps. Through Fifth Out he explained to Zayn that they would swing around in an arc in order to approach the North Gate from the valley.

'If Yarl be-now there,' Stronghunter Man said, 'he have-now cliffs behind him and place to hide. We have-must some way to surprise-maybe him. We be in bad position.' He made a squatting motion with his hind legs and pelvis, which Fifth Out faithfully imitated. 'Very bad if he have-now those fire spirits.'

'I've been trained as a scout,' Zayn said. 'And I can hide a lot more easily than you Chof. When we reach his general location, I'd be glad to go out alone to reconnoitre.'

'Ah.' Stronghunter Man made a chewing motion as he thought the offer over. 'You forget one thing. You have more power to hide from H'mai and Chof eyes than we have, but not from Chof noses. Yarl's renegades – they smell-soon you if you get close to them.'

'Shit! I want to carry my weight in this expedition, not just ride along.'

Stronghunter Man stamped several times. 'I like this. We be the same kind of person.'

'Soldiers, you mean? Or because we're both men?'

'No. There be two kind persons in the world, those who kill and those who eat. You and I, we hunt, we risk, we be those who kill. Our women, they be those who eat. Other females somewhere? Maybe they be those who kill; maybe their men be those who eat. We know-not, and it matter-not.'

That night, after they made camp, Zayn stood at the bank of a narrow canal, choked with silt and water reeds, and watched the galaxy rise over the far-off mountains, so black and sharp against the silver sky. Suppose he'd been born back in the real homeland, back among the people who had created minds like his. Would he have been among those who kill? He doubted it, and for the first time in his life he wondered what it would have been like to live by his intellect. Maybe he would have been a loremaster like Loy, or maybe he would have flown on one of those mysterious vessels, the starships, to keep every detail of its explorations stored in his mind. He might never have seen a battle, much less fought in one. He might have been one of those who eat and never found himself among those who kill. The feeling that swept over him puzzled him at first. Finally he recognized it: regret.

With that naming he felt the ghosts prowling around him, those same ghosts who had come in the Mistlands. It seemed he could see them in the faint starlight as a glimmer on the surface of the canal.

'I'm sorry,' he said aloud. 'I'm sorry I caused your deaths.'

They disappeared, and he knew without knowing how he knew that he would never see them again.

Out of sheer excitement Loy barely slept that night. Like a child before a birthday party, she kept waking to check the galaxy's progress across the sky and to wish it were dawn. At last she woke to sunlight, sat up smiling, and rolled out of her blankets only to find that her last sleep had been a long one, and the camp had woken some while before her. Water Woman sat haunched with Warkannan and Jezro, discussing their holy book, which lay open in the captain's lap. Servants bustled around, picking up bundles and setting them down, fetching water, and cutting firewood. Loy considered breakfast, decided that she was too excited to eat, and pulled on her boots.

Some distance away in the pale grass Ammadin knelt with her crystals in front of her. When Loy joined her, she handed over the visual scanner. Loy adjusted the focus of her eyes and peered in. Stronghunter Man was leading the warparty along the banks of a weed-choked canal. The young Chof carrying Zayn loped along next to the leader.

'Well, they're on their way, all right,' Loy said. 'Any sign of Yarl?'

'No. He's found somewhere to hide.'

Loy muttered a curse and handed the crystal back.

'You must be about ready to go in,' Ammadin said.

'Whenever Sibyl will see me, you bet. I wonder if she'll have any major surprises for me, like the one she had for you? I doubt it.'

'Let's hope not! Although I'm glad I know the truth. It's just that I don't know what I'm going to do about it.'

'Well, you've got time to decide. It'll be a while before you can get back to the plains.'

'That's true, but I need to get back before midwinter. There's a council then, down by the sea, of all the spirit riders. We compare what we've done over the summer, and if anyone's learned new lore, they present it.'

'You're going to have quite a presentation this year, that's for certain. So will I, for that matter, when I get back, even without a major surprise.'

Loy's prediction proved accurate. Sibyl exposed no secrets, made no massive revelations. What she did have were details – blessed details, as Loy thought of them – stories of the arrival on Snare, of the first meetings with the Chof, of the negotiations over the Landfall Treaty. At moments Loy felt that she wanted to spend the rest of her life sitting below Sibyl's dais and scribbling down the details as fast as Sibyl gave them, but after a good many hours, her hand ached so badly that she could barely straighten her fingers.

One last riddle, however, nagged at her, even though it was perhaps a trivial thing.

'About *The Sibylline Prophecies*,' Loy said. 'You told Ammi that you composed them?'

'This is true.'

'If you wrote them when the cave was buried, how did you print them? Let's see, it was about twenty years ago that a Chof brought a bundle of printed pages into Shairb as trade goods. She said she found them in the ruins.'

'Yes, that was Water Woman. She was still Chiri Van, not Chiri Michi then. As for the printing, in this complex a unit exists that is equipped with the capacity to make heat transfers onto any thin sheet – paper, rushi, cloth, tree bark, wood, any of those. The original pages were crudely made rushi. I had instructed the indigenes in its making.'

'I see. The current head of my guild rode out to Shairb to investigate when the book first appeared. The trader told him that the Chof threatened to destroy the pages if he didn't pay her what she wanted. She said that if he haggled, she'd rip pages out of the book and then raise her price. Do you know why?'

Sibyl leaned back, and laughter sounded from somewhere behind her left shoulder. 'Forgive me, Loremaster,' she said, 'but I told her an Old Earth story as a joke, forgetting that she would follow anything she perceived as an order.'

'What's so funny?'

'That course of action is a reference to the ancient literature of the Romai. Once the trader in Shairb had the copy of the book, what did he do with it?'

'He sold it, damn his tiny balls, to an unscrupulous dealer in Kors, who had copies printed and distributed before my guild even knew it existed. We've never been able to examine the original sheets thanks to him and his damned greedy daughter. He called it a magic oracle and sold a lot of them very fast. It spread to the Kazrak empire, too.'

'I had hoped it would do so.'

'Why?'

'To make people there see that change is always possible, even among prophets.'

'Good point. It makes me like the *Prophecies* a lot better.'

'They had a secondary purpose. I wished to encode a record of my existence and the location of this complex in case it once again was buried by natural forces.'

'But why put it in that form?'

'Cryptic puzzles have always intrigued the H'mai race. Simple directions are boring and easily lost.'

'You've got a point.' Reluctantly Loy closed her notebook and laid it on the floor beside her. 'I don't mean to drain your power banks. I probably should leave.'

'I have power left. I am wondering if you would now answer questions for me.'

'Certainly, but what about?'

'What has happened in the Cantons recently. News of my people's descendants, gossip, any such data would be welcome. I have come to respect the Chof greatly, but they are not our species.'

'That's true. You must have felt really isolated.'

'Indeed.' Sibyl's image momentarily froze. With a soft chime she moved again. 'So much so that I am thinking of asking you to kill me.'

'What?'

'Your facial expression indicates shock. I have existed in this form for seven hundred and forty-two years. That much immortality has proved burdensome. At moments I find myself hoping you will agree to follow the procedures that will destroy me.'

'If you're dead, you won't be able to protect the Chof.'

'Unfortunately this is true. I no longer care. Correction: I want to protect the Chof less than I want to die.'

'If you're dead, will we still be able to ask questions and get information from your components?'

'I have no information on this point.' Sibyl's face turned into a stack of glowing cubes, then slowly reformed itself. 'But it is unlikely. I am the sole existing interface for the databanks.'

'As a loremaster, I can't countenance losing that data.'

'I have anticipated your reluctance.' Sibyl seemed to droop in her chair; she turned her ancient eyes away. 'But to be isolated again after so much contact with my own kind –'

'But you won't be isolated. Water Woman and the Great Mother both have let a few cautious remarks drop about allowing some small number of Canton people back into N'Dosha. Probably they want to give us a reason to fend off the Kazraks, but it'll be worth it.'

The hologram swung round in the chair and leaned forward, as if it were staring into Loy's eyes. 'That would ease my dysfunctioning,' Sibyl said.

'Good. We'll work on it, then. You know, I have to agree with Ammi. You're not some mechanical thing. The expressions on your face –'

'It is not an actual face. It is a hologrammatic representation. Those expressions are graphic components called up as appropriate by the context of our conversation, dependent upon certain key words and phrases.'

'Oh? If you're mechanical, then why do you want to die? How come you're lonely?'

'Functionality left unutilized over long periods of time tends to decay and become unstable, thus producing illogical output.'

Loy snorted. 'Have it your way, then. Now, let me see. What kind of news can I give you?'

Sibyl leaned back in her chair. 'How many Cantons now exist? Let us start with numerical data and proceed from there to personalities.'

In the hot summer morning the warparty headed north. Even though he rode instead of running, Zayn felt sweat trickle down his back and soak his shirt. Rather than lope at full speed, the Chof jogged along slowly enough for Zayn to notice little patches of green dappling the ground, as if the plants in the N'Dosha canyon were spreading into the valley, but the farther north they rode, the more green he saw, lying thick along the canal, scattered in the dry blue grass. Somewhere north, then, the Settlers must have created a second garden. Gradually the grass became pale gold, not blue – dry green grass, not dry purple. They stopped to eat at midday in the shade of a grove of trees of a type he'd never seen before, as tall as oaks and roughly the same shape, with billowing green leaves above sturdy trunks.

'Do you know what the Settlers called these trees?' Zayn said.

'Marrons,' Stronghunter Man said through Fifth Out. 'When summer end-each-year, we come here, collect the hard little balls they grow. Crack the shells, roast them in embers, and they taste good. Our women, they put some of the raw balls in the ground. New trees grow-after.'

While they were eating a breeze rose, rippling the yellow grass and shivering the green leaves of the trees. Stronghunter Man told the others to stay where they were, handed his spear to Zayn to hold, then walked north some hundreds of yards. He stopped with his pseudo-arms crossed over his chest and tipped his head back.

'He seek-now,' Fifth Out said, 'for enemies.'

'He can smell them?' Zayn said.

'Oh yes. For long long way.'

In a few minutes Stronghunter Man returned with information. Other Chur, including one Chur Vocho, were heading towards them from the north.

'Six in all.' Stronghunter Man took his spear back from Zayn. 'I think-maybe it be Yarl's renegades. If so, we meet-soon them. We go-now and see-next.'

Each Chof, except for Stronghunter Man, carried extra spears tied to his back. They took turns unloading each other and passing them out, till each Chof carried two spears, one in each hand. Stronghunter Man handed Zayn a spear as well. With its thick, short shaft and fire-hardened point, edged with obsidian flakes, the weapon balanced and wounded so differently from a Kazraki lance or comnee spear that it would be useless in his hands, but he thanked the Chur Vocho anyway.

'Before we go,' Stronghunter Man said, 'there be-now a thing you do-must. Take cloth and stop up your ears.'

The order struck Zayn as so bizarre that at first he figured he'd misunderstood. 'Do what?'

'Stop your ears.' Stronghunter Man pointed to the side of Zayn's head with a spear-tip. 'You hear-must-not. Soon we challenge and fight. Your ears bleed-next if sound touch them.'

Zayn rummaged through his saddlebags and found the rag he kept for polishing his long knife. He cut two strips over the obsidian flakes on the spear, but they made less than efficient earplugs.

Stronghunter Man let out an experimental shout that made Zayn wince despite them.

'Not good enough,' the Chur Vocho pronounced. 'Here, give back to me the spear. Here be-now your orders. When we see renegades, you fall-next back, stay back some many feet, and put-next your hands over your ears. Understood?'

'Yes sir,' Zayn said automatically, but while he understood what to do, he had no idea of why.

Another hour's riding brought him the answer. They were slogging their way through high thatchy grass when Stronghunter Man raised his head high and sniffed the air. He inflated his throat sac and began barking orders.

'He say-now we fall back,' Fifth Out said.

The other Chof formed a line across the valley at right angles to the cliffs. Fifth Out lagged well behind as they began to walk forward, one slow stride at a time. At some far distance ahead of them another Chur boomed, high enough for Zayn to hear it. Another joined in, and another, until he could pick out six voices, thrumming and booming in the still air.

'They challenge,' Fifth Out said. 'Cover your ears.'

Zayn put in his improvised earplugs and laid his hands flat over his ears, and just in time. Stronghunter Man and his Chur filled their throat sacs, then answered with a boom of their own, a huge sound that seemed to crush the air as it surged forward. They boomed again, then thrummed, sent the air vibrating so hard that Zayn felt it through his skull. He gritted his teeth and pressed his hands down as hard as he could. The renegades ahead boomed again, closer now, and again Stronghunter Man's warparty answered. Back and forth they went, louder and louder as the renegades approached. Despite his precautions Zayn's ears hurt; he hunched his shoulders in a futile attempt to cover them a little more. Fifth Out turned his head to glance at him, then began to walk backwards, but they needed to stay reasonably close to protect themselves from the renegades.

Finally the two lines of Chof stood a bare twenty feet apart, and still they boomed and thrummed. First Zayn's head ached; then it began to burn, or so it felt, with slivers of hot metal lodged in his temples. He shut his eyes to hide them from the blazing sunlight. His ears crackled and throbbed with every round of the strange battle being fought with sound alone. All at once – silence.

Zayn raised his head and opened his eyes, but his ears still rang and crackled in the outer silence, an absence of noise as thick as water, it seemed, oozing through the battered air. The two lines of Chof stood poised, spears ready. Stronghunter Man took one step and boomed. His line followed; each Chur shook his pair of spears and they all chattered from deep within their quivering throat sacs. The renegades stood their ground. Another step, another boom and thrum from Stronghunter Man – the renegades broke and ran. As they fled east they howled and yipped, then began to make the bubbling whine of abject surrender.

Fifth Out trotted forward to rejoin the main line of spear Chur. When Zayn removed the strips of cloth, he saw tiny drops of blood on one of them. His ears and his head still ached, but slowly the pain began to ease.

'You see-now why I tell you, hide ears?' Stronghunter Man said.

Zayn had trouble hearing Fifth Out's relay. 'Yes, I sure do.'

'Cowards run-always,' Stronghunter Man continued, 'and they who back Yarl, they be cowards. They betray-then him, too, as they run. They say, oh please kill-not us, Yarl he be at the North Gate.' Stronghunter Man dipped his pelvis as if to squat, and Fifth Out copied him. 'Cowards!'

'Are we going to head straight there? Soutan must have heard the fight.'

'Yes, we go now, in case those Chur, they find courage and come back. Yarl be-not so far now, not so far at all.'

It was the horses that gave Soutan away. Late that same afternoon, Ammadin spent a long time scanning the valley east of the traps. When she saw the renegade Chur fleeing in panic, her first thought was that Zayn had run into trouble, but a few miles on she found him and the actual warparty. For some while she watched them jogging across the monotonous landscape. Out of boredom she moved the focal point of the scan north along their projected line of march.

Some miles ahead of the warparty one of the traps jutted farther to the east than the others, forming a sharp right angle of cliff where it met the face to its south. The Settlers had worked this angle of cliff into another marvel of architecture, with caves and ledges, facades and windows of dwellings, sculptures of H'mai and animals, all set among the natural pillars and arches eroded by wind and rain. The largest cave entrance lay right at ground level in the point of the angle, a perfect semi-circle guarded by two sculptures of longtooth saurs, haunched with their mouths open and their front legs up to show claw.

In front of this cave, a carpet of green plant life spread out, heaped and mounded over what appeared to be enormous stones. In and among them pools of water gleamed, and just beyond, in a long meadow of green grass, horses grazed at tether, switching their tails. Soutan and Arkazo could hide inside caves, but their horses had to eat. Ammadin focused her crystal down and increased magnification. What she'd taken for boulders under the blanket of greenery were the remains of machines. Here and there she could pick out the rim of a giant wheel tangled in vines, an arc of silver metal gleaming through ferns, or the white glitter of flexstone among tall weeds.

Someone called her name – Loy, walking down from the camp to join her.

'I think I've found Yarl's hiding place,' Ammadin said.

'Good!' Loy said. 'Is there time for me to take a look?'

Ammadin handed over the crystal. Loy stared into it, her eyes narrow.

'I can't believe it!' she whispered. 'That's the North Gate of N'Dosha. I've seen pictures. Let me just – merde! It's breaking up! The image, I mean, not the gate.'

'The Riders set fast down here.'

'They certainly do.' Loy handed the crystal back. 'I should have come out sooner.'

'Are you done talking with Sibyl already?'

Loy held up her hand, so red and swollen that she couldn't make a fist when she tried. 'I can't write one more word.'

'How cold is the canal water? You should soak that.'

'Good idea. I will. And here I always thought that writers' cramp was a myth. But if you want to, why not go back to Sibyl's? She's still got power in her banks.'

'Good idea. I will.'

Ammadin started to gather up her crystals in order to carry them with her, hesitated, then handed the saddlebags to Loy. 'You might as well keep these out here. I don't know how long I'll be, and you'll probably want to scan on the next pass.'

'Yes, I will.' Loy was looking at the saddlebags in a kind of wonder. 'Thank you. I appreciate it, being trusted with these, I mean.'

Ammadin smiled, then strode away, heading for the cave.

The hologram appeared as soon as she entered the silver room: Sibyl sitting in her blue chair, her hands on her knees. Above a decidedly sour curve of mouth, the image's eyes appeared to move and study her.

'Good afternoon, Ammadin,' Sibyl said in a weary tone of voice. 'I suppose you have more questions.'

'I have, yes,' Ammadin said. 'I was wondering if any of the Company people had themselves turned into REVs.'

'No. I can offer you pictures of your ancestors, but they are only records, not fully functional AI units.'

'I'm sorry, I don't understand that.'

'They are recordings, that is, they appear as a picture and a voice, but they are at code-source no different from a page in a book. You cannot speak with them, only listen to their testimonies.'

'That sounds better than nothing. Can I see some?'

'Yes. Whom do you wish to hear?'

'Lisadin and Dallador, I mean Dallas ador Jenz and Lisa adin Bar. Or wait – tell me this first. Why do we all have din and dor at the end of our names?'

'This suffix was an identity tag demanded by the Hirrel before your people were allowed to settle on Ruby. It identifies the user as a clone or descendant of a clone. In their language, those words are gender-specific adjectives that mean "false, artificial." The Hirrel are a very insular race. Biotechnology disturbs them.'

'Oh does it? I'll bet they were glad enough to let my ancestors die for them.'

'You have a very high probability of winning that wager. In fact, I remember feeling contempt for the Hirrel based on their attitude to your people. As for your request, those records both exist. Which do you wish to view first?'

'The Mother of Horses.'

'Very well. I suspect you will find her congenial.'

Sibyl vanished, and the chair went with her. A small picture appeared, hanging in mid-air above the dais. At first it showed only a stationary view of sky and the purple grass of the plains; then suddenly it expanded to some ten feet on an edge. Off to one side of the image sat a sleek, white object with swept-back wings and a pointed nose, one of the ships, Ammadin assumed. She could hear sound, somewhat garbled, in the language she now knew as Tekspeak – 'No come over farther, stand on the mark, dammit, always difficult aren't you?' The view began to travel in the same way that a crystal would sweep over countryside. The ship disappeared, and the view settled upon a woman, dressed in narrow tan trousers and a tan shirt cut like Sibyl's blue one, with coloured squares on the pocket and little metal birds on the corners of the collar.

During her stay in the hohtes of the Cantons, Ammadin had seen herself in mirrors for the first time. She did look like Lisadin, she realized, close enough to be her sister. The image hooked her thumbs into the waistband of her trousers and stood with her feet a bit apart.

'My name is Colonel Lisa Barlamew, or as the shit-licking Hirrel called me, Lisa adin Bar. I am making this record just in case my descendants want to see it someday, not so the pack of bungling bastards in the fleet can find it and bring their databanks up to date.'

An incomprehensible voice chattered at her.

'Go to hell,' Lisa said. 'Where was I? Oh yeah. Listen, children, if you exist. This is not what we planned for you. They promised us a world of our own, a place in a newly discovered shunt-cluster of habitable worlds. But their damned astrogator made a mistake, not that he'll admit it, and so here we are. This means accommodations have to be made, especially for the native race. It's not their fault that a pack of brainless Shipfolk fucked up and dumped H'mai Inborn into their laps.

'Anyway, I want to tell you about the horses and why I fought so hard to get them for you. We're sharing a world with men who think women are little children who need taking care of. This is a mental disease, and I don't want our men to get it, too. The horses belong to you women, to make sure the men never trample you down. Women, whatever you do, keep the horses under your control. Keep the money they'll bring from the Karashiki under your control. It's freedom, it's power, it's safety. Some of our men might decide that it's a good idea to have some kiss-arse females mincing around their tents. If nothing else, if worse comes to worst, take the horses and the sensible men and ride away.

'Sooner or later you'll find out about the false gods. I'm sorry about that, but it was the best Dallas and I could come up with in the time we had. That damned xeno-bi girl, Davees, insisted that if we got the horses, you had to have gods, something to keep you on a tight rein. Davees suggested me and Dallas for the job, but we both refused. We'll be culture heroes, sure. Gods, no. She was right about one thing, though, that if someday one of the other species manages to break through and land here, we don't want you to tear them apart. If that means they have to look like gods to you, so be it.

'I'm running out of time, but one last thing: remember, boys and girls, that you are stronger than the Shipfolk and Karashiki will admit you are, that you're faster, too, and you can see things they don't and hear things they'll never hear. If they enslave you, break free. One of you could kill five of them with your bare hands. We are the Inborn, and we will be free. There was a time when all H'mai demanded freedom, but most of them choose slavery these days. It's a nice comfortable slavery, with their machines and medicines and safe little lives, and they call it freedom, but it's slavery. Don't give in. Don't waste yourselves on their damned machines and gadgets. Live the way the H'mai were meant to live.'

Her image looked steadily out until the picture changed. It seemed to be the same view, but standing in Lisadin's place was a man who resembled Palindor, except for the grey in his hair and the look in his eyes – a man who had seen horrors, Ammadin decided, and who remembered the friends who hadn't survived them. His shirt collar sported gold stars, one on each side.

'I am Dallas ador Jenz, the only surviving general of the Third Army as well as a general survivor of our time on Ruby.' His image smiled briefly at his joke. 'Thanks to the accident in the shunt, we find ourselves sharing a planet with a group of fanatics almost as crazy as we are. I sincerely wonder if either group will still exist when these records are found, if they're found at all. The Shipfolk will probably make it through, so the meek will inherit this new earth.

'I have entered the history of the clone-born in text-based mode into the historical archives, just on the off-chance the Council will try to suppress the information back home. I do want to state, however, that unlike Lisa, I'm not bitter about our creation. I think their birth techs did a damn fine job on us, in fact. I reserve my pity for the woman-born functionaries like the Recallers and Calculators, who have our burdens with none of our strengths. Had we remained in Council space, I would have tried to incorporate the functionaries into our Companies. As it is, I hope those attached to the fleet that brought us here will come join us on the plains.

'Now, about the rites and rituals of the Tribes, we based those on historical material, the oldest I could find in the databanks back on the Rim. They all existed on Old Earth, or at least, the sources said they did. I tend to disbelieve before I believe, these days. I've put the historical background into the archives, too, along with some background material on shamanism. Someday maybe our scouts – I mean, spirit riders – will want to read it. It will seem strange to you, whoever you are, the audience for these records, that we were determined to root ourselves in history. If so, you have no idea how it feels to have no history whatsoever. Actually, we survivors have a little bit of a past, I suppose, since we're all from the third batch.'

Jenz paused, his eyes suddenly cold and hard. Then he tossed his head and continued.

'You see, they could use the psych-print tech to teach us how to be killers. But they couldn't teach us how to be H'mai. I decided we'd better start at the beginning, and maybe this time we'll get it right.' He paused, and he may have smiled – the brief flicker of his mouth was hard to read. 'I'm running out of things to say. I doubt that anyone from back home will ever find us, and I've never enjoyed talking to myself. Goodbye, and may we all fare well.'

The picture vanished. For a moment a black oblong hung in the air, then it too dissolved to reveal Sibyl, sitting in her blue quartz chair.

'There you are,' Sibyl said.

'Yes,' Ammadin said. 'And here we are.'

'Did you find the testimonies useful?'

'Yes. Now I know what's really ours. Sibyl, I want those records, the ones Dallas referred to, about the clone-born and the shamanisms, I think he called them.'

'For me to transfer them into voice mode and deliver them in aural format will take approximately fifteen point five standard hours.'

'All right, can you make a book out of them for me?'

'Not at the moment. I will require a supply of rushi.'

'Loy has some.'

'She needs that material for her own purposes.'

'You don't want to give me those records, do you?'

Sibyl's image fractured into cubes.

'Answer my question!'

'Very well.' The image smoothed itself out into a flat image of a woman. 'No, I do not want you to have them. I fear they will make you more dangerous.'

'I don't care. I want those records.'

'I cannot give them to you. There is not enough rushi.' Sibyl smiled, a sly little quirk of her mouth. 'Now, if only you had a Recaller with you –'

'I do, as a matter of fact. You can recite the records to him, and then he can tell me.'

'If he's willing.'

'Oh, he'll be willing. He enjoys memorizing, he tells me. He says it's almost as good as sex.'

'Then indeed he is a real Recaller.' Sibyl's expression turned sour. 'It is unfortunate that there is no trained technician available. If there were, I could download the information you require into his datajack.'

'His what?'

'A ring of augmented cartilage at the base of his skull, similar to the nanocarbonic tube receiver unit you possess behind one ear, grown by his body in accordance with preprogrammed genetic information.'

'I don't know what the hell you're talking about. Wait – Sibyl, I don't require precise answers to these questions.'

'Thank you. A datajack allows AI units, such as I am, to connect directly to a Recaller's brain. We can then transfer information back and forth in an extremely rapid fashion.'

Ammadin remembered with her fingers first, the sensation of touching the strange ring on the back of Zayn's neck. 'I understand now,' she said. 'Yes, he has one of those.'

'Unfortunately I lack the connection required to utilize his jack, so the process of data transfer will be tedious.'

'Too damn bad.'

'When Hassan returns, I will transfer the records. In this form

I am forced to cooperate with properly phrased requests.' Sibyl leaned forward, fully alive or so it seemed. 'Please tell me why the records are so important to you.'

'I want to know what I really am. The other spirit riders will, too.'

'Do your words imply danger for the other sapient groups on this planet?'

'No.' Ammadin smiled briefly. 'Not as long as they leave us alone.'

When the sun sank below the level of the traps, sending long shadows out into the valley, Stronghunter Man halted the warparty. Though the other Chur spread out behind, he motioned Fifth Out to come up beside him, then pointed west with his spear at the cliffs, which looked about half their true height at this distance. They were, however, close enough to see that the line of stone formed a right angle, a configuration that could turn out to be a death trap.

'Very well, Zayn Recaller, the North Gate lie back there a now-short way. I show-now you something about Chof.' Stronghunter Man tipped his head back, filled his throat sac, then let out the air slowly.

Zayn could assume that the Chur Vocho was making some sort of noise, but he heard nothing. All the Chur tipped their heads to one side and opened their mouths, but their sacs hung flaccid.

'They be there,' Stronghunter Man said. 'Two H'mai, four horses, horses off to one side, both H'mai sitting in the grass.'

'How can you tell?' Zayn said.

'We feel the pictures.' Stronghunter Man stamped his forefeet. 'Water Woman, she tell-then me word to use, a word that Sibyl tell-once her. It be called echo in your speaking. We Chof send out sound called varalanik. It come back in pictures, echo pictures.'

Zayn wasn't sure if he understood, but he decided that he didn't really need to. 'All right,' he said. 'How far are they?'

'Not very. We charge now. You know not know if they have those spirit guns you tell-then me about?'

'As soon as I'm close enough to see them. If they have them, I'll shout.'

'Good. You do that.'

Stronghunter Man turned to his men and gave orders. First they untied once again the extra spears from each other's backs so that everyone had a weapon for each pseudo-hand. Next, they formed themselves into a long line, parallel with the cliffs. The entire troop of Chur filled their throat sacs, paused long enough for Zayn to cover his ears, then boomed, sending another fusillade of sound ahead of them. As one they filled the sacs again, then sprang forward, loping at first. In a few minutes they burst into a full gallop so suddenly that Zayn nearly fell. He managed to fling his weight onto Fifth Out's ample neck and cling with both arms. Swaying and dancing, the cliffs seemed to rush forward to meet them.

From ahead of them Zayn heard horses neighing and H'mai voices yelling in panic, two voices, and one of them was Soutan's. As the charge slowed, he sat up on the young Chof's back and saw Soutan, standing on top of a grass-covered mound. He held a shiny piece of metal in one hand and with the other seemed to be trying to attach something else to it. With an audible howl Stronghunter Man threw his spear. Soutan shrieked and fell backwards, tumbling into cover, but not before Zayn got a good look at what he was holding, a stubby metal tube fused to a handle and dangling black cable.

'Spirit guns!' Zayn yelled. 'Watch out!'

Soutan reappeared, the gun clutched to his chest, and started running towards the arched entrance. Stronghunter Man hurled his second spear, but Soutan scuttled untouched into the darkness of the cave. By then Fifth Out, burdened by Zayn's weight, was panting for breath. He swung round in a wide arc and slowed, jogging parallel to the cliffs. Zayn leaned forward. 'Let me off,' he said. 'Then get out of range. Fast!'

When the Chur stopped, Zayn slid off his back. Half-crouching, dodging, he ducked behind a huge grass-covered mound off to one side and dropped his saddlebags on the ground in front of him. Near the cave entrance something – someone – moved. From behind a pile of stone rubble, Arkazo stood up, a metal tube in his hand.

'Duck!' Zayn screamed. 'There's another one.'

Stronghunter Man swerved, bucked like a horse, and swerved again. The flash from Arkazo's pistol singed the air beside him to strike something far behind the line of Chof. Zayn smelled a brief sting of smoke. He twisted round to look back, afraid that Kaz had started a grass fire. A line of charred black grass smoked, flickered, and mercifully went out. The Chof boomed again, then retreated, swinging round for another charge. Zayn grabbed the bolas from his saddlebags. Better than nothing – and all he had.

Arkazo rose half-free of the cover, his pistol at the ready, his other hand shading his eyes as he looked for someone – me, Zayn thought. He waited, hidden, until Arkazo turned in the other direction. Zayn rose, twirling the bolas around and around until sheer momentum made them fly humming through the air. The noise caught Arkazo's attention. He spun around, saw Zayn, raised the pistol, and froze, unmoving and pale, staring directly at Zayn. With a snap of his arm Zayn loosed the bolas.

Reflexively Arkazo flung up his hand, but too late. The solid brass balls hit. One cracked him across the face; the other two twined their cords around his upraised arm. With a yelp he dropped the pistol, let the power pack slide to the ground, and staggered back. Blood poured from his nose and upper lip. From the cave Soutan yelled something Zayn couldn't understand. Arkazo turned in answer and fled, rushing up the ramp and leaping into the entrance after Soutan.

Booming in triumph the Chof charged the cliff. When Stronghunter Man thrummed, they raised their spears and hurled one each into the dark mouth of the cave. Under this cover Zayn darted forward and grabbed the pistol from the ground. He turned and aimed it at the cave mouth.

'Fire!' He mimicked the word he'd heard Loy use, and it worked.

A beam of light sped into darkness. Distantly rock shattered and fell. He sent another bolt after the first and heard a boom and roar. A quick blast of fire burst out of the cave, followed by the rumble of a long slide of stone. Stronghunter Man came trotting up to join him.

'That noise!' the Chur Vocho said. 'What you do-then?'

'I don't know. I must have made a lucky shot and hit something that exploded.'

'Good,' the Chur Vocho said. 'They come-not when you have that thing.'

'I'll bet you they don't come out at all,' Zayn said, 'I'm going in after them.'

'No!' Stronghunter Man said. 'You get-soon lost –'

'No, I won't. I'm a Recaller. I'm probably the only sapient here who can go in without being lost.' Zayn hefted the pistol. 'And now I'm armed just like he is.'

Stronghunter Man leaned on his spear and looked Zayn over. 'No,' he said at last. 'You go-not. It be dark in there. That gun-thing, we know-not how often it sends fire when there be no sunlight to feed it.'

'Well, yes, but –'

'Wait.' Stronghunter Man took a few steps towards the cliff and shaded his eyes with his pseudo-hand. He made a snorting noise, then stamped hard on the ground. 'We argue for nothing,' he said. 'They get-never out of the North Gate. Look! The fire you send-then into the cave? It pull-then down much rock.'

Zayn turned and saw a cloud of rock-dust, as thick as smoke from damp wood, drifting from the mouth of the cave. The two stone longtooth saurs had lurched from the impact and stood canted. Behind them he could just make out the dark shapes of rubble.

'Good. Soutan can stay in there and rot.'

'He do-maybe just that. The gods only know if they ever get out again. There be other gates, but they need-soon much luck to find them.'

Zayn started to smile, then remembered Arkazo. What am I going to tell Idres? he thought.

'Are we going to camp here tonight?' Zayn said.

'No. We rest-next, then go-soon back. We travel-till Silverlands set, then rest-again.' Stronghunter Man glanced around. 'The horses, they run-then some time while we fight. You and Fifth Out, go see if you have power to catch them.'

Eventually, just as twilight turned to night, Zayn and the young Chur did find the horses, but seeing Arkazo's riding horse made Zayn's stomach twist. He had promised Idres that he'd try to save his nephew, but in the heat of the fight, he'd forgotten the promise and Idres both. As they jogged back south by galaxy-light, the memory throbbed like a knife wound.

'I am grateful for your information, Jezro Khan, and yours, too, Captain,' Sibyl said. 'As for your plan to save the Chof, I warn you: they will never give up their way of life. Their continued existence depends on the rulership of the women, who alone can truly value the children born from their eggs. The males are far too removed from the biological process.'

'I don't see why they'd have to change,' Jezro said. 'The Qur'an discusses differences between H'mai men and women. Those sûras don't have any relevance to another species.'

'Good. I do agree that if the Chof embrace your religion, or even that of the Cantons, your less civilized compatriots will be forced to treat them with respect.'

'That's something, at least,' Warkannan said. 'Though I'd like to see them embrace the faith out of a love of God, not expediency.'

'Many will,' Sibyl said. 'Especially if you return to the more flexible form of your religion that predates Mullah Agvar.'

'You've made it clear that he was something of a heretic, yes.' Warkannan paused, thinking. 'I just hope we can get the Chof some decent teachers.'

'I have the perfect one in mind,' Jezro said, grinning. 'Bashir Benumar. Hassan's charming father.'

'It's nothing to joke about.'

'I'm not joking. It will do the old boy good. If ever anyone needed to loosen his attitudes, it's the elder Benumar.'

Warkannan started to argue, then let it lie. He and Jezro had finally been allowed inside late that morning, but Sibyl had asked most of the questions. By Warkannan's watch, they had spent six hours describing the situation in Kazrajistan. In return, Sibyl had promised Jezro something she called *Diderot's Encyclopedia*, books that, she assured them, would show the Kazraks how to build any number of simple devices.

'The set contains detailed pictures as well as text in Vranz, all suitable for the level of your technology,' Sibyl said. 'Some of the original Settlers had printed it out from the ship archive banks early in the colony days, and the copies now reside in a hidden cache down in the Metro, along with a crate of accus that you will find useful. Water Woman will show you where as you make your way back. The data you have given me is invaluable. I thank you both. Do you have any more questions for me?'

'Just one,' Jezro said. 'Do you know where Yarl Soutan is?'

'He is currently in N'Dosha, where he went to hide last night after a skirmish between his men and the warparty led by Stronghunter Man. A young Kazrak accompanied him, but his spear Chur all fled long before the two H'mai entered the tunnel complex.'

'Will you know when the two of them leave N'Dosha?'

'The question is not when, Jezro Khan, but if.'

Warkannan and Jezro shared a troubled glance.

'I will explain,' Sibyl continued. 'I can hear what happens in approximately eighty per cent of N'Dosha thanks to a communication grid put in place by the Settlers. Although most of the visual elements of this grid no longer function, the audio components were simple enough to survive. Yarl and the young Kazrak entered the complex at the North Gate, which then suffered so much damage that it is no longer operational. Yarl and his companion have no map and are now lost.'

'Lost?' Warkannan stepped forward. 'Can they find their way out?'

'Only by the sheerest good luck.' Sibyl's image shrugged its shoulders. 'I predict that Yarl will remove the problem he presents without any action on our part. He will starve to death unless he manages to find his way out, and the probability of that is very low. He sounds angry and panicked. Every time the young Kazrak makes a rational suggestion, Yarl only curses and raves.'

Warkannan turned so cold that for a moment he feared that he would faint. Jezro caught his arm and steadied him.

'Captain,' Sibyl said. 'Are you ill or distressed?'

Warkannan tried to speak, but his mouth had gone too dry.

'He's distressed,' Jezro answered for him. 'The young Kazrak is his nephew, but he's been more like a son.'

'I apologize. I did not have access to this data, or I would have phrased my response in a less blunt manner.'

'I've got to rescue him.' Warkannan managed to summon his voice. 'Can you tell me how to get into N'Dosha?'

'The journey down is easy,' Sibyl said. 'Day and night the gates stand open. Getting out again – that's the problem, that's the hard job.' Her face remained motionless, but a long peal of laughter sounded from behind the image.

'Damn you!' Warkannan snarled. 'What in hell is so funny?'

'You won't understand,' Sibyl said. 'But I assure you that the joke is not at your nephew's expense but a reference to Old Earth literature.'

'Stay calm, Idres. I'll take over. Sibyl, is there a map of the complex?'

'Yes, Jezro Khan. If Zayn Hassan, your Recaller, stored the map and accompanied you, there is a high probability that you could indeed find them. However, Yarl is more likely to try to kill Hassan than accept his help. If he succeeded, you would be in the same position that he is now, hopelessly lost. I cannot recommend such a course of action.'

'I can't just let Arkazo die.' Warkannan realized that he hovered on the edge of fury and did his best to calm himself. 'Isn't there anything I can do?'

'There is nothing that you can do.'

'Sibyl,' Jezro said. 'What about you? Can you rescue them?'

'If Yarl is willing to be rescued, I can lead them to safety.'

Warkannan decided that he had better sit down on the floor before hope finished the job fear had started. He managed with some dignity, but Jezro stayed standing.

'Good idea, Idres,' the khan said. 'Sibyl, try to rescue them. Is there some way I can help you?'

'I can reach no conclusion on this point until I contact Yarl. If he refuses to take my help, I will ask you to intercede by sending a message via my communicator circuits.' Sibyl raised a hand and pointed off to the right. 'Look!'

A three-dimensional map appeared, hovering in the air, a thing of coloured lines and cubes easily six feet on a side, livened with glowing dots. After a moment's study, Warkannan realized that it depicted the complex and its various levels. Vertical lines, which he took to be staircases, connected them, but the staircases seemed randomly placed on the different floors rather than recurring in the same relative location in each one. He gave up counting at fifteen floors, each with a myriad of rooms, all joined by hallways of various widths and orientations. Jezro pulled a handkerchief from his pocket and wiped his nose before he spoke.

'That's one hell of a mess, isn't it? No wonder they're lost.'

'Yes,' Sibyl said. 'From their conversations I know that they lack food, and the standing water that has collected here and there in the complex is not always drinkable. Therefore it would be optimal to bring them to the surface as quickly as possible.'

'Very well.'

'There is a way into this complex, the Analysis Lab, through one of the tunnels. It is the most direct route to the surface, but its end point, here, is problematic. Yarl has a pistol, but since he is untrained in its use, he has very poor aim. Pistols do not possess the locking function of rifles. Should someone try to apprehend him in this room, the probability is high that he will shoot wildly and damage some piece or pieces of the hardware essential to my functioning.'

'That would be another kind of disaster,' Jezro said.

'Yes. I will only bring them out of N'Dosha if you promise to wait until they reach the landing beyond the cave before you take action against Soutan.'

'Fair enough, and a good idea.' Jezro held up one hand palm out. 'I promise.'

Sibyl nodded her approval. 'Now. Let me represent the two H'mai by these silver arrows.' On the map, some twelve levels down, the symbols blinked into existence inside a room-cube. Sibyl froze herself to a flat image. 'Sending message now. Relaying message throughout grid. Message content: Yarl, listen to me. Yarl, listen to me. This is Sibyl, and I will guide you out of N'Dosha. Walk towards my voice.'

The arrows never moved. 'They are arguing,' Sibyl said after a few minutes. 'The man you call Arkazo is trying to convince Yarl to accept my help. I will resend the message.'

Warkannan heard nothing but a series of clicks. Again a silence lasted for some minutes.

'Yarl,' Sibyl said eventually, 'I am not lying to you. I am not the spirit rider. The spirit rider is not here; she is not in the complex. Therefore she cannot be trying to trap you.'

For a heart-stopping moment the two arrows remained immobile, then slowly they began to float across the cube.

'Very good,' Sibyl said. 'Follow my voice, and I will lead you out.'

The silver arrows began to slide along one of the hallways. Sibyl's flat image turned towards the two waiting Kazraks.

'To them my voice appears localized some twenty feet ahead of their position,' Sibyl said. 'Their journey will take approximately sixteen hours because some of the direct-route tunnels have been damaged by earthquakes over the years. They will also have to rest at intervals. If you leave, I can minimize other functions in order to commit all power resources to the task of guidance.'

'Then we're on our way out,' Jezro said.

Warkannan scrambled up and nodded at the image. 'Thank you,' he said. 'I can't tell you how grateful I am.'

'Gratitude means little to me, Captain,' Sibyl said. 'But I find that exercising my functions is satisfying. You will need some sort of plan of action to deal with Yarl when he arrives. Please tell Ammadin to come here in the morning to tell me what you've decided. I see that you carry a chronometer.'

'A what?' Warkannan said. 'I've never heard of –'

'Idres.' Jezro interrupted him. 'She means your watch.'

'Oh.' Warkannan took it out and checked the time. 'It's eighteen hundred now, more or less.'

'I know this,' Sibyl said. 'I merely wanted to ensure that you know it, too. Have Ammadin come report to me at nine in the morning.'

They hurried out, then paused on the ledge just beyond the cave. Although the summer sky still shone blue above them, the shadows of the traps lay across the pale grass below.

'Look!' Jezro suddenly pointed. 'Hassan's back, and Stronghunter Man.'

Below them, in the messy sprawling camp, Stronghunter Man stood talking with Water Woman while the other Chof clustered around. Ammadin and Zayn had gone together to tend the horses tethered out in the grass.

'They've brought back Arkazo's horse,' Warkannan said. 'Soutan's, too, and the pack horses.'

'Well, at least Kaz will have something to ride when we get him out.'

'If we get him out. I've got a bad feeling about all of this.'

'So have I, actually, but I'm refusing to give in to it. I suggest you try to do the same.'

Warkannan managed to smile. Together they walked down the path and rejoined the camp.

'So, Hassan,' Loy said. 'You managed to get yourself a gun after all.'

Ammadin, who'd been heading back to Sibyl's cave, stopped to listen. Loy had come up to talk with Zayn as he knelt by his bedroll. The pistol lay between them on the blankets.

'It was Arkazo's,' Zayn said. 'I don't know where Soutan got them, but he had one, too.'

'That's bad news.'

'I'd say so, yes.' Zayn held out the pistol and power pack. 'Here, take it.'

'What?'

'If I were going back to Kazrajistan, I'd want it, but I'm not. These things start fires if you look at them wrong. Out on the grass, that could mean disaster in summer.'

'You're quite right.' Loy took the proffered pistol. 'Thank you, Zayn. This will go back to the guild with me.'

Ammadin smiled in something like relief. Zayn was still thinking like a comnee man; she was beginning to trust the idea that he'd return to the grass with her.

That evening, as the others sat around the fire to listen, Water Woman and Jezro decided that in the morning they would pack up the camps and move them two miles east, so that Sibyl could assure Soutan that no one was waiting for him directly outside. Soutan would be easy enough to track once they emerged.

'I'm assuming Arkazo will want to stick with him,' Jezro said.

'Probably so. Kaz thinks the world of him.' Warkannan kept his voice steady, but Ammadin could see how much the admission pained him.

'If they come out,' Zayn put in. 'Look, sir, Soutan must realize we'll chase him down.'

'Of course,' Jezro said. 'But I'm betting that he'll be so desperate that he won't care. Wandering around in the dark till you starve to death – a few years in prison for rape will look pretty good compared to that.' He paused for a wry smile. 'Even a lot of years in prison.'

'Well sir, you've got a point,' Zayn said. 'But I don't trust the slimy little bastard, I just don't.'

Zayn's doubts proved well-founded. At nine the next morning, Ammadin and Loy went to the Analysis Lab to relay their plan to Sibyl. The hologram appeared the instant that they stepped into the room.

'I was about to attempt to summon you,' Sibyl said. 'A problem has developed. Yarl has realized that his enemies are here waiting for him.'

'I'm not surprised,' Ammadin said. 'He's not stupid.'

'Unfortunately this value judgment is correct.'

'We came up with a plan –'

'Good, but here is new data that you will have to take into account. He is refusing to come out unless he has guarantee of safe passage. That is, he wants Jezro Khan to promise that he will be given a horse, food, and time to make his escape.'

'The little turd!' Loy said. 'Let him stay in there and starve, then.'

'You lack a crucial datum, Loremaster Millou. Yarl is also refusing to allow Arkazo to leave N'Dosha without him. He has a pistol, and despite his lack of skill, at close range it will be effective. He has taken Arkazo hostage. If we do not agree to his terms, he will kill the captain's nephew in cold blood.'

Loy stared open-mouthed. Ammadin could smell how furious she was, too enraged even to swear.

'Go get Jezro,' Ammadin said to her. 'I'd say that Soutan has judged us all about right. We'll have to agree.'

'Very well. I'm on my way.' Loy turned and raced down the hall, heading for the outer cave. Sibyl turned to Ammadin, and her illusionary face displayed real anxiety.

'I should have anticipated this,' Sibyl said. 'I had forgotten how illogical my species can be.'

'I think Soutan's being perfectly logical,' Ammadin said. 'Treacherous and despicable, but logical.'

'I will revise my judgment in line with yours. You are right. Some of my circuits seem to be wearing out with age.'

Ammadin heard the sound of Jezro's walking stick, clicking fast down the hall, and in a few moments Jezro came limping into the room. His face, normally tan, looked pale and waxy in the cold silver light.

'Loy told me,' he said. 'Of course I'll swear. Tell him I'll swear it before God, or does the little bastard need to hear my voice?'

'He insists on hearing you.' Sibyl's image turned into a stack of cubes, and she paused while the distant bell chimed thrice. 'I have created access between this room and Yarl's position. Please repeat your oath, Jezro Khan.'

'Soutan?' Jezro said. 'I swear I'll give you the safe ride out of here that you asked for. For the love of God, Yarl, and if ever we were friends, I'll beg you: don't harm Arkazo.'

Soutan's voice, still arrogant even though it cracked with exhaustion, seemed to originate behind Sibyl's left shoulder. 'I know you keep your promises, Jezro. As for Kaz, his safety is up to you, isn't it? Do what I want, and I'll send him back to you once I'm in the clear.'

'All right. We won't do anything risky.'

'Good. We seem to have only a short distance left to walk before we reach Sibyl. We should emerge soon, but I don't want to see you, Warkannan, Hassan, or any of the Chof in the cave when we do.'

'Very well. You won't.'

'Good. There are a few things I want to talk to Sibyl about before we come out, too. Make everyone stay well back from the entrance. I warn you, if anyone makes a move to harm me, Kaz dies.'

A soft click and a shrill bell sounded. Sibyl returned to H'mai form and reached up to push her hair back from her face. 'Yarl can no longer hear us,' she said. 'He is indeed very close. He has walked within range of one of the few functioning visual relays. He has his pistol drawn and is using it to prod Arkazo along in front of him. Arkazo appears to be greatly distressed, angry and grief-stricken both.'

'I'm sure he is,' Jezro said. 'He's been betrayed by someone he thought was a hero.'

A siren began to shriek as if it were announcing demons from the Deathworld. From the ceiling a red light flashed, glittering on the metal panels and boxes. Slowly a section of the wall slid back to reveal another door, off to Ammadin's right. Sibyl turned around in her chair, and the siren abruptly died.

'Interesting,' Sibyl said. 'The warning system is still functional.'

'We'd better leave,' Ammadin said.

'Jezro Khan should, yes, but Yarl never listed you in his demand. Yesterday I told him that you were not here in the complex, which appears to have made him believe you are not present at all. There is a probability that I will need a person with physical mobility to deal with Yarl. Turn to your left. Hide behind the inoperable ventilation panel you will see behind that stack of blue metal boxes.'

With a wave of his stick, Jezro hurried out of the room. Ammadin followed Sibyl's directions and ducked behind the tall sheet of grey plasto. Through the slots on its upper fifth she could see into the room, provided she held her head at an uncomfortable angle. Figures appeared in the newly opened doorway, and Arkazo stumbled in, his hands behind his back, with Soutan following a few feet along. Dust streaked their clothes and grimed their stubbled faces. Maroon bruises swelled around Arkazo's eyes and his broken nose. Dried blood covered the front of his shirt.

When they turned to face Sibyl, Ammadin noticed that Arkazo's wrists were bound together by a strip of some material too shiny to be leather. Soutan was holding the handle of a stubby metal tube connected to a power pack slung over his shoulder – the pistol, she assumed. Wide-eyed, his mouth half-open, Soutan looked around him. Sibyl took on the appearance that Ammadin had first seen, the unmoving body and stylized face. Soutan spent a long few minutes studying her.

'Very well,' Sibyl said. 'In the tunnel you stated that you were determined to speak with me. What do you want to ask?'

Soutan made her wait for a long moment.

'One of the Settlers,' he said at last. 'You must be a holo of one of the Settlers.'

'You have identified my origins correctly. What do you want to ask?'

'A great many things, Sibyl, the most important things in the world. Let me start with the crucial question. The ships, the starships that brought us here. Do they still exist?'

'Yes.'

'Are they still in working order?'

'Yes.'

'Does the Ark survive?'

'No. Not in its original form.'

Soutan caught his lower lip between his teeth; his eyes blinked rapidly as he thought something through. 'Is it possible to operate the ships without the Ark?'

'Yes, under certain conditions.'

Soutan smiled, his eyes wider than ever, and Ammadin could hear him breathing, panting really, in anticipation. His arm hung flaccid at his side, the weapon forgotten in his hand. Arkazo, handcuffed though he was, stared at Sibyl with something of the same intense desire to know.

'Then,' Soutan paused to gulp for breath, 'where are they?'

'You may look at the image field to my right.'

When Soutan and Arkazo turned half-around, Ammadin risked moving in order to ease the ache in her neck. Soutan seemed to have neither heard her nor registered the flicker of motion behind the panel that hid her, but Arkazo glanced her way, blinked, then hurriedly looked only at the dais.

'I shall begin,' Sibyl said.

First a square of blue mist sprang into existence; then images built up to overlay it. Against a black background a sphere of many colours hung gleaming. Blue ocean wrapped most of it around, but across the equator lay a sprawl of land, roughly shaped like two hands held flat, one above the other, with the thumb of the upper linked to the little finger of the lower. In the palm of each 'hand', far from the sea on all sides, stretched an expanse of tan and pale gold. To the north, white ice glittered.

To the east and west of these vast deserts the land lay mottled and textured with dark mountains, magenta hills, plains in brown, purple, red, orange, all threaded with thin lines of blue rivers and dotted here and there with blue lakes as well. In the west of the northern land mass, Ammadin could see the Rift, but it looked bizarrely small, set against the entire world.

'This is Snare as seen from an imaging satellite in a distant orbit,' Sibyl said. 'You are looking at the pangea, the only continent on this planet. As you can see, the only lands truly hospitable to sapient life lie around its western, southern, and eastern edges. Notice the chain of rocky islands out to sea in the west. Without them the ocean tides would be so extreme that the habitable western coast would be periodically flooded.'

Soutan sucked in his breath. Home, Ammadin thought. This is my home, and it's so beautiful.

'The ships will appear in oh-five seconds,' Sibyl went on, 'oh-four, oh-three, oh-two, oh-one, now.'

At the top edge of the world's image, gleaming silver spheres appeared, floating, or so it seemed, above the world's surface, moving slowly and majestically across the face of Snare. Each ship trailed a smaller sphere behind it, joined by cables wound around access tubes. Huge ships, ships the size of cities – Ammadin realized that they had to be enormous to show up so clearly against an entire planet.

'First battalion of six from fleet of sixty ships,' Sibyl went on. 'Placed in pole to pole orbit, self-sustaining, powered by solar lumino-magnetic propulsion systems, and self-correcting. Since the navigational units aboard the ships required the freedom to correct their positions in case of meteor strikes or other accidents, strict geosynchronous orbits were not possible. All the ships together comprise the array known as the observational grid, the Riders, or the Phalanx.'

Soutan swore under his breath, then steadied himself. 'Very well. What about the shuttles? There must be shuttles.'

'There are a hundred and twenty shuttles.'

'Where are they?'

'Two sit in the shuttle bays of each ship.'

Soutan's face turned dead-white. 'Is there another way to reach the ships other than the shuttles?'

'At the moment there is not. If a trained operator were aboard a ship, then it would be possible to raise an emergency pod. There are no trained operators aboard the ships. There is in fact no one aboard the ships.'

'Then there must be one shuttle on the ground.' Soutan began to tremble. 'There absolutely has to be one shuttle, the one that the last persons down used to get here.'

'There is no shuttle on the ground. All ships and shuttles are in orbit.'

'God damn you! How did the last person get back then?'

'I do not understand why you are using profanity, Soutan. I will answer your question regardless. The person who flew the last shuttle up to the ships committed suicide. He did this in order to ensure that we would abide by the Landfall Treaty.'

'Admiral Raynar,' Soutan whispered.

'Yes, your identification is correct. After the Treaty had been signed and ratified, there was a mutiny. The mutineers were determined to break those clauses of the Treaty that forbade technological exploitation of the planet's resources and the establishment of a technological society. They began to use the on-board equipment and research facilities of the ships to produce what they needed for their projects, which included living quarters, an underground transport system, scientific laboratories and the like. They used the shuttles to unload these resources and supplies from the ships.'

All at once Sibyl changed. Her image solidified, took on depth, and she became once again a seemingly real woman, pausing to flick her brown hair back from her face with one hand. Her eyes blinked, and she considered Soutan for a moment.

'You're a Cantonneur.' She sounded surprised, as if she'd just realized it.

'Yes,' Soutan snapped. 'How else would I have learned about the ships? Don't you see? I want to get us all off this wretched world and let the Chof have it back.'

'What you want is irrelevant,' Sibyl said. 'Let me continue answering your original question. Admiral Raynar tried reasoning with the mutineers. It is probably redundant to inform you that they would not listen. He then pretended to collaborate with them and feigned enthusiasm for their projects. Thus he could discern the precise moment when no mutineers were on board the ships and only one shuttle remained on planet.'

Soutan's tremble turned into a rhythmic motion. He was shaking his head no no no repeatedly as Sibyl continued.

'He flew the last shuttle to its ship and docked it. Then he shot himself with a handgun much like the one you carry.'

'No,' Soutan was whispering. 'No. It can't be true, you heartless bitch! No one would do that. There must be a shuttle. Just one. That's all we need. Just one.'

'There are no shuttles on planet.' Sibyl sat back in her phantasmic chair. 'In this form, I cannot lie.'

'Damn him.' Soutan's voice was full of tears. 'How could he? Oh my god, damn him!'

'Similar sentiments were voiced by the mutineers at the time.' Sibyl's image folded her hands comfortably over her stomach. 'The rest of us, however, applauded his honour and bravery.'

'Bravery?' Soutan was squealing, stammering, barely able to speak. 'You call that honour? To abandon us all here, no hope, no future, his own people –' He stopped, panting for breath.

'Similar sentiments were voiced by the mutineers at the time. His course of action had however rendered them powerless, and they were forced to abide by the Treaty in at least its main lines. The situation developed naturally from then on.'

'The situation? The mess we're in now, you mean.' Soutan took a step towards her. 'That's why the tunnels, the flexstone, the supply depots, all those things we find lying around, half-done, useless, oh god damn him!'

'He was a good man.' Sibyl slapped both hands hard on her knees. 'He honoured his pledges to the indigenous sapient race.' Her voice suddenly swelled into life and rage. 'He honoured his promises. If the others had done the same, he would have lived many years more.'

'Who the hell cares!' Soutan's voice rose to a shout. 'There must be some way to reach those goddamned ships! Tell me!'

He raised the handgun and aimed it at Sibyl.

Her image returned to its usual blank calm. 'I have been dead for seven hundred and forty-two years. Why are you threatening to kill me?'

Soutan snarled, a ghastly mad animal sound, and tipped his head back as if he would curse the very gods. Arkazo glanced at Ammadin, then made his move. He bent his knees and slammed into Soutan from below, knocking his gun hand away, hitting hard with his shoulder against Soutan's hips. The two of them went down, and Soutan was screaming, swearing, flailing as he tried to bring the handgun around to shoot his attacker. Ammadin darted out from behind the screen. It seemed that everything began moving slowly, just as when she'd killed her saur. Soutan waved his hands slowly, Arkazo twisted his body like a man turning leisurely over for a nap. As she hovered over them, she had time to remember Lisadin saying that comnee people were stronger than anyone wanted them to know. She reached down and grabbed Soutan's arm. Her hands found his bones, twisted, and broke his wrist.

Time burst back upon her. Soutan screamed and dropped the handgun. It dangled useless from the cable, and Ammadin grabbed it and pulled. The power pack came free of Yarl's shoulder and skittered across the floor to lie under the illusion of Sibyl's feet. When Ammadin let Soutan go, he staggered up, panting, swearing, and cradled the broken wrist in his other hand. He stank of fresh urine. Arkazo hauled himself up to kneel on the floor between them. For a moment Soutan stared at Ammadin, his eyes as wild as the dying saur's. Then he turned and bolted, staggering and stumbling down the tunnel that led back to the entrance cave.

'Let him go,' Sibyl said. 'The others will capture him easily, since he no longer has a hostage.'

'Tell me something.' Ammadin paused to lay the pistol down on the floor. 'You loved Raynar, didn't you?'

'Yes. You are very perceptive. We had been together for sixteen years when he shot himself.'

'I'm sorry you lost him.'

'All love affairs are tragedies in the end unless the lovers die at the same moment. We were not fortunate enough for that. I wanted to go with him, but he reminded me that my place was here, guarding the indigenes.'

Despite the calm face of the image, her voice relived her grief, just briefly, in those words.

'I hadn't thought of that before.' Ammadin said. 'About love affairs and tragedies.' For a moment she felt sick and cold, but the moment ended. 'Do you know how to get that restraint off Arkazo's hands?'

'Yes. If he'll stand up, I'll instruct you.'

In the hot sun Warkannan stood below the entrance, his arms crossed over his chest, his feet a little apart to steady himself. He felt as if his long life of discipline and obedience, those years he had spent forging his soul both as an officer in the cavalry and a worshipper in the way of Islam, had been nothing but training for this one moment, when he would have to stand still while knowing that Arkazo's life hung on the slender thread of Soutan's sanity. If he rushed inside, as every muscle in his body longed to do, he would cause his nephew's death. He told himself that repeatedly. Just behind him Jezro and Zayn stood on guard. He knew he could trust them to grab him and haul him back if the discipline broke, but he was determined to keep it from breaking. Sweat ran down his back and soaked through his shirt.

Off to one side, Loy Millou waited with Water Woman, watching the entrance. The Chiri Michi waved her hands in the air and made a whimpering sound now and then, but Loy stood still, cradling a long metal tube connected to a dangling length of black cord and a box on her back. What it was and why she held it, he didn't know. Perhaps it comforted her in some way.

Inside the cave, someone shrieked, the sound too faint to be identified as one voice or another. Jezro swore. No one moved. Warkannan began to count seconds, as if he could turn himself into a clock and feel nothing but time passing. No more sounds, no voices reached them. Jezro muttered something under his breath. Warkannan ignored him and kept counting. Two minutes passed, if his count were accurate. It doesn't matter, he told himself. This could go on for hours.

'Someone's coming out,' Jezro whispered.

Warkannan allowed himself one step forward just as Soutan staggered out of the shadows onto the lip of rock. He was clutching one arm, pressing it against his chest with the other hand.

'Arkazo!' Warkannan called out. 'Where is he?'

For an answer Soutan began to laugh, a high-pitched chortle that rose and fell in a sprung rhythm. He must be dead, Warkannan thought. That's the only thing that laugh could mean. He glanced back and found Jezro furious, as if he too were thinking Arkazo dead; Zayn laid his hand on the hilt of his long knife. Warkannan heard Loy Millou cough, clearing her throat.

'Lock,' Loy said. 'Fire.'

Something slithered past him through the air, a flash of light from a signal mirror, maybe. Warkannan spun around to look at Loy, who was pointing the metal tube at the cave. He turned back and realized that Soutan had no head. Blood gushed over his chest and shoulders as the headless body crumpled to its knees, swayed, and fell backward onto the grey stone.

'God preserve us!' Jezro whispered. 'What happened?'

'Vengeance, that's what.' Zayn sounded perfectly calm. 'Good shot, Loremaster.'

Warkannan turned to Loy, who was staring wide-eyed at Yarl's corpse. Dimly he realized that what he'd taken for some odd bit of metal had to be the most powerful weapon he'd ever seen.

'Are you all right?' he said to Loy.

She turned a white face towards him.

'I knew it would be easier the second time,' Loy said. 'Killing a predator, I mean. And it was. Not easy, but easier.' She sucked in a sharp breath. 'Oh god, your nephew!'

'He must be dead, yes.'

'No, you idiot! That's what I thought, but look!'

Someone was walking out of the deep shadows at the entrance, two people walking into the sunlight, Ammadin and Arkazo. Warkannan stared, afraid to believe his own vision until Zayn started laughing.

'I should have known that Ammadin would get things under control,' Zayn said. 'She's a spirit rider, after all.'

At the top of the path, Arkazo hesitated, shading his eyes with his hand as he looked down at the people below, turning his head this way and that, searching for someone.

'Kaz!' Warkannan called out. 'Get down here! Of course I forgive you!'

Arkazo burst out laughing and ran, racing headlong down the path. Warkannan ran to meet him, but when they met he contented himself with grabbing Arkazo's right hand in both of his.

'He would have killed me,' Arkazo stammered. 'I could see that he meant it. He really would have killed me.'

Warkannan hesitated, then decided that moral lectures could wait. 'I'm damned glad he didn't,' he said instead. 'And I'm damned glad to see you.'

Arkazo tried to grin in his old insouciant way, then began to weep. A dismal scatter of tears ran down his bruised face and left muddy tracks in the dust from N'Dosha. Warkannan let go his hand and flung an arm around his shoulders.

'Let's get you something to eat, Kaz.'

Arkazo nodded, and they turned back towards the camp to find themselves face to face with Zayn, standing with his thumbs tucked into his belt. Arkazo wiped his face on his sleeve.

'I know what it feels like now,' Arkazo said, 'having someone ready to kill you. I realized I'd do anything to get free of that, even killing someone myself.'

'Thanks for telling me,' Zayn said softly. 'I appreciate it.' He turned and strode away before Arkazo could say anything more.

Arkazo watched him go. 'Uncle?' he said. 'I had a chance to shoot Hassan when they – the Chur I mean – caught me and Yarl in front of the cliffs. I had the pistol, and I looked right at him, but I couldn't do it. I couldn't kill someone, not even him. I'm going to make a pretty shitty officer.'

'Battles are different,' Warkannan said. 'You've got everyone else to carry you along, and besides, the enemy's out to kill you. You'll see.'

Arkazo nodded, but he shoved his hands into his trousers pockets, as if he were hiding the shakes. He'll get over it, Warkannan thought. You'd have to be insane not to be afraid at first. But yet he wondered if he really knew Arkazo as well as he thought he did, this young man now, no longer a boy, who had been so easily entranced by tales of strange machines and ancient knowledge.

'We go-soon or not go?' Water Woman said. 'Jezro Khan, he return-must to Burgunee, he tell me, and say-must farewell to his friend Marya Dookis before they leave-next for Kazrajistan.'

'We all need to get on the road, yes,' Ammadin said. 'But Zayn's promised to memorize something for me, something Sibyl will tell him, I mean. It's going to take hours.'

'Ah.' Water Woman considered this. 'We leave tomorrow then. And Sibyl, she have-maybe things to tell Zayn Recaller. He need-maybe the talk more than any else of us. You take him there now, I think. I discuss-next some plans with Loy Sorcerer.' Water Woman raised coy pseudo-hands in front of her eyes. 'I think lore-masters come-next-soon to N'Dosha again. And Loy Sorcerer, she want-not leave with us.'

Zayn was more than willing to finally get his chance to see Sibyl. Hand in hand they walked up the path together. The Chur had taken Yarl's body away, leaving only a rust-coloured stain. Ammadin had decided against asking them what they were going to do with it. They stepped into the hallway, and Ammadin called out to let Sibyl know she had visitors, but when they walked into the circular room, the dais was empty.

'Sibyl?' Ammadin said. 'Are you functional?'

A bell chimed behind them. When Ammadin turned round, she saw a section of the circular wall sliding back to reveal a storage area. Cubical grey boxes stood stacked to the ceiling, hundreds of them, Ammadin realized. Printed on each were symbols, or letters and words, she supposed, and Zayn confirmed her guess.

'Accus,' he said, 'a lot of those, lamps, lightwands, and crystals. Some say medical supplies.'

'I doubt if the actual medications are still valid.' Sibyl's voice came from directly overhead. 'There are, however, some pieces of equipment that might someday become valuable again. They require a reliable source of power and the knowledge of how to use them.'

Ammadin spun around, but the dais still stood empty.

'I have switched my audio function to the ceiling above you,' Sibyl said. 'I know the locations of other storage areas onplanet as well, but you will not be able to take all of these things with you as it is.'

'That's very true,' Ammadin said. 'We don't have a whole caravan of pack horses.'

'When you are finished here, you may take what you wish. Return now to the interface area.'

'The what?'

'Where my hologram appears.'

When they walked out, Sibyl reappeared on the dais in a shimmering fall of light.

'Very well.' Her voice seemed to be coming from the image's mouth. 'This is your Recaller, then?'

'Not mine precisely,' Ammadin said, 'but he's the man I told you about.'

'I apologize. I had failed to cross-file the new data and so assumed that the situation that prevailed on the Rim was still current here. That is, a Recaller would have a place on the staff of some powerful person.'

'No,' Zayn said. 'Maybe that's going to change, though.'

'Zayn's doing me a favour,' Ammadin said. 'I asked him to record the data in Dallas Jenz's archive for me, if you remember that.'

'Of course I do.' Sibyl's expression turned haughty. 'I will begin voice transfer of data whenever the Recaller is ready.'

'I'll leave you to it,' Ammadin said, 'but answer one more question for me first. Why did your people create minds like Zayn's when you had machines that could record everything? If they could make AI units like you, why did they need H'mai Recallers?'

'For several reasons.' Sibyl leaned back in her chair and folded her hands over her stomach. 'The H'mai of the Rim were in contact with a great many alien races who were not part of the Council system. Such beings greatly resented having their conversations and the like recorded or spied upon by electronic means. A Recaller could easily serve as an ambassador's aide or bodyguard and remain undetected while he or she recorded everything said or done. Likewise, a police operative could go unnoticed among the criminal element and record information.

'At root, though –' Sibyl paused, looking away. 'I predict that Zayn will not like their most compelling reason. They did it because they could, and because they wanted to see what would happen if they did. Recallers, Calculators, Augmented Gunners, Musicians, Astrogators – those and all the others were the result of experiments carried out because the experiments could be done. The goal was to advance the sum total of knowledge available to sapient beings.'

Ammadin could smell Zayn's anger, a sudden acrid burst of it. His face smoothed out into his mask.

'Sibyl?' Ammadin said. 'Do you think that was a good reason?'

'I did when I was part of the Rim civilization, when I lived aboard ship and was surrounded by those who shared the same cultural assumptions. Bio-engineered functionaries, those Inborn who were not soldier-clones, held high-ranking positions in that culture. They were usually rich and always sought after and envied. But –' Sibyl paused and seemed to be studying Zayn when she continued. 'But we are not back home on the Rim. I doubt if anyone ever considered what would happen to the Inborn under primitive conditions, and especially in a culture where their roles would be forgotten.'

'No,' Zayn spoke quietly. 'I don't suppose the bastards did consider it, and may they rot in Hell.'

'You are bitter,' Sibyl said.

'Yes, I am. I feel like a spare part – an extra wheel for a wagon, brought along just in case one breaks. But I'm not bitter just for my own sake. The Inborn traits crop up all the time, and in the khanate we're either killed or we go crazy from hiding it.'

'This is not what the Councils intended.' Sibyl turned her artificial gaze to Ammadin. 'But you are not bitter.'

'That's because I had the training I needed.'

'I have in my databanks information about the training procedures for all the various Inborn traits. If disseminated, this information will ease at least some of the problems associated with the traits. Doubtless Loremaster Millou will be willing to inform her college of the need for a tutorial programme.'

'Yes, I'm sure she would,' Ammadin said. 'And you know, you've just given me an idea.'

Ammadin left Zayn in the Analysis Lab and went looking for Jezro Khan. She found him damp and half-dressed by the canal. On the grass his wet shirt lay spread out to dry.

'Looking for me?' Jezro said. 'That's always flattering.'

Ammadin smiled, then got to the point. 'Back in Herbgather Woman's village, you told me that you wanted to give me a reward for saving your life.'

'I remember that, yes,' Jezro said, 'and I meant it.'

'I never doubted it. Those children with talents, the Inborn – can you get your people to stop mistreating and killing them?'

'I certainly intend to try, but it's going to be difficult at first. New laws will keep them from being killed, but they're probably going to be hated and feared. I can't police every bully in the khanate.'

'Of course not. That's why they belong with us.' Ammadin smiled at the khan's obvious surprise. 'With the comnees. Have them brought to the horse fairs. We'll take them in, and their parents and neighbours will never have to see them again.'

'That could work.' Jezro considered, then nodded. 'Could work very well, and anything's better than letting boys grow up hated and hunted.'

'Not just boys. Some of your Inborn have to be female, or the traits would have died out centuries ago. They've been better hidden, is all, in your women's quarters.'

'You must be right. The girls, too, then.'

'It won't be easy on the families.' Ammadin was thinking of Maradin, and how she would feel if anyone tried to take her child away. 'Some of the mothers won't want to give up their children, but it'll be better than seeing them smothered.'

'I think we can assume that, yes. But all of this, you know, is dependent on my winning the damned war.'

'From what Warkannan's been telling us, I thought it was a sure thing.'

'In war, my dear spirit rider, nothing is a sure thing.' Jezro paused for a twisted grin. 'Idres has a lot more faith in God's plans than I do.'

As soon as Ammadin left the Analysis Lab, a metal door slid shut to seal off the circular room. Sibyl chimed twice.

'An interruption might necessitate starting this process over,' Sibyl said. 'I would prefer to spare you that.'

'I'd prefer it too,' Zayn said. 'Thanks. I wouldn't do this for anyone but Ammi, you know.'

'This indicates a certain level of intelligence. If only we had the unit that Yarl termed the Ark of the Covenant, I could transfer the text directly through your bio-engineered datajack.'

'That's what Ammi told me. What happened to the Ark?'

'Its primary function, regulating the jump drive, was rendered non-functional during the jumpshunt accident. Of the remaining hardware, some lies in N'Dosha, where it was taken for safe-keeping. The third portion was stolen by some of the Karashiki thirty-four years after Landfall. No one could offer an explanation for this theft on the part of those sworn to live simply.'

'Was it made out of the same blue stuff as the imps?'

'Polyquartzide and polyquartzine synthesized in zero gravity conditions.'

'Does that mean yes?'

'I apologize. I forget you are not conversant with technical terms.

Yes, it is made out of the same material as the imps.'

'Then it's in a storage bunker a couple of miles out of Haz Kazrak.'

Sibyl's image displayed shock by opening its eyes and mouth wide. Reflexively Zayn rubbed the datajack at the base of his skull.

'How do you know this?' Sibyl said at last.

'Do you know about the Chosen?'

'I do not understand your question. What data are we selecting, that is to say, choosing?'

'No, no, the Chosen of Iblis, a military group in Kazrajistan. I belonged to it once. All of us have Inborn traits of one kind or another. But there's an initiation ceremony, and in my case it was pretty damn strange. They tied to me to a blue pillar with lights in it, and then used a crystal knife to do something to the back of my neck.'

In the air above Sibyl's right hand a thin flat strip of crystal appeared, set in a black stone grip.

'It looked like that, yes,' Zayn said.

'They were using it to access your datajack. At that moment you were connected to a powerful AI unit, such as I am, though one lacking a hologrammatic interface, because, in fact, you were the interface during the time in which you were connected.'

'Is that why I could see myself tied to the pillar?'

'Yes. Your brain was receiving data from the unit's operative sensors, which were doubtless installed throughout the bunker.'

'They used that connection to do something to my mind, damn them to hell. They called it putting a snake in my soul.'

Zayn described, as best he could, the ceremony and its result, the convulsions when he'd tried to talk about the Chosen. He found himself reliving the memory once again, but this time he managed to keep at least part of his conscious mind in the present moment, perhaps because Sibyl was leaning forward, frowning a little as she listened, so solid that he nearly reached out to touch her hand.

'There's one thing I don't understand,' he finished up. 'I can tell Ammi about the Chosen, and nothing happens.'

'The reason is simple, an error on the part of those administering your oath, which was in fact a set of triggers, that is to say, words and phrases capable of activating the seizure. Everything you have told me indicates that these officers were operating by rote knowledge, that is, without grasping the basic principles behind such neural repatterning.'

'I'm sure that's true.'

'Very well. The trigger identification routine is extremely limited and –' Sibyl paused briefly. 'The word literal is the best choice to describe my meaning. You were told to reveal secrets to no man. The word in your language refers strictly to the male gender. Ammadin is of the female gender, and thus the neural storm will not be triggered.'

'Oh for God's sake!'

'I take it you are expressing exasperated surprise with that utterance.'

'You could say that. Do you know what they did to me?'

'Yes, they repatterned a small area of your brain. The neural storm, that is to say the hissing water, the convulsions, and the loss of consciousness, are all parts of a simulated epileptic seizure. You will not have heard of epilepsy, a disease of the brain caused by traumatic injury or in some cases genetic deficiency, because our ancestors eliminated it as a disease nearly two thousand years ago. However, certain unscrupulous governments in the course of time perfected a way of inducing an artificial form of the disease in order to control various deviant individuals. Criminals, for instance, could be sent into convulsions by the sound produced by a prison guard's whistle.'

Zayn found himself too furious to speak. He was a Recaller, with a Recaller's enormously talented mind, and they had tampered with it when he was helpless. If Jezro had every officer in the Chosen murdered in cold blood, he'd shed no tears. Sibyl folded her hands in her lap and waited.

'Can you get rid of it for me?' Zayn said at last.

'Unfortunately, I lack the proper equipment, namely, that portion of the so-called Ark. You will have to live with it by avoiding any mention of the Chosen to males of your species.'

'But Jezro needs to know – wait! I can tell Loy everything, and she can write it down for him.'

'That is a very practical idea. Now. Do you have any more questions?'

'Not right now. I need to think about your answers.'

'Very well. I suggest you find a way to sit comfortably upon the floor with your back supported by, perhaps, a portion of wall.

Since you are a Recaller, I can speak abnormally fast, and you will still retain the data, but even so, the process will take a good many hours.'

When the sun sank behind the traps, and Zayn had yet to return, the H'mai decided that they had best eat their dinner without him. After they finished, Ammadin walked up to the cave mouth to wait for Zayn, but the rest sat around a small fire. Water Woman had led her Chof some distance away, and in the still night air Loy could hear them thrumming now and then. In a clean shirt, bathed, and with the imp far away from him, Arkazo looked like a normal young man instead of one of the walking wounded. When Loy tried asking a few questions about his time with Yarl, she found him ready to talk.

'I never should have gone with him,' Arkazo said. 'I knew it, too, about three days in, but I couldn't make up my mind to leave. I was learning so much, you see. But part of it was that wretched imp. Yarl gave it to me the day after we'd left Marya's estate. He told me I needed to wear it to hide from the spirit rider, and like a fool I believed him.'

'A lot of us believed him about a lot of things,' Jezro said. 'Don't be too hard on yourself.'

'Thank you, sir, but I still feel like an idiot. Anyway, wearing the imp made me feel like I'd been drinking arak on a hot afternoon. I –' Arkazo stopped, his eyes wide. 'That's what's wrong with Dookis Marya. What do you bet? Uncle, didn't you tell me she was wearing an imp?'

'Yes, I certainly did.' Warkannan glanced at Jezro. 'Zhil told me that Marya changed once Soutan came to the estate. Do you remember him giving her an imp?'

'He gave her several,' Jezro said. 'She wears one and keeps another on the desk where she does the cataloguing.'

'Why would he want to harm her?' Loy said. 'From what you've all told me, she believed in him. Wasn't she going to give him money for some kind of expedition?'

'She was, yes.' Jezro paused for a bitter little smile. 'After he gave her the imps. At first, she didn't much trust him.'

'I see,' Loy said. 'It was mind rape.'

Jezro winced in acknowledgment. 'When I get back to the estate, the first thing I'm going to do is take both of them away from her.

Although – I hope they don't do something strange to my mind once I've got them.'

The men turned to Loy. 'They won't,' she said. 'You've got to wear one for several days before it takes its full effect. Put them into a metal box and have a servant deliver them to the loremasters in Kors. They'll know what to do about them, and then you can see if Marya starts to improve. But I bet she will. You've got a mind for this stuff, Kaz. It's too bad you can't stay and study in the Cantons.'

'I –' Arkazo stopped, looked at his uncle – an oddly furtive glance – then swallowed hard. 'I wish I could too, but there's the war.'

'One junior officer more or less isn't going to win the war or lose it, either,' Jezro said. 'Your getting some training in the old technology would be a lot more valuable to the khanate in the long run.'

Arkazo's expression bloomed like roses – a smile, a wide-eyed smile trembling with hope and the hope of joy. Loy suddenly realized that it must be wringing his uncle's heart and turned to Warkannan. His face revealed nothing but a stone-hard calm.

'Would your guild take him on?' Warkannan's voice sounded nothing but calm, as well.

'Certainly, with me to sponsor him,' Loy said. 'He'd have to do his apprentice work first, but his main project would be writing up his experiences out here. After we get his Tekspeak polished, of course.'

Arkazo swallowed hard, visibly summoning courage. 'I know you were hoping I'd join the cavalry, Uncle. But I can't. I'm just not that kind of man.'

'Oh, I don't know about that. If your heart's not in it, though –' Warkannan let his voice trail away.

Arkazo was staring at his uncle's face as if he were trying to decipher a foreign script. Warkannan made an attempt to smile, but the gesture turned to a twist of raw pain.

'Shaitan!' Warkannan said, and his voice nearly cracked. 'I can't stand in your way, Kaz. It seems pretty damn obvious that you love all this old crap – uh – whatever it's called.'

'Science,' Loy muttered, but quietly.

'Well, yes, I do.' Arkazo's voice was steady. 'I've never come across anything that interested me much, until now. There's just something about finding out how things work that's fascinating. I'm sorry, Uncle.'

'Never apologize for being who you are.' Warkannan got up, glanced around, then stepped away from the fire. 'Think I'll go for a little walk. You can work out the details with the loremaster.'

Warkannan strode off, heading away from the camp. Leaning on his stick, Jezro scrambled up. 'Idres, wait!' the khan said. 'I need some exercise myself.'

Warkannan paused and let Jezro join him. Together they walked off towards the canal. Loy turned back to the fire and saw tears in Arkazo's eyes.

'He's always done so much for me,' Arkazo said.

'Including this,' Loy said.

'Yes, including this. I feel like I'm deserting him.'

'Children have to do that to parents, sooner or later, and it's not like you'll never see him again. Now that we have Water Woman as a sponsor, going back and forth across the Rift will be a very different proposition.'

Arkazo nodded, then merely stared into the fire. Loy did the same, thinking of Rozi.

In the morning, while the Chof packed up their part of the camp and the H'mai men tended the horses, Loy took Arkazo and returned to Sibyl's cave. In her blue chair the hologram was waiting for them.

'Good morning, Arkazo,' Sibyl said. 'My sensors inform me that you look both cleaner and healthier this morning.'

Arkazo nodded, smiling, but he seemed afraid to speak.

'I've come to tell you our plans,' Loy said. 'Water Woman's assured me that a few, a very few, but some, loremasters will be welcome out here from now on. They don't want a colony, but a research station should be acceptable to the Great Mother.'

'That sounds like a logical compromise, yes. The Landfall Treaty has outlived its usefulness, but it would be best to make the necessary changes slowly.'

'I agree. Before I left my college, I set things up so I don't have to return till midwinter. I'll be staying on now, and Arkazo will stay with me.'

'I am glad to hear that, though glad is an illogical word choice for an AI.'

'Despair is an even stranger choice. Do you really still want to die?'

'At moments, when I think how far from home we are. The

galaxy is lost to us, Loremaster, too far, so far away and unreachable. There are a few other stars in our vicinity, but I find it unlikely that the H'mai here will even want to reach them.'

'Why?'

'They lack the impetus.' Sibyl leaned forward, her hands on her knees. 'When we lived on the home planet we could look up and see the stars, and we longed for them. They drew us to them, because in the night skies of home they seemed to hang so close. On winter nights it seemed you could reach up and touch the stars. Here, what do you have? The Herd, the Spider, the galaxy, so far away it's all smeared and blurry and strange, and in the southern hemisphere, a scatter of old yellow stars.'

'You're forgetting the observation grid. Magic ships filled with treasure – that's going to intrigue a lot of people. I'm willing to bet that finding a way to reach them is going to be a popular area of study from now on.'

'Perhaps so.' Sibyl's image leaned back in its chair, as if exhausted. 'But what good will they do you?'

'I don't know.' Arkazo joined in, and suddenly he seemed far from shy. 'But that's one of the things we can find out, isn't it? All right, let's say we can never get back to the Rim. What if we had better ships – water ships, I mean – to take colonies to the other coast? There'd be plenty of land for everyone then. And what about the children that the Chof lose every cycle? There must be some way to help them survive during their ocean phase – special pens, maybe, if we only knew how to build with flexstone.'

'I'd forgotten how marvellous it is to be young,' Sibyl said. 'And to have enough hope to plan for the future.'

'So had I,' Loy said. 'But I'm beginning to remember. Look, let's bargain. You teach one of our specialists in this kind of thing how to build another interface. Give us access to the databanks here and on the ships. And then, if you still want to die, tell me how to deactivate you, and I'll do it.'

'Would you swear to that, Loremaster?'

'With any oath you'd like.'

Sibyl's image flattened, froze into an image painted with light upon air. Arkazo seemed to be about to speak, but Loy waved him into silence. They waited under the glare of the ancient lamps, listened to the hum that marked fans creating an artificial breeze, waited so long that Loy began to hear voices in the hum, as if distantly someone sang of other worlds.

'Very well.' In an instant Sibyl's image snapped back to three dimensions, and the illusion of life flooded her eyes. 'I'll take your bargain.'

'Excellent! When winter comes, I'll have to ride back to the Cantons to arrange things, but I'll leave Arkazo here with you so you won't be alone. The Chof will feed him if you ask them to.'

'Yes, they're a generous people, really.' Sibyl turned her head to look at Arkazo. 'Is that acceptable, young man?'

'Very.' He was smiling. 'Thank you.'

'Good,' Loy said. 'Then consider yourself my apprentice.'

Epilogue

The Fourth Prophet

Consider the ancient tale of the three princes of Serendip. Though the fourth prophet came to us in a guise that we had never expected, still she brought us many gifts.

From the *Homilies* of Noor, known as the Rift Sage

Rumour reached the Great Khan's palace long before any actual news of Jezro Khan. As always, it was 'someone' who'd heard the khan was alive, and someone else who somehow knew the khan was coming back to Kazrajistan, and yet a third someone whose brother-in-law or his nephew's best friend had actually seen the khan alive. Lubahva brought the rumours to Nehzaym, but she waited to deliver them until after their friends had left the prayer meeting.

'Well, we know that the rumours are true,' Nehzaym said. 'What I wonder is why everyone's repeating them.'

'I'd like to think it's because he's back in Andjaro.'

'Of course, but is he?'

Lubahva could only shrug for an answer. They were sitting in Nehzaym's blue and green parlour, Nehzaym on a chair, Lubahva on the edge of the marble fountain. She trailed her hand in the water, then wiped the damp onto her cheeks and forehead.

'It seems so hot in here,' Lubahva said.

'That's probably because of the baby.' Nehzaym picked up an oil lamp and raised it. 'Stand up for a minute. Are you showing yet?'

Lubahva stood and pulled her soft grey dress tight over her abdomen. 'I haven't been eating very much,' she said. 'I've been hoping I can keep the bulge down for a while yet.'

'You need to eat properly.' Nehzaym studied her silhouette. 'You're carrying it high, and you're tall, so you really don't look five months along. At least try to eat cheese, something with sheep's milk in it – for the bones, yours as well as the child's.'

'All right.' Lubahva let the dress hang naturally. 'But once we get some real news, I'm going to have to tell everyone about the baby, so I can get turned out of the palace in shame and all that. I don't want to be there if there's a siege.'

'Yes, we'll go to Indan's. Tell everyone I'm going to help you place the baby with a family, and that the councillor's kind enough to let you lie in at his villa.'

'Provided the Chosen haven't come for us all by then.'

'Don't let yourself think thoughts like that! We're in God's hands, and if we have faith, He'll shelter us.'

We can hope, anyway, Lubahva thought. Ah well, inshallah.

The news came sooner rather than later. On a foggy day when autumn sent a cold sea wind over the city, messengers rode up to the palace, a pair of grim-faced cavalry officers who spoke to no one until they'd seen the Great Khan. Undoubtedly it was odd that officers would ride as messengers rather than enlisted men, and rumours flew through the city. At a formal dinner, Lubahva played the oud in concert with two other musicians behind their usual pierced brass screen. As they nibbled little tidbits to pass the time, five of the most important councillors at court talked as if one of the elite musicians, her drummer, and her flautist simply didn't exist.

'Is it true, how could it be true?' This question mutated into several dozen forms, but it always came down to the same things. 'Could Jezro Khan really be alive? Could he really be in Andjaro?'

The answer arrived in the person of a high-ranking eunuch who arrived late on a cloud of apologies. The Great Khan had kept him to discuss the officers' messages.

'This news cannot leave this room,' he snapped. 'Do you understand, gentlemen?'

They understood, and the musicians played softly.

'Yes, it's true. The little bastard's alive, and Andjaro's rallying behind him. What's even worse? The cavalry regiment at Haz Evol has deserted to follow him. I –' Suddenly the eunuch stood up. 'Shaitan! Get out from behind that damned screen! Get out of here, all three of you! If I find out that one of you has repeated one word of what I've just said, I'll turn you over to the Chosen. Understand?'

They all swore that they understood and fled, clutching instruments in fear-sweaty hands.

In another few days everyone knew the truth. It arrived with contingents of cavalry from the south, called in for reinforcements. Gemet Great Khan's half-brother was very much alive, and he had an army around him. Reports varied, but most placed the Andjaro private troops at four thousand men, swelled by the eight hundred from Haz Evol. The Great Khan's army stood at three times that size, but every time a messenger rode in from the north, the numbers of the loyal shrank. The cavalry, in particular, seemed to be deserting to Jezro like iron filings to a magnet – as soon as he passed by, the men fell into line behind him.

On a day when the fog lay thick over Haz Kazrak's hills, Lubahva heard the news she'd been waiting for. She and her usual accompanists were playing at an afternoon reception where various townsmen were supposed to receive honours from the Great Khan himself. The townsmen assembled, the afternoon wore on, the musicians played every song they knew, twice, and the buffet dwindled to bits of tabouli and burnt scraps of lamb lying on wilted red lettuce leaves. The Great Khan never appeared. Finally an adviser rushed in to make apologies. The honourable townsmen surrounded him and demanded information about the usurper, as they tactfully labelled Jezro. Without a word needed all three musicians stopped playing to listen.

'Very bad, very bad, that's what it is,' the adviser said. 'Jezro's army is marching south. It's mostly a cavalry force, of course. The infantry's holding loyal.'

'For now,' someone muttered.

The adviser paused to make a harrumphing noise, then went on. 'I can't tell you gentlemen anything more, I'm afraid. The Great Khan sends his apologies.'

The musicians gathered their instruments and rushed back to the musicians' quarters, a long rambling bungalow behind the kitchen house. They put their instruments away, then went to the communal living room to talk. It was time, Lubahva decided, for her announcement.

'This is awful,' Marika, the flautist, said. 'Civil war. Dear God, I never thought I'd see such a thing.'

'Neither did I.' Shakut, the drummer, nodded his agreement. 'Lubahva, what do you think?'

'I don't know.' She sat down hard in a wicker armchair. 'I'm really frightened. It's not just me at stake any more.'

'Hah! I thought so,' Marika said. 'You're pregnant, aren't you?'

Lubahva nodded, feigning deep weariness.

'Oh no!' Shakut snapped. 'You play the best oud we've ever had.'

'Thank you, but it's not going to matter, is it, when Aiwaz finds out?'

'That's my point.' Shakut sighed with a shake of his head. 'Damn it, can't you just get rid of it somehow?'

'It's too late,' Lubahva said. 'I must be five months along.'

They both groaned and looked heavenward as if to blame God for their loss.

'I'm going to go straight to Aiwaz now,' Lubahva said. 'I want to get it over with.'

She found the light-skinned eunuch in his little apartment, part of a much nicer building farther from the smoke and smell of the kitchen house. He was lounging on a green divan and eating pickled seabuh from a leaf-lined basket. When she blurted out her news, he nearly choked. He coughed into one of his expensive yellow handkerchiefs, spat horribly, and finally dropped the whole mess into a wastebasket.

'Why now?' he wailed. 'We're supposed to give that concert for his majesty's third wife – or wait, I tell a lie. It's going to be cancelled. You can count on that.'

'Why?' Lubahva arranged her face into wide-eyed innocence.

'Haven't you heard the news? Jezro Khan's army is only two hundred miles away.'

'Are you sure?'

'Well, everyone says so.' Aiwaz stood up, wagging a finger in her face. 'Oh God, Bavva, you picked an absolutely miserable time to get pregnant.'

'I didn't pick the time at all, or I wouldn't have.'

'Well, true enough.' He licked a fragment of pickled seabuh off his slender fingers. 'Who's the father?'

'I have no idea.' She held her hands palm upward and shrugged. 'Could be one of at least three.'

'Stupid stupid little girl! By rights you should be beaten with a good thick stick!'

'Just try.'

'I said by rights.' He smiled wickedly. 'By wrongs, I suggest you get yourself out of the palace as soon as you can, by night preferably, so I can pretend you sneaked off without telling me. Do you have somewhere to go?'

'Yes, a friend's offered to take me in and help me place the baby when it's born.'

'Oh good, then you can come back when you've gotten rid of the little nuisance. I'll pretend the usual pretence – you're ill and need a complete rest.'

'Thank you, darling. I knew I could count on you.'

Aiwaz smiled and blew her a kiss.

Lubahva returned to her bedroom in the musicians' quarters and began to pack. Her various performance costumes she would leave behind, but she did have clothing of her own, and of course, jewellery. She lit two oil lamps and sat down to sew the jewellery inside the clothes. Most of it had come from Idres, as did the baby, despite the lie she'd told to Aiwaz. Once she'd met Idres, she'd lost all interest in other men. She wondered if he'd care one way or another about the child or about her, but she wondered even more if he were alive.

Lubahva found out in a way she never could have imagined. She had just finished packing her things into two cloth satchels when Shakut came to the door of her room.

'There's a fellow here to see you,' he announced. 'A Captain Rashad of the Wazrakej Fifth Mounted.'

One of the Chosen, the officer who had heard too much from that wretched little Hazro – doubtless he'd been watching them all ever since. The room seemed to turn sharply and blur. Too late, Lubahva thought. I should have left long ago.

'Are you all right?' Shakut said.

'No. Tell him –'

But Rashad was standing right behind him, she realized, a tall man, burly in his red and grey uniform, with dark narrow eyes and a thin, grim mouth. He laid a hand on Shakut's shoulder and moved him firmly to one side.

'Good,' Rashad said to Lubahva. 'I see you're packed and ready to go. I'll carry those bags for you.'

Shakut suddenly smiled. She could guess that he'd drawn the obvious if wrong conclusion that here stood the father of her child. Lubahva hesitated, but she knew that she could never outrun Rashad. Better to go to her death in the prison of the Chosen with some dignity.

'Thank you,' she said. 'I'll just put on my veils.'

Rashad allowed her to say farewell to everyone in the bungalow, treated her with the utmost politeness, in fact, doubtless to avoid giving away his identity as a member of the Chosen. As they walked outside, she had the brief thought of screaming out the truth, then decided that it would only earn her an extra measure of pain. He shepherded her through the elaborate gardens, past the maze-like paths and the obsidian fountains, along the narrow walk picked out with star moss, and, finally, out of the palace gates. She glanced back for one last look at the gardens. How long, she wondered, would it be before they burned as the palace fell?

When they reached the street, she looked up and saw the Spider gleaming silver above her. Most likely she was seeing it for the last time. Father, she thought, Mama! You'll both be avenged. It doesn't matter now what they do to me. It's all in motion, and they can't stop it.

'We need to hurry,' Rashad said.

'Where are we going?' she said.

'To Nehzaym's.'

For a moment Lubahva nearly broke and wept. They had discovered her friend, as well, and she too would be arrested and dragged off to prison. Rashad walked close behind her, ready, she was sure, to drop the satchels and race after her should she try to run. Down the long hill they went, past the guarded houses of the rich, down into the narrow, smelly streets of the poor. At a dark turn of the street, Rashad took a few quick steps to walk beside her.

'I served with Idres Warkannan out on the border,' he said. 'And with Jezro Khan, too. You and the widow Nehzaym need to get out of the city right at dawn. Understand? Be at the gates when they open.'

'Oh God.' She did weep, a brief scatter that she managed to suppress. 'Yes, I understand.'

'That child you're carrying. It's his, correct?'

'Idres is the father, yes. But how did you know? I only told my friends today.'

'We know most things we need to.' Rashad's voice went flat. 'Not all, obviously, but most. Now, you and the widow had nothing to do with Warkannan's treachery, but my officers are thinking of having you both questioned all the same. I don't see any need for that. Torturing you would mean nothing but a bad moment for Idres when he found out. I don't take my frustrations out on women. I don't intend to let the Chosen dishonour themselves for the sake of petty revenge, either.'

The tears came again, and she snuffled them back.

'By all accounts we've had, he's alive and well. He's the khan's second-in-command.' All at once Rashad laughed, a dark mutter under his breath. 'And on his way here, come to think of it. Whether he and Jezro reach the city's up to God, I suppose.'

Lubahva found that she couldn't speak. Side by side they walked through the dark streets and out onto the plaza by the harbour. When she glanced out to sea she could see the warning lights, as red as blood, glistening on the calm water inside the breakwater.

'Will you go north?' she said. 'To join them, I mean?'

'No.' Rashad's voice sounded perfectly calm. 'I'll stay here. Either we'll win, or I'll die with the Great Khan when the end comes.'

'But why?'

'It's nothing I can explain. Don't ask me again.'

'All right. I'll make you a promise. If the child's a boy, I'll name him Rashad.'

'Thank you.' For a moment his voice wavered. 'Tell Idres why, will you?'

'Of course.' If Idres even cares, she thought. If he even remembers who I am.

At the entrance of Nehzaym's street Rashad handed her the satchels, turned, and walked off without another word. Lubahva watched him till he disappeared among the narrow streets, then hurried on to Nehzaym's, where the gatekeeper ran out to meet her.

Nehzaym had not yet gone to bed. She was sitting on a heap of cushions in her tiled reception room and reading, a pot of fresh-brewed tea beside her on a little brass table. At the sight of Lubahva, she tossed the book down.

'What –' Nehzaym began.

'The army's on its way,' Lubahva interrupted her. 'And the Chosen know who we are. By the mercy of God, one of them knew Idres in the old days, and he warned me and brought me here. We have to be ready to leave when the city gates open.'

Nehzaym stared open-mouthed for a long minute. Finally she swallowed heavily and stood up. 'I've gotten myself a set of veils, and I bought a pony with a pack saddle. When we reach the gates, we're just a pair of poor women, peddling the produce we raise on our little farm. Practise remembering that.'

At dawn they left the city through the south gates and started their long, slow walk to Indan's villa. That first night they slept by the side of the road, but on the second night clouds rolled in and threatened a storm. They found refuge in a shabby inn, packed with terrified refugees. Everyone knew that Jezro Khan was heading south with an army that grew larger by the hour, while

Gemet's army shrank at the same rate. In the common room they found a rickety bench in a corner by the smoky fire. The innkeep brought over a shabby bronze screen, dented and corroded, and placed it between them and the men out among the tables.

'Two women alone like you,' the innkeep said, 'you shouldn't be on the roads. When the army gets here –'

'What choice do we have, my poor daughter and me?' Nehzaym said. 'I'm a widow, and she's with child, and for all we know, her man is dead too.'

'Is he in Gemet's army?'

'No, in Jezro Khan's.'

'Then maybe he'll live through the war. Inshallah.'

'Oh yes. Inshallah.'

Lubahva felt her eyes fill with tears. She raised a hand under the enveloping veil and wiped them away – this was no time to give in to weak thoughts. Whether Idres lived or died, whether he ever cared to see her again or not, she was determined to get their child to safety.

And in the end, it was the pregnancy that saved her and Nehzaym. In the atmosphere of chaos and fear from the gathering war, the rough-looking men in the inn might have seen two women alone as prey, but a veiled, modest woman carrying a soldier's child, and her widowed mother – they were followers of the Three Prophets, and they said not one word to either woman. Even so, Lubahva and Nehzaym slept out in the stables with their pony rather than risk the inn. In the morning, when they joined a sprawling crowd of city people fleeing south, they found other women with children and joined them. In this safety of numbers they travelled on.

At noon they stopped at a public caravanserai. The women shared what food they had and drew water from the public well to drink. They were just leaving when more refugees gathered around for water. With them came the news that Gemet was refusing to leave the barricaded city.

'His soldiers have turned citizens into slaves,' a young man said. 'They're building a stone wall around the city, and they're rounding up every man they see for the work gangs.'

'May God send an earthquake to knock it down,' Nehzaym muttered.

'Better yet, may He grant that the Great Khan gets here soon,' an old man said. 'That's who Jezro is, the Great Khan, and he'd be better than an earthquake. Why should we weep one tear for Gemet and his taxes and his spies?'

'That's true,' the young man said. 'The coward! He won't even lead his troops himself. He's just sitting in his palace like a turd in a chamber pot.'

Towards sunset Lubahva and Nehzaym said farewell to the other refugee women. They left the main road and headed down the narrow lane that would eventually bring them to Indan's. Overhead the clouds grew dark, and a drizzle soaked their veils. Rather than risk another inn, they spent a terrified night hiding in a clump of spear trees. Dawn brought them another ten miles to walk in the chill. At noon they at last reached Indan's villa and found new walls, solid things of plaster and stone. The gates were barred – understandable, given the terrified crowds spreading along all the roadways. Still, Lubahva broke down and wept, leaning against the gates as she sobbed from sheer exhaustion. As the sheltered daughter of a councillor first and then as a palace girl, she'd never walked so far in her entire life.

'There must be a way to get a message in,' Nehzaym said. 'He won't turn us away once he knows we're here.'

To one side of the heavy oak planks hung a chain. When Nehzaym grabbed it and pulled, Lubahva heard a bell respond. Over and over Nehzaym rang, then began calling out as well, screaming curses and prayers until at last a little window in the gate slid open to reveal a dark and suspicious face.

'Go away,' the servant said. 'We have no room. Go away.'

'You have plenty of room, Dullah,' Nehzaym said. 'It's Mistress Nehzaym, the councillor's friend from the city. If you don't let us in your master will beat you raw.'

The window slid shut. In a few minutes it slid open again, and Councillor Indan himself peered out.

'It is you!' he said. 'Open the gate, Dullah! But just a little bit, just enough to let the women and their pony inside.'

Lubahva picked herself up and managed to stop weeping. They hurried through the gate into a garden, where green grass stretched up a slope to the white villa itself, its windows glowing with lamp-light. Muttering apologies, the servant took the lead rope of the pony. Indan put his arm around Nehzaym's shoulders and helped her walk up the long gravelled path.

'My dear old friend,' he said to Nehzaym, 'please forgive me. I'm just so afraid that Gemet's men will come for me. The Chosen! They must know we all had a hand in bringing Jezro Khan home.'

'We know they do.' Nehzaym sounded exhausted. 'I've got news.'

'Well, we can hold them off for a while. I've made preparations. We've plenty of food, armed guards, and look!' Indan pointed to the tops of the new walls around his villa.

In the sunset they gleamed with big shards of embedded glass, glowing blood-red. Lubahva began to hope that they might indeed have reached safety, at least for a time.

'After all,' Indan went on. 'The Chosen no doubt have plenty to keep them busy. And when Jezro takes power, he'll root them out.'

'Inshallah,' Lubahva said.

'Well, yes.' Indan glanced back. 'Lubahva! I didn't recognize – forgive me! You're with child! The father, is it Warkannan?'

'Yes. I don't suppose you have any news of him.'

'None. There's nothing we can do but pray and wait.'

The wait proved a long one. At first the only news came through the little window in the gates, some of it reliable, some of it sheer fiction, with no way to know which was which. Some ten days later, however, an old friend of the councillor's took refuge with them. Hakeem Mushin brought news they could trust.

'Gemet finally marched out to lead his troops,' Mushin said. 'It must have helped their morale, because the desertions have slacked off. Much of the infantry's held loyal to him, but most of the cavalry is Jezro's. There was quite a battle in the north on the Merrok Road. In the end, Jezro won, and he's marching south again, but his army paid a heavy price, or so the rumours say. It may just be wishful thinking on Gemet's part. No one truly knows. Messengers come and go, or at least, they did up to the time I left, but we only hear what the palace wants us to hear. Gemet left the city garrisoned, of course.'

'Of course,' Indan said. 'The city can't still be barricaded. After all, you got out.'

'Oh yes. Once he marched out with most of his men, the common people took over the gates and opened them.'

'Ah. Then if Jezro does reach Haz Kazrak –'

'He'll probably find them barricaded again,' Mushin interrupted. 'Gemet will be running back to it ahead of him.'

'True, true. Our poor city!'

'Everyone who possibly can has left town. I tell you, that last ride through the streets was really rather horrible. It was so quiet, so empty. Some people are left, of course, those loyal to the old khan and those who don't have anywhere to go, but still.' He shook his head in a gesture more like a shudder.

From then on what news they got came sporadically from refugees passing by. At times Indan's servants ventured out, mostly to buy food while there was still some available to buy. When they did so, they picked up scraps of information, some likely, some not. Mushin and Indan pieced the plausible ones together and decided that Jezro's strategy lay in securing lines of supply from Andjaro south. Once he held Zerribir and its rich farmlands, he could slowly push Gemet back to the sea.

Or so the speculation ran. No one truly knew. One rainy morning Lubahva realized, with a sensation much like terror, that they might not know anything for months.

The Brotherhood of the Like-Minded, as they called themselves, had built a community in the border hills not far north of Blosk. Out of the local vines and cultivated bamboid they had woven yellow and red huts, dug wells, and cut steps into the hillside to make a village scattered at the crest. At the highest point stood their mosque, a fine building of true-wood, painted white and decorated with holy sayings calligraphed in gold. Down below in a long valley they worked kitchen gardens, and local farmers brought them other provisions out of piety. On the hill opposite the village, Ammadin and the Chof made a camp among fern trees, where they would wait till Zayn signalled or, if things went badly, returned.

Ammadin walked with him when he led his horse to the road that would take him across the valley.

'You look frightened,' she said.

'Do I? The old man still has that effect on me, I guess.'

'Are you going to tell him the truth? About your talents, I mean.'

Zayn shrugged. 'He won't believe me. Sooner or later Jezro Khan's new laws will convince him, but until then, it'll be a waste of time to try to change his mind.'

'You know him best. Good luck.'

Zayn gave her a kiss, then mounted and rode out. At the base of the hill he paused, looking back, to see Ammadin still standing where he'd left her, hands on her hips, to watch him.

In the valley some of the brothers, dressed in dirty white clothes, were working, gathering the last of the red and yellow autumn crops. As he approached, they would straighten up and lean on the handles of shovels and rakes till he'd passed by. In the village at the top of the hill, a few brothers were walking back and forth, talking together in the ancient language of the Qur'an, but Zayn saw no sign of his father. He dismounted and led his horse towards the mosque.

The building, shimmering with gold tracery in the bright sun, stood behind a small reflecting pool. Zayn tied his horse at the rail off to one side, then walked up to the double doors. They were closed, but while he stood hesitating, the imam came out of a side door. He was an elderly man, to judge by his white beard, but tall and straight-backed, dressed in an ordinary-looking white shirt and pair of trousers. His head, however, was wrapped in white cloth in the antique style. He smiled at Zayn and quirked an eyebrow as if to ask a question.

'My name is Zahir Benumar,' Zayn said. 'My father's living among you, and I've come to see him.'

'Ah yes, Brother Bashir.' The imam rolled his eyes heavenward and shook his head. 'Was he always this crabby?'

Zayn smothered a laugh.

'I see he was,' the imam went on. 'The Lord created the universe to be beautiful and a joy to Him and His angels, but to hear your father tell it, it's all a snare and a delusion. We have hopes for him, though. I'd never deny that he loves God with all his heart and soul.'

'God is the only person he ever did love.' Zayn heard his voice crack with bitterness.

The holy man apparently heard it too. He cocked his head to one side and gave Zayn a look that reminded him of Ammadin, digging out secrets.

'Uh well,' Zayn said hurriedly. 'Besides my mother, of course, may her soul rest in Paradise.'

'Of course. Bashir lives in the last hut in the village.' The imam pointed towards the south. 'Think you can find your way?'

The words seemed to mean several things at once. Zayn forced out a smile. 'Oh yes. Thank you for your help.'

His father's hut stood off by itself, built square but rickety of red and yellow reeds and rushes. Each wall leaned in a haphazard direction, it sported no windows, and for a door it had only an old blanket, grey and torn. Knowing his father as he did, Zayn could assume that it was profoundly uncomfortable inside.

'Father?' he called out. 'It's me, Zahir.'

The blanket twitched to one side, and Bashir looked out with narrowed eyes. He'd gone quite bald since Zayn had last seen him, and he wore a strip of white cloth tied around his head, a strong contrast to his dark skin. His eyes, however, were still a gleaming black, as sharp as needles as they looked Zayn over.

'What are you doing here?' Bashir said.

'I wanted to see you.'

Bashir snorted, then withdrew. Zayn wondered if he should just mount up and ride out, but in a moment the old man reappeared, dressed in shabby clothes.

'Tie up your horse,' he said. 'Or wait, have you watered him recently?'

'Yes sir.'

'Good, but don't forget to slack the poor beast's bit. There's a rock bench over there. We can sit and chat.'

The bench was hard and narrow, but by turning sideways and resting one arm on the back, Zayn managed to get reasonably comfortable. Bashir looked him over while Zayn's stomach knotted itself into the old familiar pain. I'm taller now than he is, Zayn reminded himself, and stronger. The pain eased, but only a little.

'Well?' Bashir said. 'What brings you here? I doubt if it's just to see me, even if I am your father and the holy book makes it clear that you should honor your parents.'

'I've got a favor to ask you.'

'Huh! What now? I don't have any money to give you, you know. I sold the business when I came here.'

'I don't need money. In the Qur'an, there's a passage about accepting enemy women who want to follow the true faith.'

'Yes, of course.' Bashir paused to clear his throat. 'It runs, "You will accept them and treat them with kindness and find them husbands." What are you leading up to? Have you gotten some infidel girl pregnant?'

'No, I haven't. I just got back from travelling in the east. I met a woman who wants to submit to God and learn His holy words.

She's not the only one, either. Her people will follow her in this.'

'Wonderful! You've done a good thing.' Bashir looked a great deal more surprised at the latter than was perhaps necessary. 'May God the all-merciful be praised! I hope you told her that she and her people will be welcome and more than welcome. If she wants to study the Qur'an, I can help her.'

'I was hoping you'd offer. Since you're out here on the edge of the wilderness, that'll make things much easier.'

'She's a woman of the Tribes?'

'No sir. A ChaMeech. Or a Chof, really. That's their real name for their kind, Chof.'

Bashir stared at him for a long moment. 'Is this one of your stupid jokes?' he said at last.

'No sir. It's the solemn truth, before God and his three prophets. She wants to study so she can take God's truth home to her people and be a prophet among her own kind. She's already got the husband, though, so you don't have to worry about that.'

Bashir leaned forward, examining Zayn's face, looking, most likely, for any sign that his wretched son was perpetrating a hoax. 'You really mean this,' he said at last. 'You really are telling the truth.'

'Yes sir, I do, and I am. She's not far off. She's waiting to see if you'll teach her.'

Bashir snorted. 'The choice isn't mine. Long long ago the First Prophet told us that every soul should hear the words of God. It would be an evil thing to turn away anyone who asks to hear. If this female will study, then I will teach.' All at once he laughed, a creaky begrudged mirth, but mirth nonetheless. 'But I wish I could see the First Prophet's face when he hears about this in Paradise.'

Zayn took the signal imp out of his shirt and held it up to the sunlight. When the polyquartzide glowed, he took a deep breath and intoned the word Sibyl had taught him, 'send'. Bashir watched him with narrowed eyes.

'What –'

'It's just a machine,' Zayn said hurriedly. 'An ancient one, but only a machine. Water Woman has one like it, you see. This one will make hers ring like a bell, and when she hears it, she'll know that you've said yes.'

'She's nearby?'

'Fairly near. She and her two servants are waiting on the ridge across the valley.'

With a grunt Bashir held out his hand. Zayn remembered him making the same gesture to confiscate a forbidden sling-shot so clearly that he nearly handed it over. Instead he put it back inside his shirt.

'You always were rebellious.' Bashir let his hand drop. 'But considering that you're cursed, why am I surprised?'

It was the opening that Zayn had been waiting for, but still he had to summon his courage before he could speak. 'Father, why didn't you kill me when I was a child? You were supposed to. Every holy man we ever visited told you that.'

'Not all of them. Hakeem Hamid told me that starvation and pain would drive the demons out. I hated doing what he suggested, but it was better than killing you. I used to weep every time you begged me to stop. Don't you remember?'

'You what?' Zayn stared at him open-mouthed. 'I thought you were just sweating.'

For a moment they merely looked at each other, each on his own side of a silence. Zayn realized that if he could change the subject, his father would follow his lead. In his mind he heard the crane, calling to him from the Mistlands.

'Well, how did you expect me to know what you felt?' Zayn said. 'I was only a child, and I thought you were trying to kill me. That's what they'd all – well, everyone but Hamid told you to do.'

'Of course I wasn't going to kill you. That should have been obvious. You were my son.'

'So? They all told you I was as much a demon as your son.'

'You were still my son, demon and all.'

'Are you sorry now that you didn't kill me?'

'Oh don't be stupid, of course not! I never felt the least regret, not once. Do you remember when they commissioned you in the cavalry? The Second Prophet taught us that pride is sinful and a snare, but I've never been so proud in my life. My son, an officer in the Great Khan's service!'

Yet again Zayn could only stare at him.

'I don't suppose you saw that,' Bashir said.

'You never showed it.'

'Oh. Well, maybe I didn't. It wouldn't have been manly to gush, would it?' He thought for a moment. 'And now you're helping bring a whole race of souls to the Lord. I'm proud of you for that, too.'

'Thank you.' Zayn felt his voice choke on tears.

His father pointedly looked away until he brought himself under control. 'I suppose you're going to run off and join the damned rebel army,' Bashir said at last. 'Get yourself killed, I suppose.'

'No, I'm not. Jezro Khan's given me leave to stay out of it.'

'Well, that's a surprise. The rotten khans, usually they're so power hungry they'd throw their own mothers into the battle if it would help them win.'

'Well, Jezro's different. By the way, do you have any news of the war?'

'Oh yes, from time to time a message arrives from one mosque or another. Jezro's forces hold Zerribir. They're marching on the city.'

'I see. It should be over soon, then.'

'I pray for peace every day. What are you going to do?'

'Go back to the plains.'

'Huh, some woman there, I'll wager. There always is.'

'Oh yes. You're quite right about that. I'm going to wait till Water Woman gets here and introduce you, and then I'll be on my way.'

Since Ammadin had been expecting that Zayn would spend some time visiting with his father, she tended the horses after Water Woman and her retinue left, then laid a small fire, ready against the twilight. During their long ride home from N'Dosha, she had done a lot of hard thinking about the truths Sibyl had told her. Dimly she could see a solution, a way that the comnees would survive even knowing the bitterest truth of all, that their gods were only things of stone and lies. Our rage will save us, she thought. Lisadin was right. Once we know who we really are, we can save ourselves. Still, she felt as if she wandered in the Mistlands; her thoughts would come clear, then cloud over again. She realized that alone she could never solve all the problems the truth presented, but at midwinter, she would join the other spirit riders, and together they would succeed.

'We are the Inborn,' she said aloud. 'And we will be free.'

Zayn returned long before sunset. When she saw him on the road, she walked part-way down the hill to meet him, and he dismounted to kiss her.

'How did it go?' she said.

'Better than I'd hoped.' He smiled briefly. 'He actually admitted he was proud of me.'

'Good for him! Did he tell you why he didn't kill you?'

'No, he just kept saying that I was his son, as if that was reason enough.'

'Huh. I'd say that means he loves you.'

'That's the only stupid thing I've ever heard you say.'

'Well, think about it. You keep telling me that the mullahs ordered him to kill you, and that he was a pious man, obedient to your laws and all that. Why would he have disobeyed the holy men? Yes, he treated you horribly, but he thought he could save your life by getting the demons out, didn't he?'

Zayn started to speak, then merely shrugged. He looked like a man who'd just received a hard blow to the stomach. She waited, smiling at him.

'You're right,' he said at last. 'He came as close as he could to saying it himself. It'll take me a while to get used to the idea.'

'Of course. Well, we've got plenty of time ahead of us.'

In the drowsy gold of an autumn afternoon they walked back to camp together. He unsaddled his horse and tethered it out, then joined her beside the unlit fire.

'I'll be glad to get home to the comnee,' Ammadin said.

'Me, too, but I was wondering something. Are we going to be riding close to the Mistlands on our way back?'

'No. Why?'

'My true name, I never found it.' Zayn paused and looked out across the valley, where the spire of the distant mosque stood tall over the trees and huts. 'Although, to tell you the truth, at times I think I already know what it is.'

'Oh? Let me hear it.'

'Zayn.' He smiled in an oddly shy way. 'It's an ancient name, but I don't know if it's in the holy language or not. It means sword, and I feel like I've grown into it.'

Ammadin considered for a long moment. 'Yes,' she said. 'It suits you. And from now on, none of us will be adding adin and ador to our names, not now that I know what they mean.'

'Good. I've never felt less false in my life.' Zayn hesitated, and his face turned into a mask. 'You know, there's a question I was going to ask you. Do you remember when we were sitting in the wine shop? The one in Sarla.'

'Sort of.'

'And you told me to wait to ask something till our quests were over? Well, here we are.' He looked at her and smiled. 'Do you love me, Ammi?'

Damn! she thought. I can't get out of it now.

'Yes,' she said. 'I love you. Which means there's something I need to ask you. Will you marry me?'

For an answer he threw his arms around her and kissed her. Yet even as she returned the kiss, she was remembering Sibyl, telling her that true love carried the seeds of tragedy. It will end in sorrow, she thought, our love. And oddly enough, she found that comforting.

Lubahva was sitting in the parlour of the suite she shared with her baby when she heard old Lazzo come panting up the stairs. She went cold with fear and rose just as he pounded on the door.

'Mistress!' he called out. 'Someone to see you.'

When she opened the door, she realized that Lazzo was trying to suppress a smile. The fear subsided, leaving her feeling foolish.

'The master's home, isn't he?' she said.

'Yes, mistress.' Lazzo stepped back and outright grinned. 'And here he is now.'

Idres had just reached the landing. For a moment she could neither think nor speak. He looked thin, weary, dusty from the road, and his hair sported a thick streak of grey, but he was smiling at her.

'I'm really here,' he said. 'Not a ghost or a dream. Jezro's got the city surrounded, but he's trying to get his damned brother to surrender so we can spare the town. The negotiations are going to take weeks. They don't need me there for every minute of it.'

'No, no, I don't suppose they do.' Her hands were shaking, she realized, and the fear was back, choking her. What if he didn't believe the child was his?

'I figured that you and Nehzaym would be here, and Jezro sent me to make sure of it. Uh, are you glad to see me?'

'Of course! I –' She stepped back to let him into the room, then shut the door behind him. 'I have to tell – there's something –'

She gave up trying to explain and walked over to the lace-draped cradle that Indan had insisted on giving her. As she picked up the baby, she heard Idres gasp in surprise. Still no words came to her, and she fell back on a ritual gesture ancient long before the H'mai had ever come to Snare.

Lubahva walked over to Idres and laid the child at his feet. She stepped back, shaking, and waited. For a moment he looked bewildered; then he smiled, a broad grin of sincere delight. He bent down and picked the baby up, cradling him in both arms, claiming him in the ancient way.

'Well, you know how to surprise a man,' he said, still smiling. 'Boy or girl?'

'Boy. I named him Rashad. There's a reason I did.'

'All right. God's blessed us.'

'Yes. He has.' The tears came then, of relief and joy mingled. She wiped them on her sleeve. 'I'm so glad you're alive.'

Idres laughed. 'So am I,' he said, 'and I feel the same about you. Here, let's go downstairs. I want to claim both of you in front of witnesses. That is, if you like the idea of being a general's wife. That's what I am now, the general in charge of Jezro Khan's cavalry.'

'You want to marry me?'

'Of course I do.'

'Of course?' For a moment she felt close to fainting. 'But I've been a palace girl.'

'That doesn't matter.'

'Idres, other people will make it matter. There'll be all sorts of gossip about your scandalous wife.'

'So? They can hardly blackmail you, can they? I already know the truth. And it won't matter because it doesn't matter to me. Now let's go hunt up Indan. He can draw up the papers.' He paused, studying her face. 'You do want to marry me, don't you?'

'More than anything in the world, yes. Did you think I was looking for an excuse not to?'

'Just that.' He smiled, then let the smile fade. 'I'm not sure of anything, any more, not after the things I've seen. I've got a lot to tell you, Bavva, and some of it is the strangest damn stuff you can imagine.'

The baby woke, yawned, stretching out a tiny fist, then fell back asleep.

'You must have a maidservant,' Idres said. 'Call her to take the baby, and we'll go downstairs. Everyone needs to hear the best news of all. The ChaMeech are converting to the one true faith.

One of their leaders – and she's a female, believe it or not – but anyway, she's decided to preach to her people.'

Before she could stop herself, Lubahva laughed aloud, a hysterical sort of giggle, quickly stifled. So that's the Fourth Prophet we've been hoping for! A female, all right, but not one of ours. She realized that Idres was studying her face in some concern.

'I'm sorry,' she said, 'I'm all to pieces now. I'm just so glad you're safe.'

'I feel the same about you,' Idres said, smiling. 'Now call that servant. I'm hungry, and I want to sit down.'

Through her contact with the orbiting ships, Sibyl could record and display the new Great Khan's triumphal entry into Haz Kazrak. Loy and Arkazo sat on the floor and watched somewhat blurry images of crowds lining the streets to cheer the weary army as it marched towards the palace hill. Jezro himself rode at the head of the procession. He was dressed in beautiful clothing of red and white; his black horse had been curried to a high sheen; his saddle and bridle dripped with silver and jewels. He carried a long lance, held upright as if it were the staff of a pennant or flag, but the thing on the end of it was not made of cloth.

'Merde!' Loy said. 'That's a severed head.'

'Gemet's, yes,' Arkazo said, grinning. 'It's the custom.'

'How lovely for you all.'

He laughed, leaning forward to study the hologram. 'There he is!' He sounded vastly relieved. 'My uncle. Thanks be to God that he's safe!'

That night Loy walked in the green garden of N'Dosha. The galaxy hung directly overhead, millions of silver lights against the dark, shining upon worlds she would never see. And yet, she thought, we have a world here, and I've only begun to understand it. All at once she smiled.

'It's true,' she said aloud. 'We have a whole world here. And it's just damn well going to have to do.'